Mal and Chad
BELLY FLOP!

ALSO BY

Stephen McCranie

Mal and Chad

THE BIGGEST, BESTEST TIME EVER

&

FOOD FIGHT!

Mal [and] Chad

Stephen McCranie

BELLY FLOP!

Philomel Books 🐾 **An Imprint of Penguin Group (USA) Inc.**

PHILOMEL BOOKS

A division of Penguin Young Readers Group.

Published by The Penguin Group. Penguin Group (USA) Inc., 375 Hudson Street, New York, NY 10014, U.S.A. Penguin Group (Canada), 90 Eglinton Avenue East, Suite 700, Toronto, Ontario M4P 2Y3, Canada (a division of Pearson Penguin Canada Inc.). Penguin Books Ltd, 80 Strand, London WC2R 0RL, England. Penguin Ireland, 25 St. Stephen's Green, Dublin 2, Ireland (a division of Penguin Books Ltd). Penguin Group (Australia), 250 Camberwell Road, Camberwell, Victoria 3124, Australia (a division of Pearson Australia Group Pty Ltd). Penguin Books India Pvt Ltd, 11 Community Centre, Panchsheel Park, New Delhi - 110 017, India. Penguin Group (NZ), 67 Apollo Drive, Rosedale, Auckland 0632, New Zealand (a division of Pearson New Zealand Ltd). Penguin Books (South Africa) (Pty) Ltd, 24 Sturdee Avenue, Rosebank, Johannesburg 2196, South Africa. Penguin Books Ltd, Registered Offices: 80 Strand, London WC2R 0RL, England.

Published simultaneously in Canada.
Printed in the United States of America.
Edited by Michael Green.
Design by Richard Amari.
Library of Congress Cataloging-in-Publication Data is available upon request.

ISBN 978-0-399-25658-5
3 5 7 9 10 8 6 4

For Kait

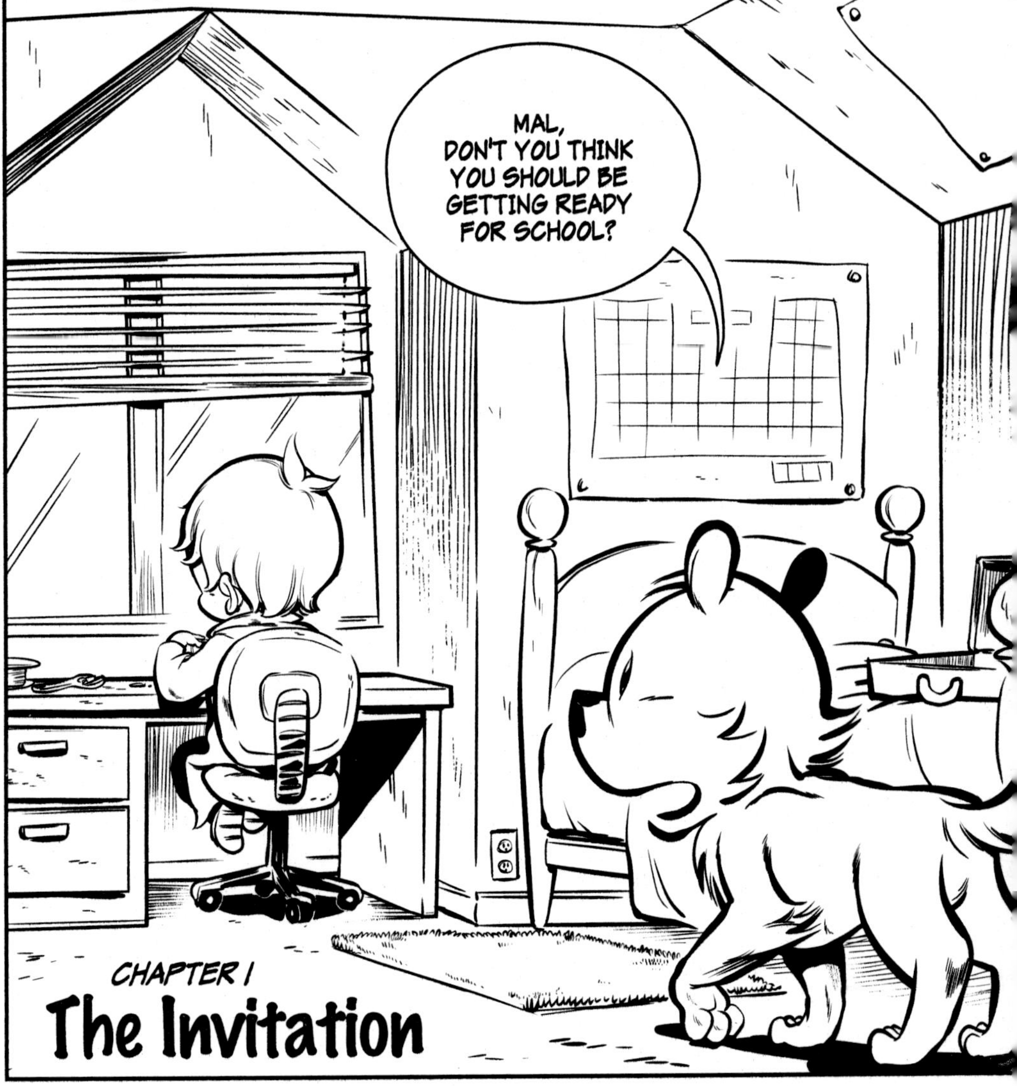
MAL, DON'T YOU THINK YOU SHOULD BE GETTING READY FOR SCHOOL?

CHAPTER 1

The Invitation

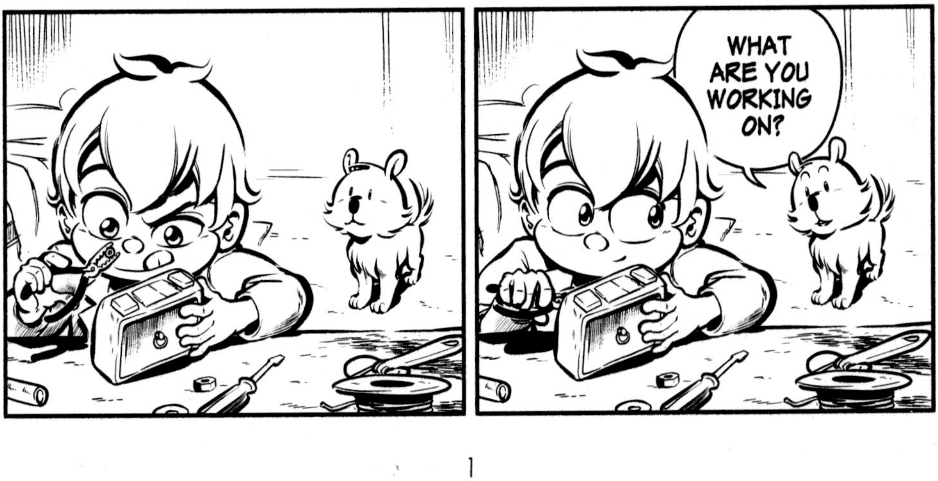
WHAT ARE YOU WORKING ON?

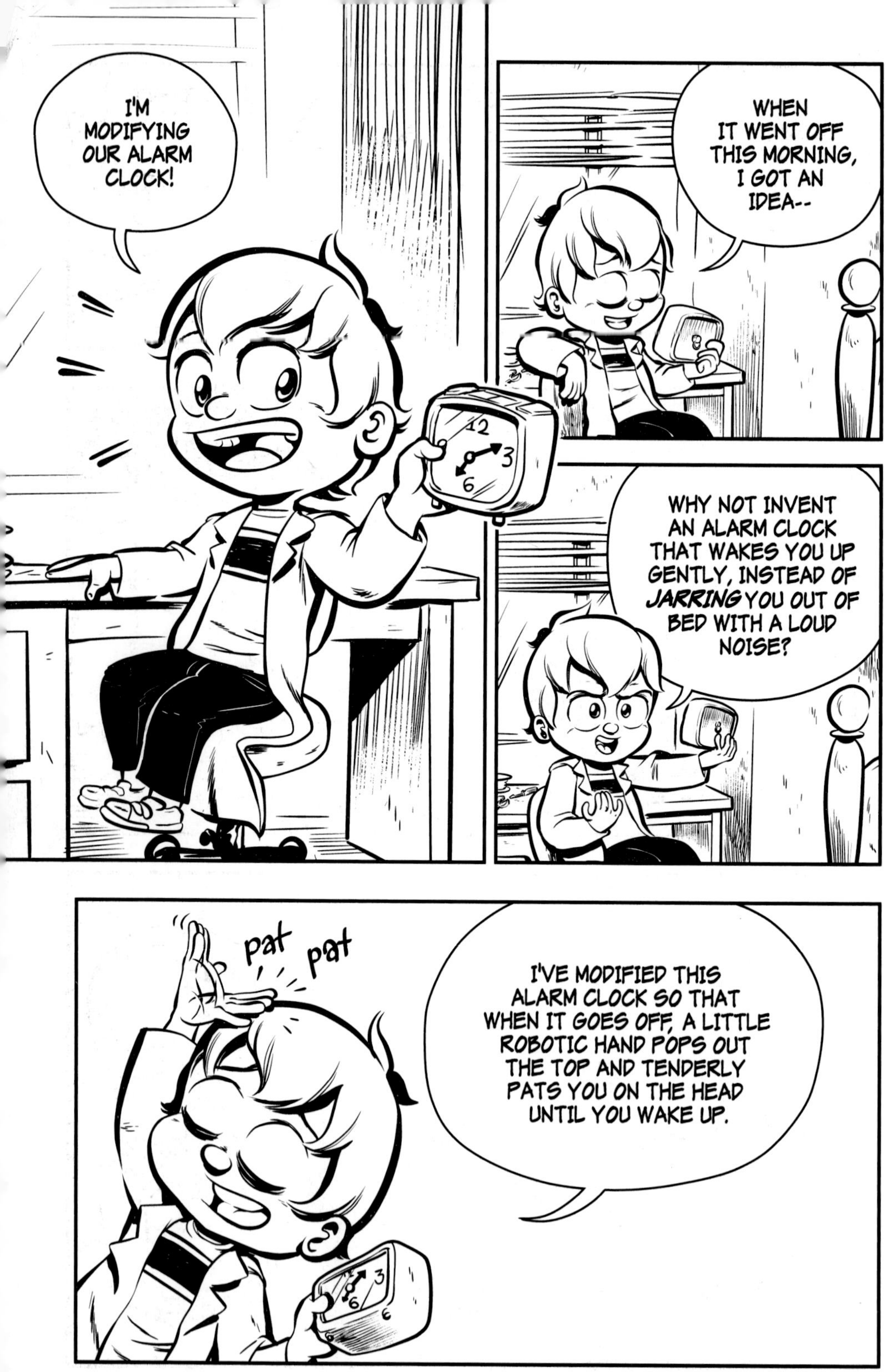
I'M MODIFYING OUR ALARM CLOCK!
WHEN IT WENT OFF THIS MORNING, I GOT AN IDEA--
WHY NOT INVENT AN ALARM CLOCK THAT WAKES YOU UP GENTLY, INSTEAD OF *JARRING* YOU OUT OF BED WITH A LOUD NOISE?
pat pat
I'VE MODIFIED THIS ALARM CLOCK SO THAT WHEN IT GOES OFF, A LITTLE ROBOTIC HAND POPS OUT THE TOP AND TENDERLY PATS YOU ON THE HEAD UNTIL YOU WAKE UP.

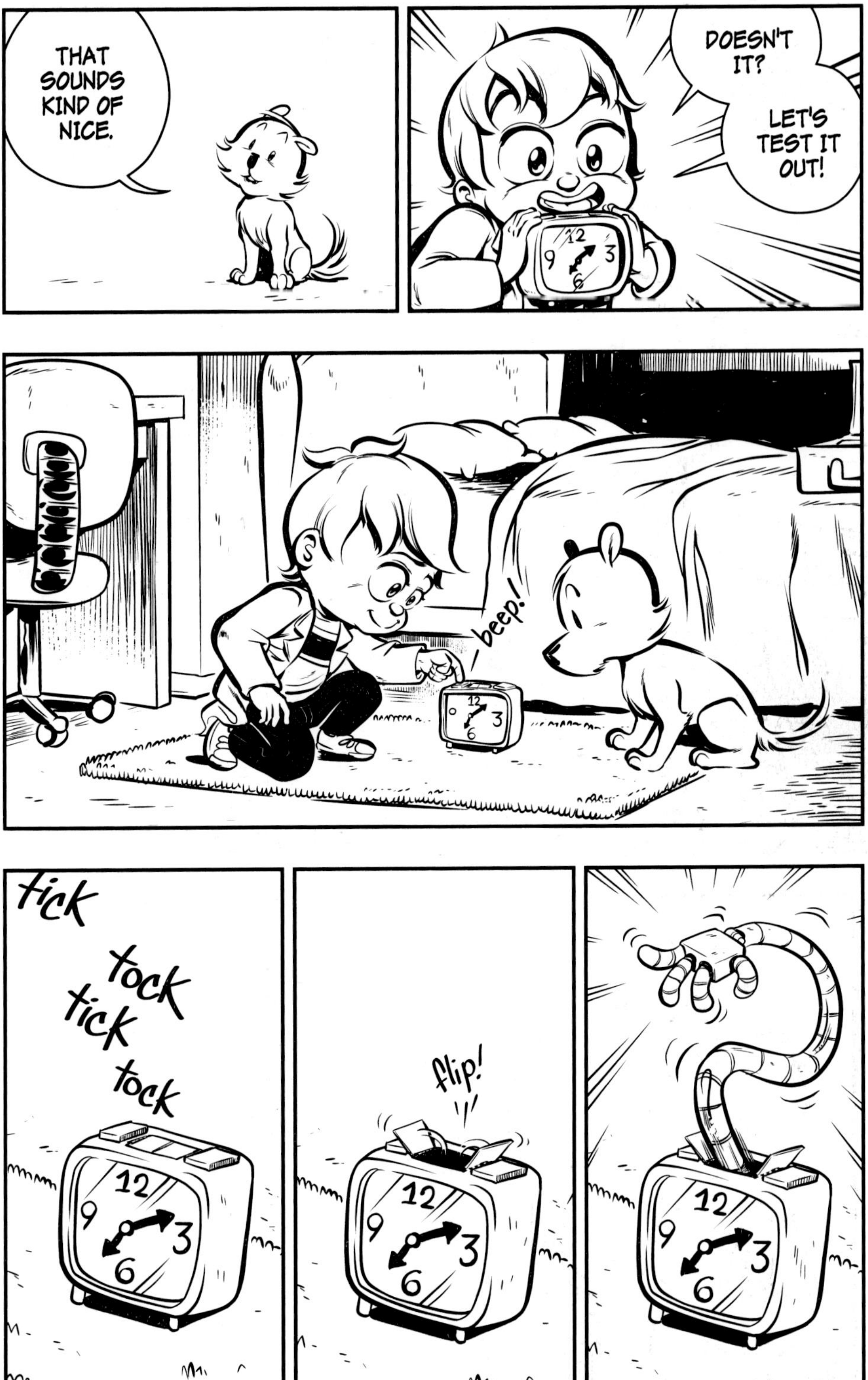
THAT SOUNDS KIND OF NICE.
DOESN'T IT?
LET'S TEST IT OUT!
beep!
tick
tock
tick
tock
flip!

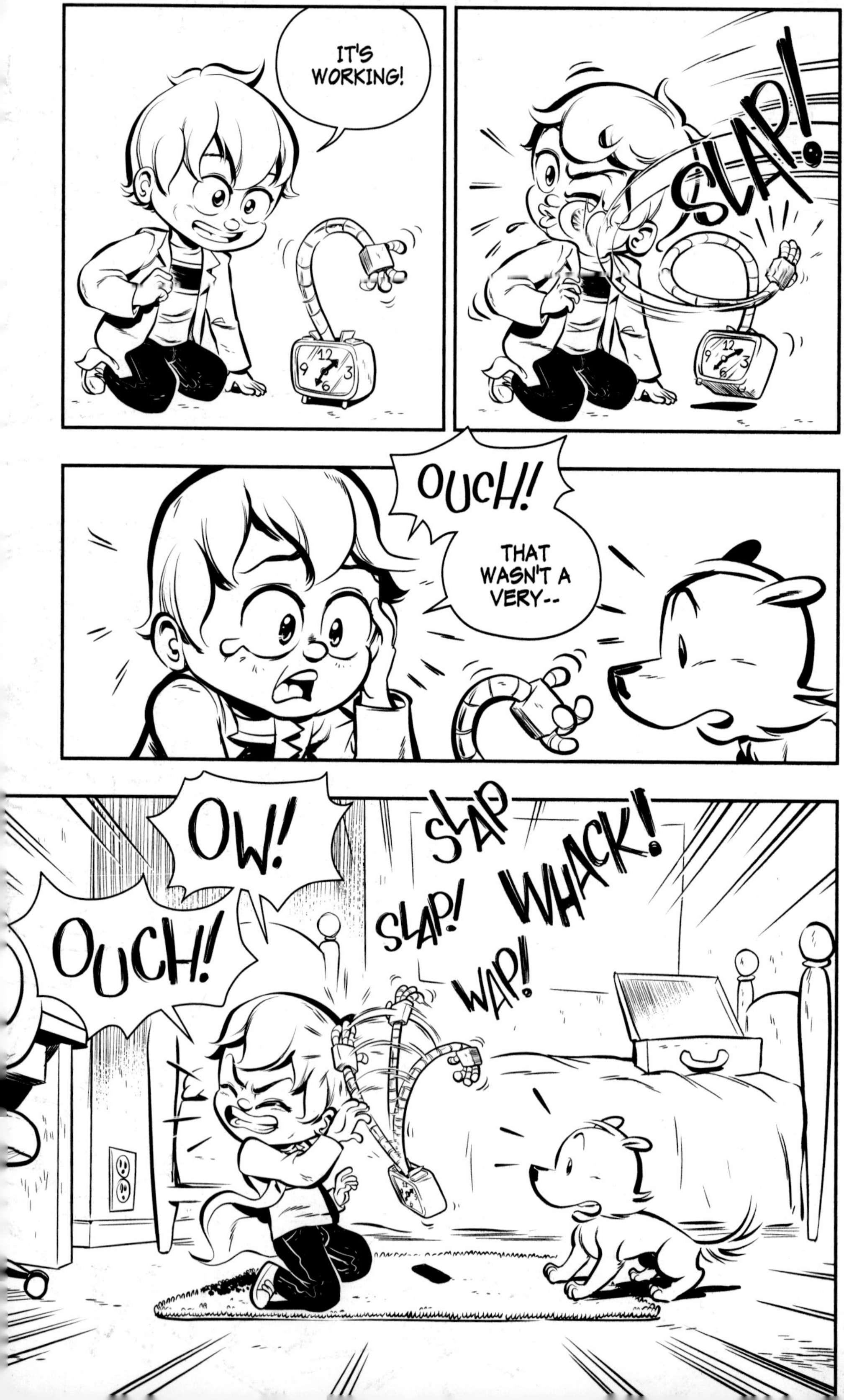
IT'S WORKING!
SLAP!
OUCH!
THAT WASN'T A VERY--
OW!
OUCH!
SLAP
SLAP!
WHACK!
WAP!

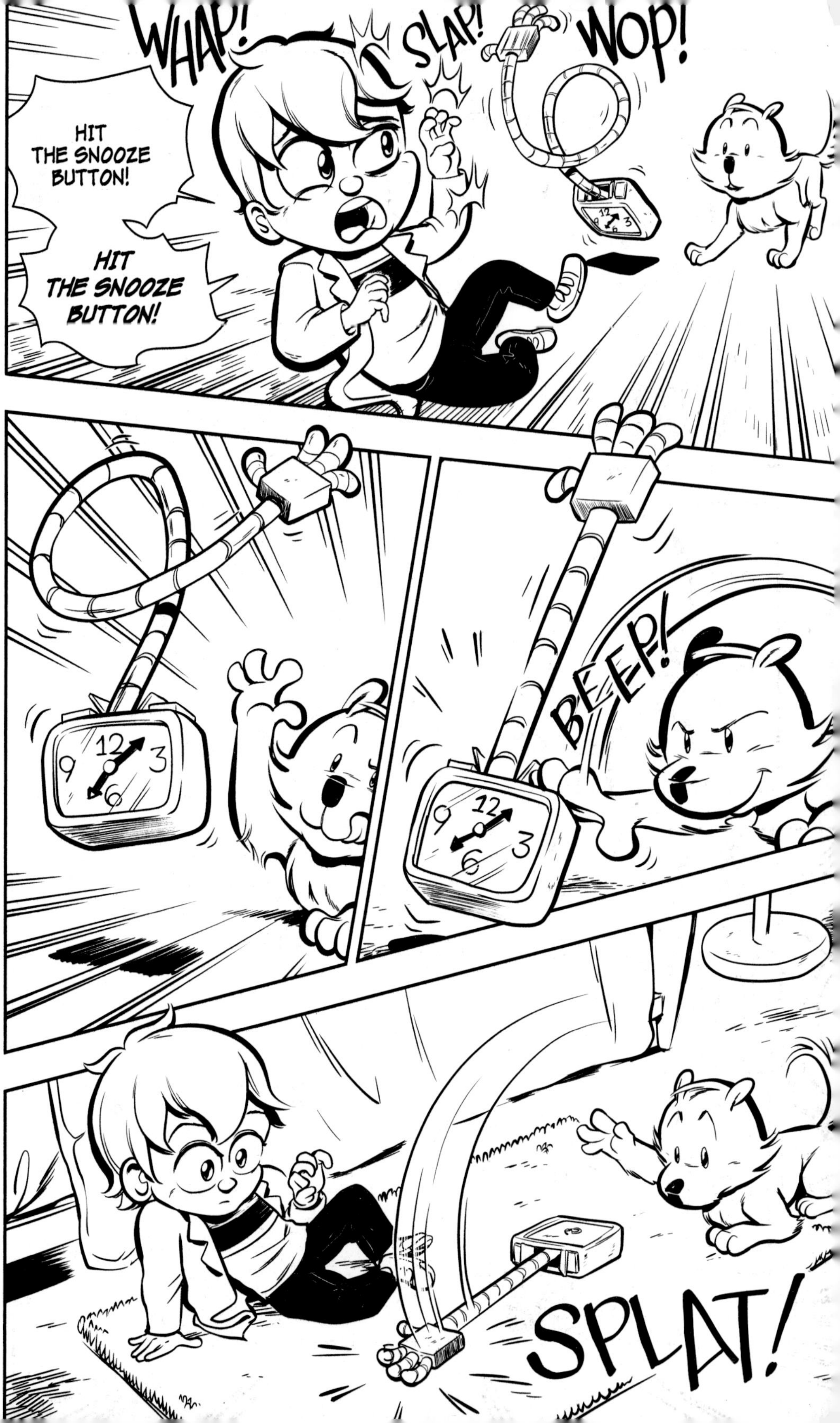
WHAP!
SLAP!
WOP!
HIT THE SNOOZE BUTTON!
HIT THE SNOOZE BUTTON!
BEEP!
SPLAT!

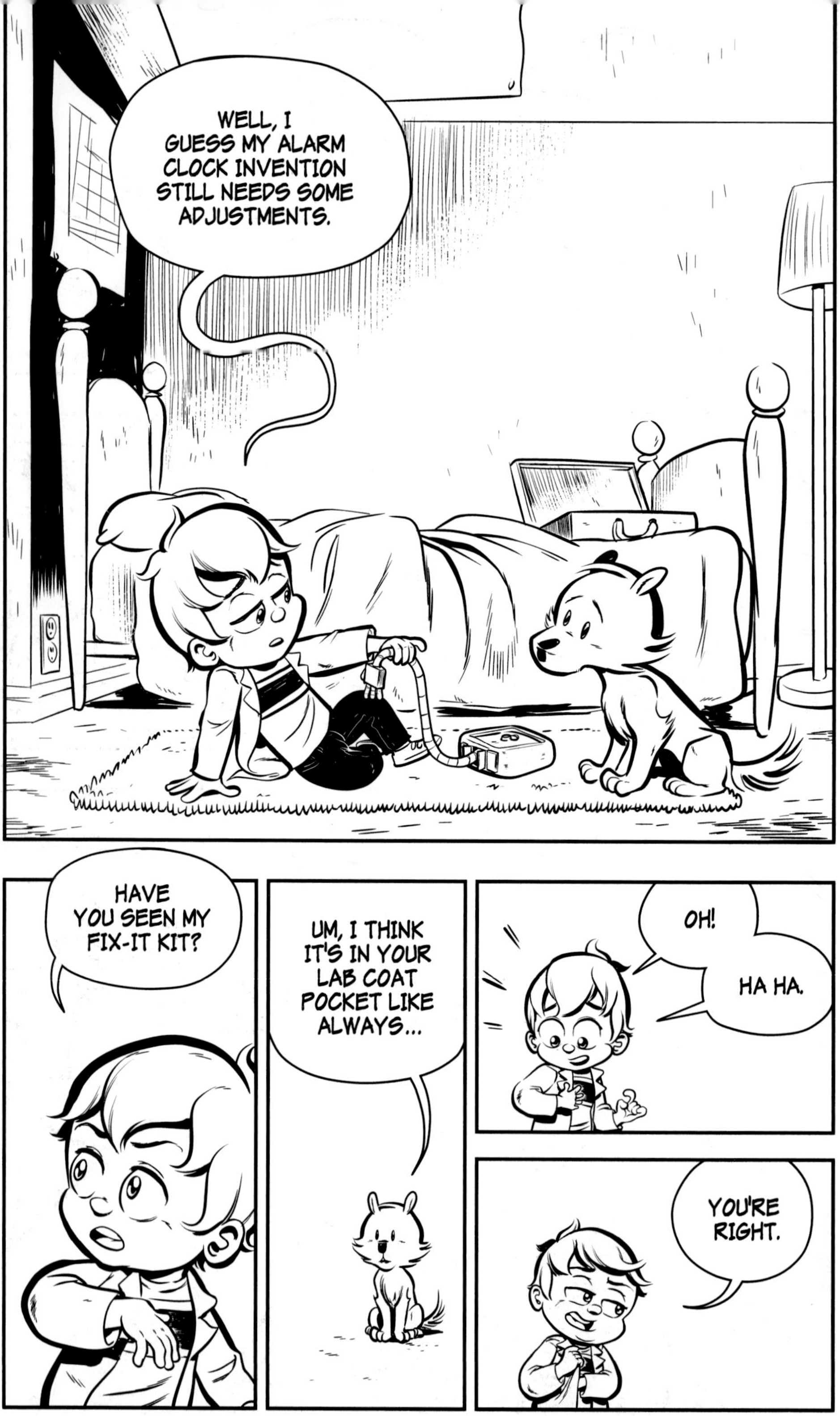
WELL, I GUESS MY ALARM CLOCK INVENTION STILL NEEDS SOME ADJUSTMENTS.
HAVE YOU SEEN MY FIX-IT KIT?
UM, I THINK IT'S IN YOUR LAB COAT POCKET LIKE ALWAYS...
OH!
HA HA.
YOU'RE RIGHT.

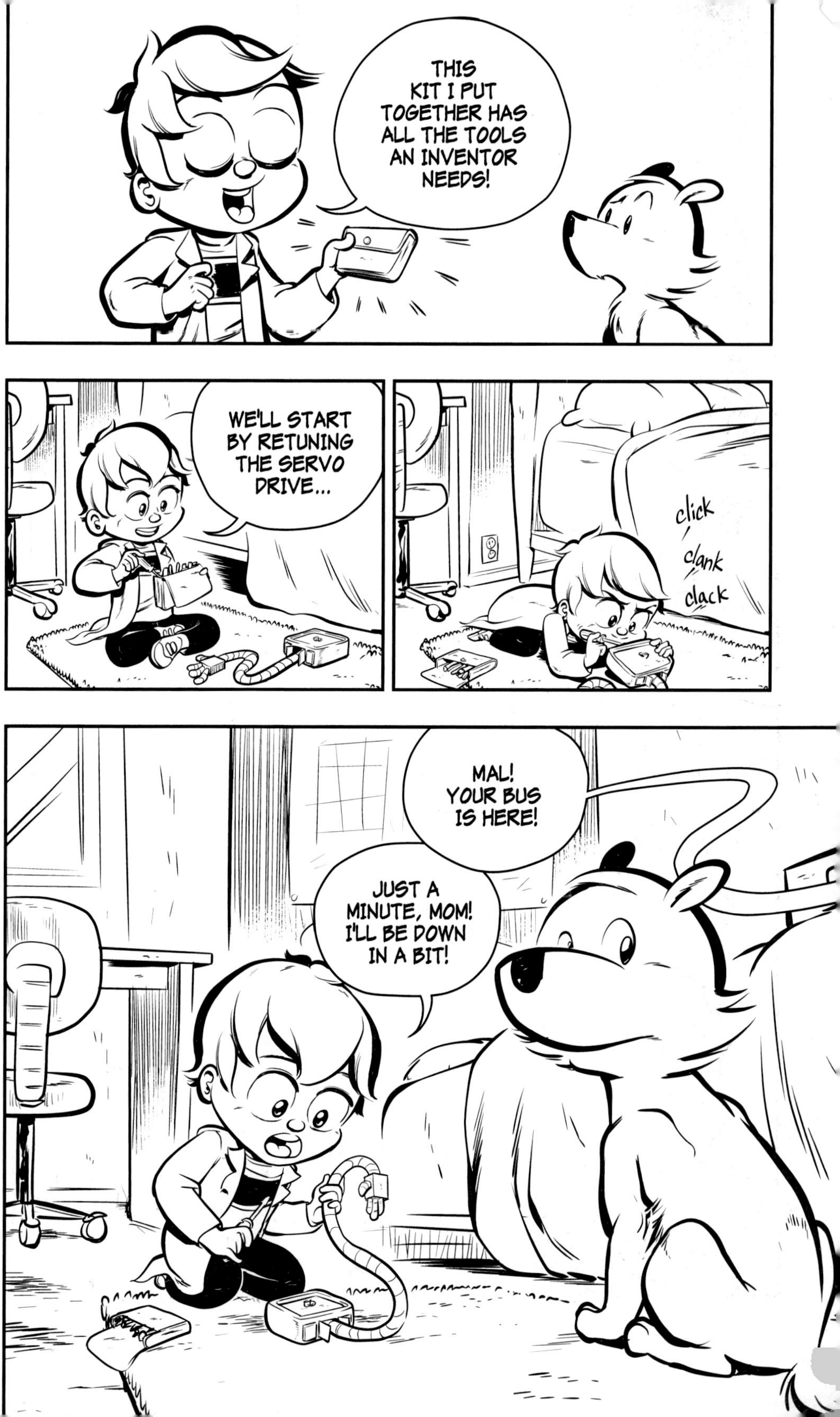
THIS KIT I PUT TOGETHER HAS ALL THE TOOLS AN INVENTOR NEEDS!
WE'LL START BY RETUNING THE SERVO DRIVE...
click
clank
clack
MAL! YOUR BUS IS HERE!
JUST A MINUTE, MOM! I'LL BE DOWN IN A BIT!

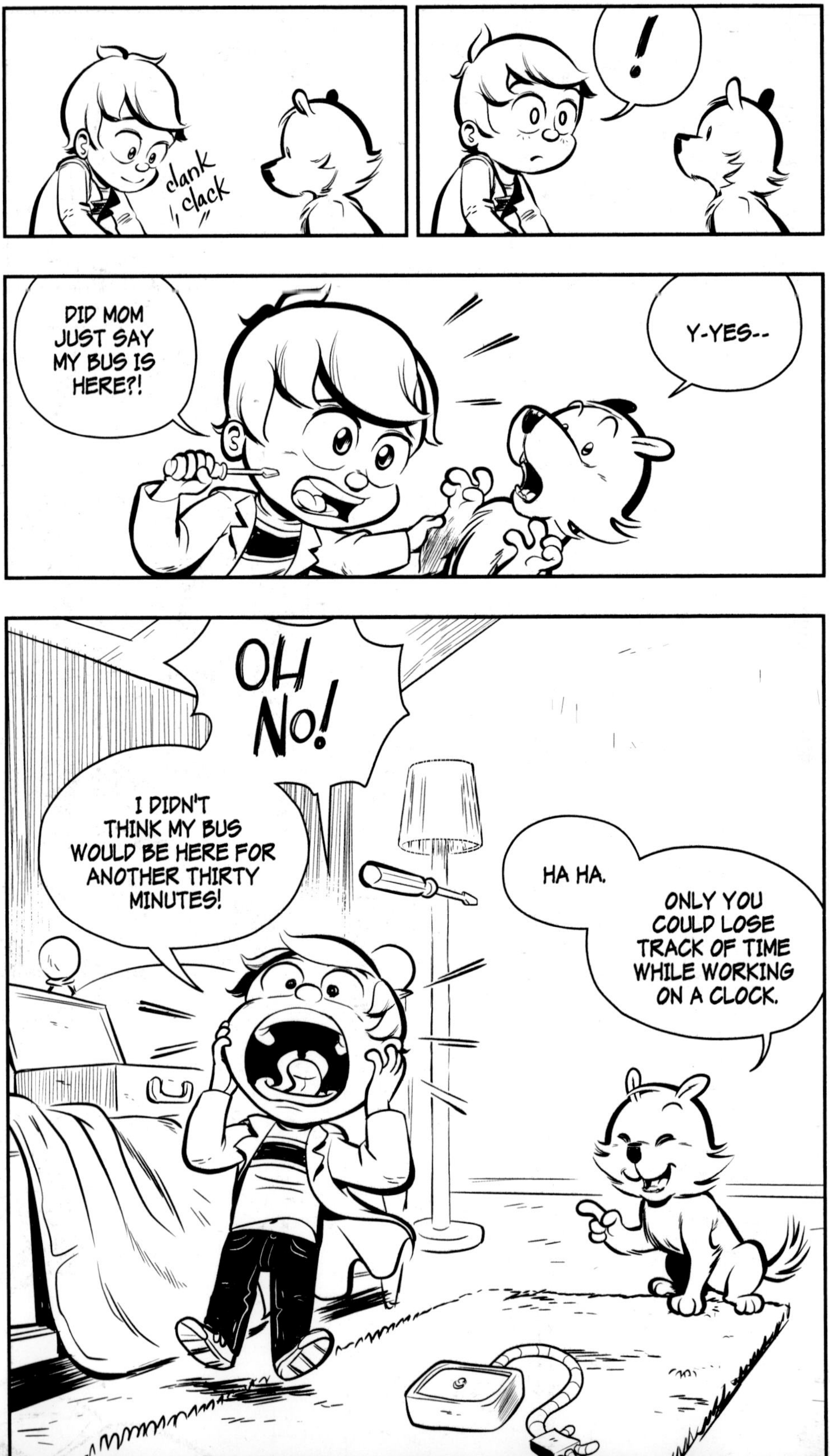
clank clack
!
DID MOM JUST SAY MY BUS IS HERE?!
Y-YES--
OH NO!
I DIDN'T THINK MY BUS WOULD BE HERE FOR ANOTHER THIRTY MINUTES!
HA HA.
ONLY YOU COULD LOSE TRACK OF TIME WHILE WORKING ON A CLOCK.

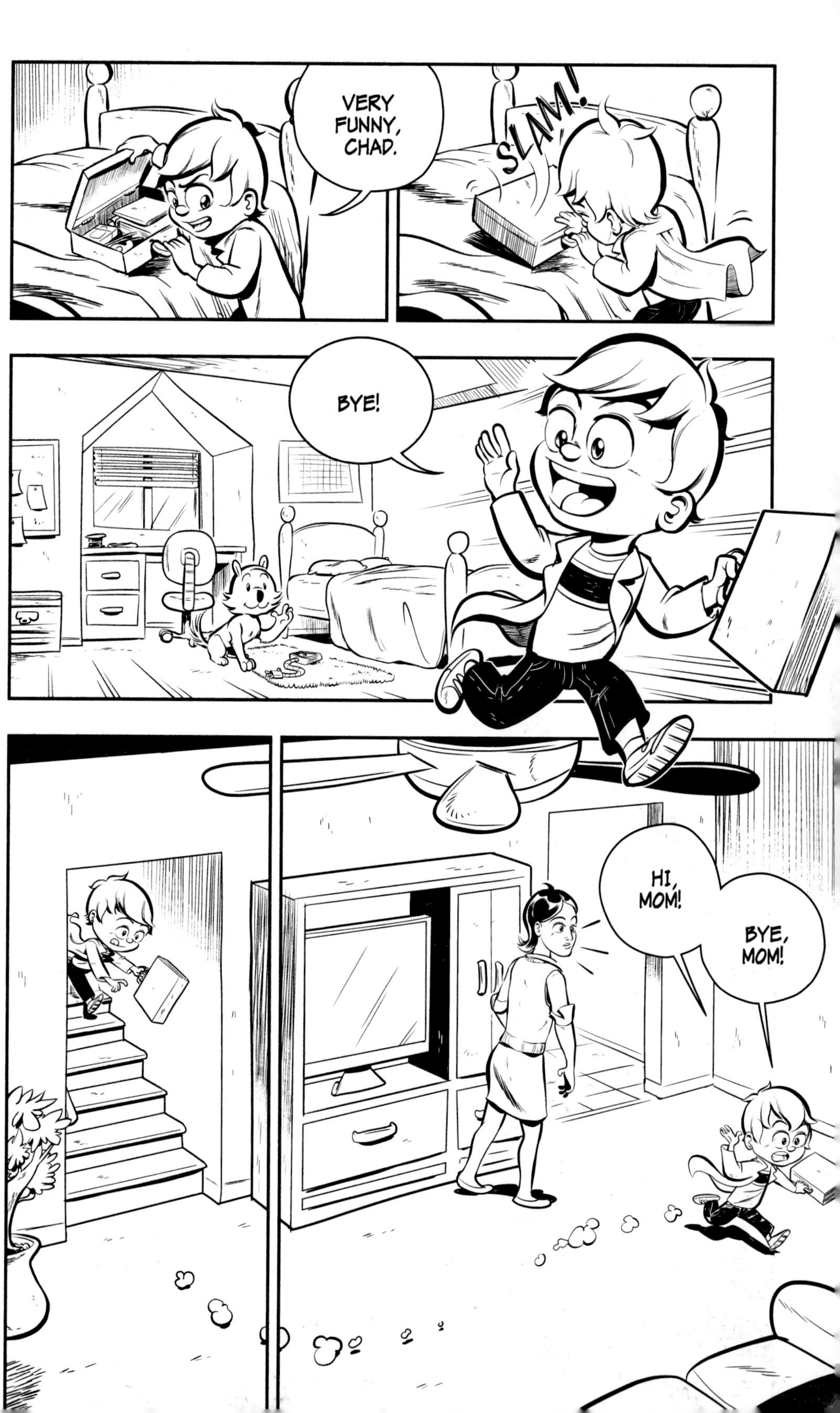
VERY FUNNY, CHAD.
SLAM!
BYE!
HI, MOM!
BYE, MOM!

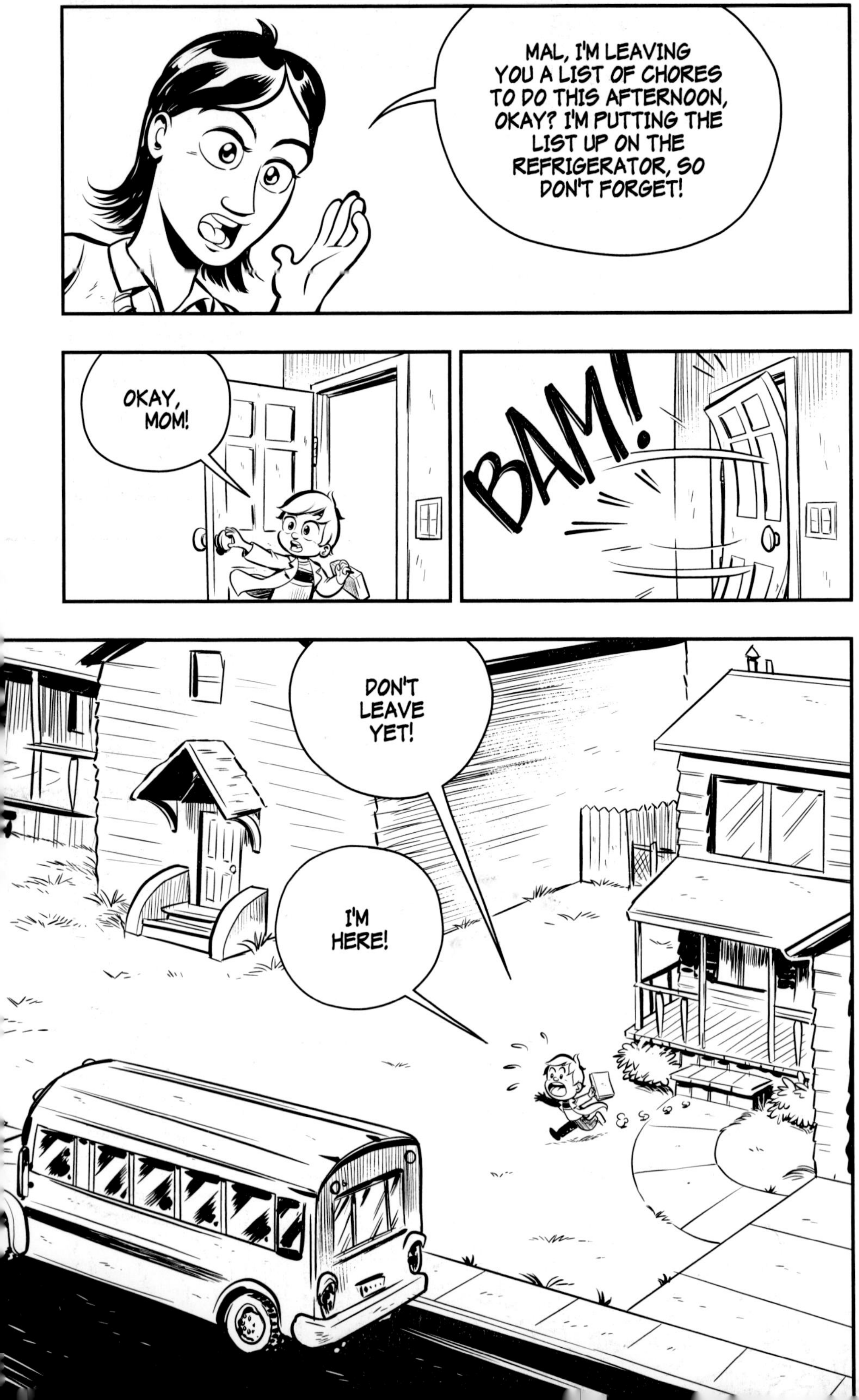
MAL, I'M LEAVING YOU A LIST OF CHORES TO DO THIS AFTERNOON, OKAY? I'M PUTTING THE LIST UP ON THE REFRIGERATOR, SO DON'T FORGET!
OKAY, MOM!
BAM!
DON'T LEAVE YET!
I'M HERE!

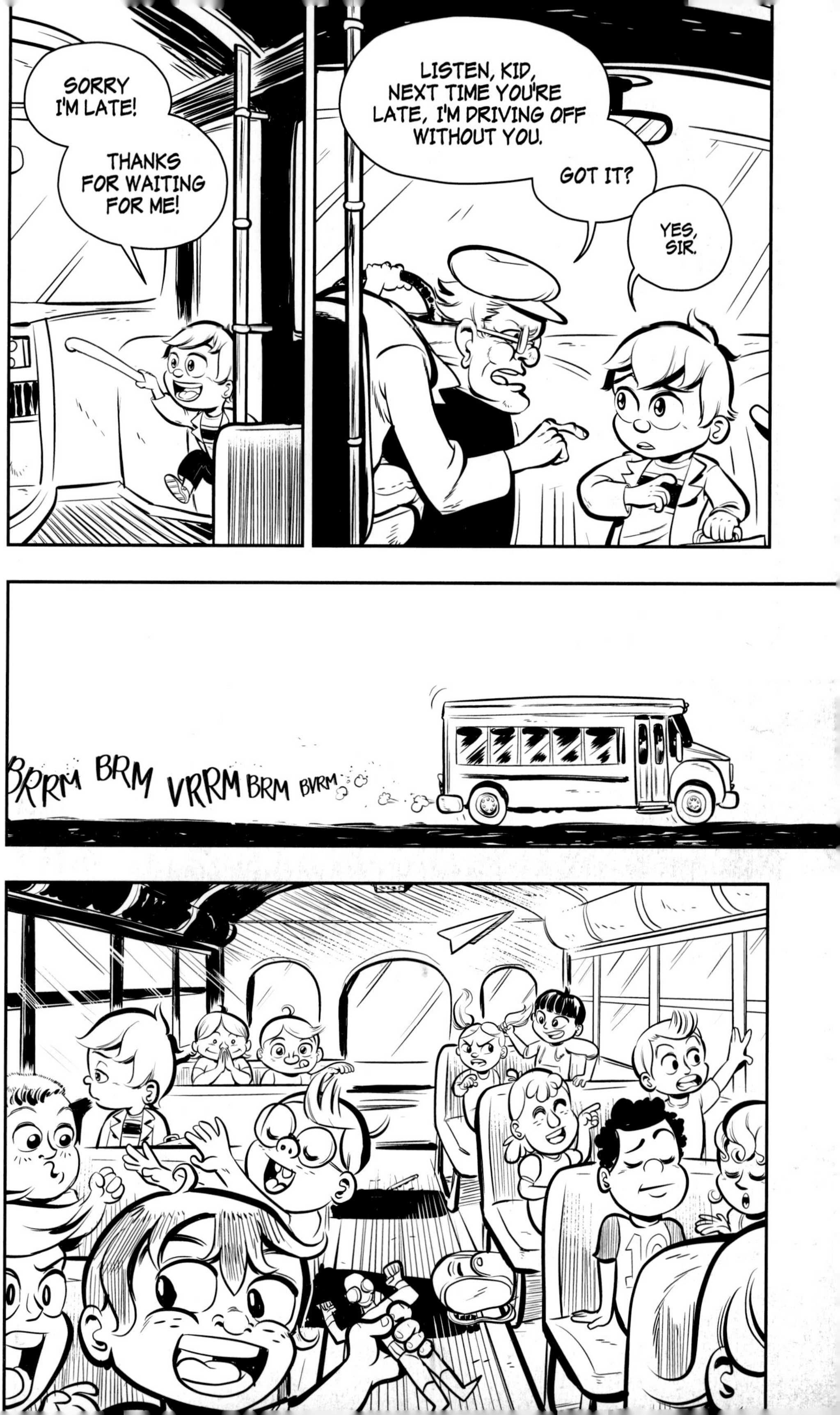
SORRY I'M LATE!
THANKS FOR WAITING FOR ME!
LISTEN, KID, NEXT TIME YOU'RE LATE, I'M DRIVING OFF WITHOUT YOU.
GOT IT?
YES, SIR.
BRRM BRM VRRM BRM BVRM

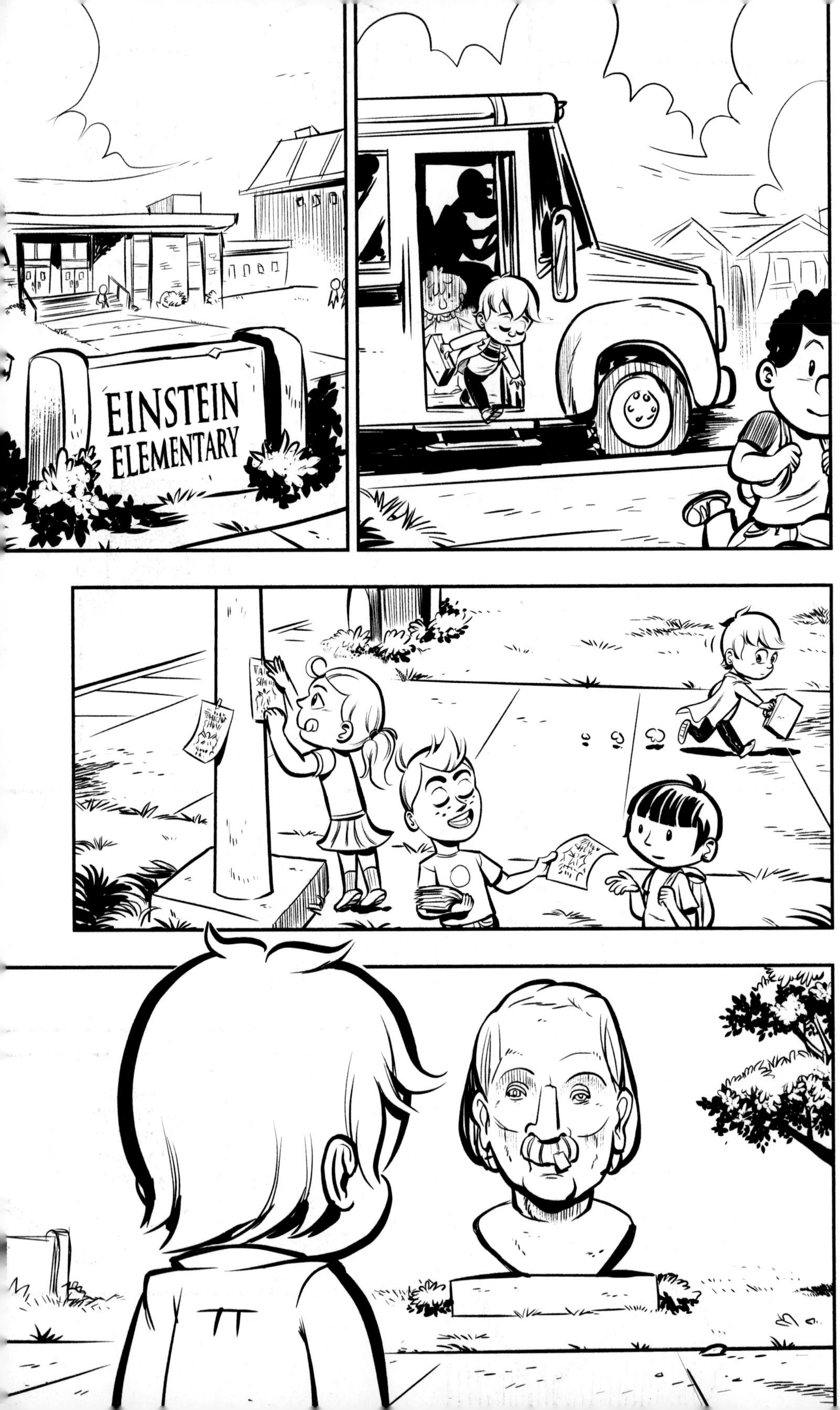
EINSTEIN
ELEMENTARY

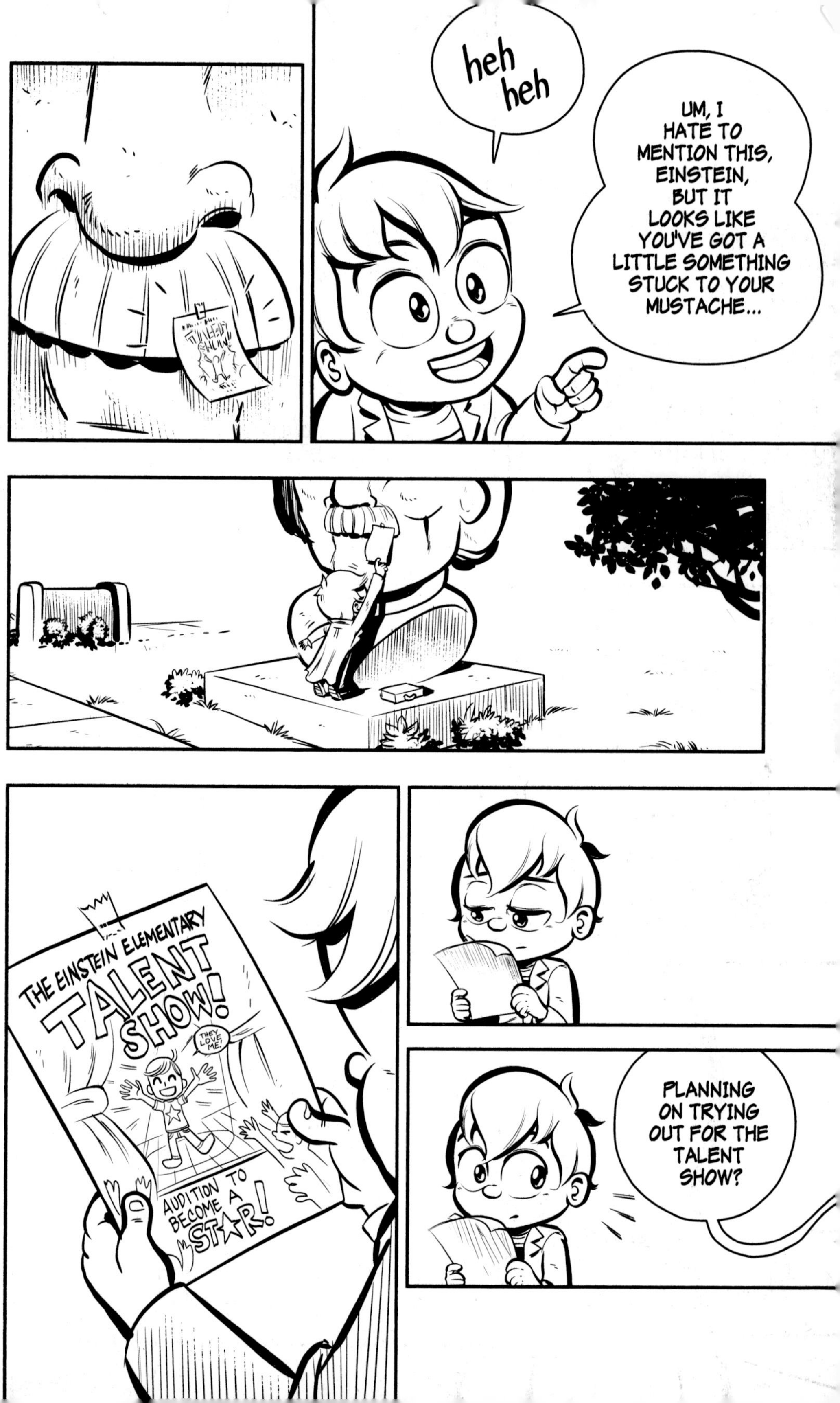
heh heh
UM, I HATE TO MENTION THIS, EINSTEIN, BUT IT LOOKS LIKE YOU'VE GOT A LITTLE SOMETHING STUCK TO YOUR MUSTACHE...
THE EINSTEIN ELEMENTARY TALENT SHOW!
THEY LOVE ME!
AUDITION TO BECOME A STAR!
PLANNING ON TRYING OUT FOR THE TALENT SHOW?

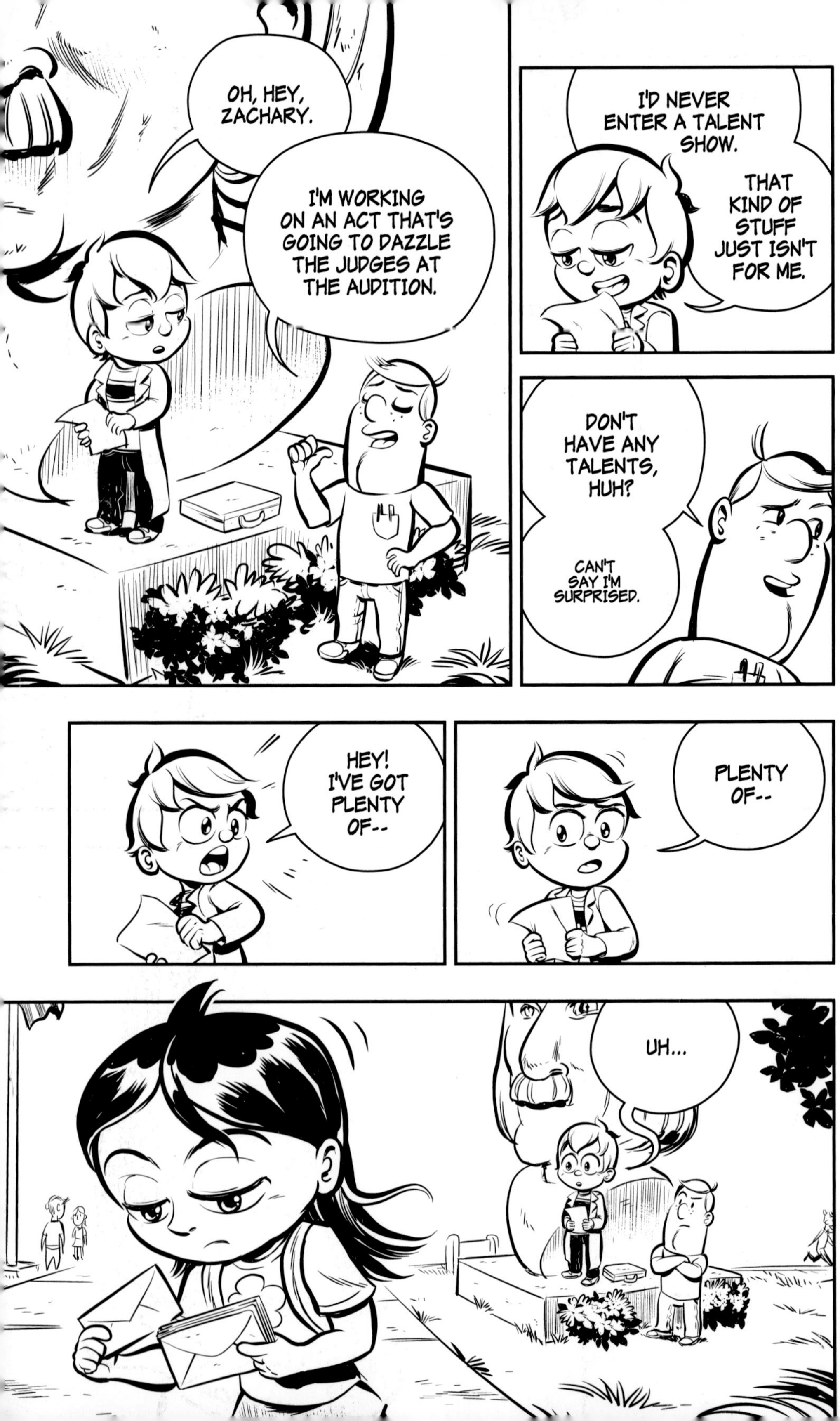
OH, HEY, ZACHARY.
I'M WORKING ON AN ACT THAT'S GOING TO DAZZLE THE JUDGES AT THE AUDITION.
I'D NEVER ENTER A TALENT SHOW.
THAT KIND OF STUFF JUST ISN'T FOR ME.
DON'T HAVE ANY TALENTS, HUH?
CAN'T SAY I'M SURPRISED.
HEY! I'VE GOT PLENTY OF--
PLENTY OF--
UH...

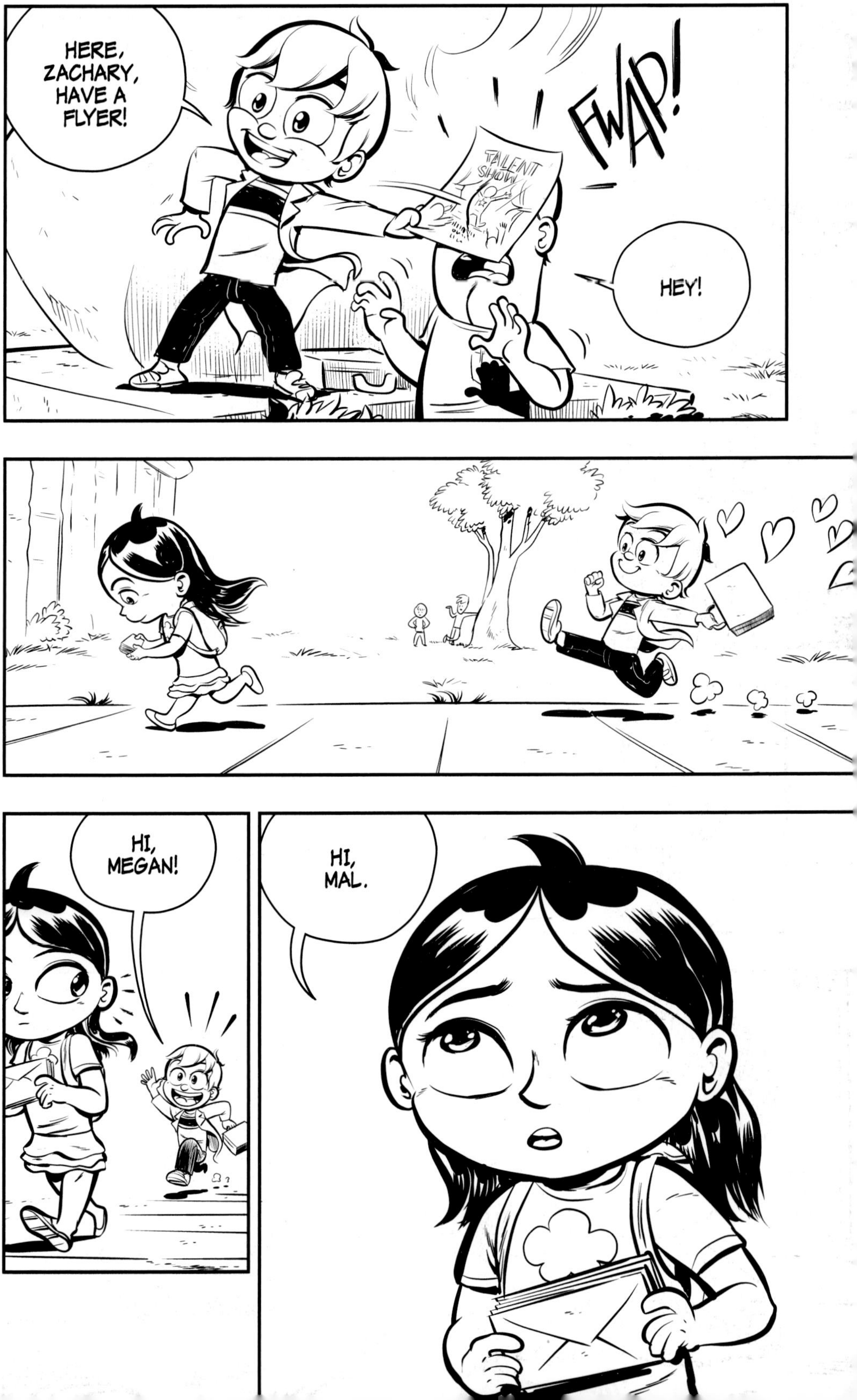
HERE, ZACHARY, HAVE A FLYER!
TALENT SHOW
FWAP!
HEY!
HI, MEGAN!
HI, MAL.

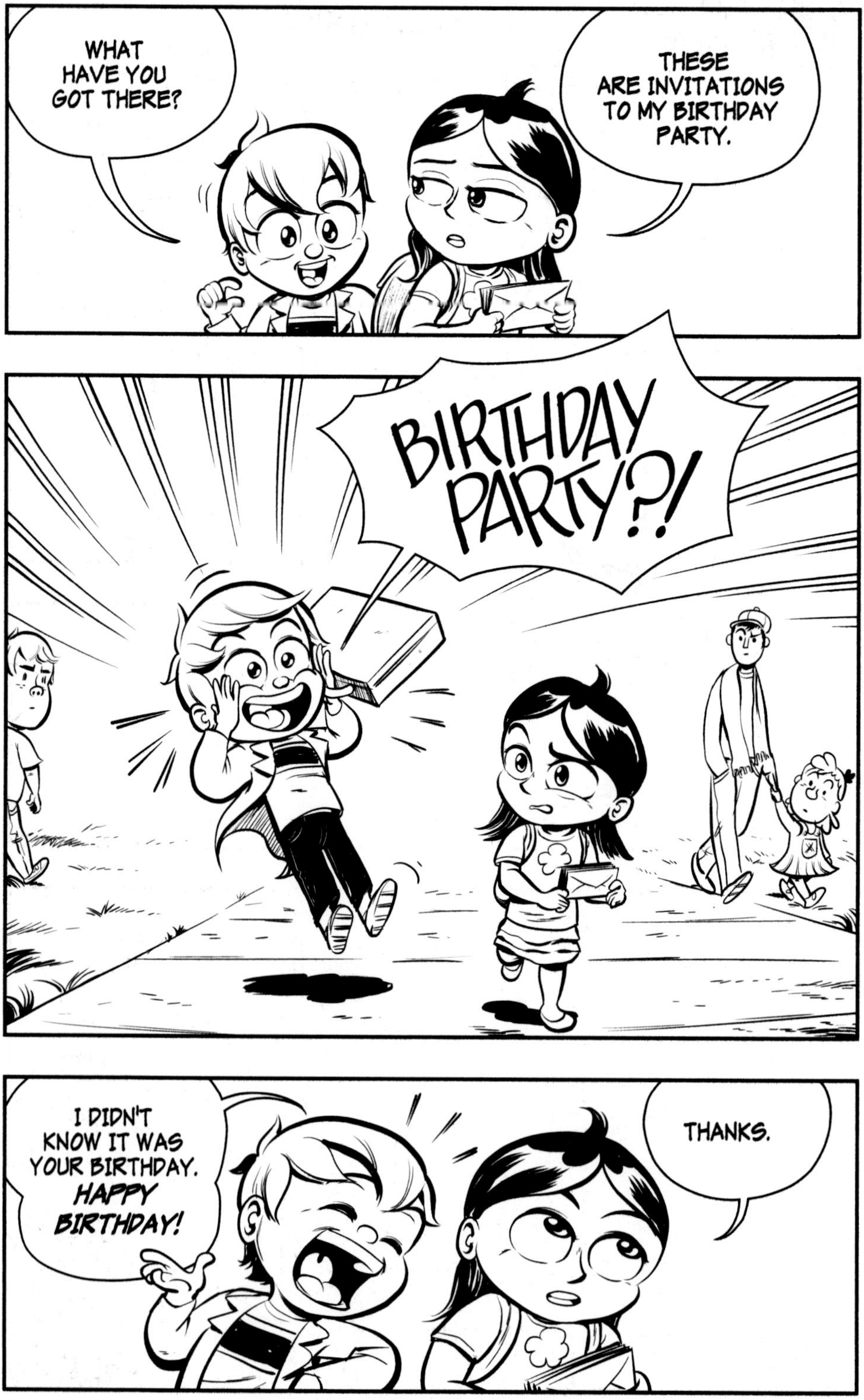
WHAT HAVE YOU GOT THERE?
THESE ARE INVITATIONS TO MY BIRTHDAY PARTY.
BIRTHDAY PARTY?!
I DIDN'T KNOW IT WAS YOUR BIRTHDAY. HAPPY BIRTHDAY!
THANKS.

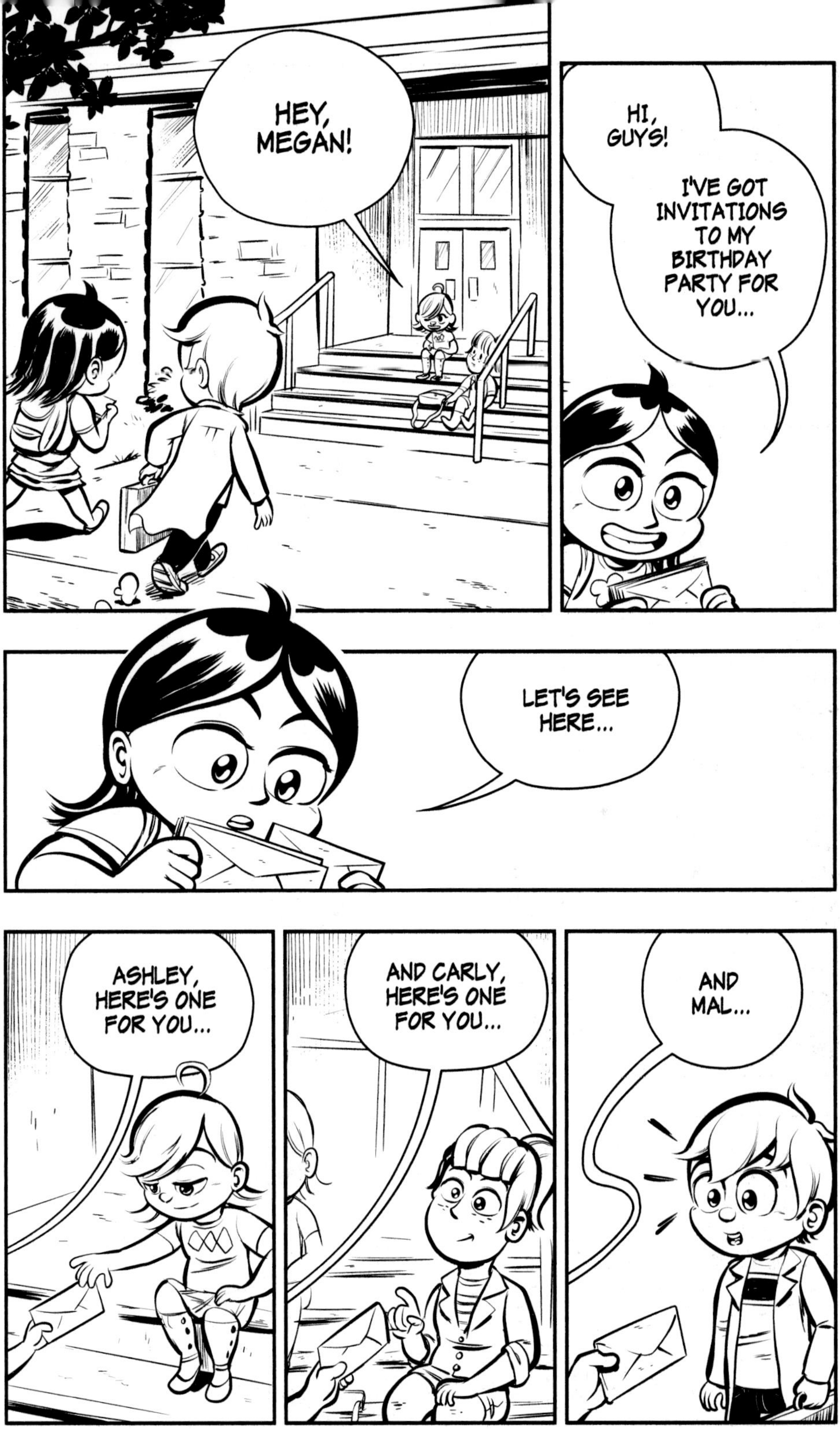
HEY, MEGAN!
HI, GUYS!
I'VE GOT INVITATIONS TO MY BIRTHDAY PARTY FOR YOU...
LET'S SEE HERE...
ASHLEY, HERE'S ONE FOR YOU...
AND CARLY, HERE'S ONE FOR YOU...
AND MAL...

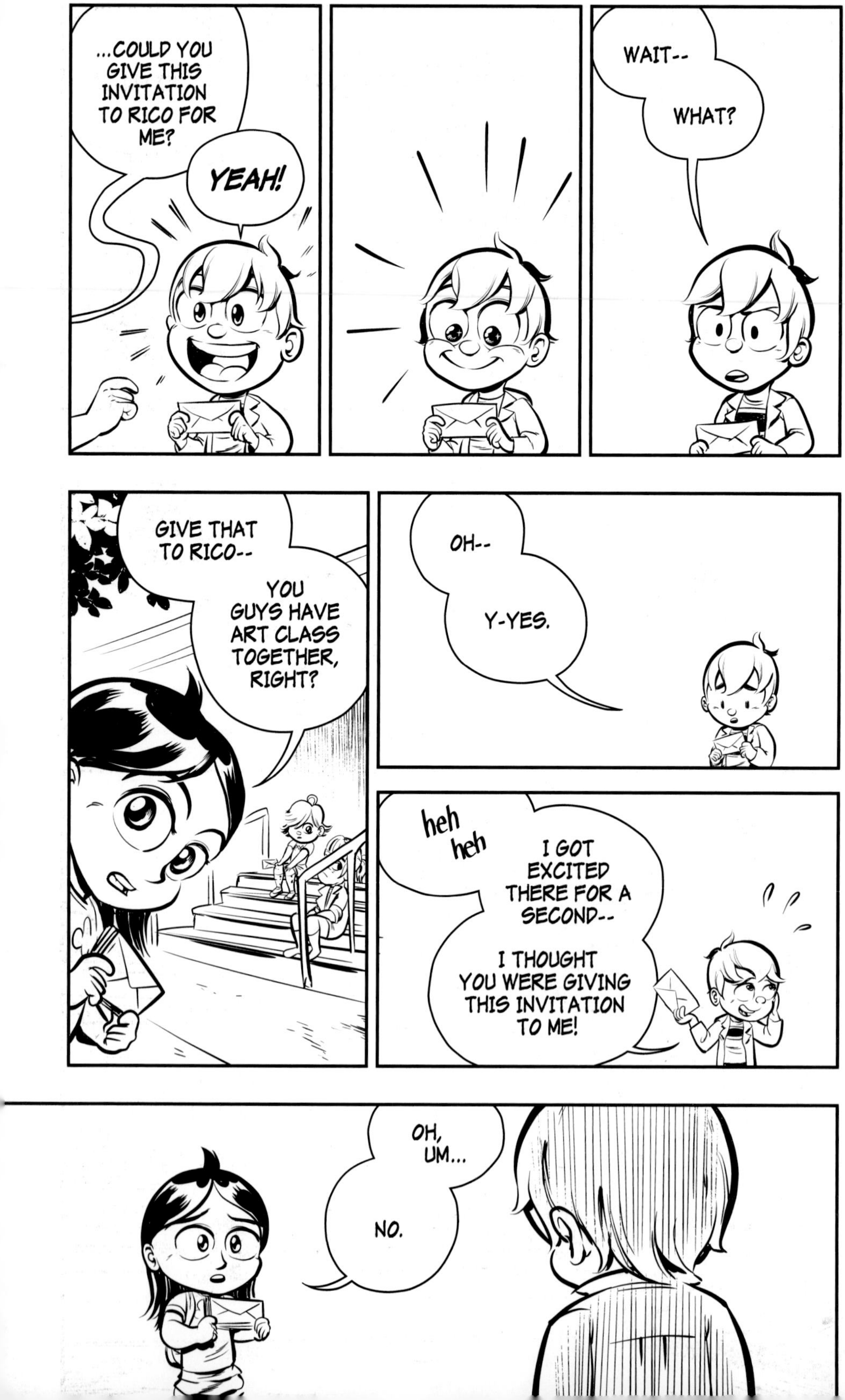
...COULD YOU GIVE THIS INVITATION TO RICO FOR ME?
YEAH!
WAIT--
WHAT?
GIVE THAT TO RICO--
YOU GUYS HAVE ART CLASS TOGETHER, RIGHT?
OH--
Y-YES.
heh heh
I GOT EXCITED THERE FOR A SECOND--
I THOUGHT YOU WERE GIVING THIS INVITATION TO ME!
OH, UM...
NO.

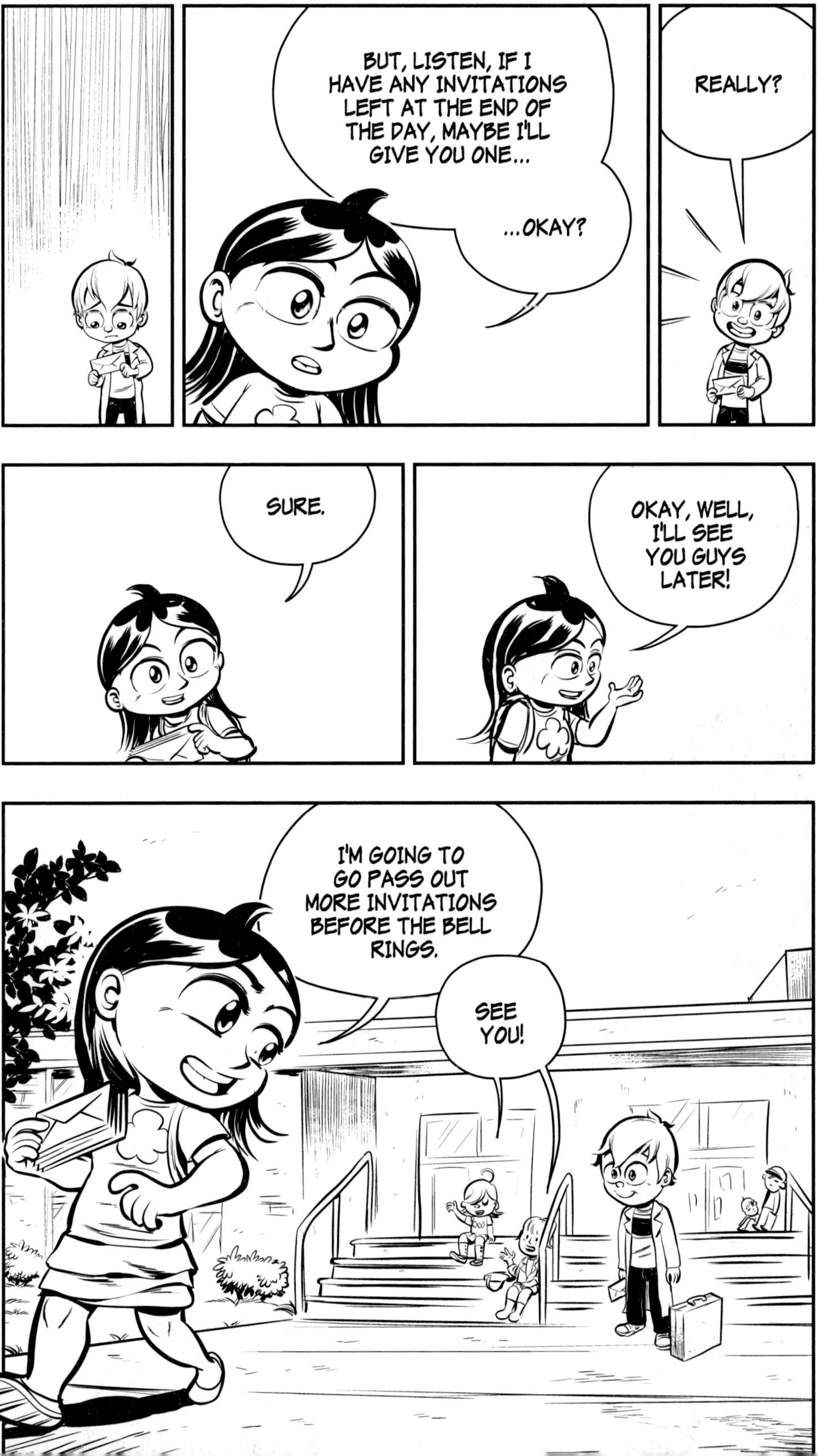
BUT, LISTEN, IF I HAVE ANY INVITATIONS LEFT AT THE END OF THE DAY, MAYBE I'LL GIVE YOU ONE...
...OKAY?
REALLY?
SURE.
OKAY, WELL, I'LL SEE YOU GUYS LATER!
I'M GOING TO GO PASS OUT MORE INVITATIONS BEFORE THE BELL RINGS.
SEE YOU!

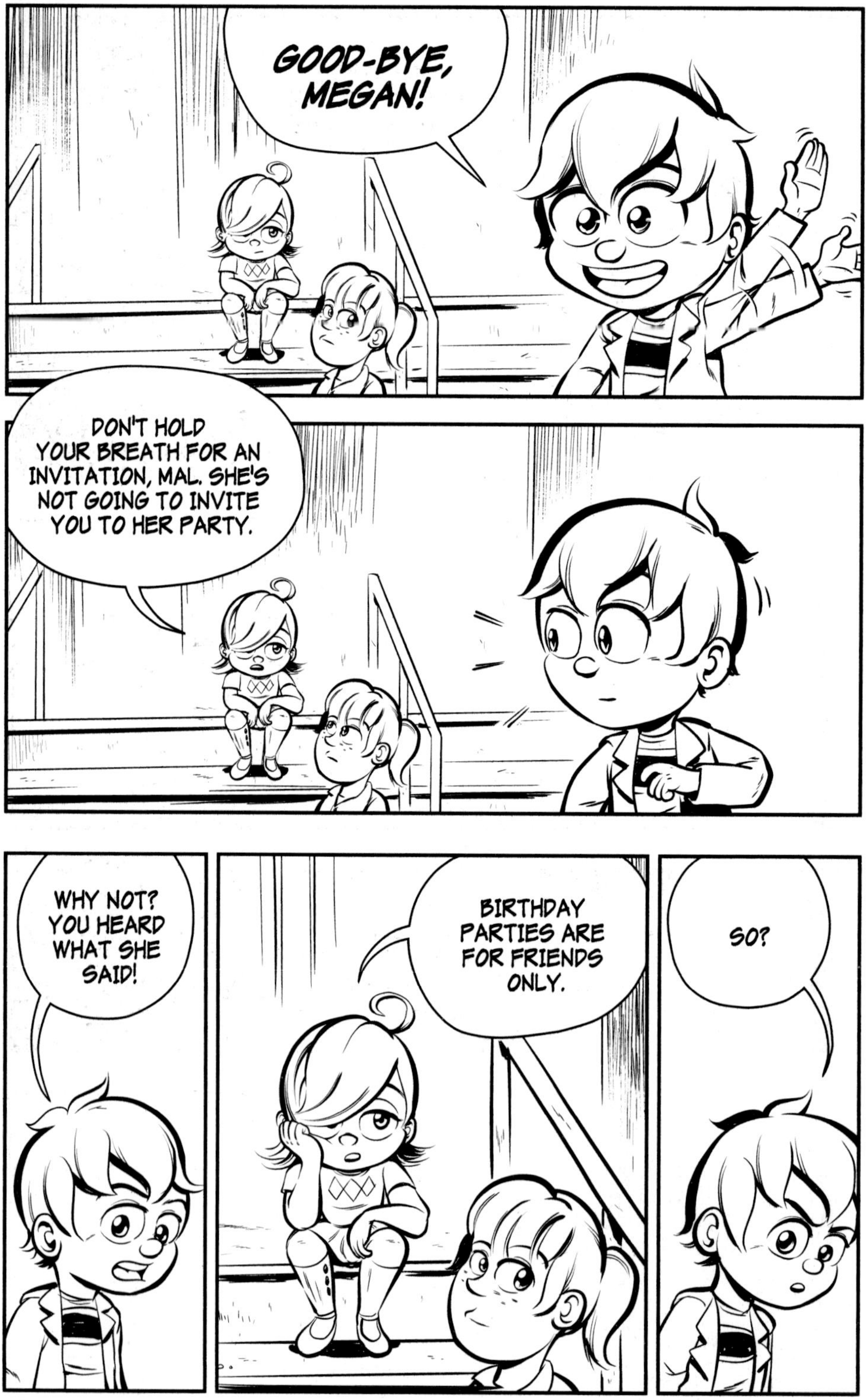
GOOD-BYE, MEGAN!
DON'T HOLD YOUR BREATH FOR AN INVITATION, MAL. SHE'S NOT GOING TO INVITE YOU TO HER PARTY.
WHY NOT? YOU HEARD WHAT SHE SAID!
BIRTHDAY PARTIES ARE FOR FRIENDS ONLY.
SO?

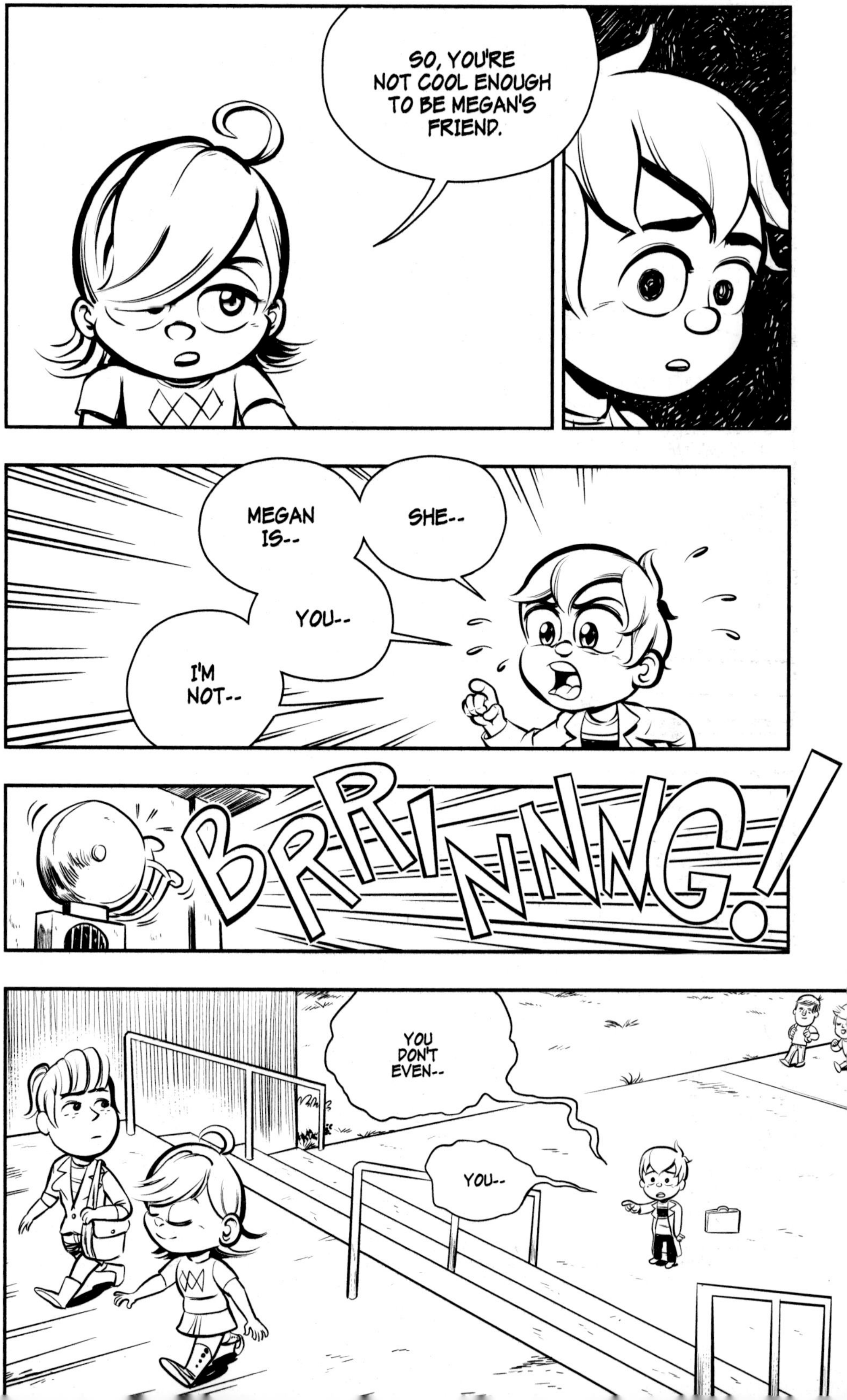
SO, YOU'RE NOT COOL ENOUGH TO BE MEGAN'S FRIEND.
MEGAN IS--
SHE--
YOU--
I'M NOT--
BRRINNNG!
YOU DON'T EVEN--
YOU--

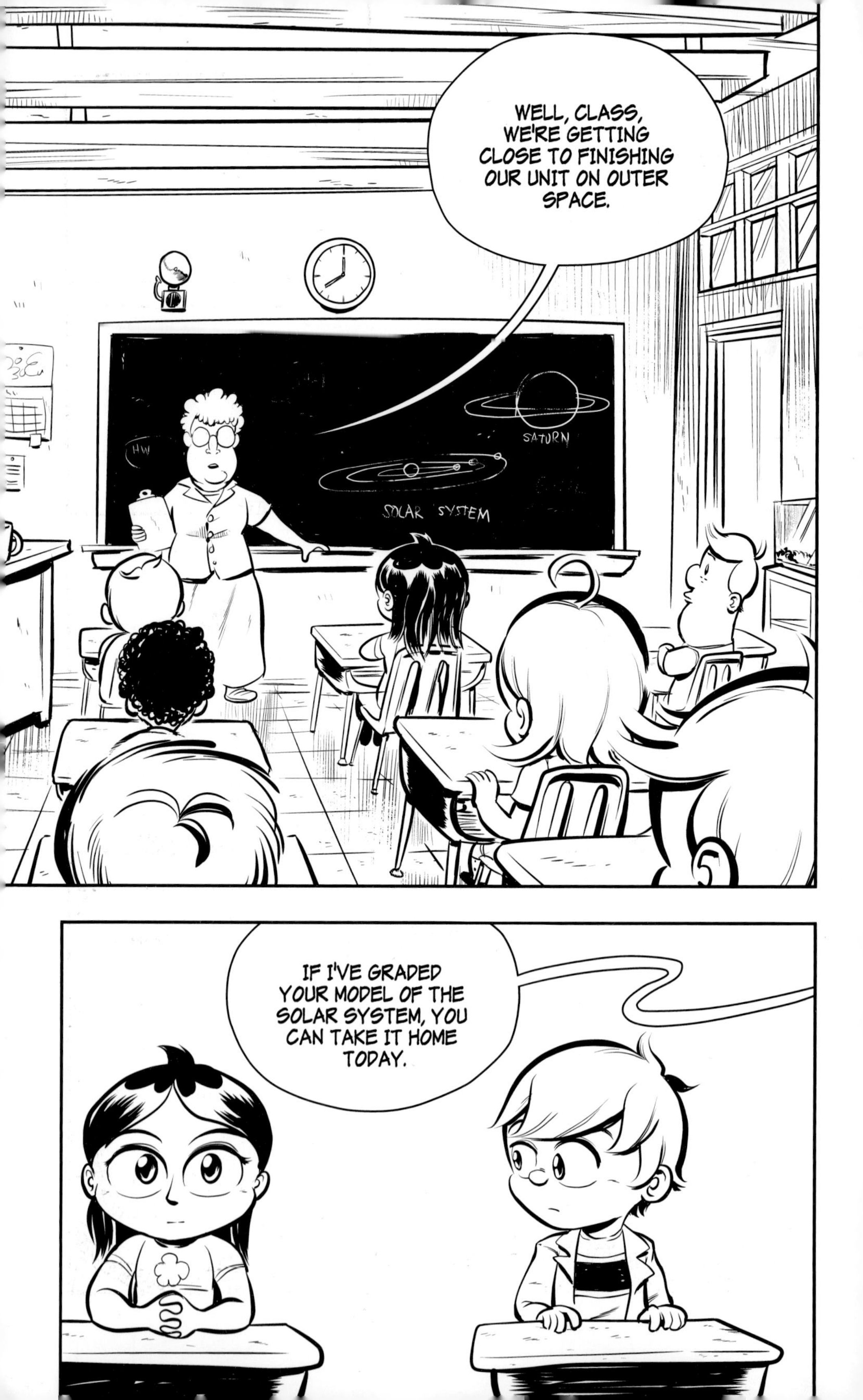
WELL, CLASS, WE'RE GETTING CLOSE TO FINISHING OUR UNIT ON OUTER SPACE.
SATURN
SOLAR SYSTEM
HW
IF I'VE GRADED YOUR MODEL OF THE SOLAR SYSTEM, YOU CAN TAKE IT HOME TODAY.

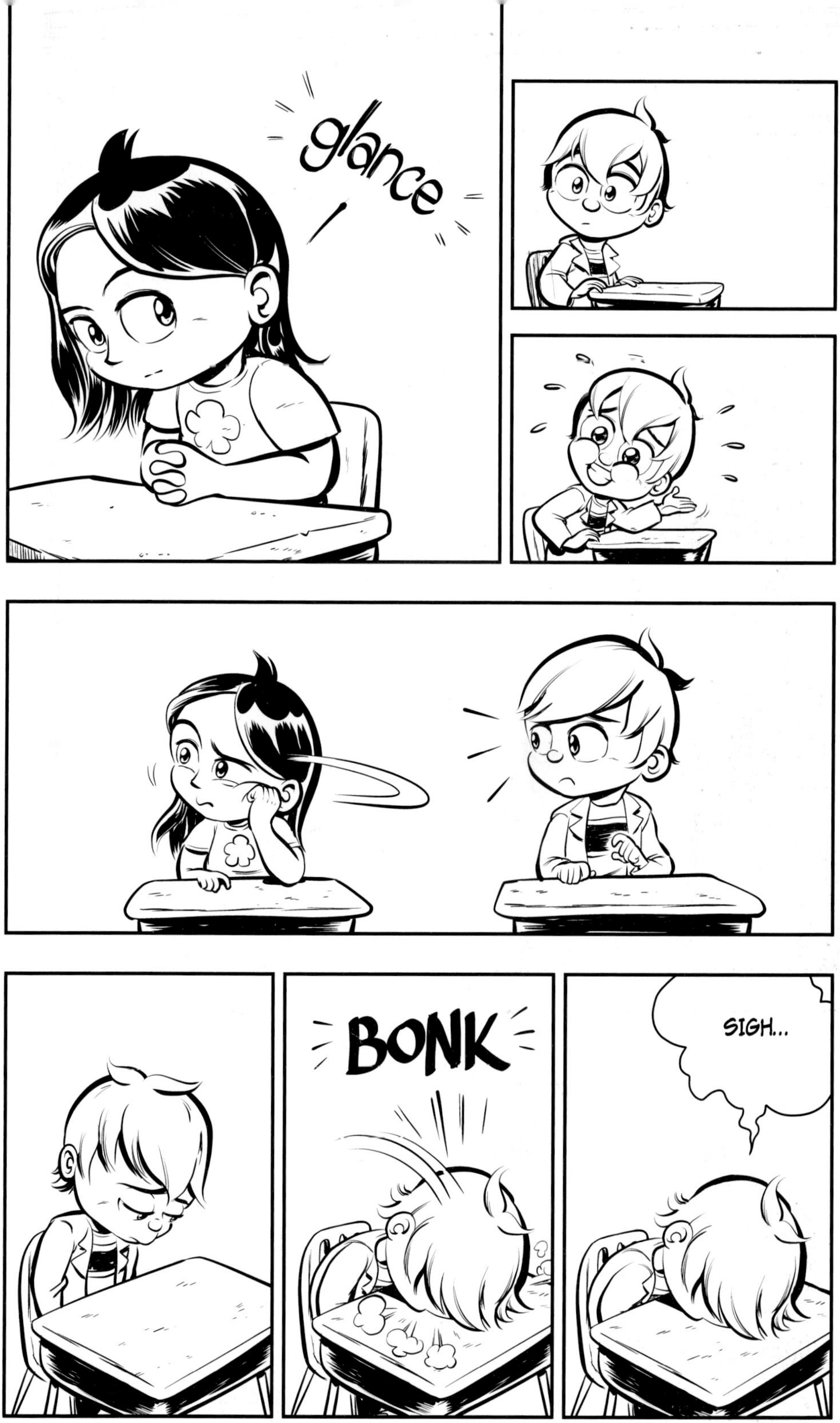
glance
BONK
SIGH...

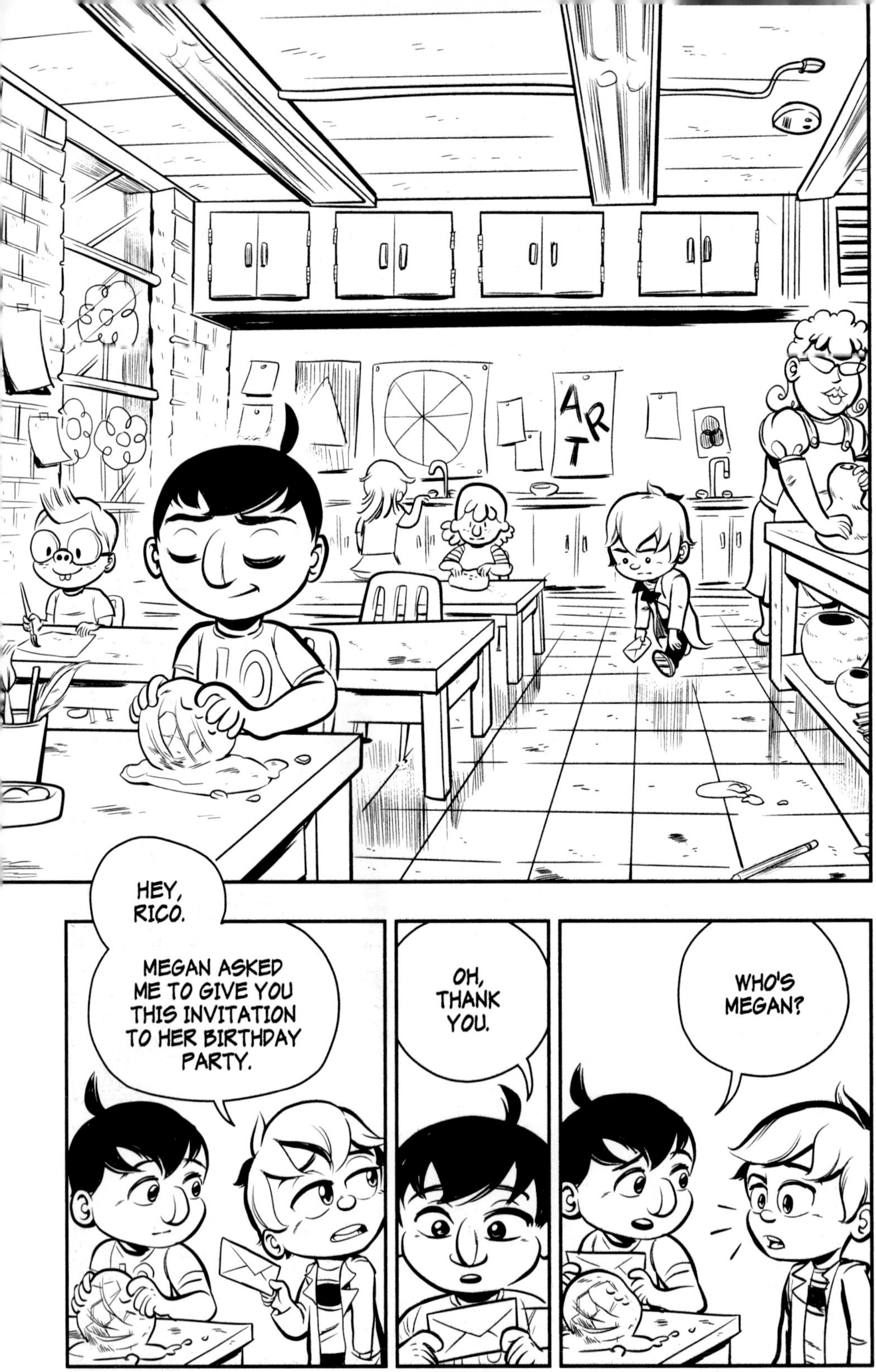
ART
HEY, RICO.
MEGAN ASKED ME TO GIVE YOU THIS INVITATION TO HER BIRTHDAY PARTY.
OH, THANK YOU.
WHO'S MEGAN?

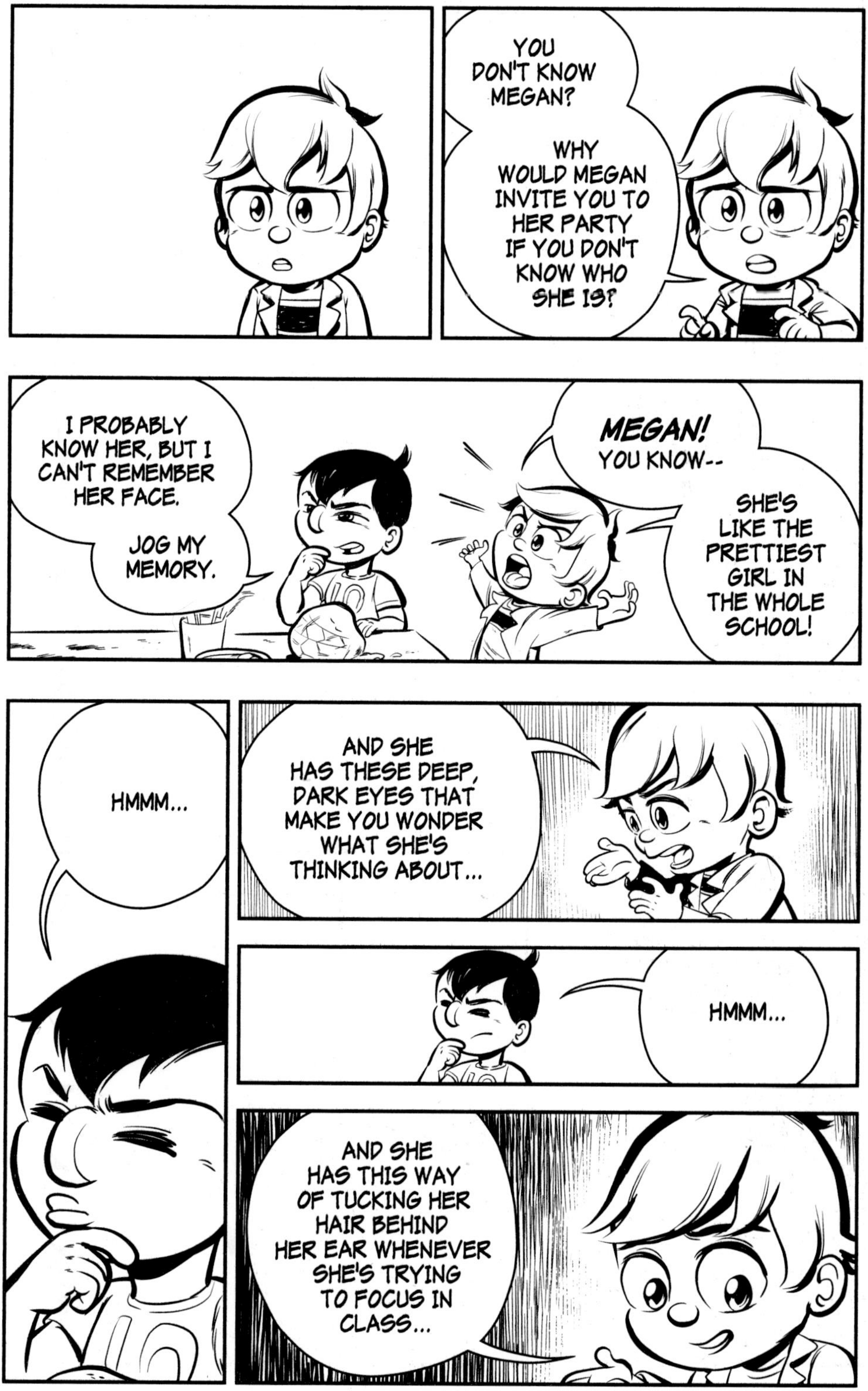
YOU DON'T KNOW MEGAN?
WHY WOULD MEGAN INVITE YOU TO HER PARTY IF YOU DON'T KNOW WHO SHE IS?
I PROBABLY KNOW HER, BUT I CAN'T REMEMBER HER FACE.
JOG MY MEMORY.
MEGAN! YOU KNOW--
SHE'S LIKE THE PRETTIEST GIRL IN THE WHOLE SCHOOL!
HMMM...
AND SHE HAS THESE DEEP, DARK EYES THAT MAKE YOU WONDER WHAT SHE'S THINKING ABOUT...
HMMM...
AND SHE HAS THIS WAY OF TUCKING HER HAIR BEHIND HER EAR WHENEVER SHE'S TRYING TO FOCUS IN CLASS...

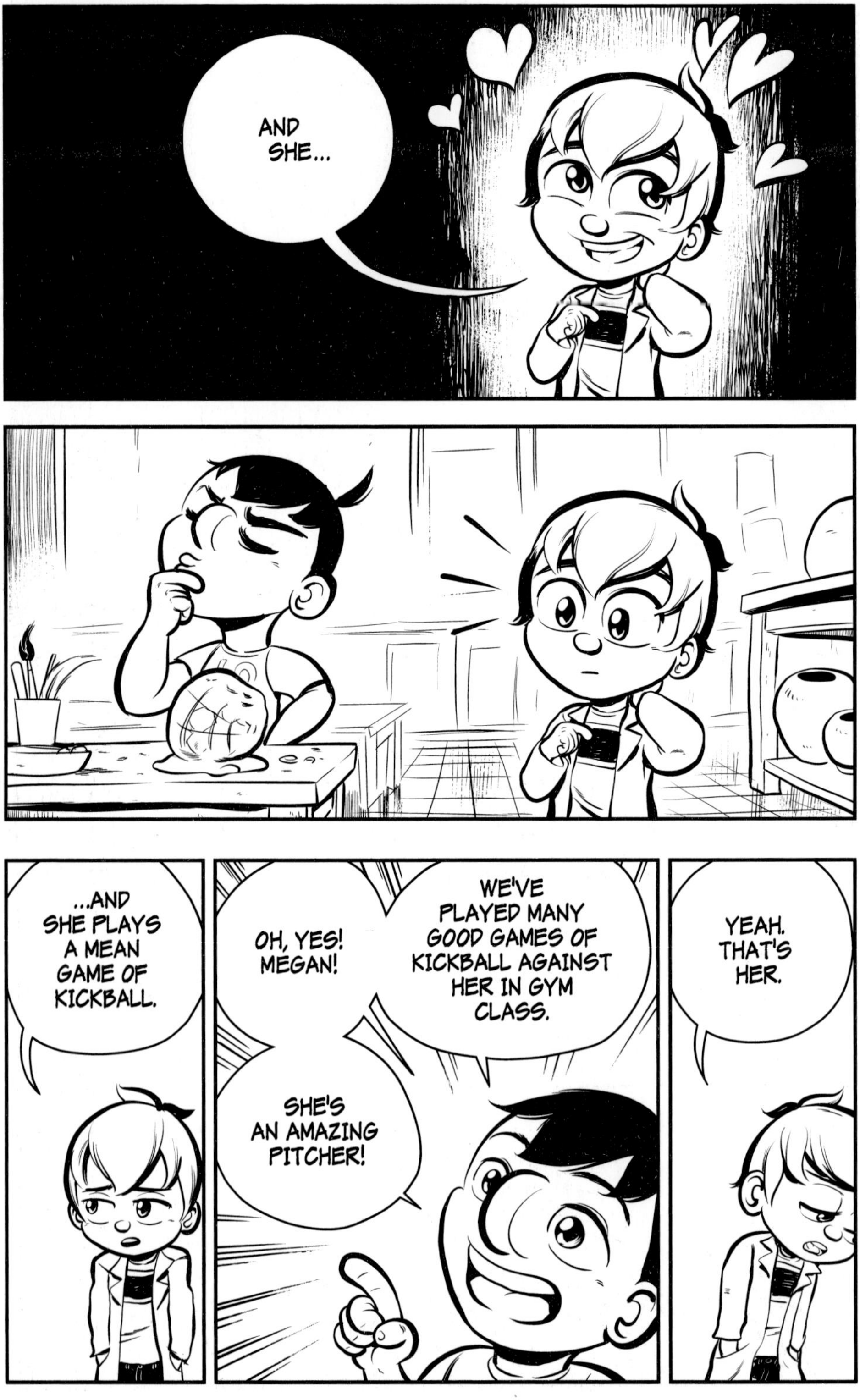
AND SHE...
...AND SHE PLAYS A MEAN GAME OF KICKBALL.
OH, YES! MEGAN!
WE'VE PLAYED MANY GOOD GAMES OF KICKBALL AGAINST HER IN GYM CLASS.
SHE'S AN AMAZING PITCHER!
YEAH. THAT'S HER.

WELL, EINSTEIN, MEGAN BARELY EVEN LOOKED AT ME TODAY, MUCH LESS GAVE ME AN INVITATION TO HER BIRTHDAY PARTY.

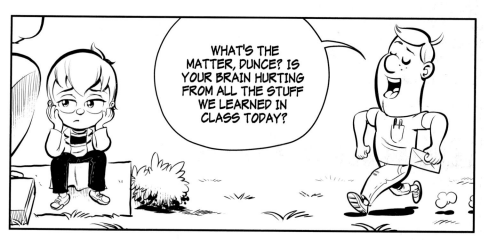

WHAT'S THE MATTER, DUNCE? IS YOUR BRAIN HURTING FROM ALL THE STUFF WE LEARNED IN CLASS TODAY?

I'M FINE. I'M JUST HAVING A TOUGH DAY, THAT'S ALL.

!

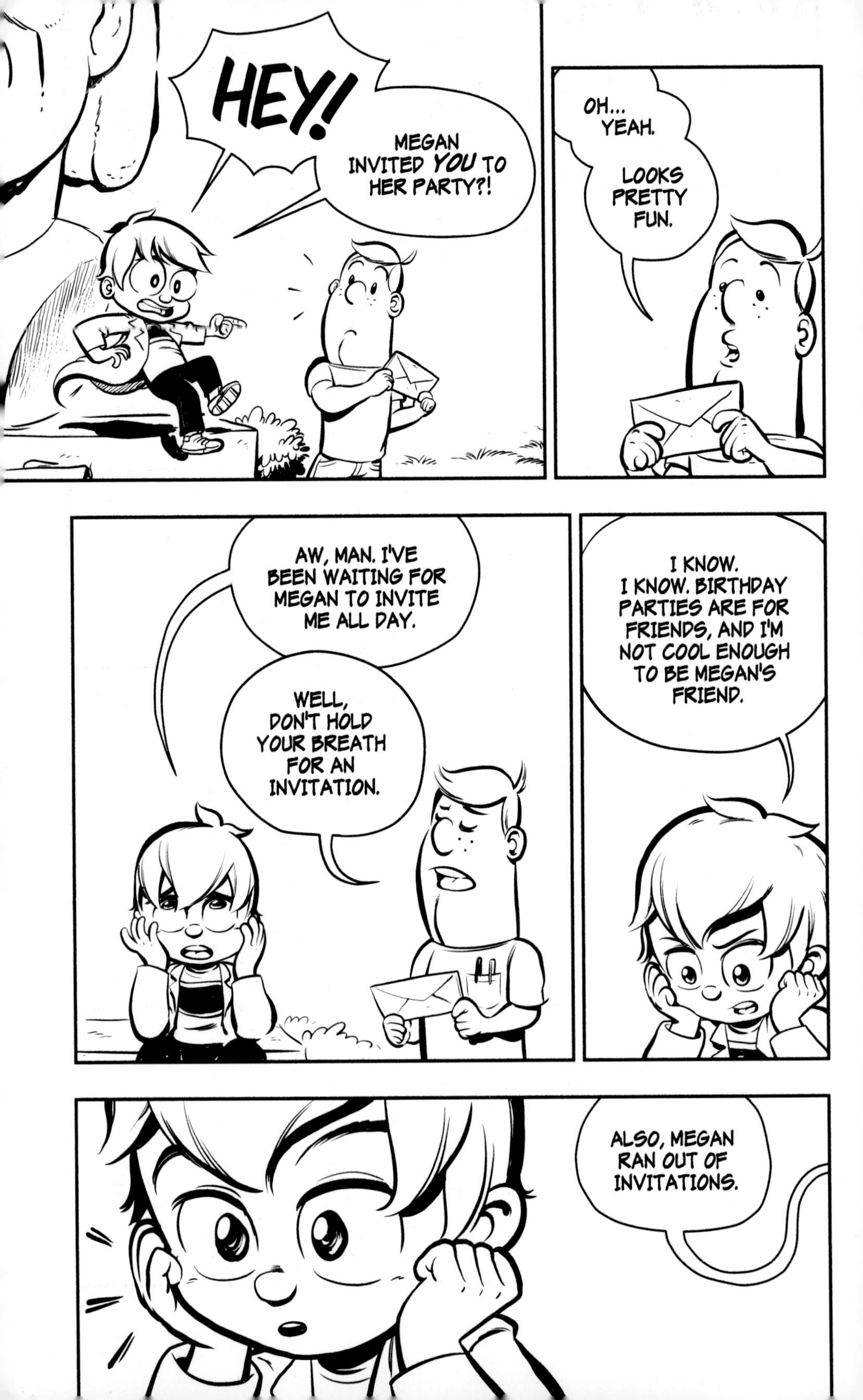
HEY!
MEGAN INVITED YOU TO HER PARTY?!
OH... YEAH.
LOOKS PRETTY FUN.
AW, MAN. I'VE BEEN WAITING FOR MEGAN TO INVITE ME ALL DAY.
WELL, DON'T HOLD YOUR BREATH FOR AN INVITATION.
I KNOW. I KNOW. BIRTHDAY PARTIES ARE FOR FRIENDS, AND I'M NOT COOL ENOUGH TO BE MEGAN'S FRIEND.
ALSO, MEGAN RAN OUT OF INVITATIONS.

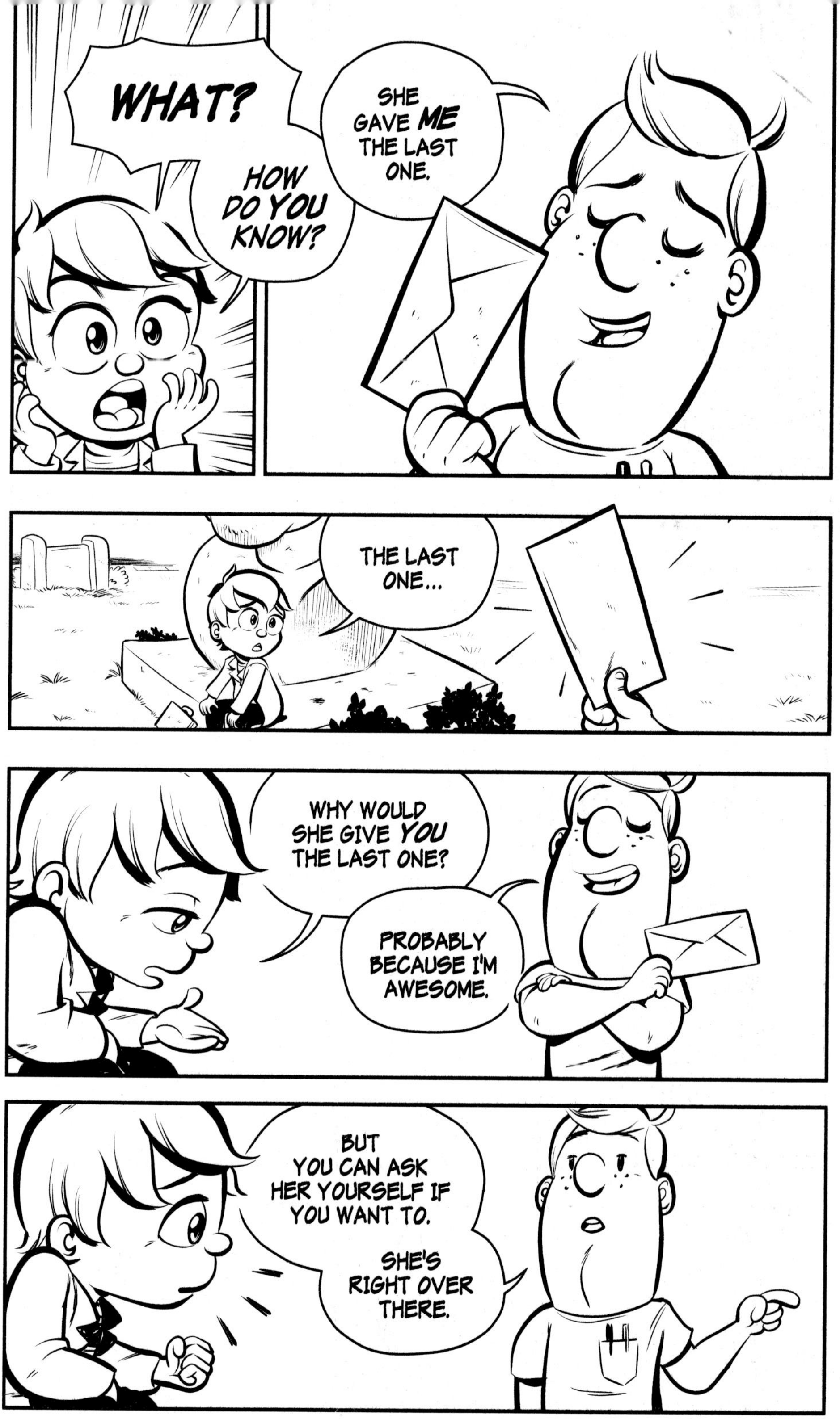
WHAT?
SHE GAVE ME THE LAST ONE.
HOW DO YOU KNOW?
THE LAST ONE...
WHY WOULD SHE GIVE YOU THE LAST ONE?
PROBABLY BECAUSE I'M AWESOME.
BUT YOU CAN ASK HER YOURSELF IF YOU WANT TO.
SHE'S RIGHT OVER THERE.

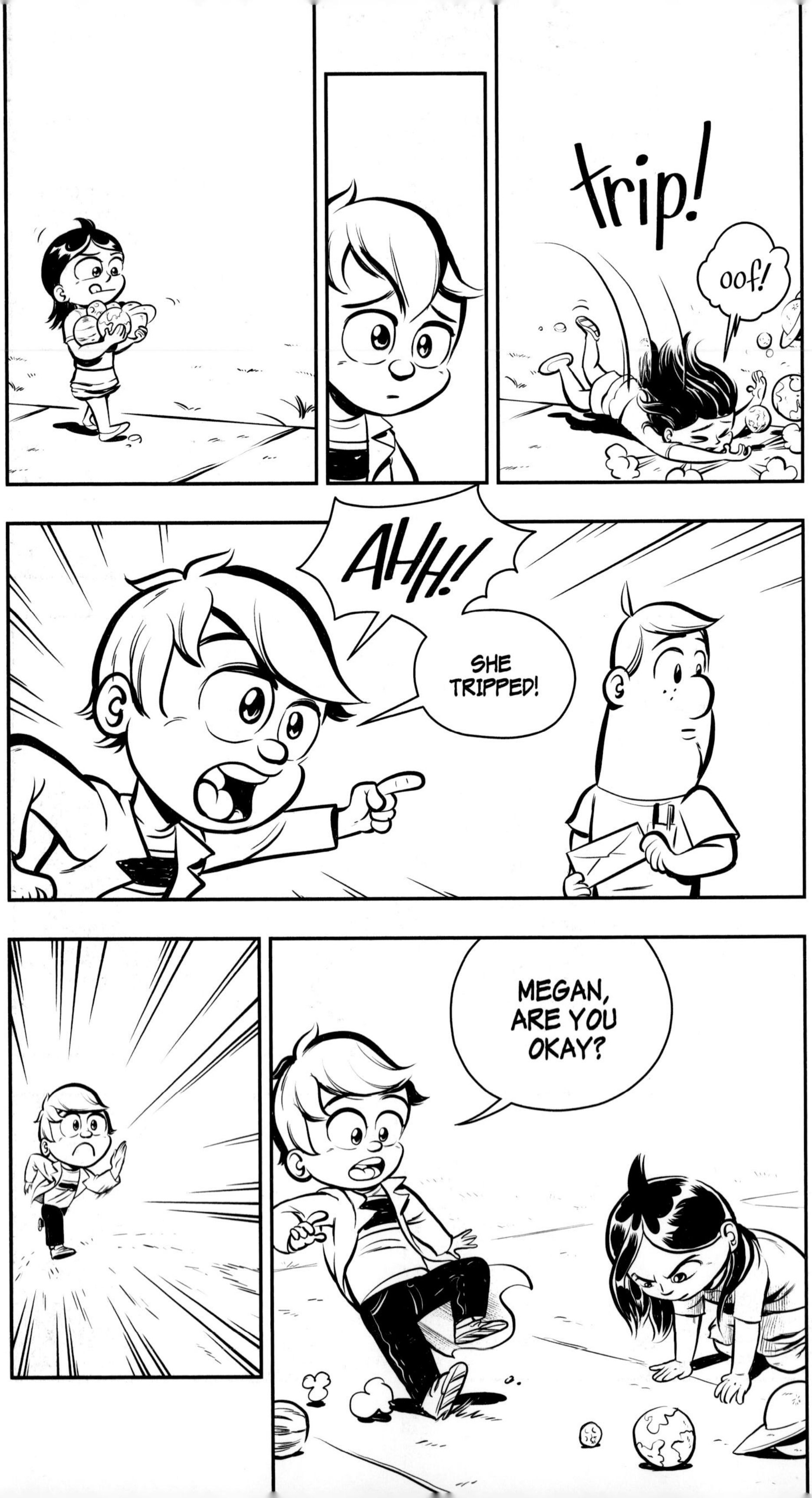
trip!
oof!
AHH!
SHE TRIPPED!
MEGAN, ARE YOU OKAY?

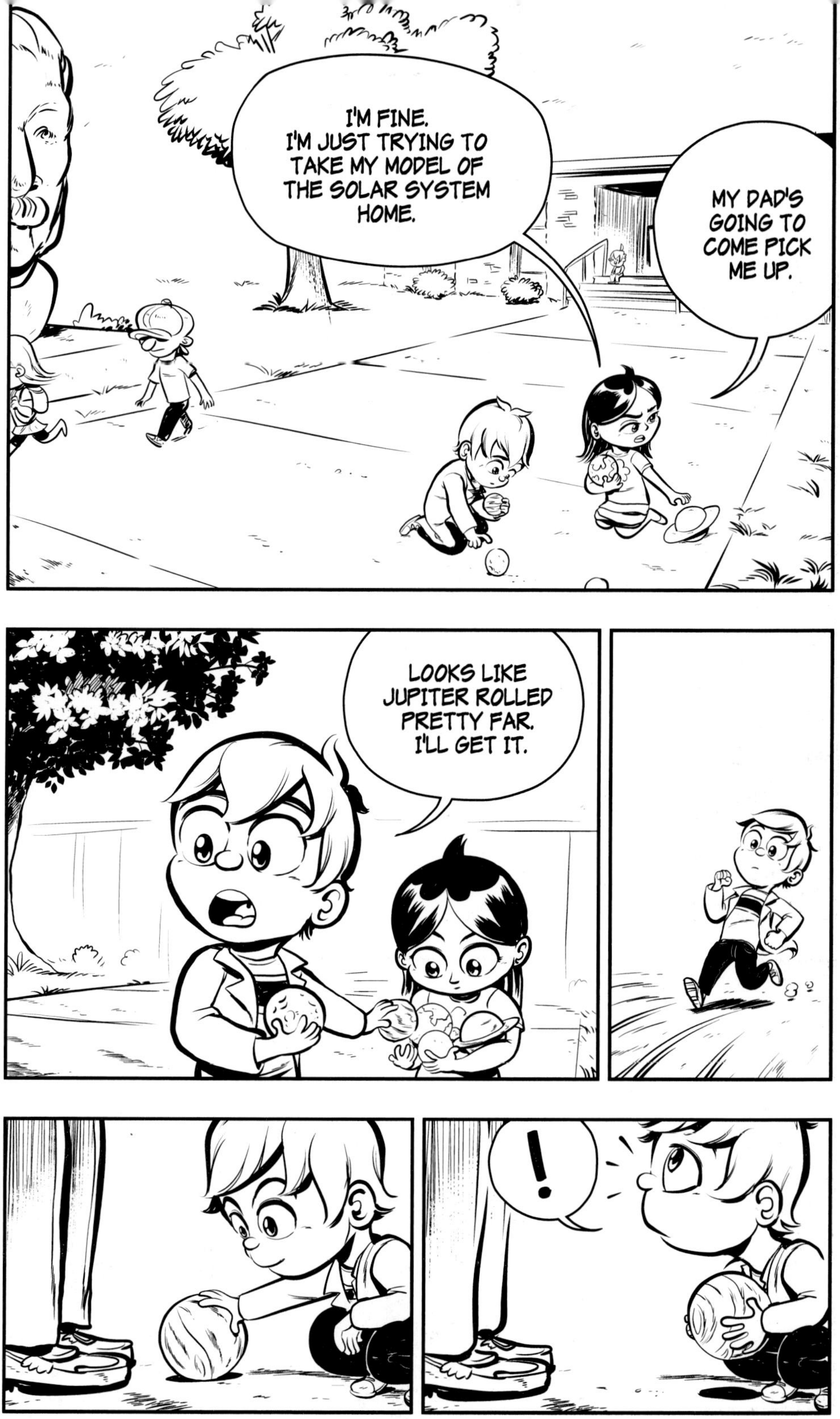
I'M FINE. I'M JUST TRYING TO TAKE MY MODEL OF THE SOLAR SYSTEM HOME.
MY DAD'S GOING TO COME PICK ME UP.
LOOKS LIKE JUPITER ROLLED PRETTY FAR. I'LL GET IT.
!

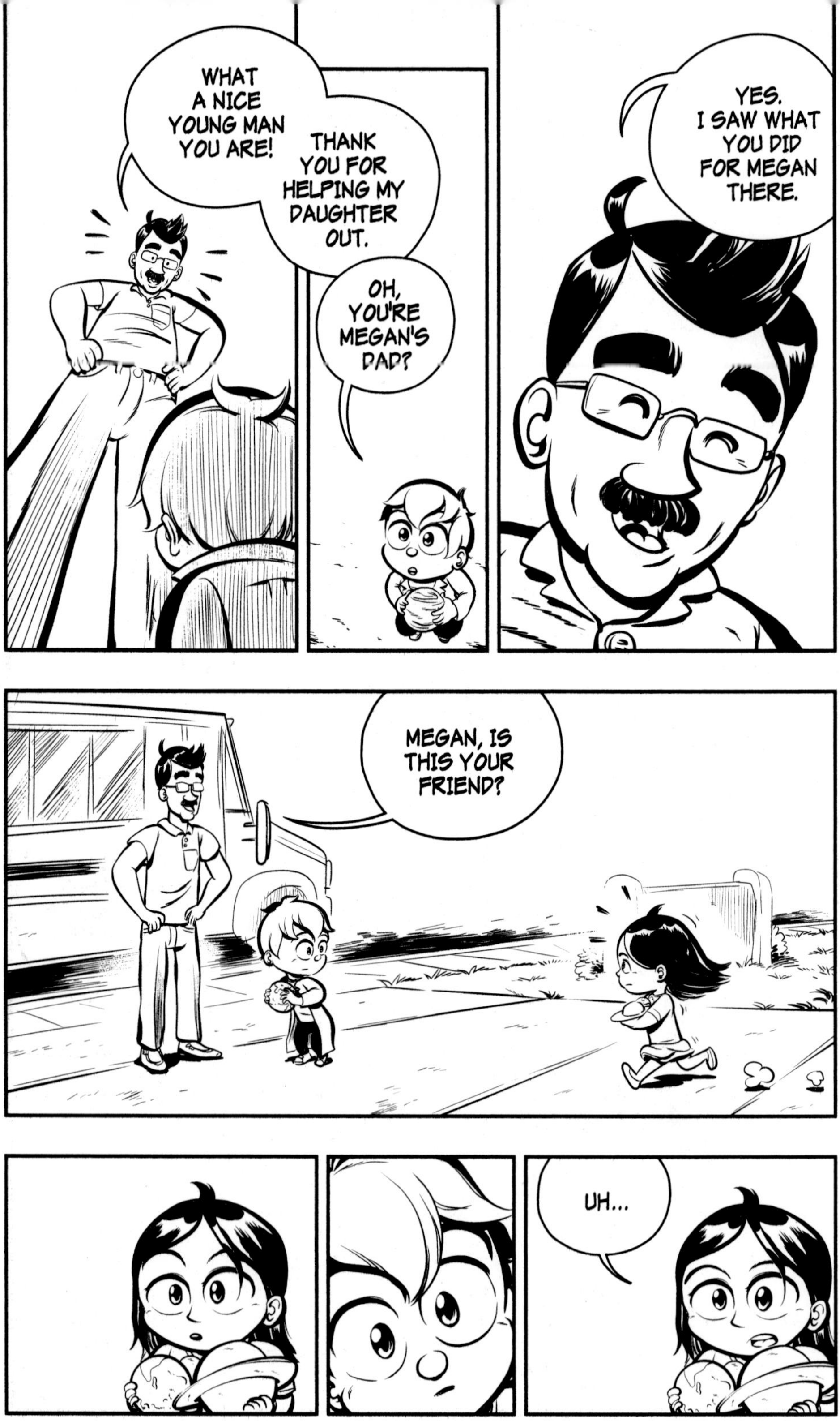
WHAT A NICE YOUNG MAN YOU ARE!
THANK YOU FOR HELPING MY DAUGHTER OUT.
OH, YOU'RE MEGAN'S DAD?
YES. I SAW WHAT YOU DID FOR MEGAN THERE.
MEGAN, IS THIS YOUR FRIEND?
UH...

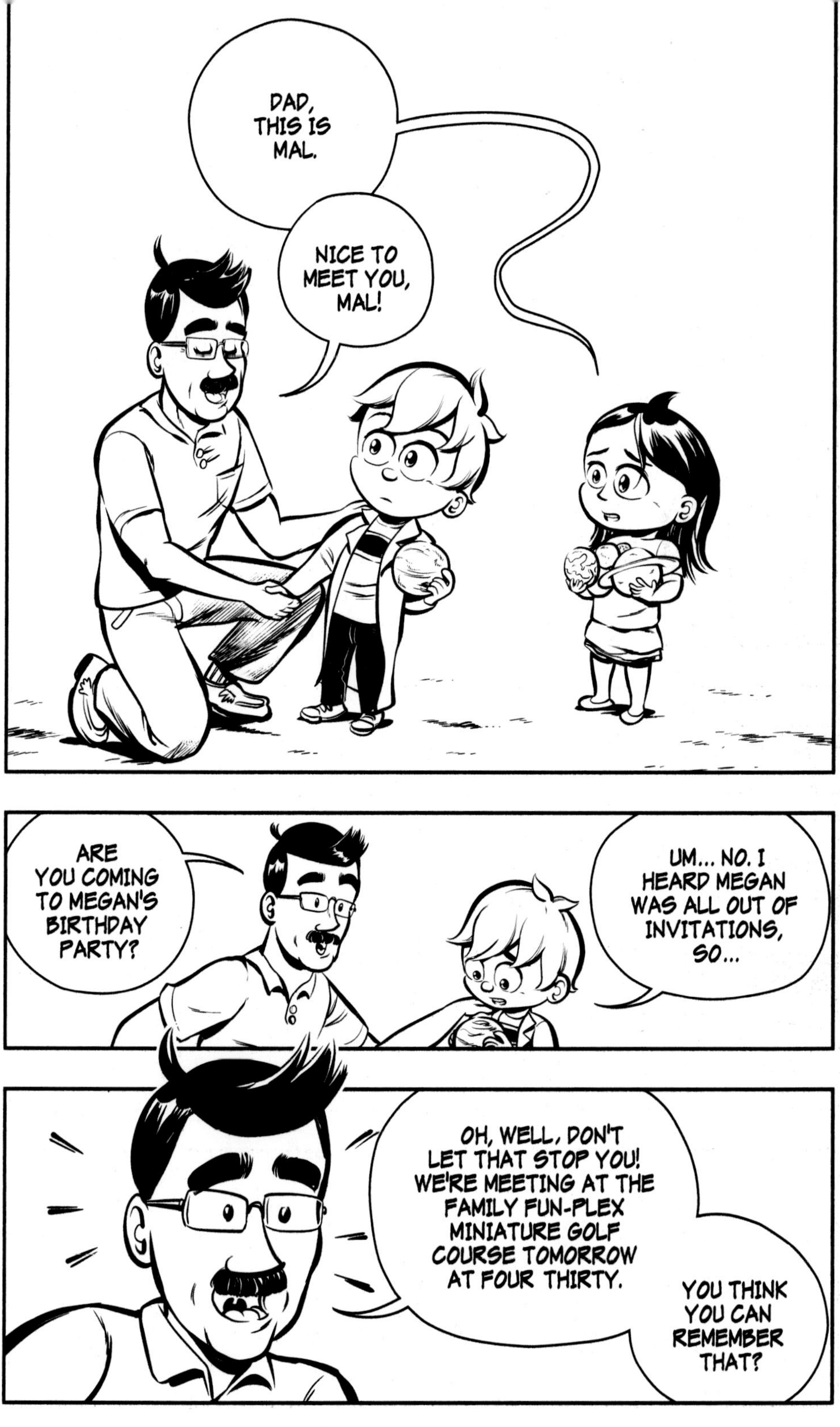
DAD, THIS IS MAL.
NICE TO MEET YOU, MAL!
ARE YOU COMING TO MEGAN'S BIRTHDAY PARTY?
UM... NO. I HEARD MEGAN WAS ALL OUT OF INVITATIONS, SO...
OH, WELL, DON'T LET THAT STOP YOU! WE'RE MEETING AT THE FAMILY FUN-PLEX MINIATURE GOLF COURSE TOMORROW AT FOUR THIRTY.
YOU THINK YOU CAN REMEMBER THAT?

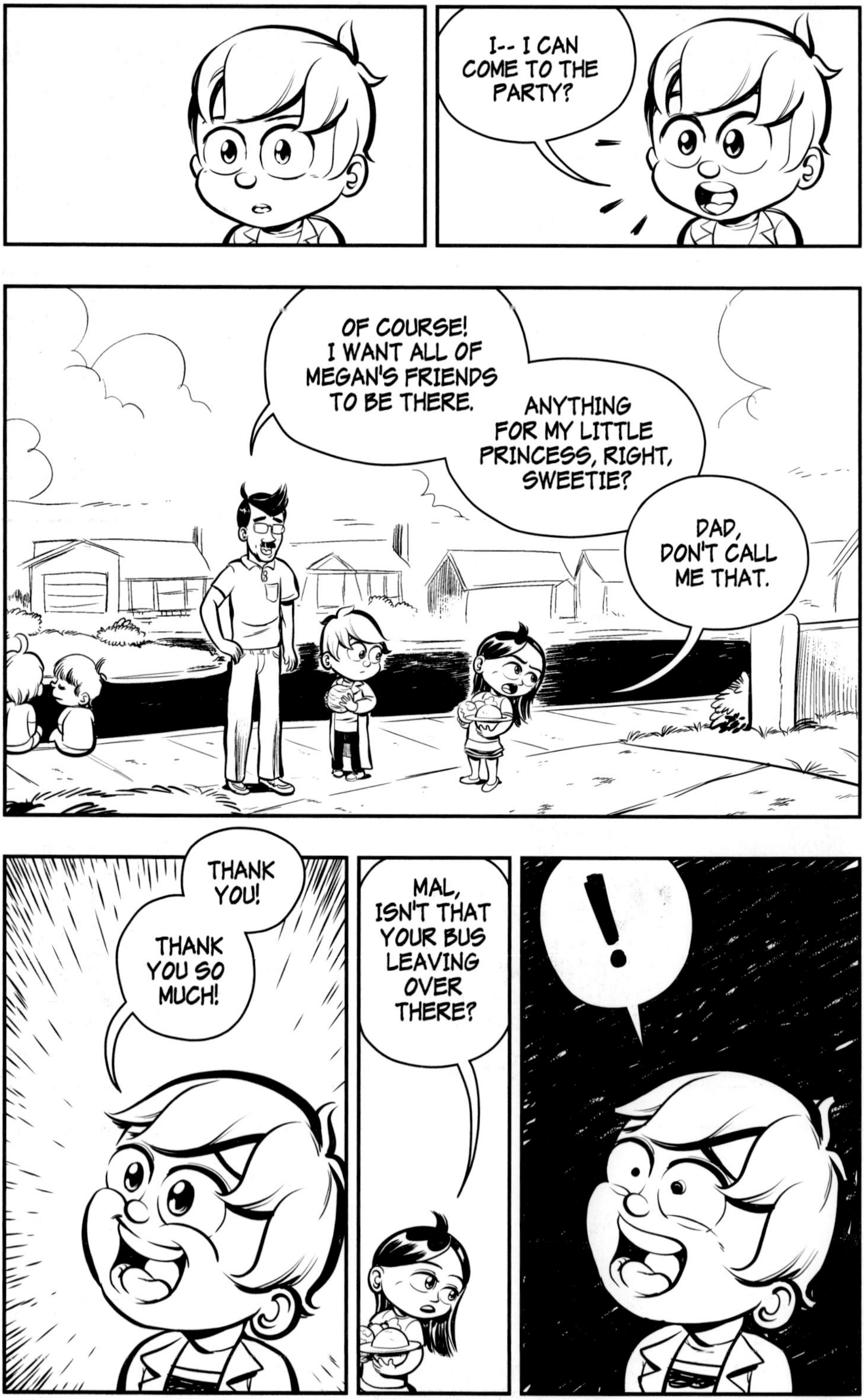
I-- I CAN COME TO THE PARTY?
OF COURSE! I WANT ALL OF MEGAN'S FRIENDS TO BE THERE.
ANYTHING FOR MY LITTLE PRINCESS, RIGHT, SWEETIE?
DAD, DON'T CALL ME THAT.
THANK YOU!
THANK YOU SO MUCH!
MAL, ISN'T THAT YOUR BUS LEAVING OVER THERE?
!

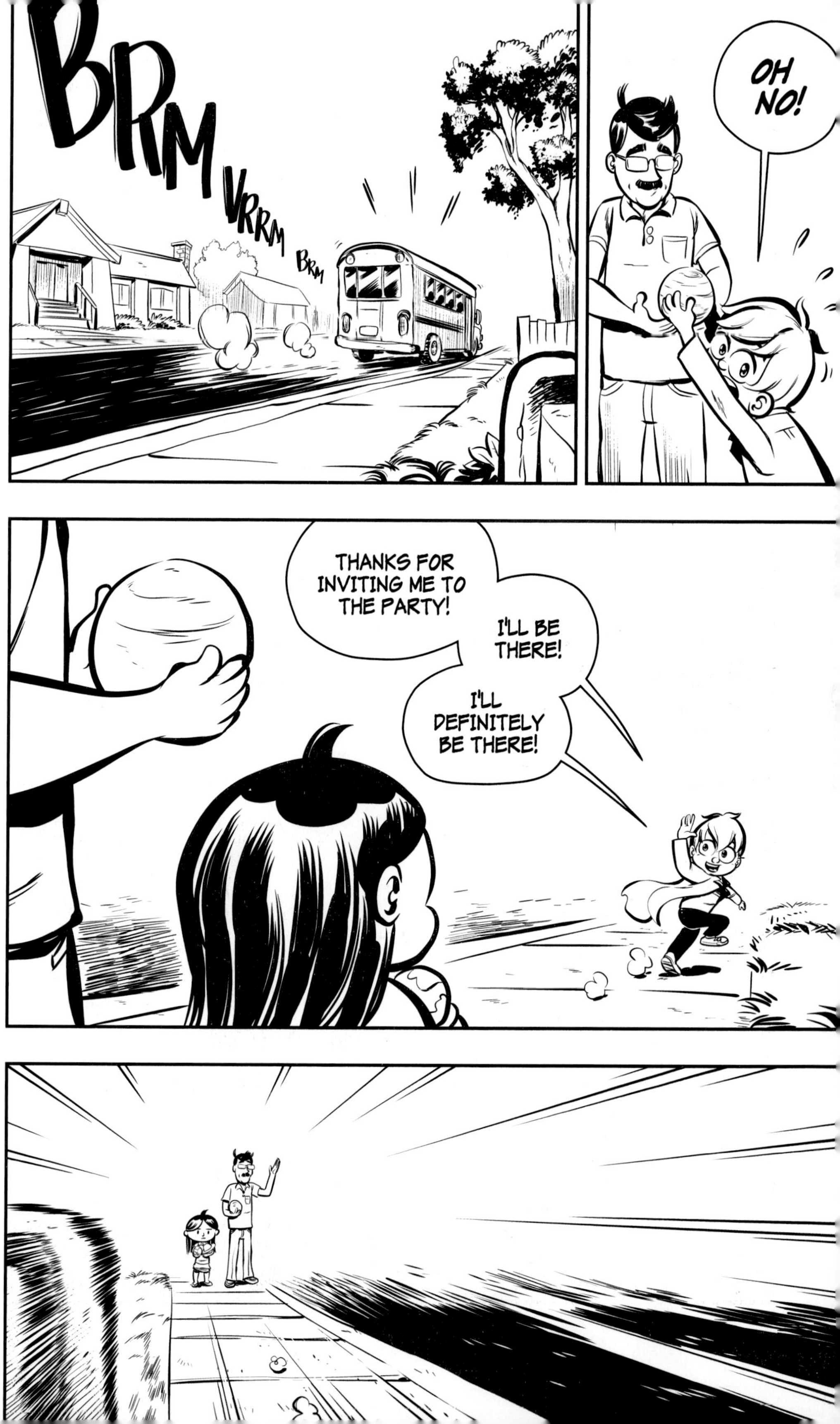
BRM
VRRM
BRM
OH NO!
THANKS FOR INVITING ME TO THE PARTY!
I'LL BE THERE!
I'LL DEFINITELY BE THERE!

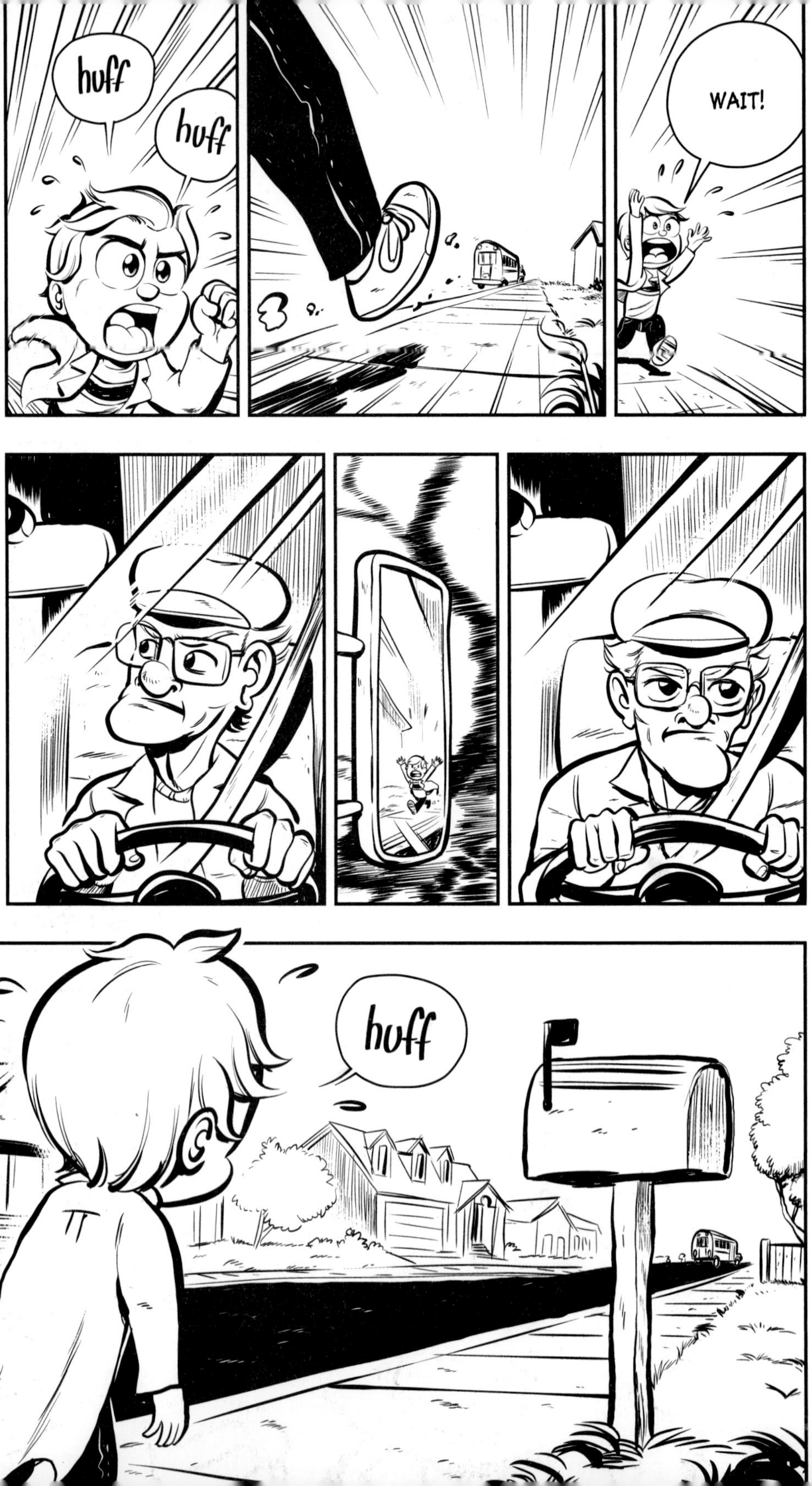
huff
huff
WAIT!
huff

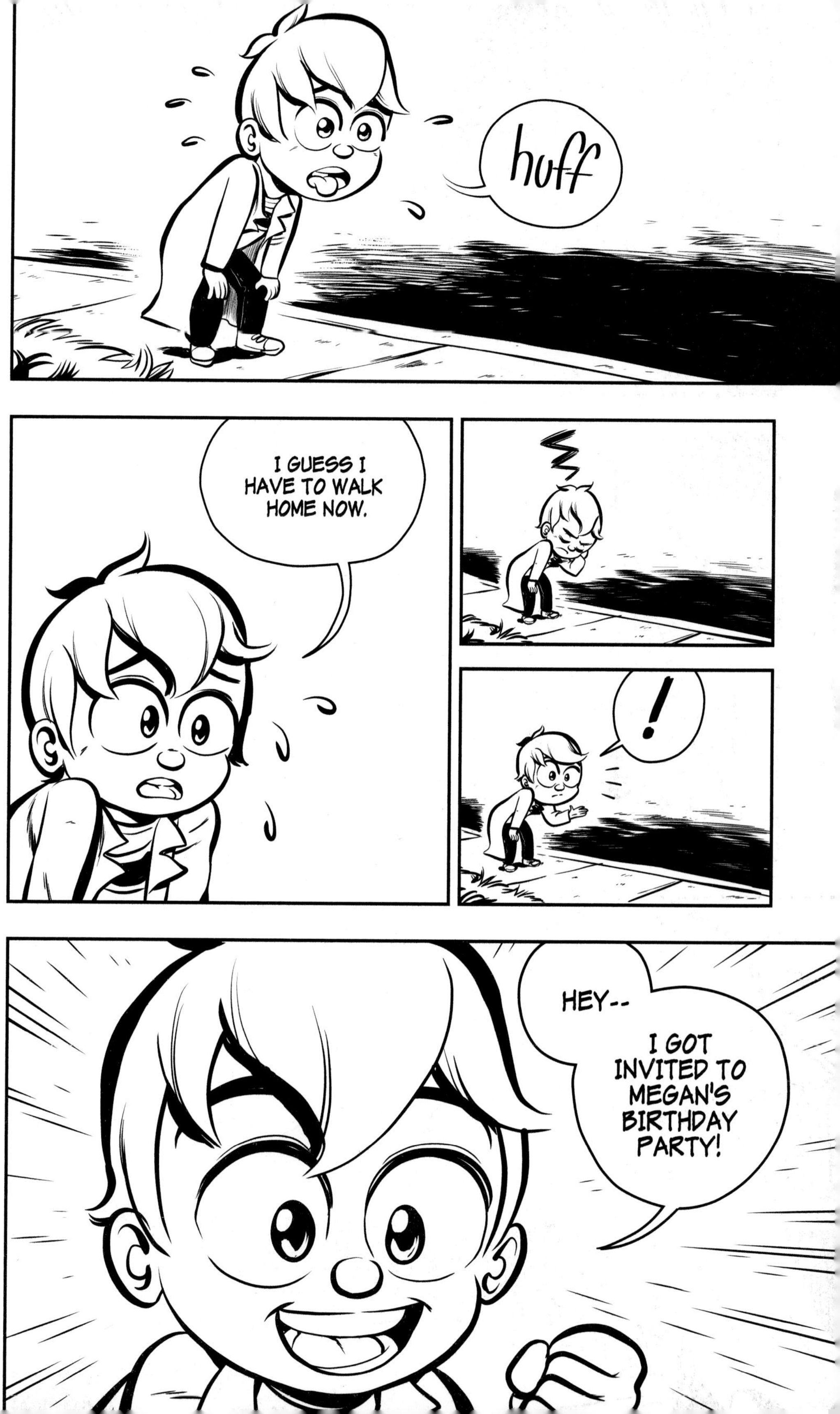
huff
I GUESS I HAVE TO WALK HOME NOW.
!
HEY--
I GOT INVITED TO MEGAN'S BIRTHDAY PARTY!

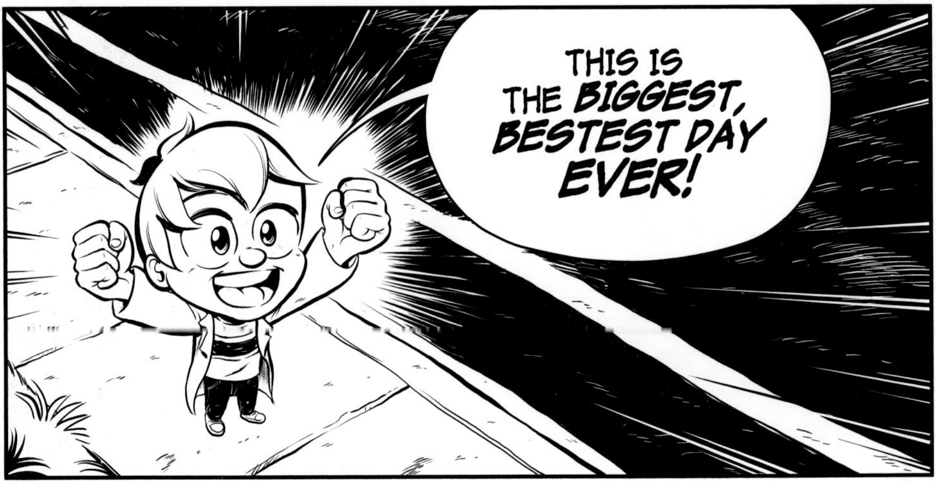
THIS IS THE BIGGEST, BESTEST DAY EVER!

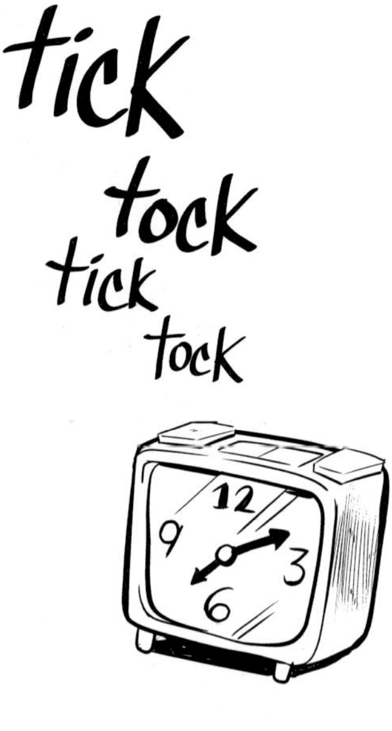
tick
tock
tick
tock
12
9
3
6

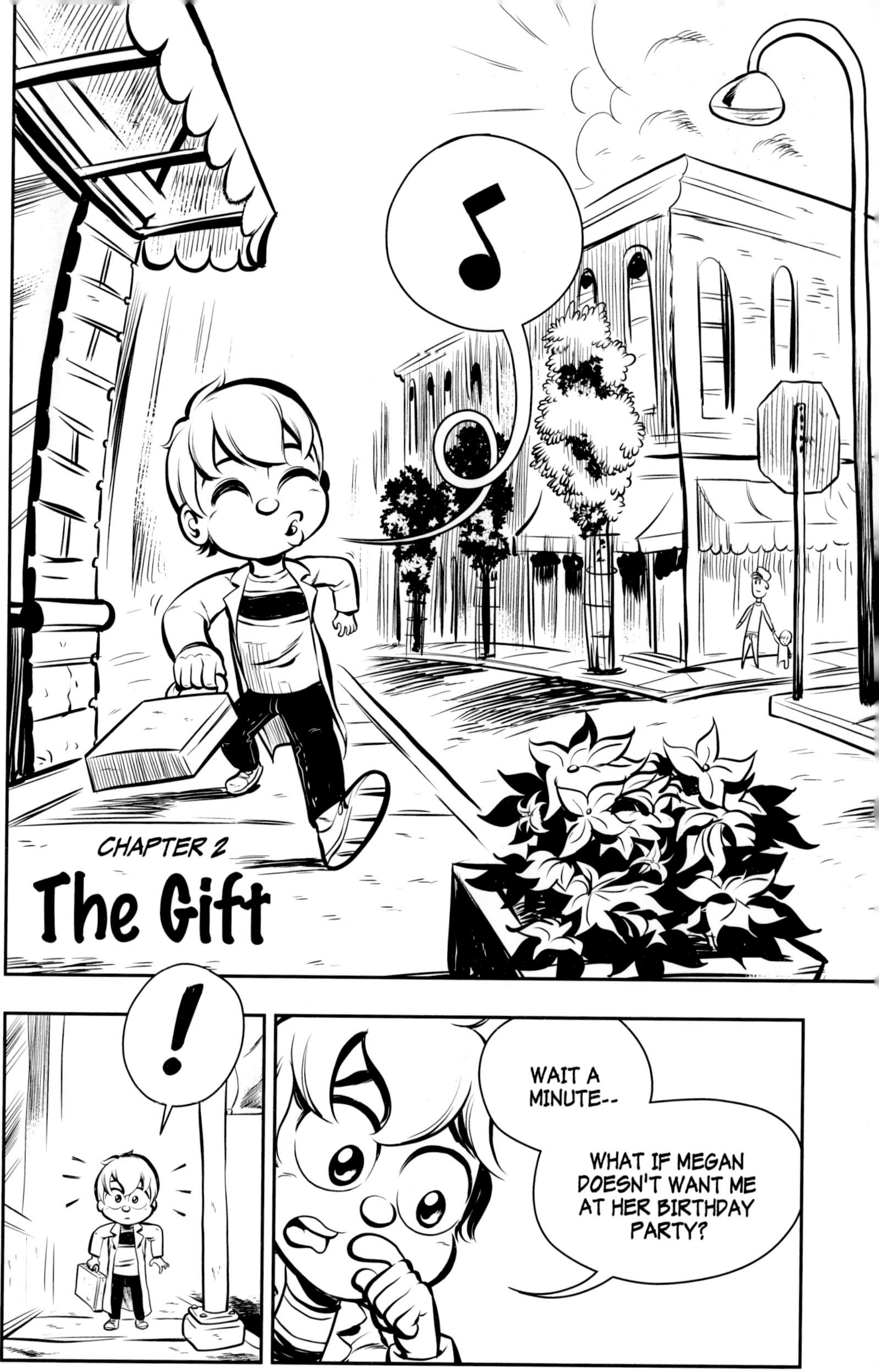
CHAPTER 2
The Gift
!
WAIT A MINUTE--
WHAT IF MEGAN DOESN'T WANT ME AT HER BIRTHDAY PARTY?

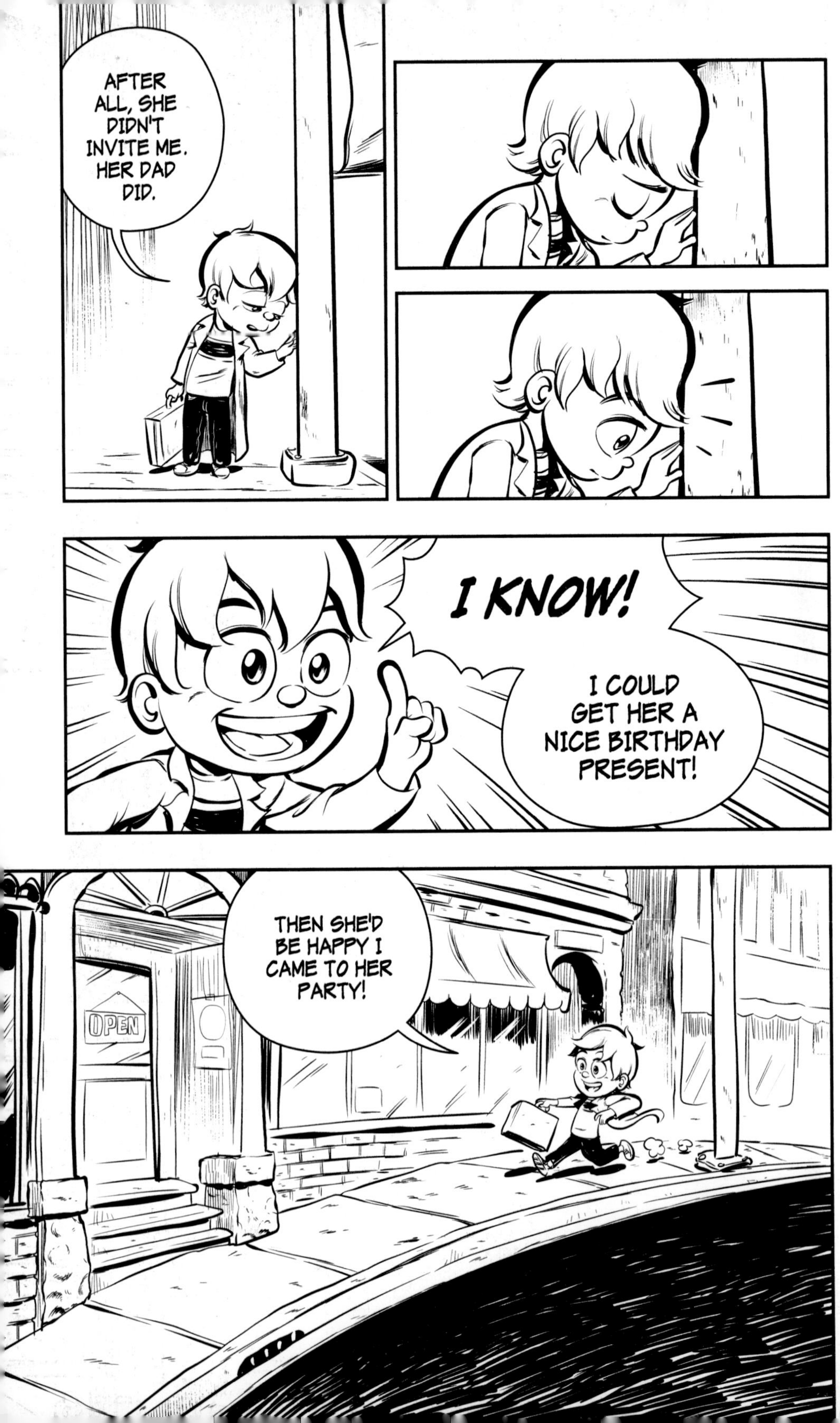
AFTER ALL, SHE DIDN'T INVITE ME. HER DAD DID.
I KNOW!
I COULD GET HER A NICE BIRTHDAY PRESENT!
OPEN
THEN SHE'D BE HAPPY I CAME TO HER PARTY!

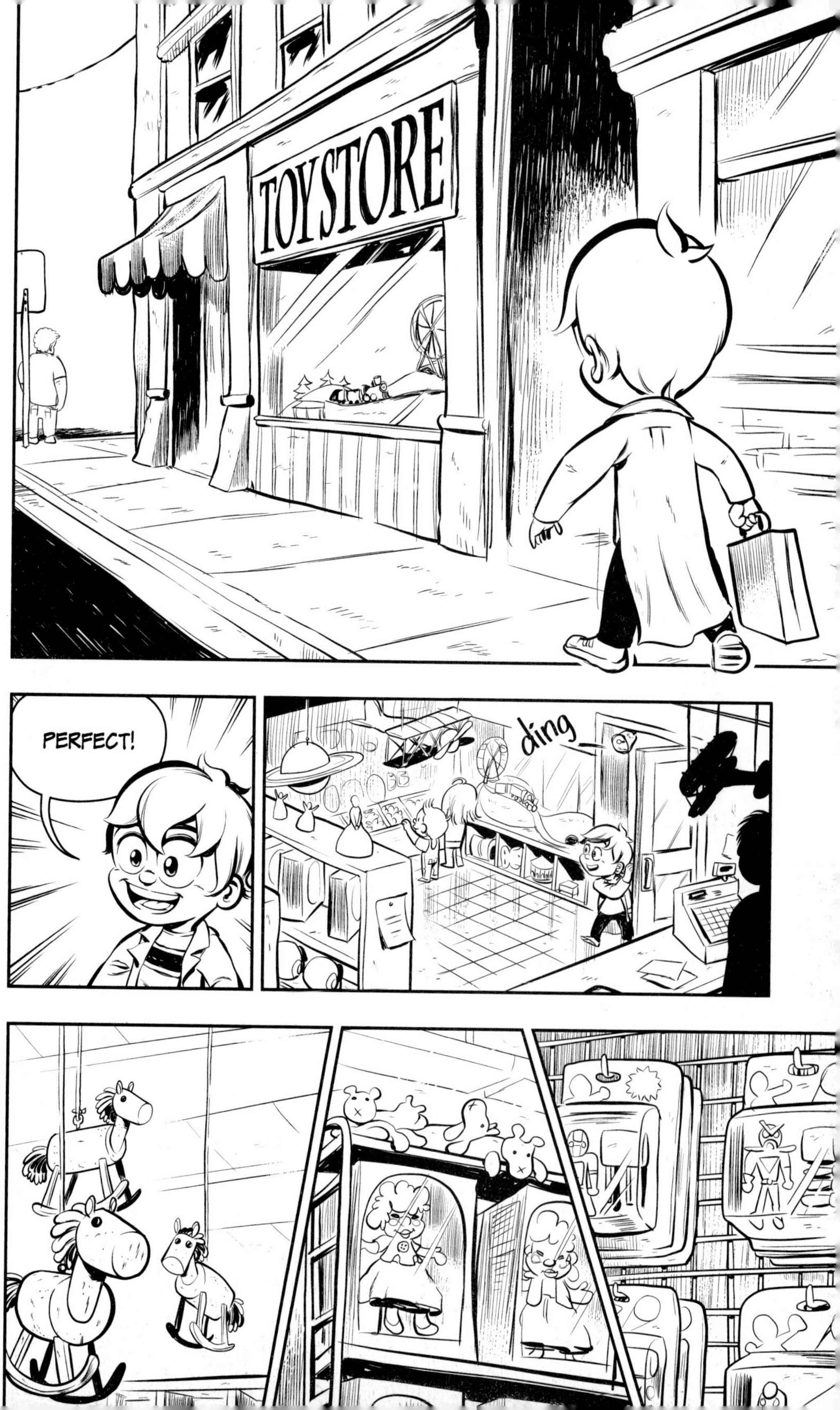
TOYSTORE
PERFECT!
ding

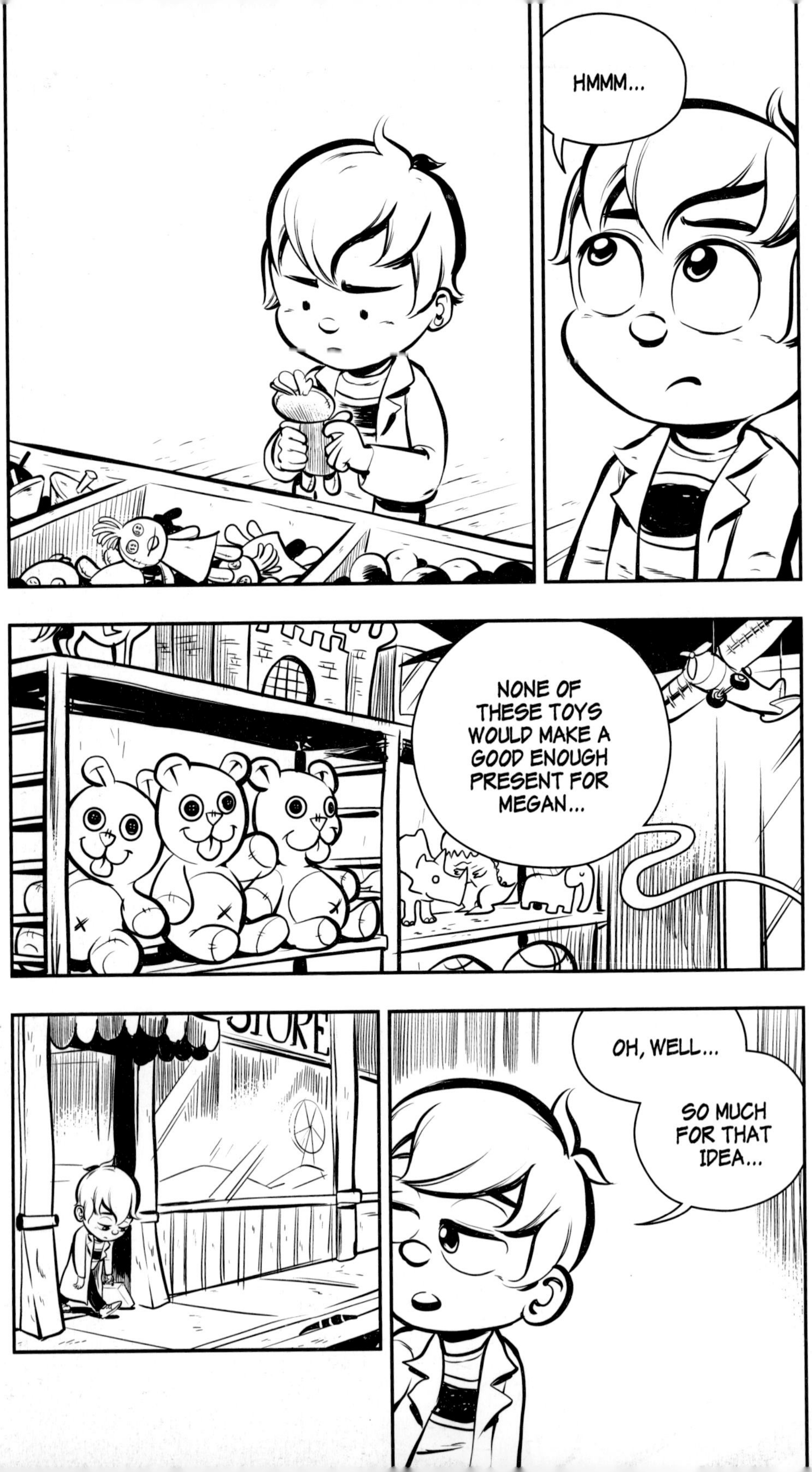
HMMM...
NONE OF THESE TOYS WOULD MAKE A GOOD ENOUGH PRESENT FOR MEGAN...
STORE
OH, WELL...
SO MUCH FOR THAT IDEA...

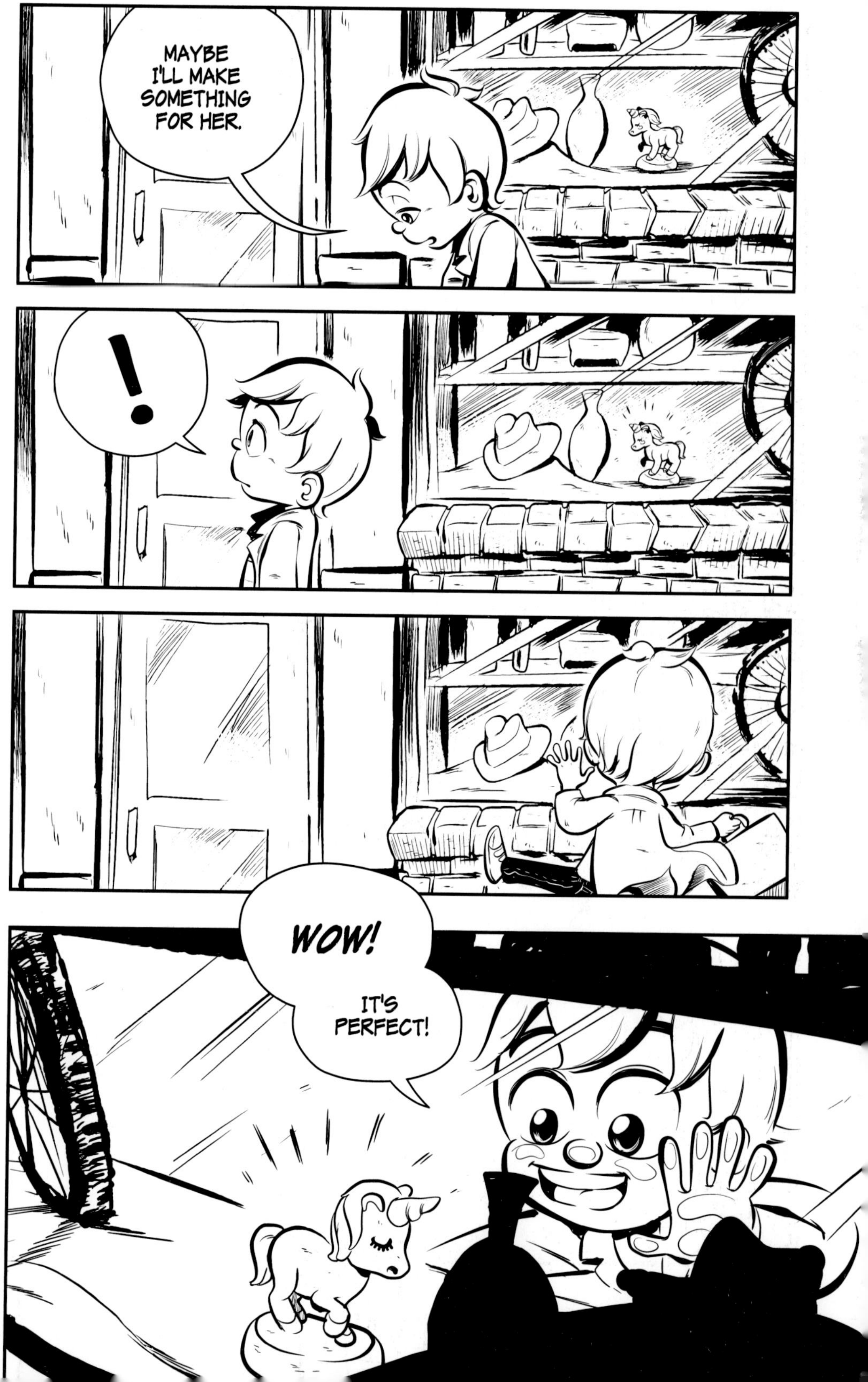
MAYBE I'LL MAKE SOMETHING FOR HER.
!
WOW!
IT'S PERFECT!

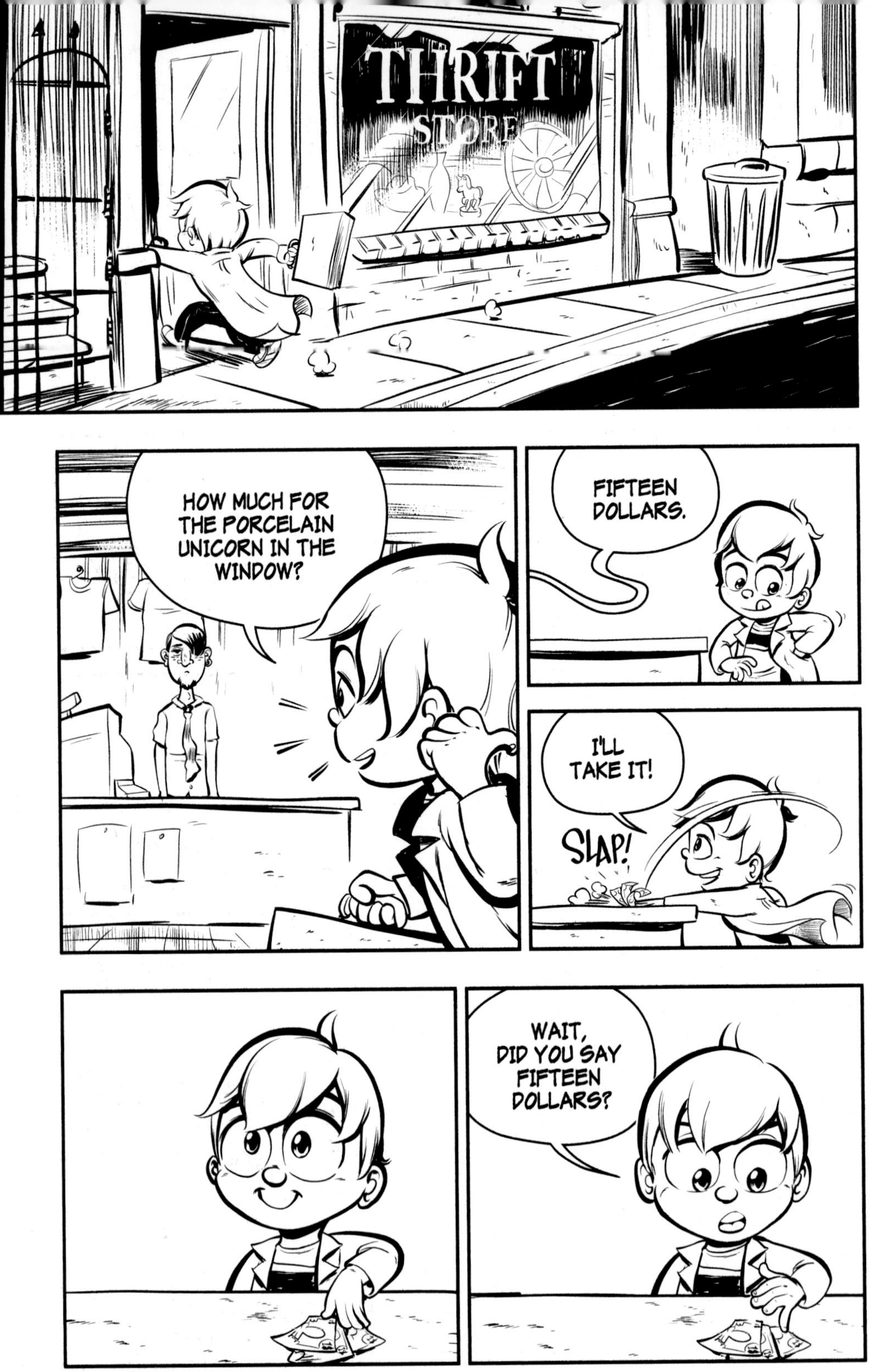
THRIFT STORE
HOW MUCH FOR THE PORCELAIN UNICORN IN THE WINDOW?
FIFTEEN DOLLARS.
I'LL TAKE IT!
SLAP!
WAIT, DID YOU SAY FIFTEEN DOLLARS?

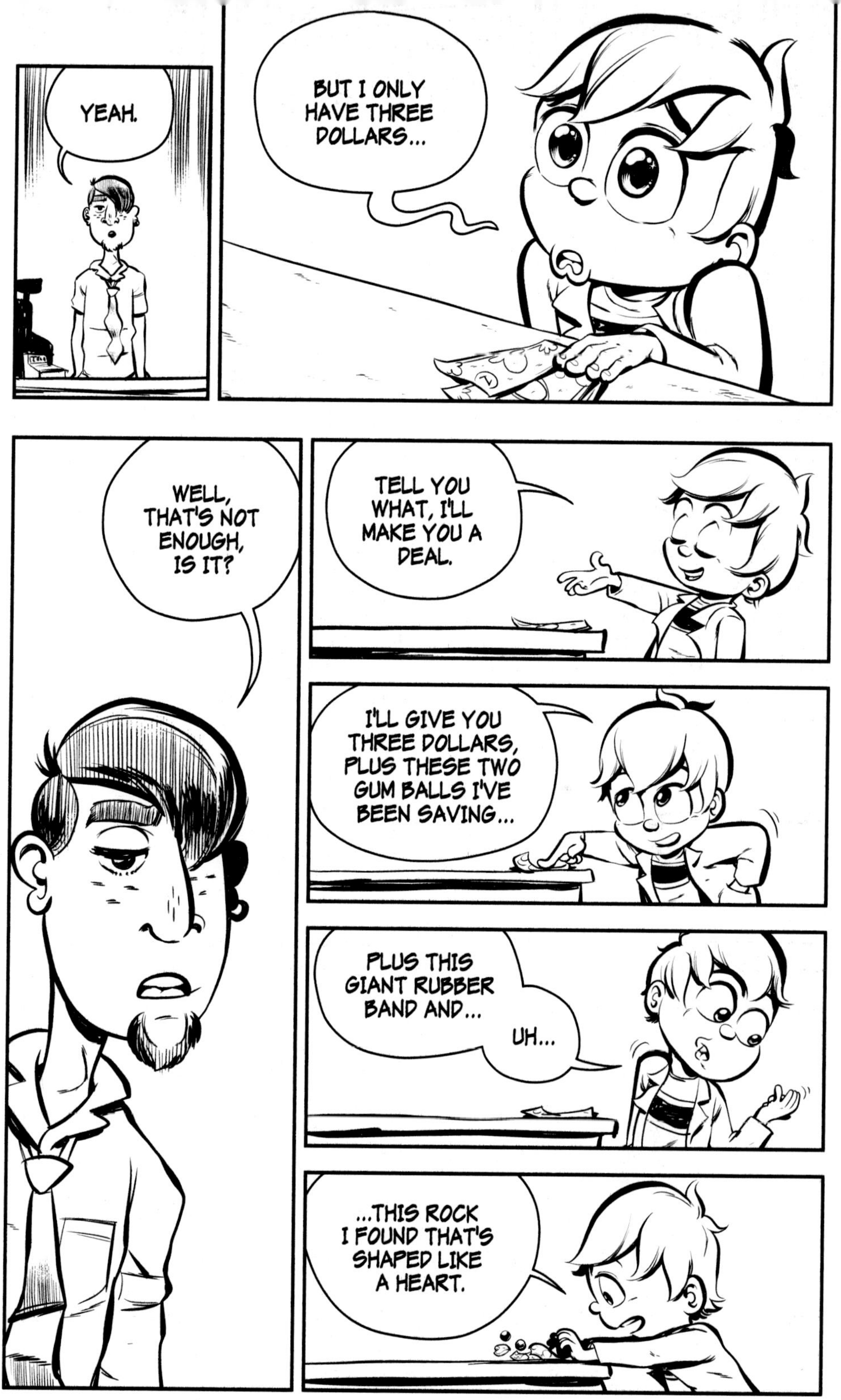
YEAH.
BUT I ONLY HAVE THREE DOLLARS...
WELL, THAT'S NOT ENOUGH, IS IT?
TELL YOU WHAT, I'LL MAKE YOU A DEAL.
I'LL GIVE YOU THREE DOLLARS, PLUS THESE TWO GUM BALLS I'VE BEEN SAVING...
PLUS THIS GIANT RUBBER BAND AND...
UH...
...THIS ROCK I FOUND THAT'S SHAPED LIKE A HEART.

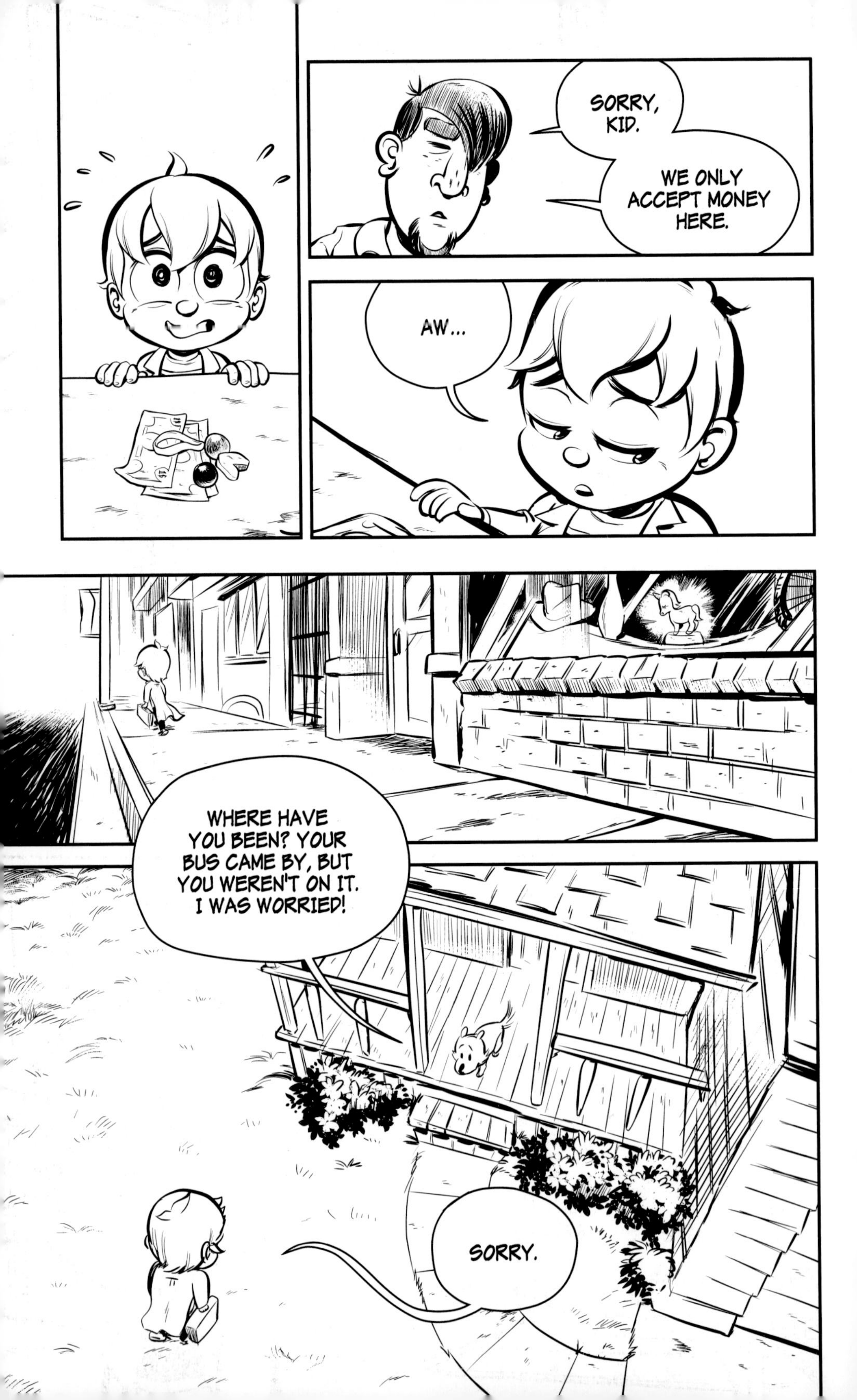
SORRY, KID.
WE ONLY ACCEPT MONEY HERE.
AW...
WHERE HAVE YOU BEEN? YOUR BUS CAME BY, BUT YOU WEREN'T ON IT. I WAS WORRIED!
SORRY.

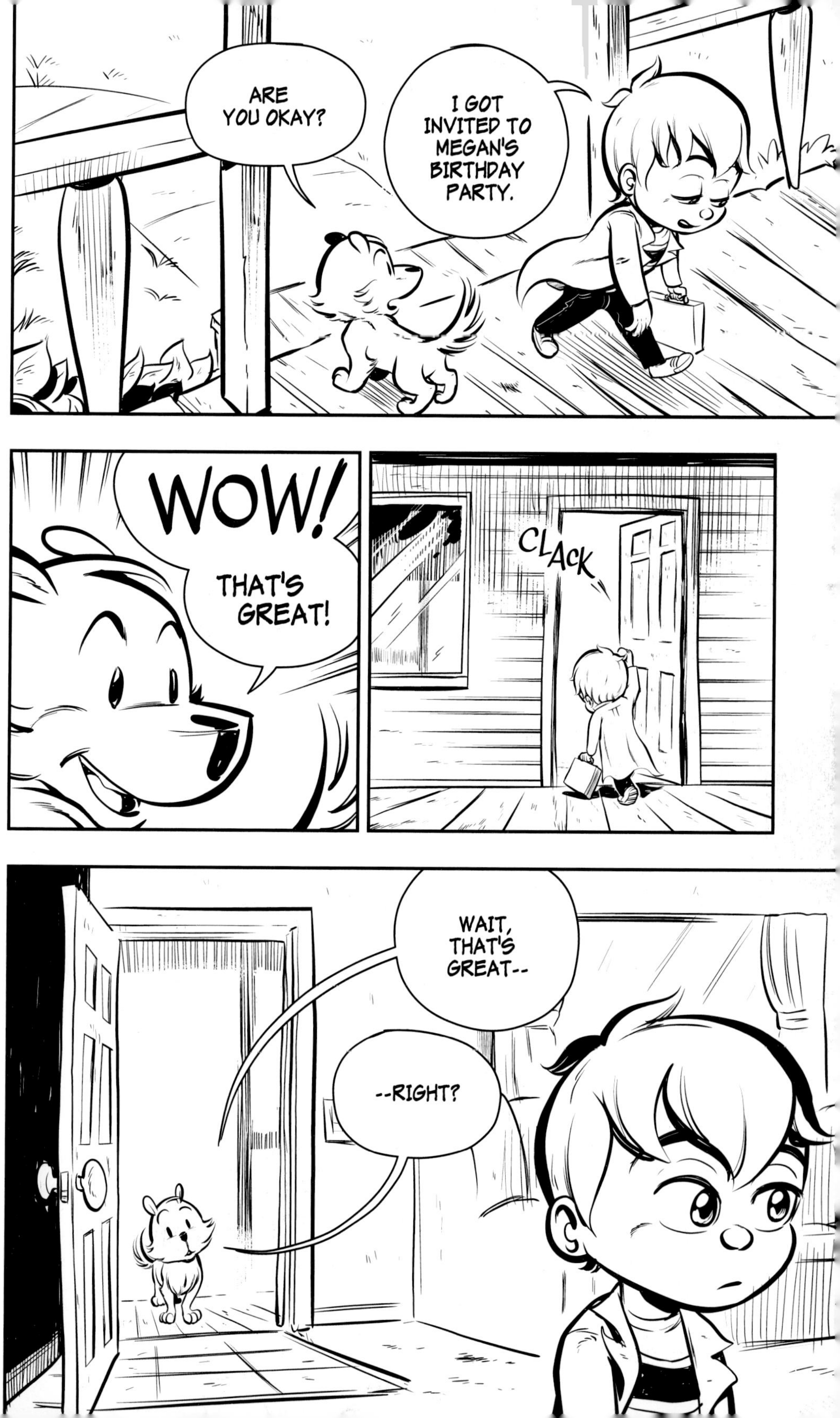

ARE YOU OKAY?
I GOT INVITED TO MEGAN'S BIRTHDAY PARTY.
WOW!
THAT'S GREAT!
CLACK
WAIT, THAT'S GREAT--
--RIGHT?

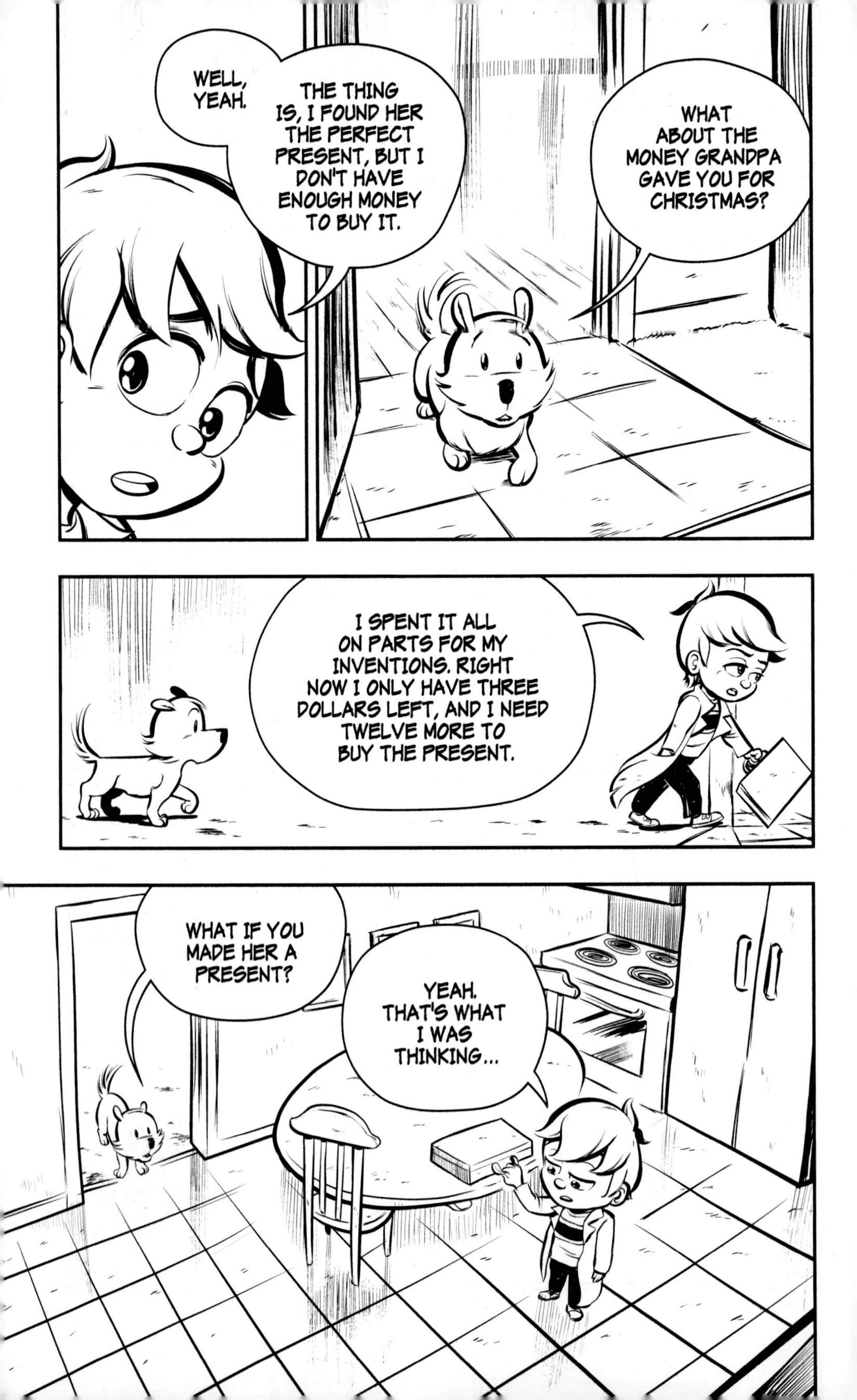
WELL, YEAH.
THE THING IS, I FOUND HER THE PERFECT PRESENT, BUT I DON'T HAVE ENOUGH MONEY TO BUY IT.
WHAT ABOUT THE MONEY GRANDPA GAVE YOU FOR CHRISTMAS?
I SPENT IT ALL ON PARTS FOR MY INVENTIONS. RIGHT NOW I ONLY HAVE THREE DOLLARS LEFT, AND I NEED TWELVE MORE TO BUY THE PRESENT.
WHAT IF YOU MADE HER A PRESENT?
YEAH. THAT'S WHAT I WAS THINKING...

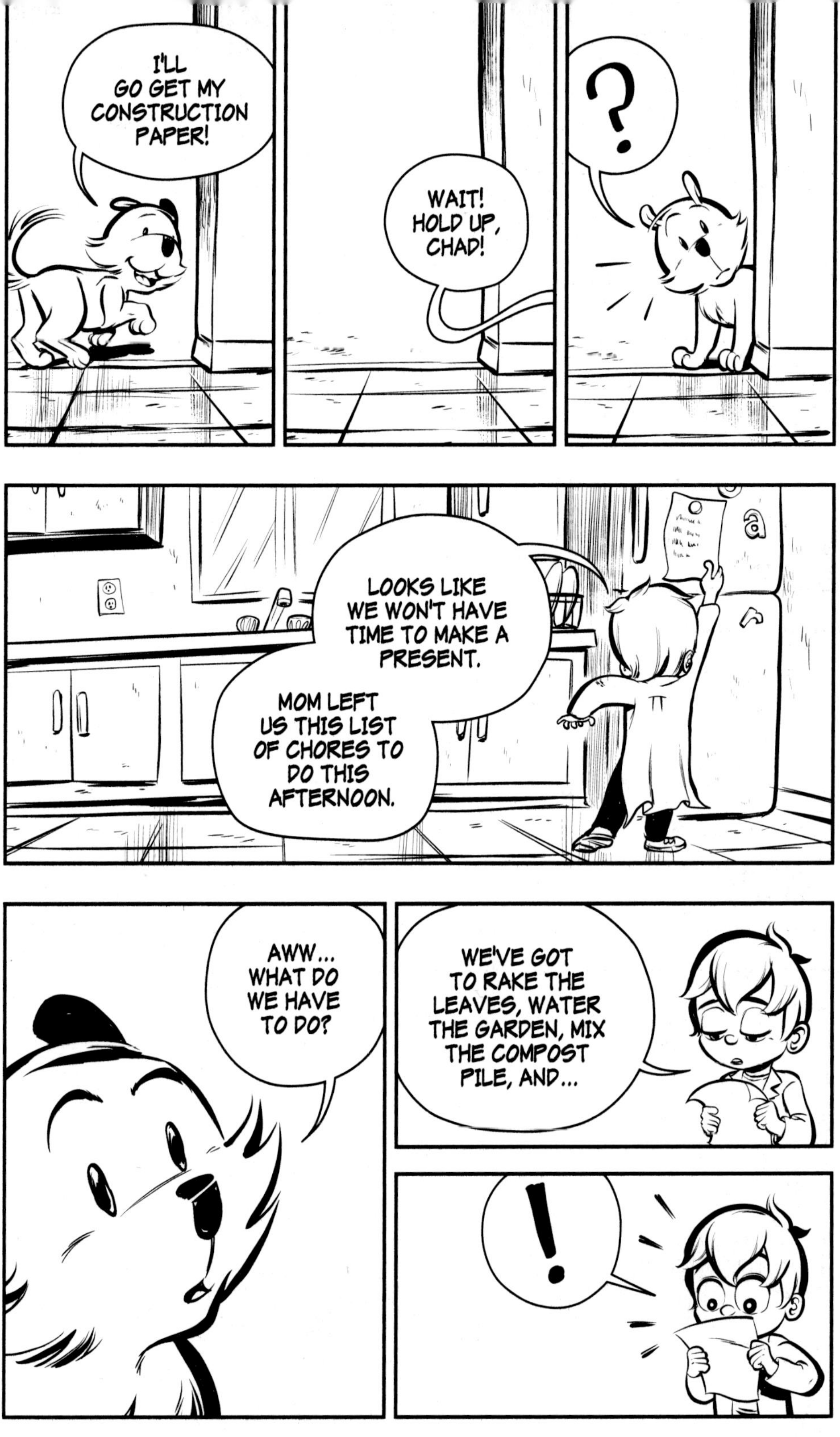
I'LL GO GET MY CONSTRUCTION PAPER!
WAIT! HOLD UP, CHAD!
?
LOOKS LIKE WE WON'T HAVE TIME TO MAKE A PRESENT.
MOM LEFT US THIS LIST OF CHORES TO DO THIS AFTERNOON.
AWW... WHAT DO WE HAVE TO DO?
WE'VE GOT TO RAKE THE LEAVES, WATER THE GARDEN, MIX THE COMPOST PILE, AND...
!

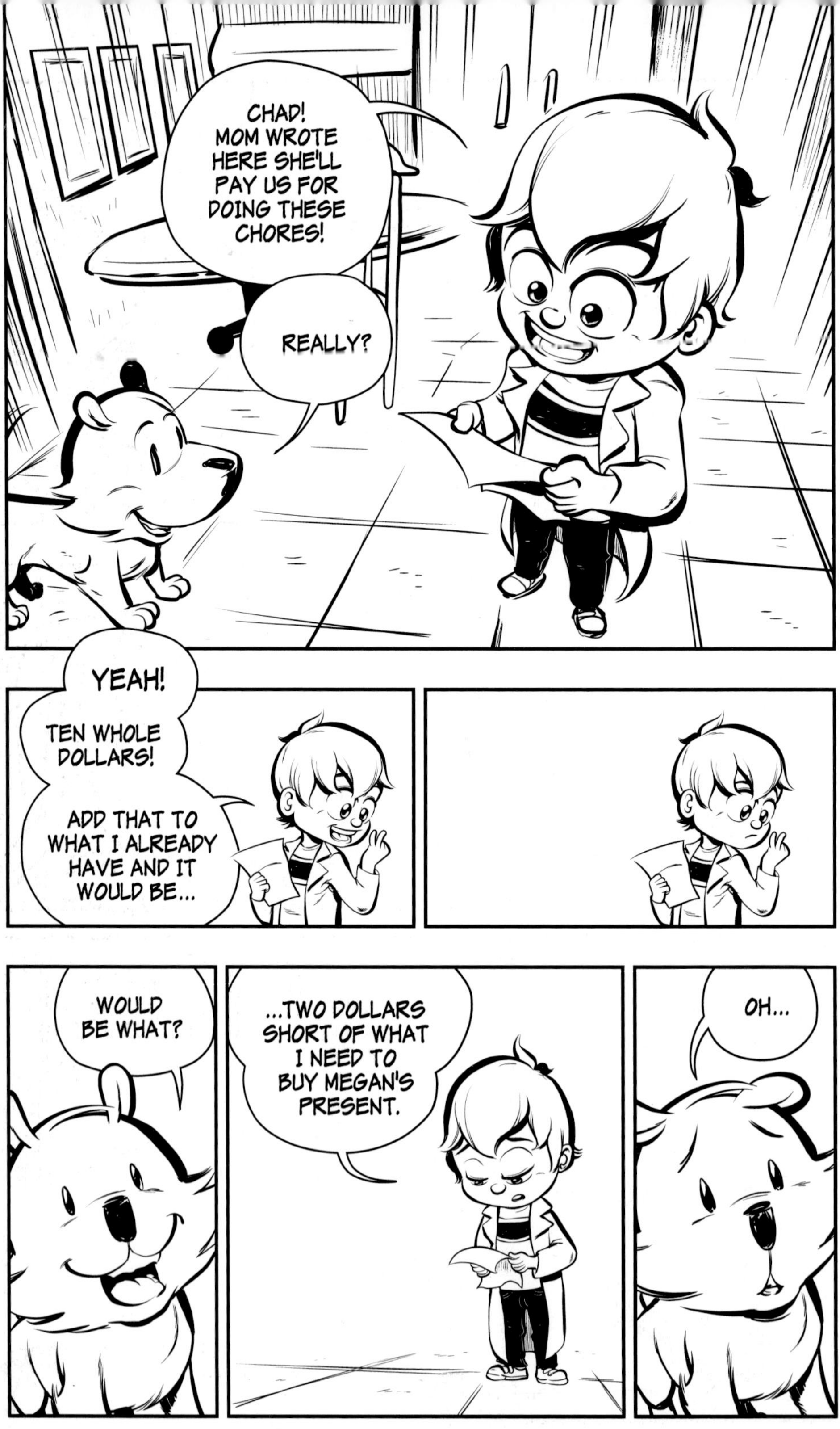
CHAD! MOM WROTE HERE SHE'LL PAY US FOR DOING THESE CHORES!
REALLY?
YEAH!
TEN WHOLE DOLLARS!
ADD THAT TO WHAT I ALREADY HAVE AND IT WOULD BE...
WOULD BE WHAT?
...TWO DOLLARS SHORT OF WHAT I NEED TO BUY MEGAN'S PRESENT.
OH...

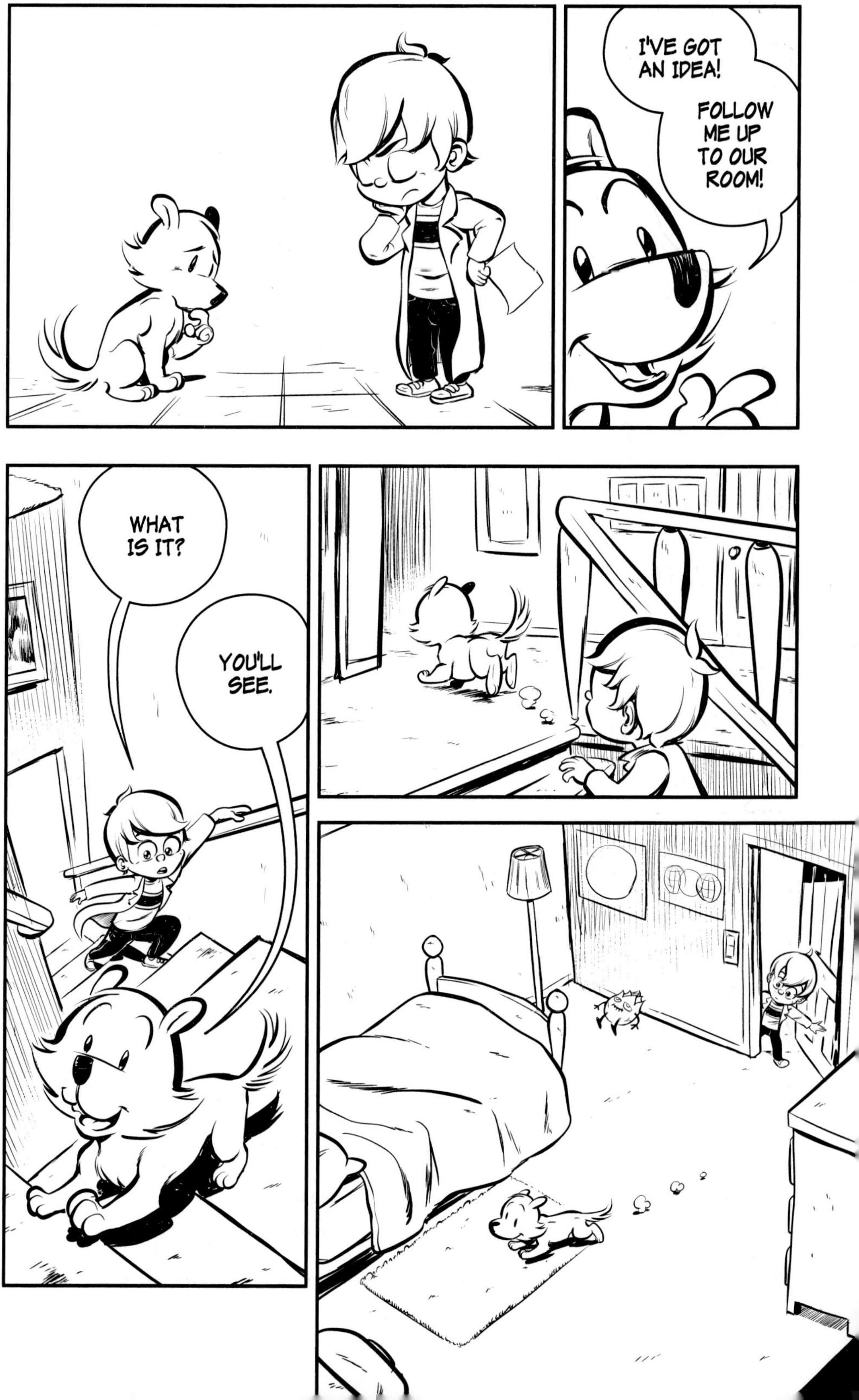
I'VE GOT AN IDEA!
FOLLOW ME UP TO OUR ROOM!
WHAT IS IT?
YOU'LL SEE.

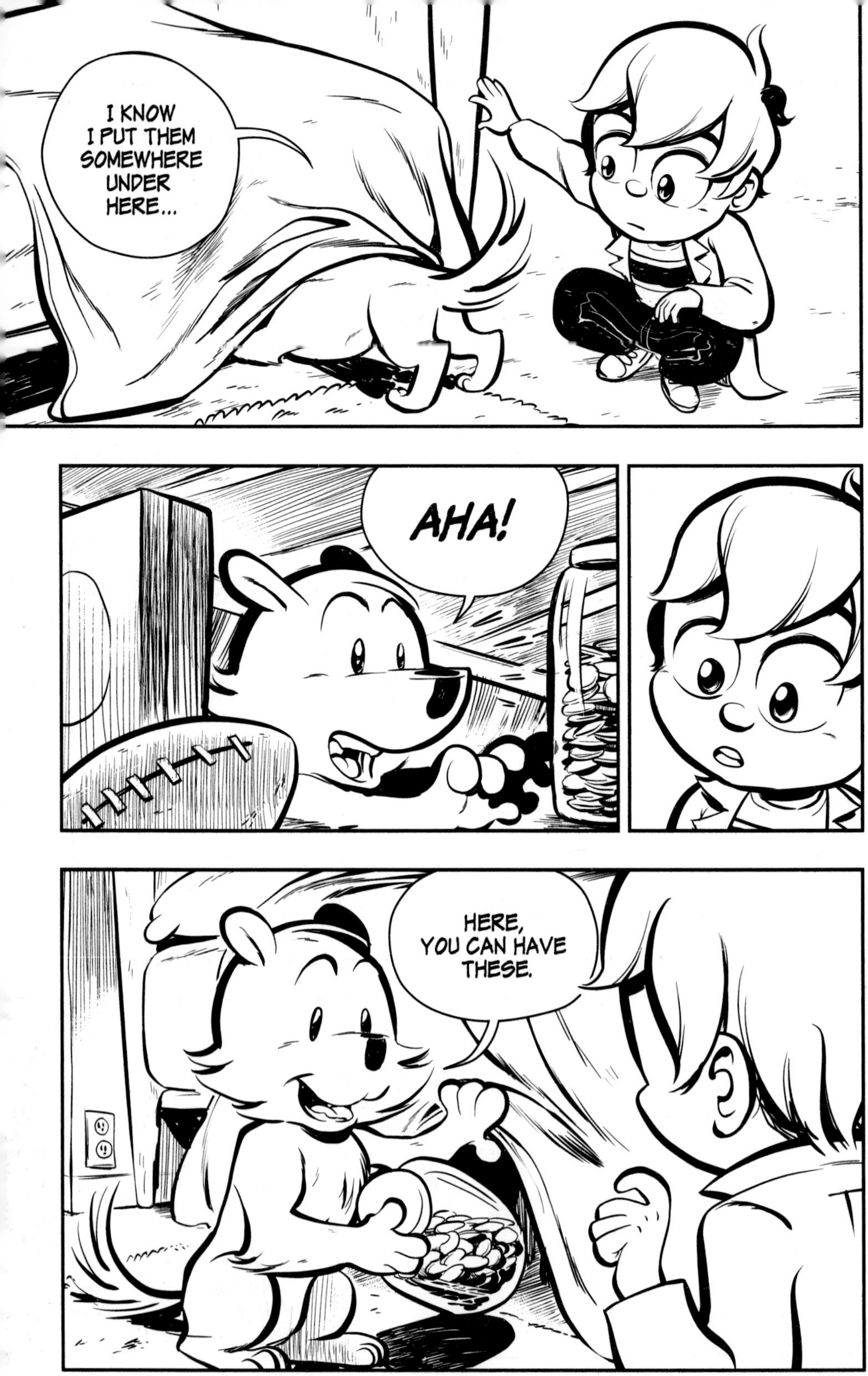
I KNOW
I PUT THEM
SOMEWHERE
UNDER
HERE...
AHA!
HERE,
YOU CAN HAVE
THESE.

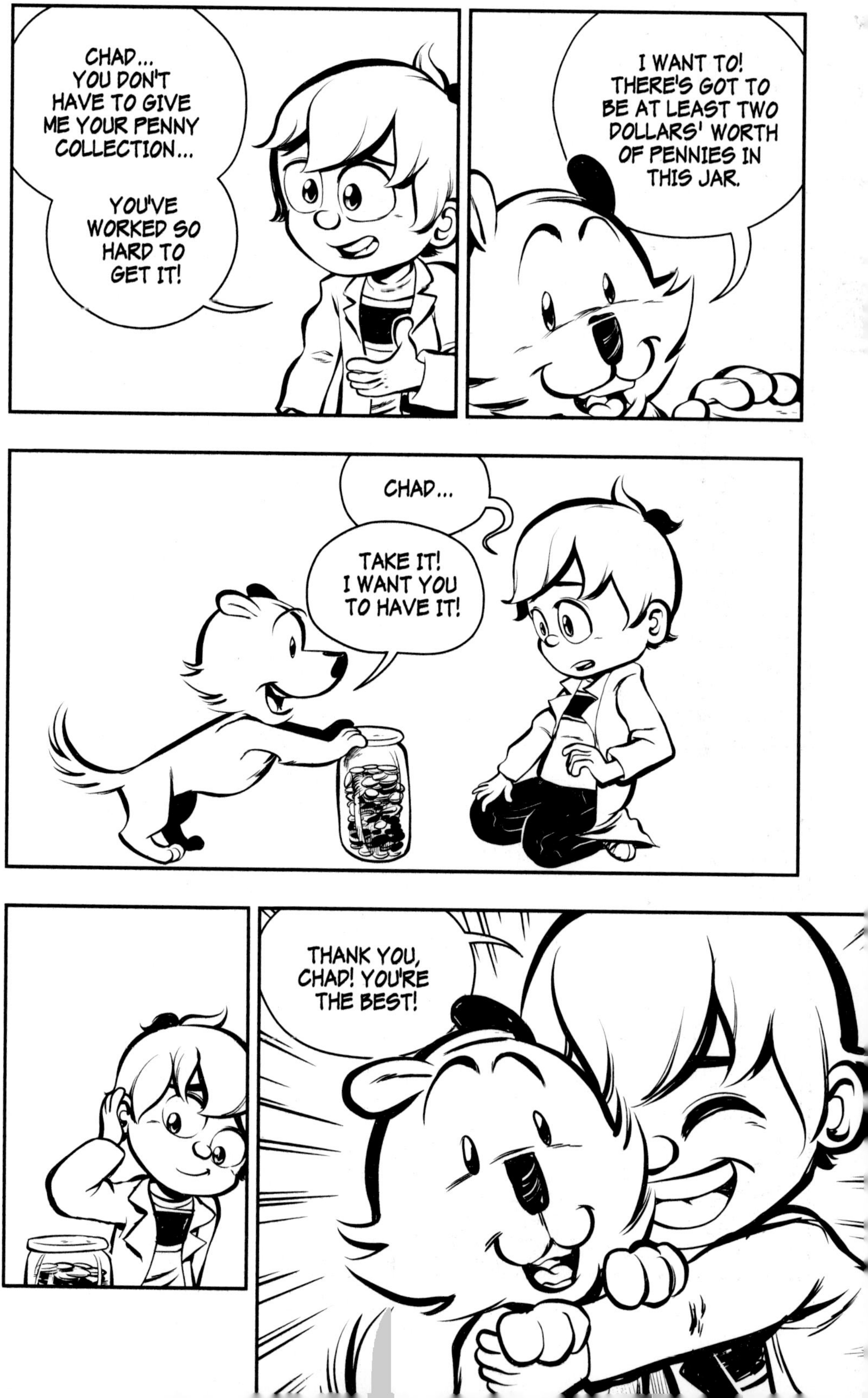
CHAD... YOU DON'T HAVE TO GIVE ME YOUR PENNY COLLECTION...
YOU'VE WORKED SO HARD TO GET IT!
I WANT TO! THERE'S GOT TO BE AT LEAST TWO DOLLARS' WORTH OF PENNIES IN THIS JAR.
CHAD...
TAKE IT! I WANT YOU TO HAVE IT!
THANK YOU, CHAD! YOU'RE THE BEST!

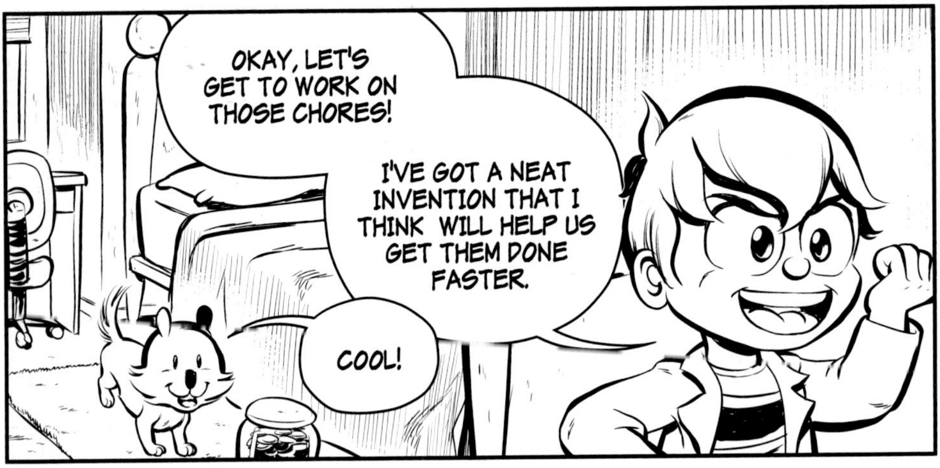
OKAY, LET'S GET TO WORK ON THOSE CHORES!
I'VE GOT A NEAT INVENTION THAT I THINK WILL HELP US GET THEM DONE FASTER.
COOL!

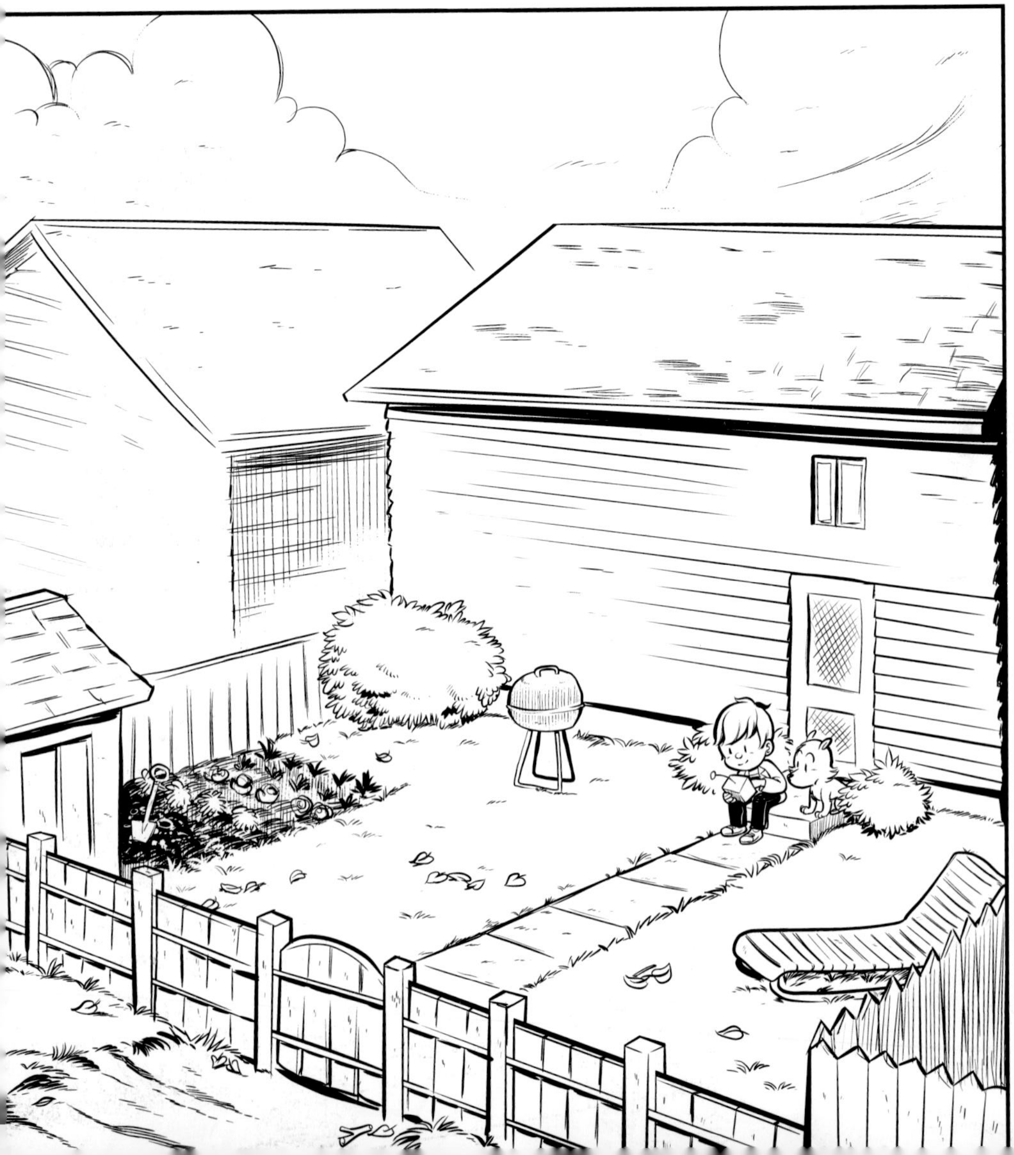

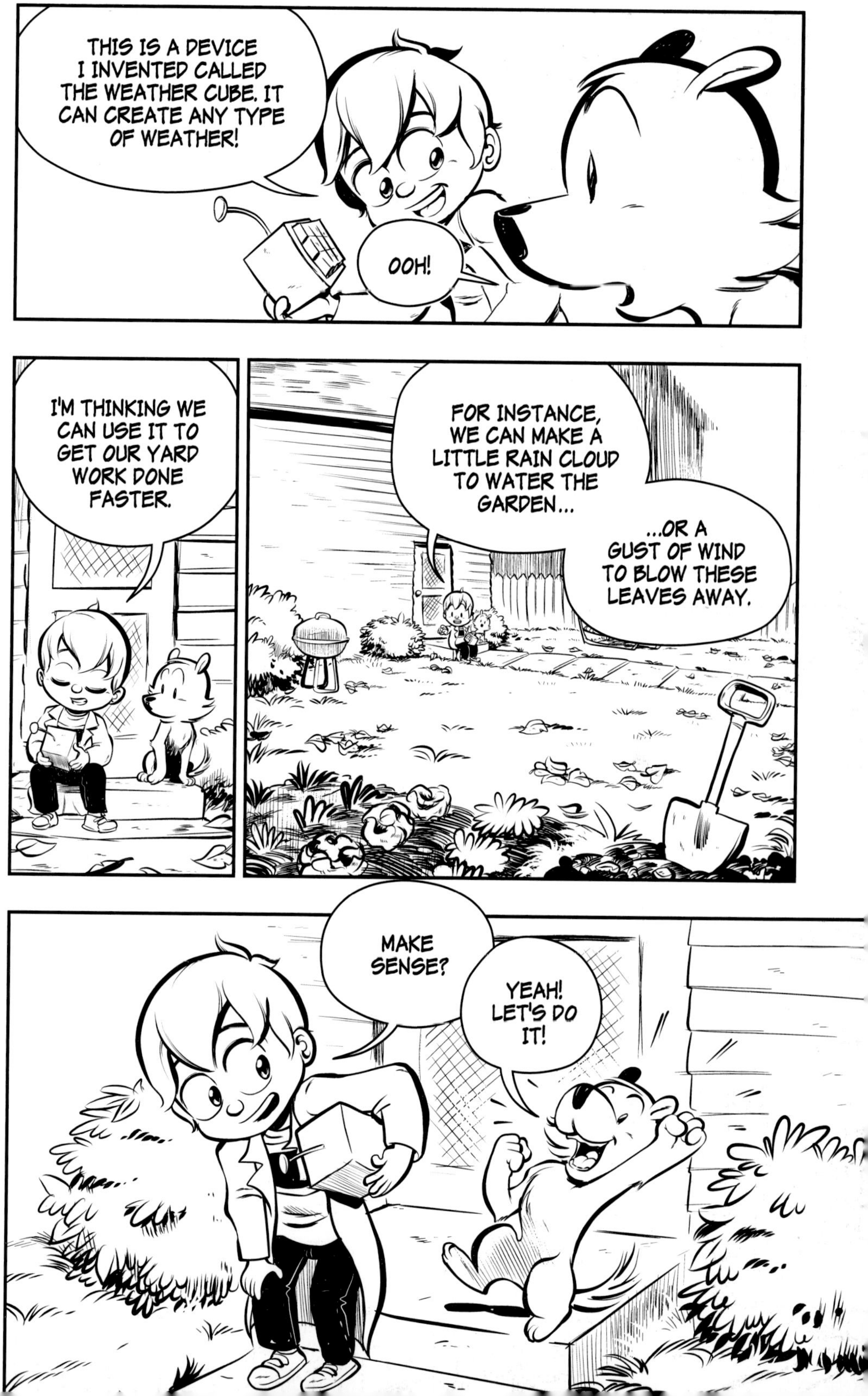
THIS IS A DEVICE I INVENTED CALLED THE WEATHER CUBE. IT CAN CREATE ANY TYPE OF WEATHER!
OOH!
I'M THINKING WE CAN USE IT TO GET OUR YARD WORK DONE FASTER.
FOR INSTANCE, WE CAN MAKE A LITTLE RAIN CLOUD TO WATER THE GARDEN...
...OR A GUST OF WIND TO BLOW THESE LEAVES AWAY.
MAKE SENSE?
YEAH! LET'S DO IT!

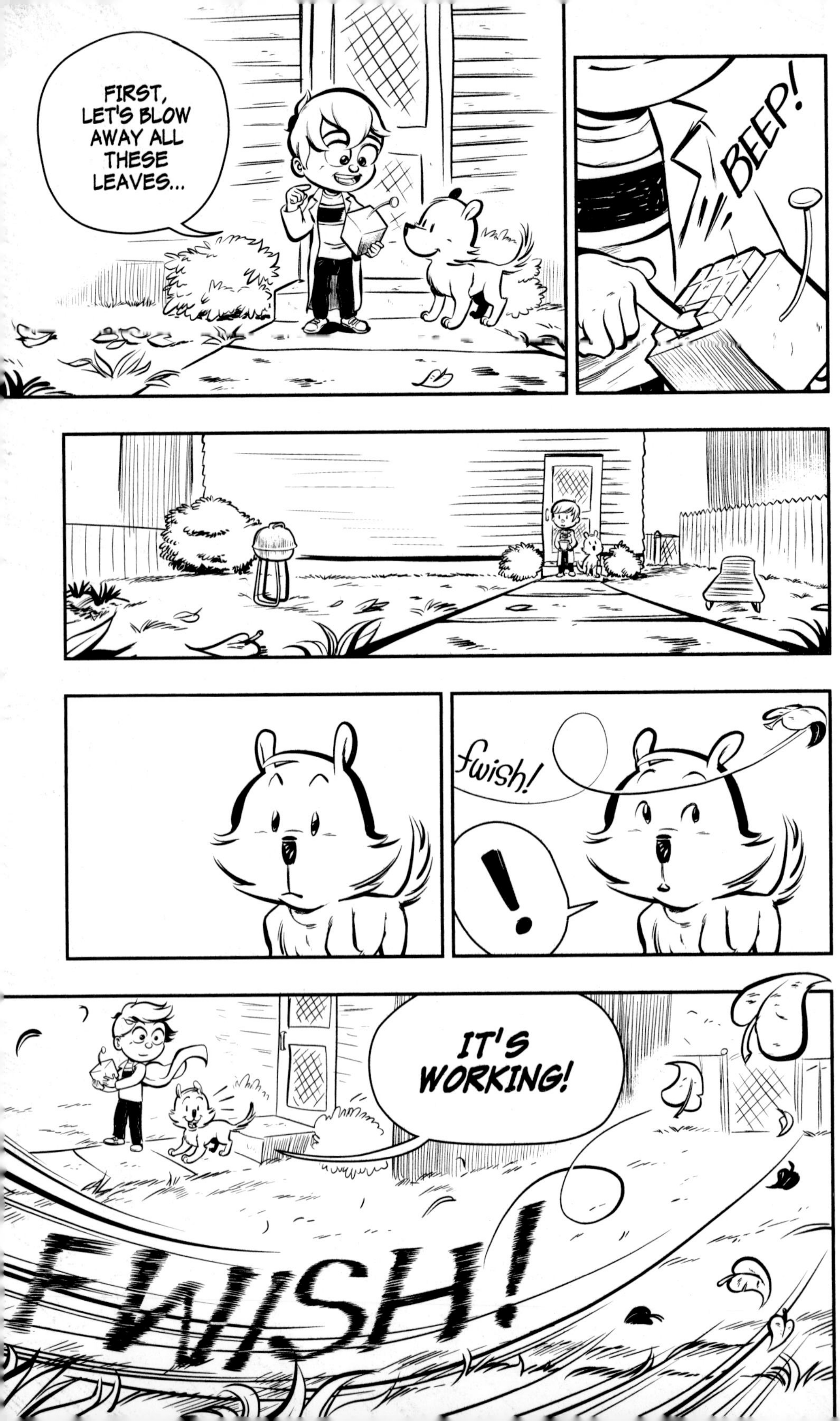
FIRST, LET'S BLOW AWAY ALL THESE LEAVES...
BEEP!
fwish!
!
IT'S WORKING!
FWISH!

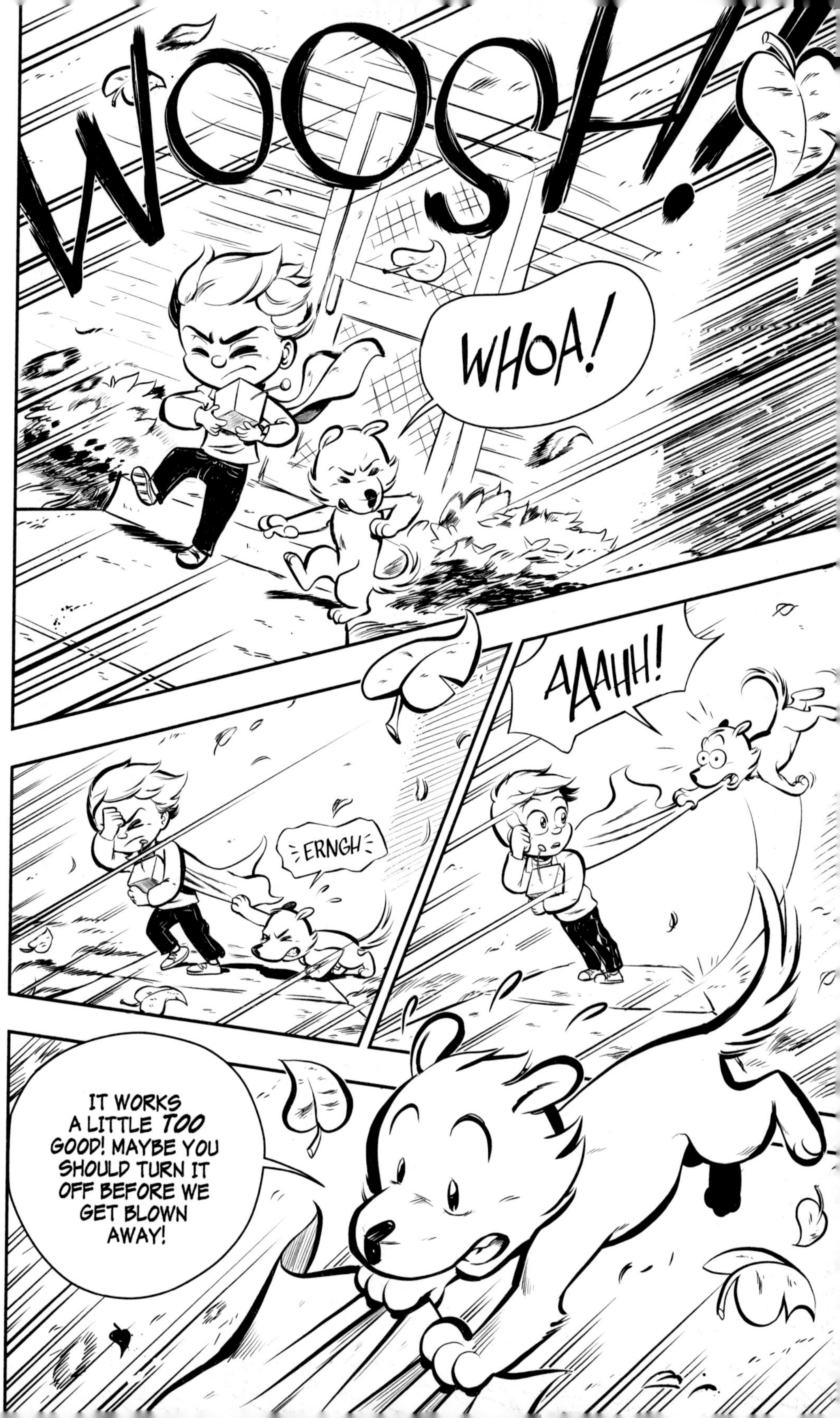
WOOSH!
WHOA!
ERNGH
AAAHH!
IT WORKS A LITTLE *TOO* GOOD! MAYBE YOU SHOULD TURN IT OFF BEFORE WE GET BLOWN AWAY!

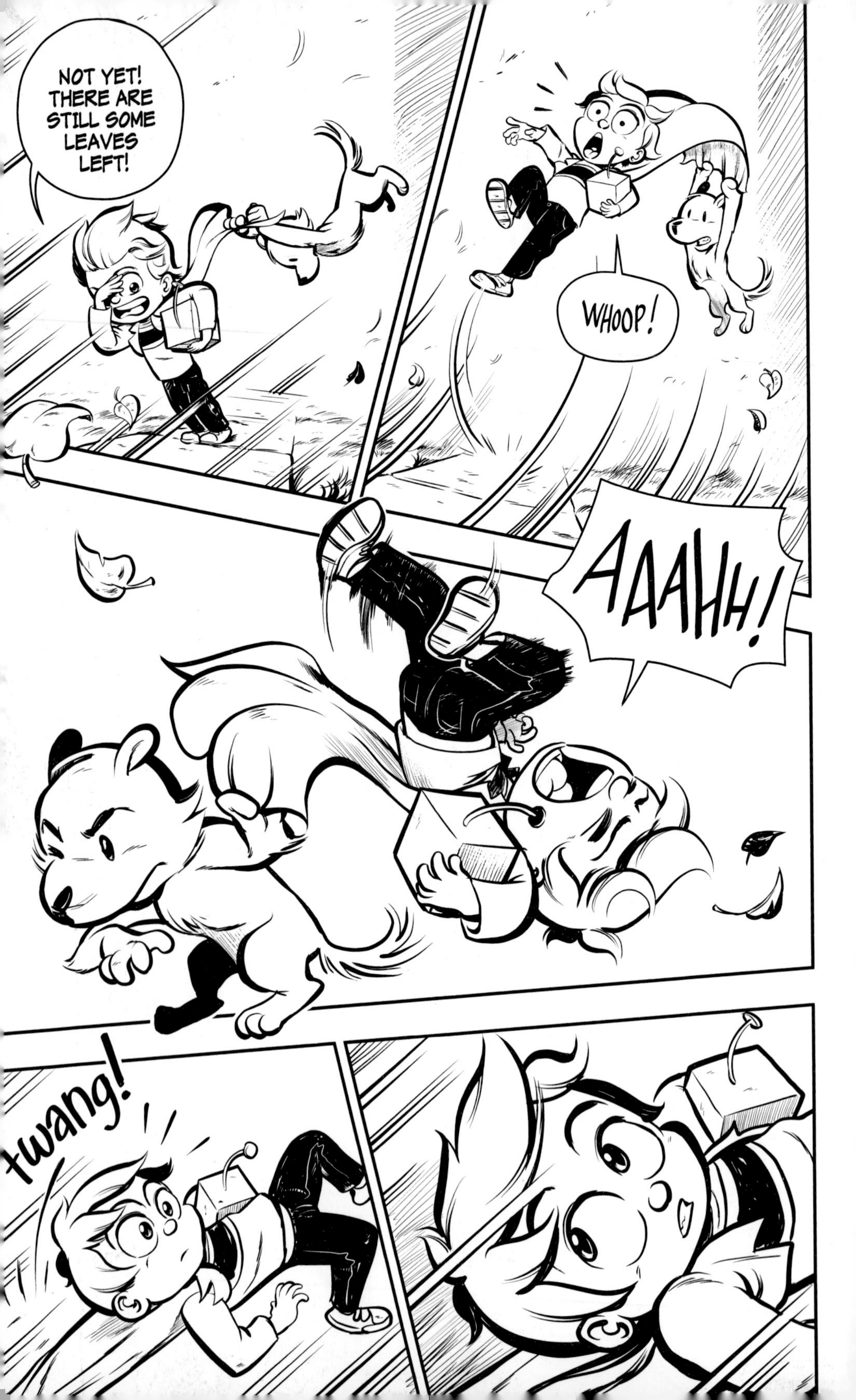
NOT YET! THERE ARE STILL SOME LEAVES LEFT!
WHOOP!
AAAHH!
twang!

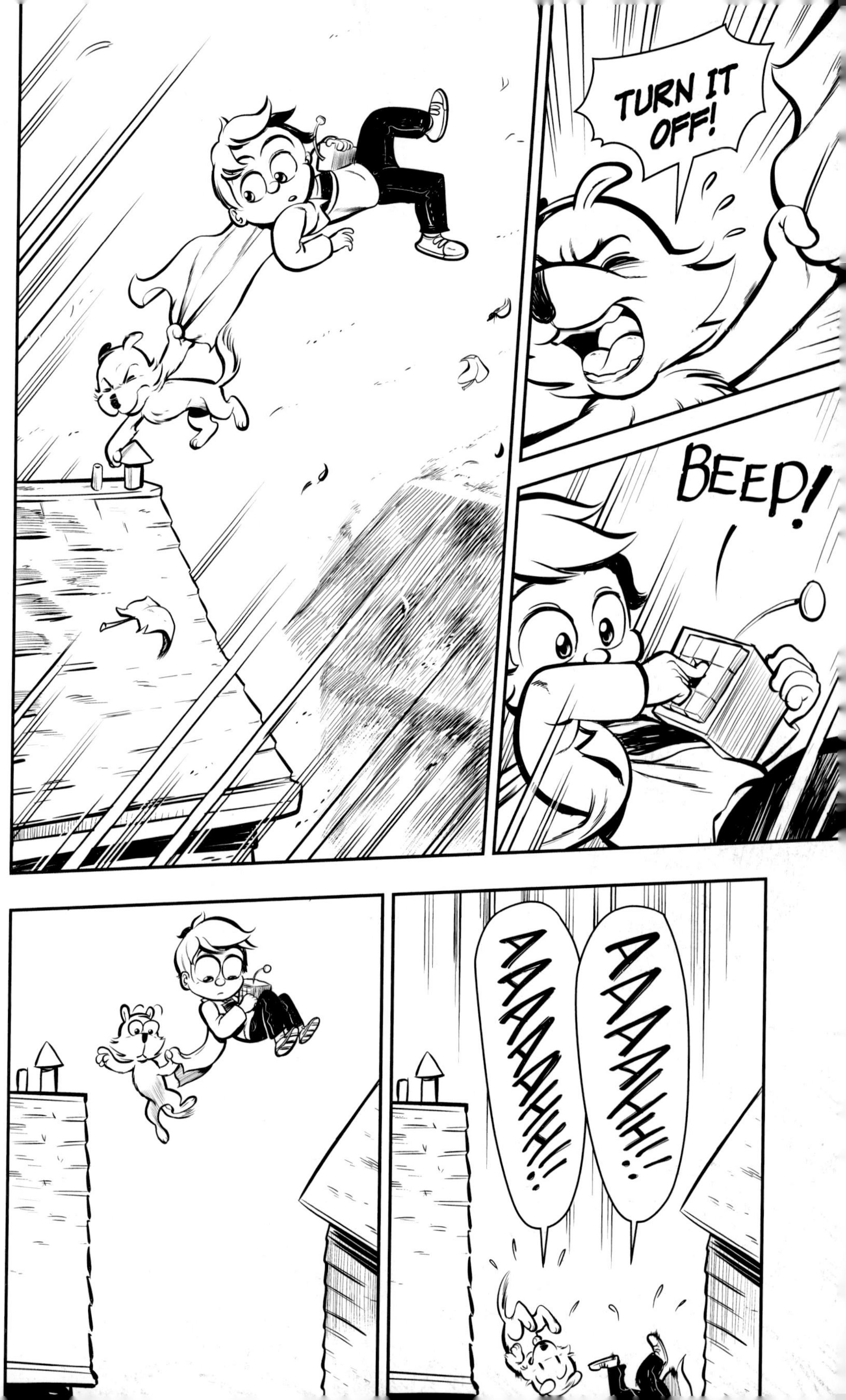
TURN IT OFF!
BEEP!
AAAAAAHH!!!
AAAAAAHH!!!

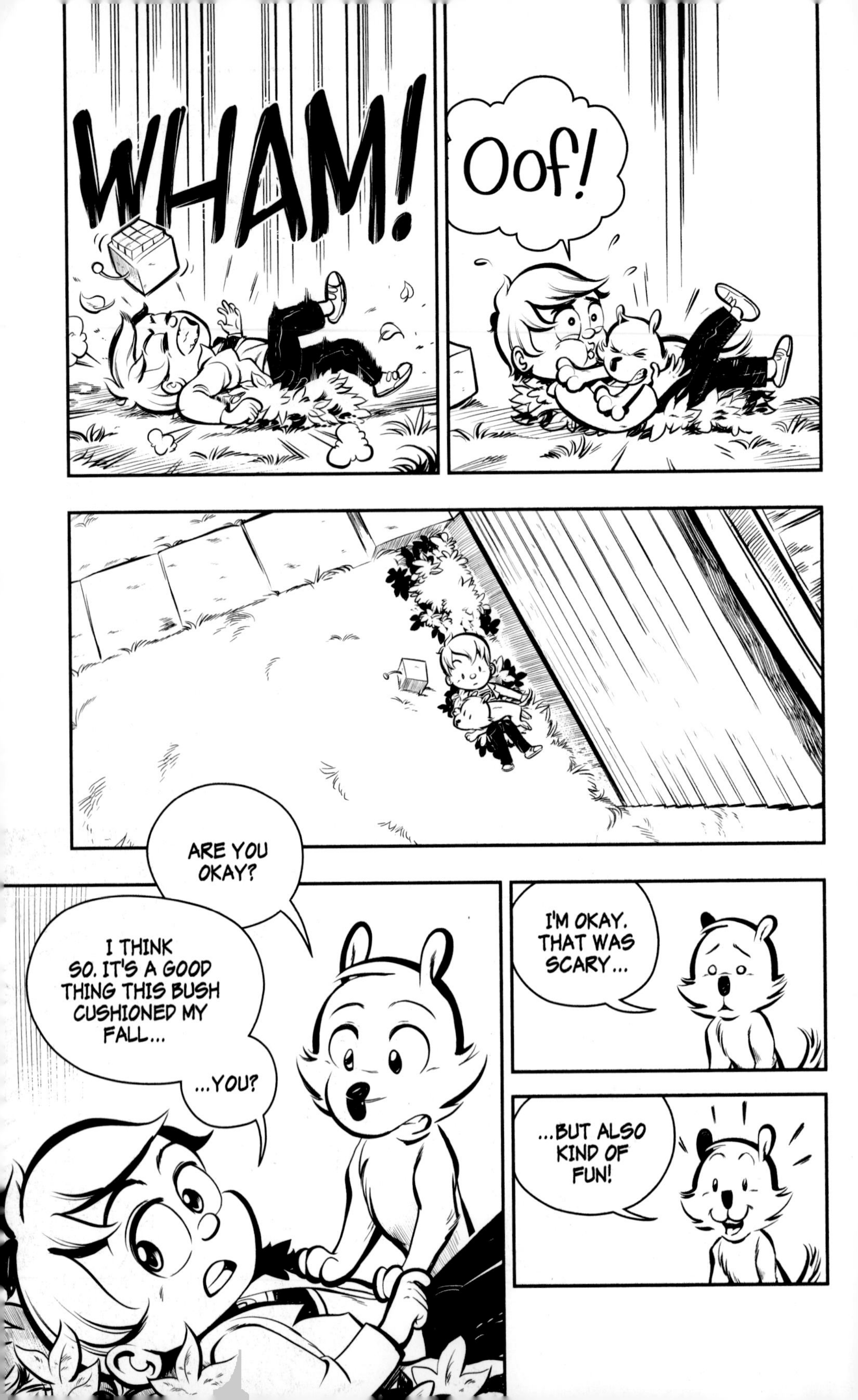
WHAM!
Oof!
ARE YOU OKAY?
I THINK SO. IT'S A GOOD THING THIS BUSH CUSHIONED MY FALL...
...YOU?
I'M OKAY. THAT WAS SCARY...
...BUT ALSO KIND OF FUN!

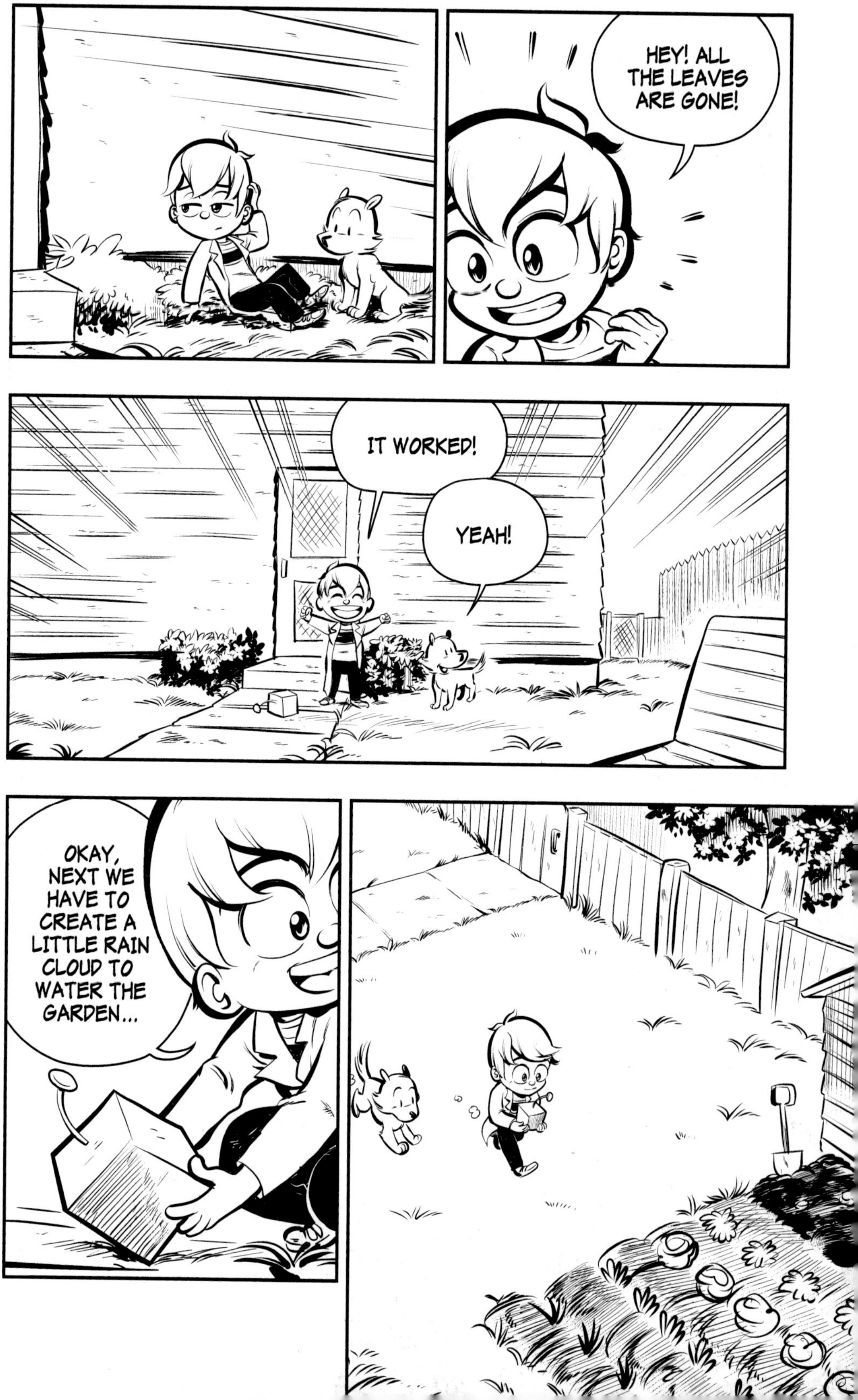
HEY! ALL THE LEAVES ARE GONE!
IT WORKED!
YEAH!
OKAY, NEXT WE HAVE TO CREATE A LITTLE RAIN CLOUD TO WATER THE GARDEN...

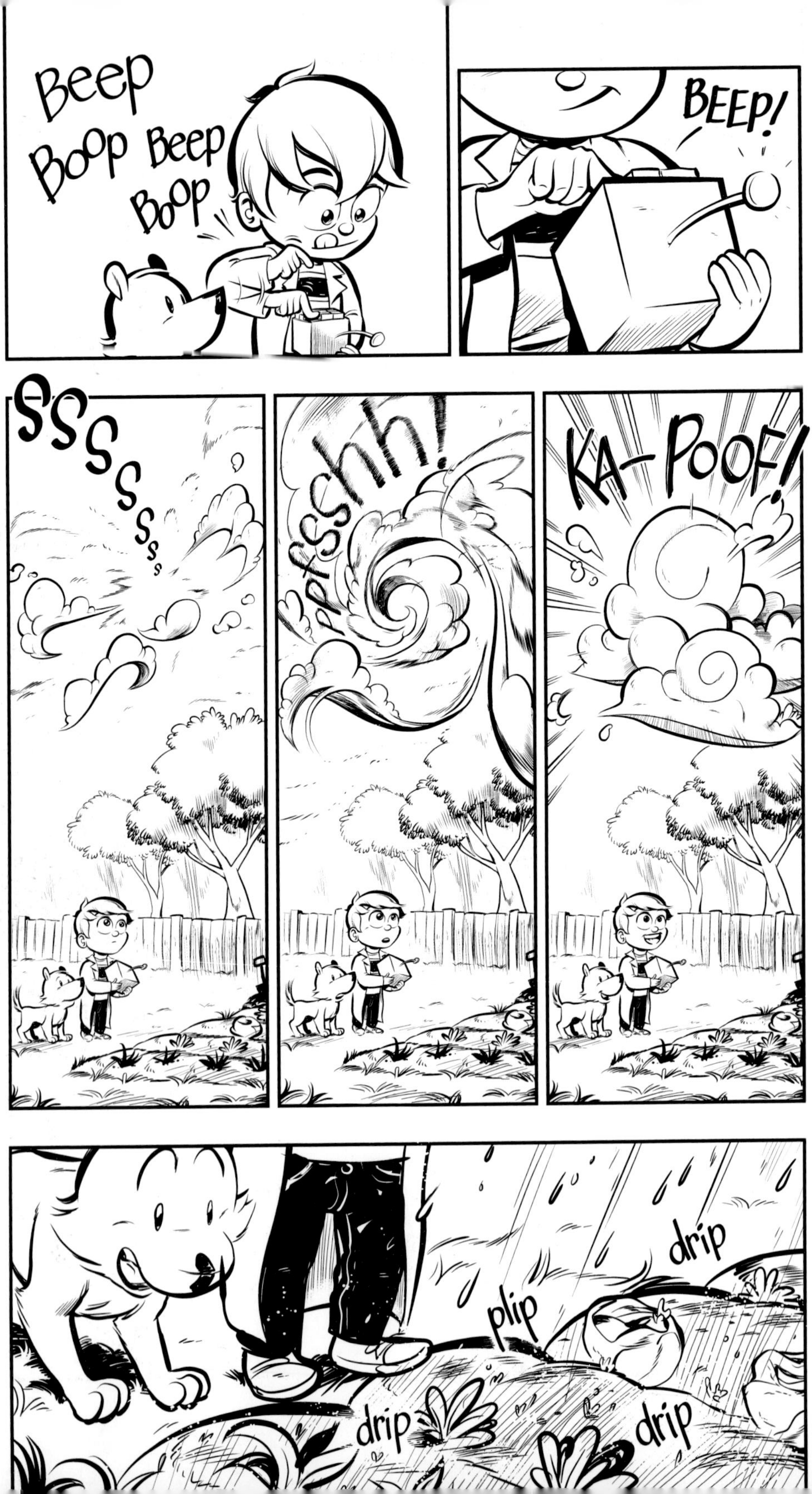
Beep
Boop Beep
Boop
BEEP!
SSSSSsss
pfsshh!
KA-POOF!
drip
plip
drip
drip

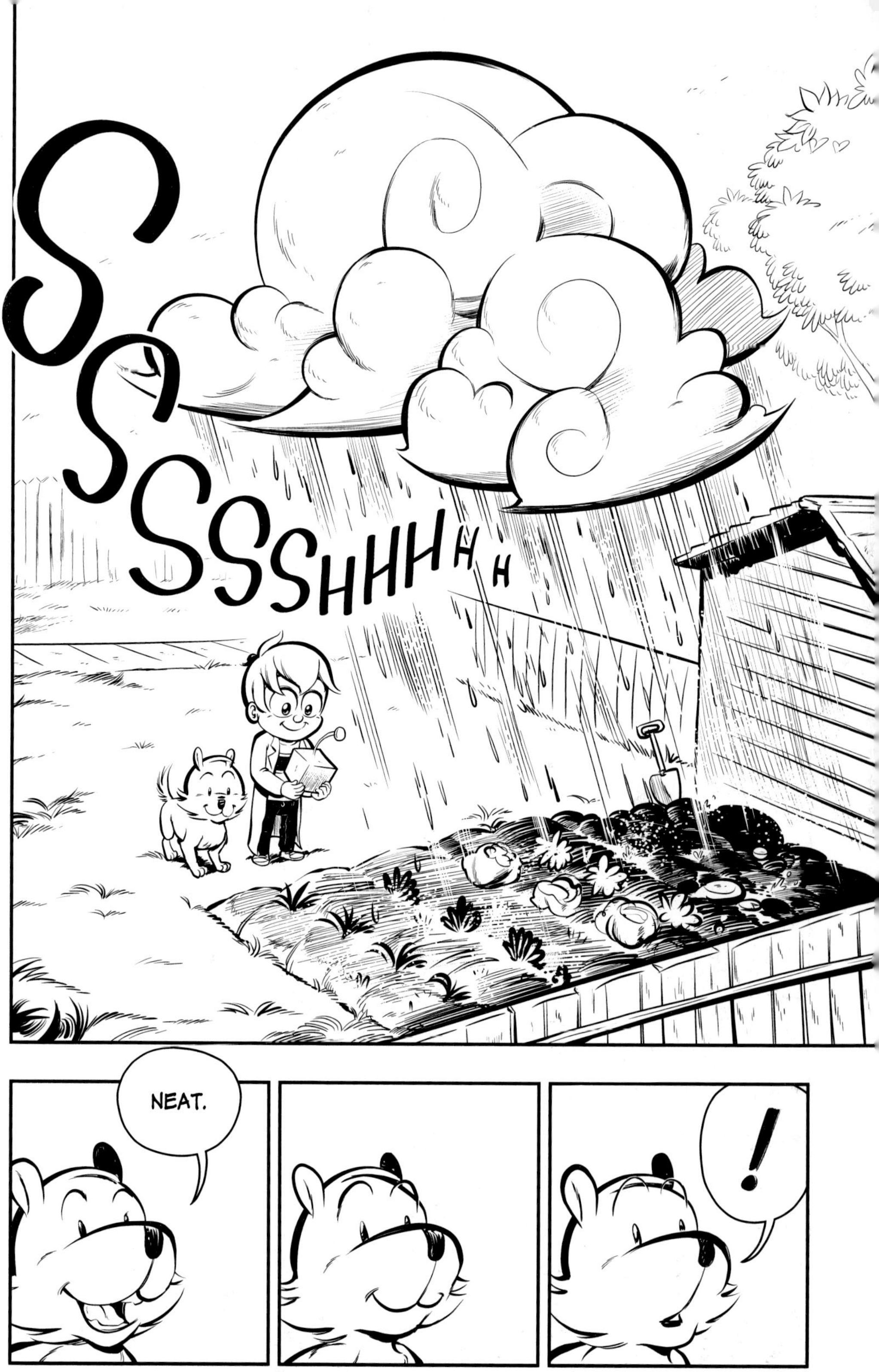
SSSSSSHHHHHH
NEAT.
!

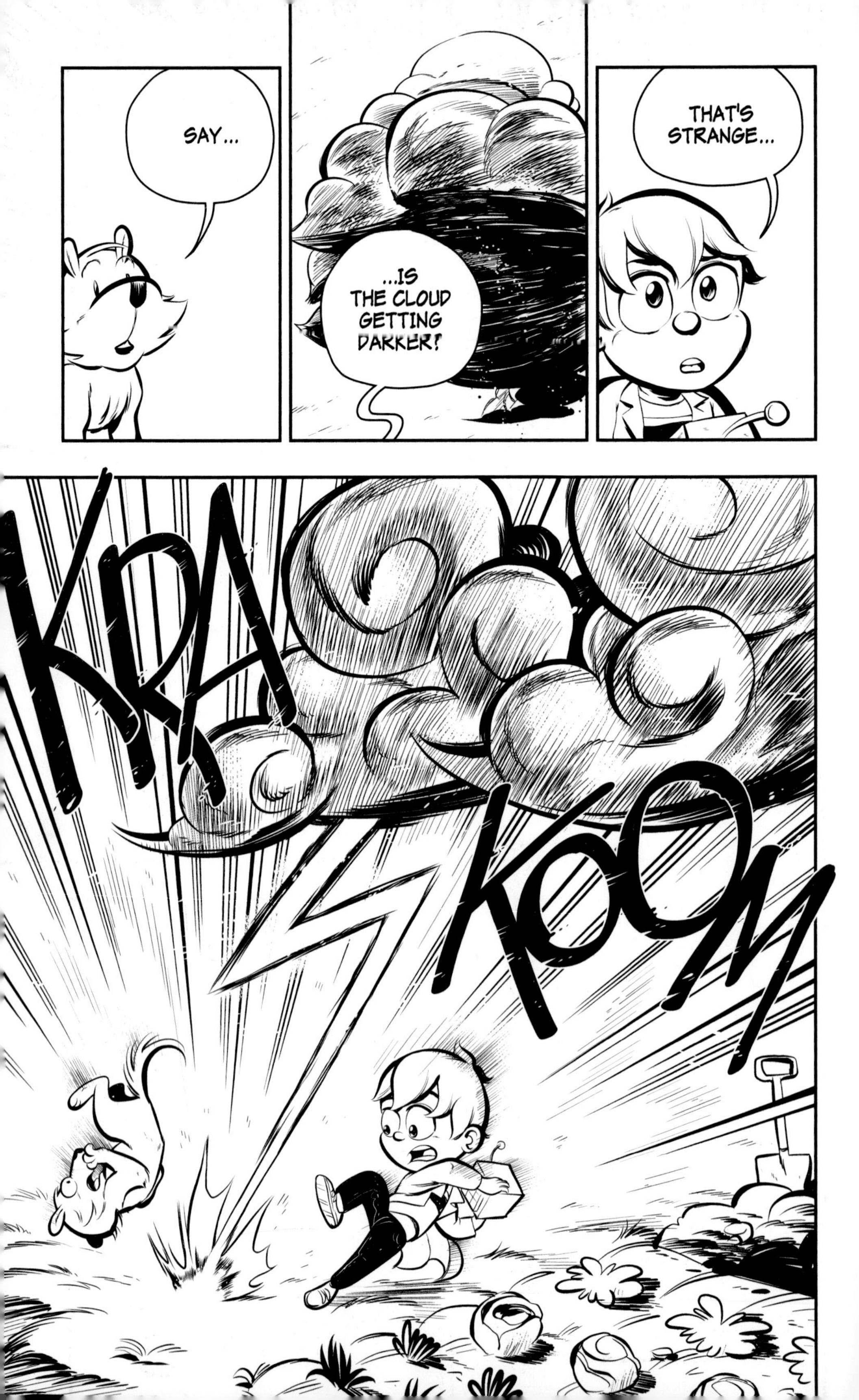
SAY...
...IS THE CLOUD GETTING DARKER?
THAT'S STRANGE...
KRA
KOOM

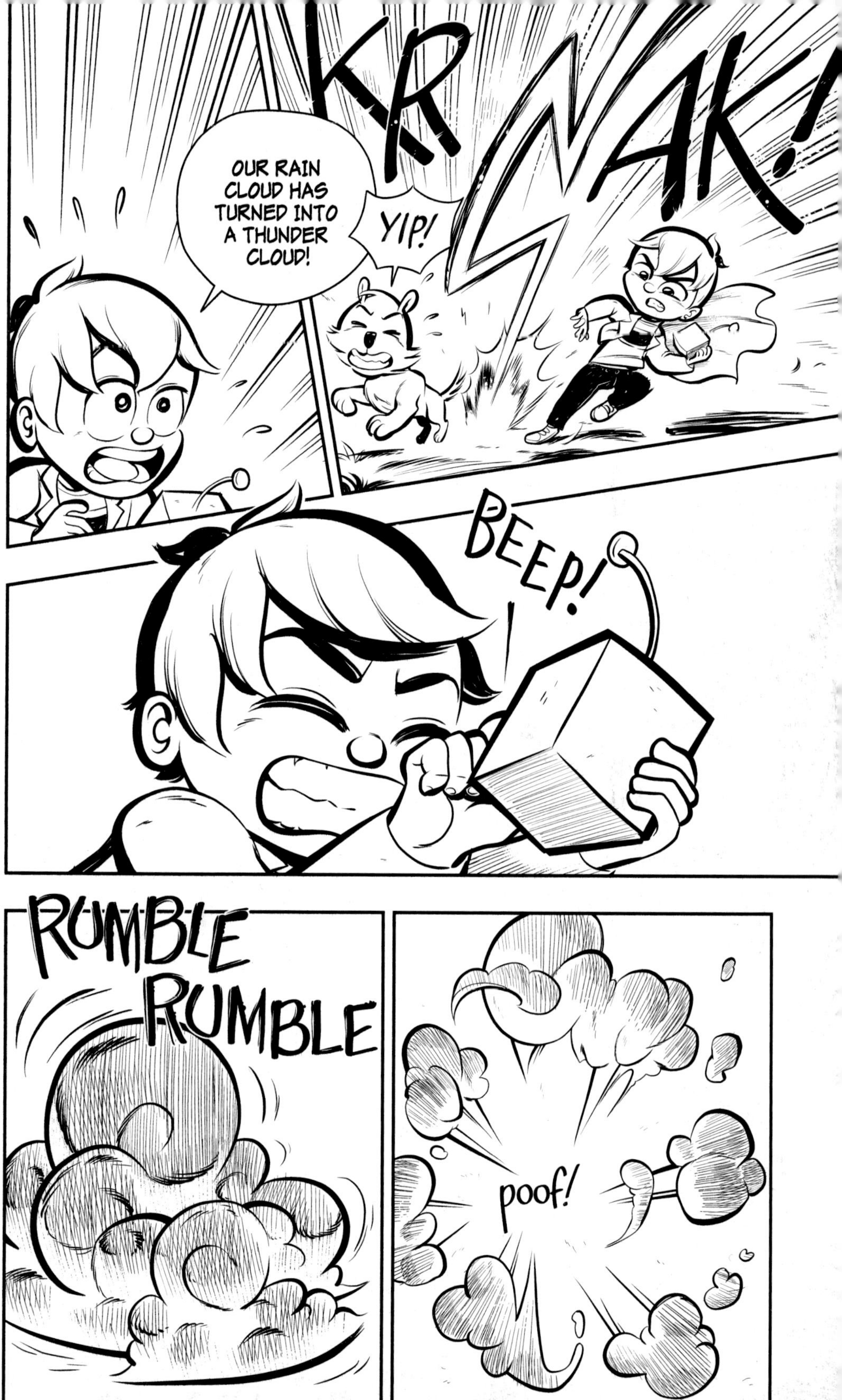
KRSNAK!
OUR RAIN CLOUD HAS TURNED INTO A THUNDER CLOUD!
YIP!
BEEP!
RUMBLE
RUMBLE
poof!

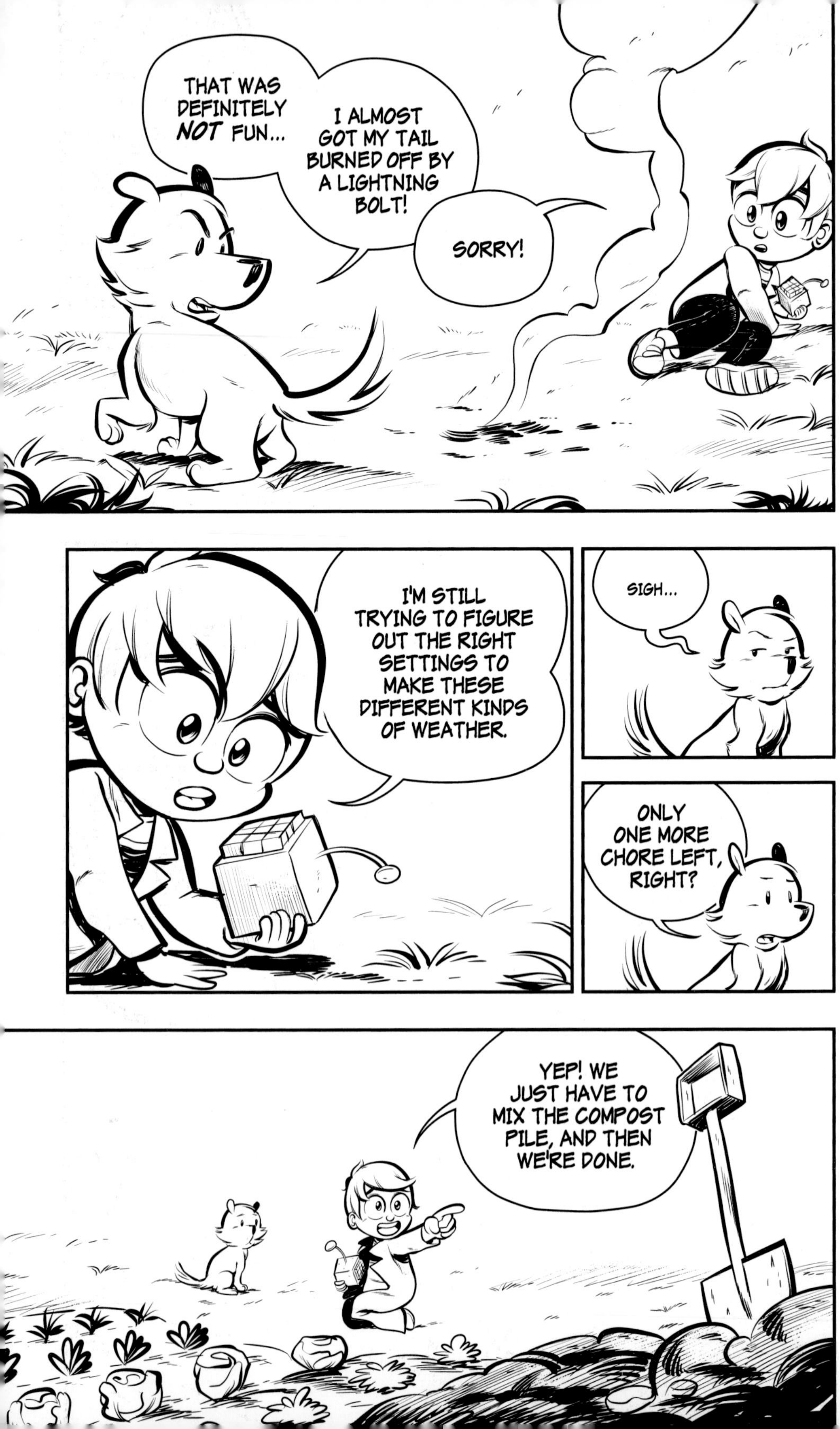
THAT WAS DEFINITELY *NOT* FUN...
I ALMOST GOT MY TAIL BURNED OFF BY A LIGHTNING BOLT!
SORRY!
I'M STILL TRYING TO FIGURE OUT THE RIGHT SETTINGS TO MAKE THESE DIFFERENT KINDS OF WEATHER.
SIGH...
ONLY ONE MORE CHORE LEFT, RIGHT?
YEP! WE JUST HAVE TO MIX THE COMPOST PILE, AND THEN WE'RE DONE.

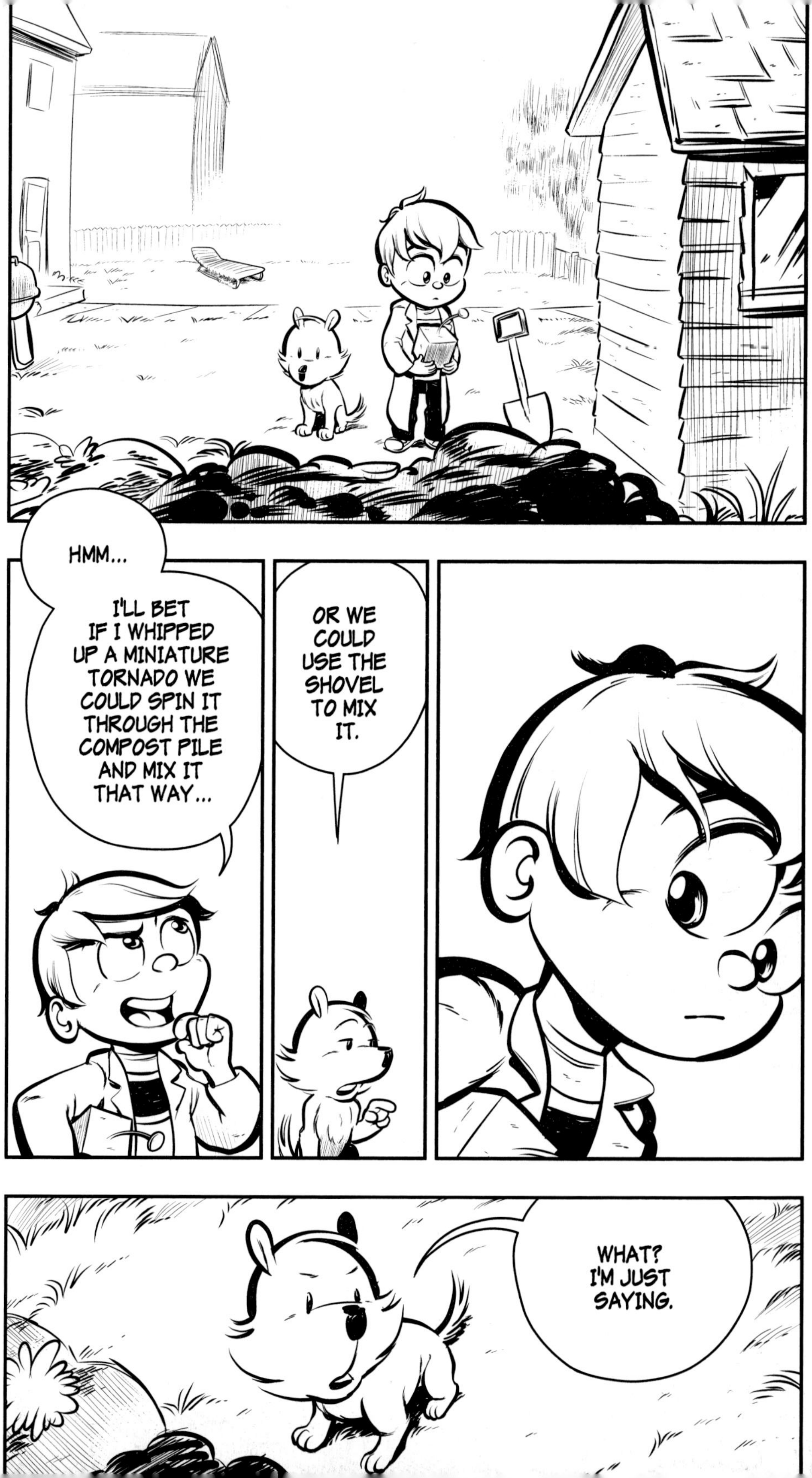
HMM...
I'LL BET IF I WHIPPED UP A MINIATURE TORNADO WE COULD SPIN IT THROUGH THE COMPOST PILE AND MIX IT THAT WAY...
OR WE COULD USE THE SHOVEL TO MIX IT.
WHAT? I'M JUST SAYING.

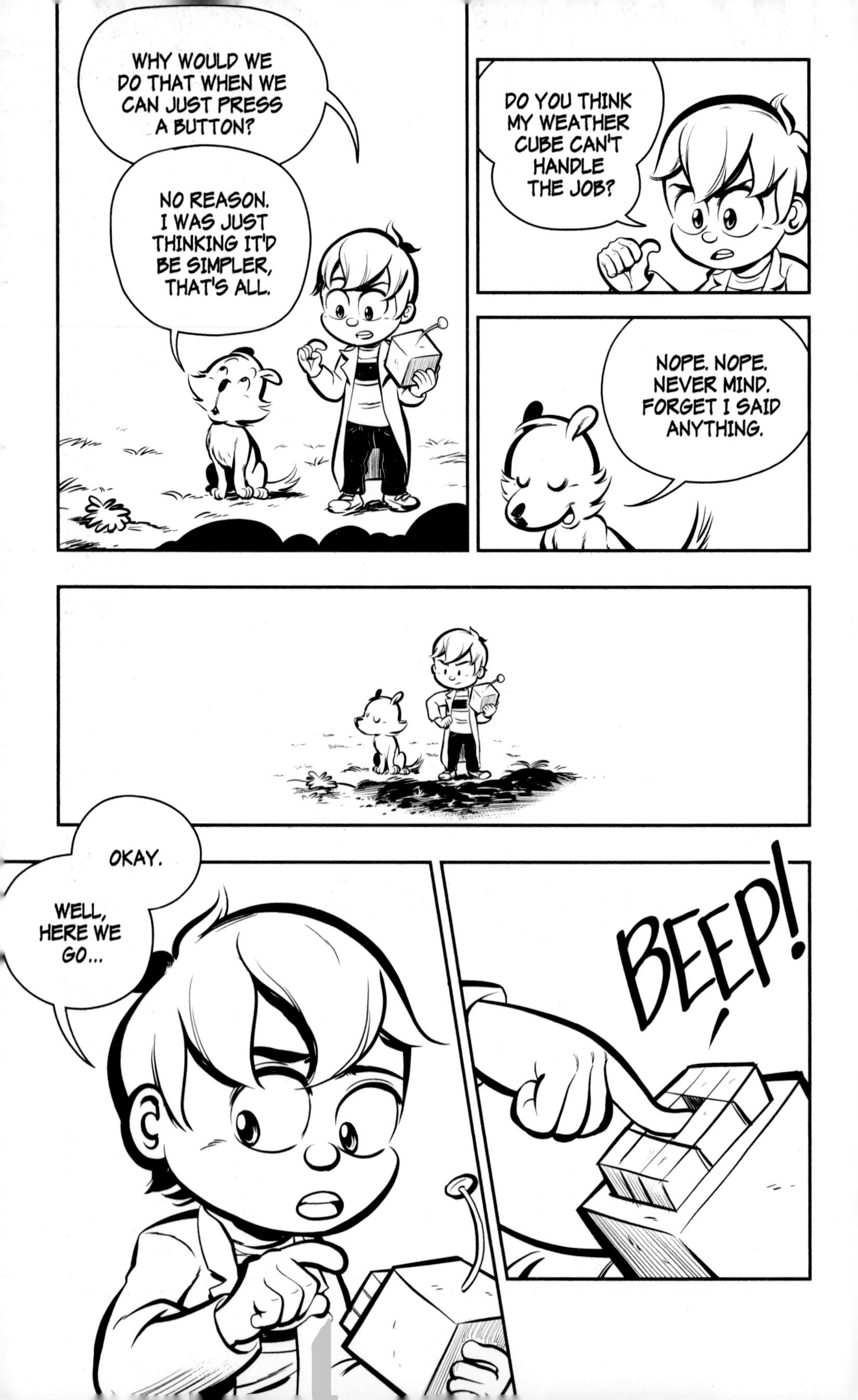
WHY WOULD WE DO THAT WHEN WE CAN JUST PRESS A BUTTON?
NO REASON. I WAS JUST THINKING IT'D BE SIMPLER, THAT'S ALL.
DO YOU THINK MY WEATHER CUBE CAN'T HANDLE THE JOB?
NOPE. NOPE. NEVER MIND. FORGET I SAID ANYTHING.
OKAY.
WELL, HERE WE GO...
BEEP!

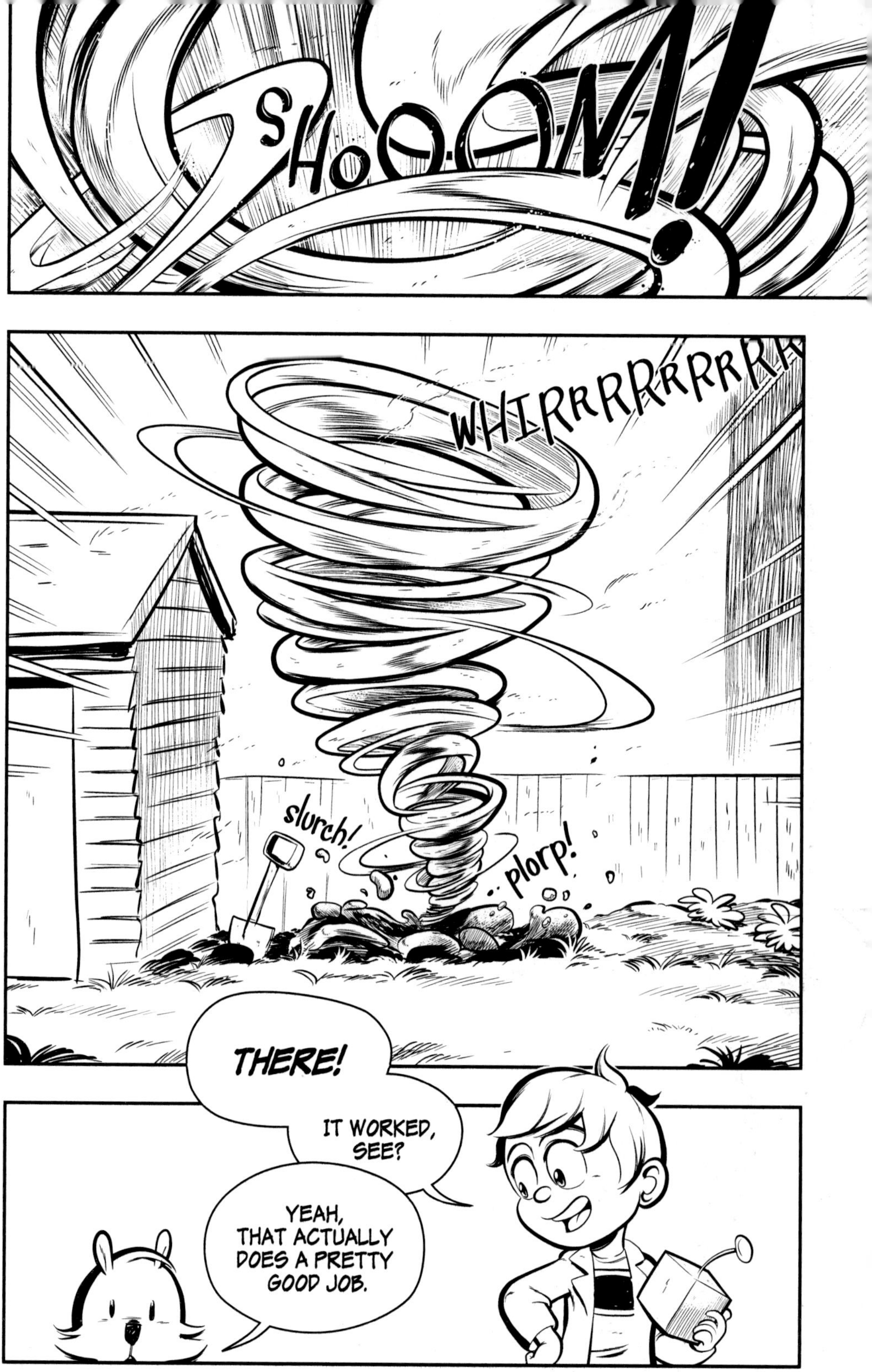
SHOOOM!
WHIRRRRRRRRR
slurch!
plorp!
THERE!
IT WORKED, SEE?
YEAH, THAT ACTUALLY DOES A PRETTY GOOD JOB.

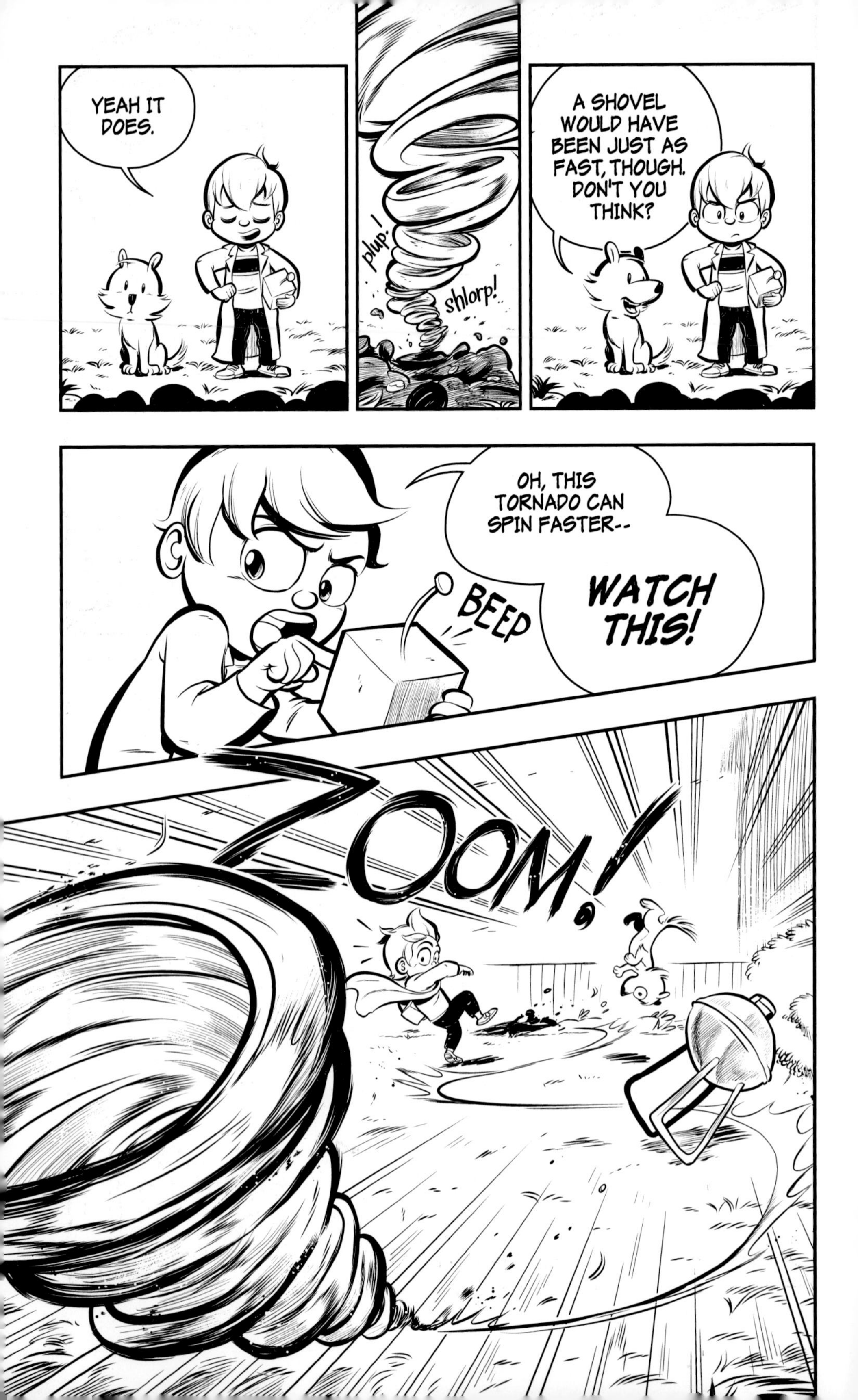
YEAH IT DOES.
plup!
shlorp!
A SHOVEL WOULD HAVE BEEN JUST AS FAST, THOUGH. DON'T YOU THINK?
OH, THIS TORNADO CAN SPIN FASTER--
WATCH THIS!
BEEP
ZOOM!

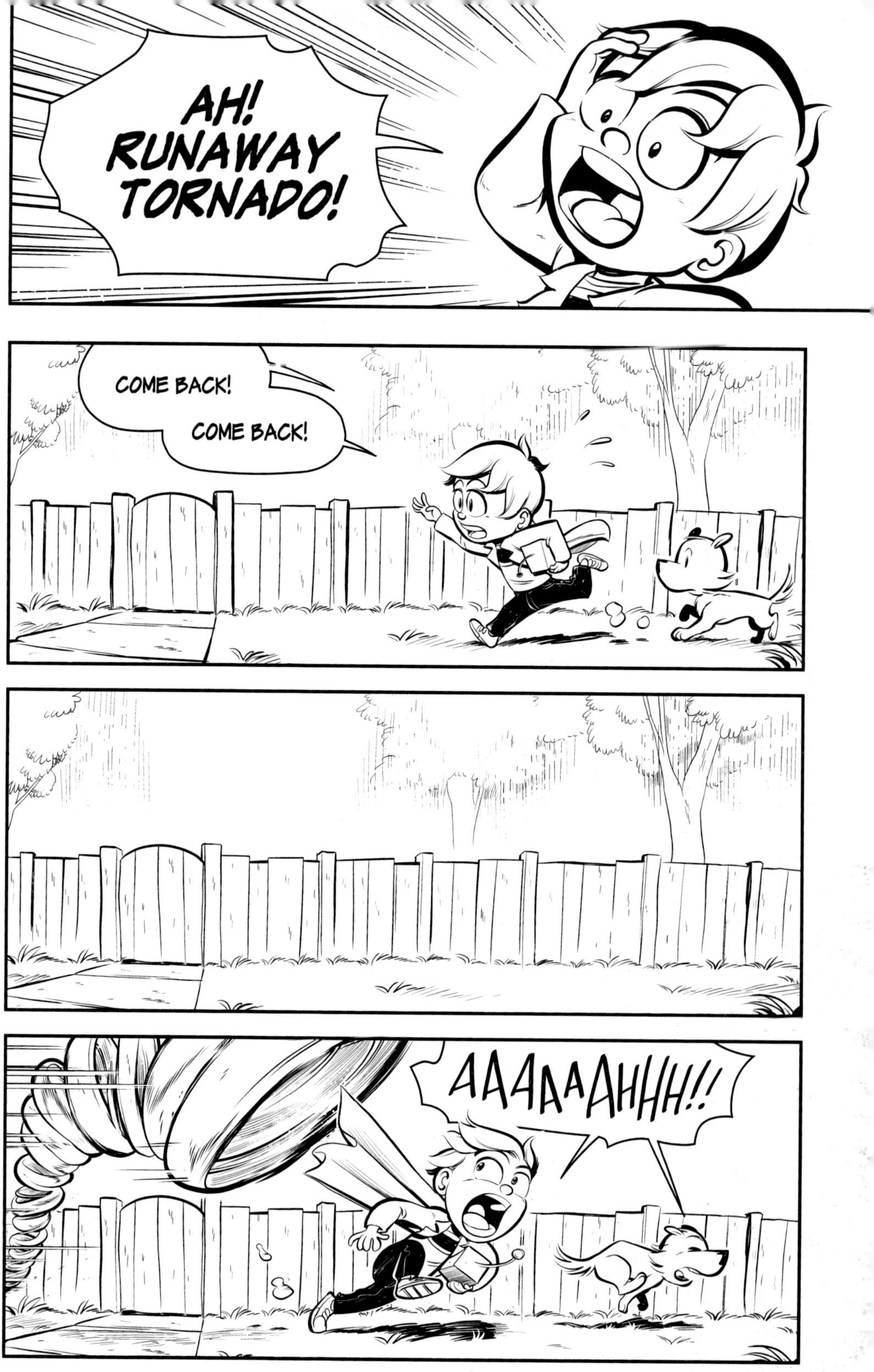
AH! RUNAWAY TORNADO!
COME BACK!
COME BACK!
AAAAAAHHHH!!

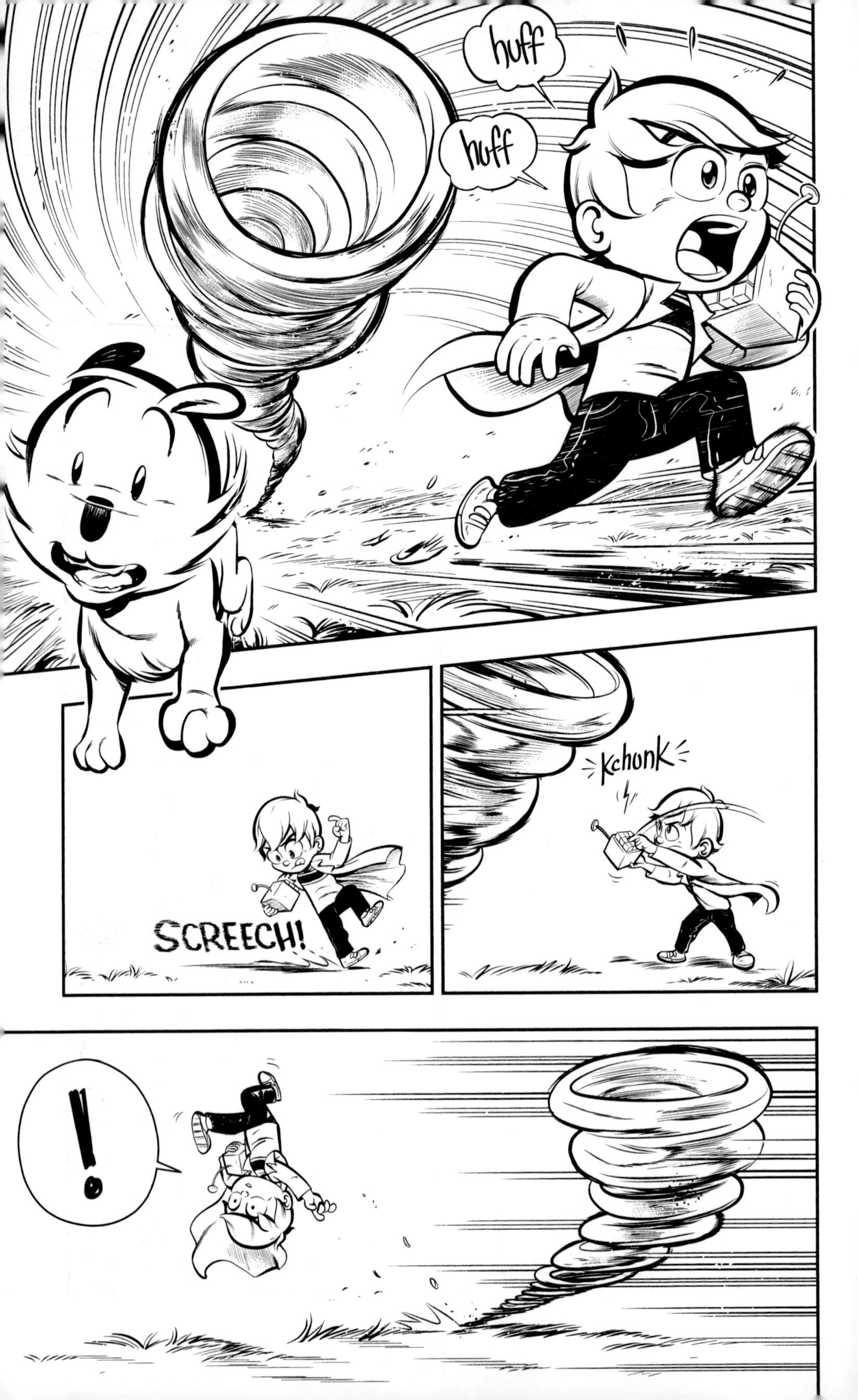

huff
huff
SCREECH!
Kchonk
!

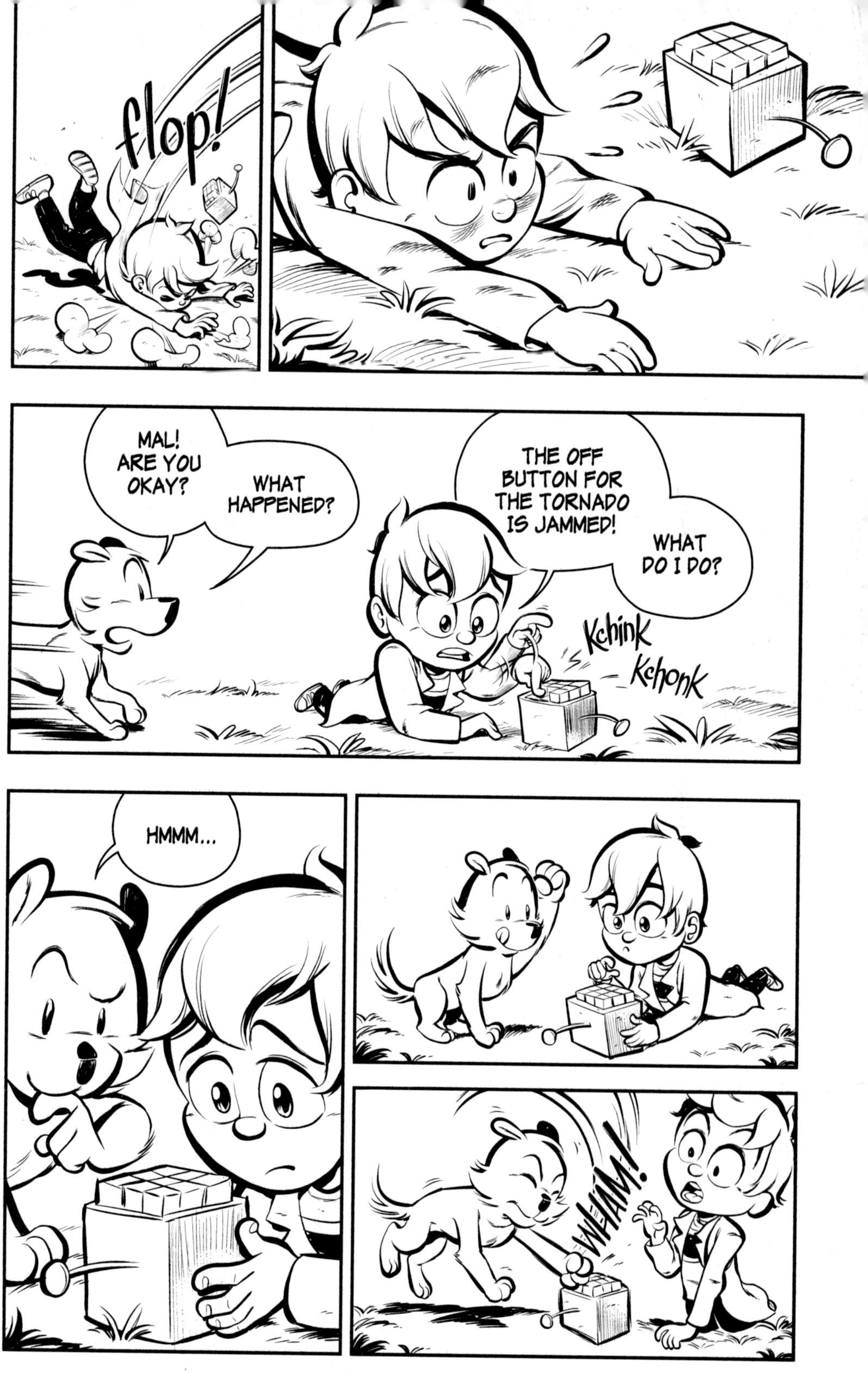
flop!
MAL! ARE YOU OKAY?
WHAT HAPPENED?
THE OFF BUTTON FOR THE TORNADO IS JAMMED!
WHAT DO I DO?
Kchink
Kchonk
HMMM...
WHAM!

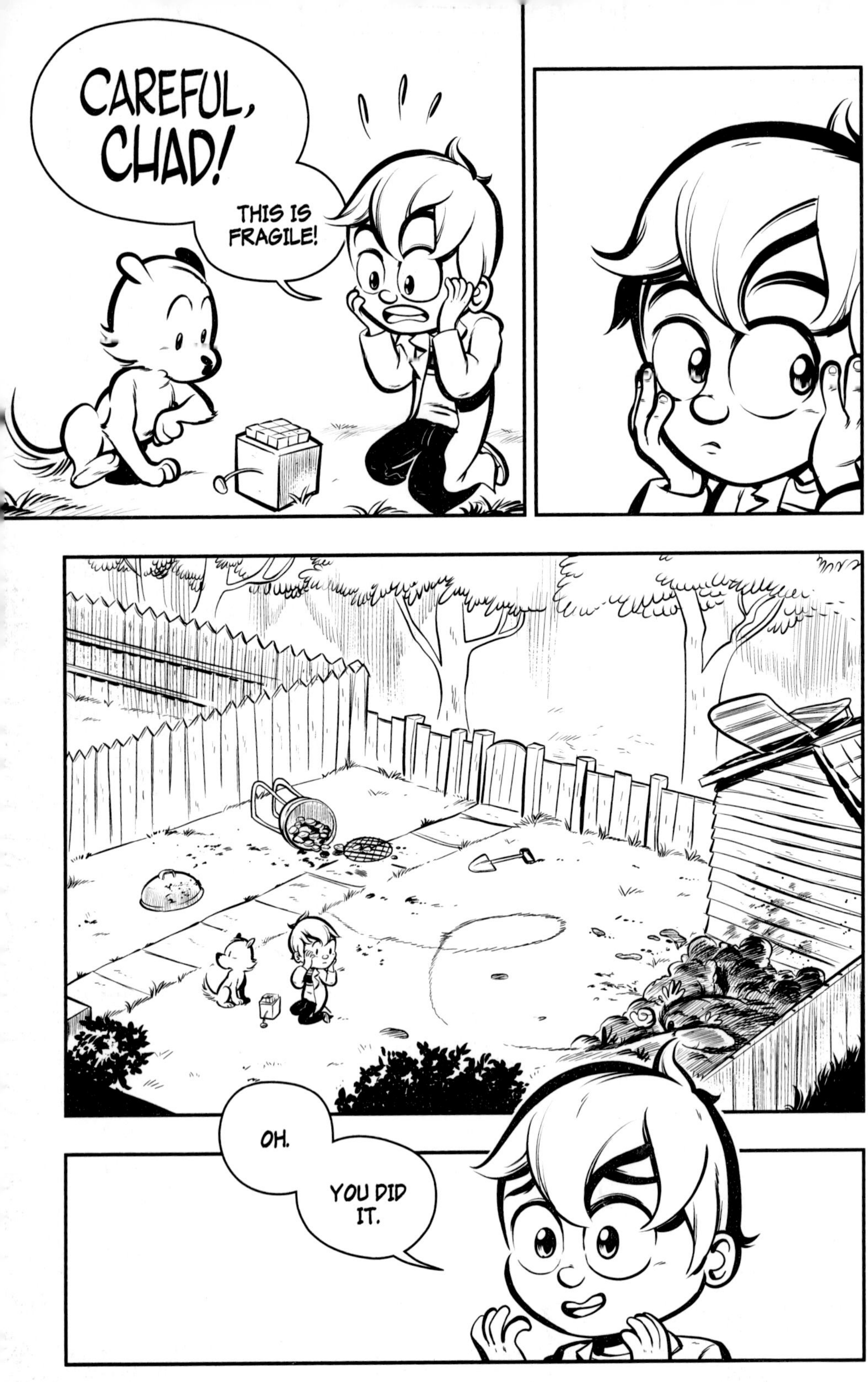
CAREFUL, CHAD!
THIS IS FRAGILE!
OH.
YOU DID IT.

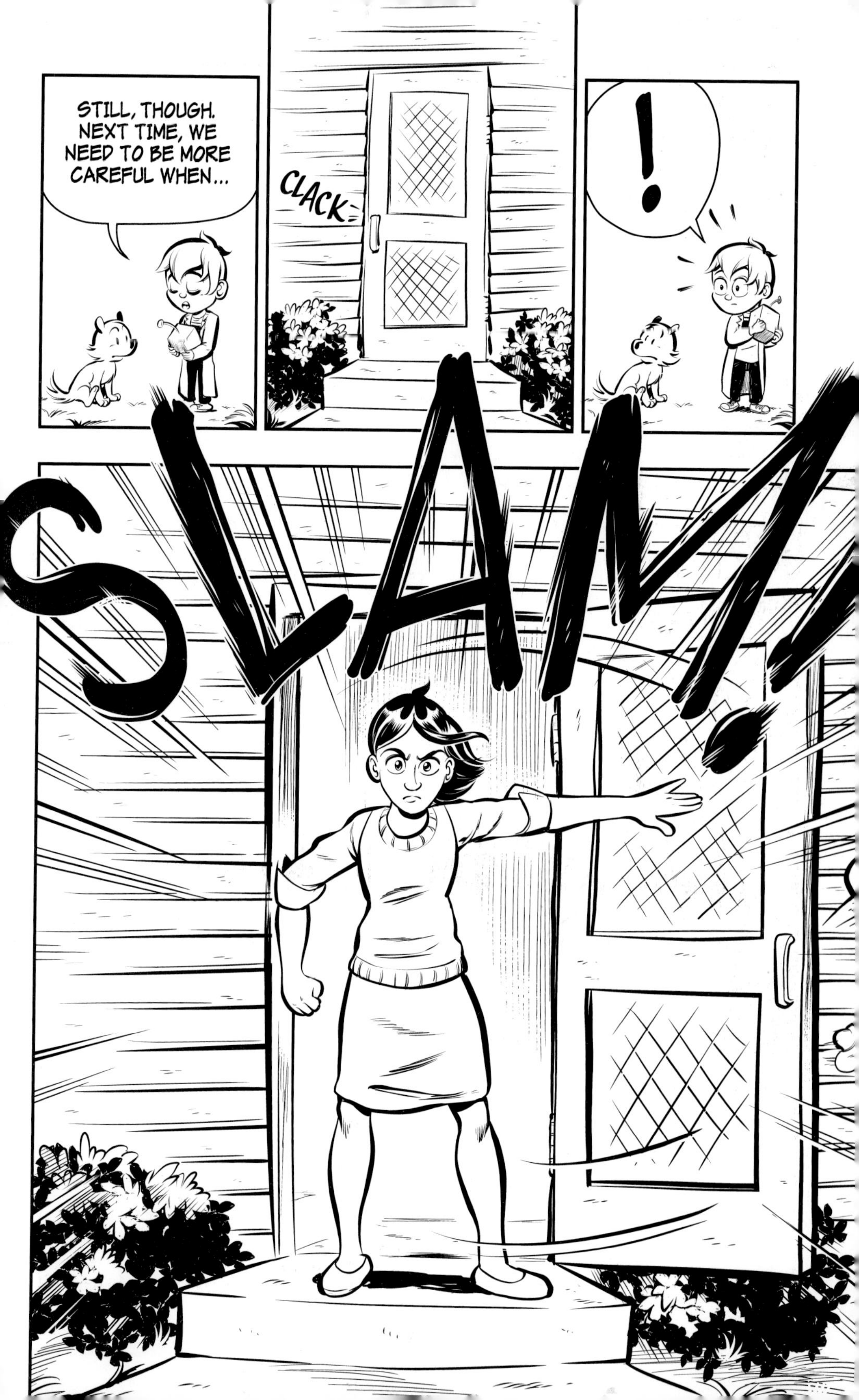
STILL, THOUGH. NEXT TIME, WE NEED TO BE MORE CAREFUL WHEN...
CLACK
!
SLAM!

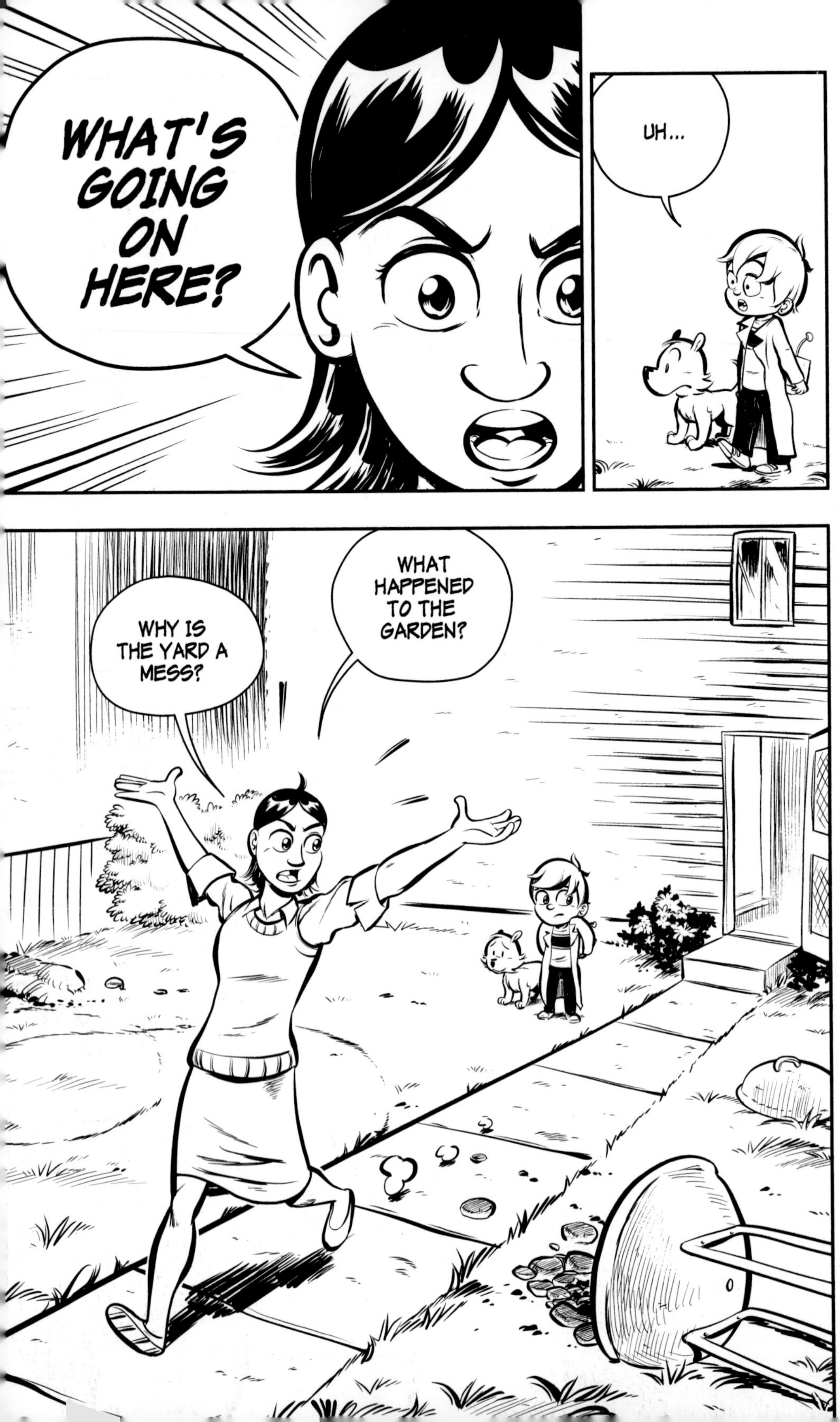
WHAT'S GOING ON HERE?
UH...
WHY IS THE YARD A MESS?
WHAT HAPPENED TO THE GARDEN?

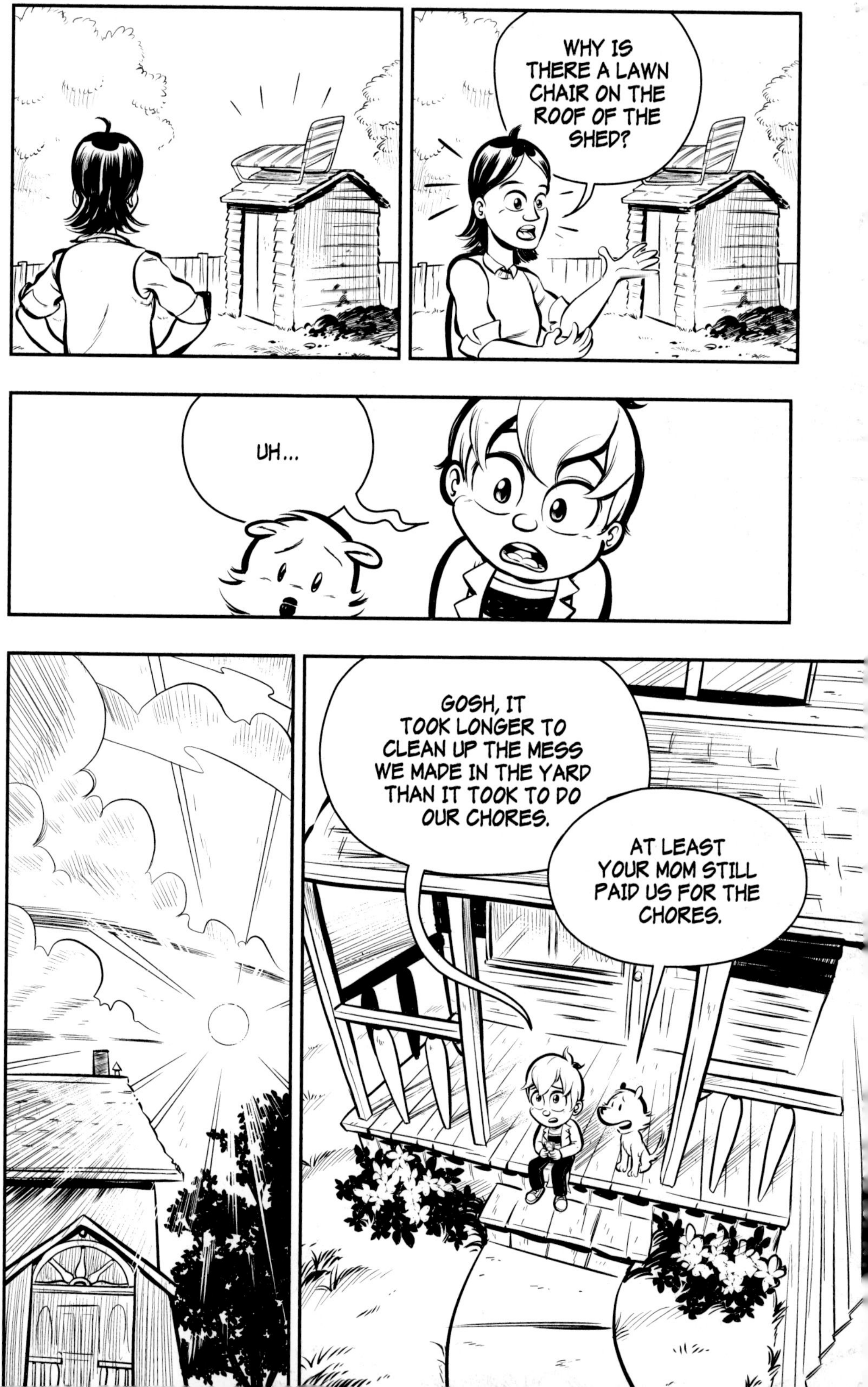
WHY IS THERE A LAWN CHAIR ON THE ROOF OF THE SHED?
UH...
GOSH, IT TOOK LONGER TO CLEAN UP THE MESS WE MADE IN THE YARD THAN IT TOOK TO DO OUR CHORES.
AT LEAST YOUR MOM STILL PAID US FOR THE CHORES.

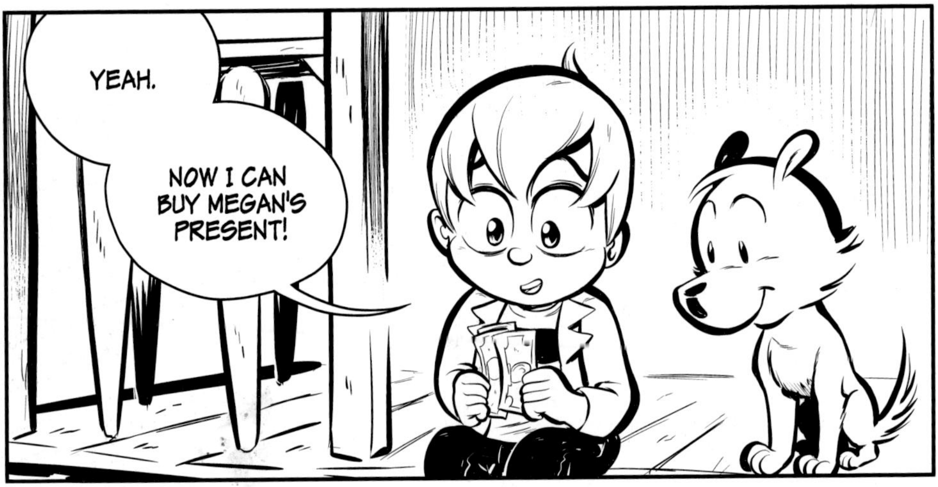
YEAH.
NOW I CAN BUY MEGAN'S PRESENT!

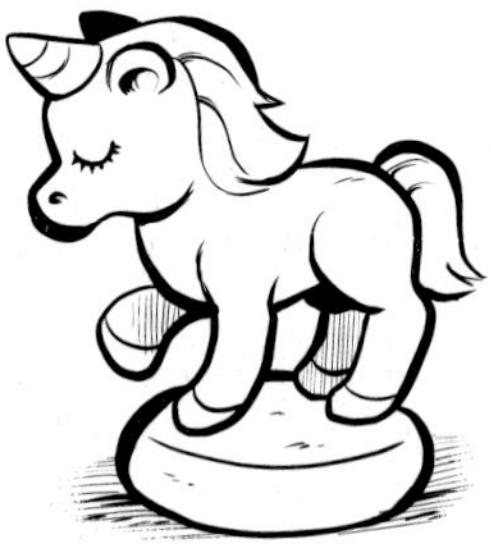

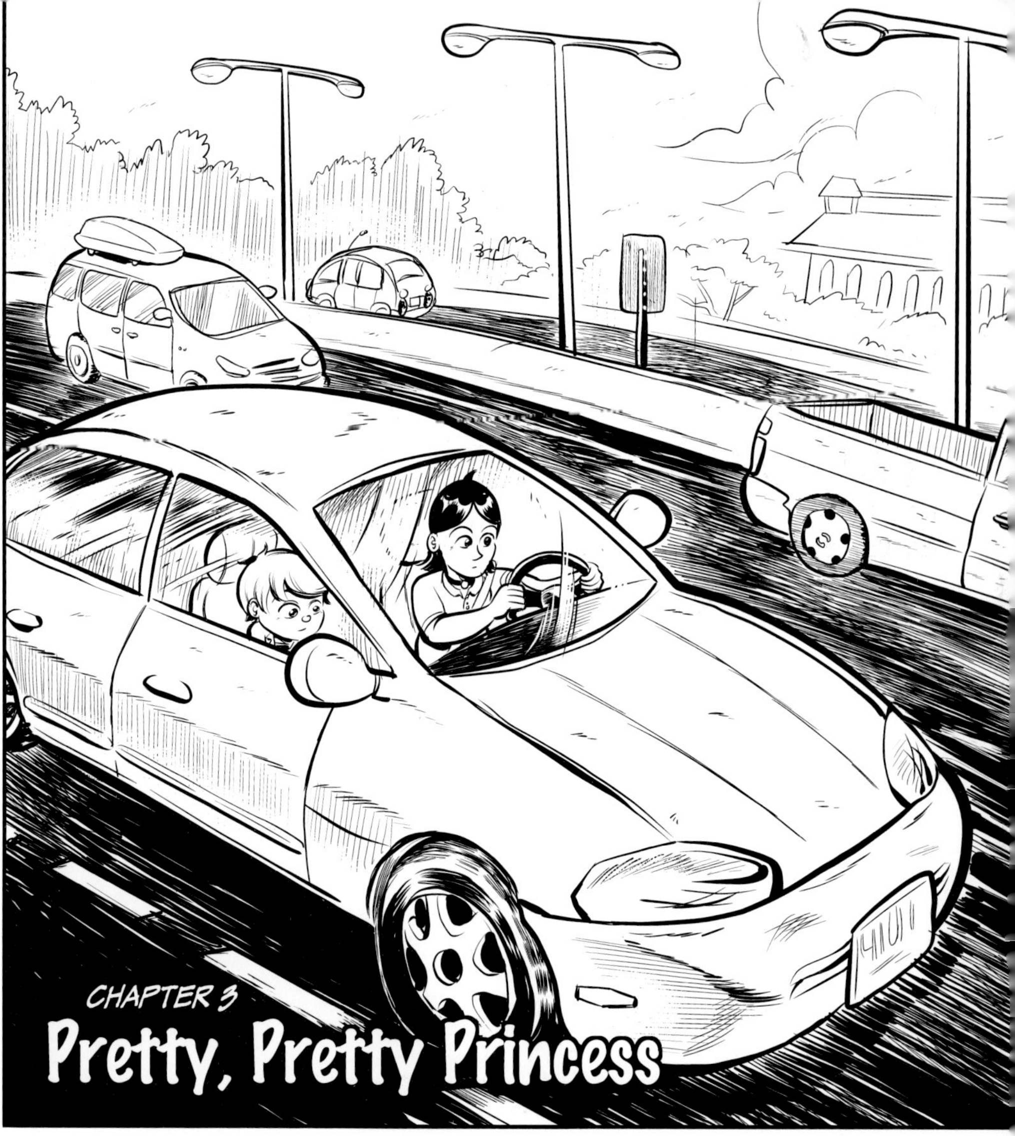

CHAPTER 3
Pretty, Pretty Princess

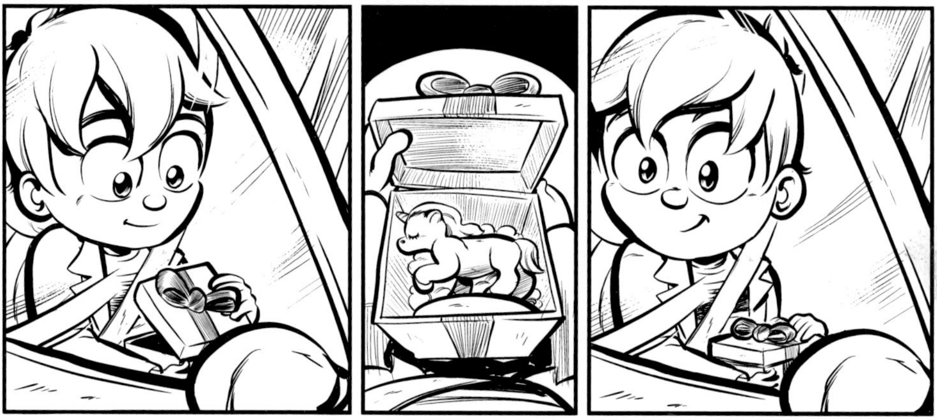

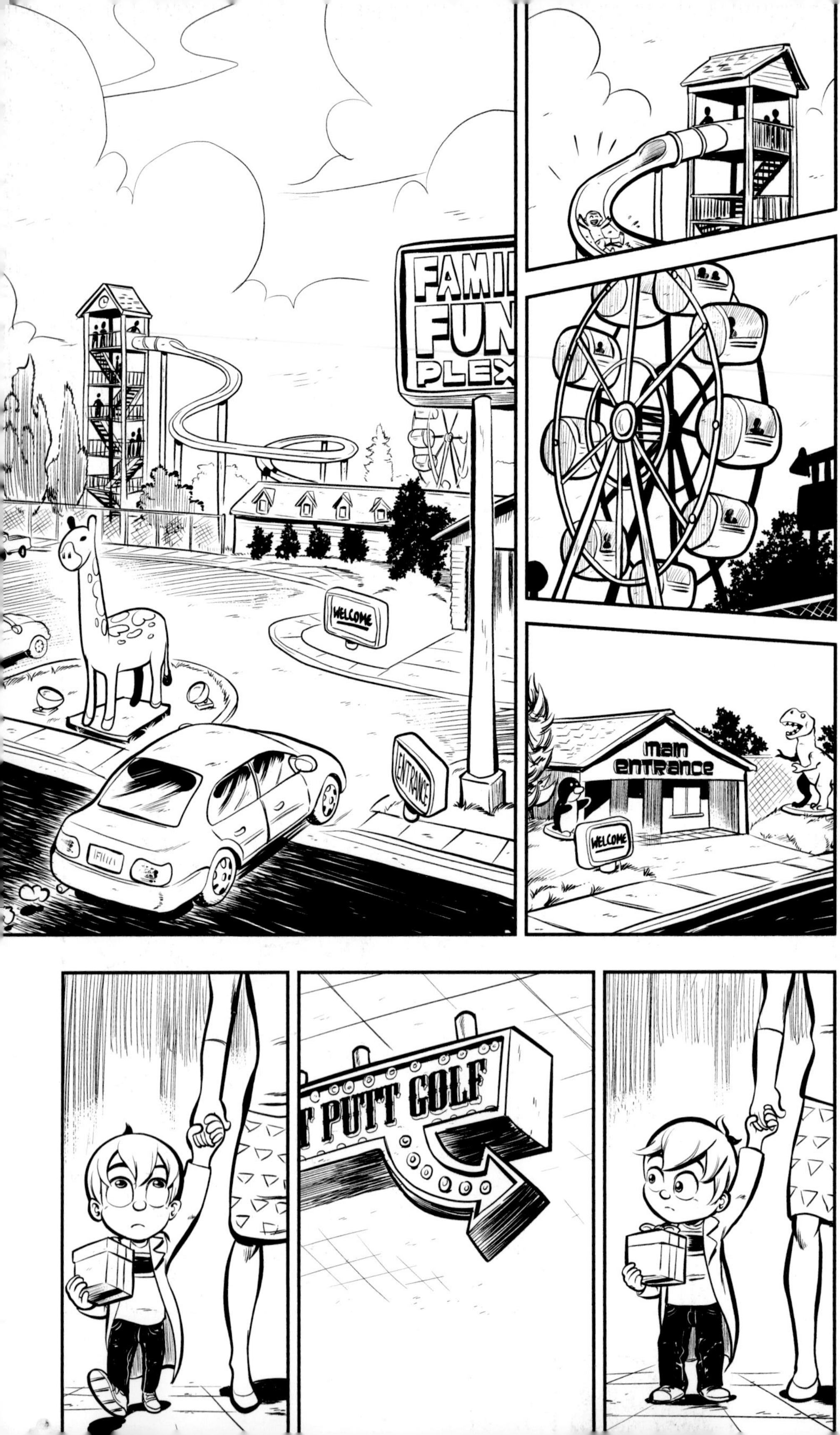
FAMI
FUN
PLEX
WELCOME
ENTRANCE
Main Entrance
WELCOME
PUTT GOLF

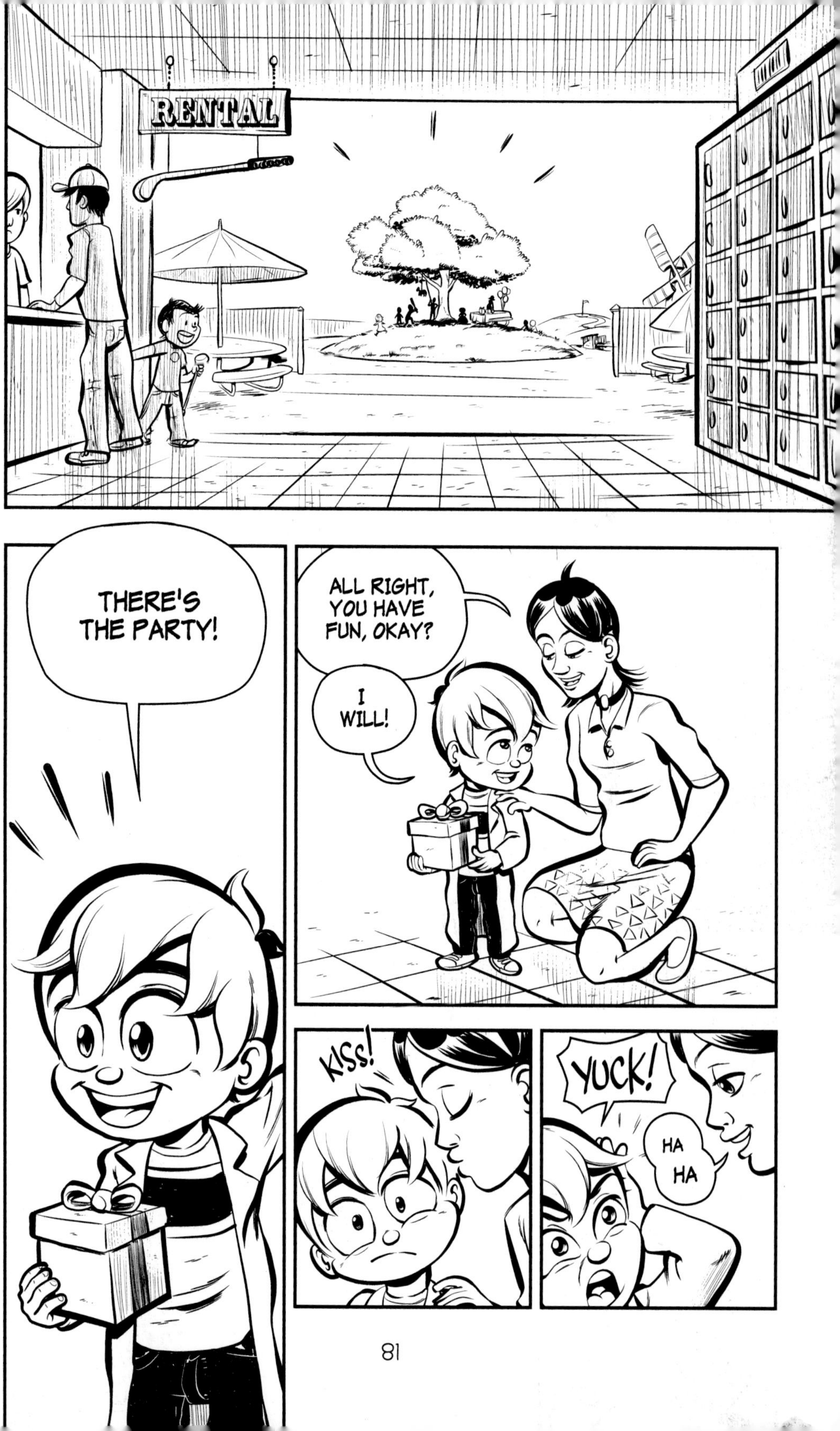
RENTAL
THERE'S THE PARTY!
ALL RIGHT, YOU HAVE FUN, OKAY?
I WILL!
KISS!
YUCK!
HA HA

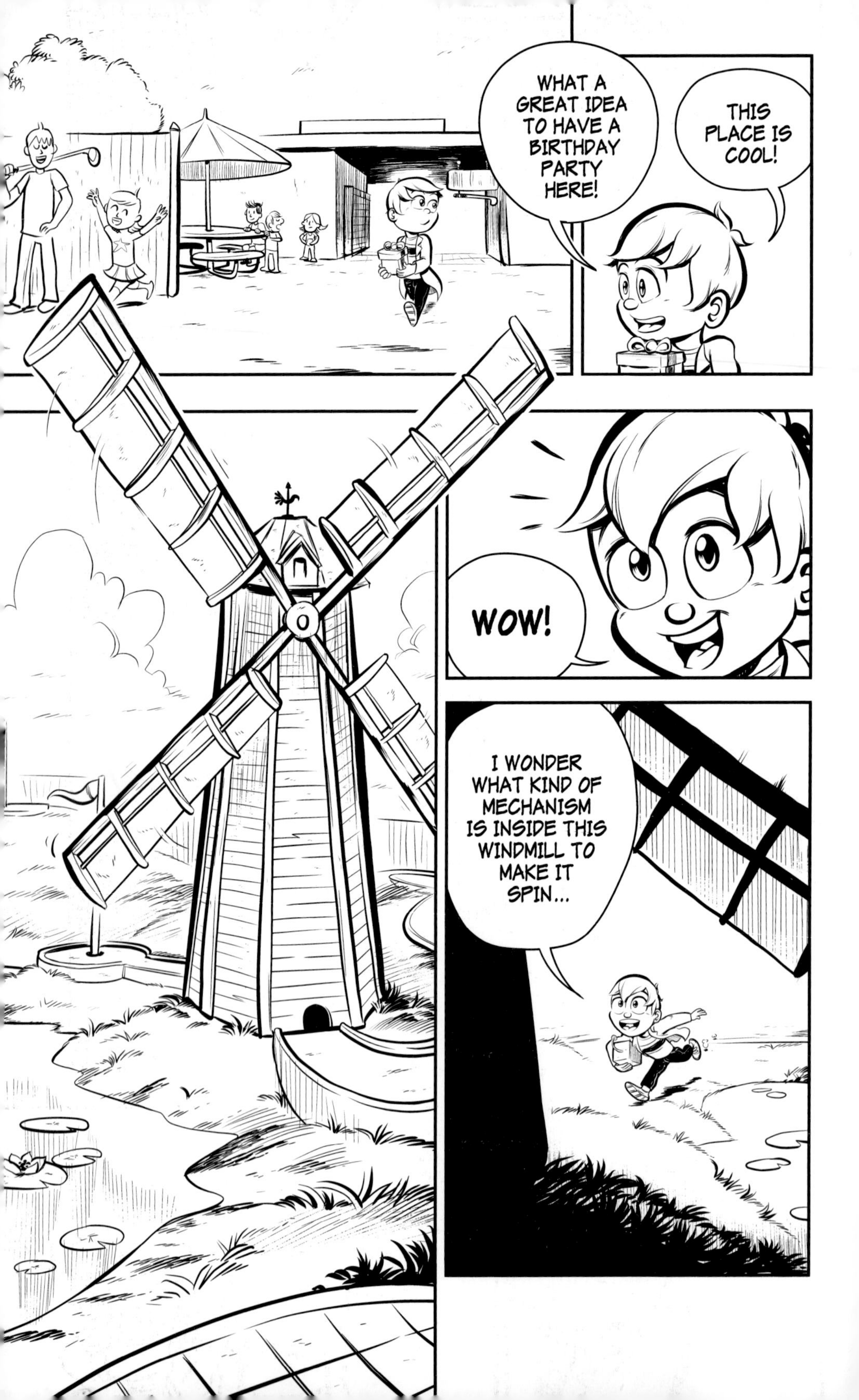
WHAT A GREAT IDEA TO HAVE A BIRTHDAY PARTY HERE!
THIS PLACE IS COOL!
WOW!
I WONDER WHAT KIND OF MECHANISM IS INSIDE THIS WINDMILL TO MAKE IT SPIN...

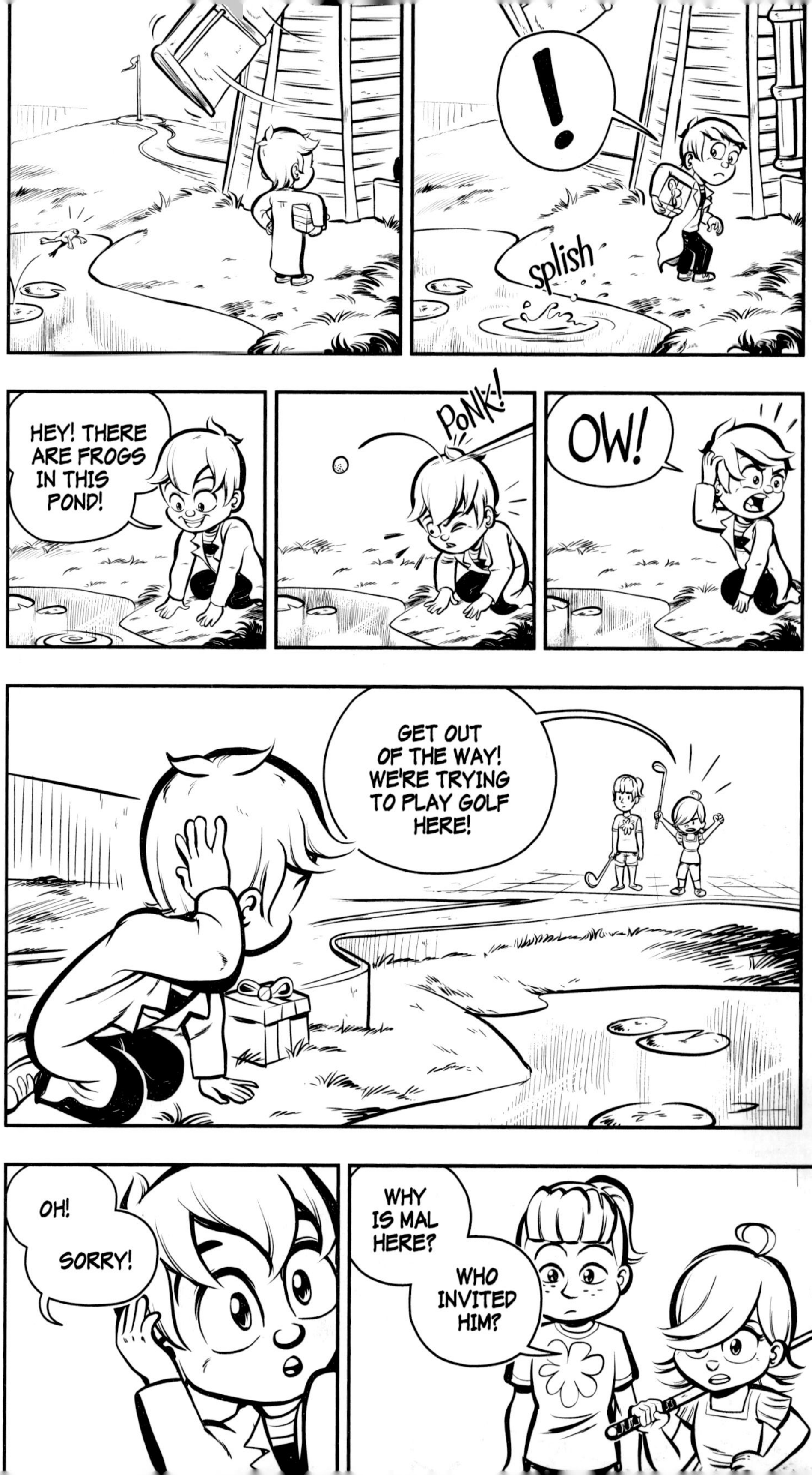
!
splish
HEY! THERE ARE FROGS IN THIS POND!
PONK!
OW!
GET OUT OF THE WAY! WE'RE TRYING TO PLAY GOLF HERE!
OH!
SORRY!
WHY IS MAL HERE?
WHO INVITED HIM?

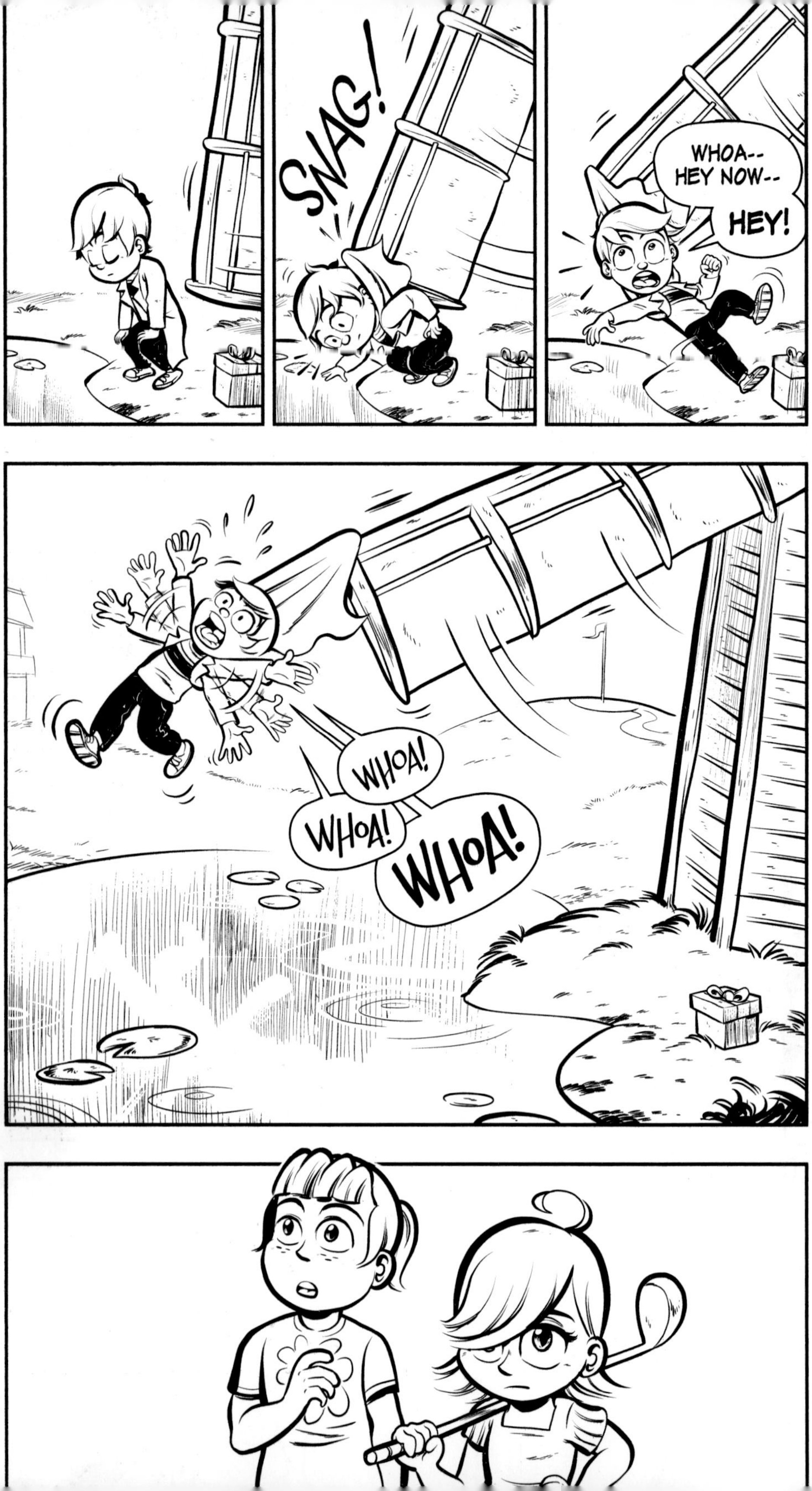

SNAG!
WHOA-- HEY NOW--
HEY!
WHOA!
WHOA!
WHOA!

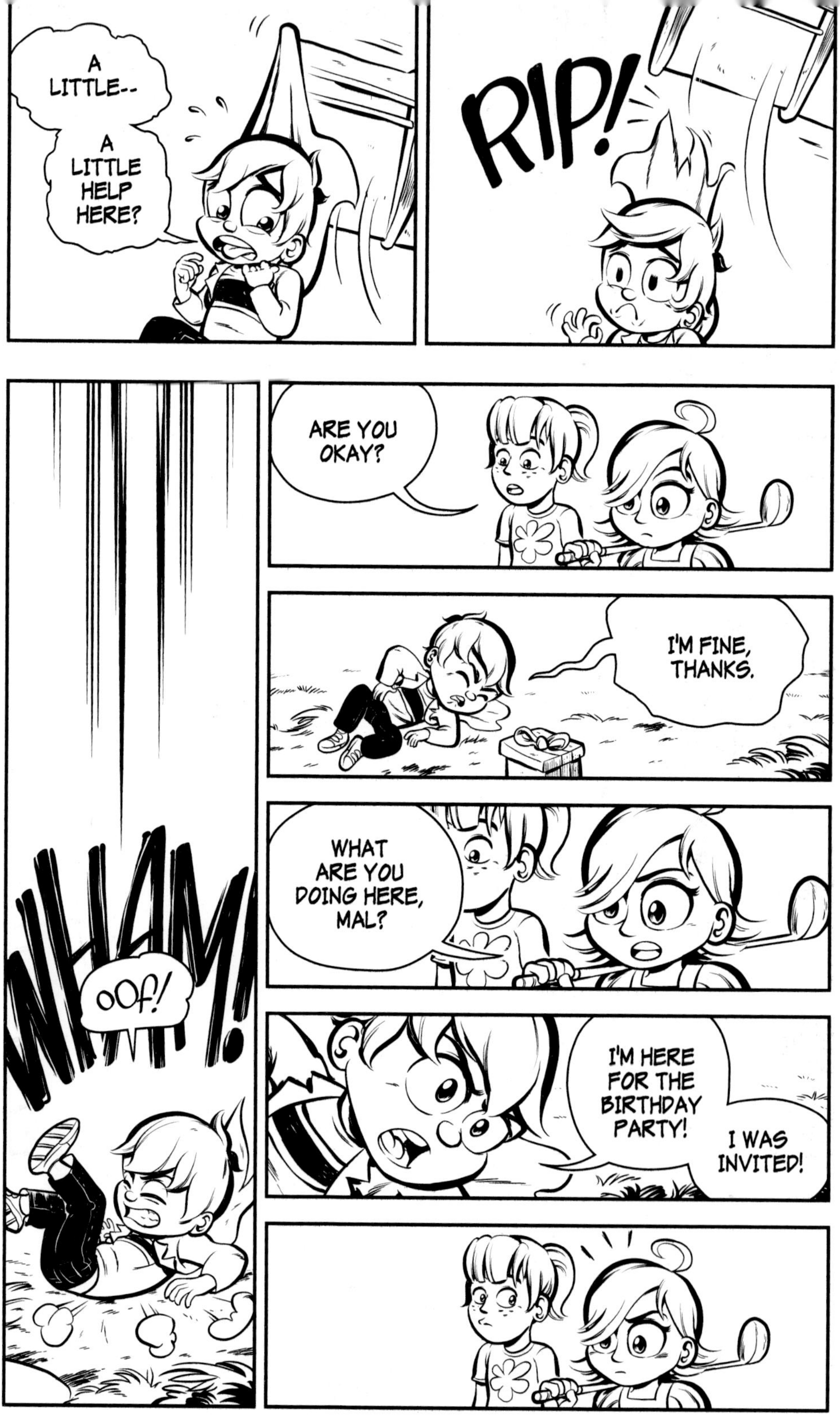
A LITTLE--
A LITTLE HELP HERE?
RIP!
WHAM!
OOF!
ARE YOU OKAY?
I'M FINE, THANKS.
WHAT ARE YOU DOING HERE, MAL?
I'M HERE FOR THE BIRTHDAY PARTY!
I WAS INVITED!

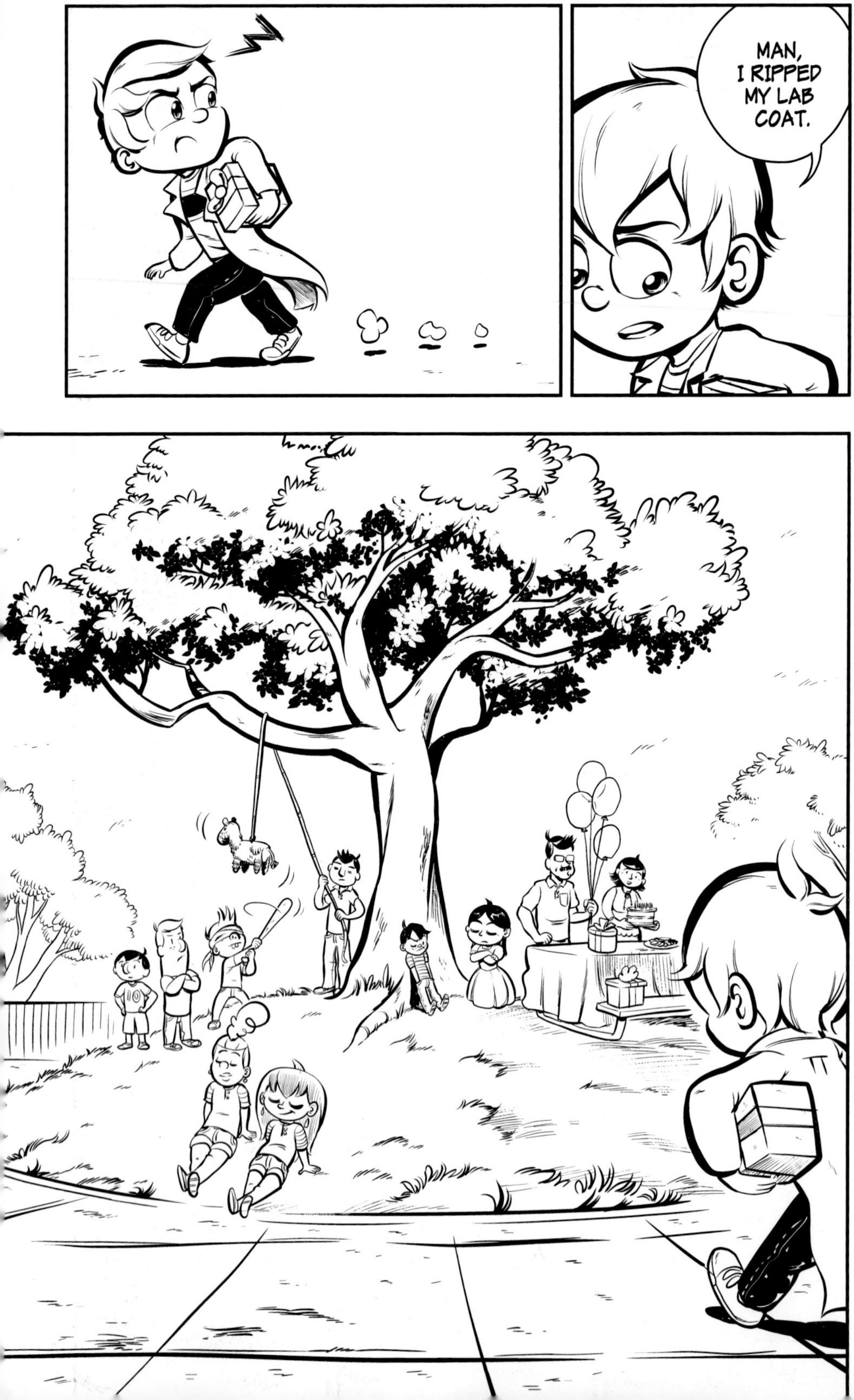
MAN, I RIPPED MY LAB COAT.

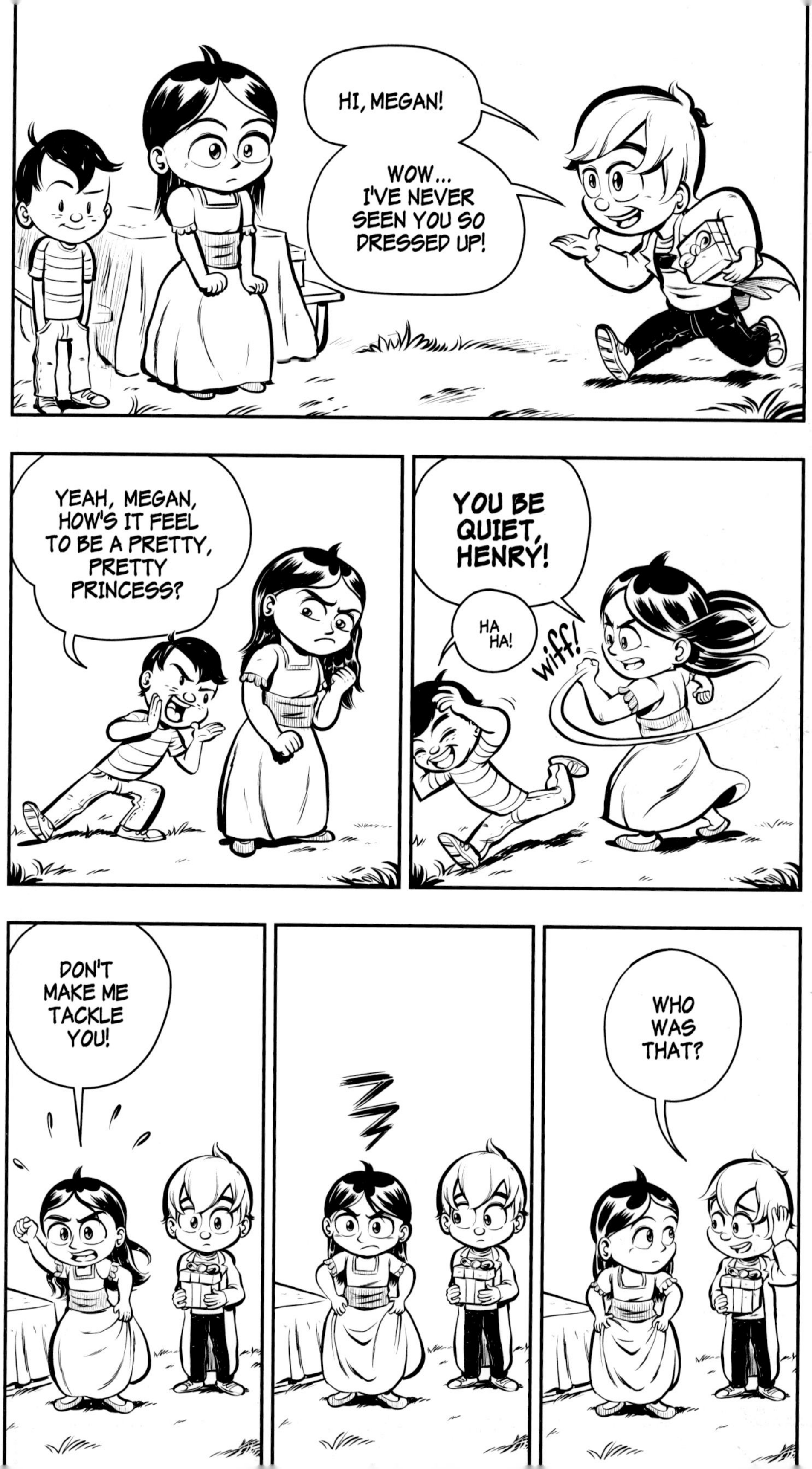
HI, MEGAN!
WOW... I'VE NEVER SEEN YOU SO DRESSED UP!
YEAH, MEGAN, HOW'S IT FEEL TO BE A PRETTY, PRETTY PRINCESS?
YOU BE QUIET, HENRY!
HA HA!
wiff!
DON'T MAKE ME TACKLE YOU!
WHO WAS THAT?

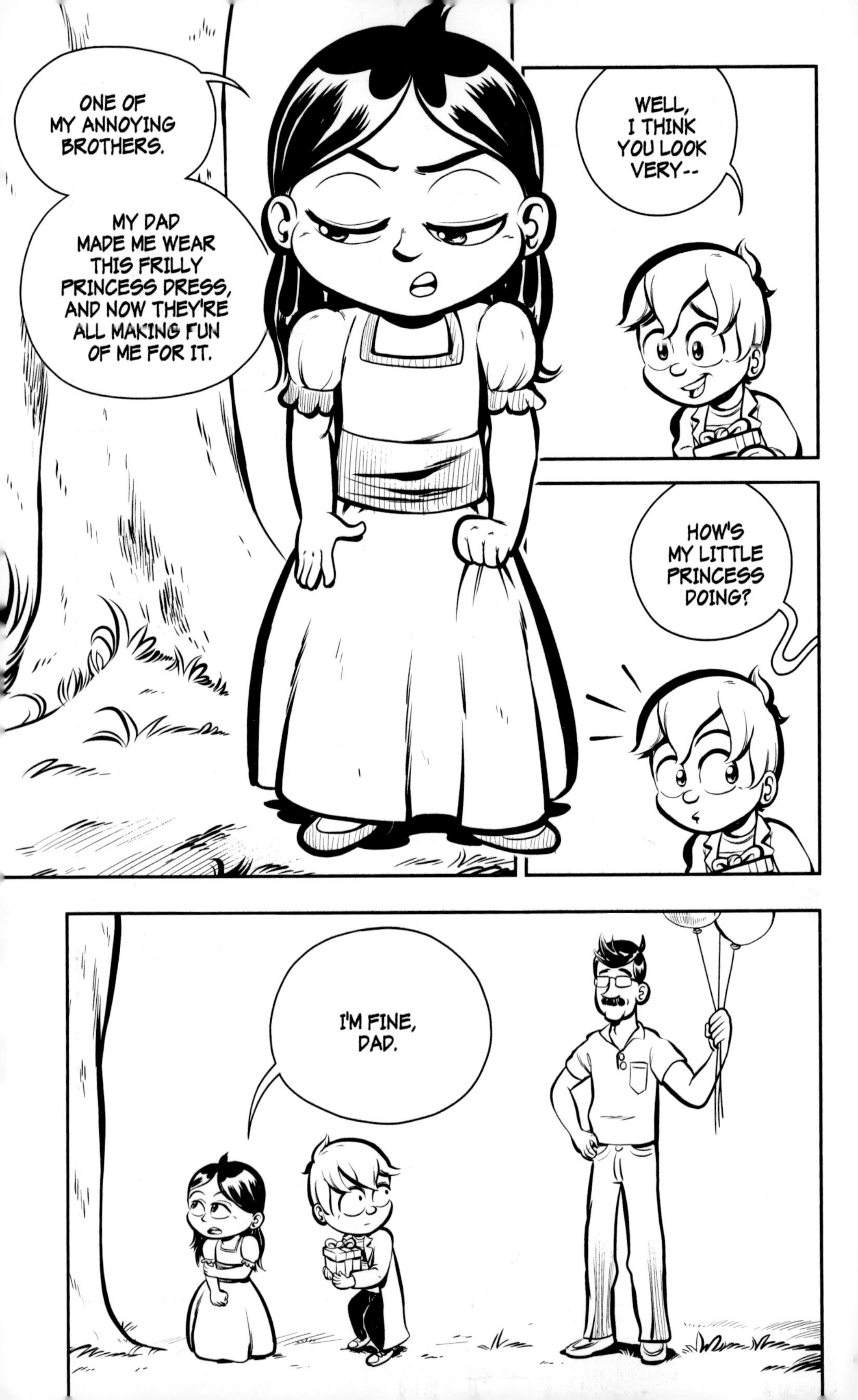
ONE OF MY ANNOYING BROTHERS.
MY DAD MADE ME WEAR THIS FRILLY PRINCESS DRESS, AND NOW THEY'RE ALL MAKING FUN OF ME FOR IT.
WELL, I THINK YOU LOOK VERY--
HOW'S MY LITTLE PRINCESS DOING?
I'M FINE, DAD.

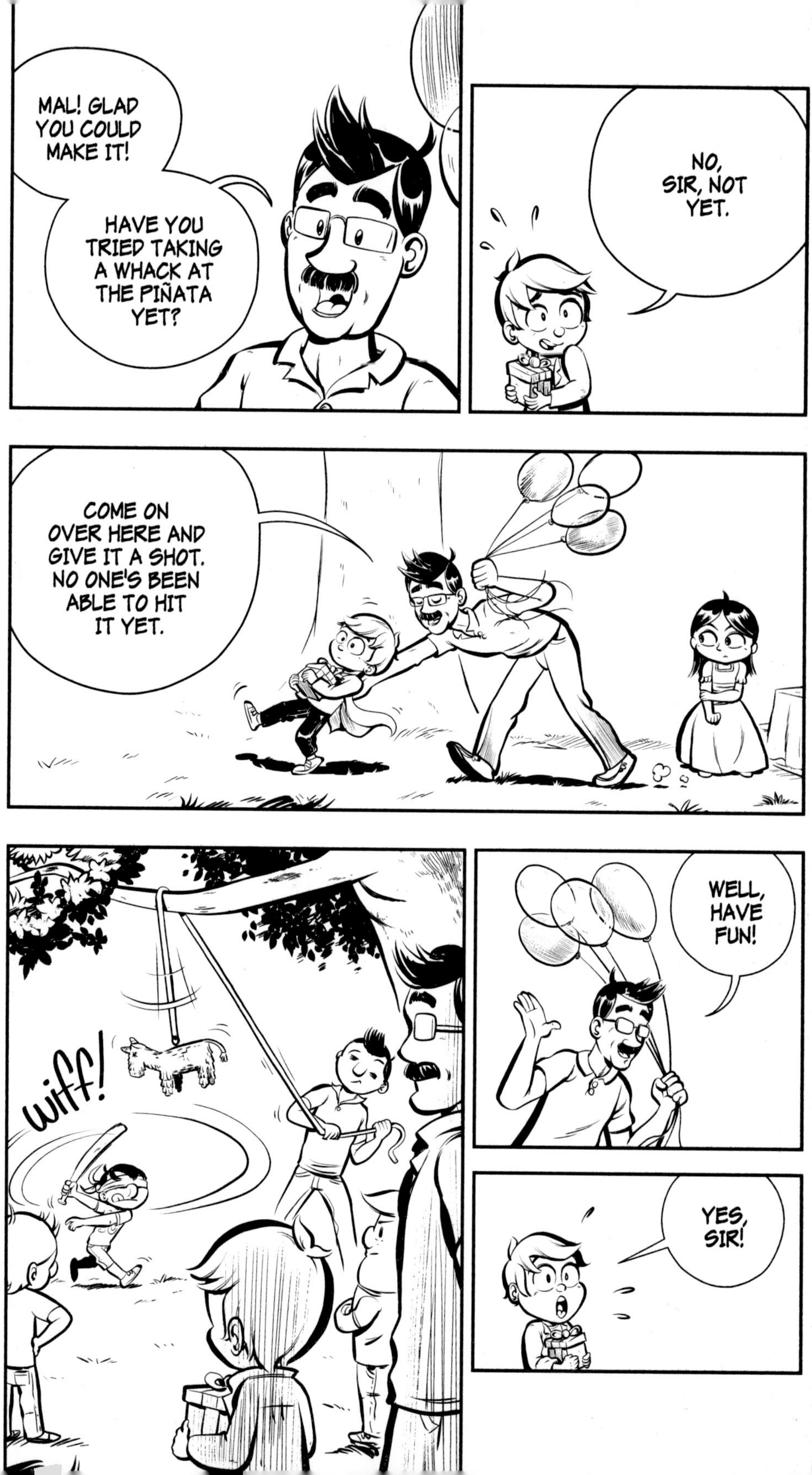
MAL! GLAD YOU COULD MAKE IT!
HAVE YOU TRIED TAKING A WHACK AT THE PIÑATA YET?
NO, SIR, NOT YET.
COME ON OVER HERE AND GIVE IT A SHOT. NO ONE'S BEEN ABLE TO HIT IT YET.
wiff!
WELL, HAVE FUN!
YES, SIR!

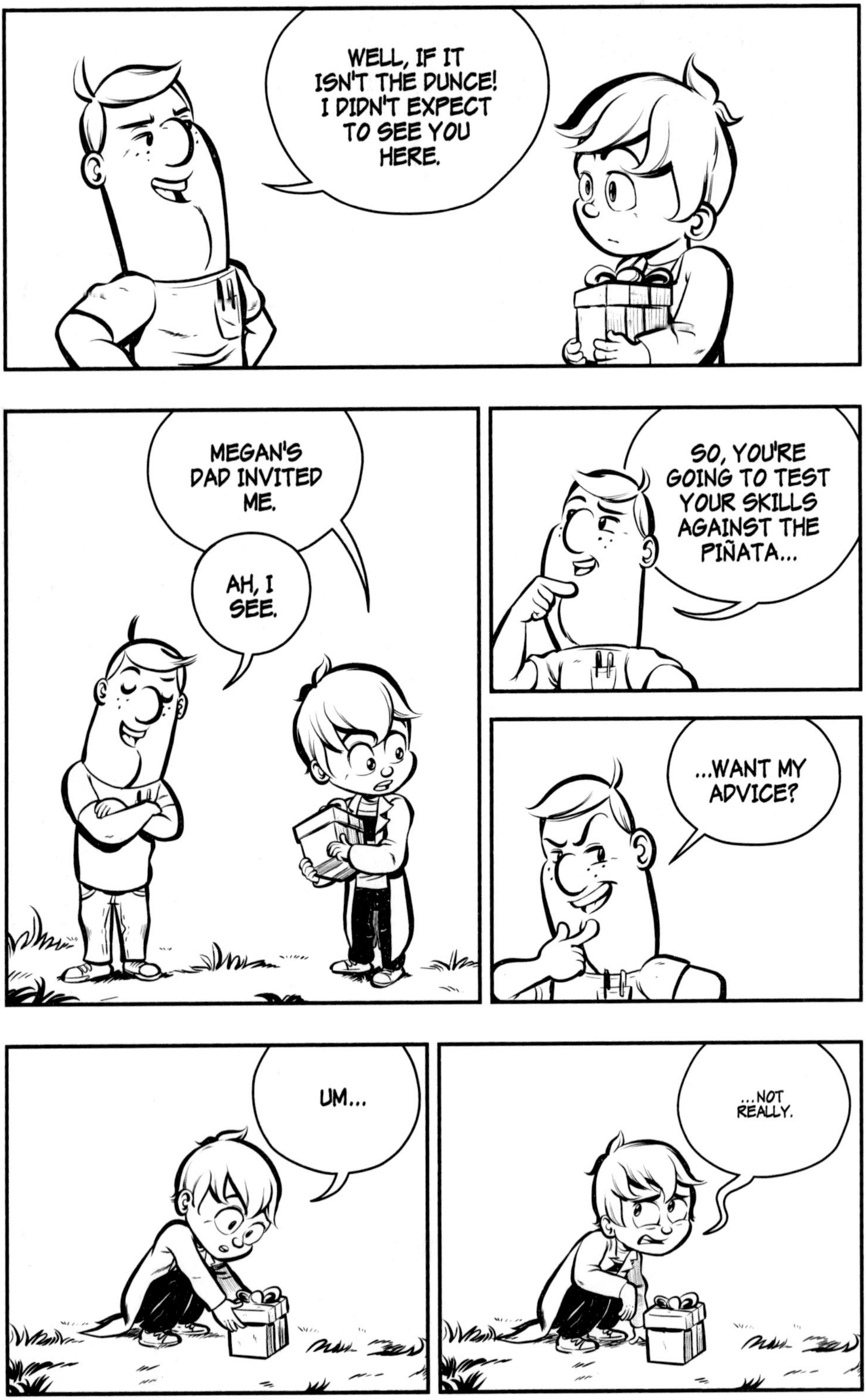
WELL, IF IT ISN'T THE DUNCE! I DIDN'T EXPECT TO SEE YOU HERE.
MEGAN'S DAD INVITED ME.
AH, I SEE.
SO, YOU'RE GOING TO TEST YOUR SKILLS AGAINST THE PIÑATA...
...WANT MY ADVICE?
UM...
...NOT REALLY.

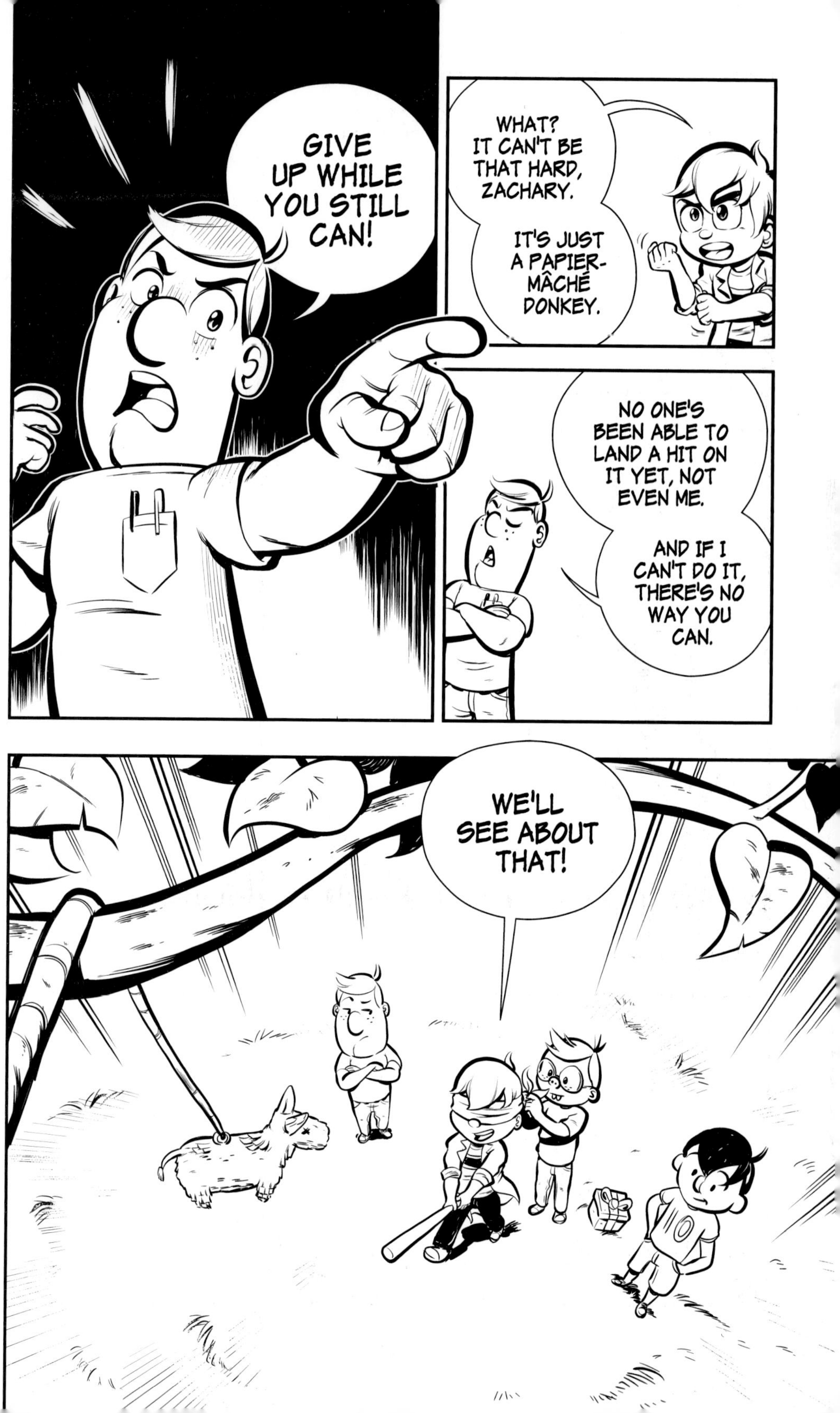
GIVE UP WHILE YOU STILL CAN!
WHAT? IT CAN'T BE THAT HARD, ZACHARY.
IT'S JUST A PAPIER-MÂCHÉ DONKEY.
NO ONE'S BEEN ABLE TO LAND A HIT ON IT YET, NOT EVEN ME.
AND IF I CAN'T DO IT, THERE'S NO WAY YOU CAN.
WE'LL SEE ABOUT THAT!

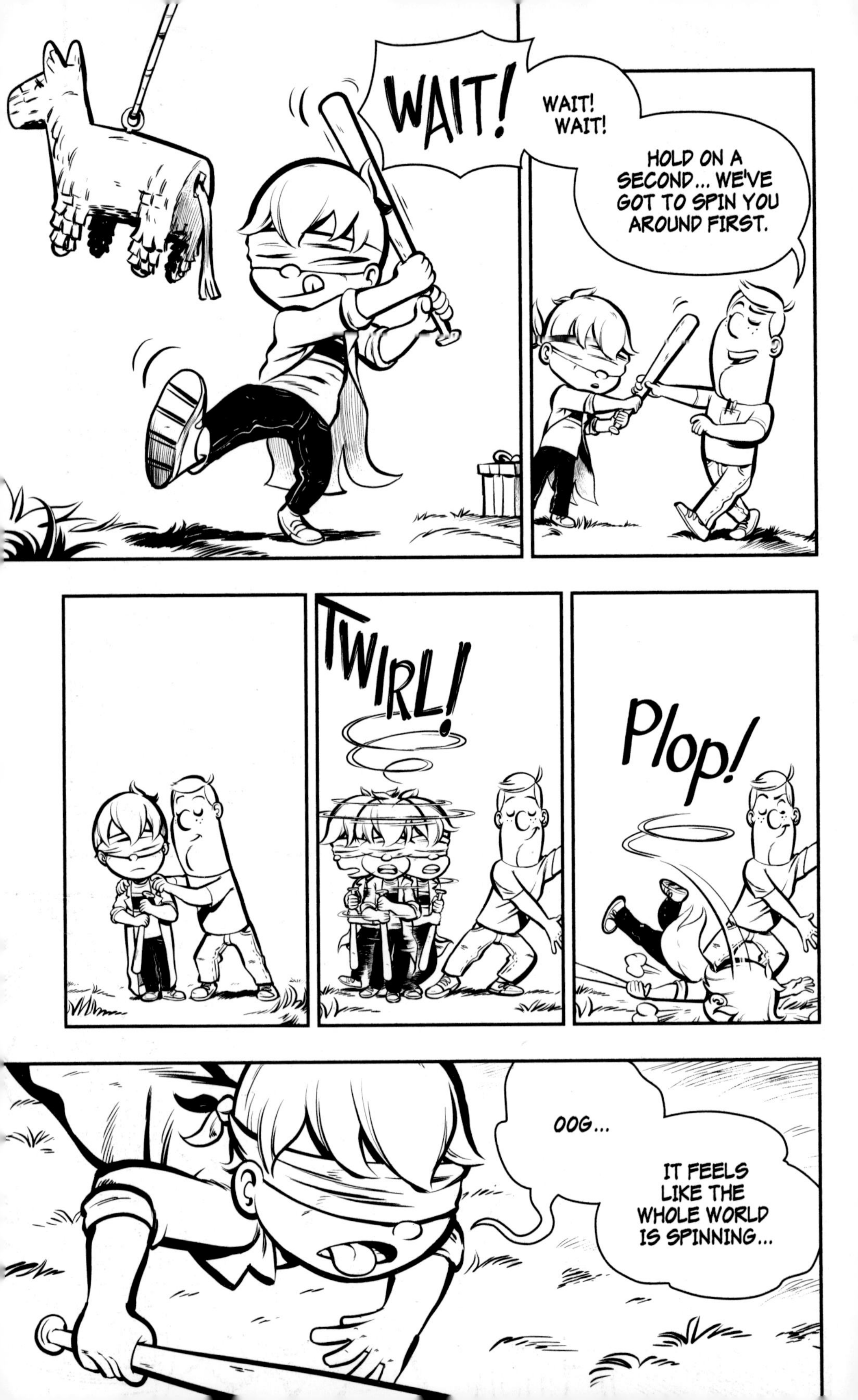
WAIT!
WAIT! WAIT!
HOLD ON A SECOND... WE'VE GOT TO SPIN YOU AROUND FIRST.
TWIRL!
Plop!
OOG...
IT FEELS LIKE THE WHOLE WORLD IS SPINNING...

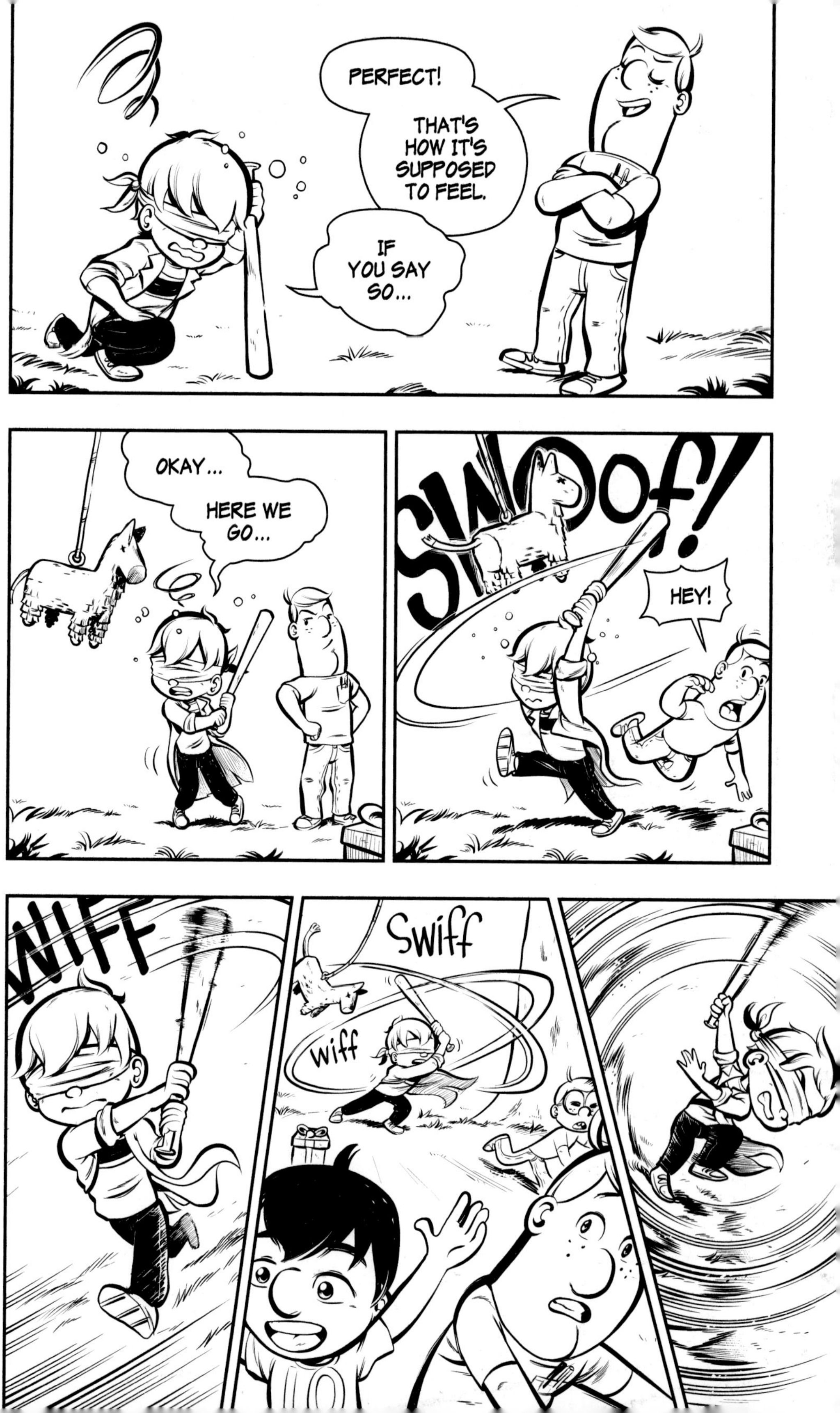
PERFECT!
THAT'S HOW IT'S SUPPOSED TO FEEL.
IF YOU SAY SO...
OKAY...
HERE WE GO...
SWOOF!
HEY!
WIFF
Swiff
wiff

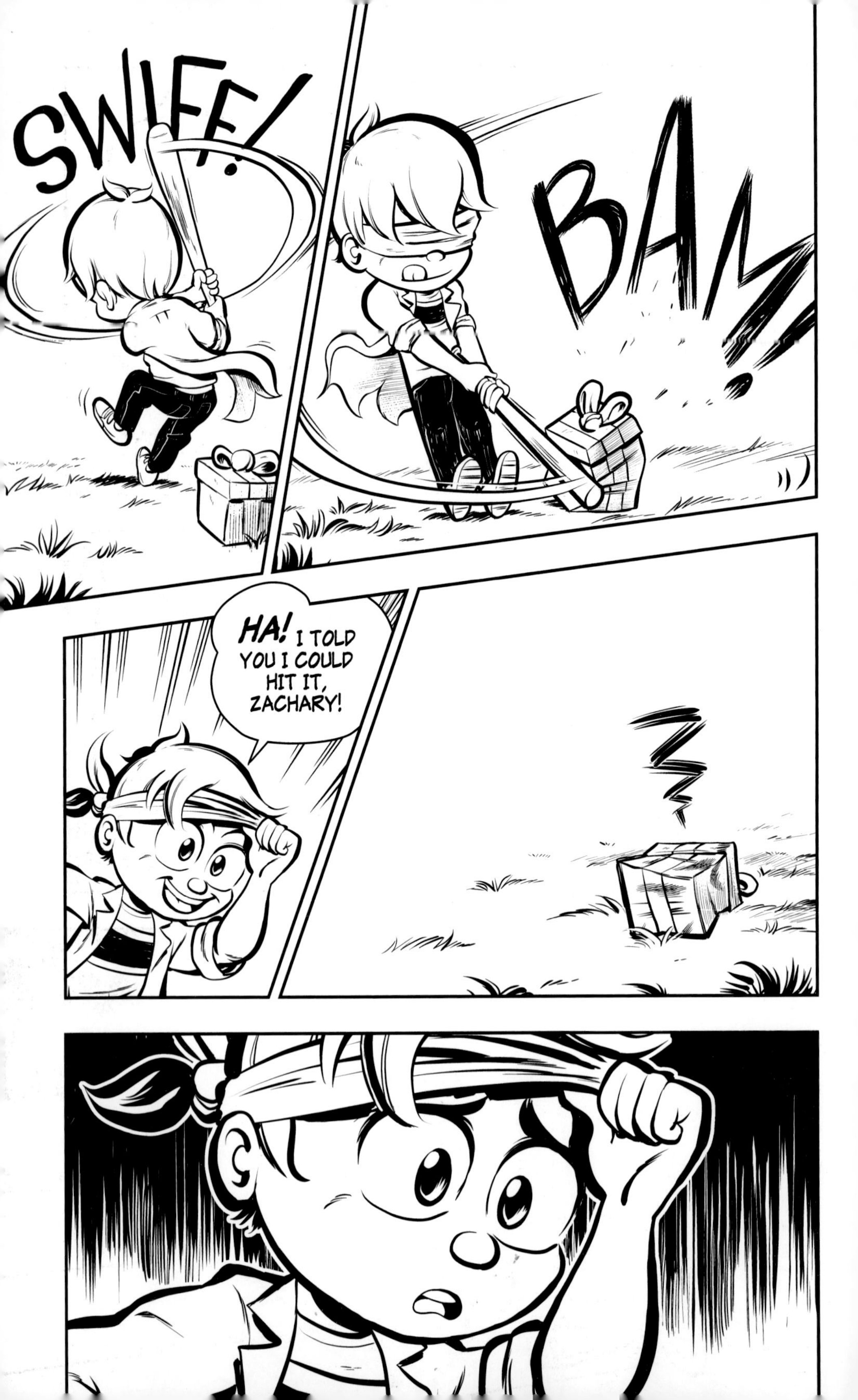
SWIFF!
BAM!!
HA! I TOLD YOU I COULD HIT IT, ZACHARY!

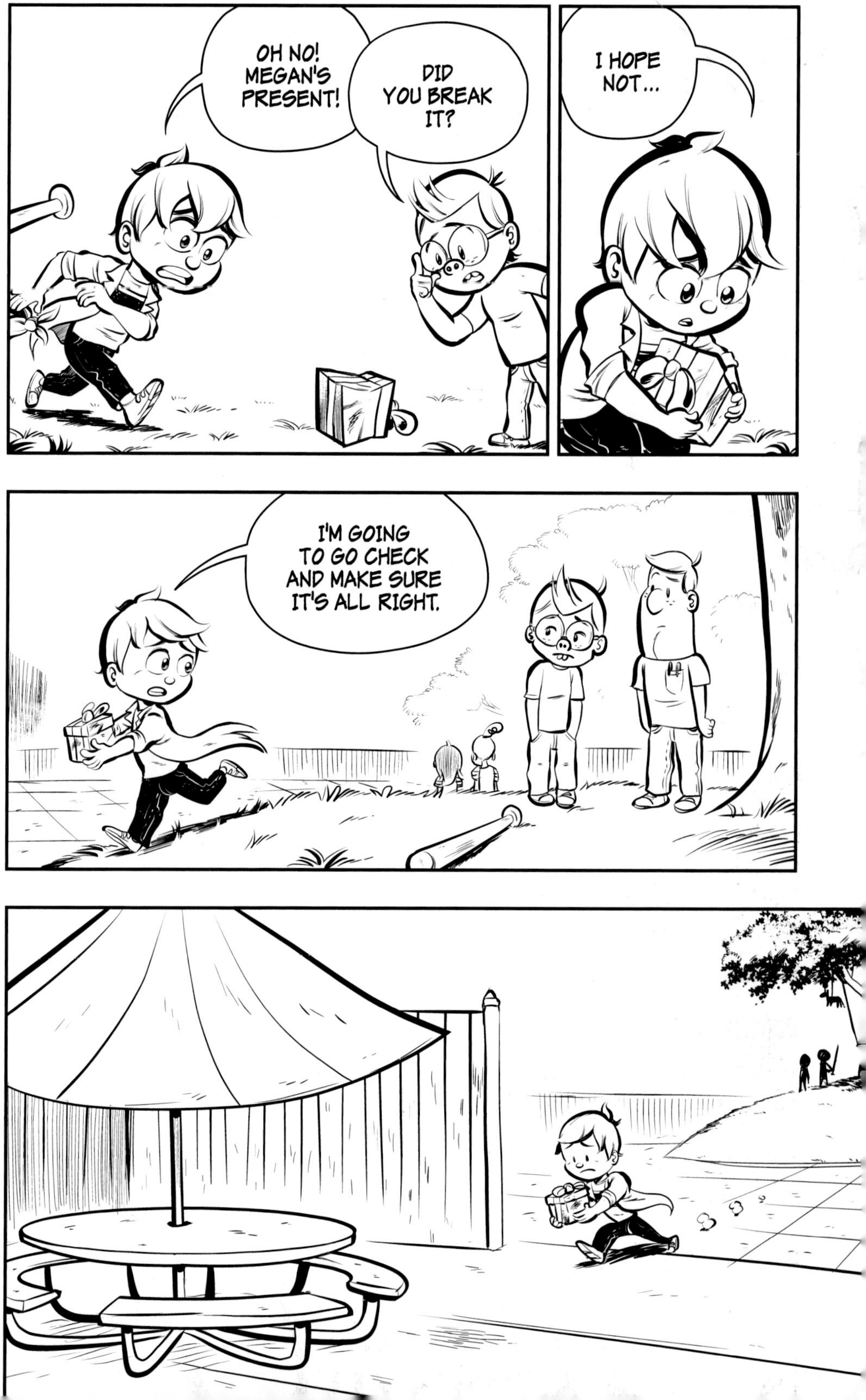
OH NO! MEGAN'S PRESENT!
DID YOU BREAK IT?
I HOPE NOT...
I'M GOING TO GO CHECK AND MAKE SURE IT'S ALL RIGHT.

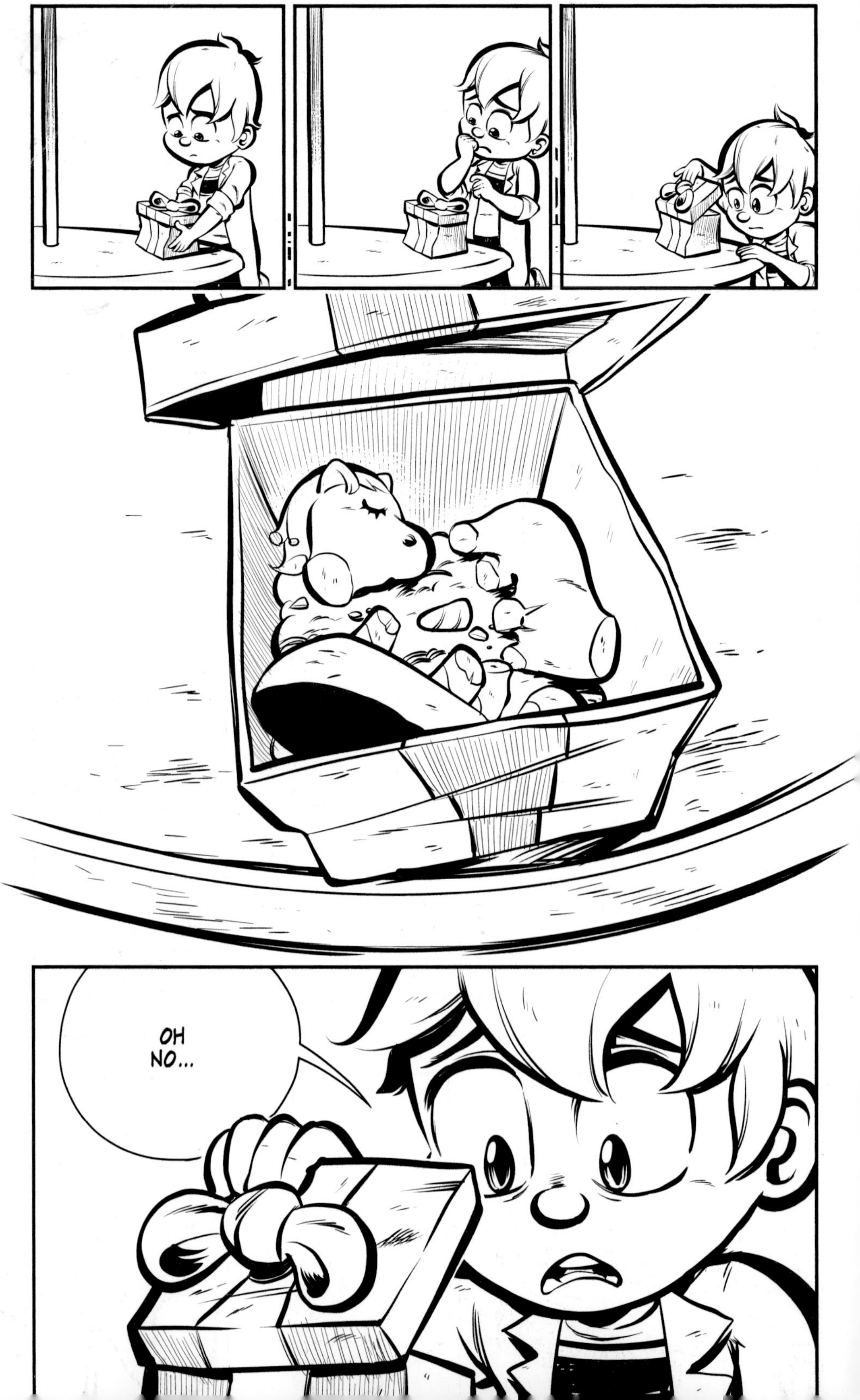
OH
NO...

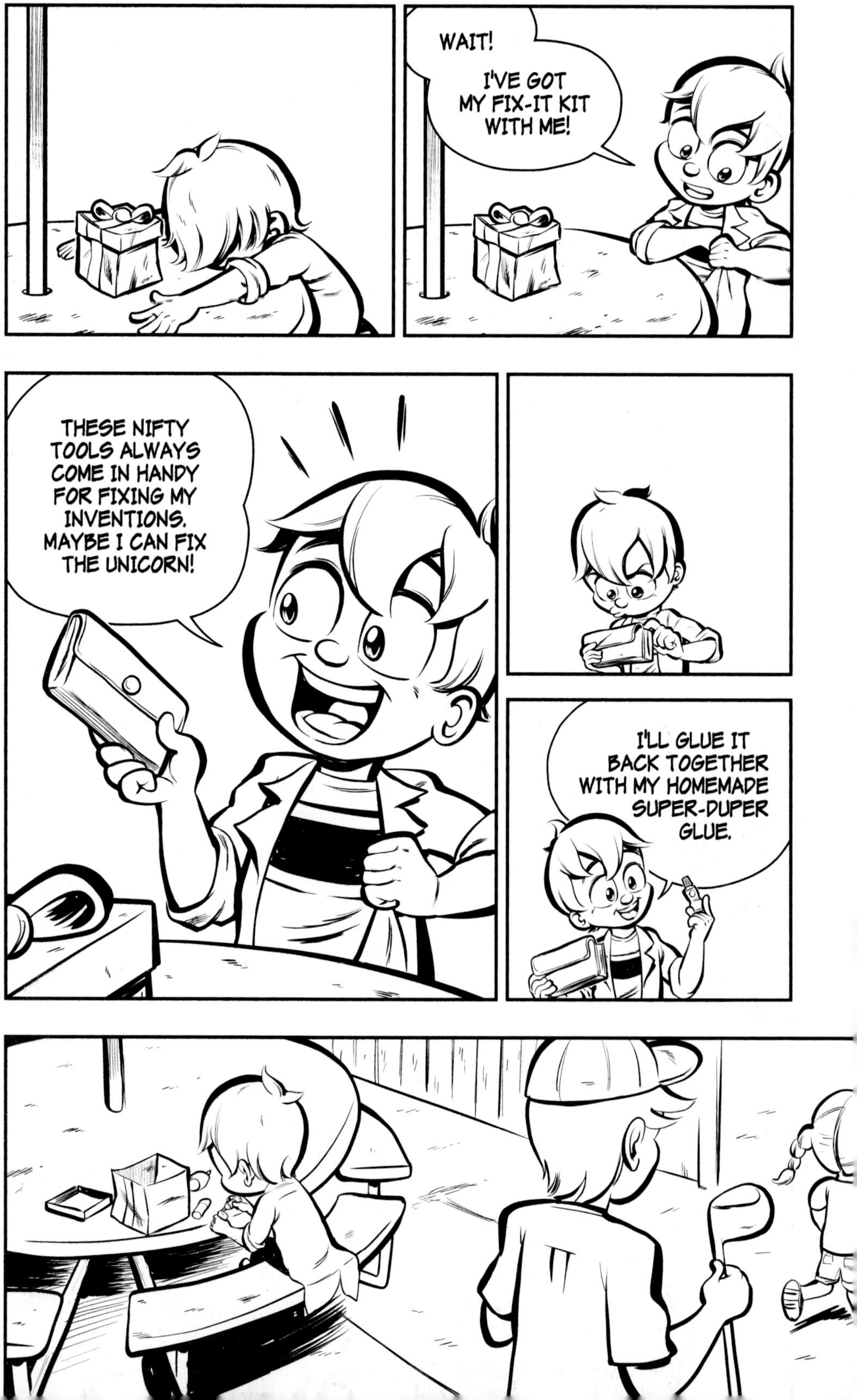
WAIT!
I'VE GOT MY FIX-IT KIT WITH ME!
THESE NIFTY TOOLS ALWAYS COME IN HANDY FOR FIXING MY INVENTIONS. MAYBE I CAN FIX THE UNICORN!
I'LL GLUE IT BACK TOGETHER WITH MY HOMEMADE SUPER-DUPER GLUE.

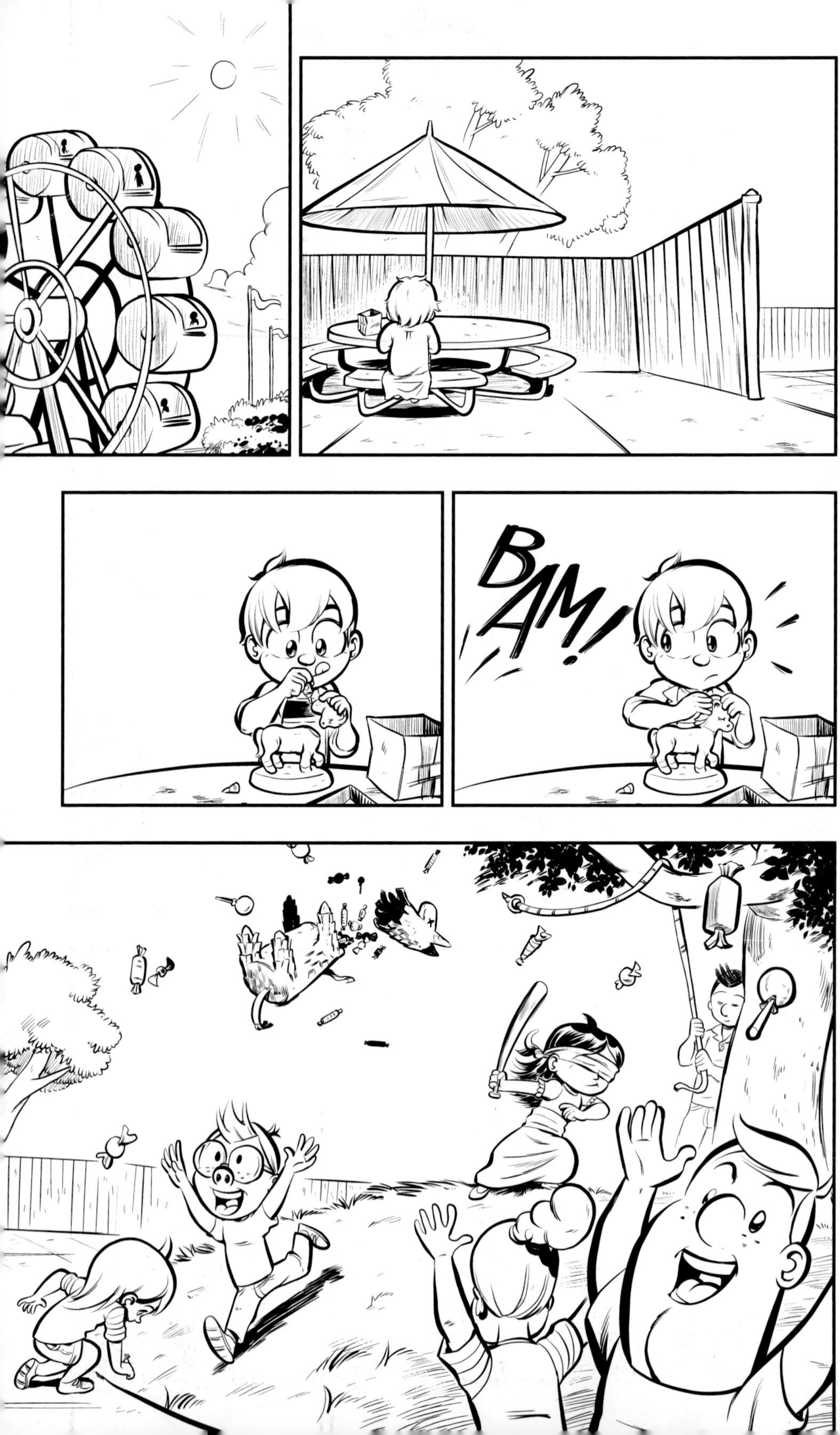
BAM!

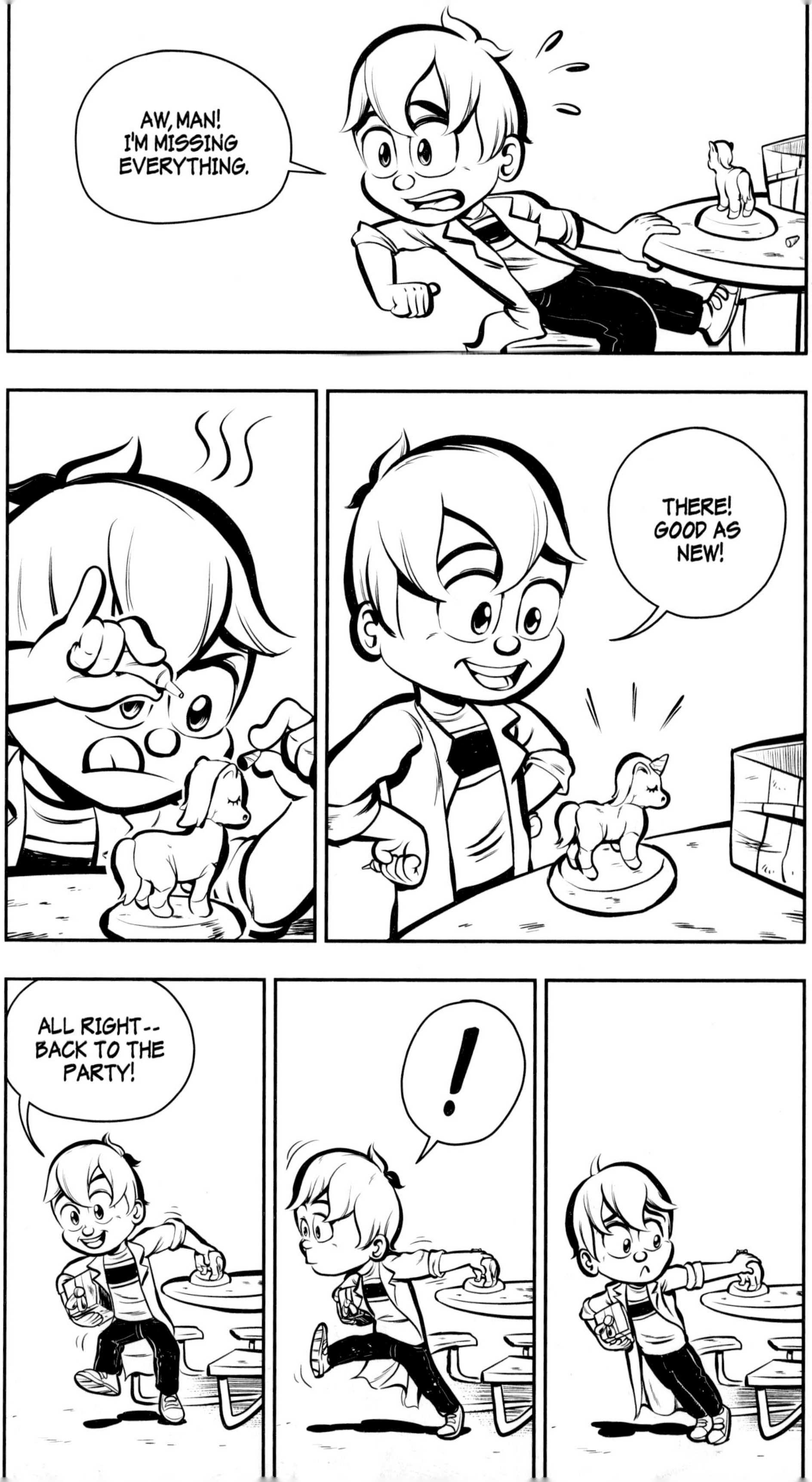
AW, MAN! I'M MISSING EVERYTHING.
THERE! GOOD AS NEW!
ALL RIGHT-- BACK TO THE PARTY!
!

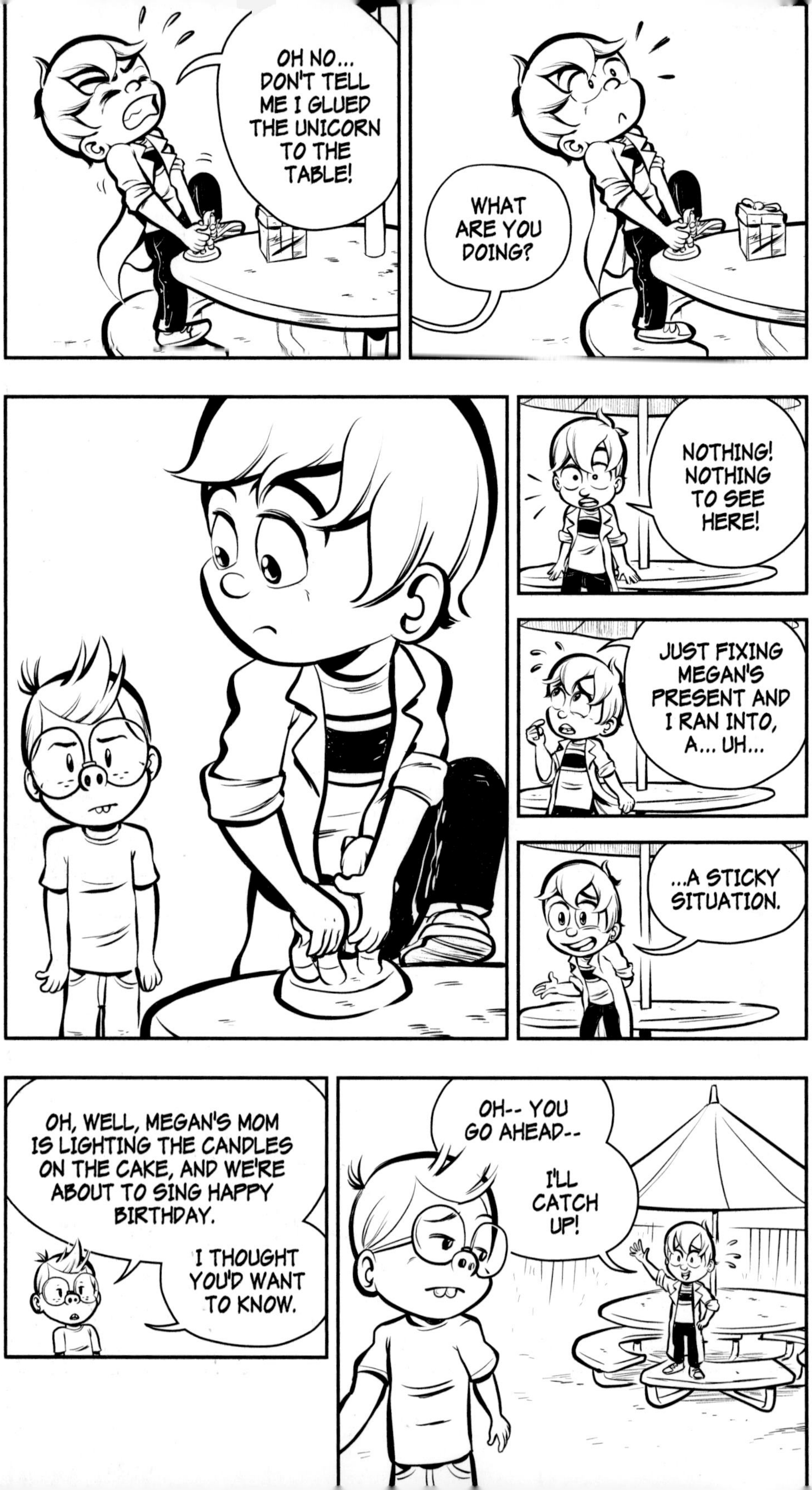
OH NO... DON'T TELL ME I GLUED THE UNICORN TO THE TABLE!
WHAT ARE YOU DOING?
NOTHING! NOTHING TO SEE HERE!
JUST FIXING MEGAN'S PRESENT AND I RAN INTO, A... UH...
...A STICKY SITUATION.
OH, WELL, MEGAN'S MOM IS LIGHTING THE CANDLES ON THE CAKE, AND WE'RE ABOUT TO SING HAPPY BIRTHDAY.
I THOUGHT YOU'D WANT TO KNOW.
OH-- YOU GO AHEAD--
I'LL CATCH UP!

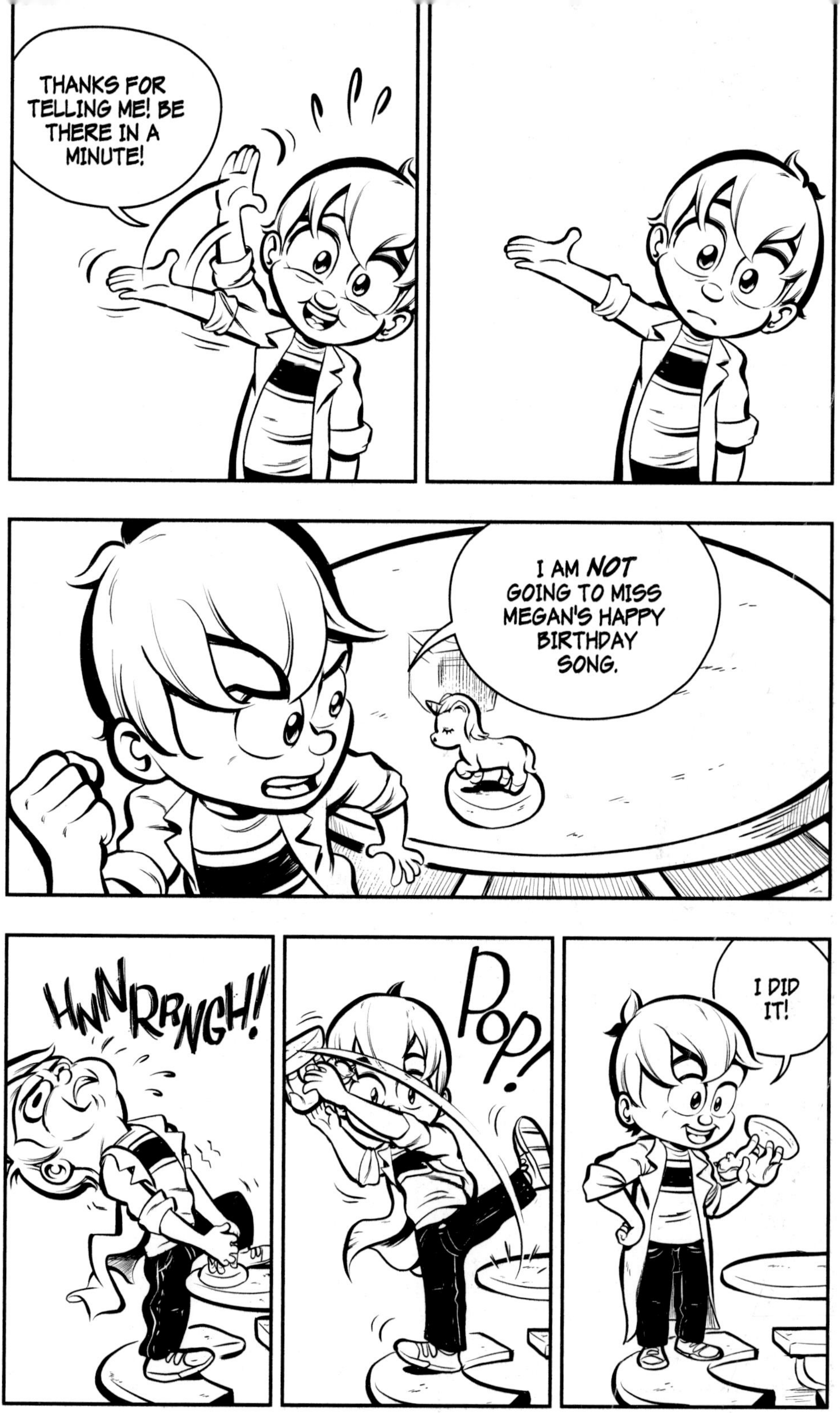
THANKS FOR TELLING ME! BE THERE IN A MINUTE!
I AM *NOT* GOING TO MISS MEGAN'S HAPPY BIRTHDAY SONG.
HNNRRNGH!
POP!
I DID IT!

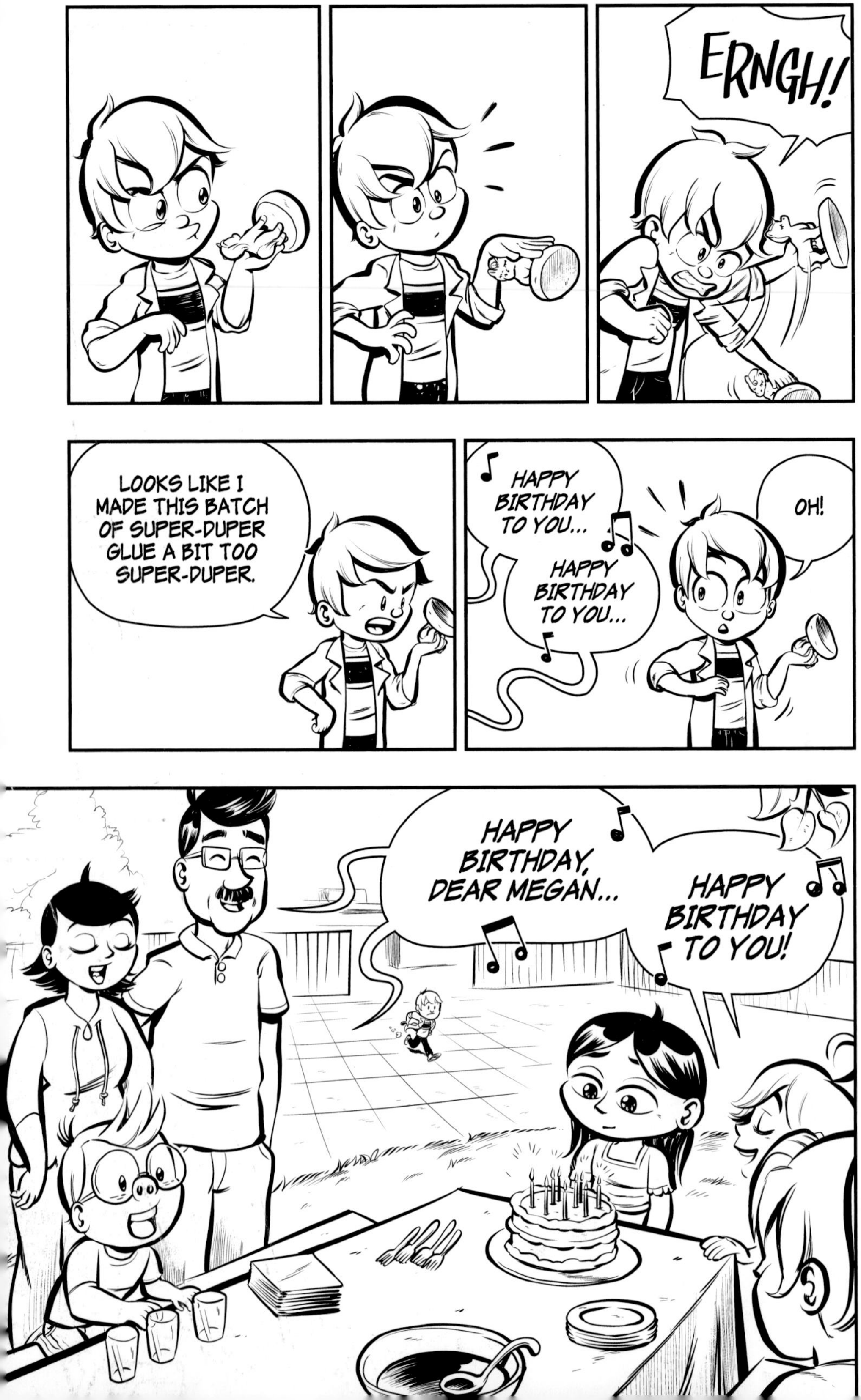
ERNGH!
LOOKS LIKE I MADE THIS BATCH OF SUPER-DUPER GLUE A BIT TOO SUPER-DUPER.
HAPPY BIRTHDAY TO YOU...
HAPPY BIRTHDAY TO YOU...
OH!
HAPPY BIRTHDAY, DEAR MEGAN...
HAPPY BIRTHDAY TO YOU!

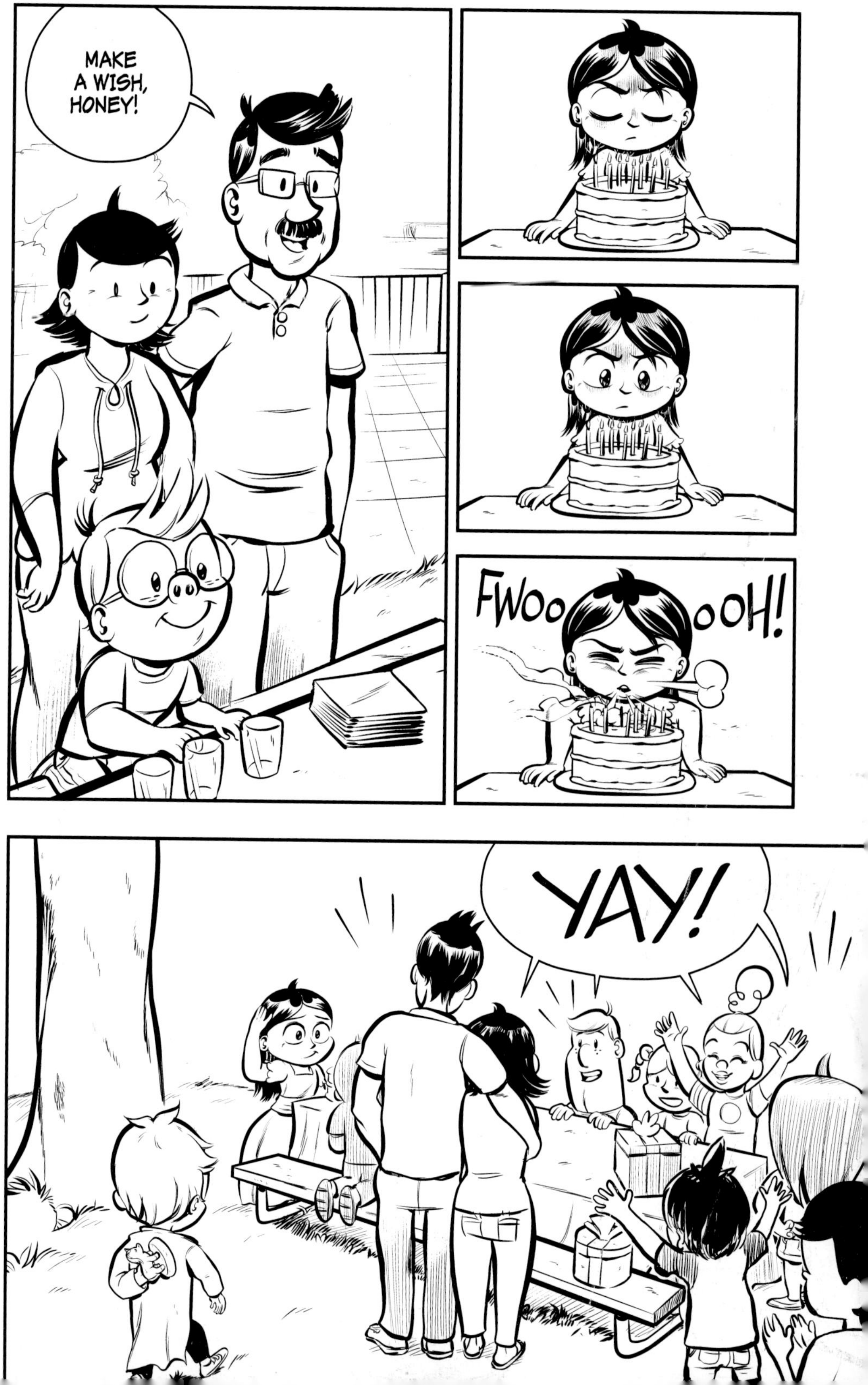
MAKE A WISH, HONEY!
FWOOOOH!
YAY!

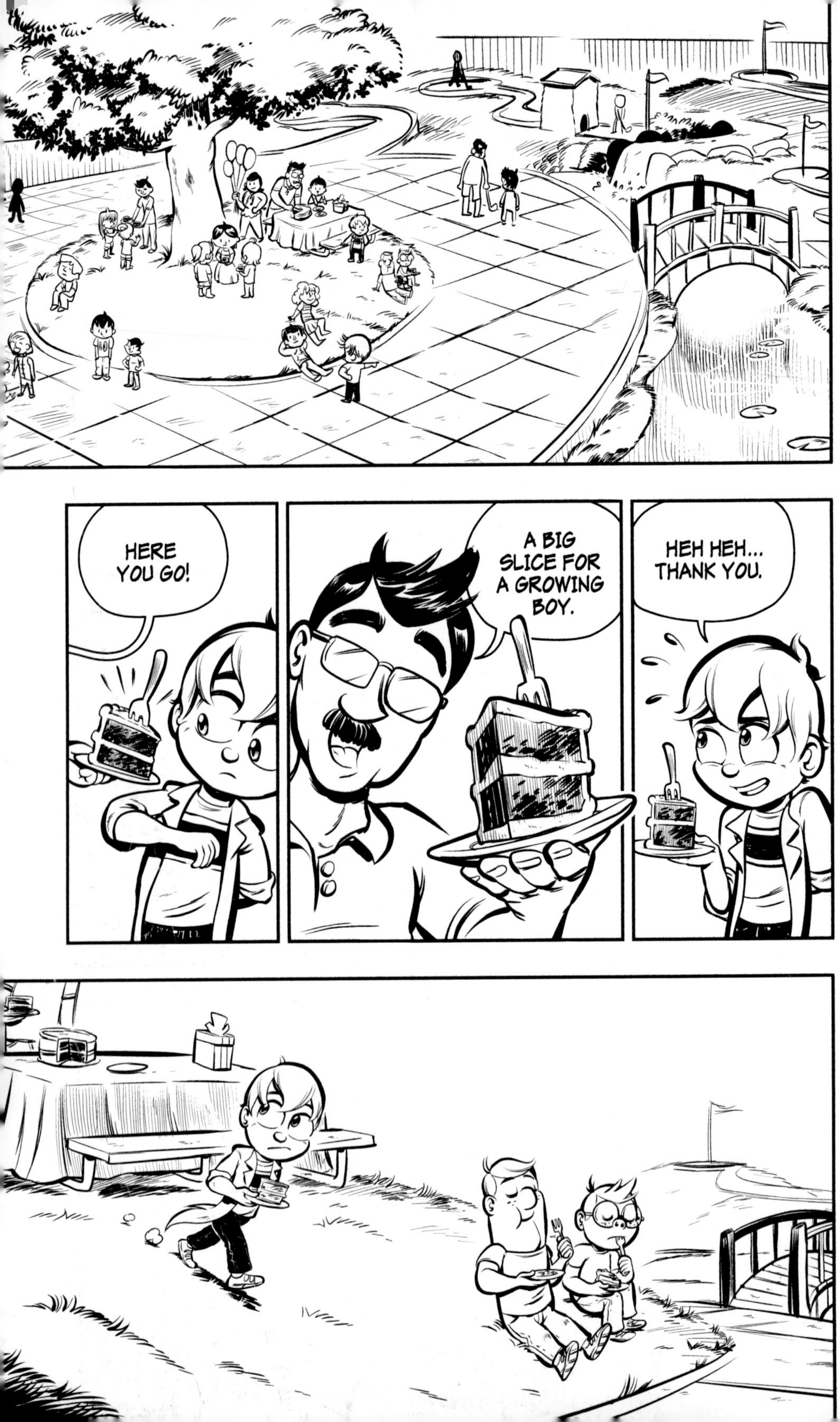
HERE YOU GO!
A BIG SLICE FOR A GROWING BOY.
HEH HEH... THANK YOU.

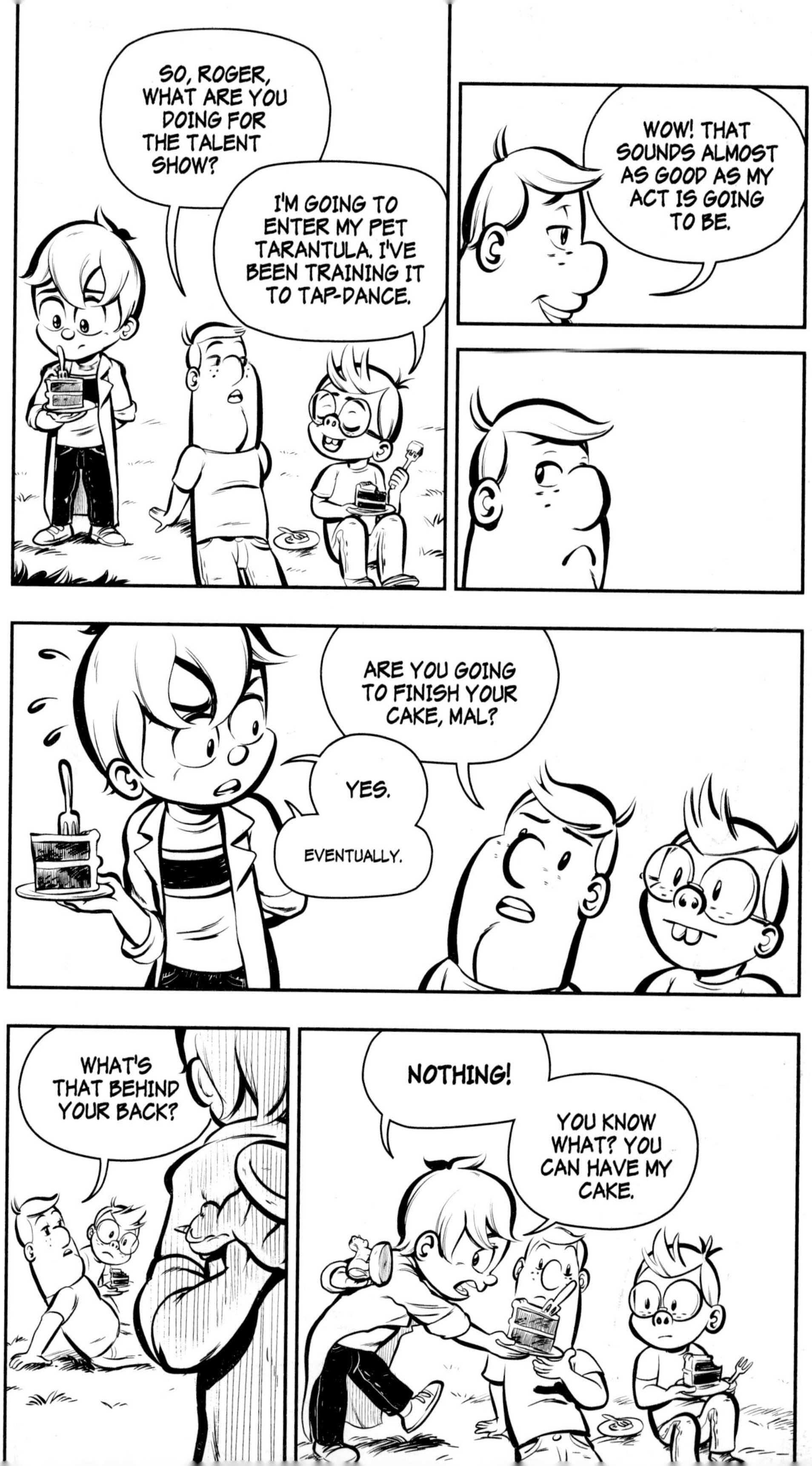
SO, ROGER, WHAT ARE YOU DOING FOR THE TALENT SHOW?
I'M GOING TO ENTER MY PET TARANTULA. I'VE BEEN TRAINING IT TO TAP-DANCE.
WOW! THAT SOUNDS ALMOST AS GOOD AS MY ACT IS GOING TO BE.
ARE YOU GOING TO FINISH YOUR CAKE, MAL?
YES.
EVENTUALLY.
WHAT'S THAT BEHIND YOUR BACK?
NOTHING!
YOU KNOW WHAT? YOU CAN HAVE MY CAKE.

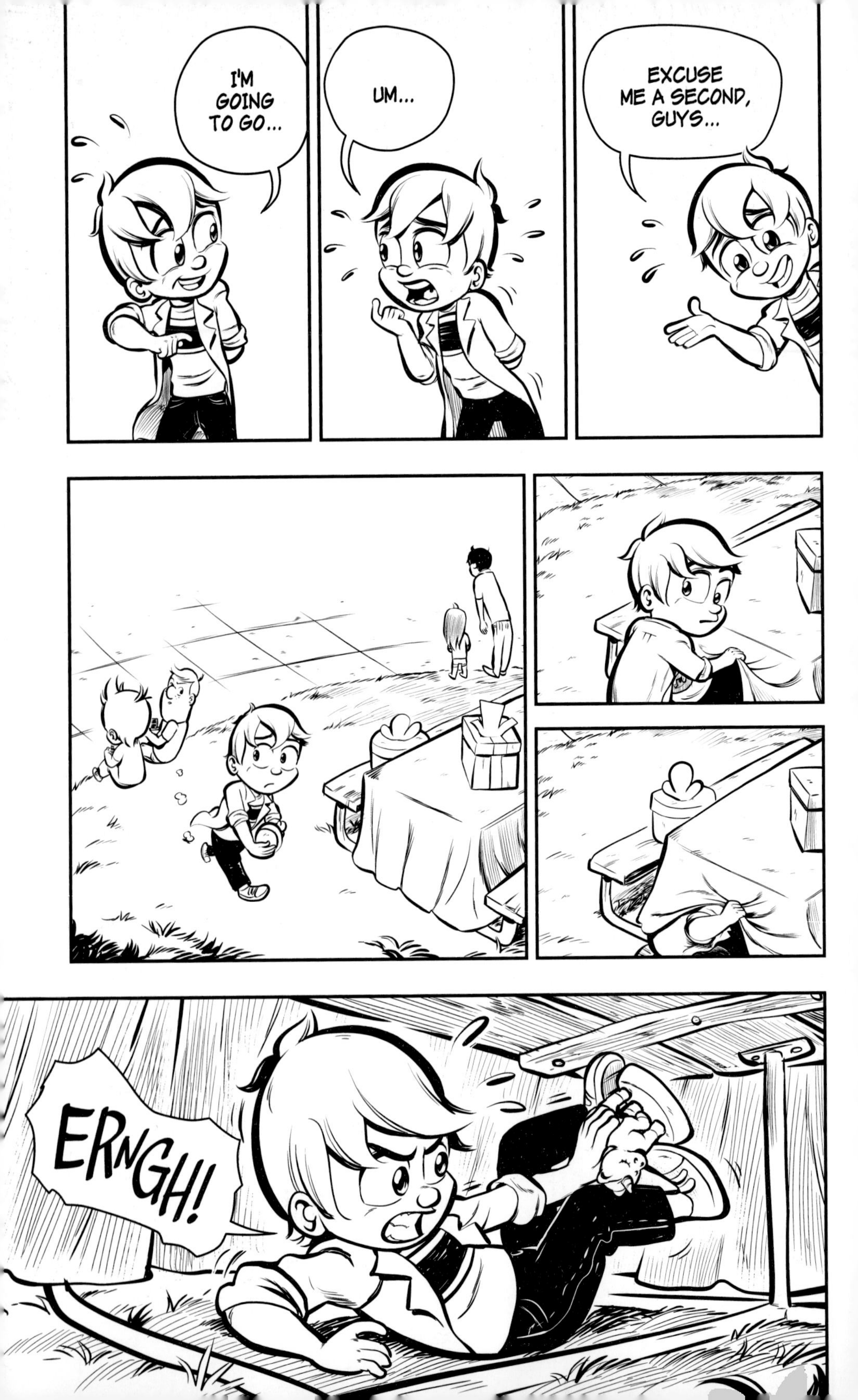
I'M GOING TO GO...
UM...
EXCUSE ME A SECOND, GUYS...
ERNGH!

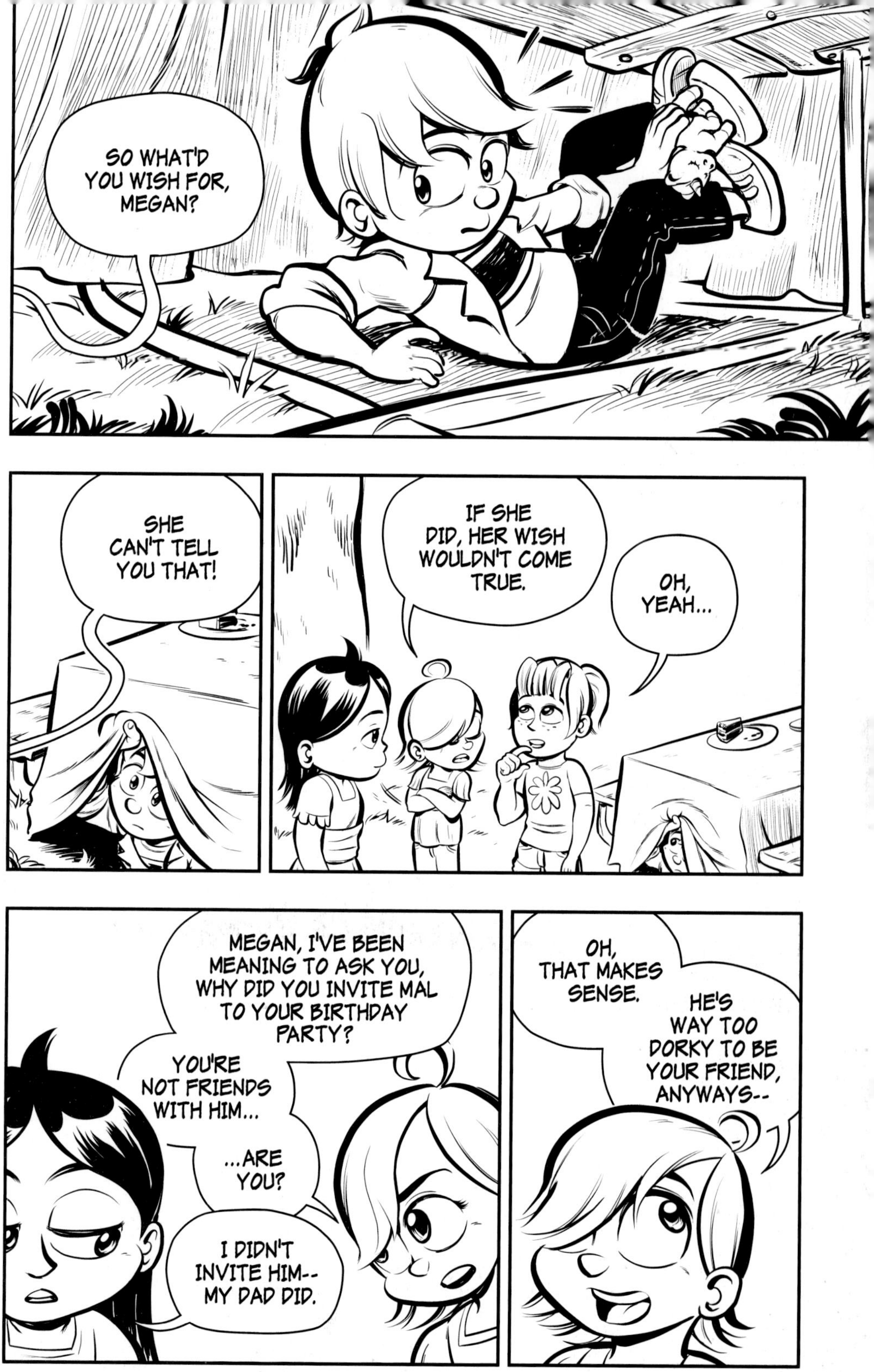
SO WHAT'D YOU WISH FOR, MEGAN?
SHE CAN'T TELL YOU THAT!
IF SHE DID, HER WISH WOULDN'T COME TRUE.
OH, YEAH...
MEGAN, I'VE BEEN MEANING TO ASK YOU, WHY DID YOU INVITE MAL TO YOUR BIRTHDAY PARTY?
YOU'RE NOT FRIENDS WITH HIM...
...ARE YOU?
I DIDN'T INVITE HIM-- MY DAD DID.
OH, THAT MAKES SENSE.
HE'S WAY TOO DORKY TO BE YOUR FRIEND, ANYWAYS--

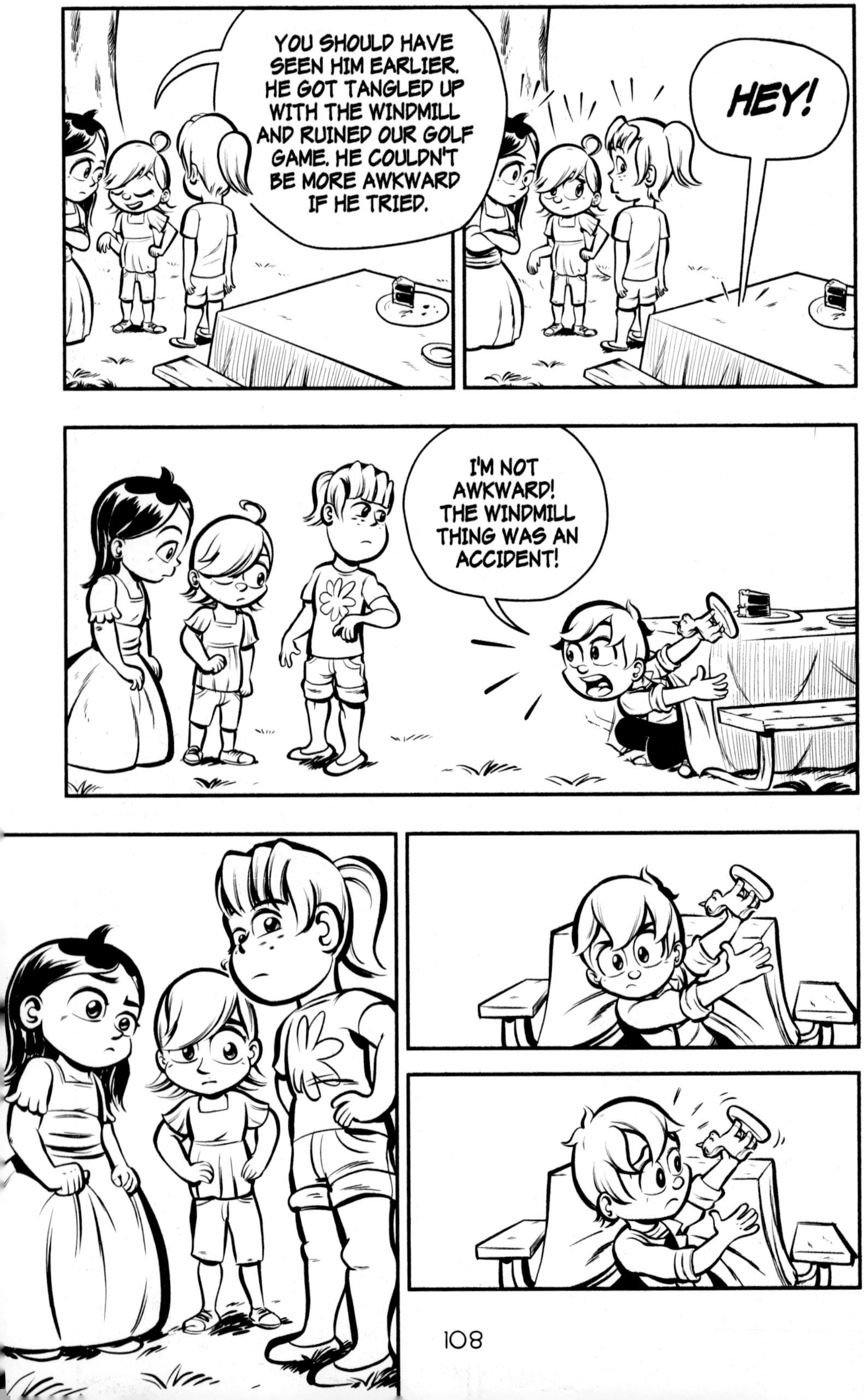
YOU SHOULD HAVE SEEN HIM EARLIER. HE GOT TANGLED UP WITH THE WINDMILL AND RUINED OUR GOLF GAME. HE COULDN'T BE MORE AWKWARD IF HE TRIED.
HEY!
I'M NOT AWKWARD! THE WINDMILL THING WAS AN ACCIDENT!

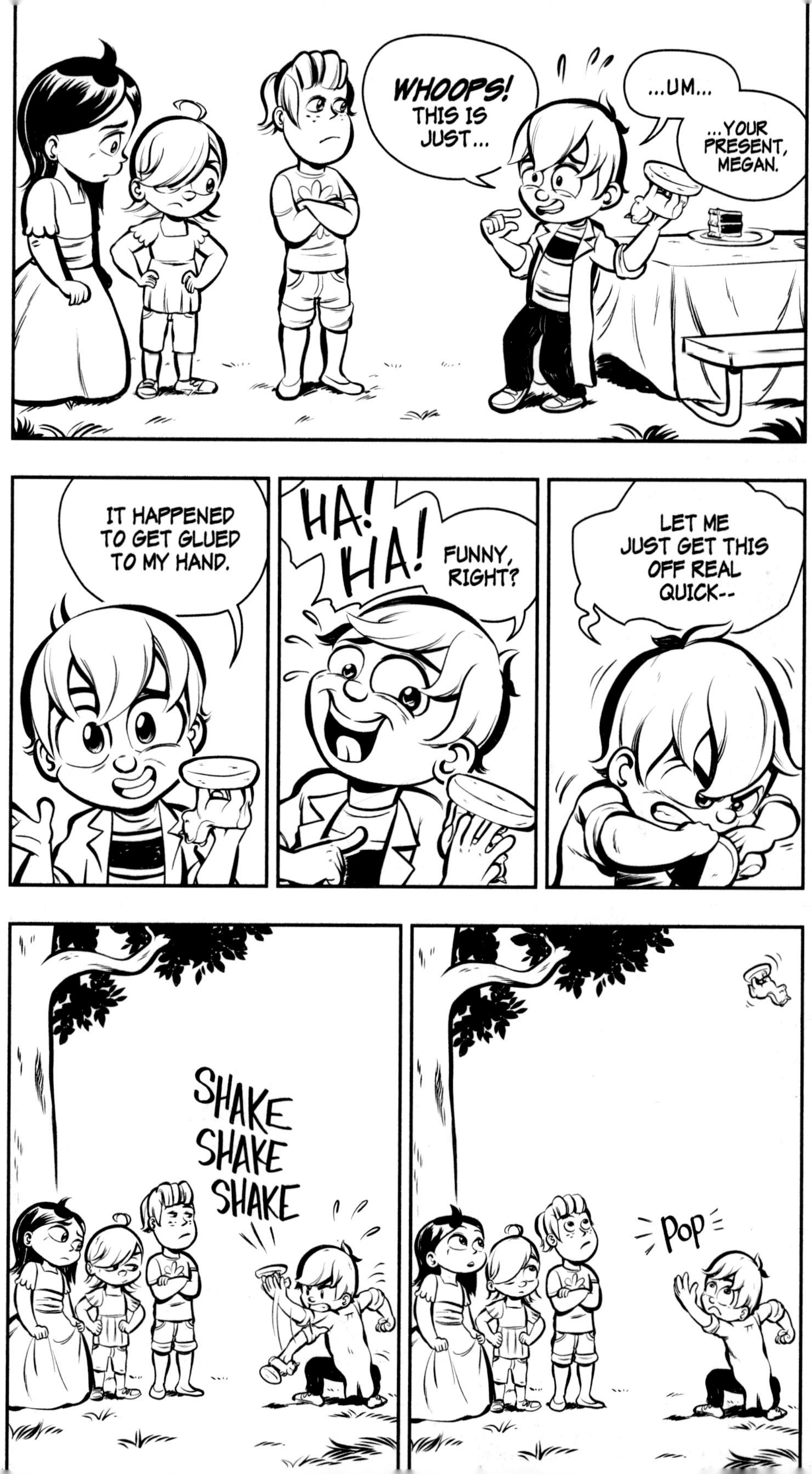
WHOOPS! THIS IS JUST...
...UM...
...YOUR PRESENT, MEGAN.
IT HAPPENED TO GET GLUED TO MY HAND.
HA! HA!
FUNNY, RIGHT?
LET ME JUST GET THIS OFF REAL QUICK--
SHAKE SHAKE SHAKE
POP

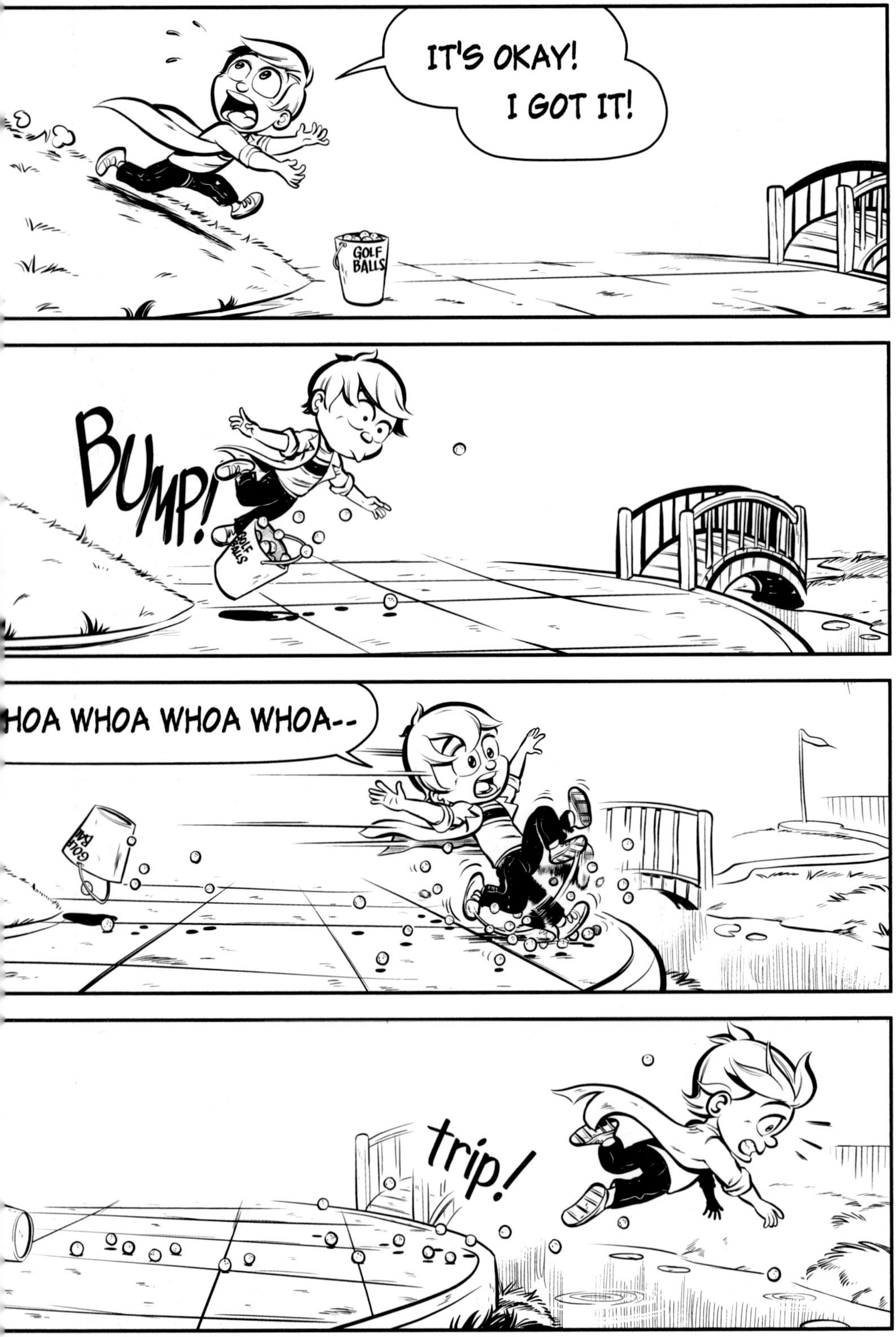
IT'S OKAY!
I GOT IT!
GOLF BALLS
BUMP!
GOLF BALLS
HOA WHOA WHOA WHOA--
trip!

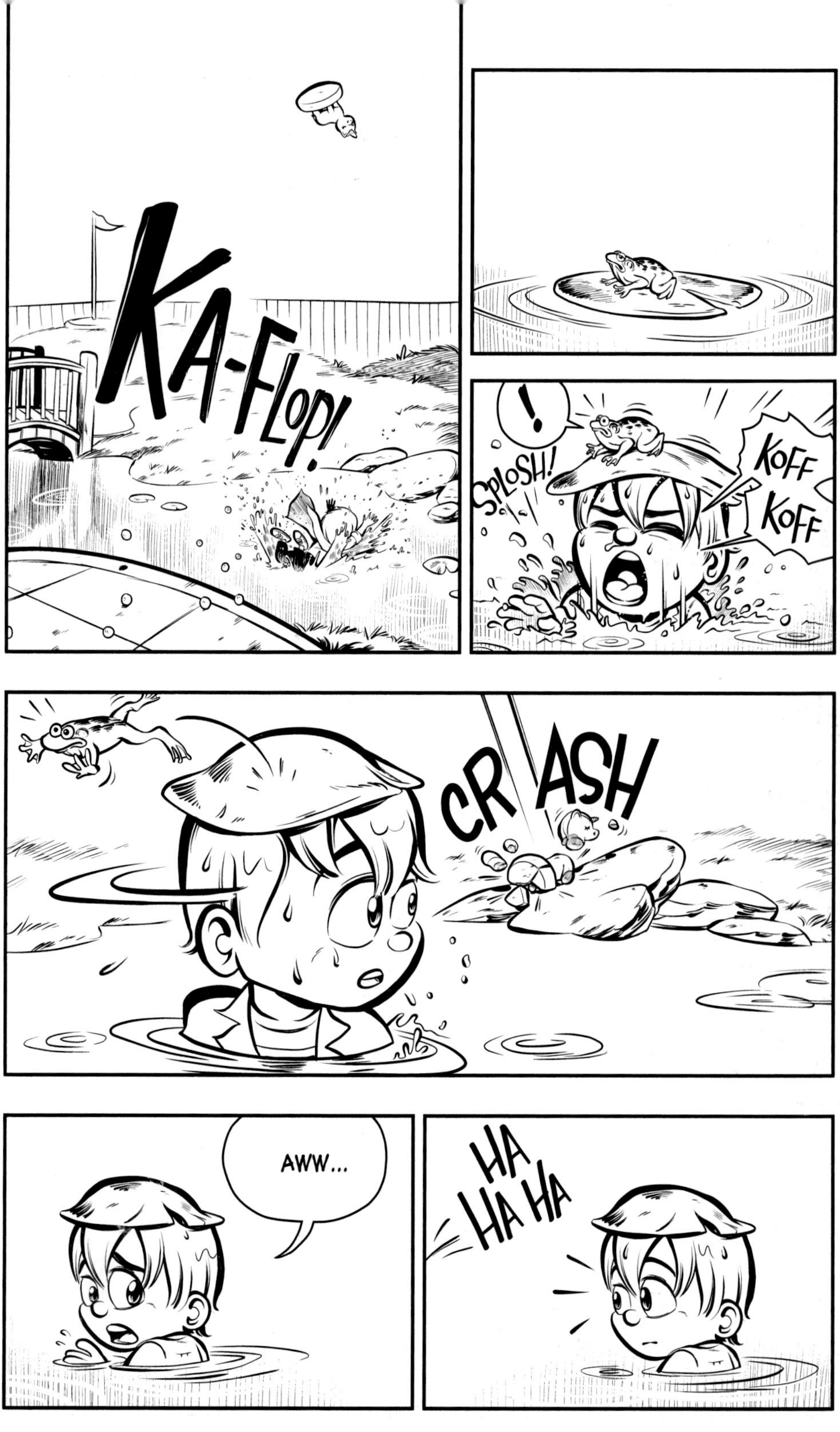
KA-FLOP!
!
SPLOSH!
KOFF KOFF
CRASH
AWW...
HA HA HA HA

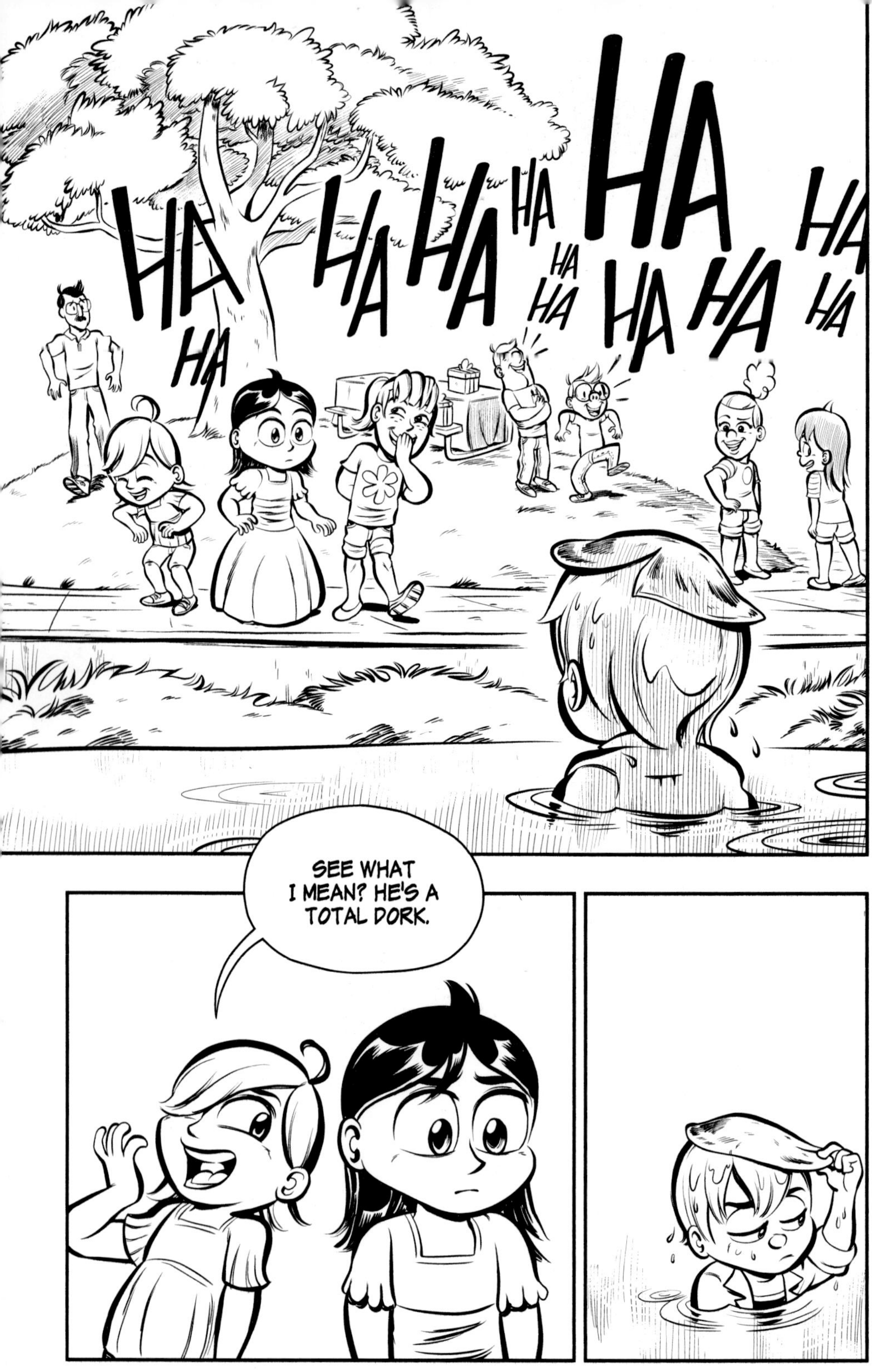
HA HA
HA HA HA HA
HA
HA HA
HA
HA HA HA
HA HA
SEE WHAT I MEAN? HE'S A TOTAL DORK.

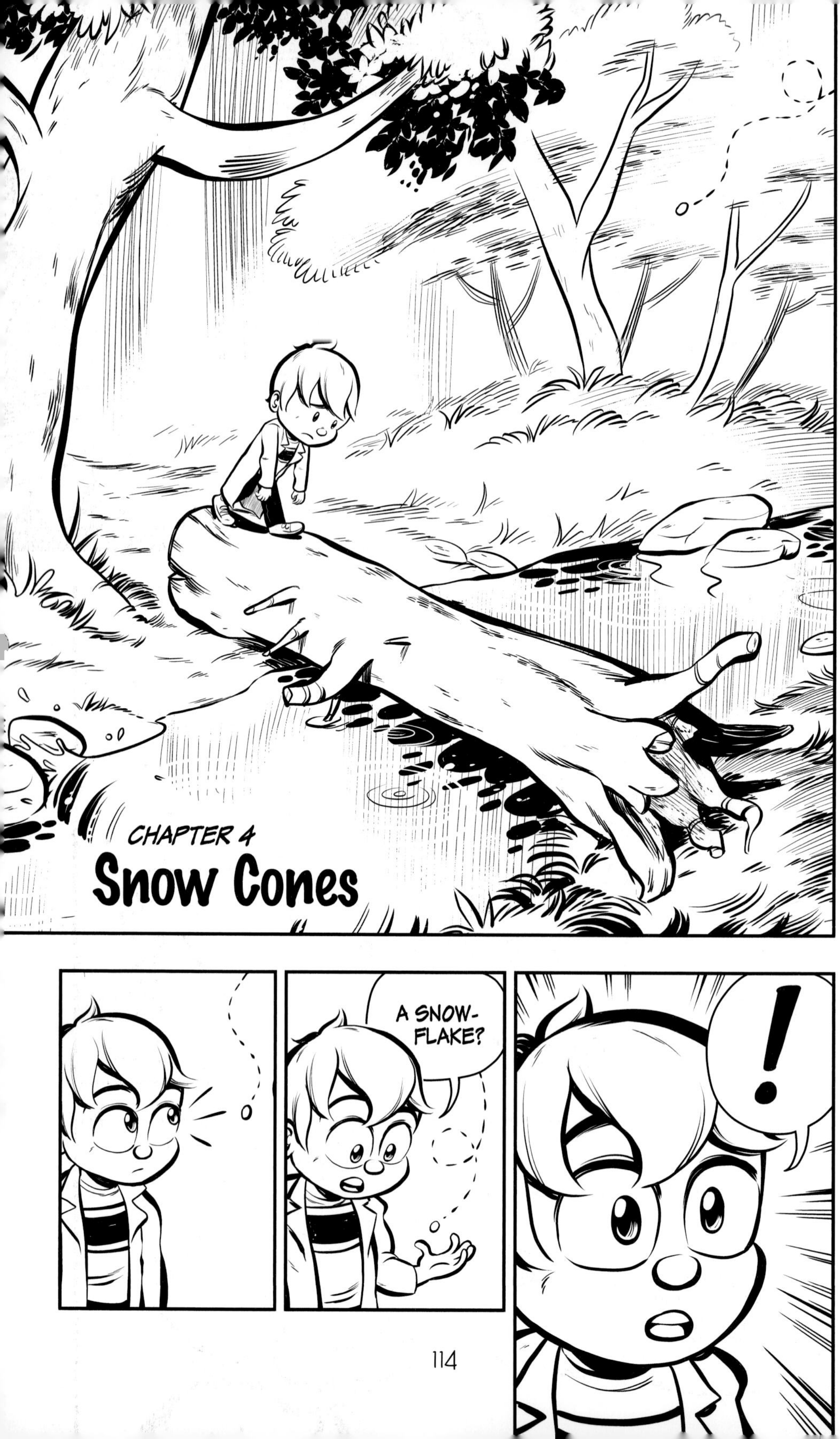
CHAPTER 4
Snow Cones
A SNOW-FLAKE?
!

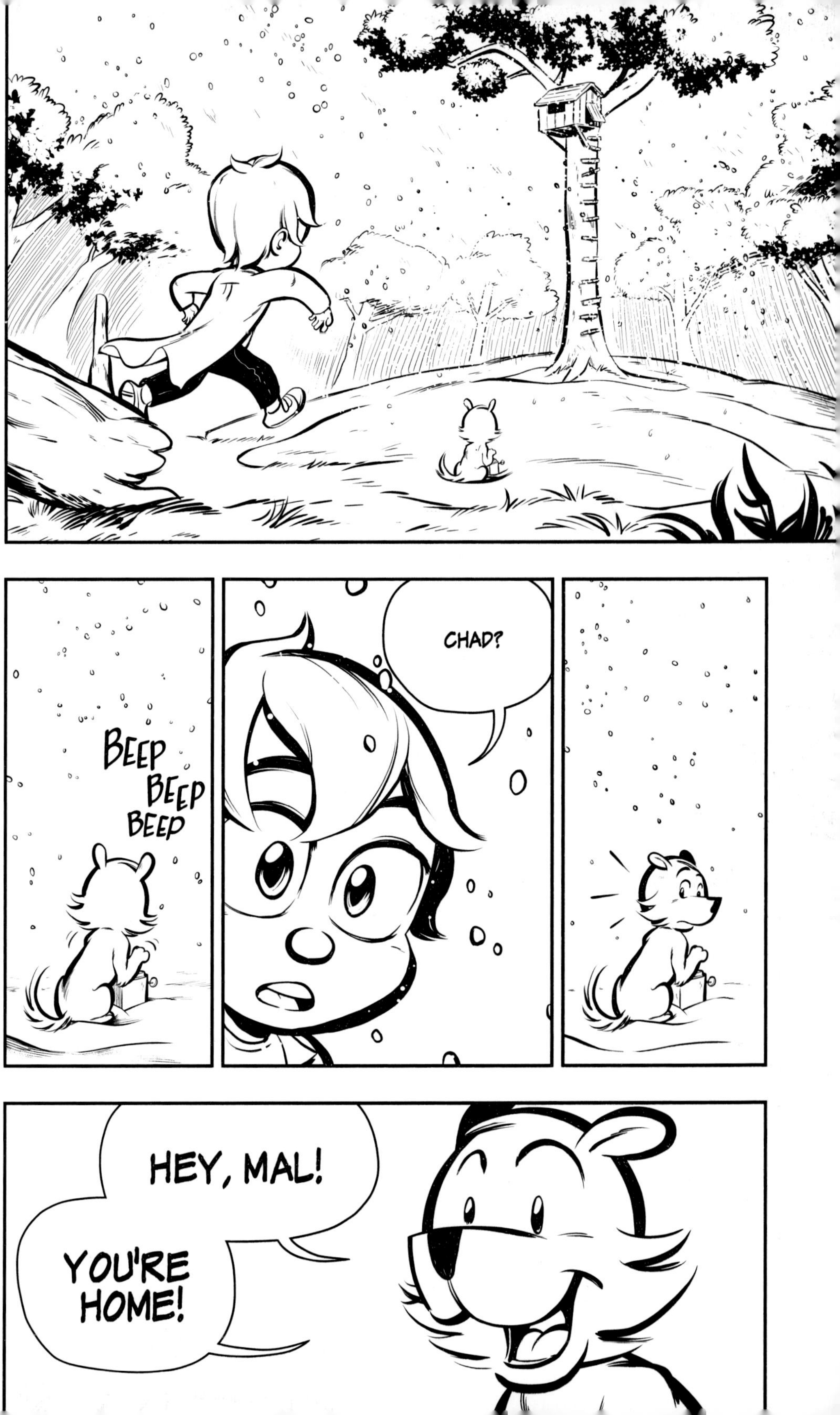
BEEP
BEEP
BEEP
CHAD?
HEY, MAL!
YOU'RE HOME!

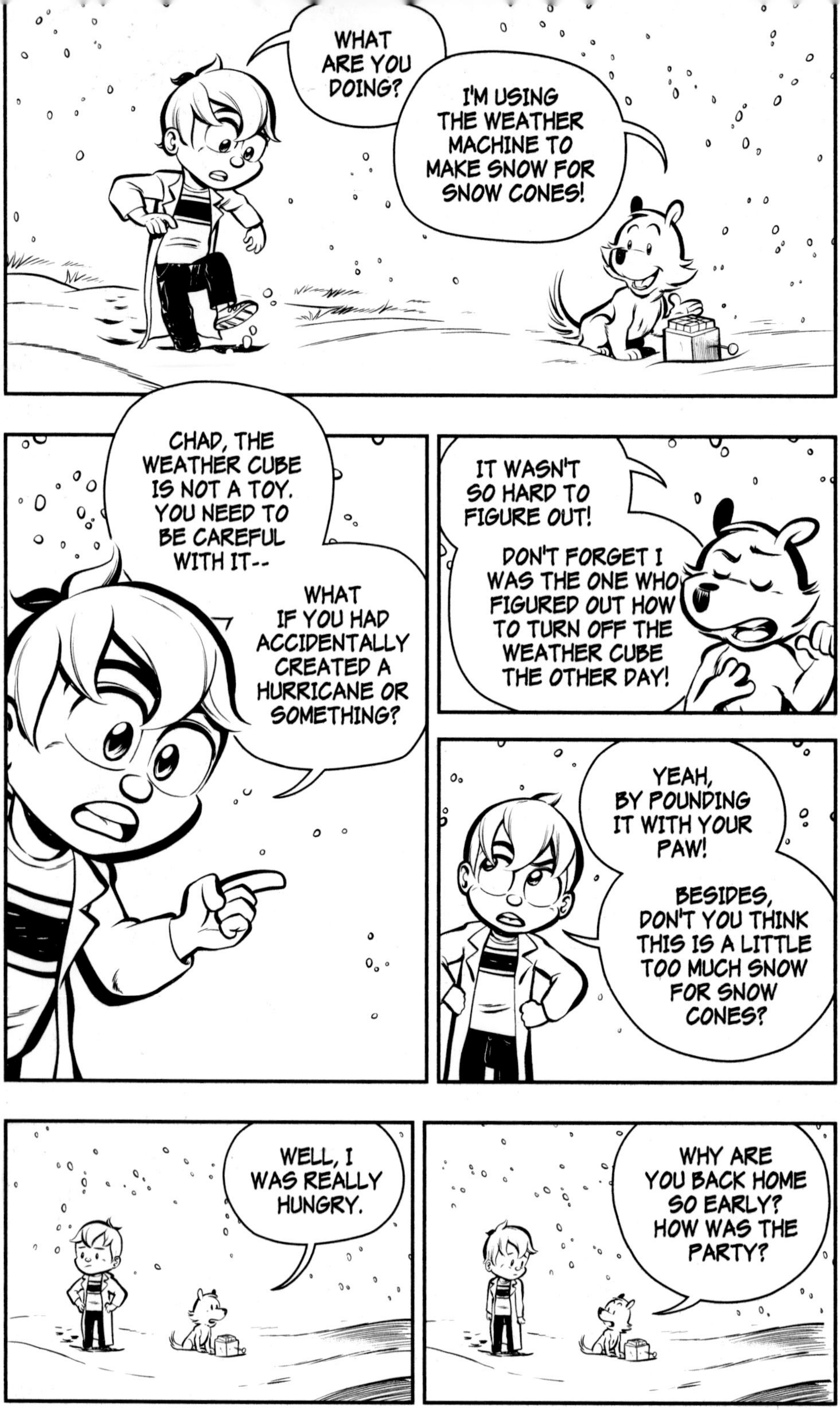
WHAT ARE YOU DOING?
I'M USING THE WEATHER MACHINE TO MAKE SNOW FOR SNOW CONES!
CHAD, THE WEATHER CUBE IS NOT A TOY. YOU NEED TO BE CAREFUL WITH IT--
WHAT IF YOU HAD ACCIDENTALLY CREATED A HURRICANE OR SOMETHING?
IT WASN'T SO HARD TO FIGURE OUT!
DON'T FORGET I WAS THE ONE WHO FIGURED OUT HOW TO TURN OFF THE WEATHER CUBE THE OTHER DAY!
YEAH, BY POUNDING IT WITH YOUR PAW!
BESIDES, DON'T YOU THINK THIS IS A LITTLE TOO MUCH SNOW FOR SNOW CONES?
WELL, I WAS REALLY HUNGRY.
WHY ARE YOU BACK HOME SO EARLY? HOW WAS THE PARTY?

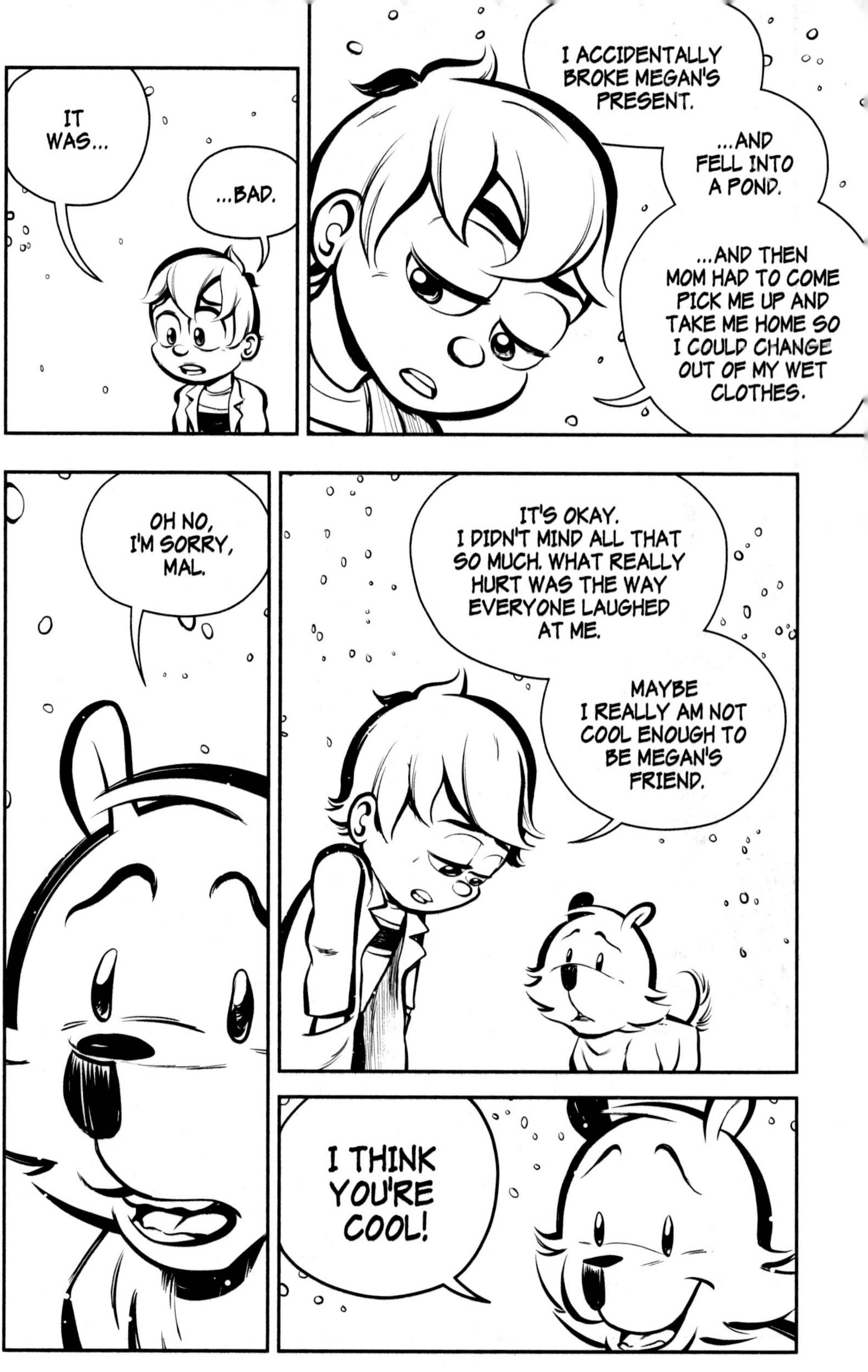
IT WAS...
...BAD.
I ACCIDENTALLY BROKE MEGAN'S PRESENT.
...AND FELL INTO A POND.
...AND THEN MOM HAD TO COME PICK ME UP AND TAKE ME HOME SO I COULD CHANGE OUT OF MY WET CLOTHES.
OH NO, I'M SORRY, MAL.
IT'S OKAY. I DIDN'T MIND ALL THAT SO MUCH. WHAT REALLY HURT WAS THE WAY EVERYONE LAUGHED AT ME.
MAYBE I REALLY AM NOT COOL ENOUGH TO BE MEGAN'S FRIEND.
I THINK YOU'RE COOL!

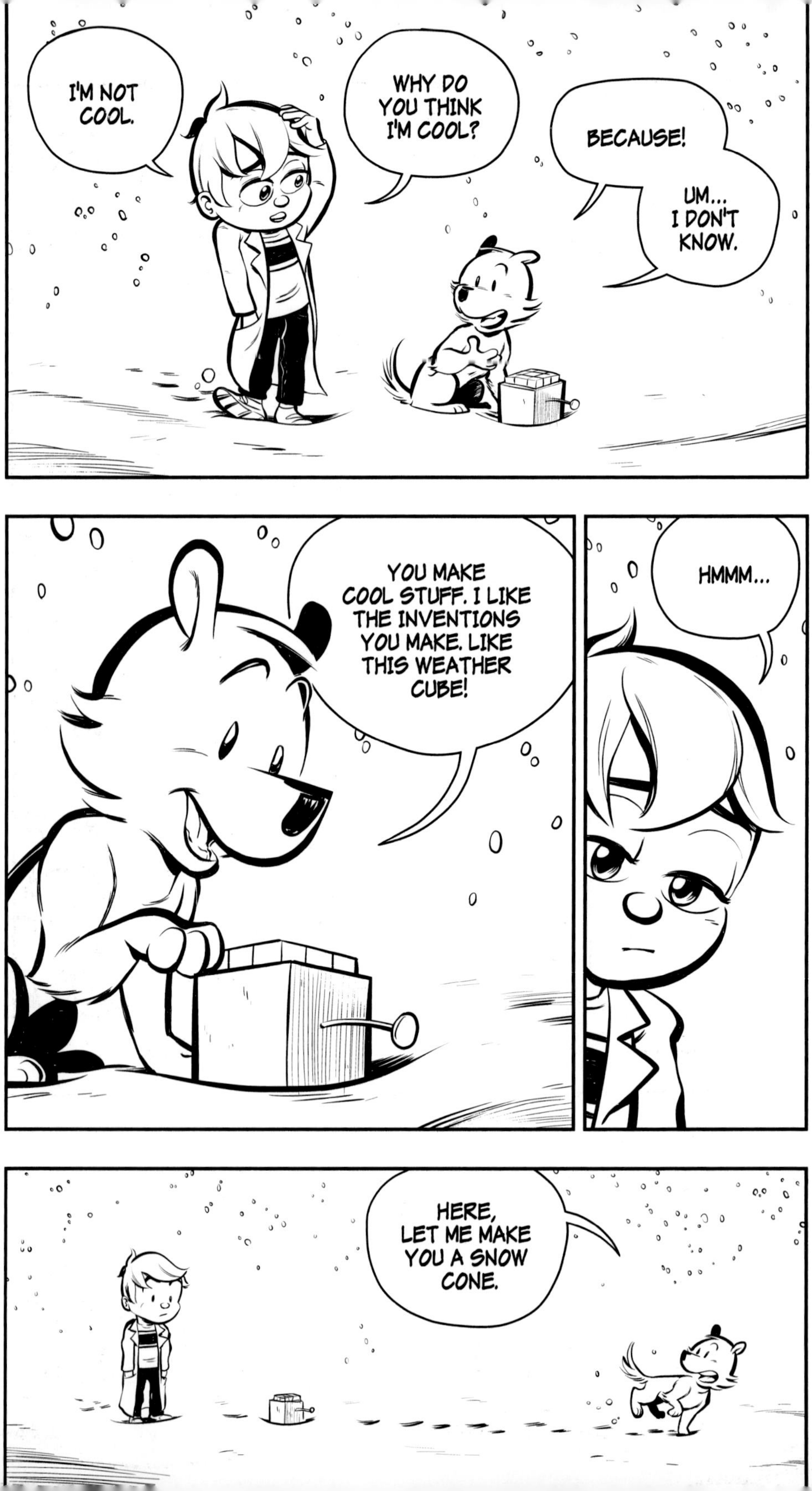
I'M NOT COOL.
WHY DO YOU THINK I'M COOL?
BECAUSE!
UM... I DON'T KNOW.
YOU MAKE COOL STUFF. I LIKE THE INVENTIONS YOU MAKE. LIKE THIS WEATHER CUBE!
HMMM...
HERE, LET ME MAKE YOU A SNOW CONE.

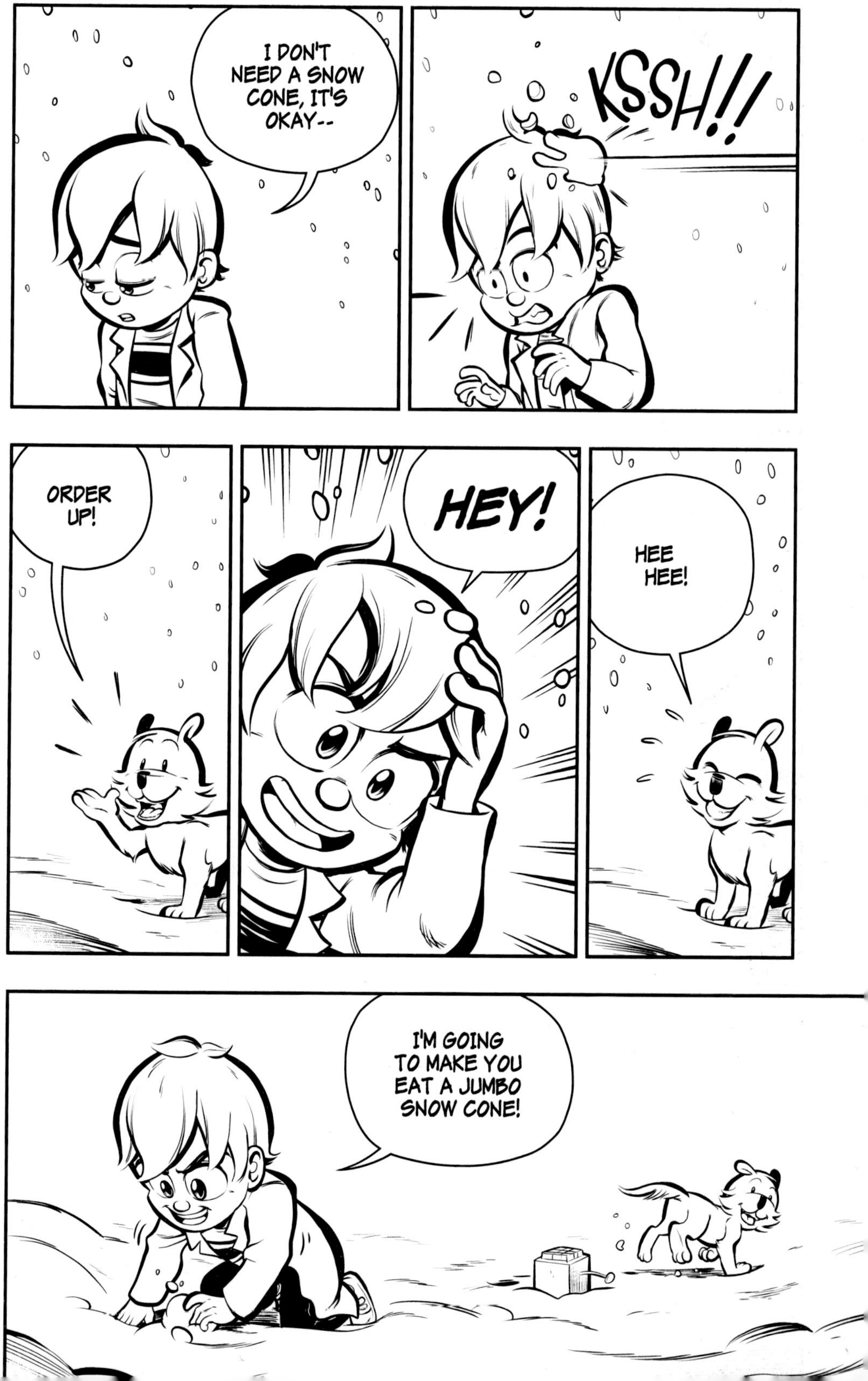

I DON'T NEED A SNOW CONE, IT'S OKAY--
KSSH!!!
ORDER UP!
HEY!
HEE HEE!
I'M GOING TO MAKE YOU EAT A JUMBO SNOW CONE!

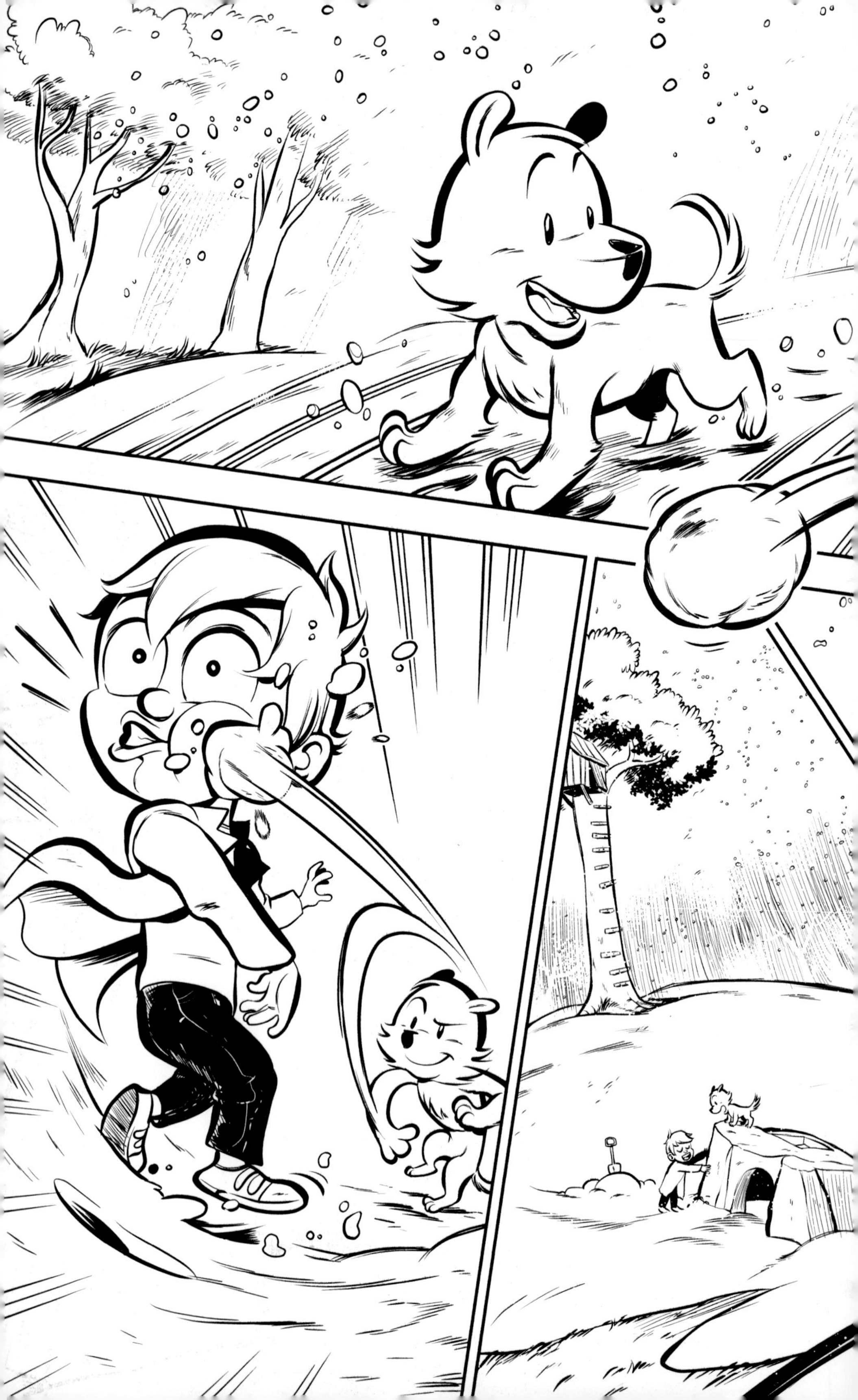

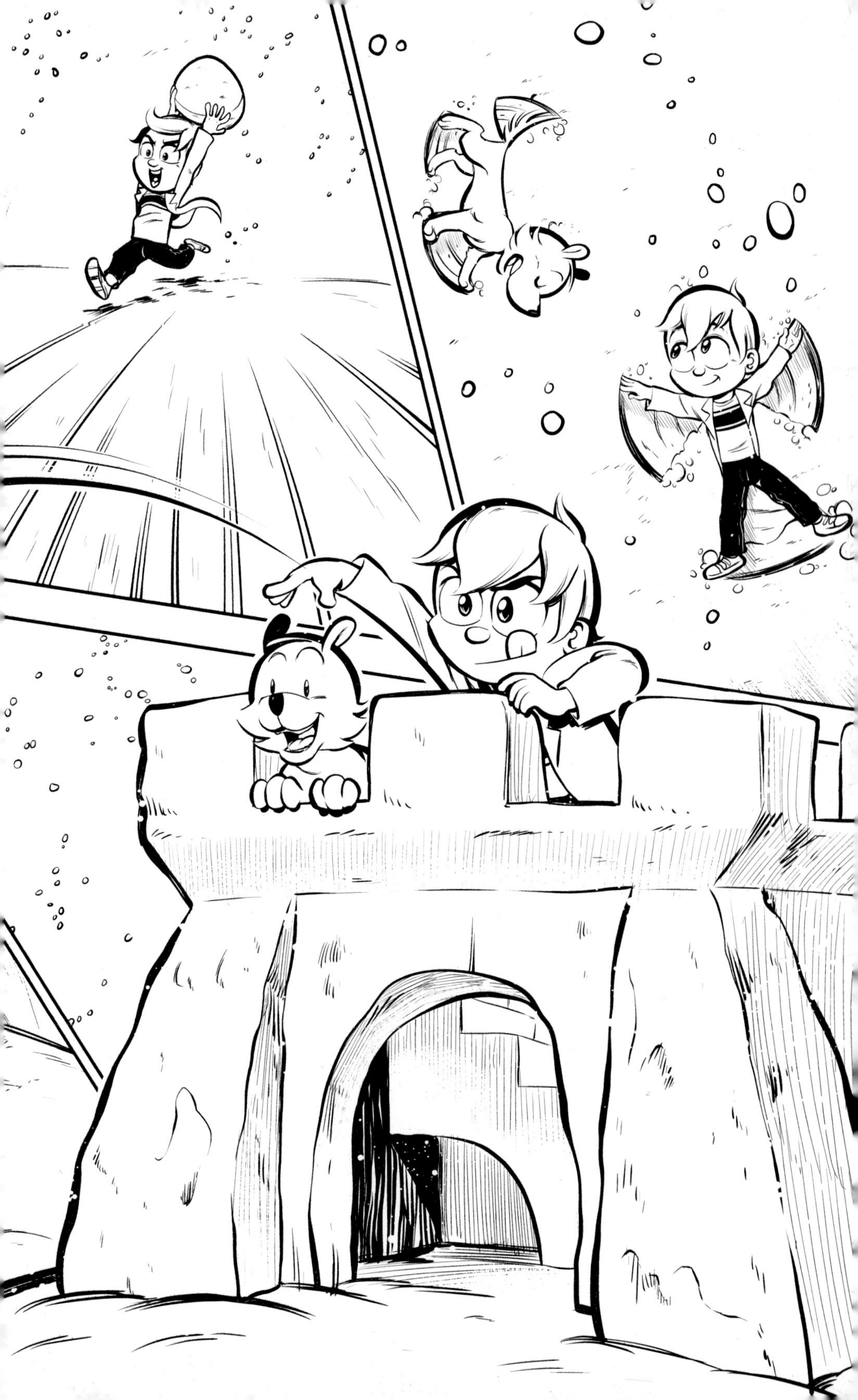

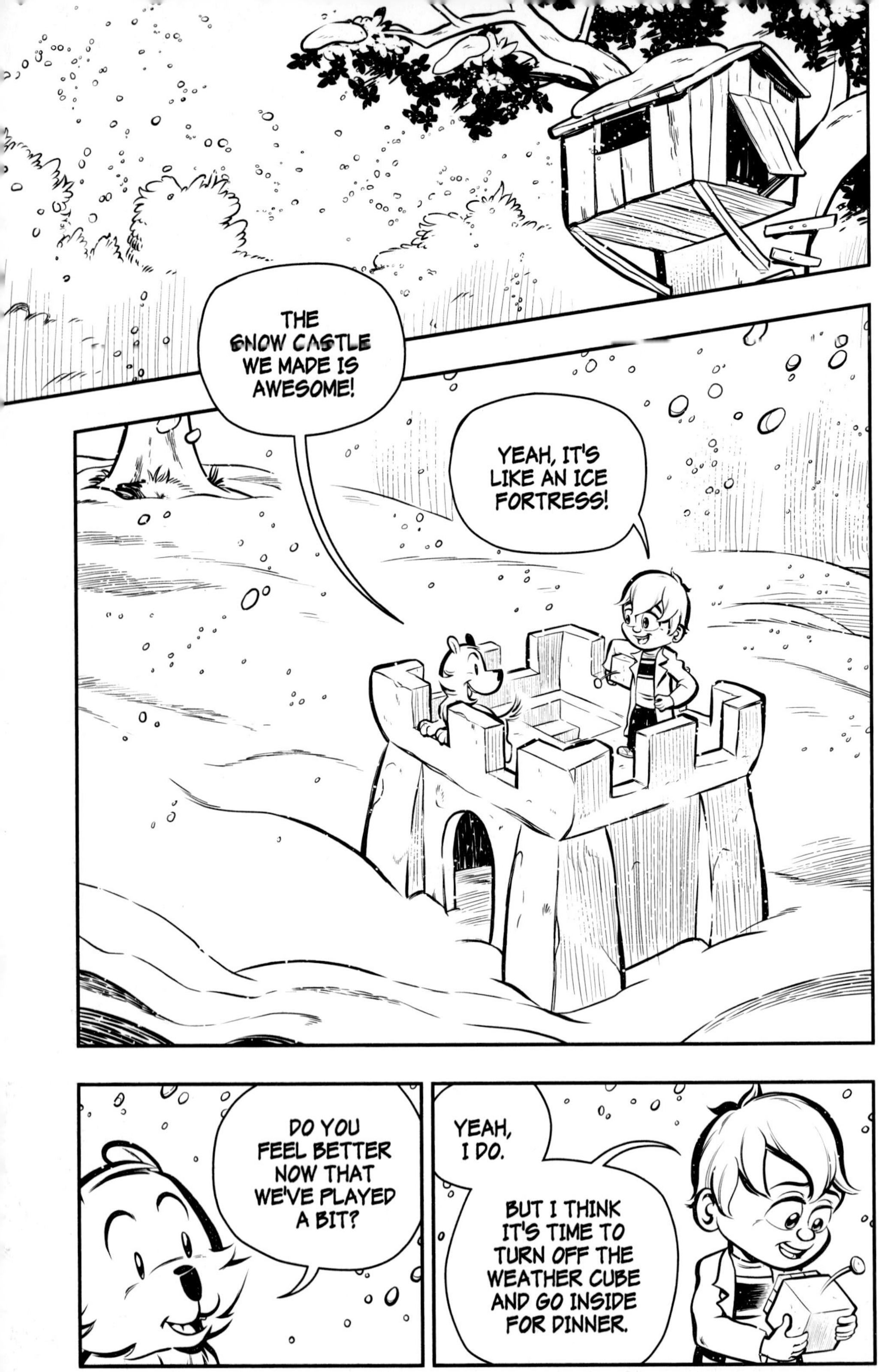
THE SNOW CASTLE WE MADE IS AWESOME!
YEAH, IT'S LIKE AN ICE FORTRESS!
DO YOU FEEL BETTER NOW THAT WE'VE PLAYED A BIT?
YEAH, I DO.
BUT I THINK IT'S TIME TO TURN OFF THE WEATHER CUBE AND GO INSIDE FOR DINNER.

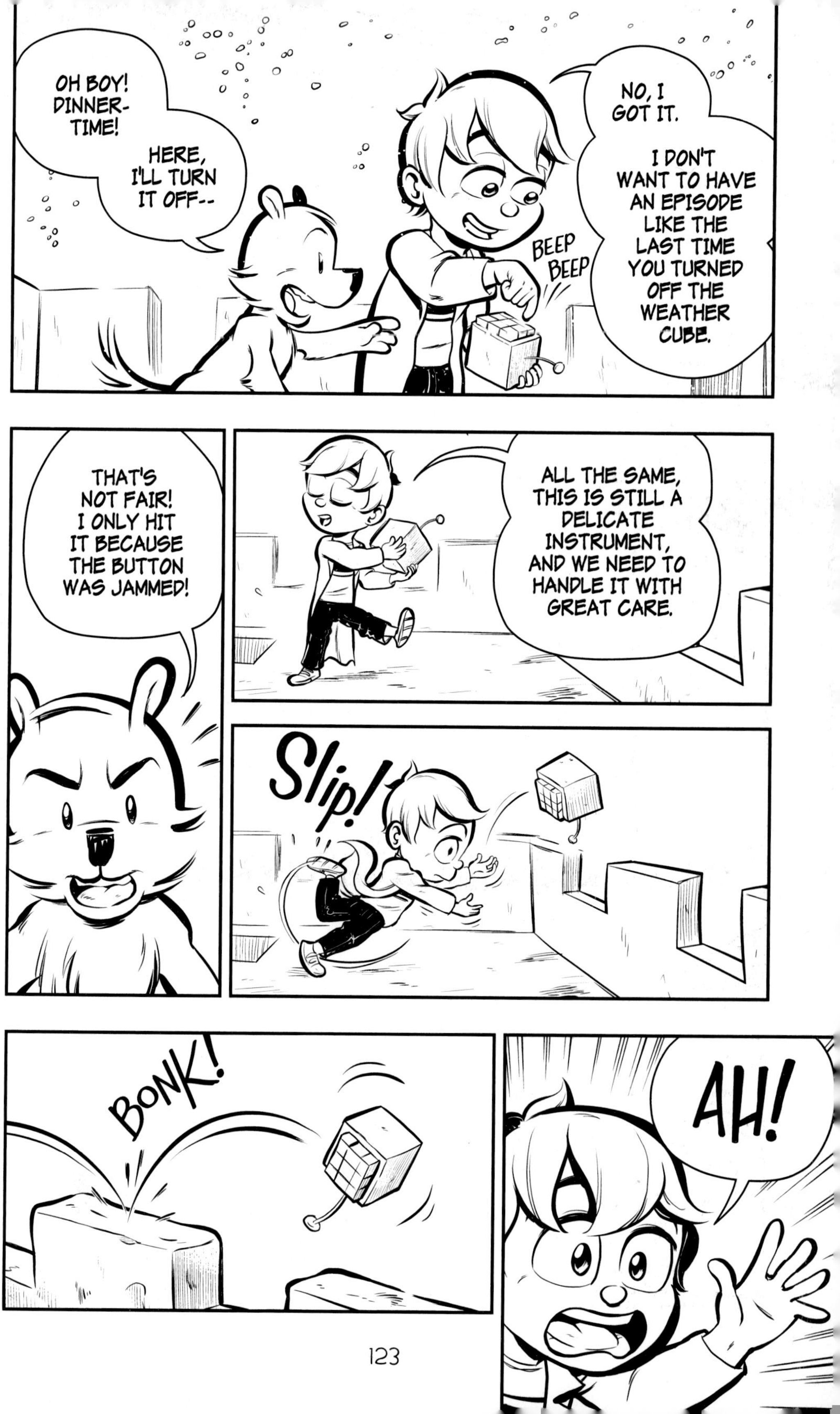
OH BOY! DINNER-TIME!
HERE, I'LL TURN IT OFF--
BEEP BEEP
NO, I GOT IT.
I DON'T WANT TO HAVE AN EPISODE LIKE THE LAST TIME YOU TURNED OFF THE WEATHER CUBE.
THAT'S NOT FAIR! I ONLY HIT IT BECAUSE THE BUTTON WAS JAMMED!
ALL THE SAME, THIS IS STILL A DELICATE INSTRUMENT, AND WE NEED TO HANDLE IT WITH GREAT CARE.
Slip!
BONK!
AH!

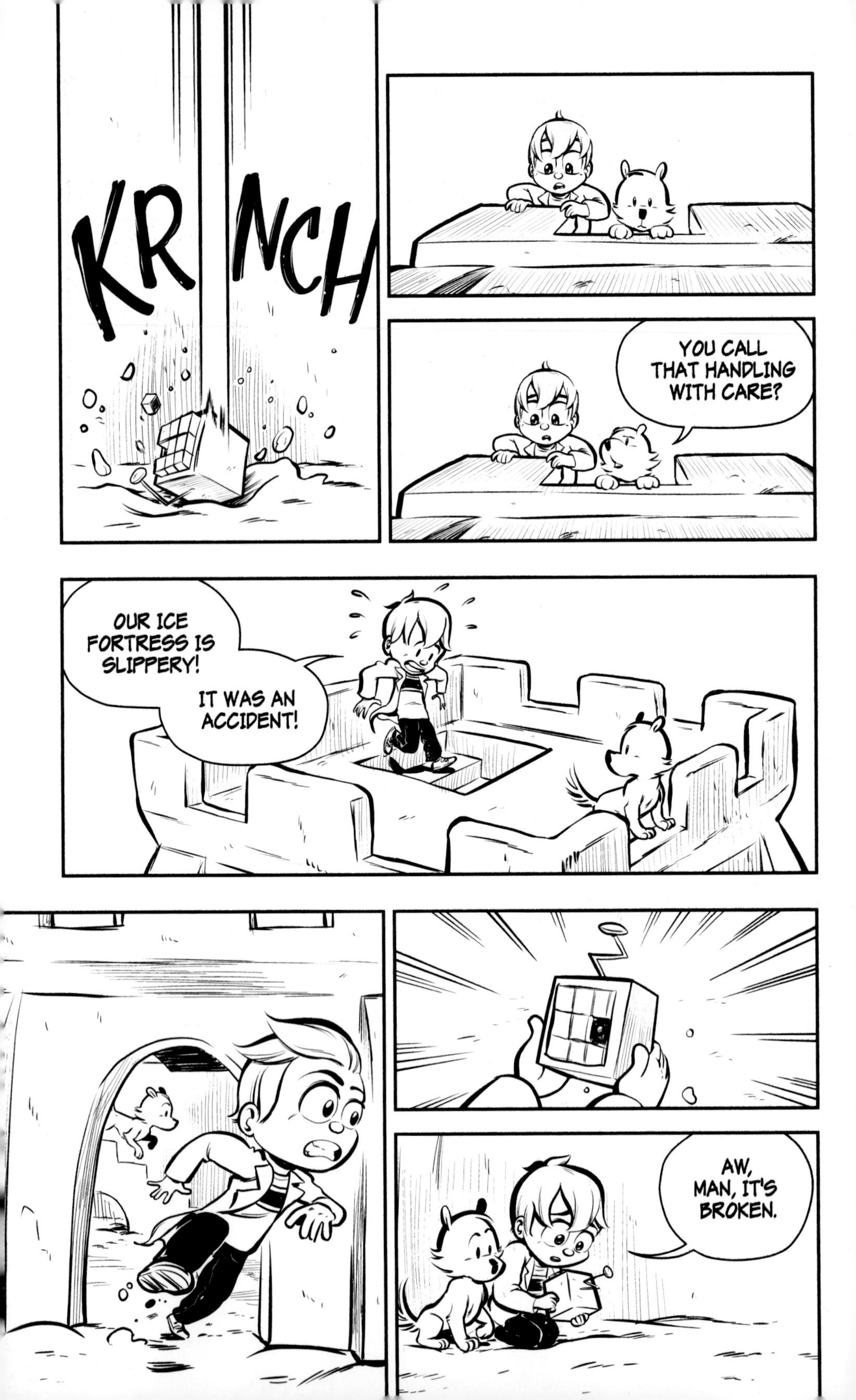
KRNCH
YOU CALL THAT HANDLING WITH CARE?
OUR ICE FORTRESS IS SLIPPERY!
IT WAS AN ACCIDENT!
AW, MAN, IT'S BROKEN.

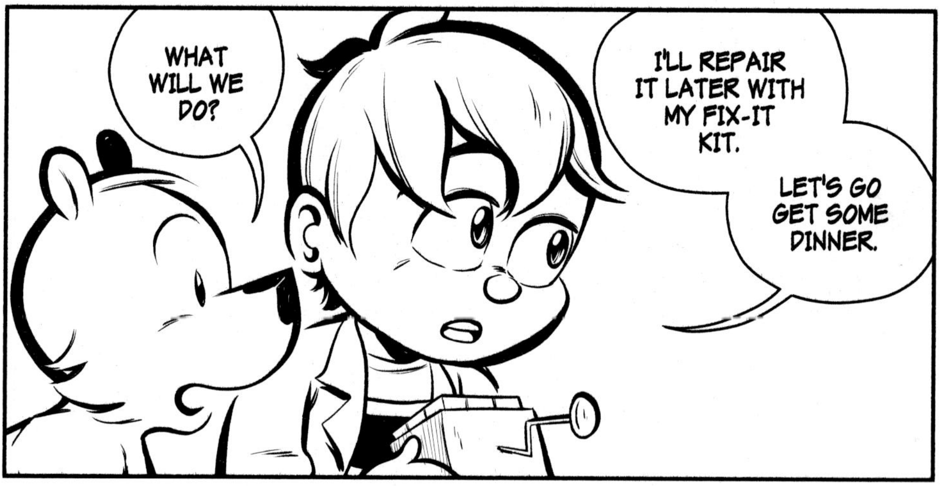
WHAT WILL WE DO?
I'LL REPAIR IT LATER WITH MY FIX-IT KIT.
LET'S GO GET SOME DINNER.

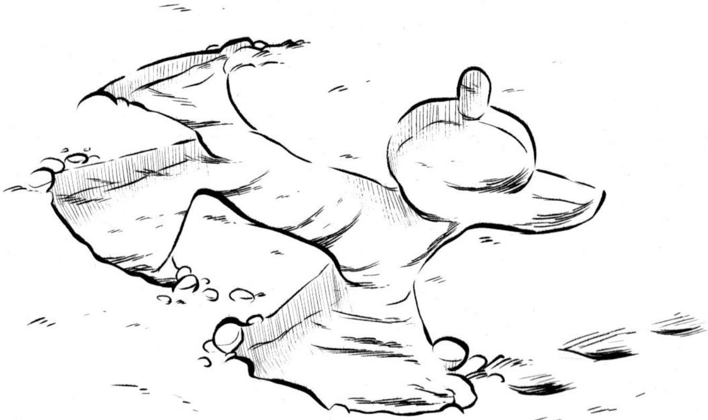

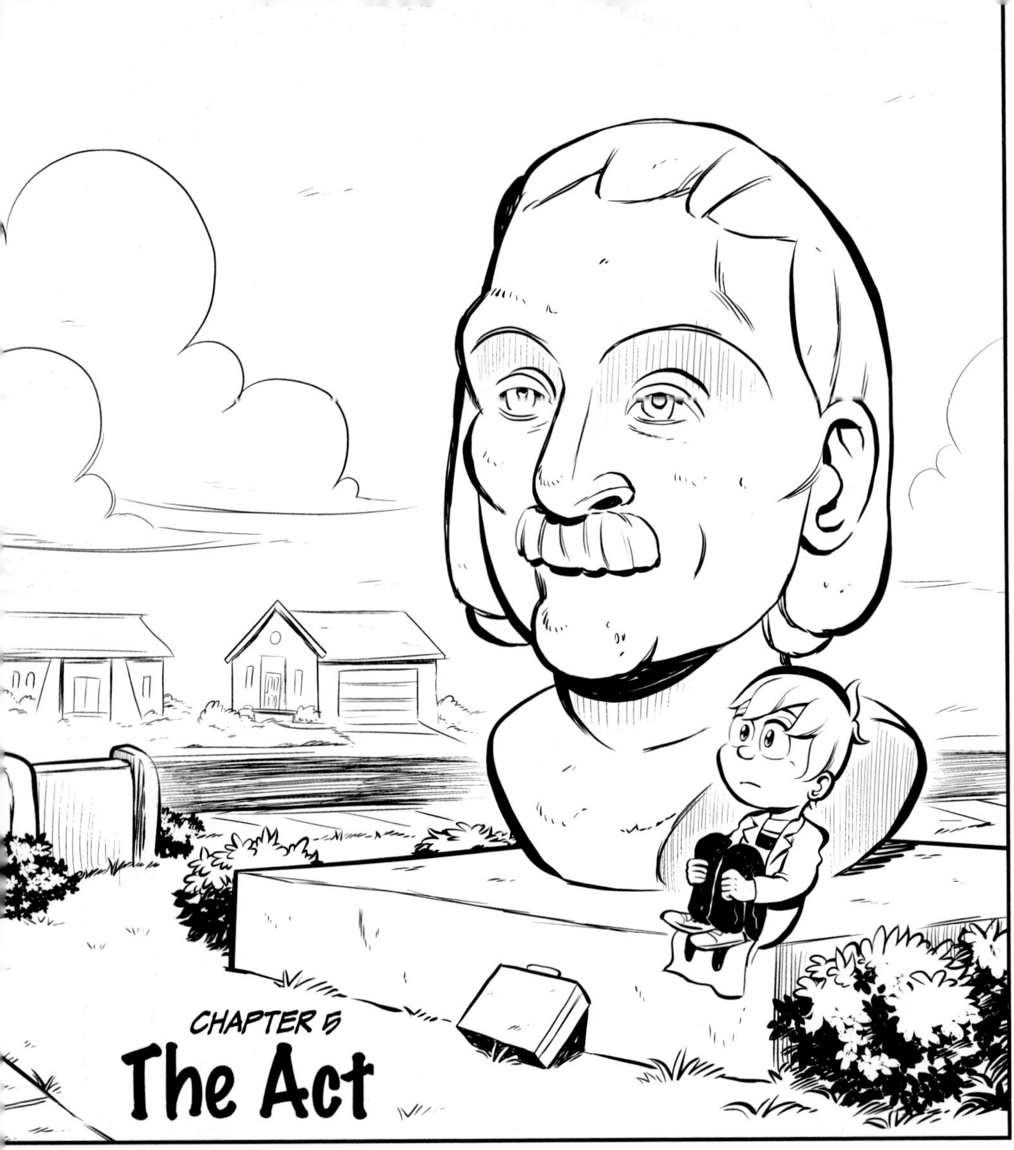
CHAPTER 5
The Act

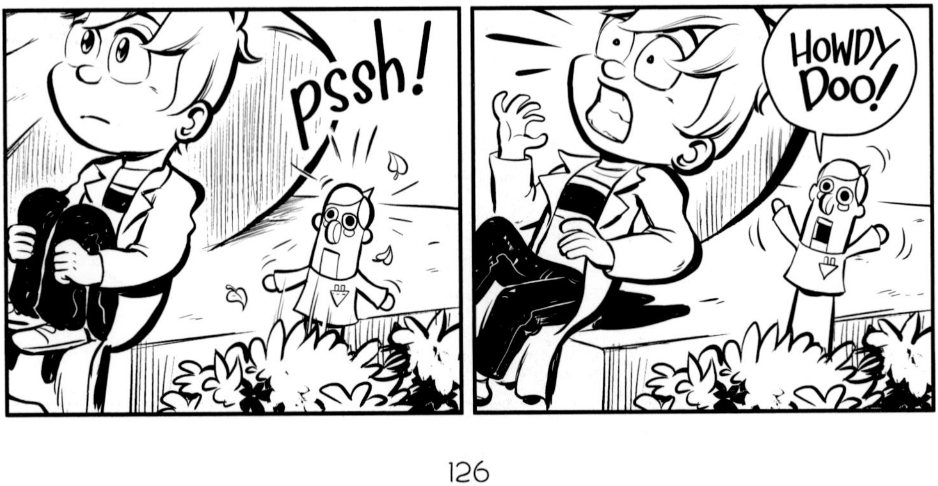
PSSH!
HOWDY DOO!

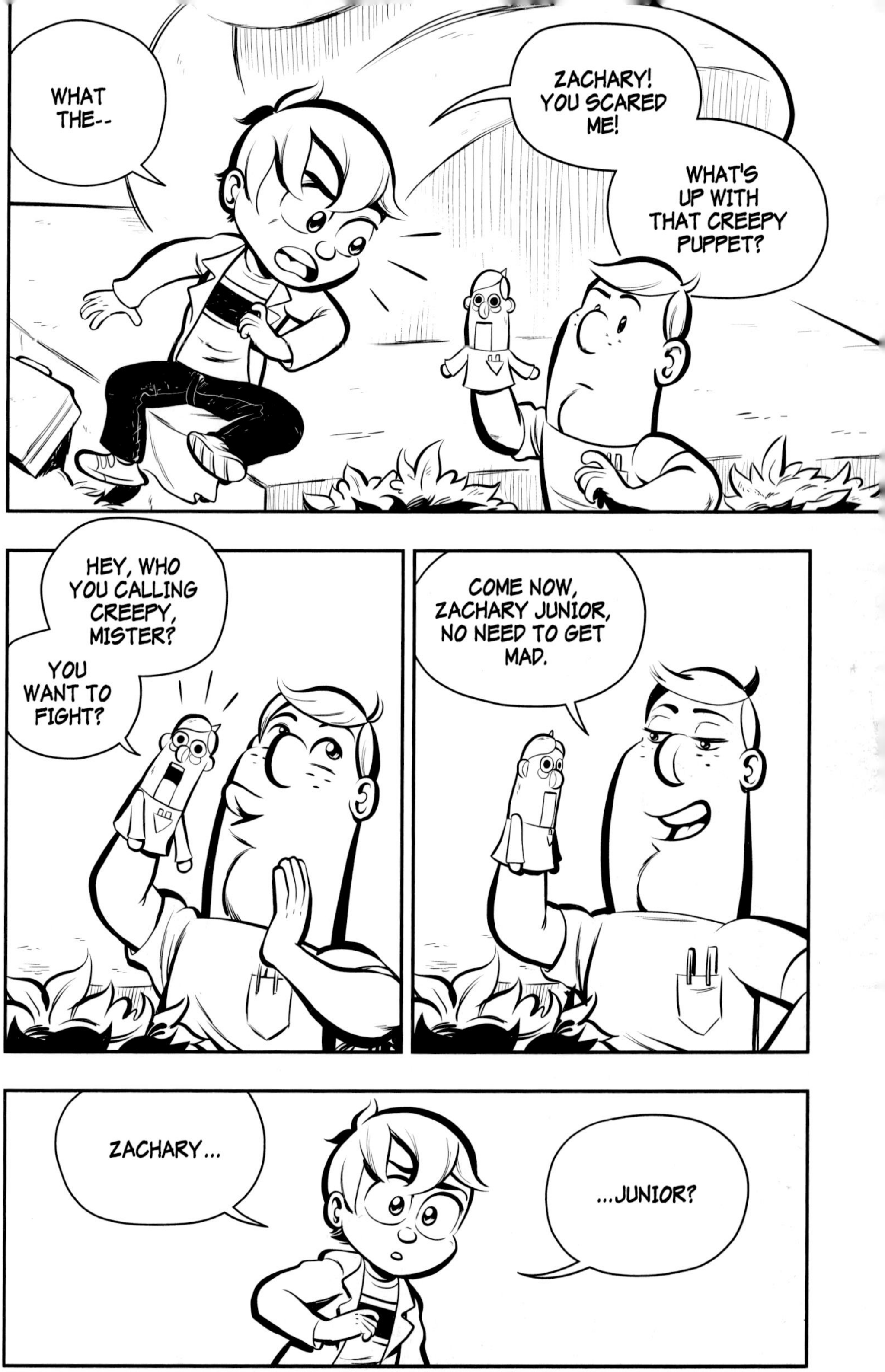
WHAT THE--
ZACHARY! YOU SCARED ME!
WHAT'S UP WITH THAT CREEPY PUPPET?
HEY, WHO YOU CALLING CREEPY, MISTER?
YOU WANT TO FIGHT?
COME NOW, ZACHARY JUNIOR, NO NEED TO GET MAD.
ZACHARY...
...JUNIOR?

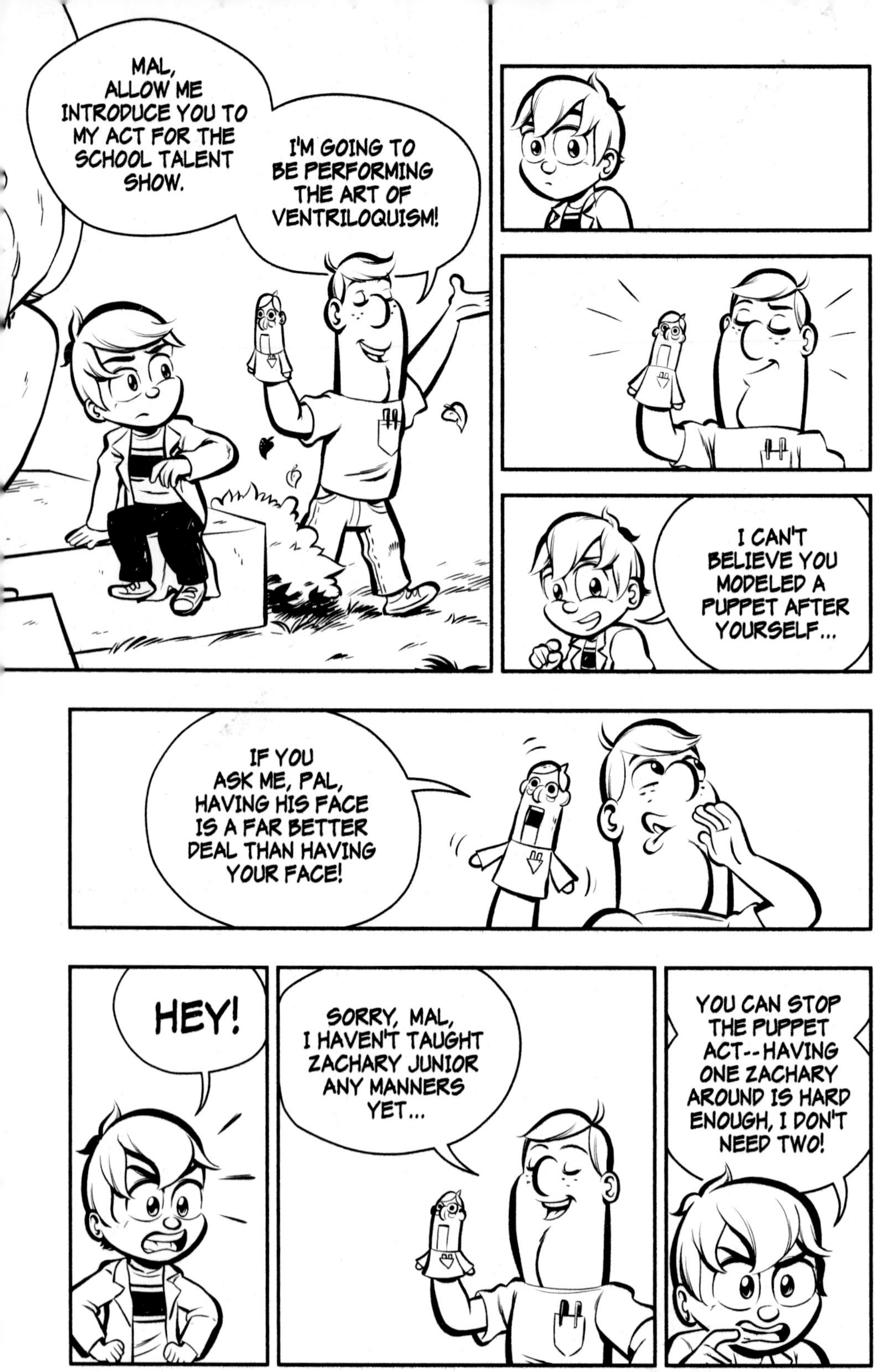
MAL, ALLOW ME INTRODUCE YOU TO MY ACT FOR THE SCHOOL TALENT SHOW.
I'M GOING TO BE PERFORMING THE ART OF VENTRILOQUISM!
I CAN'T BELIEVE YOU MODELED A PUPPET AFTER YOURSELF...
IF YOU ASK ME, PAL, HAVING HIS FACE IS A FAR BETTER DEAL THAN HAVING YOUR FACE!
HEY!
SORRY, MAL, I HAVEN'T TAUGHT ZACHARY JUNIOR ANY MANNERS YET...
YOU CAN STOP THE PUPPET ACT--HAVING ONE ZACHARY AROUND IS HARD ENOUGH, I DON'T NEED TWO!

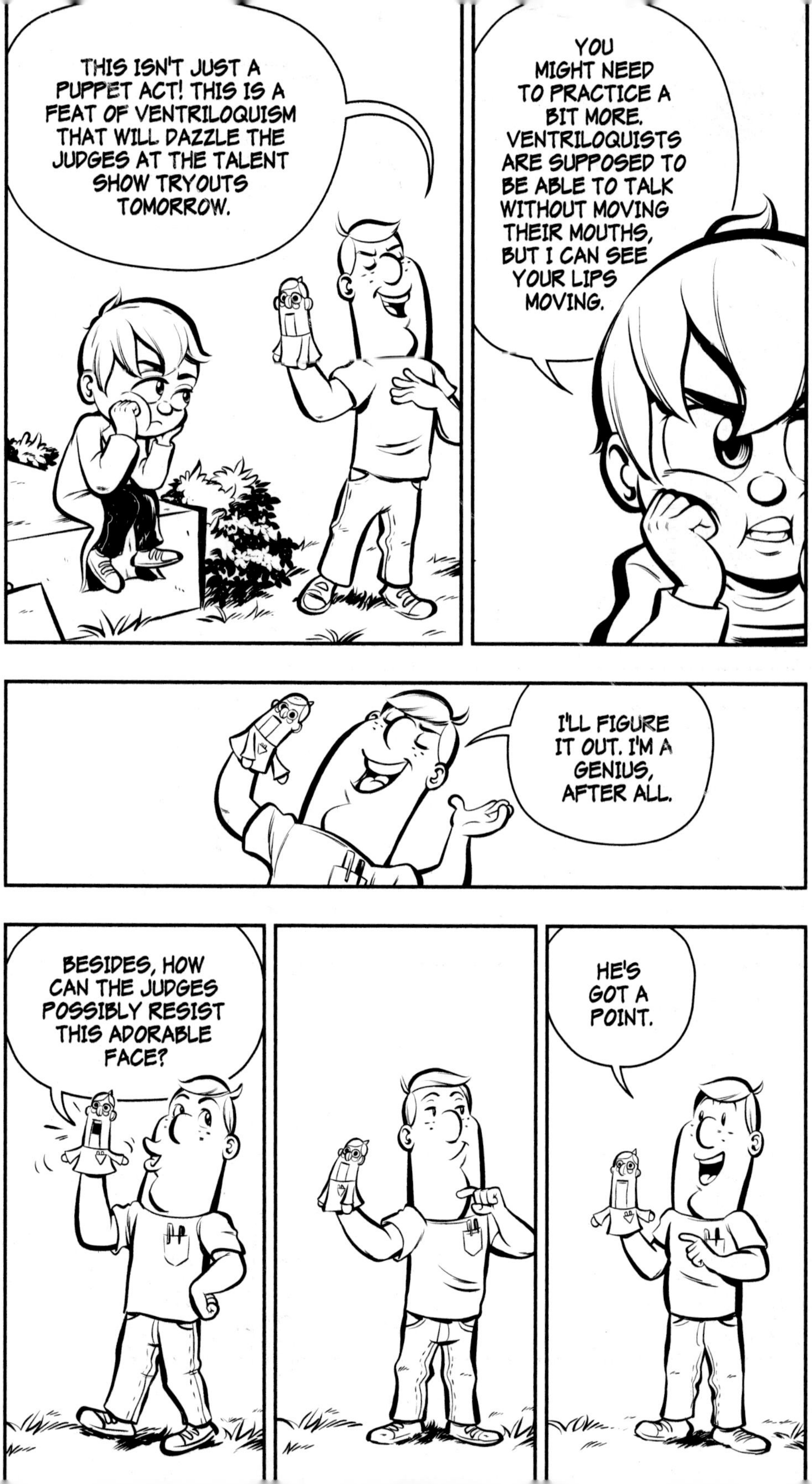
THIS ISN'T JUST A PUPPET ACT! THIS IS A FEAT OF VENTRILOQUISM THAT WILL DAZZLE THE JUDGES AT THE TALENT SHOW TRYOUTS TOMORROW.
YOU MIGHT NEED TO PRACTICE A BIT MORE. VENTRILOQUISTS ARE SUPPOSED TO BE ABLE TO TALK WITHOUT MOVING THEIR MOUTHS, BUT I CAN SEE YOUR LIPS MOVING.
I'LL FIGURE IT OUT. I'M A GENIUS, AFTER ALL.
BESIDES, HOW CAN THE JUDGES POSSIBLY RESIST THIS ADORABLE FACE?
HE'S GOT A POINT.

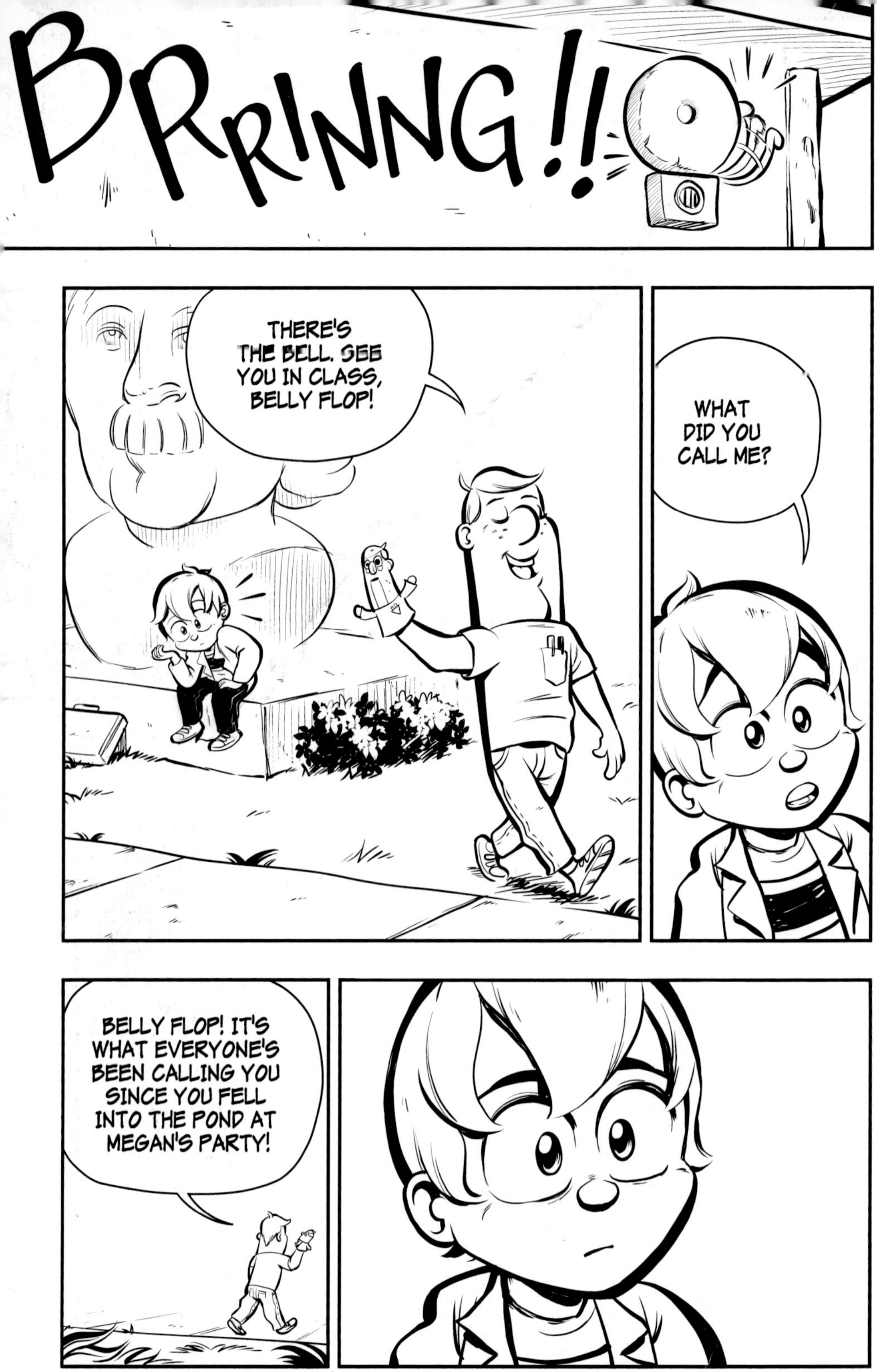
BRRINNG!!!
THERE'S THE BELL. SEE YOU IN CLASS, BELLY FLOP!
WHAT DID YOU CALL ME?
BELLY FLOP! IT'S WHAT EVERYONE'S BEEN CALLING YOU SINCE YOU FELL INTO THE POND AT MEGAN'S PARTY!

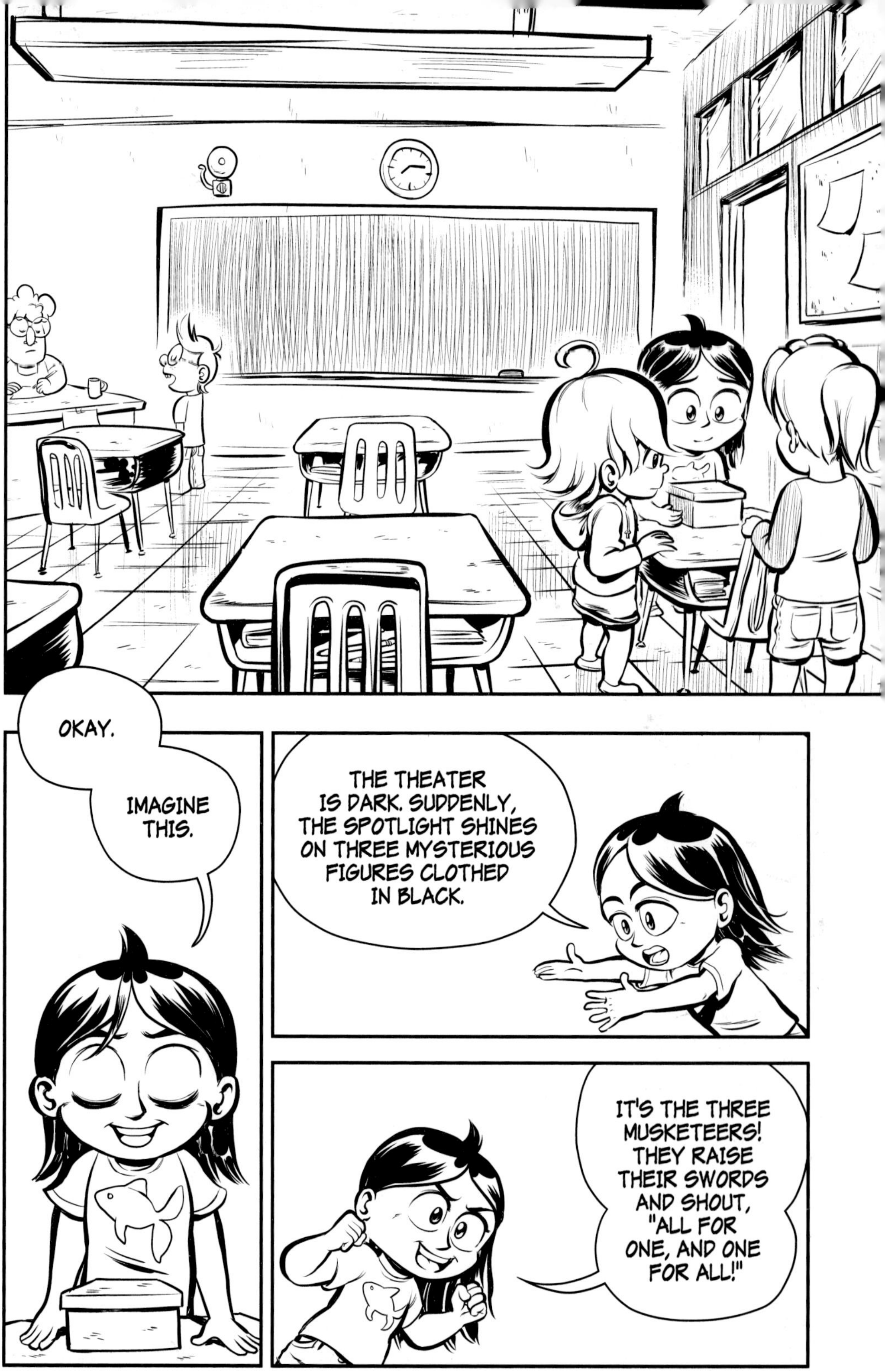
OKAY.
IMAGINE THIS.
THE THEATER IS DARK. SUDDENLY, THE SPOTLIGHT SHINES ON THREE MYSTERIOUS FIGURES CLOTHED IN BLACK.
IT'S THE THREE MUSKETEERS! THEY RAISE THEIR SWORDS AND SHOUT, "ALL FOR ONE, AND ONE FOR ALL!"

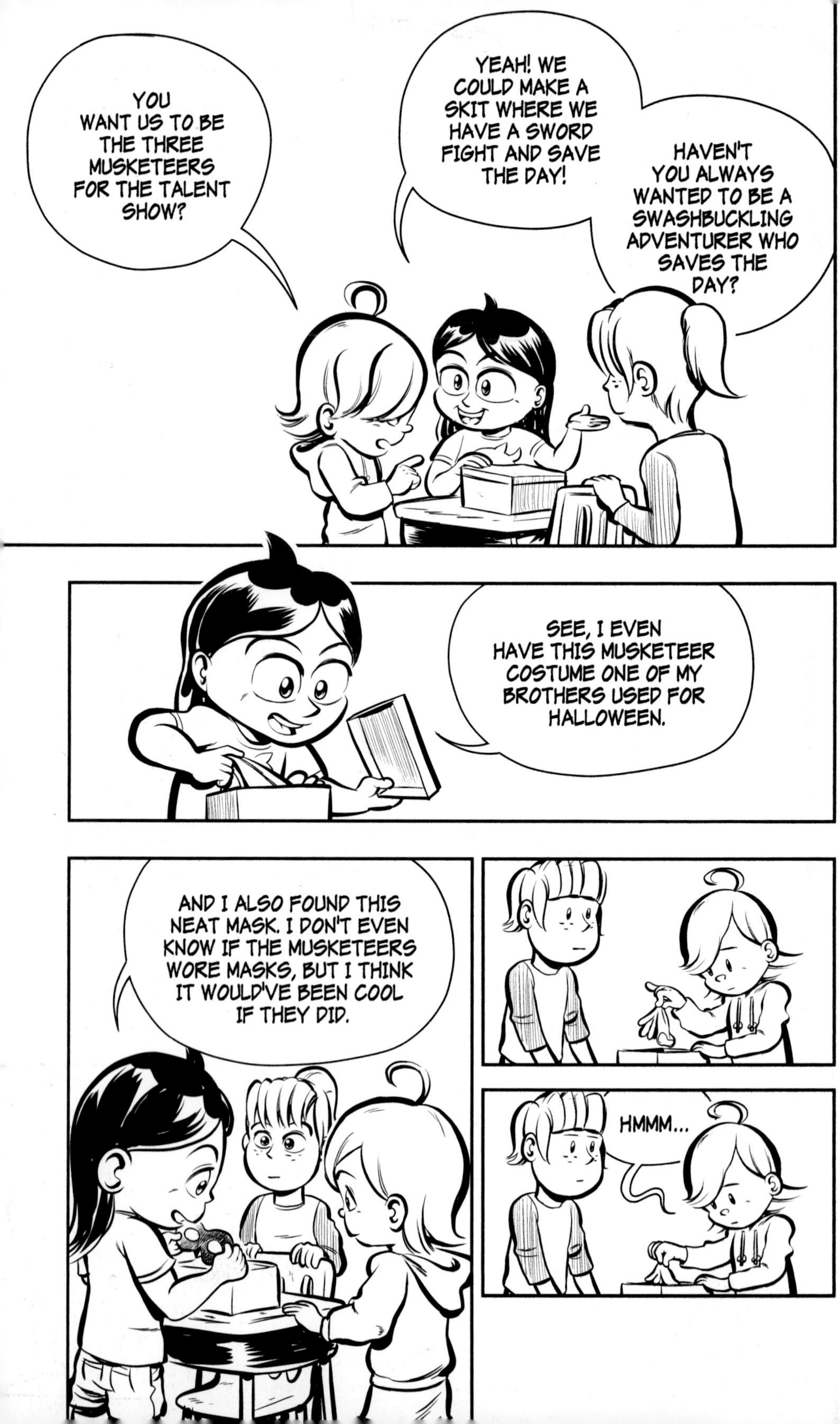
YOU WANT US TO BE THE THREE MUSKETEERS FOR THE TALENT SHOW?
YEAH! WE COULD MAKE A SKIT WHERE WE HAVE A SWORD FIGHT AND SAVE THE DAY!
HAVEN'T YOU ALWAYS WANTED TO BE A SWASHBUCKLING ADVENTURER WHO SAVES THE DAY?
SEE, I EVEN HAVE THIS MUSKETEER COSTUME ONE OF MY BROTHERS USED FOR HALLOWEEN.
AND I ALSO FOUND THIS NEAT MASK. I DON'T EVEN KNOW IF THE MUSKETEERS WORE MASKS, BUT I THINK IT WOULD'VE BEEN COOL IF THEY DID.
HMMM...

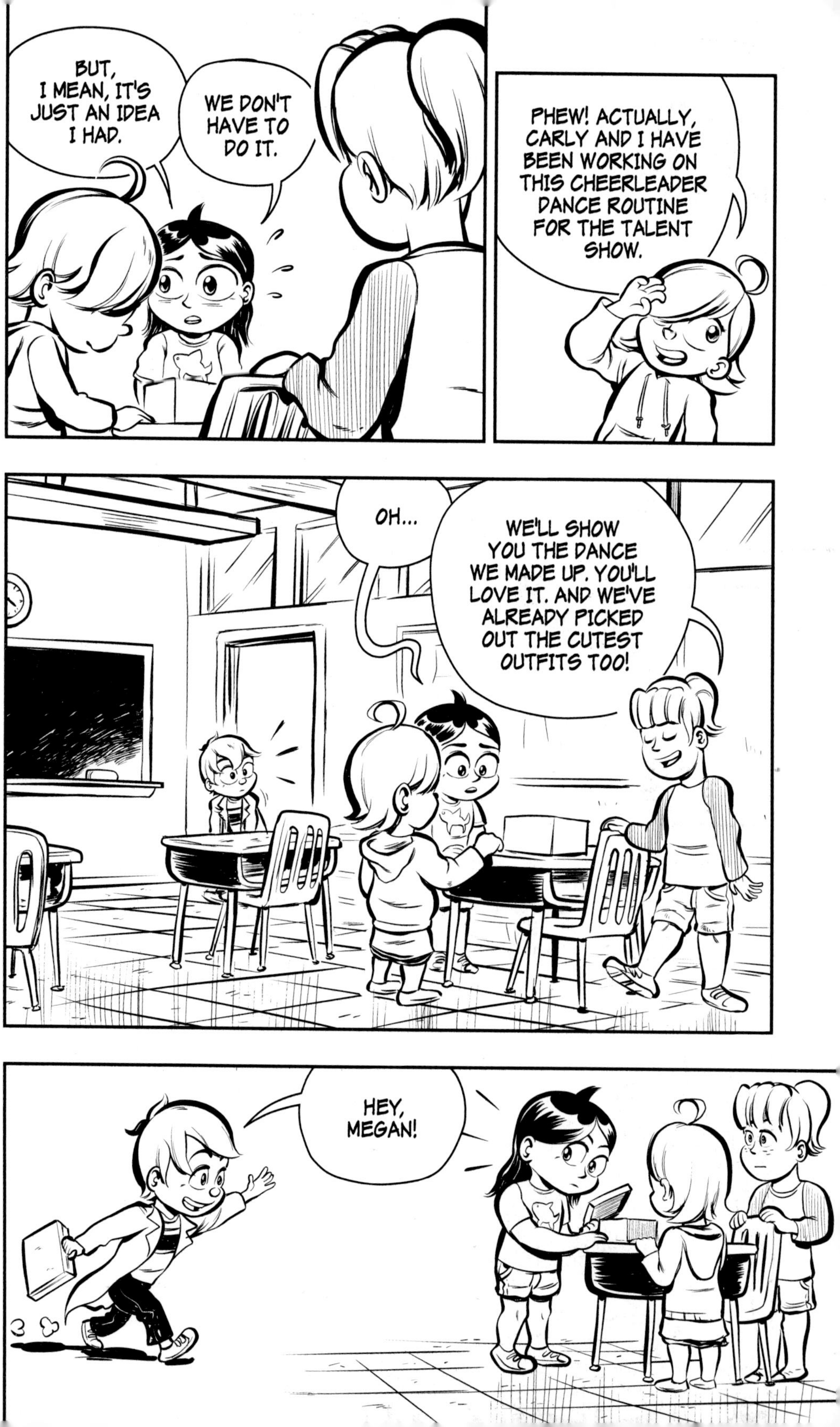
BUT, I MEAN, IT'S JUST AN IDEA I HAD.
WE DON'T HAVE TO DO IT.
PHEW! ACTUALLY, CARLY AND I HAVE BEEN WORKING ON THIS CHEERLEADER DANCE ROUTINE FOR THE TALENT SHOW.
OH...
WE'LL SHOW YOU THE DANCE WE MADE UP. YOU'LL LOVE IT. AND WE'VE ALREADY PICKED OUT THE CUTEST OUTFITS TOO!
HEY, MEGAN!

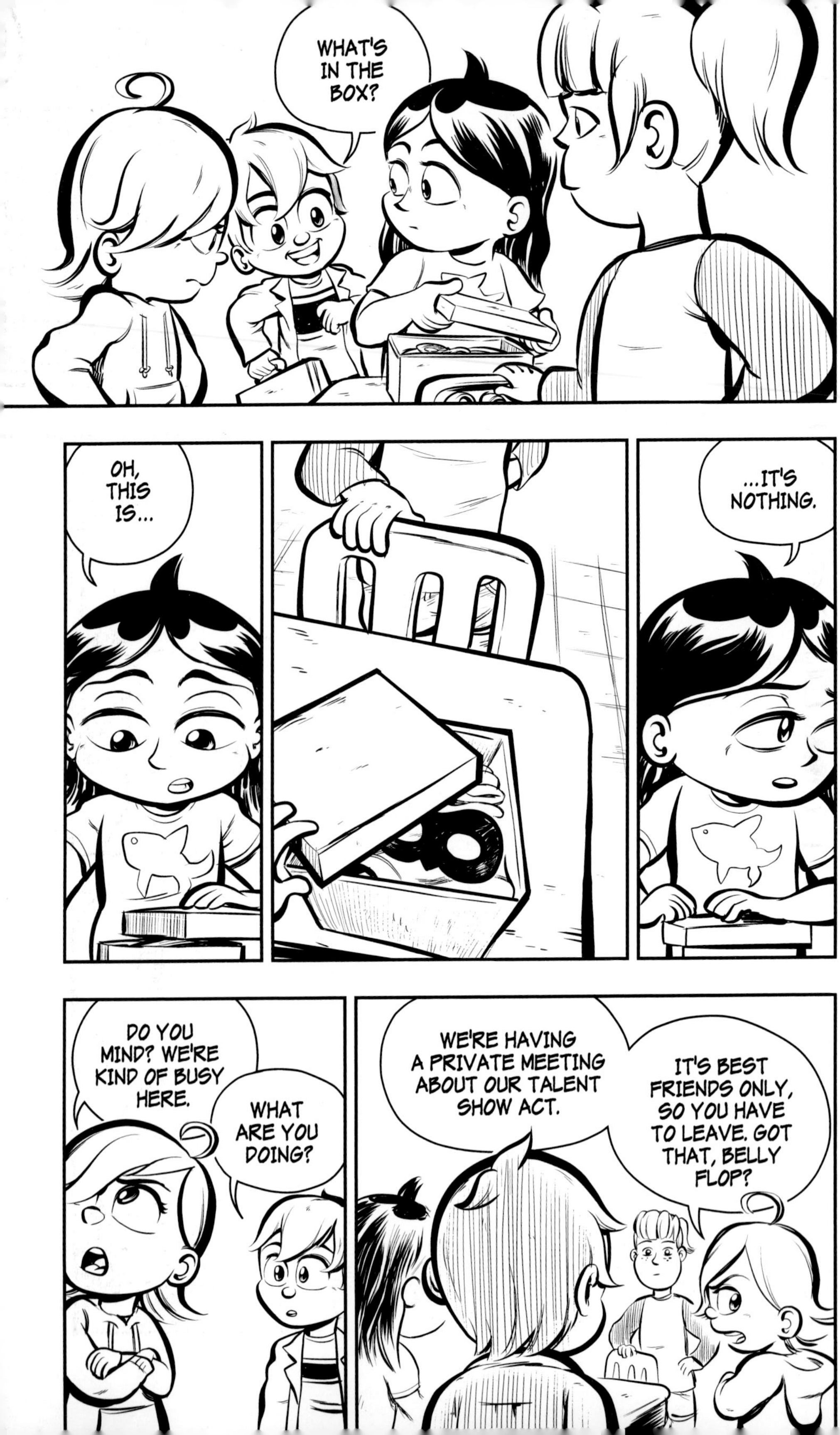
WHAT'S IN THE BOX?
OH, THIS IS...
...IT'S NOTHING.
DO YOU MIND? WE'RE KIND OF BUSY HERE.
WHAT ARE YOU DOING?
WE'RE HAVING A PRIVATE MEETING ABOUT OUR TALENT SHOW ACT.
IT'S BEST FRIENDS ONLY, SO YOU HAVE TO LEAVE. GOT THAT, BELLY FLOP?

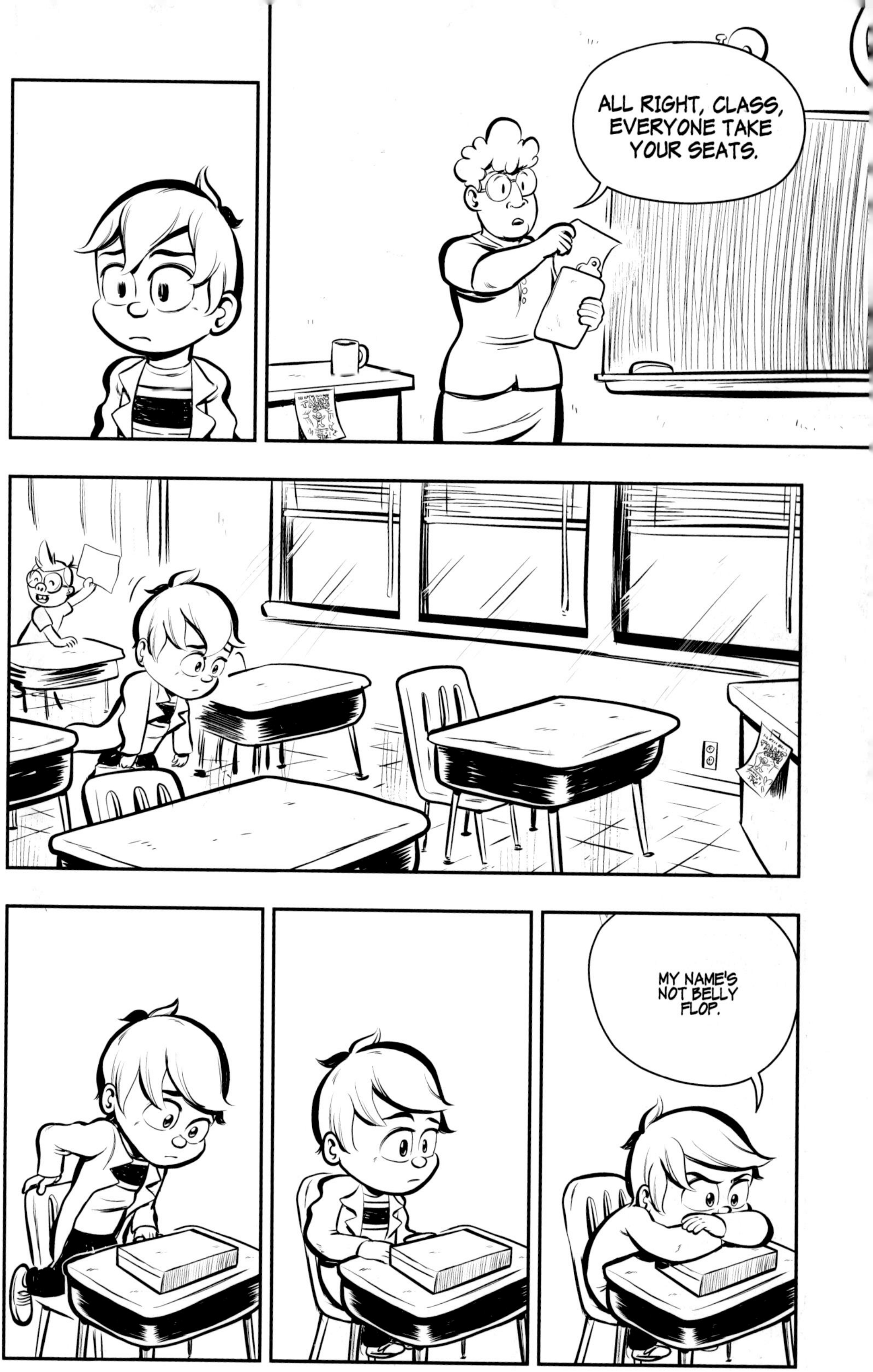
ALL RIGHT, CLASS, EVERYONE TAKE YOUR SEATS.
MY NAME'S NOT BELLY FLOP.

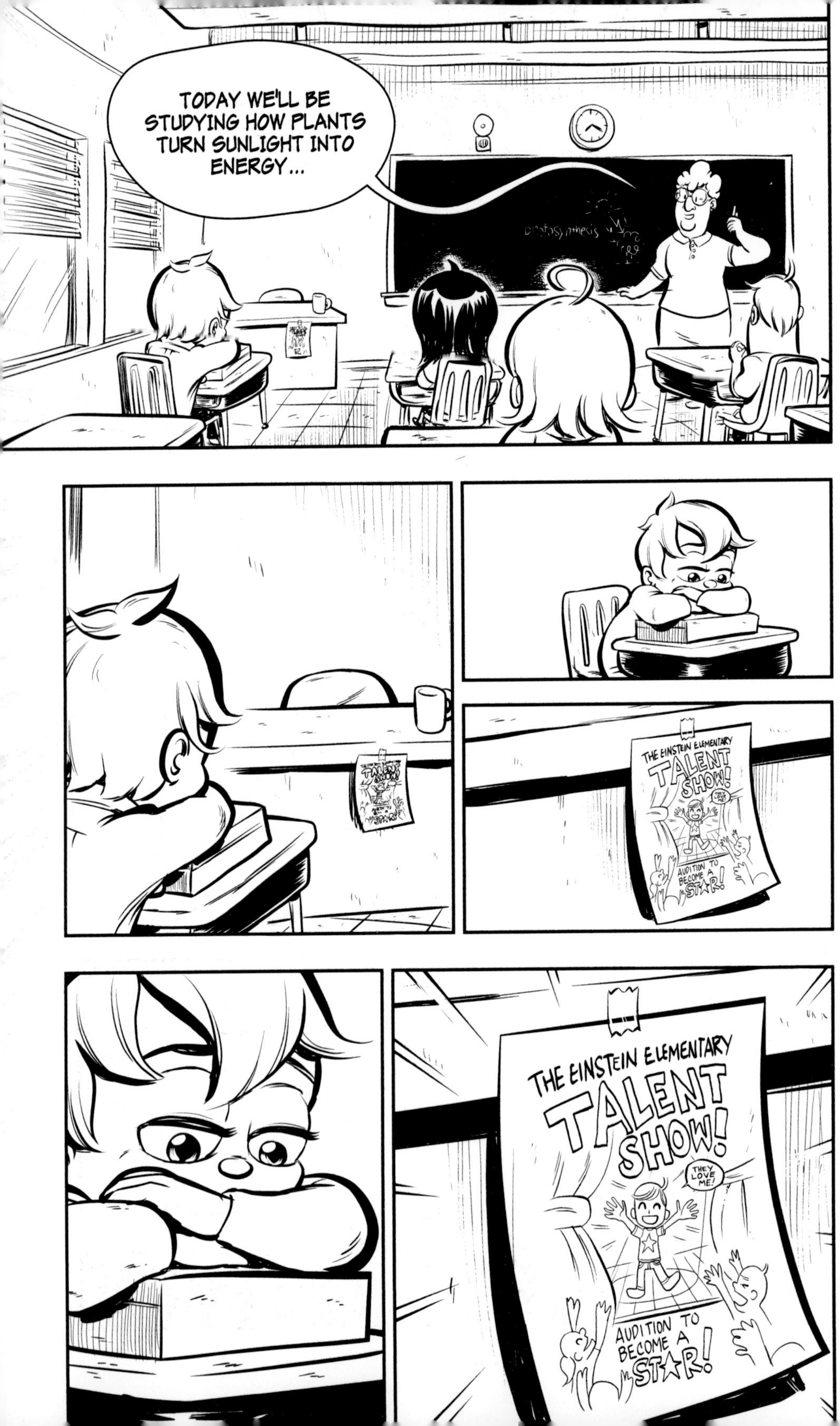
TODAY WE'LL BE STUDYING HOW PLANTS TURN SUNLIGHT INTO ENERGY...
THE EINSTEIN ELEMENTARY
TALENT SHOW!
AUDITION TO BECOME A STAR!
THE EINSTEIN ELEMENTARY
TALENT SHOW!
THEY LOVE ME!
AUDITION TO BECOME A STAR!

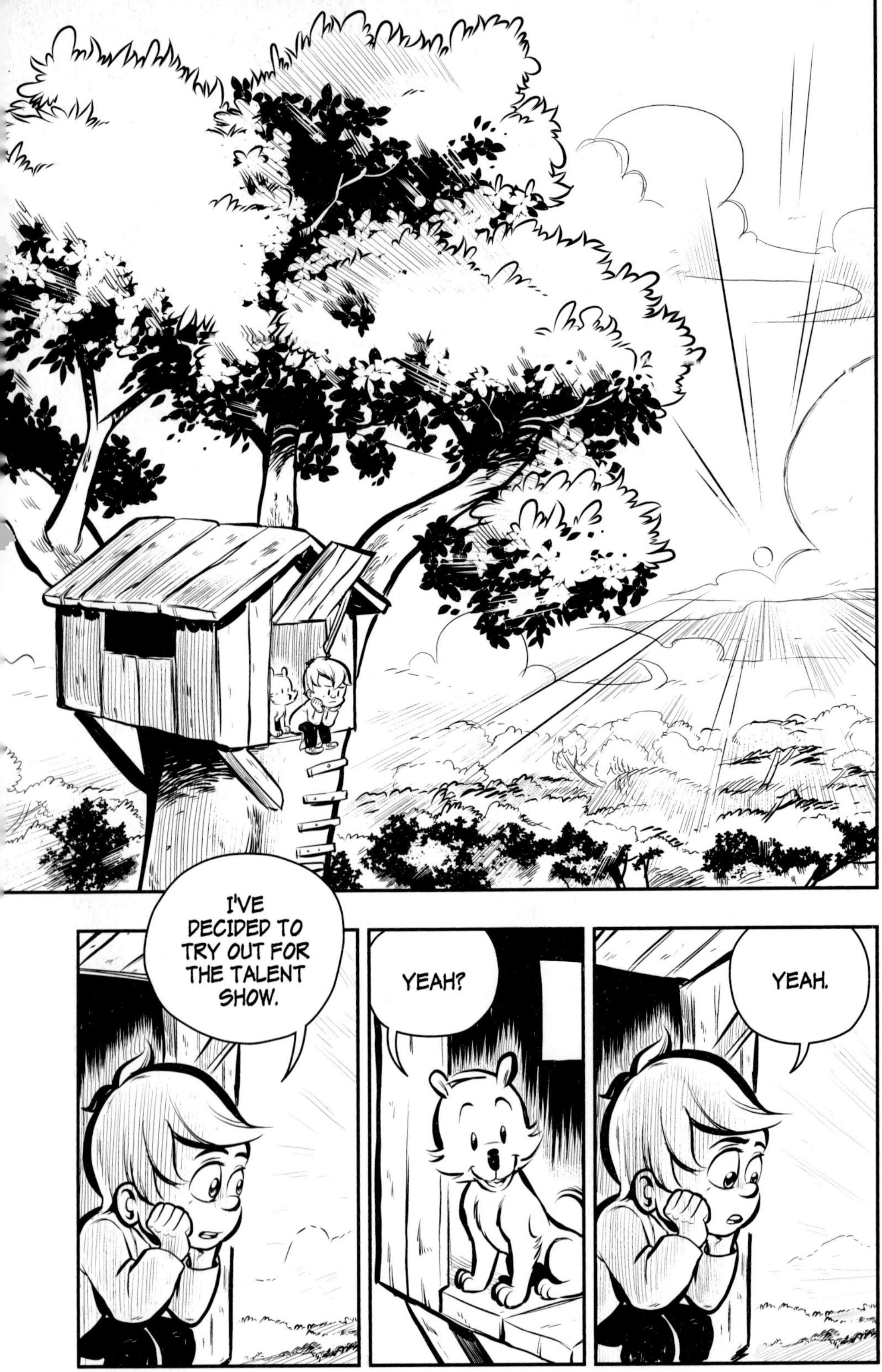
I'VE DECIDED TO TRY OUT FOR THE TALENT SHOW.
YEAH?
YEAH.

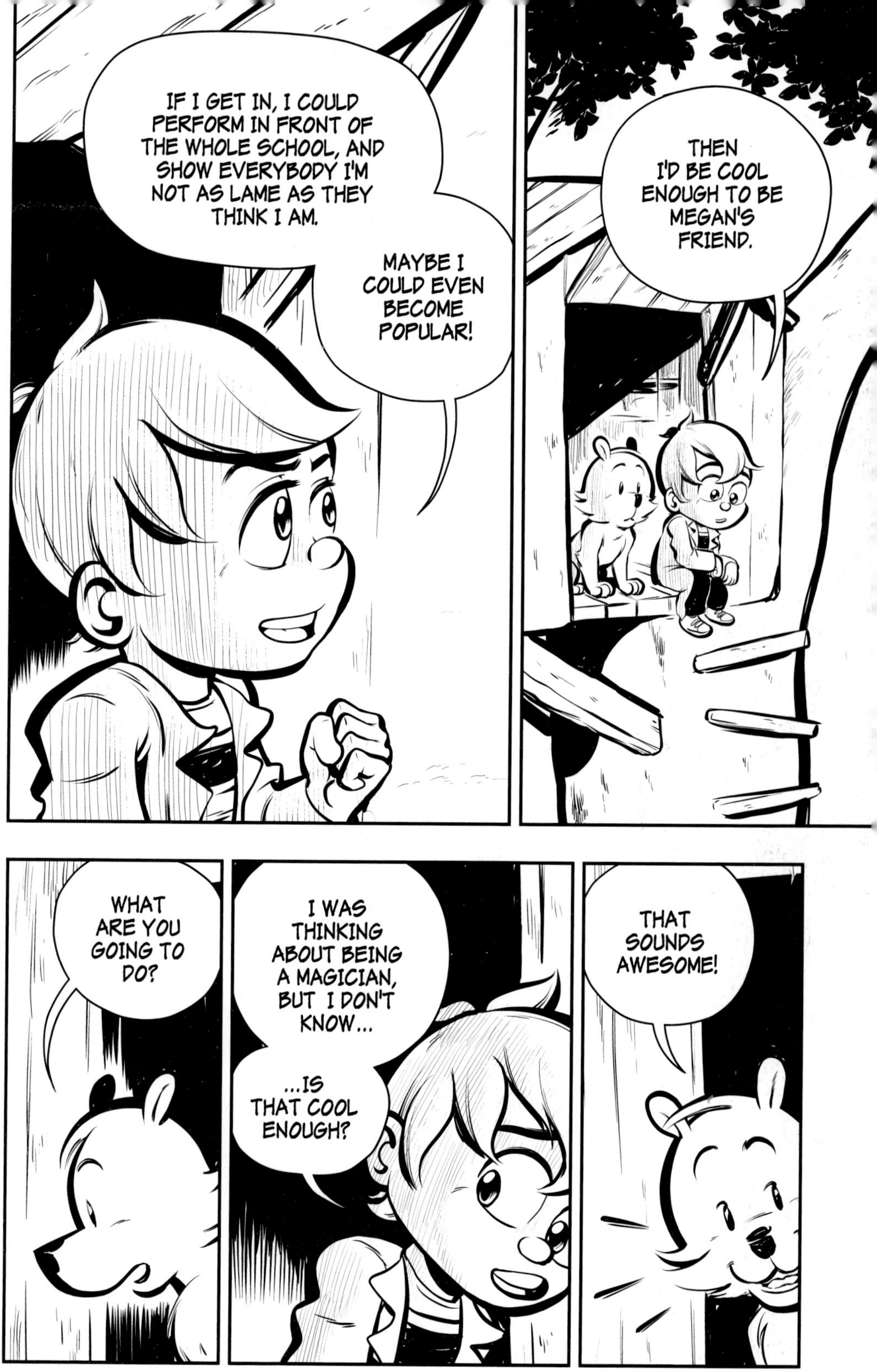
IF I GET IN, I COULD PERFORM IN FRONT OF THE WHOLE SCHOOL, AND SHOW EVERYBODY I'M NOT AS LAME AS THEY THINK I AM.
MAYBE I COULD EVEN BECOME POPULAR!
THEN I'D BE COOL ENOUGH TO BE MEGAN'S FRIEND.
WHAT ARE YOU GOING TO DO?
I WAS THINKING ABOUT BEING A MAGICIAN, BUT I DON'T KNOW...
...IS THAT COOL ENOUGH?
THAT SOUNDS AWESOME!

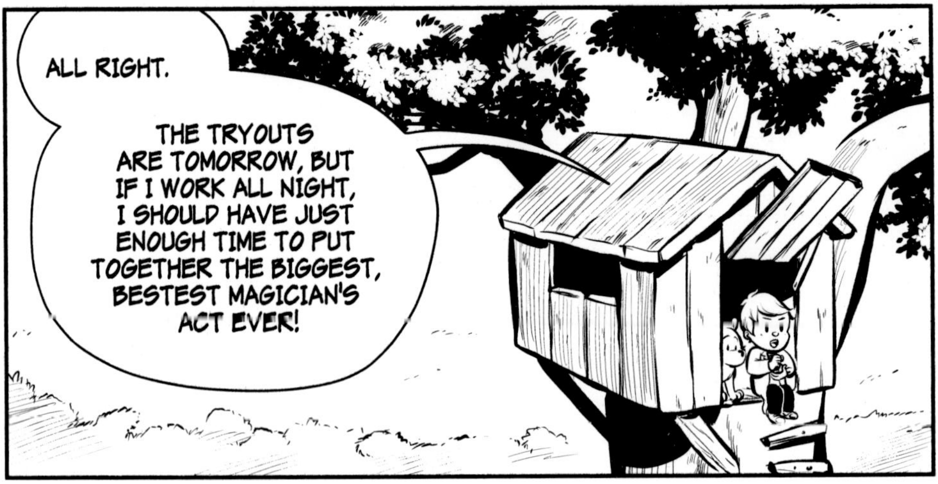
ALL RIGHT.
THE TRYOUTS ARE TOMORROW, BUT IF I WORK ALL NIGHT, I SHOULD HAVE JUST ENOUGH TIME TO PUT TOGETHER THE BIGGEST, BESTEST MAGICIAN'S ACT EVER!

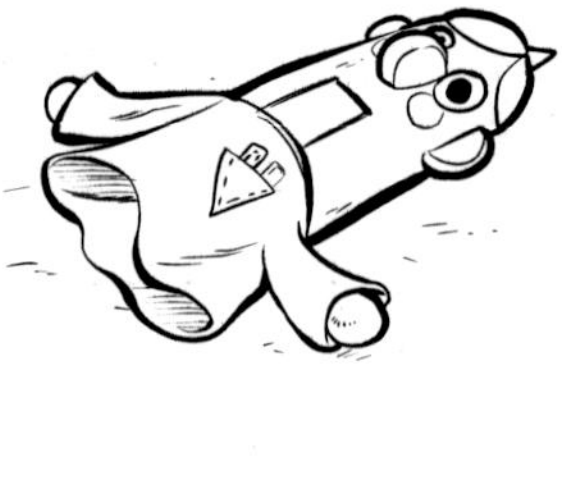

CHAPTER 6

Alakazam!

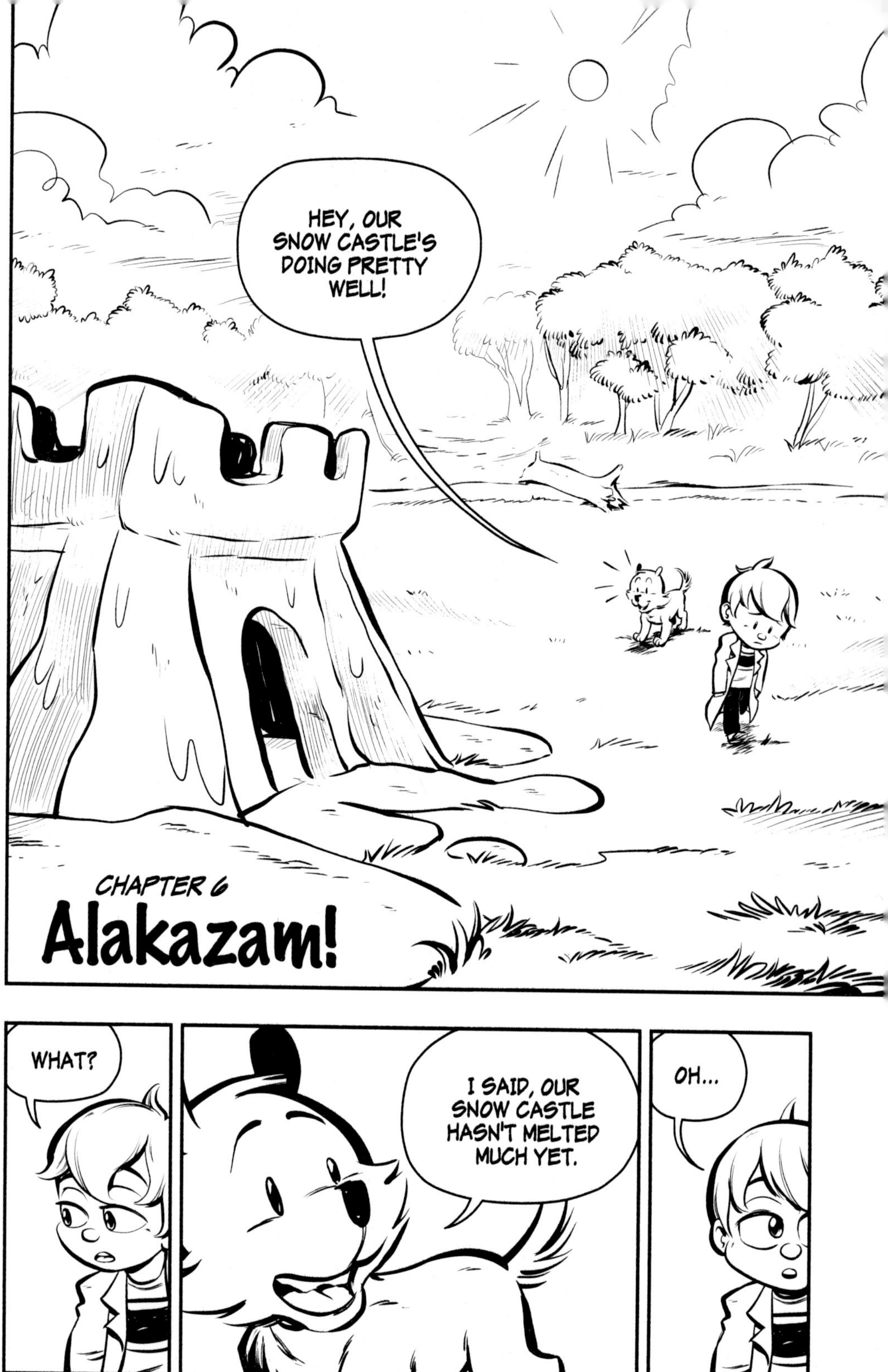
HEY, OUR SNOW CASTLE'S DOING PRETTY WELL!
WHAT?
I SAID, OUR SNOW CASTLE HASN'T MELTED MUCH YET.
OH...

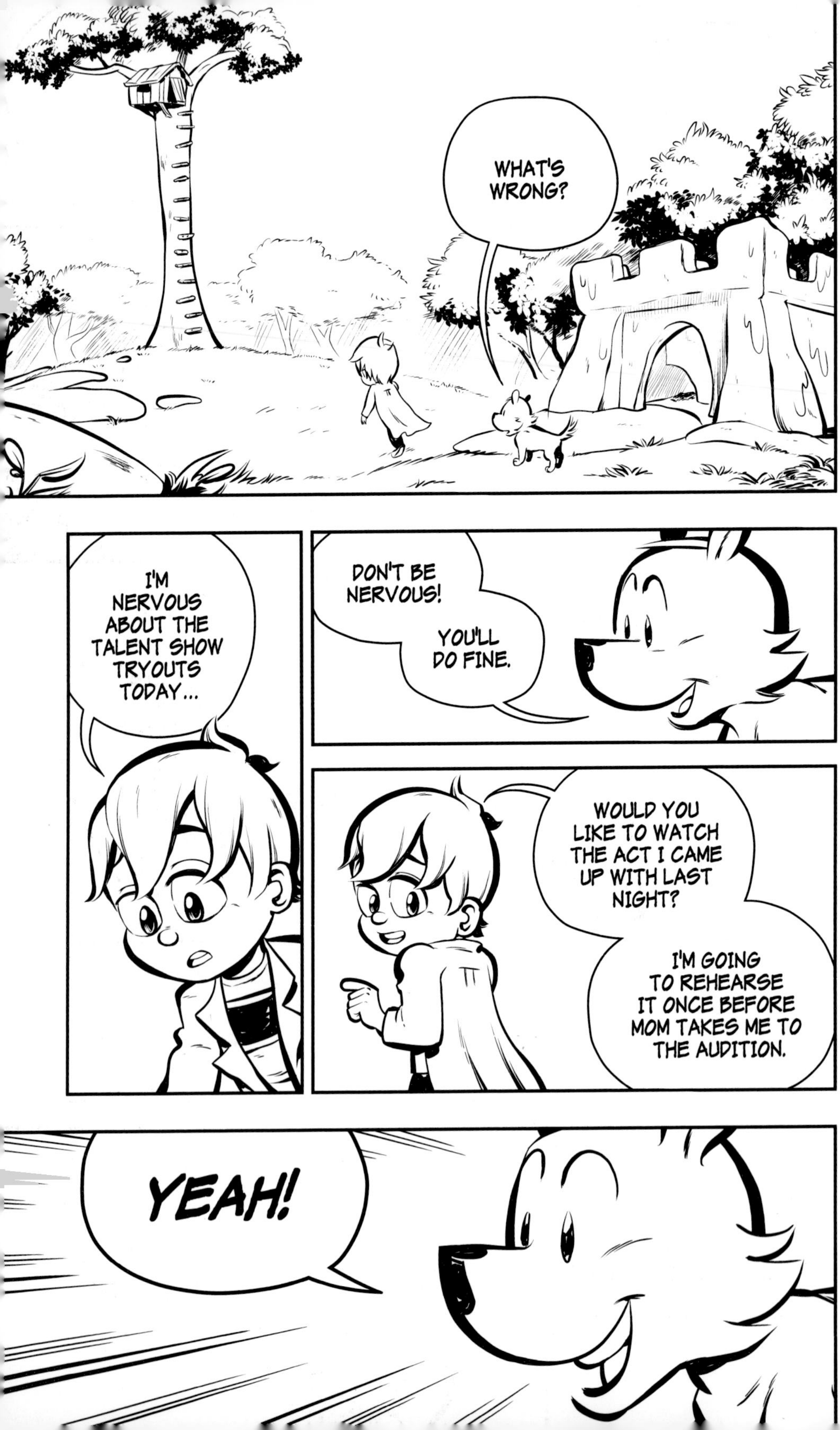
WHAT'S WRONG?
I'M NERVOUS ABOUT THE TALENT SHOW TRYOUTS TODAY...
DON'T BE NERVOUS!
YOU'LL DO FINE.
WOULD YOU LIKE TO WATCH THE ACT I CAME UP WITH LAST NIGHT?
I'M GOING TO REHEARSE IT ONCE BEFORE MOM TAKES ME TO THE AUDITION.
YEAH!

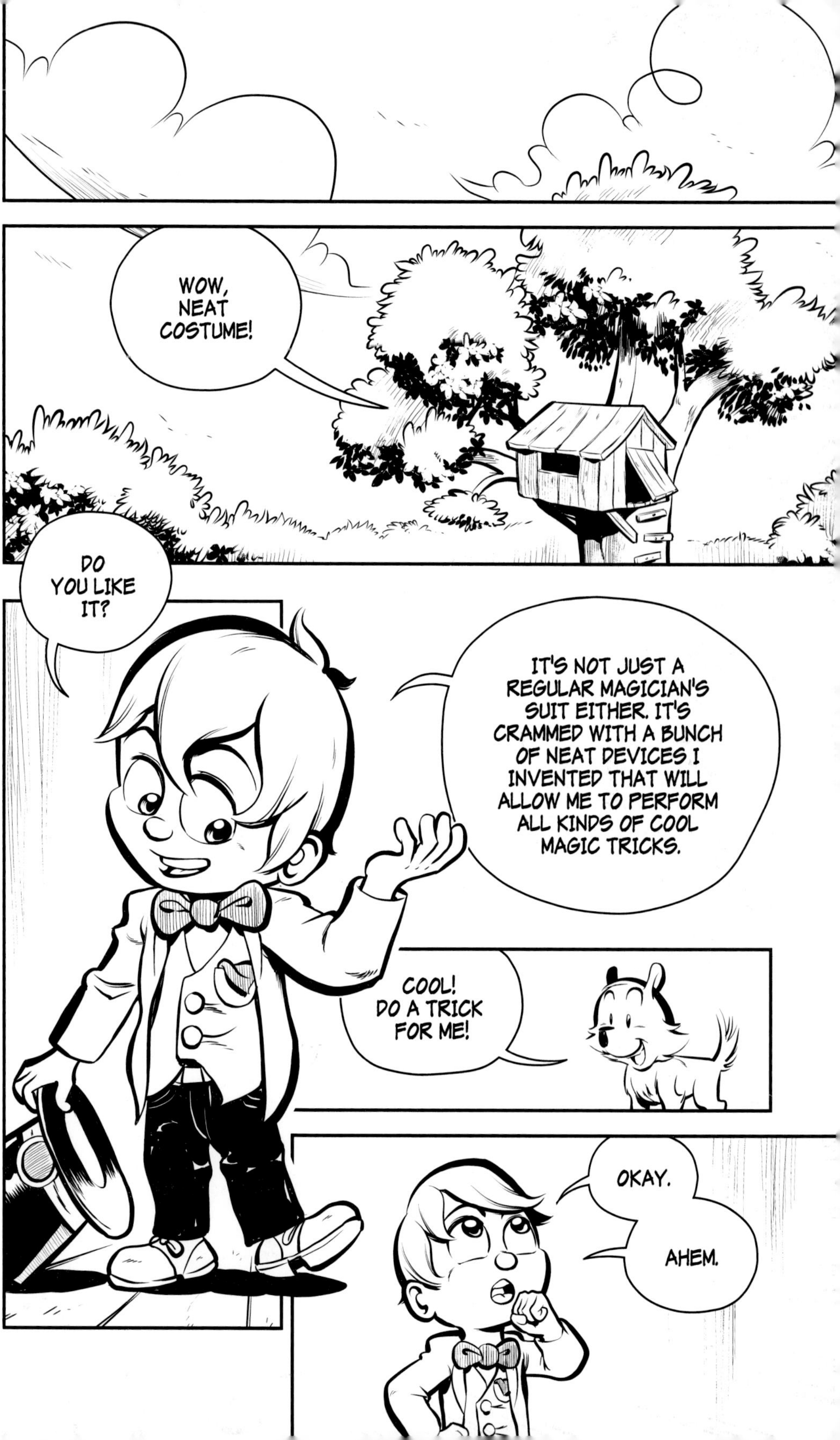
WOW, NEAT COSTUME!
DO YOU LIKE IT?
IT'S NOT JUST A REGULAR MAGICIAN'S SUIT EITHER. IT'S CRAMMED WITH A BUNCH OF NEAT DEVICES I INVENTED THAT WILL ALLOW ME TO PERFORM ALL KINDS OF COOL MAGIC TRICKS.
COOL! DO A TRICK FOR ME!
OKAY.
AHEM.

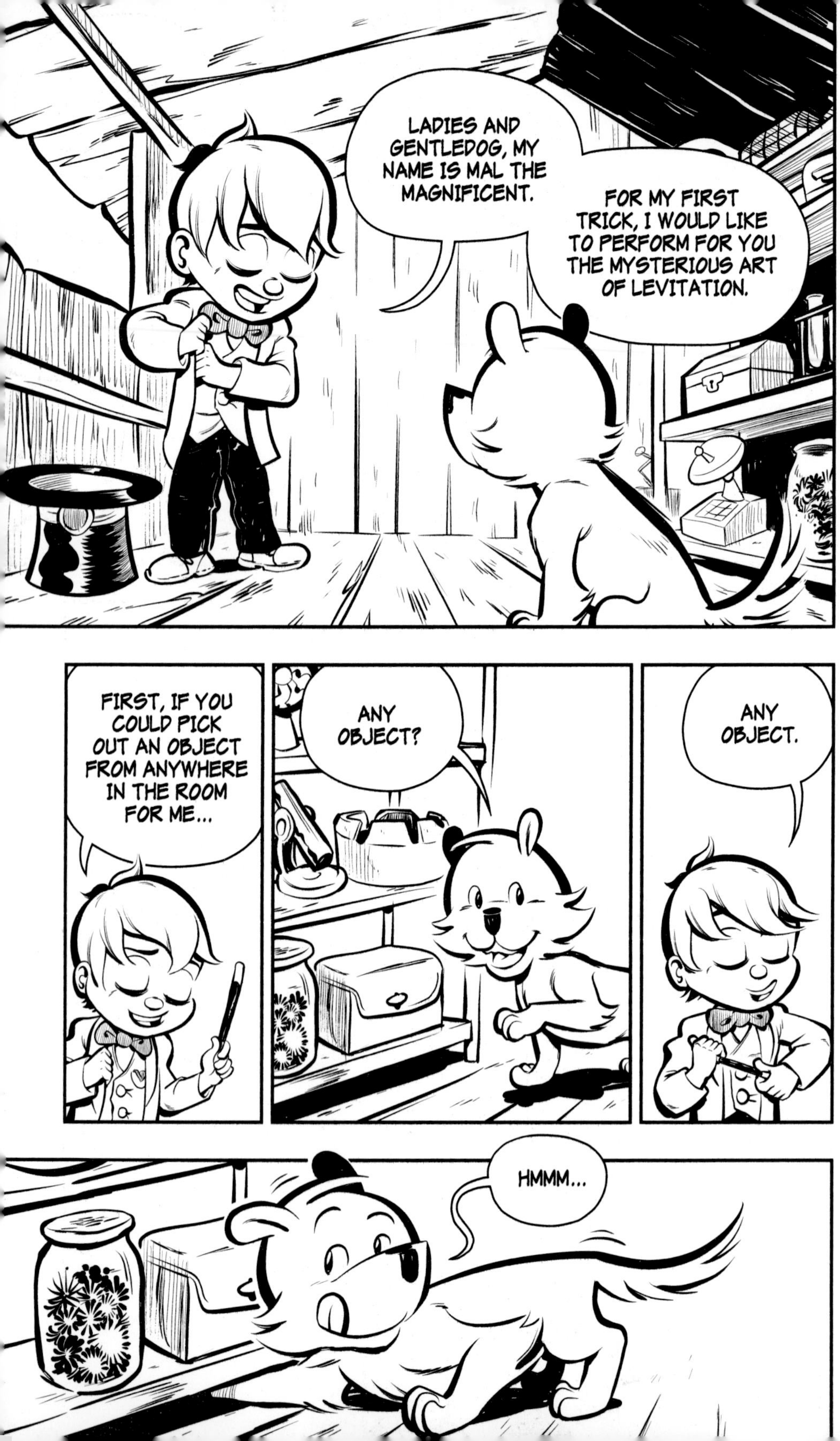
LADIES AND GENTLEDOG, MY NAME IS MAL THE MAGNIFICENT.
FOR MY FIRST TRICK, I WOULD LIKE TO PERFORM FOR YOU THE MYSTERIOUS ART OF LEVITATION.
FIRST, IF YOU COULD PICK OUT AN OBJECT FROM ANYWHERE IN THE ROOM FOR ME...
ANY OBJECT?
ANY OBJECT.
HMMM...

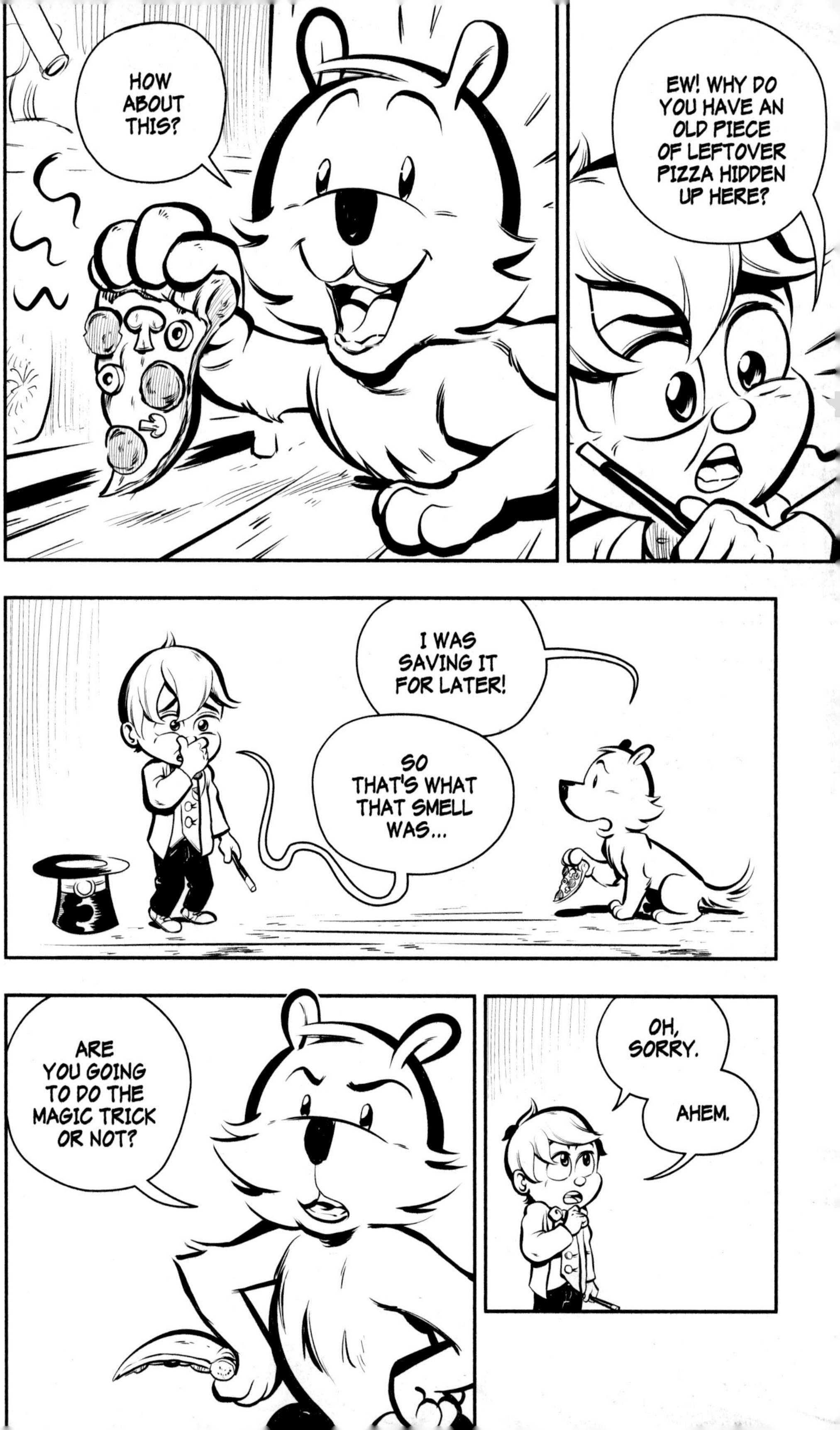
HOW ABOUT THIS?
EW! WHY DO YOU HAVE AN OLD PIECE OF LEFTOVER PIZZA HIDDEN UP HERE?
I WAS SAVING IT FOR LATER!
SO THAT'S WHAT THAT SMELL WAS...
ARE YOU GOING TO DO THE MAGIC TRICK OR NOT?
OH, SORRY.
AHEM.

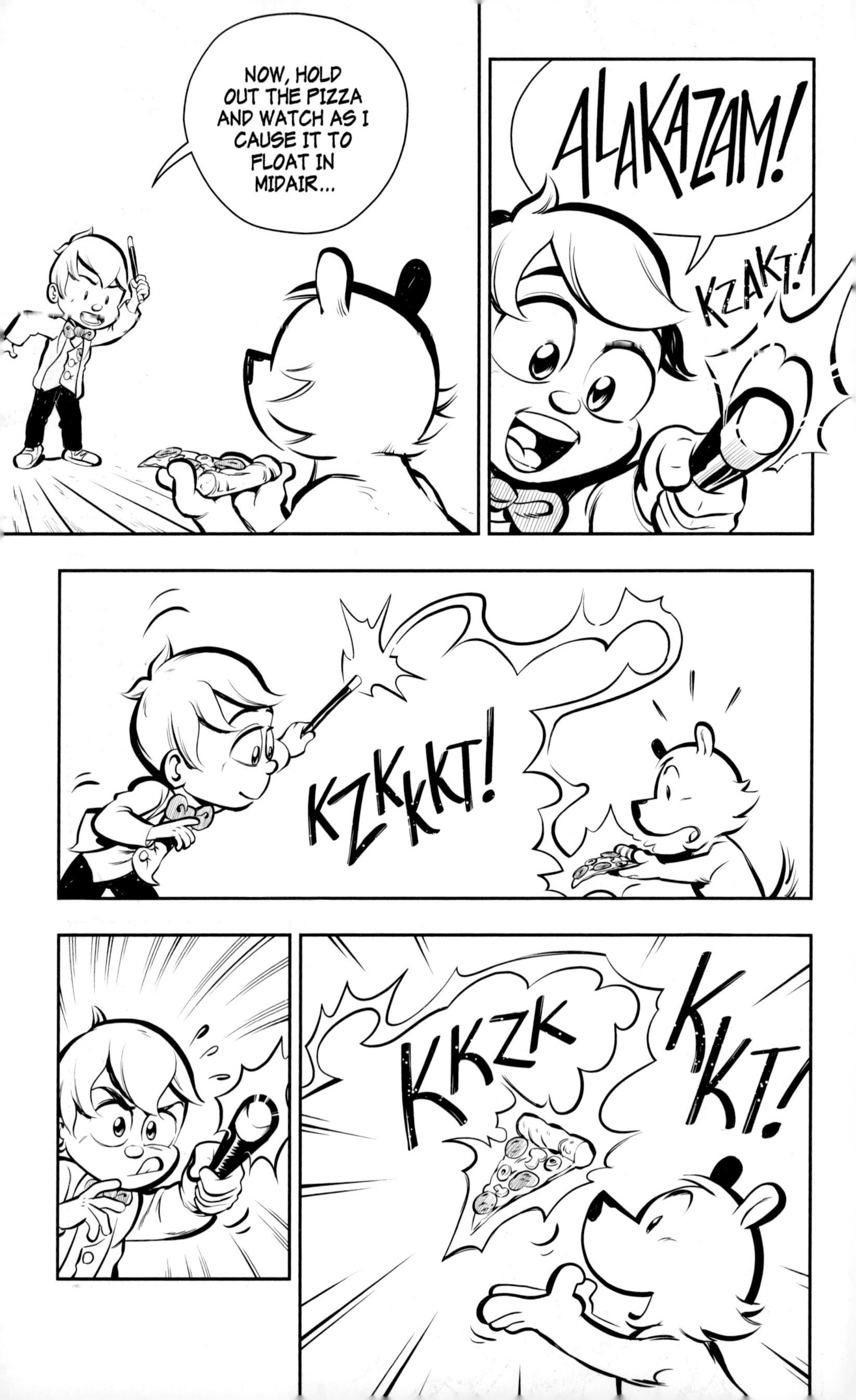
NOW, HOLD OUT THE PIZZA AND WATCH AS I CAUSE IT TO FLOAT IN MIDAIR...
ALAKAZAM!
KZAKT!
KZKKKT!
KKZK KKT!

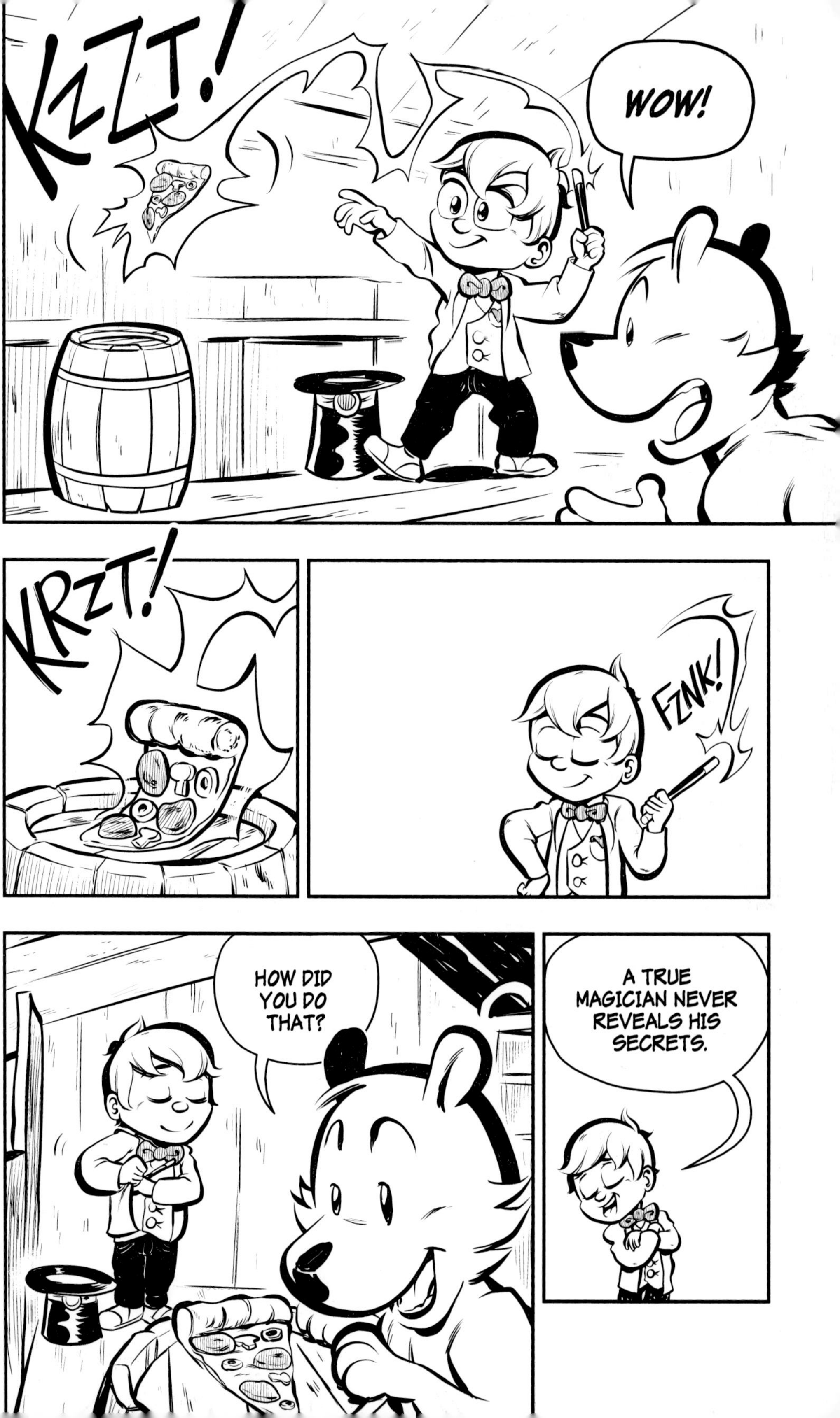
KZZT!
WOW!
KRZT!
FZNK!
HOW DID YOU DO THAT?
A TRUE MAGICIAN NEVER REVEALS HIS SECRETS.

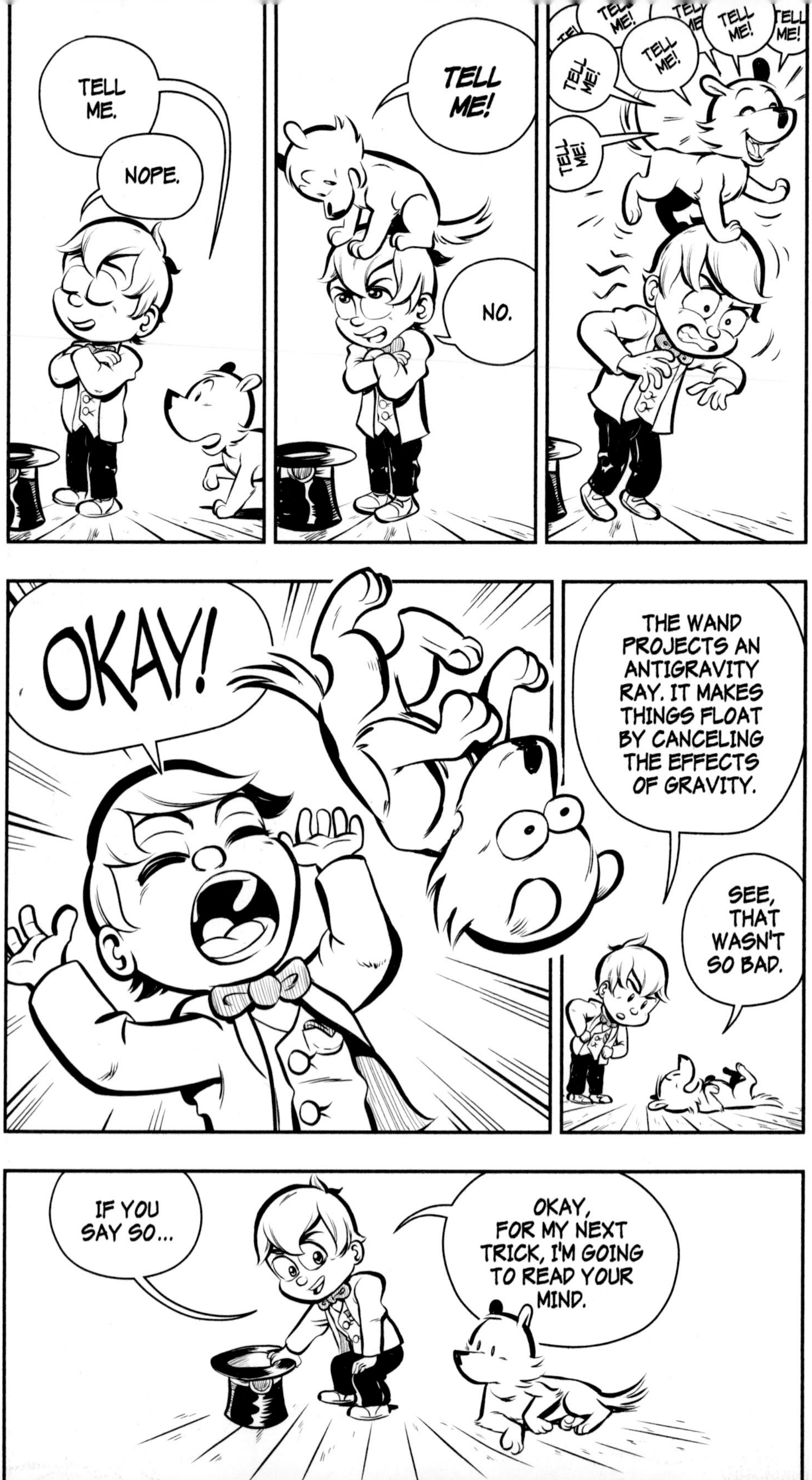
TELL ME.
NOPE.
TELL ME!
NO.
TELL ME!
TELL ME!
TELL ME!
TELL ME!
TELL ME!
OKAY!
THE WAND PROJECTS AN ANTIGRAVITY RAY. IT MAKES THINGS FLOAT BY CANCELING THE EFFECTS OF GRAVITY.
SEE, THAT WASN'T SO BAD.
IF YOU SAY SO...
OKAY, FOR MY NEXT TRICK, I'M GOING TO READ YOUR MIND.

OH, BOY!

THIS IS GOING TO BE GOOD...

EVEN *I* CAN'T READ MY OWN MIND SOMETIMES.

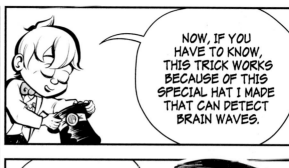

NOW, IF YOU HAVE TO KNOW, THIS TRICK WORKS BECAUSE OF THIS SPECIAL HAT I MADE THAT CAN DETECT BRAIN WAVES.

WHEN I WEAR THE HAT, IT LETS ME HEAR WHAT YOU'RE THINKING.

VWC-POM!

ALL RIGHT, I'LL START BY ASKING YOU A QUESTION AND THEN READING THE ANSWER FROM YOUR THOUGHTS.

ASK AWAY!

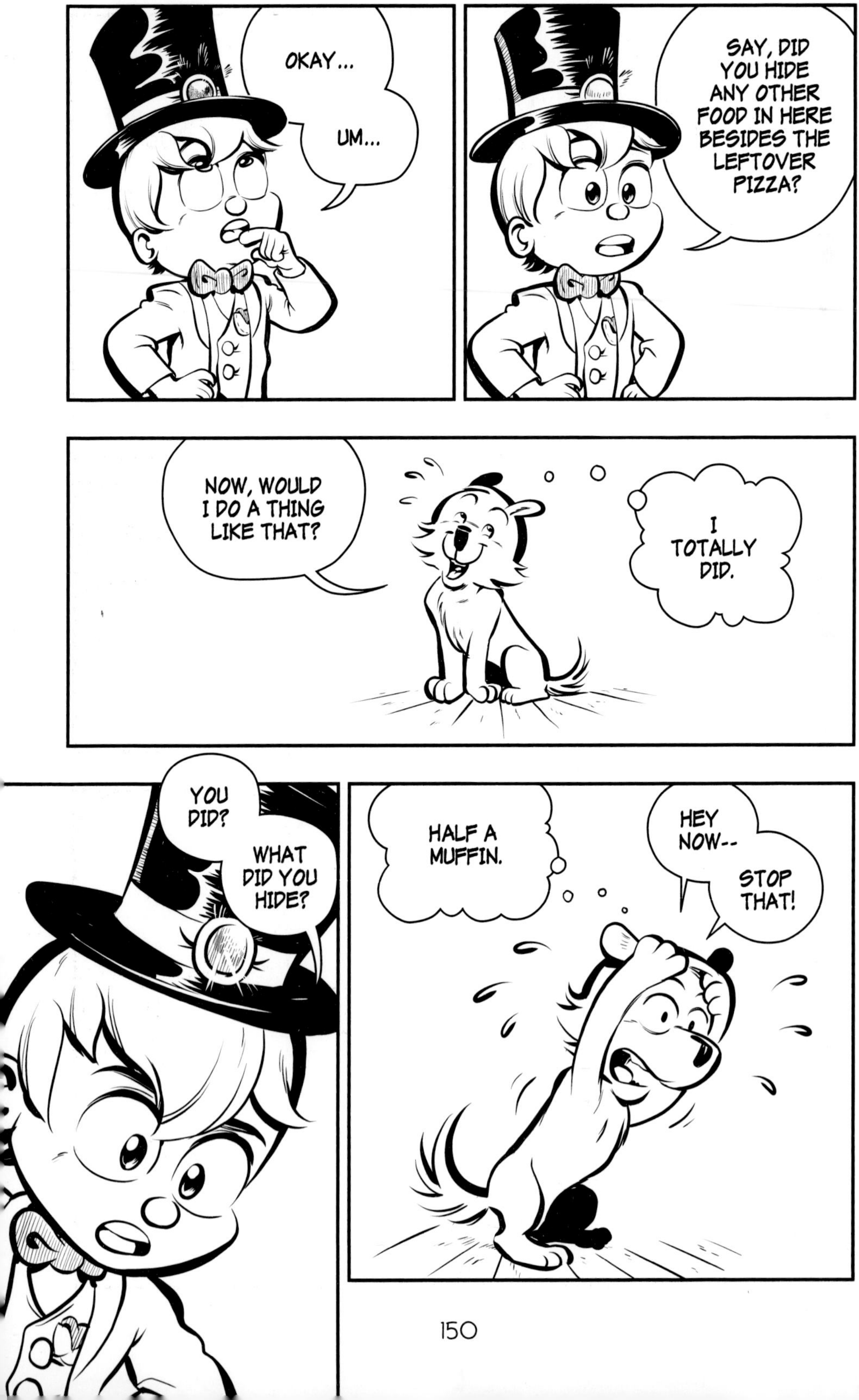
OKAY...
UM...
SAY, DID YOU HIDE ANY OTHER FOOD IN HERE BESIDES THE LEFTOVER PIZZA?
NOW, WOULD I DO A THING LIKE THAT?
I TOTALLY DID.
YOU DID?
WHAT DID YOU HIDE?
HALF A MUFFIN.
HEY NOW--
STOP THAT!

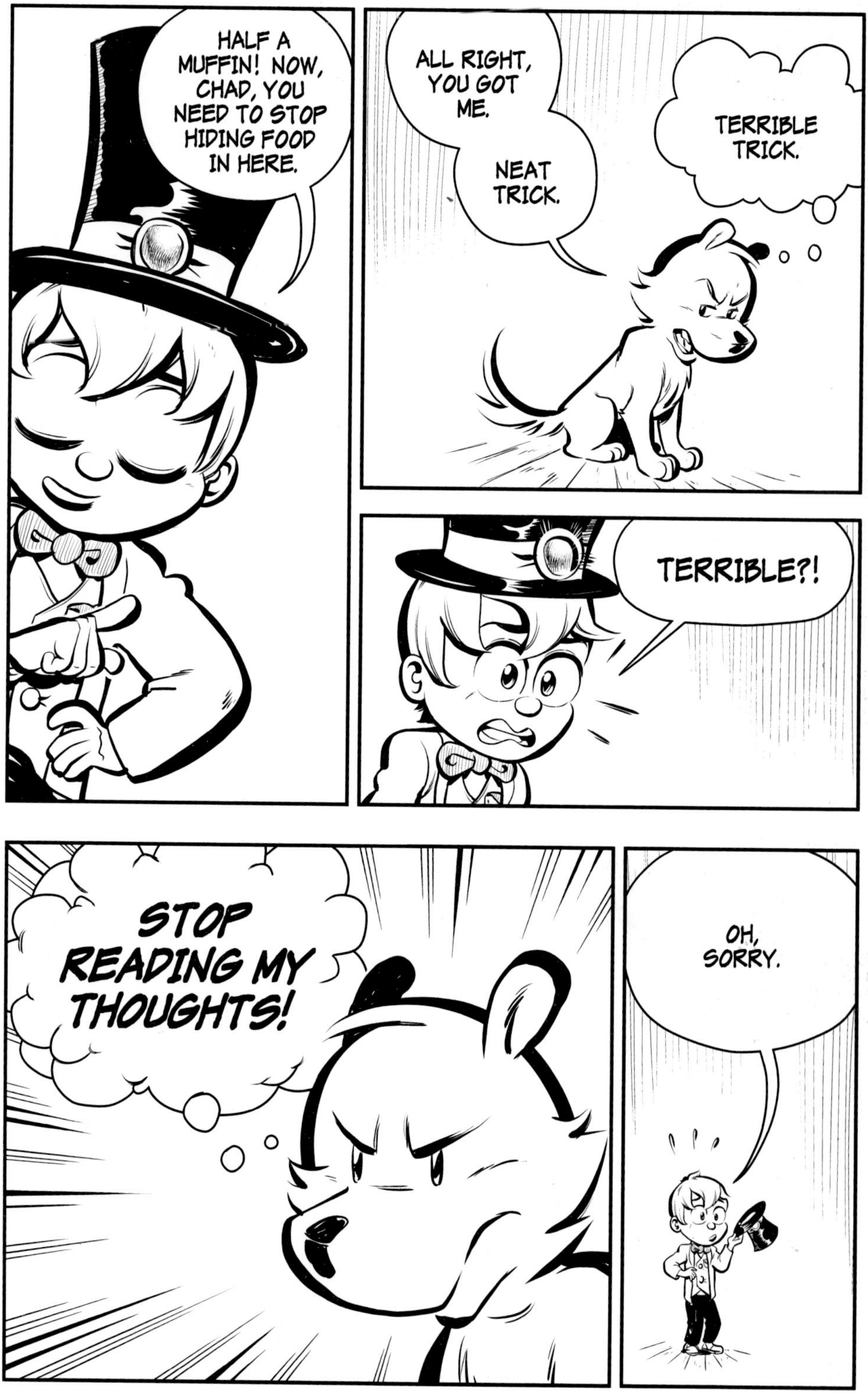
HALF A MUFFIN! NOW, CHAD, YOU NEED TO STOP HIDING FOOD IN HERE.
ALL RIGHT, YOU GOT ME.
NEAT TRICK.
TERRIBLE TRICK.
TERRIBLE?!
STOP READING MY THOUGHTS!
OH, SORRY.

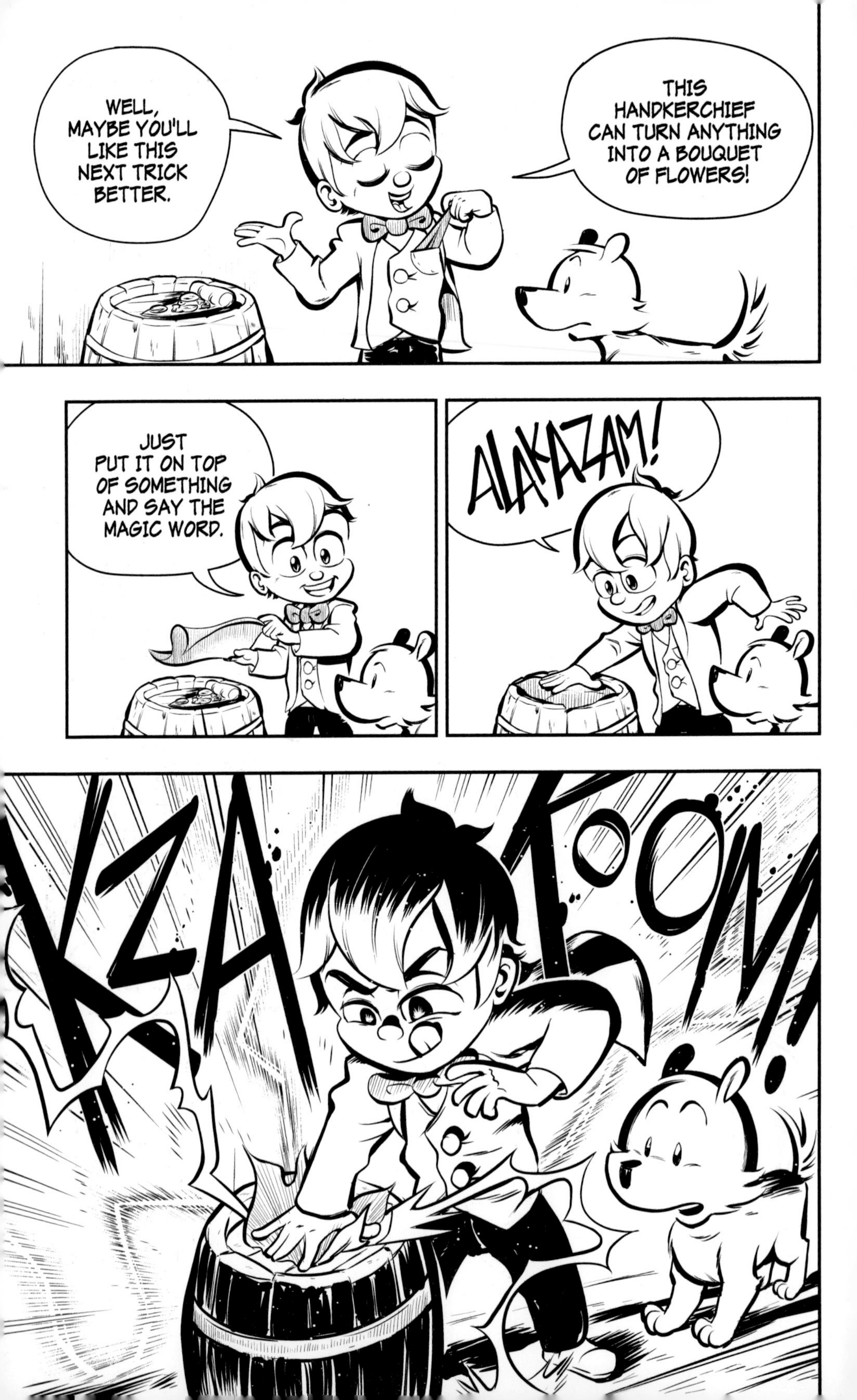
WELL, MAYBE YOU'LL LIKE THIS NEXT TRICK BETTER.
THIS HANDKERCHIEF CAN TURN ANYTHING INTO A BOUQUET OF FLOWERS!
JUST PUT IT ON TOP OF SOMETHING AND SAY THE MAGIC WORD.
ALAKAZAM!
KZA-BOOM!

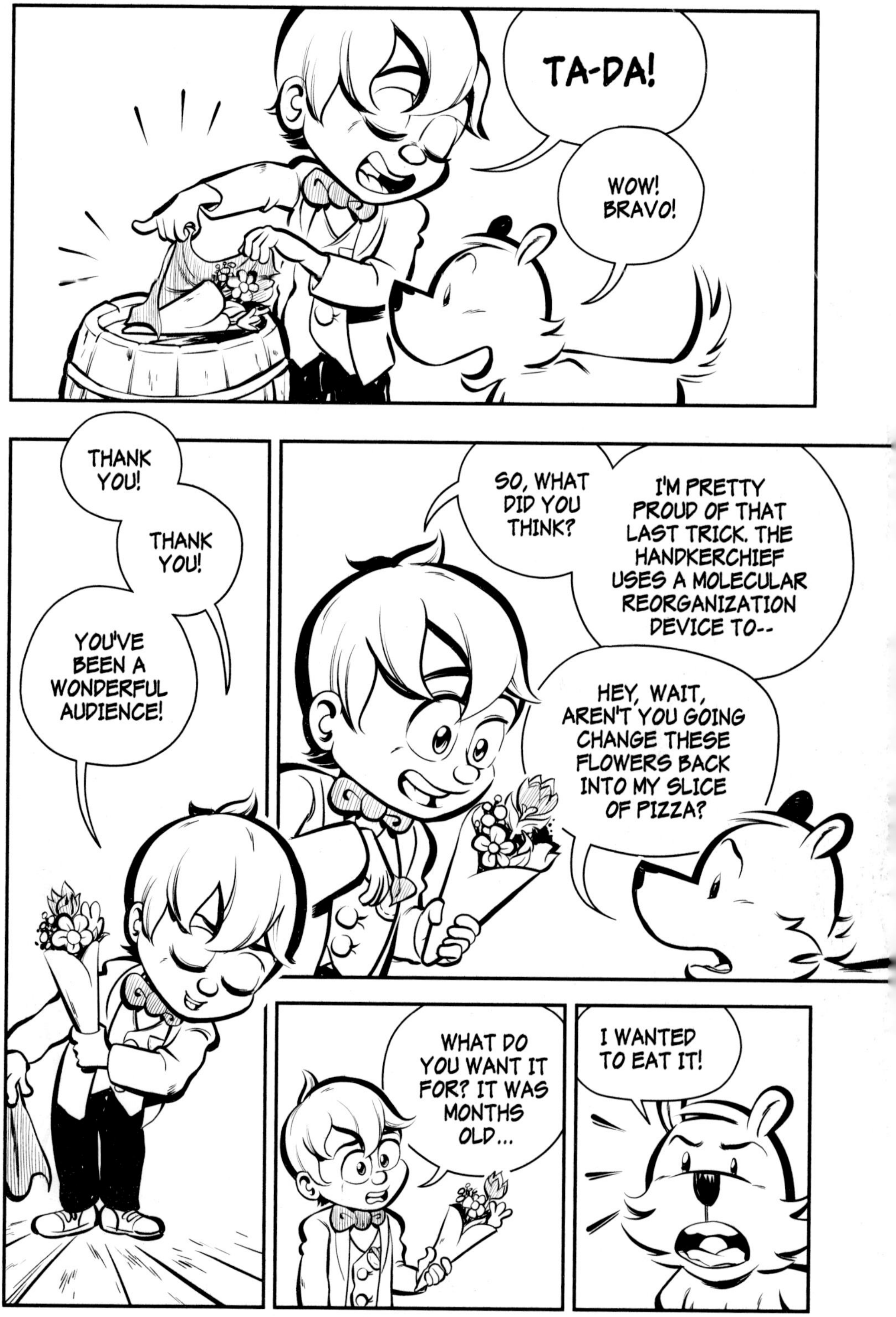
TA-DA!
WOW! BRAVO!
THANK YOU!
THANK YOU!
YOU'VE BEEN A WONDERFUL AUDIENCE!
SO, WHAT DID YOU THINK?
I'M PRETTY PROUD OF THAT LAST TRICK. THE HANDKERCHIEF USES A MOLECULAR REORGANIZATION DEVICE TO--
HEY, WAIT, AREN'T YOU GOING CHANGE THESE FLOWERS BACK INTO MY SLICE OF PIZZA?
WHAT DO YOU WANT IT FOR? IT WAS MONTHS OLD...
I WANTED TO EAT IT!

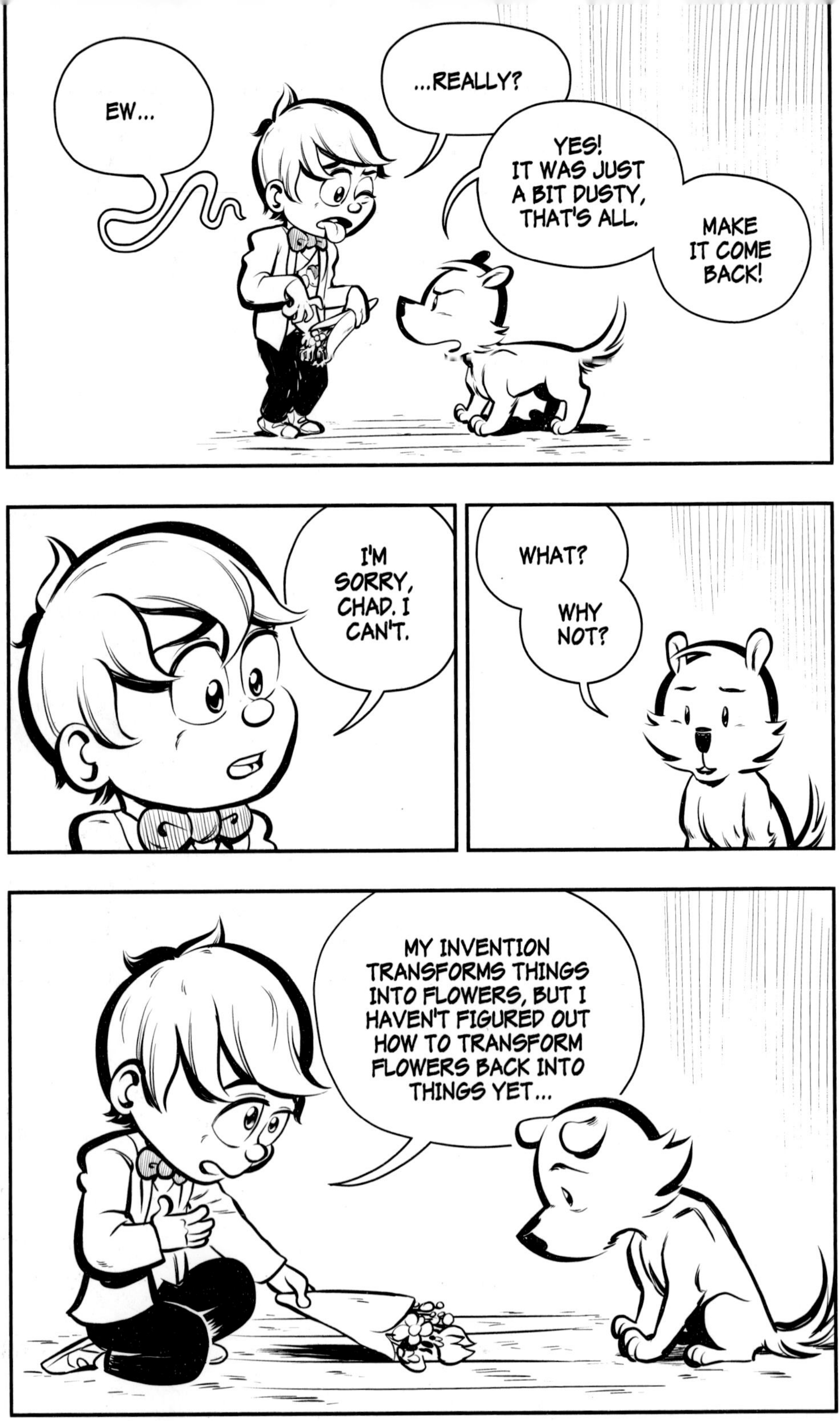
EW...
...REALLY?
YES! IT WAS JUST A BIT DUSTY, THAT'S ALL.
MAKE IT COME BACK!
I'M SORRY, CHAD. I CAN'T.
WHAT?
WHY NOT?
MY INVENTION TRANSFORMS THINGS INTO FLOWERS, BUT I HAVEN'T FIGURED OUT HOW TO TRANSFORM FLOWERS BACK INTO THINGS YET...

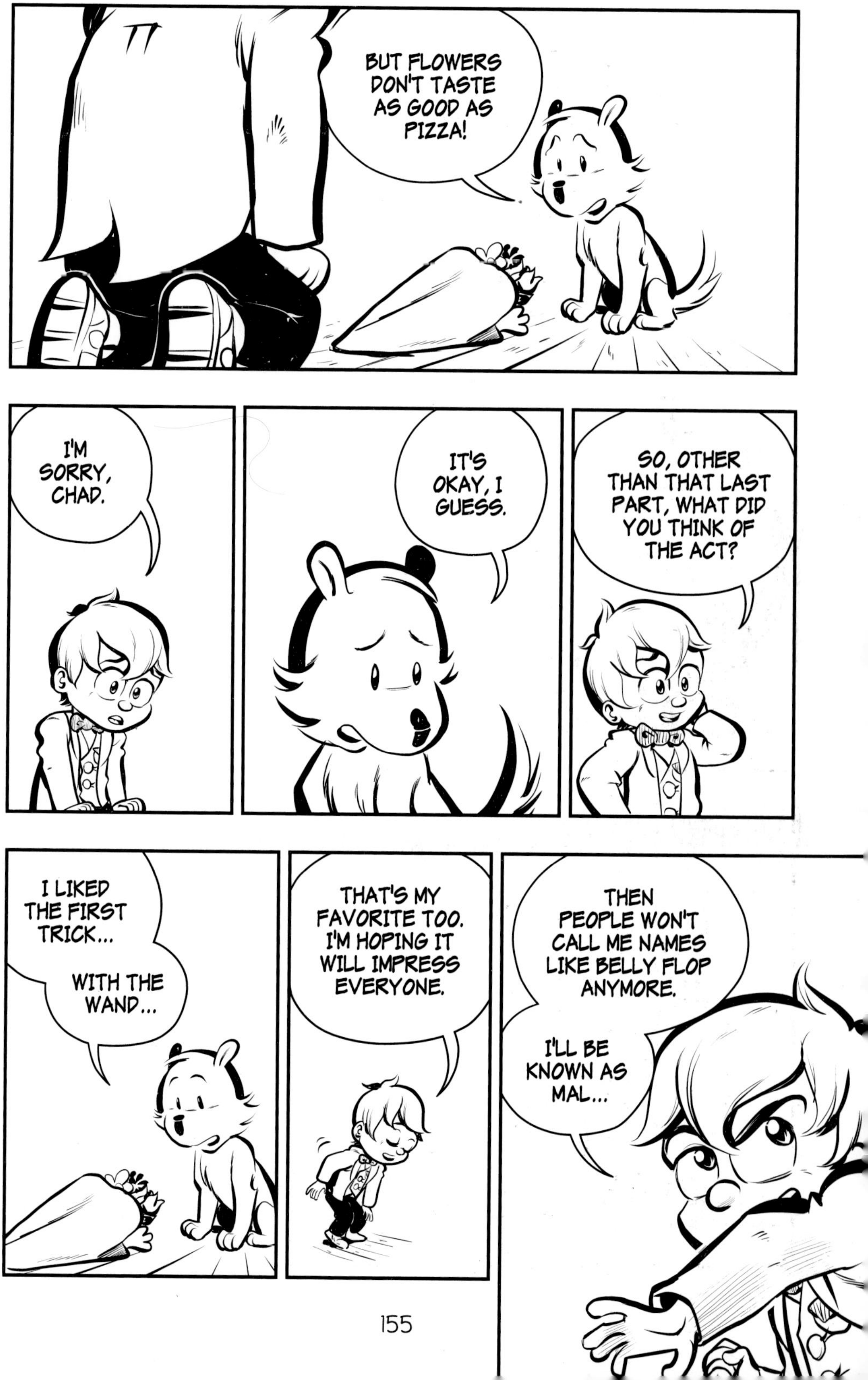
BUT FLOWERS DON'T TASTE AS GOOD AS PIZZA!
I'M SORRY, CHAD.
IT'S OKAY, I GUESS.
SO, OTHER THAN THAT LAST PART, WHAT DID YOU THINK OF THE ACT?
I LIKED THE FIRST TRICK...
WITH THE WAND...
THAT'S MY FAVORITE TOO. I'M HOPING IT WILL IMPRESS EVERYONE.
THEN PEOPLE WON'T CALL ME NAMES LIKE BELLY FLOP ANYMORE.
I'LL BE KNOWN AS MAL...

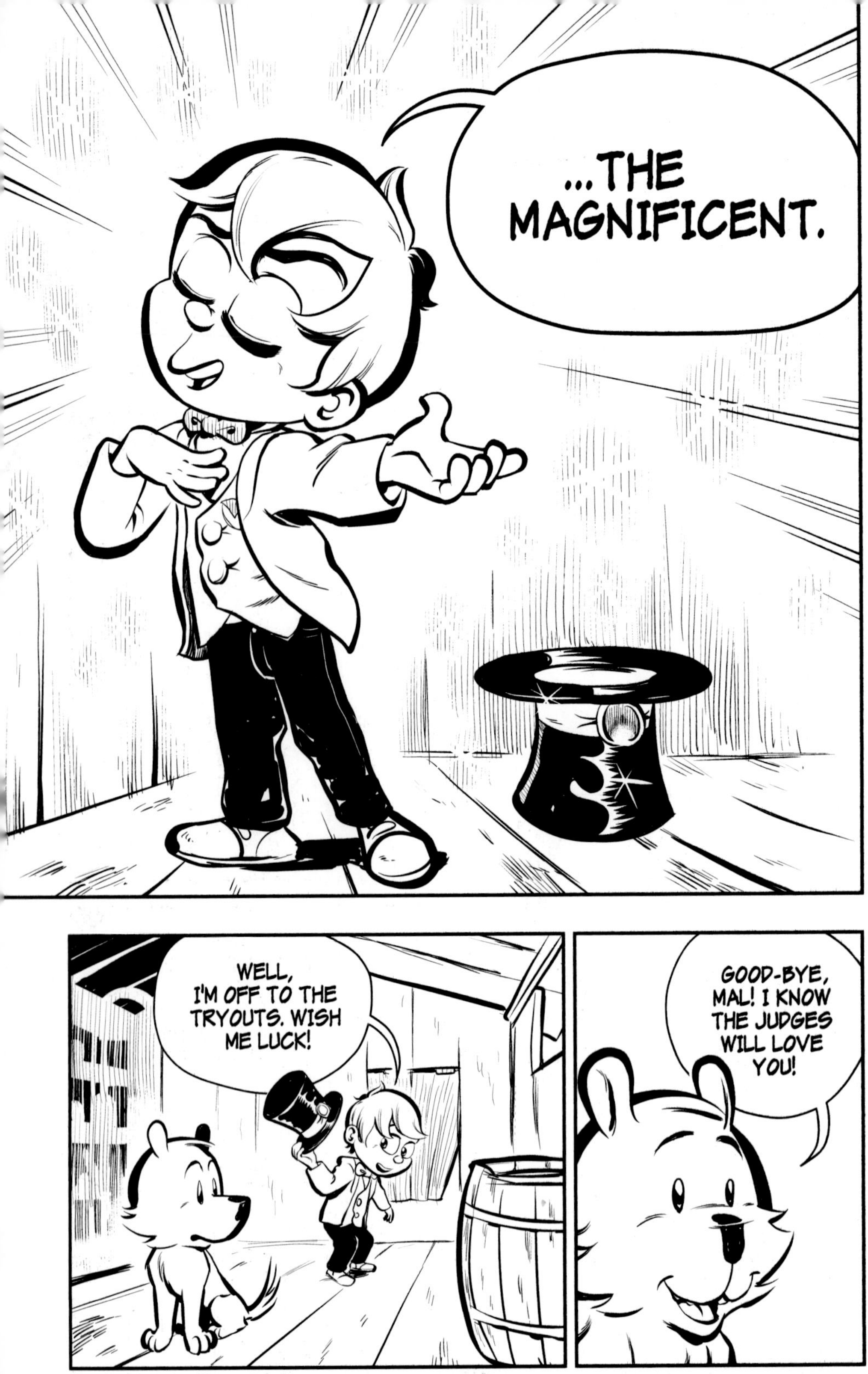
...THE MAGNIFICENT.
WELL, I'M OFF TO THE TRYOUTS. WISH ME LUCK!
GOOD-BYE, MAL! I KNOW THE JUDGES WILL LOVE YOU!

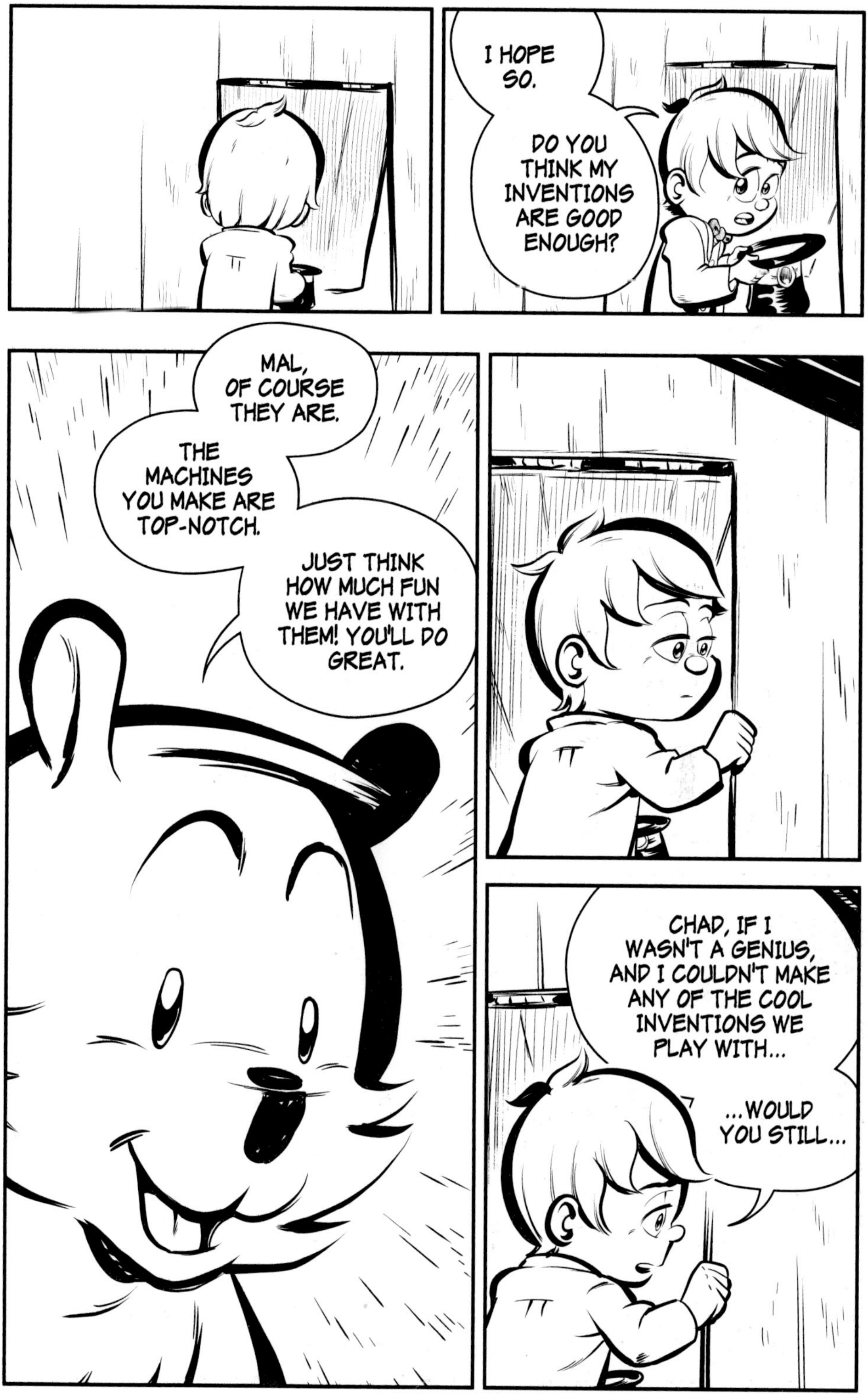
I HOPE SO.
DO YOU THINK MY INVENTIONS ARE GOOD ENOUGH?
MAL, OF COURSE THEY ARE.
THE MACHINES YOU MAKE ARE TOP-NOTCH.
JUST THINK HOW MUCH FUN WE HAVE WITH THEM! YOU'LL DO GREAT.
CHAD, IF I WASN'T A GENIUS, AND I COULDN'T MAKE ANY OF THE COOL INVENTIONS WE PLAY WITH...
...WOULD YOU STILL...

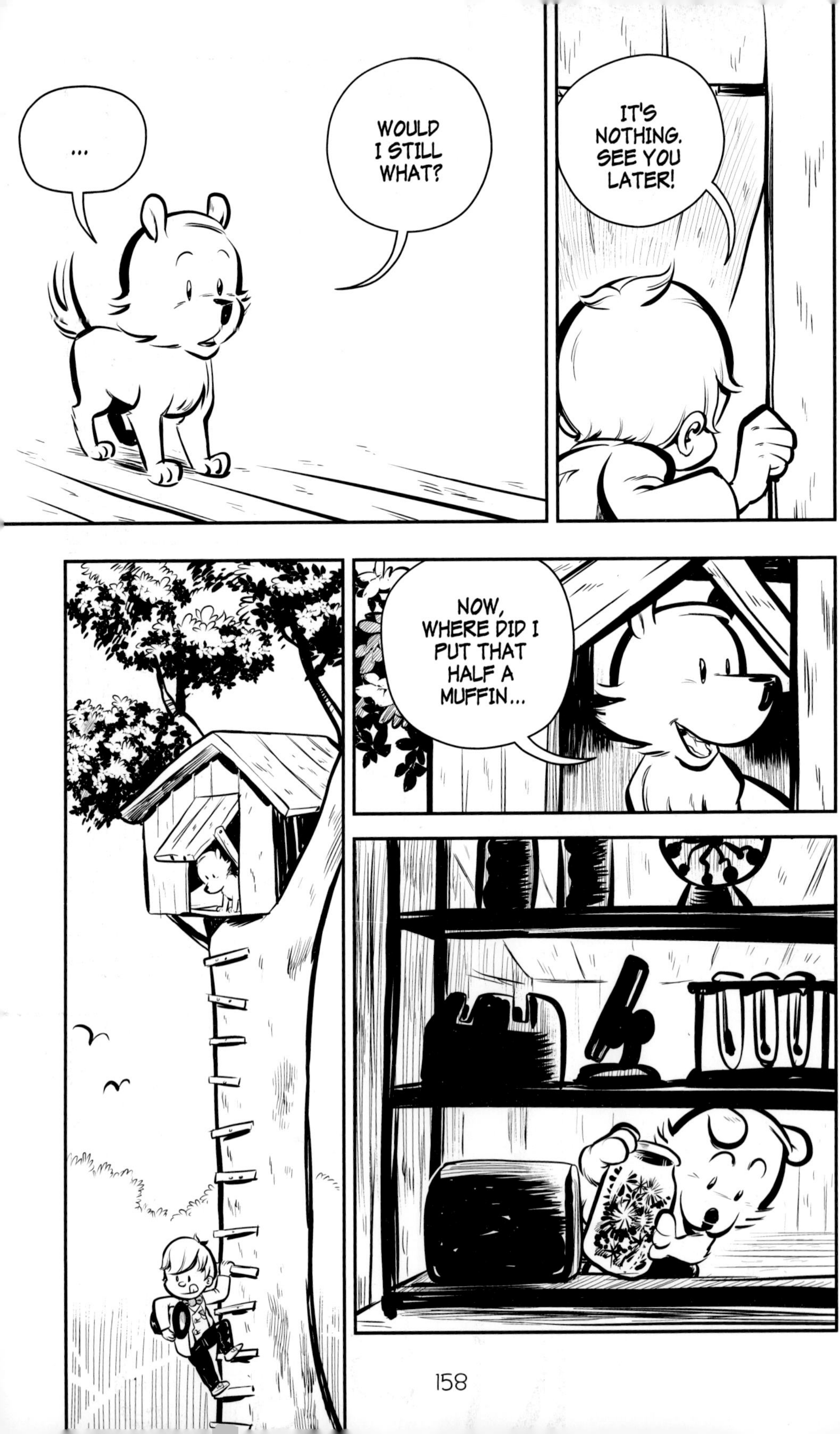
...
WOULD I STILL WHAT?
IT'S NOTHING. SEE YOU LATER!
NOW, WHERE DID I PUT THAT HALF A MUFFIN...

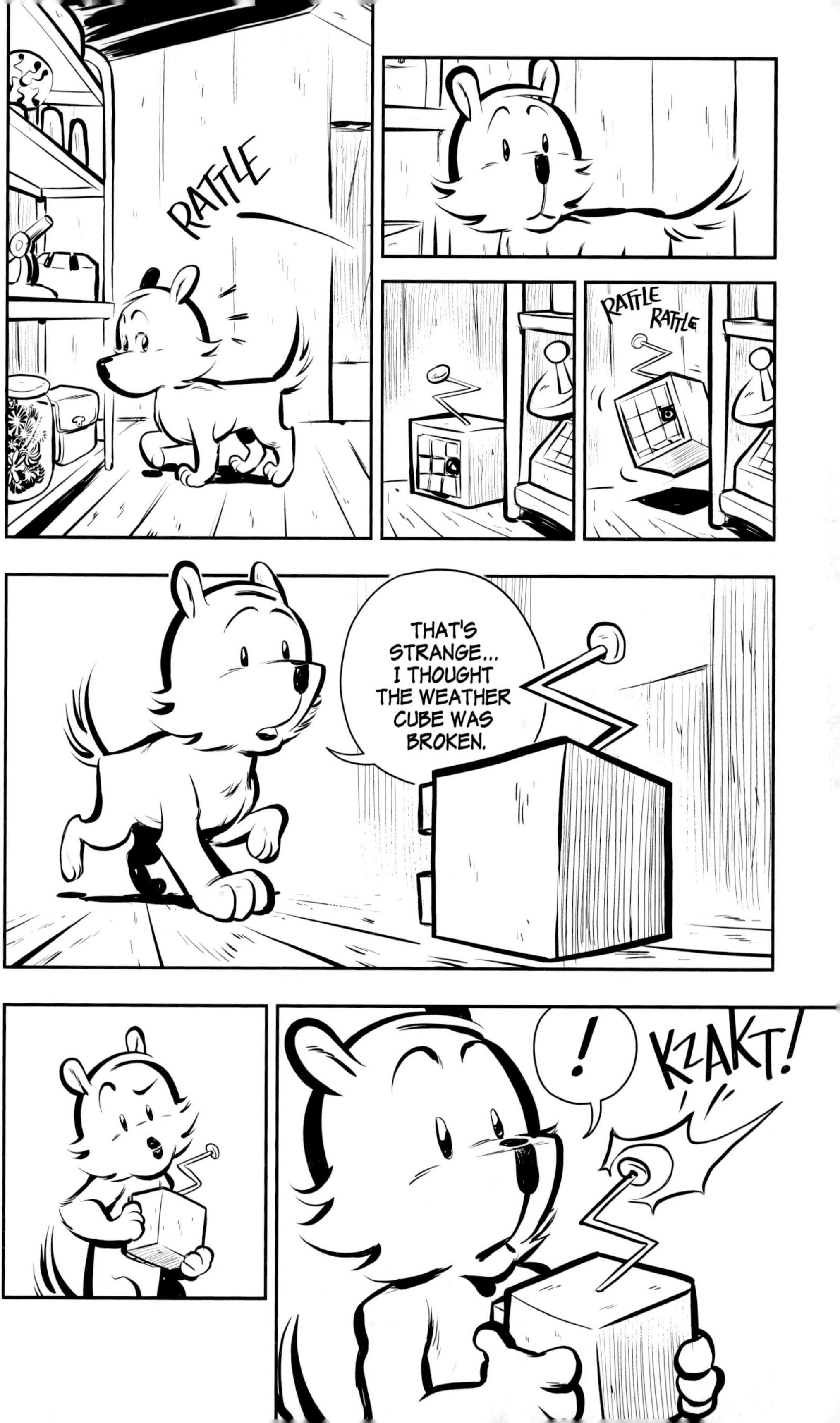
RATTLE
RATTLE
RATTLE
THAT'S STRANGE... I THOUGHT THE WEATHER CUBE WAS BROKEN.
!
KZAKT!

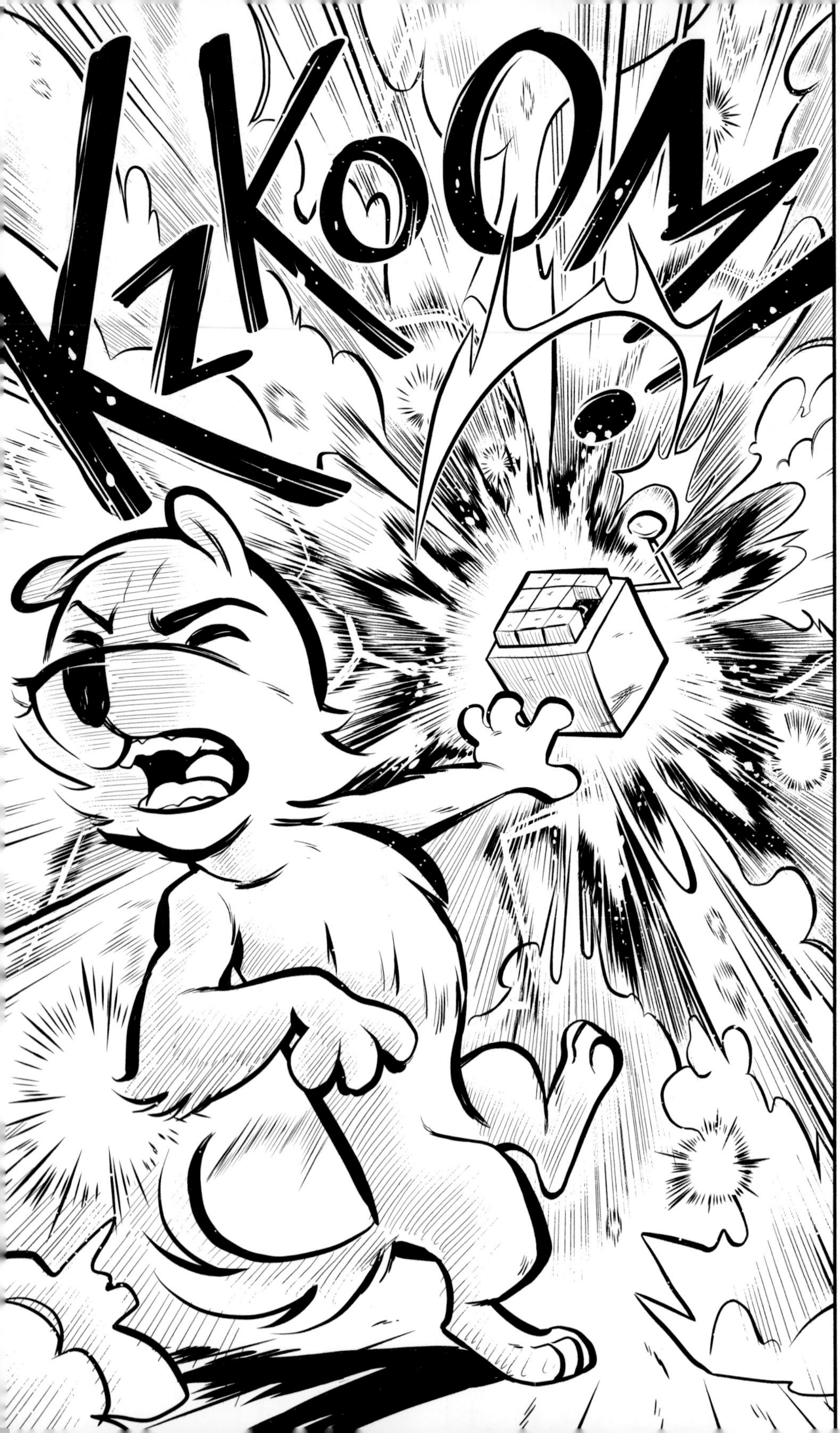
KZKOOM

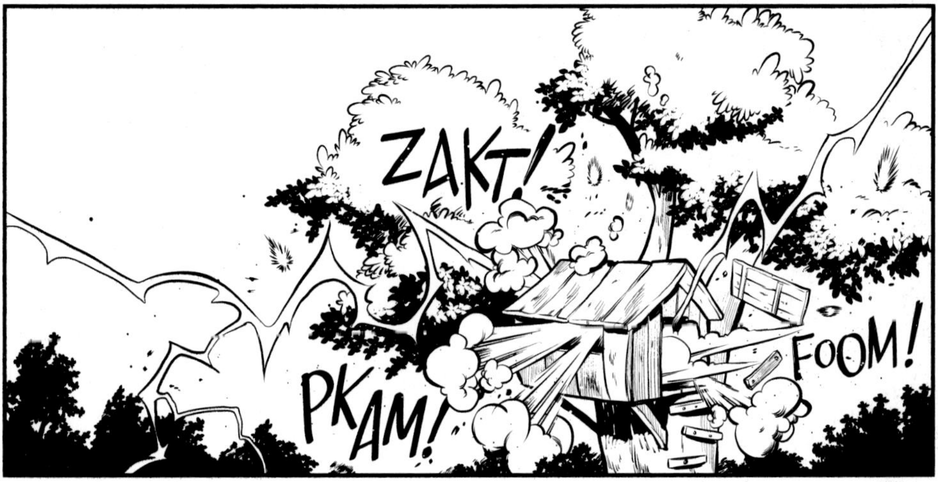
ZAKT!
PKAM!
FOOM!

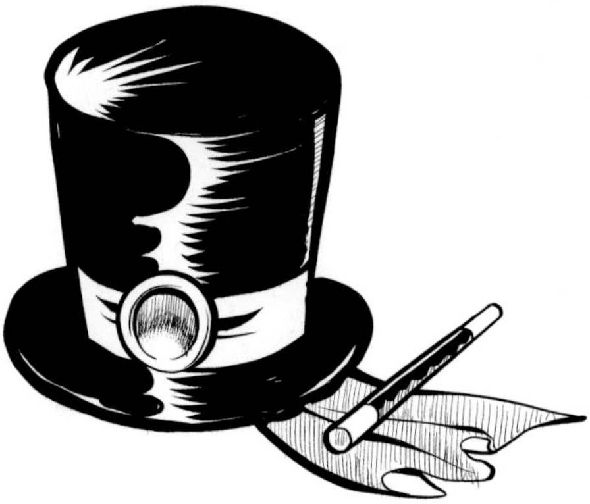

CHAPTER 7

The Talent Show

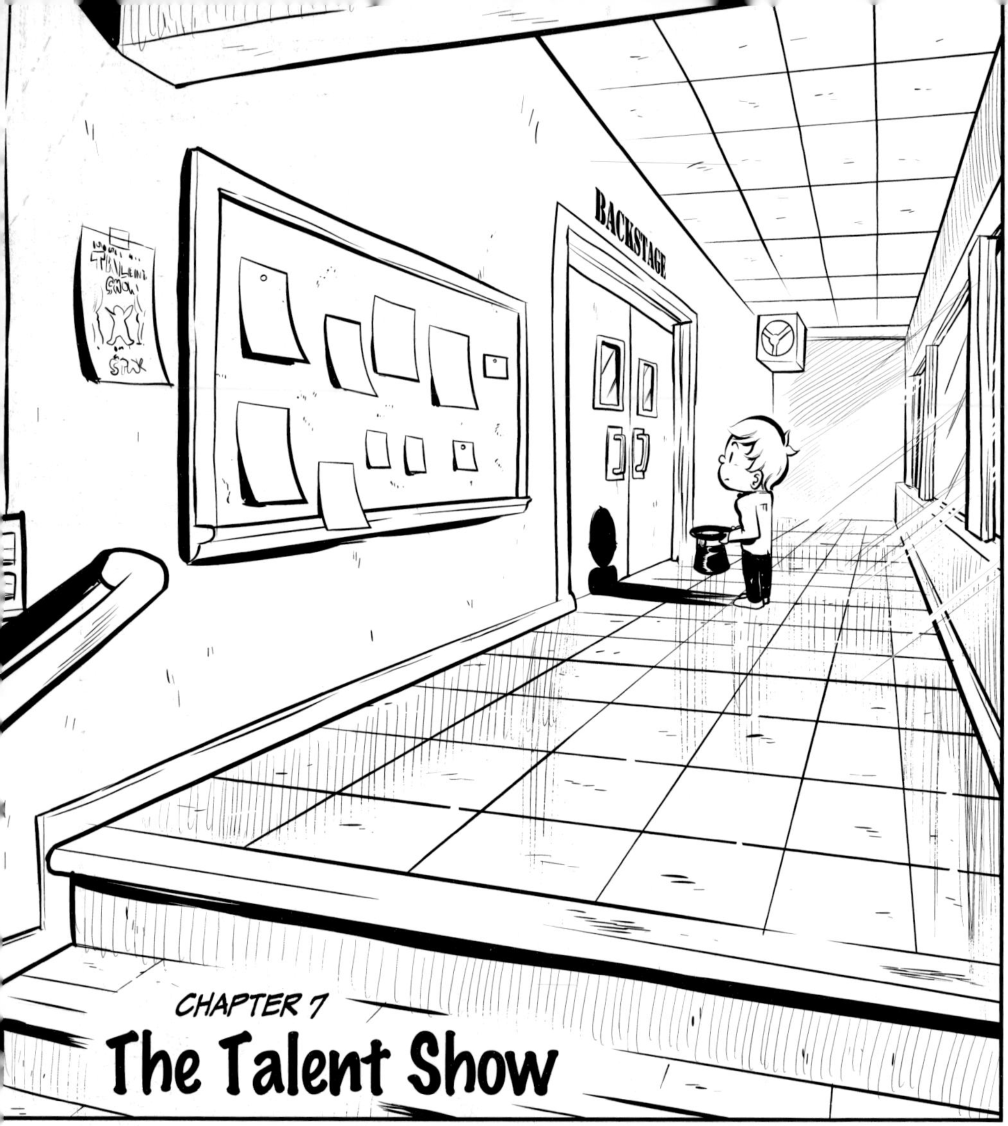
BACKSTAGE

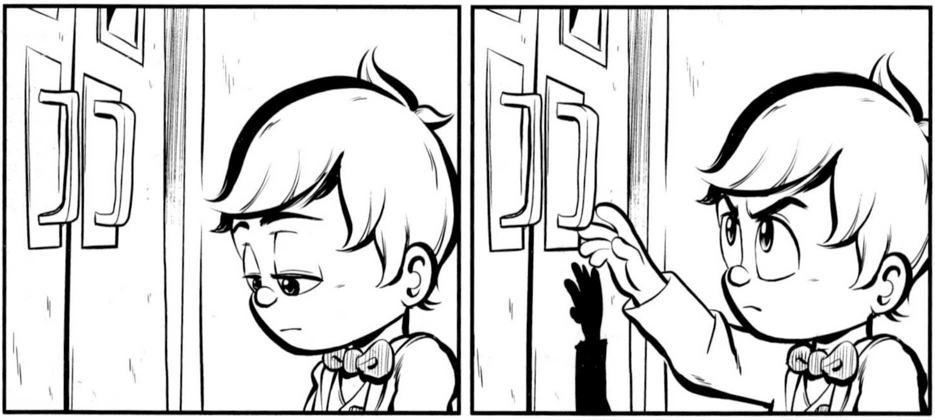

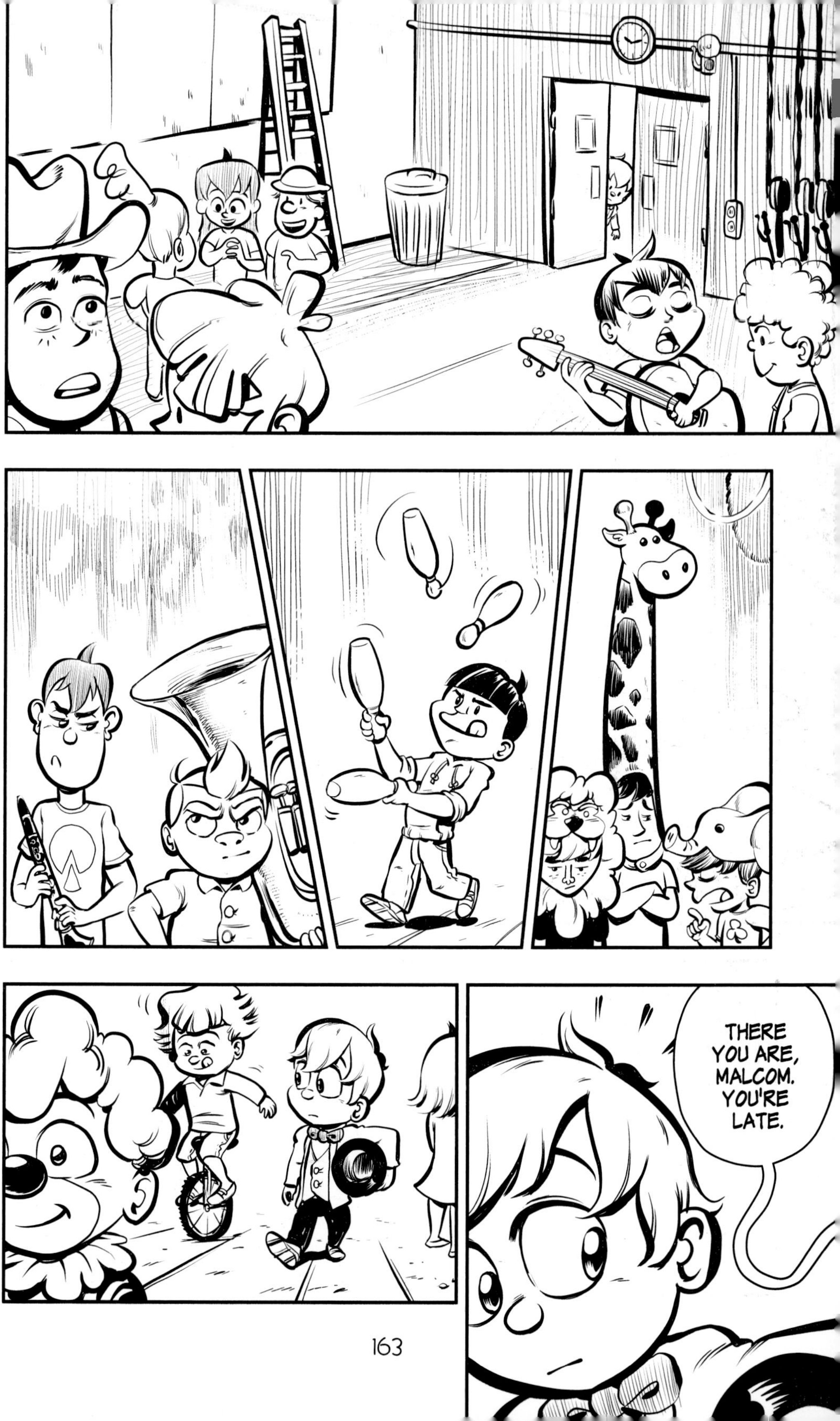
THERE YOU ARE, MALCOM. YOU'RE LATE.

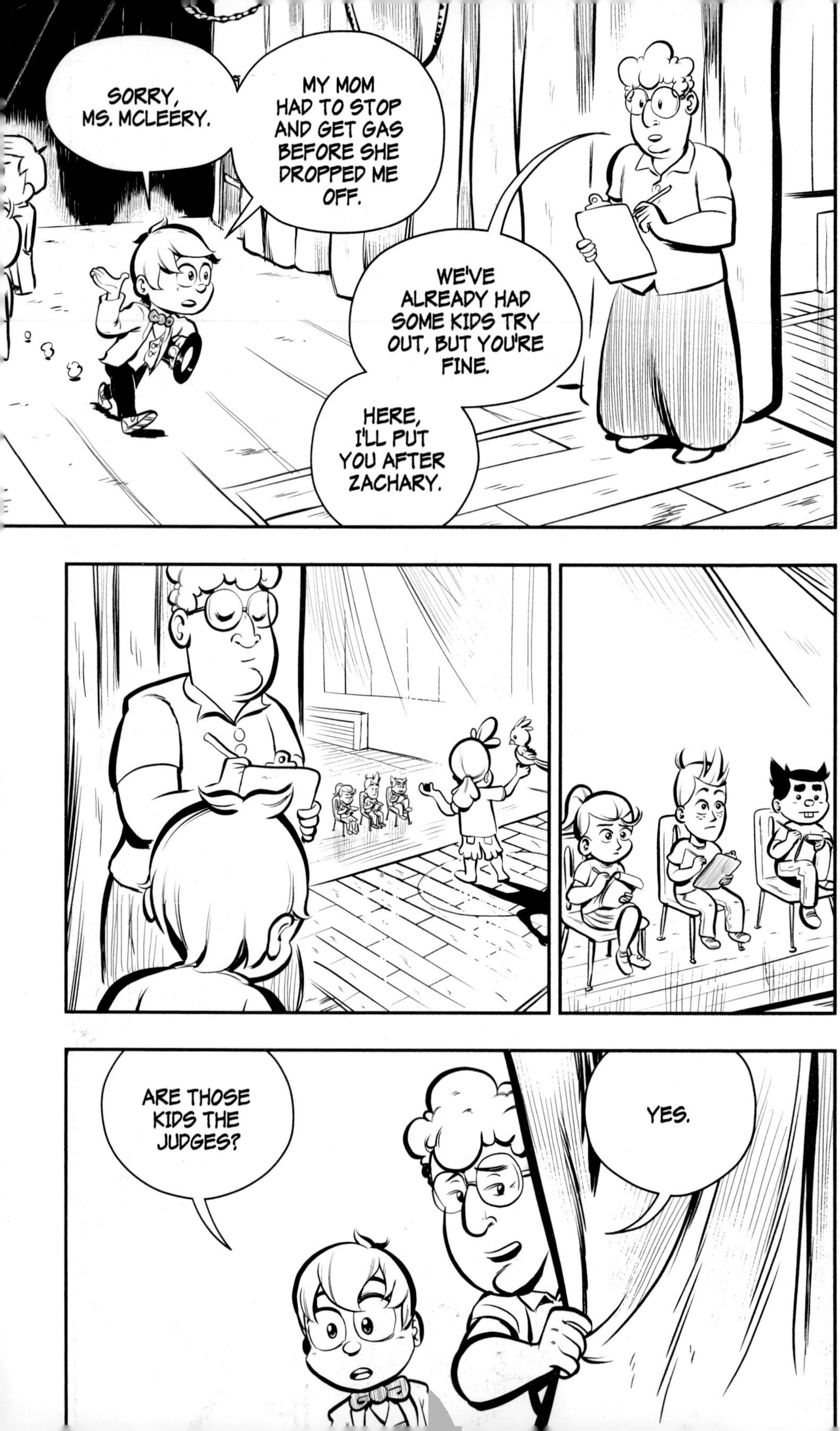
SORRY, MS. MCLEERY.
MY MOM HAD TO STOP AND GET GAS BEFORE SHE DROPPED ME OFF.
WE'VE ALREADY HAD SOME KIDS TRY OUT, BUT YOU'RE FINE.
HERE, I'LL PUT YOU AFTER ZACHARY.
ARE THOSE KIDS THE JUDGES?
YES.

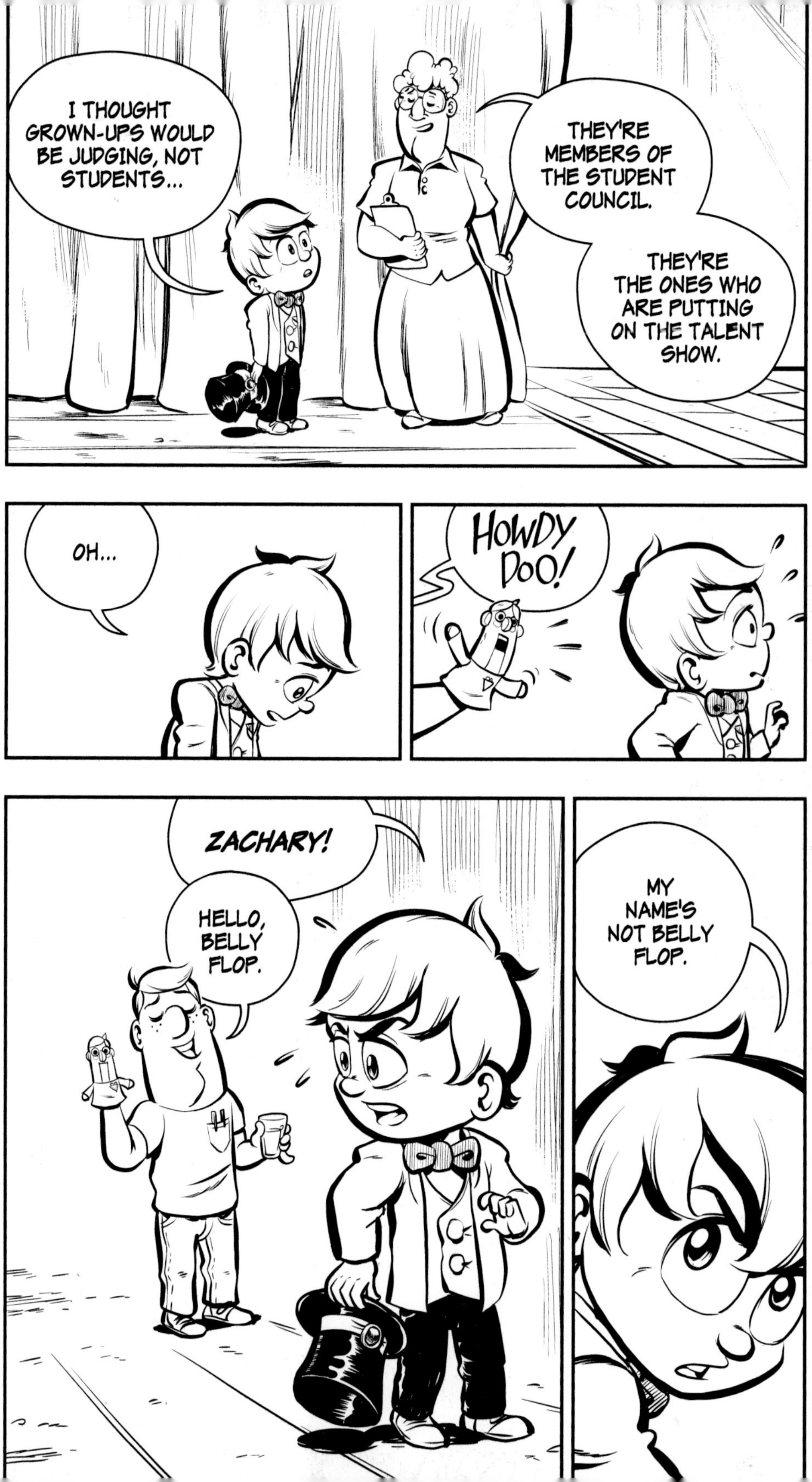
I THOUGHT GROWN-UPS WOULD BE JUDGING, NOT STUDENTS...
THEY'RE MEMBERS OF THE STUDENT COUNCIL.
THEY'RE THE ONES WHO ARE PUTTING ON THE TALENT SHOW.
OH...
HOWDY DOO!
ZACHARY!
HELLO, BELLY FLOP.
MY NAME'S NOT BELLY FLOP.

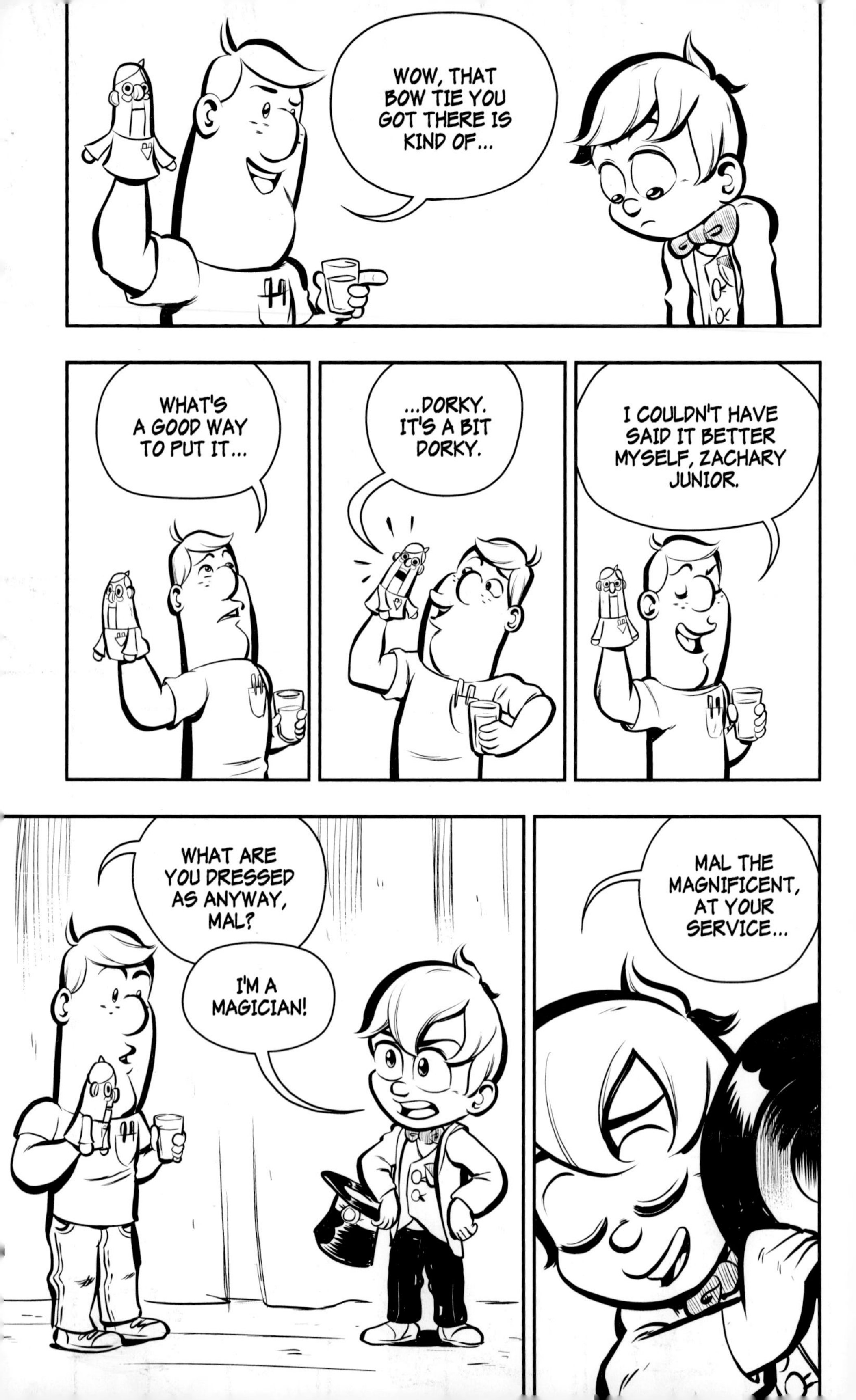
WOW, THAT BOW TIE YOU GOT THERE IS KIND OF...
WHAT'S A GOOD WAY TO PUT IT...
...DORKY. IT'S A BIT DORKY.
I COULDN'T HAVE SAID IT BETTER MYSELF, ZACHARY JUNIOR.
WHAT ARE YOU DRESSED AS ANYWAY, MAL?
I'M A MAGICIAN!
MAL THE MAGNIFICENT, AT YOUR SERVICE...

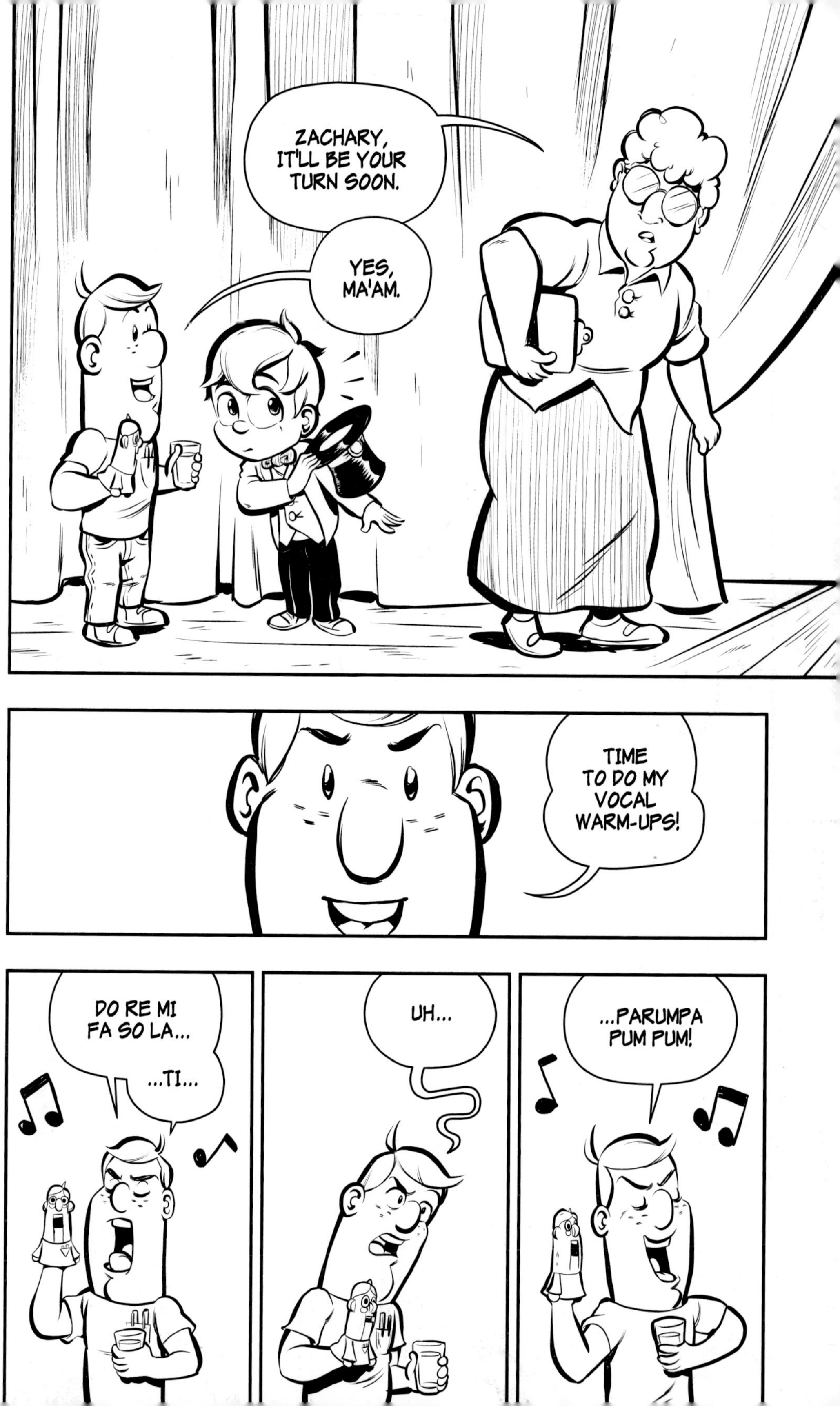
ZACHARY, IT'LL BE YOUR TURN SOON.
YES, MA'AM.
TIME TO DO MY VOCAL WARM-UPS!
DO RE MI FA SO LA...
...TI...
UH...
...PARUMPA PUM PUM!

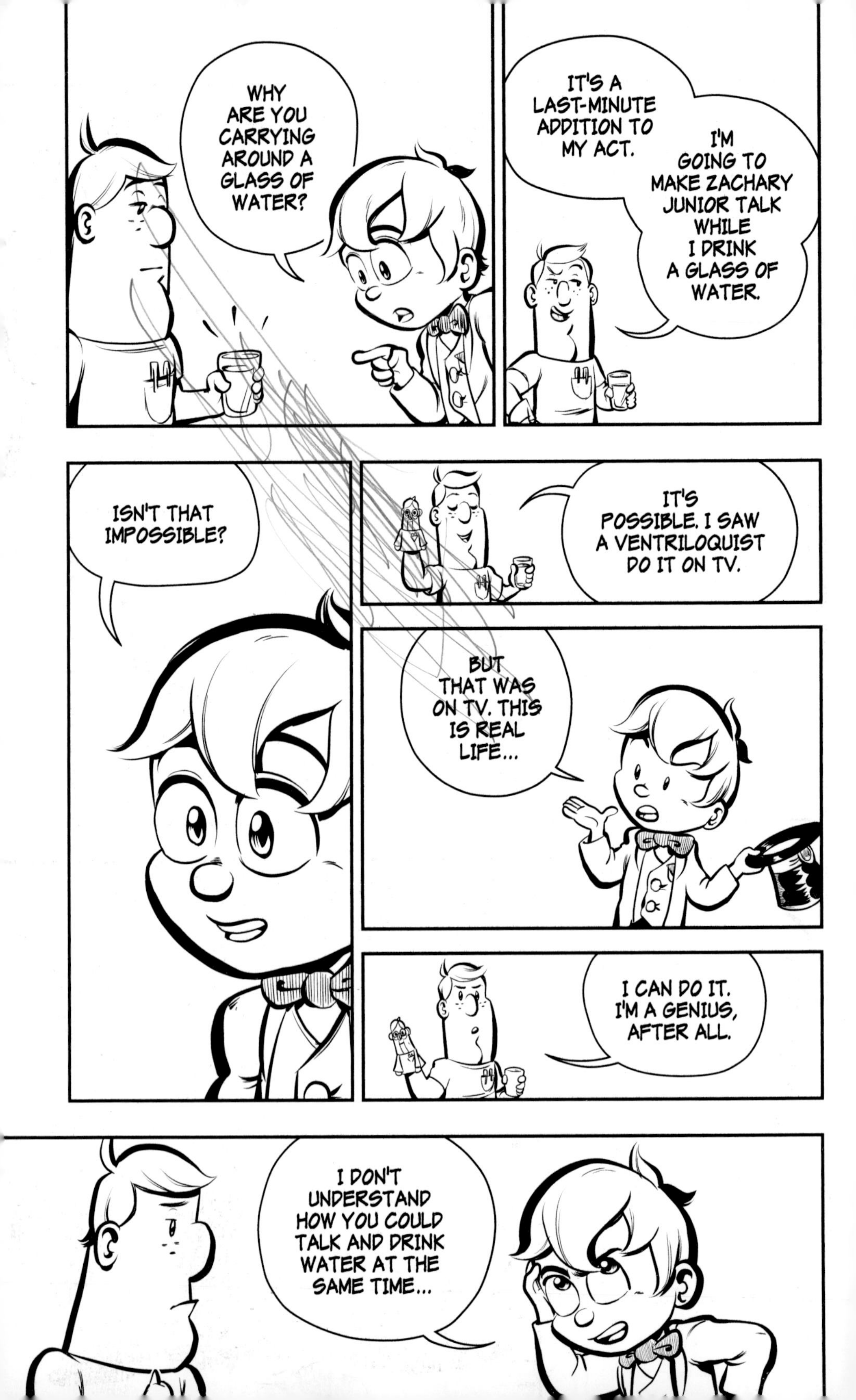
WHY ARE YOU CARRYING AROUND A GLASS OF WATER?
IT'S A LAST-MINUTE ADDITION TO MY ACT.
I'M GOING TO MAKE ZACHARY JUNIOR TALK WHILE I DRINK A GLASS OF WATER.
ISN'T THAT IMPOSSIBLE?
IT'S POSSIBLE. I SAW A VENTRILOQUIST DO IT ON TV.
BUT THAT WAS ON TV. THIS IS REAL LIFE...
I CAN DO IT. I'M A GENIUS, AFTER ALL.
I DON'T UNDERSTAND HOW YOU COULD TALK AND DRINK WATER AT THE SAME TIME...

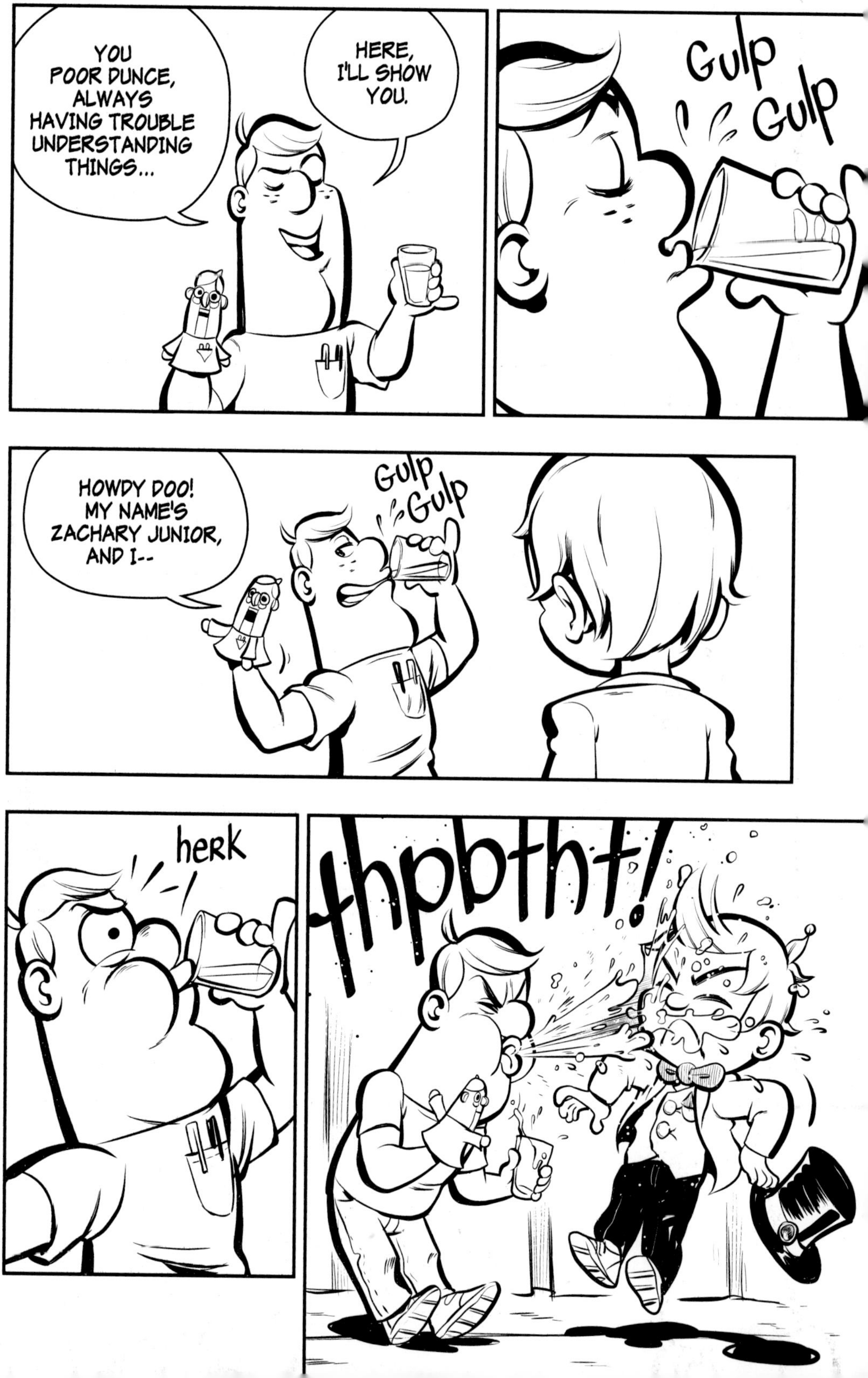
YOU POOR DUNCE, ALWAYS HAVING TROUBLE UNDERSTANDING THINGS...
HERE, I'LL SHOW YOU.
Gulp Gulp
HOWDY DOO! MY NAME'S ZACHARY JUNIOR, AND I--
Gulp Gulp
herk
thpbtht!

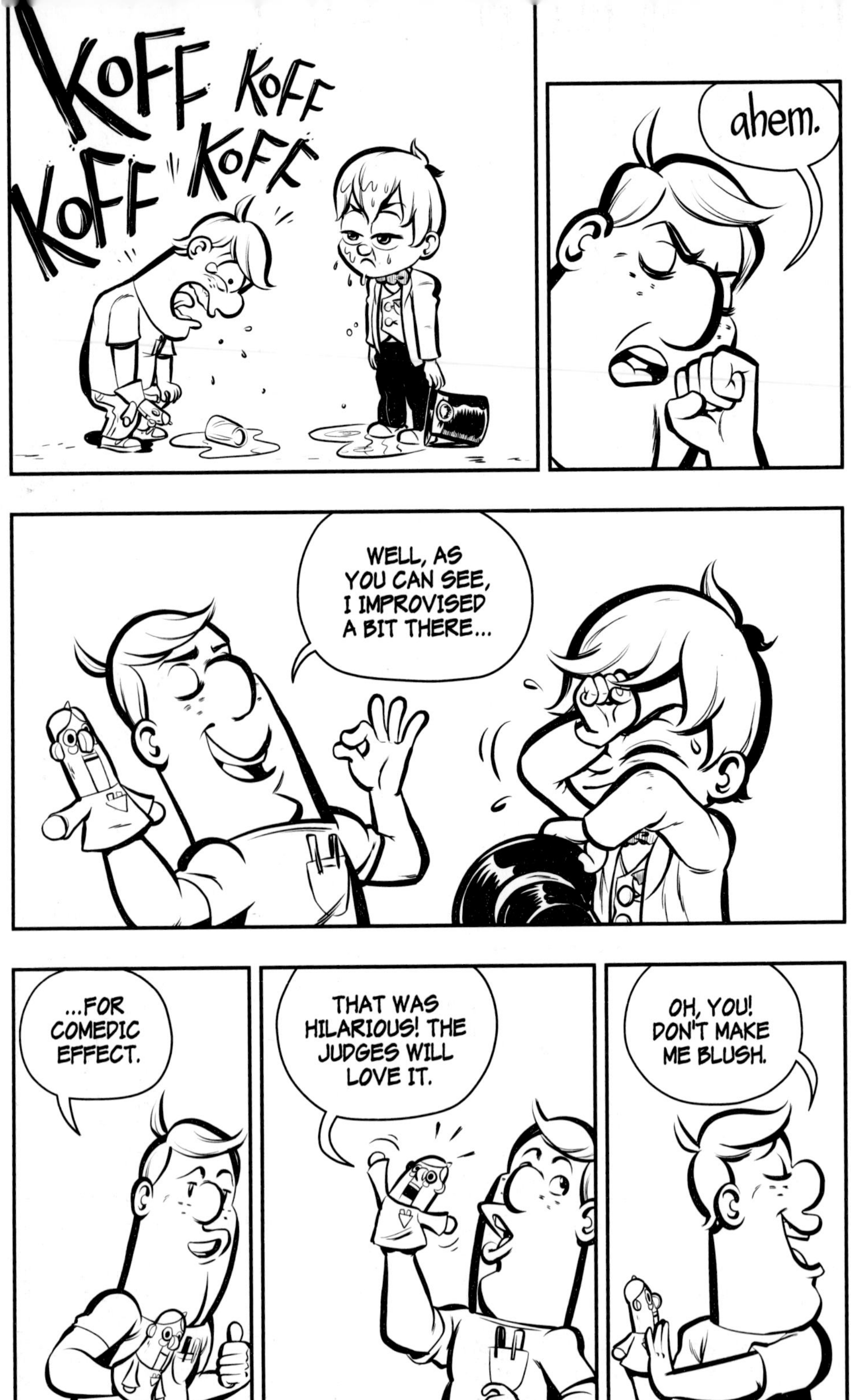
KOFF KOFF
KOFF KOFF
ahem.
WELL, AS YOU CAN SEE, I IMPROVISED A BIT THERE...
...FOR COMEDIC EFFECT.
THAT WAS HILARIOUS! THE JUDGES WILL LOVE IT.
OH, YOU! DON'T MAKE ME BLUSH.

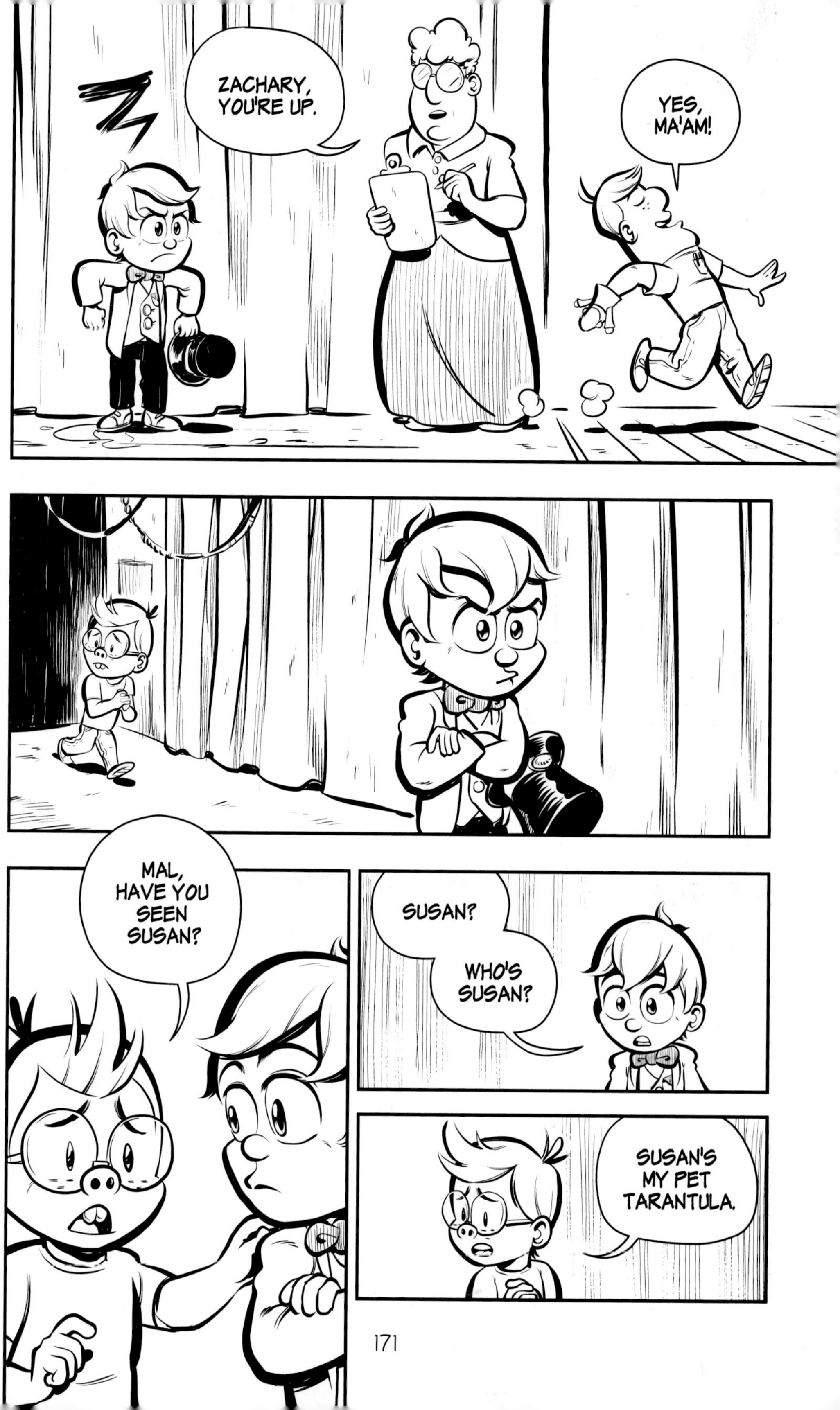
ZACHARY, YOU'RE UP.
YES, MA'AM!
MAL, HAVE YOU SEEN SUSAN?
SUSAN?
WHO'S SUSAN?
SUSAN'S MY PET TARANTULA.

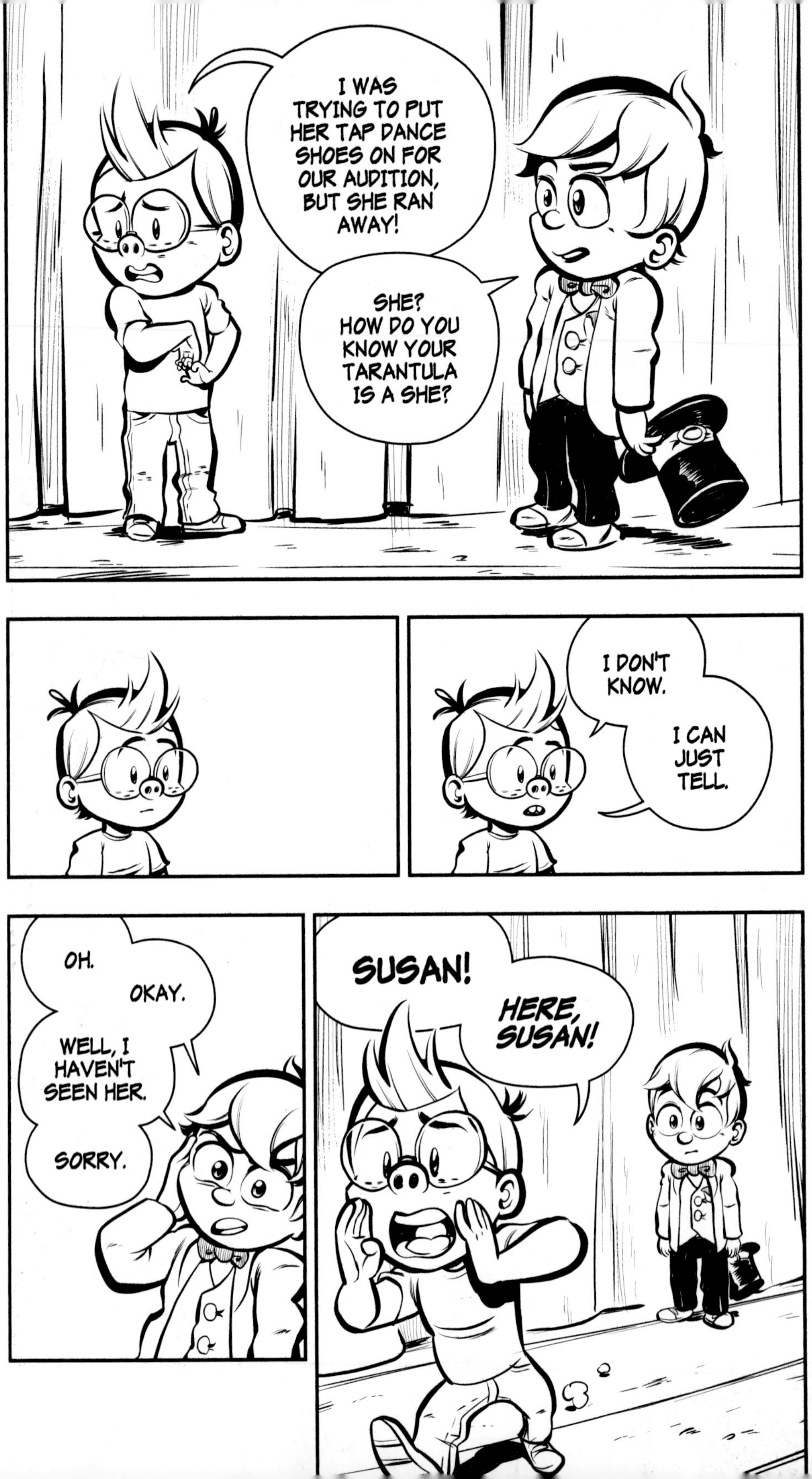
I WAS TRYING TO PUT HER TAP DANCE SHOES ON FOR OUR AUDITION, BUT SHE RAN AWAY!
SHE? HOW DO YOU KNOW YOUR TARANTULA IS A SHE?
I DON'T KNOW.
I CAN JUST TELL.
OH.
OKAY.
WELL, I HAVEN'T SEEN HER.
SORRY.
SUSAN!
HERE, SUSAN!

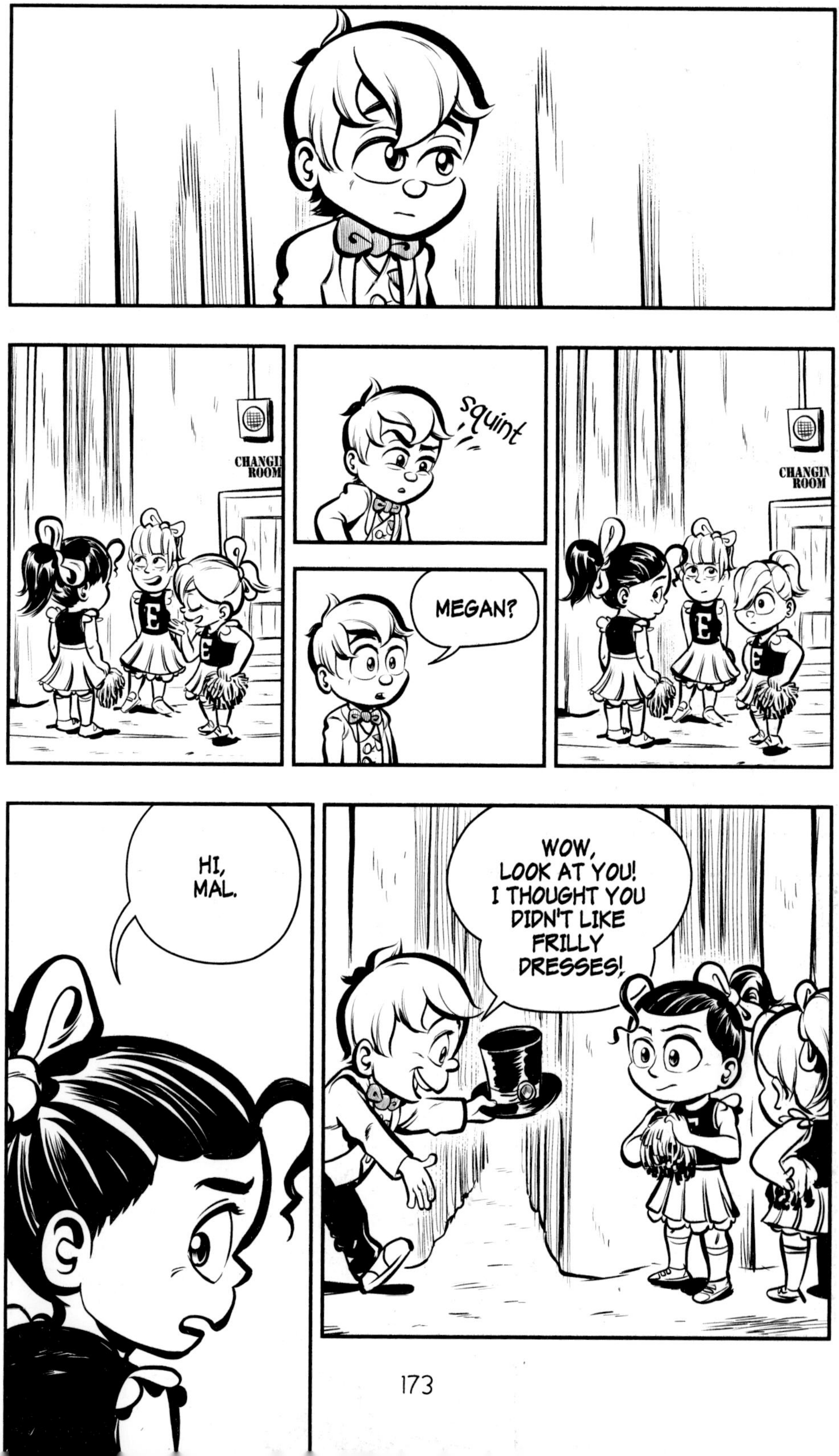
squint
CHANGING ROOM
MEGAN?
HI, MAL.
WOW, LOOK AT YOU! I THOUGHT YOU DIDN'T LIKE FRILLY DRESSES!

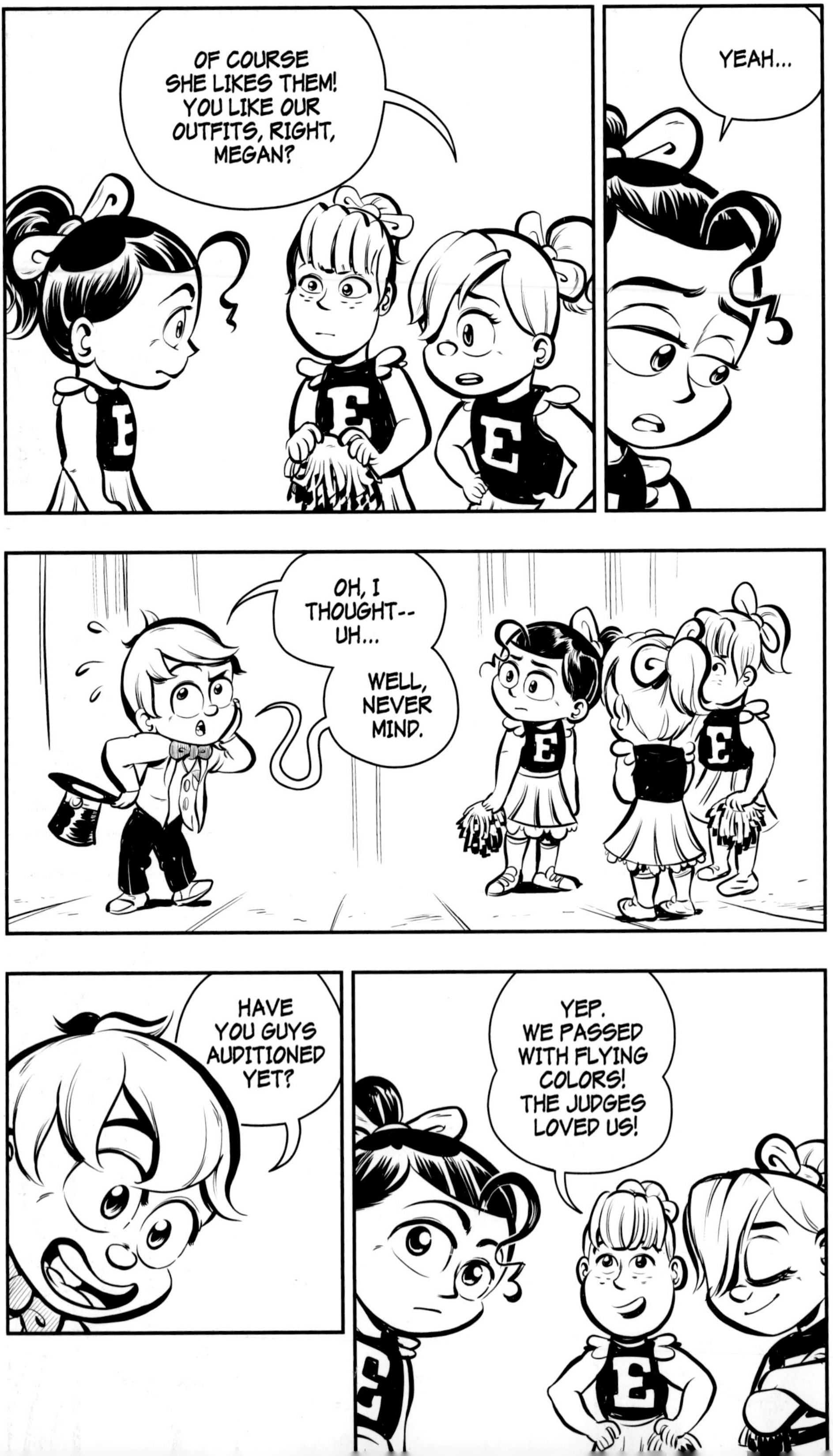
OF COURSE SHE LIKES THEM! YOU LIKE OUR OUTFITS, RIGHT, MEGAN?
YEAH...
OH, I THOUGHT-- UH...
WELL, NEVER MIND.
HAVE YOU GUYS AUDITIONED YET?
YEP. WE PASSED WITH FLYING COLORS! THE JUDGES LOVED US!

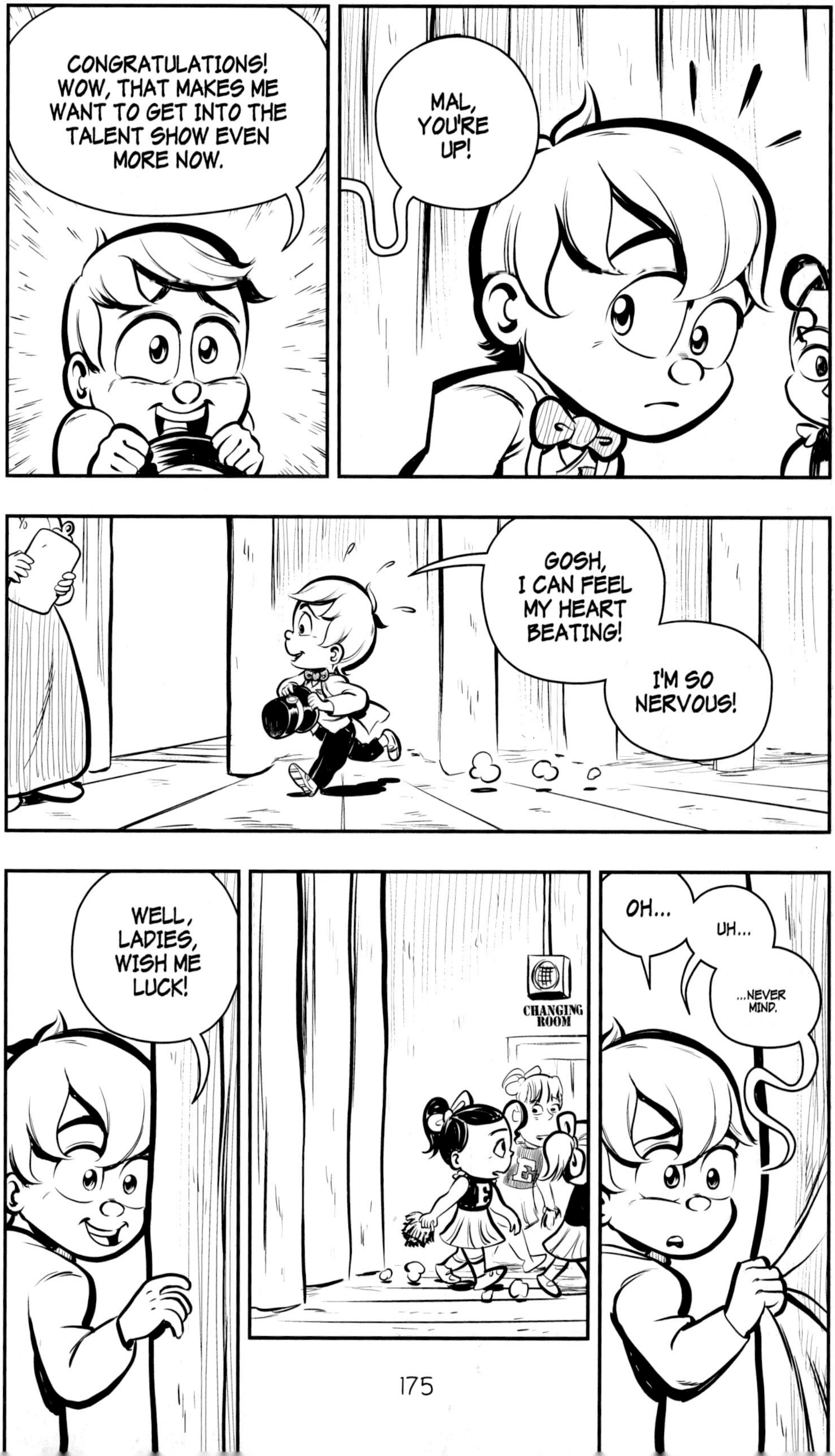
CONGRATULATIONS! WOW, THAT MAKES ME WANT TO GET INTO THE TALENT SHOW EVEN MORE NOW.
MAL, YOU'RE UP!
GOSH, I CAN FEEL MY HEART BEATING!
I'M SO NERVOUS!
WELL, LADIES, WISH ME LUCK!
CHANGING ROOM
OH...
UH...
...NEVER MIND.

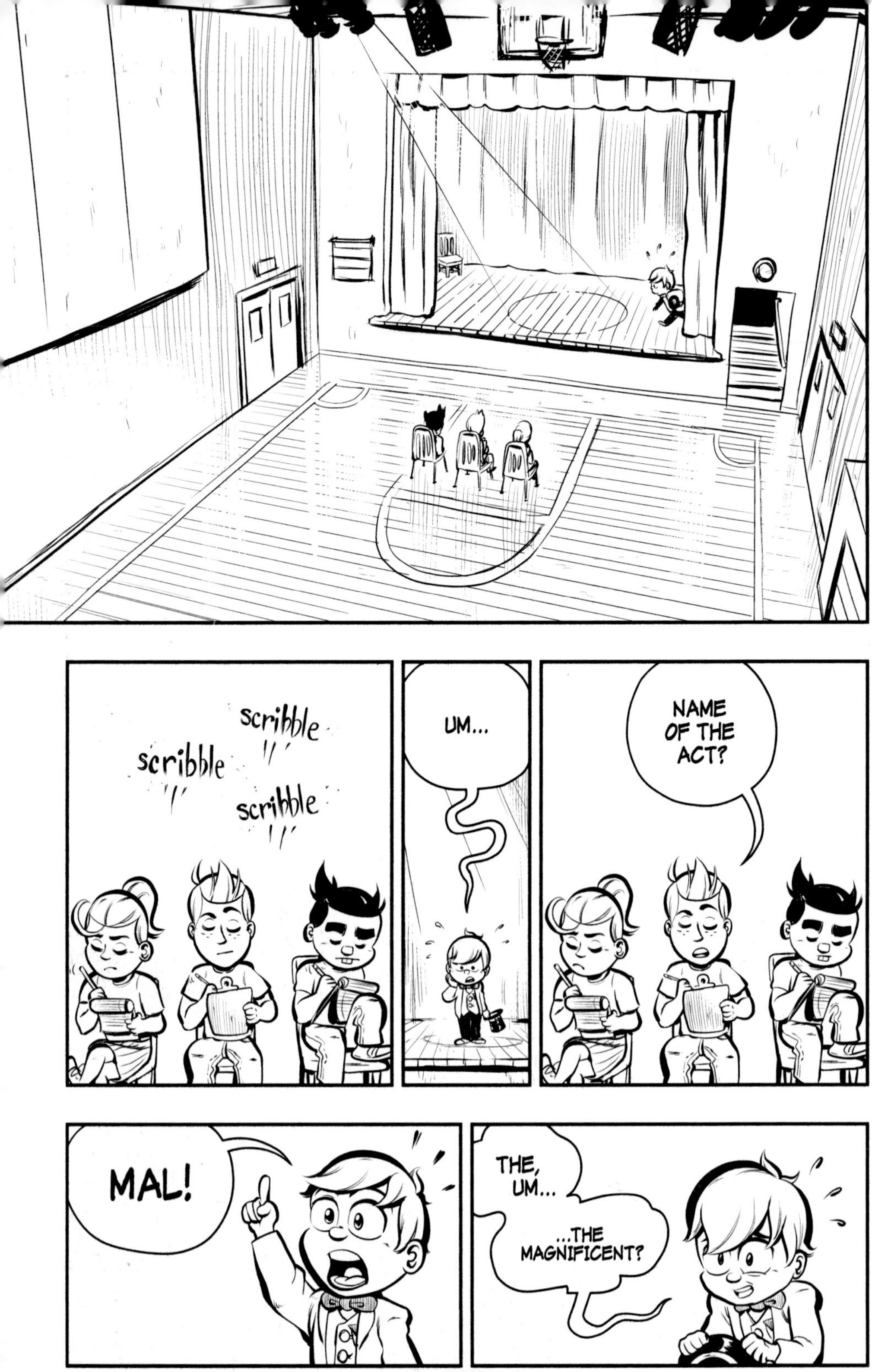
scribble
scribble
scribble
UM...
NAME OF THE ACT?
MAL!
THE, UM...
...THE MAGNIFICENT?

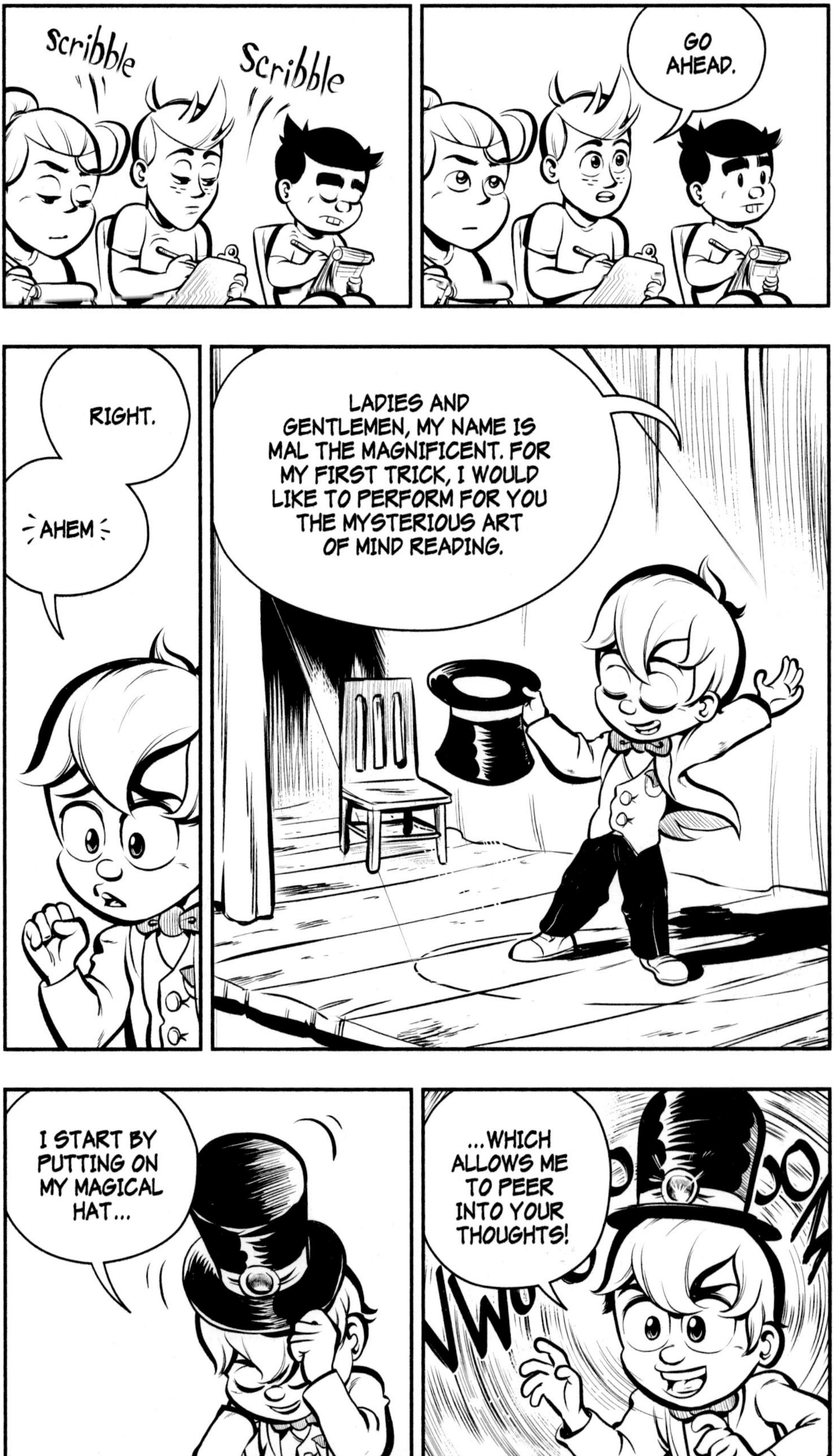
Scribble
Scribble
GO AHEAD.
RIGHT.
AHEM
LADIES AND GENTLEMEN, MY NAME IS MAL THE MAGNIFICENT. FOR MY FIRST TRICK, I WOULD LIKE TO PERFORM FOR YOU THE MYSTERIOUS ART OF MIND READING.
I START BY PUTTING ON MY MAGICAL HAT...
...WHICH ALLOWS ME TO PEER INTO YOUR THOUGHTS!

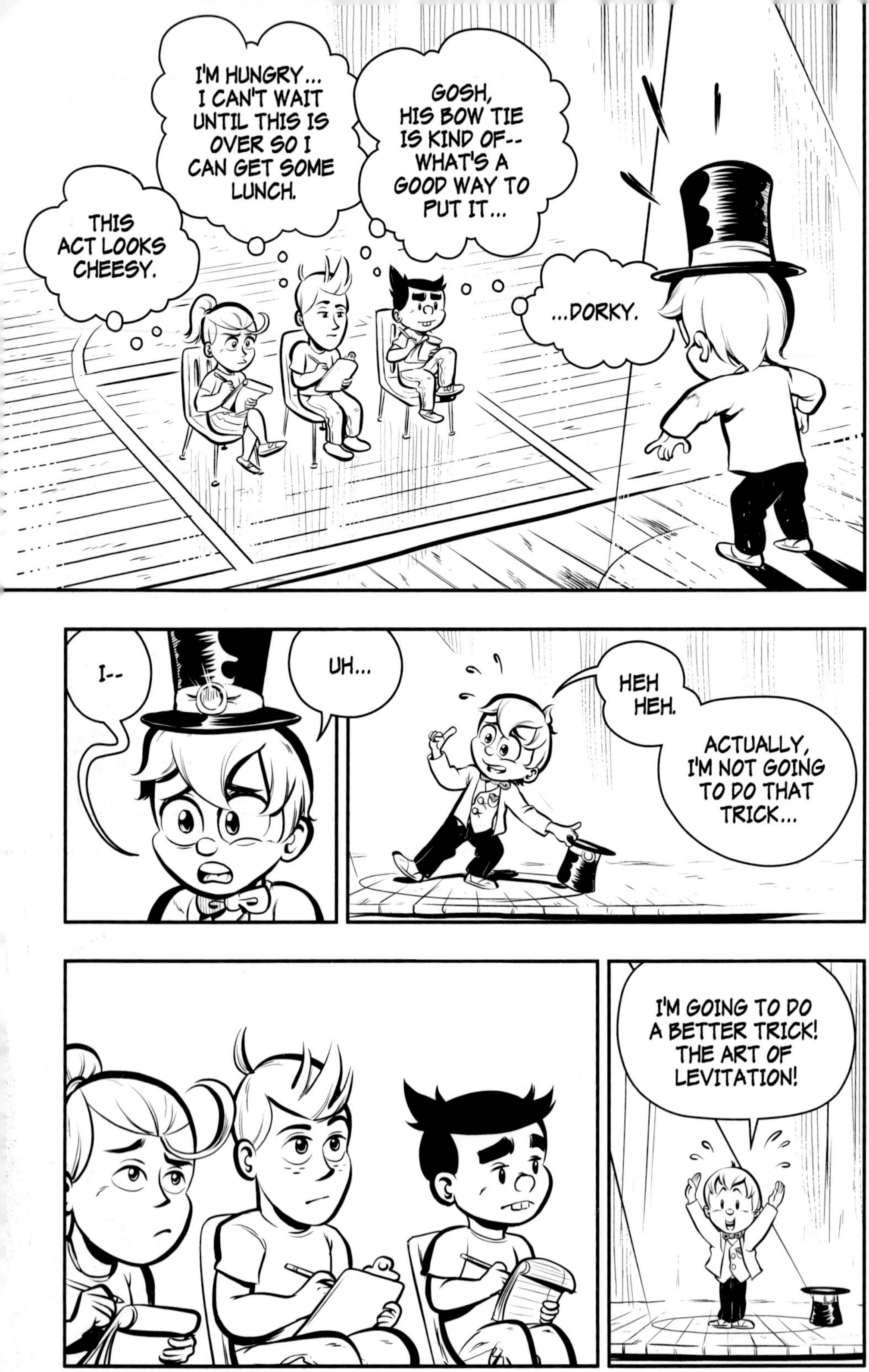
THIS ACT LOOKS CHEESY.
I'M HUNGRY... I CAN'T WAIT UNTIL THIS IS OVER SO I CAN GET SOME LUNCH.
GOSH, HIS BOW TIE IS KIND OF-- WHAT'S A GOOD WAY TO PUT IT...
...DORKY.
I--
UH...
HEH HEH.
ACTUALLY, I'M NOT GOING TO DO THAT TRICK...
I'M GOING TO DO A BETTER TRICK! THE ART OF LEVITATION!

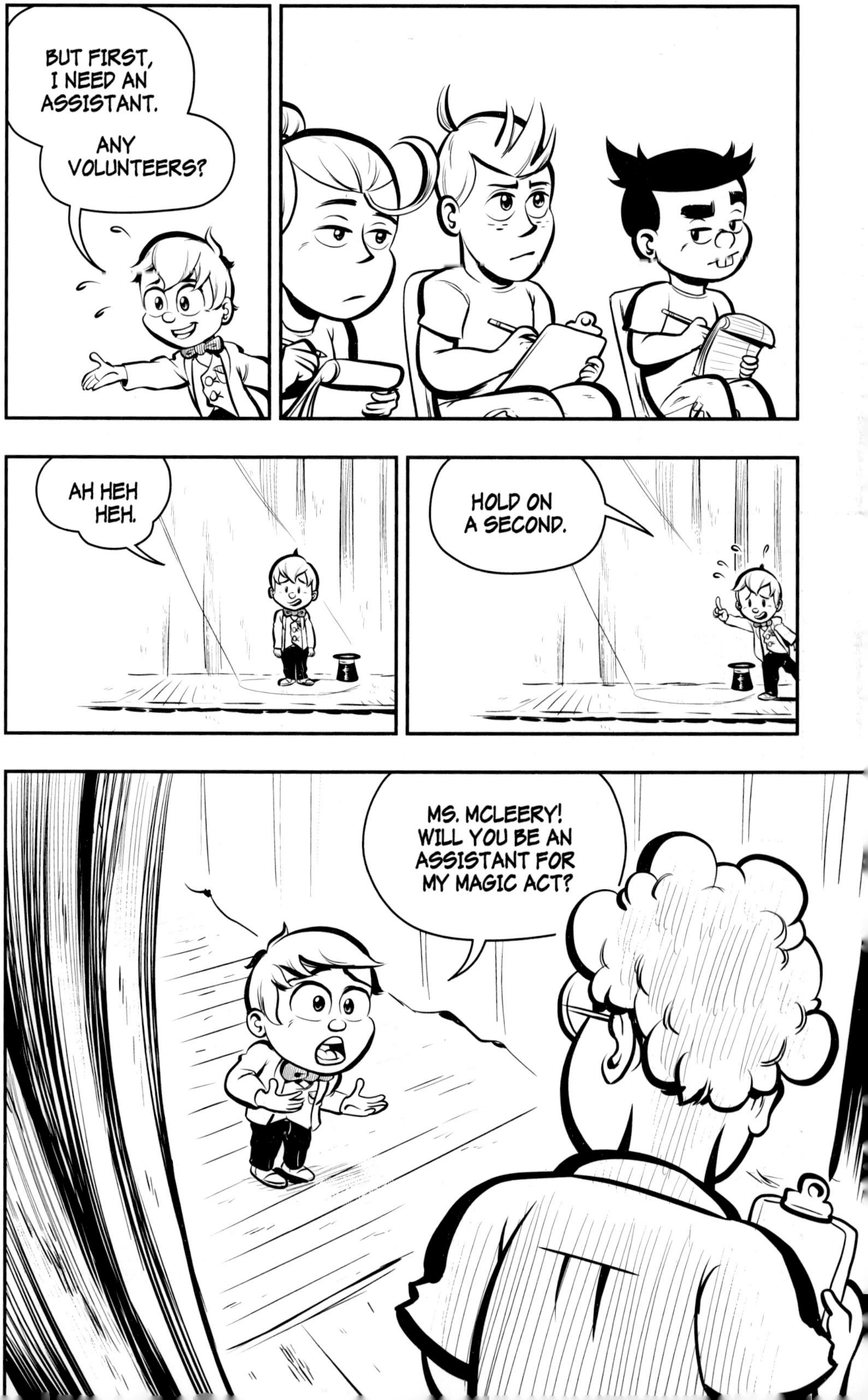
BUT FIRST, I NEED AN ASSISTANT.
ANY VOLUNTEERS?
AH HEH HEH.
HOLD ON A SECOND.
MS. MCLEERY! WILL YOU BE AN ASSISTANT FOR MY MAGIC ACT?

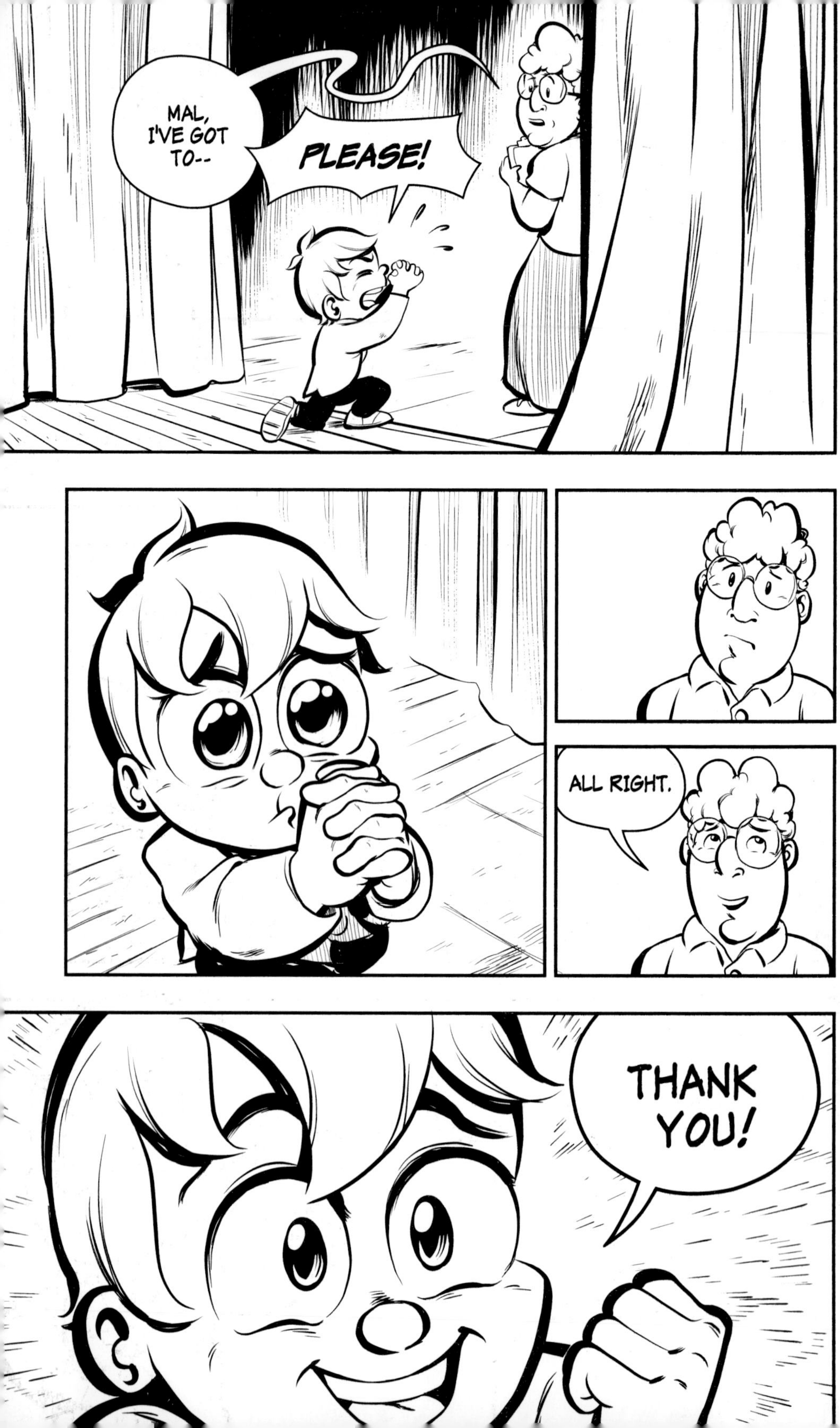
MAL, I'VE GOT TO--
PLEASE!
ALL RIGHT.
THANK YOU!

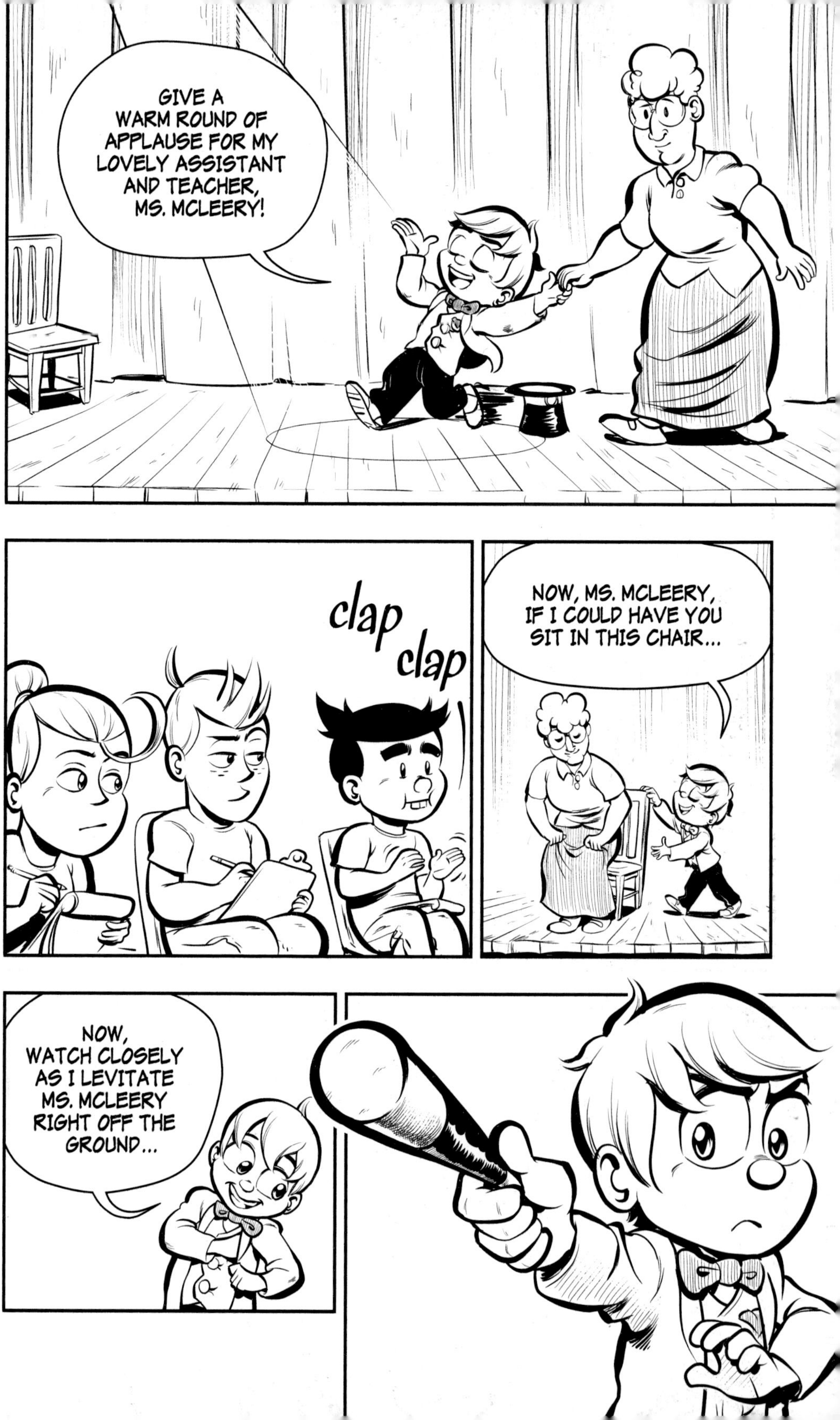
GIVE A WARM ROUND OF APPLAUSE FOR MY LOVELY ASSISTANT AND TEACHER, MS. MCLEERY!
clap
clap
NOW, MS. MCLEERY, IF I COULD HAVE YOU SIT IN THIS CHAIR...
NOW, WATCH CLOSELY AS I LEVITATE MS. MCLEERY RIGHT OFF THE GROUND...

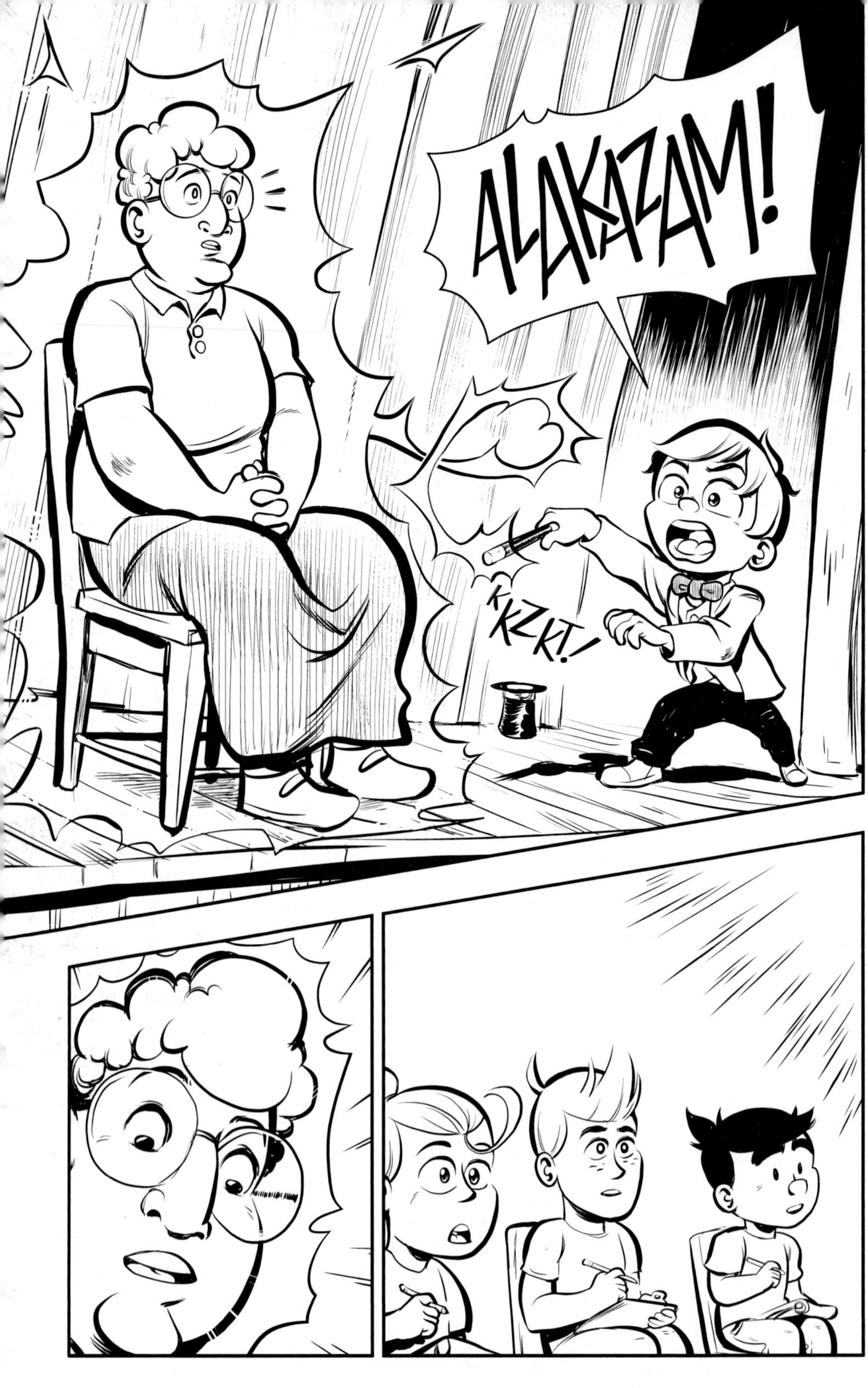
ALAKAZAM!
KKZKT!

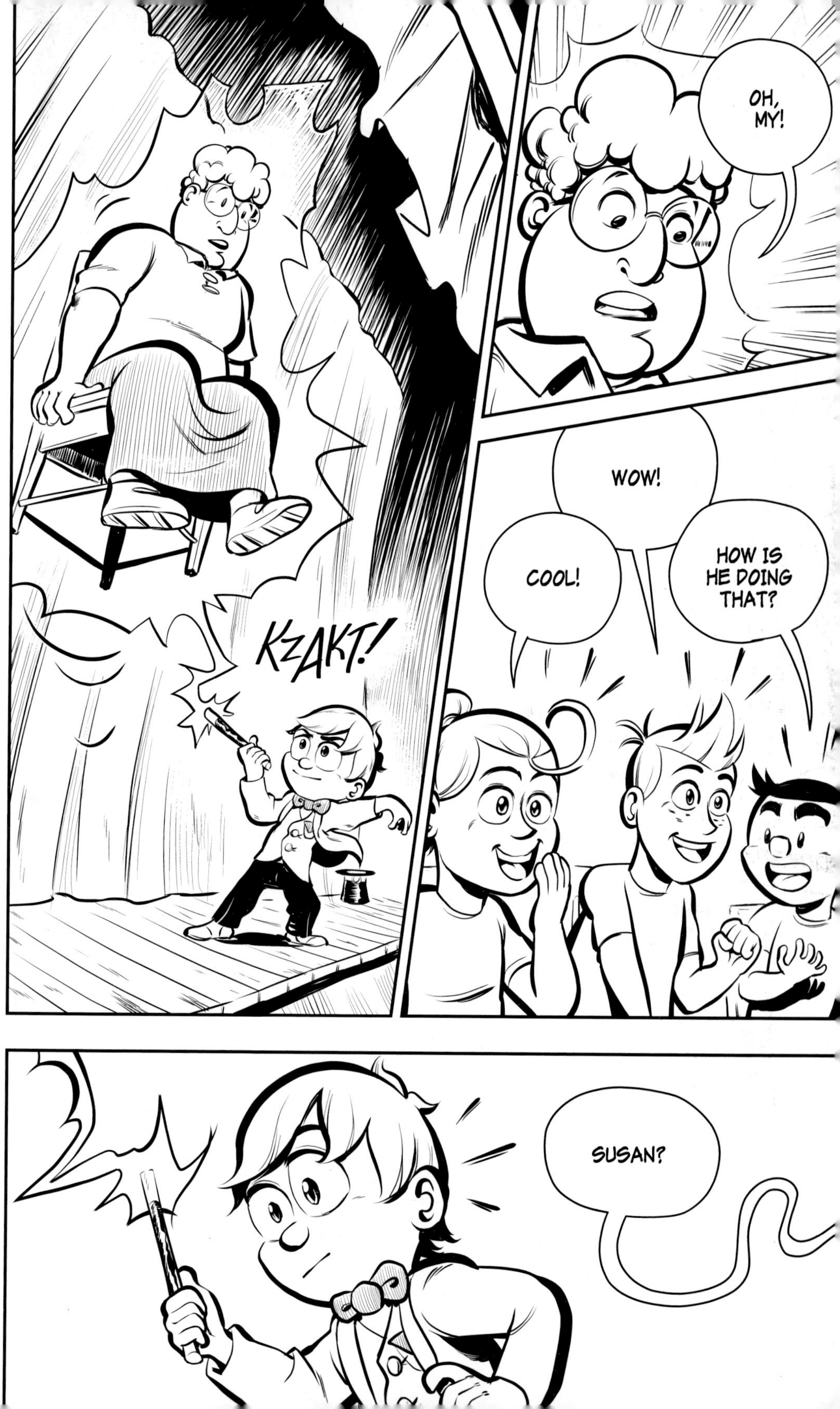

KZAKT!
OH, MY!
WOW!
COOL!
HOW IS HE DOING THAT?
SUSAN?

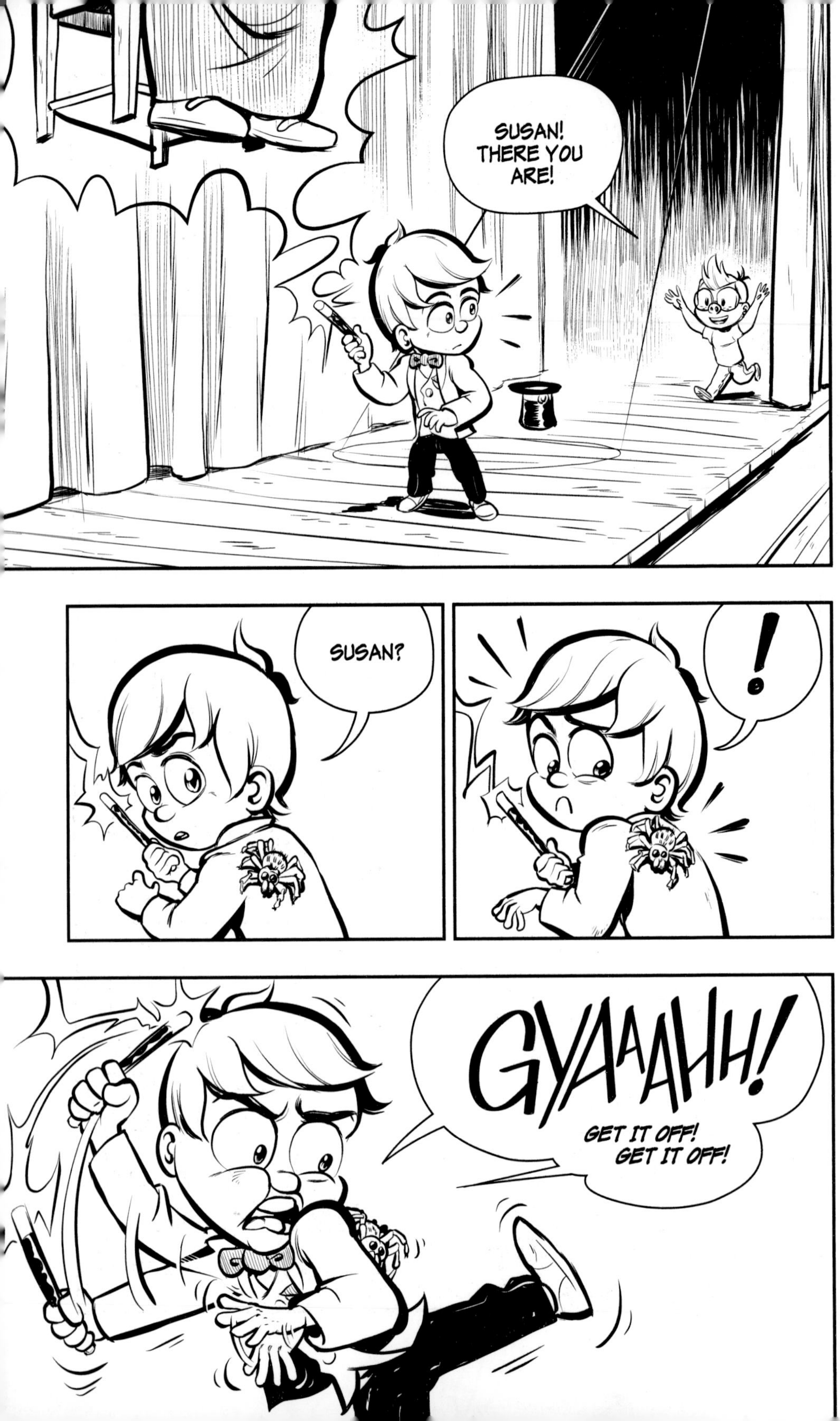
SUSAN! THERE YOU ARE!
SUSAN?
!
GYAAAHH!
GET IT OFF! GET IT OFF!

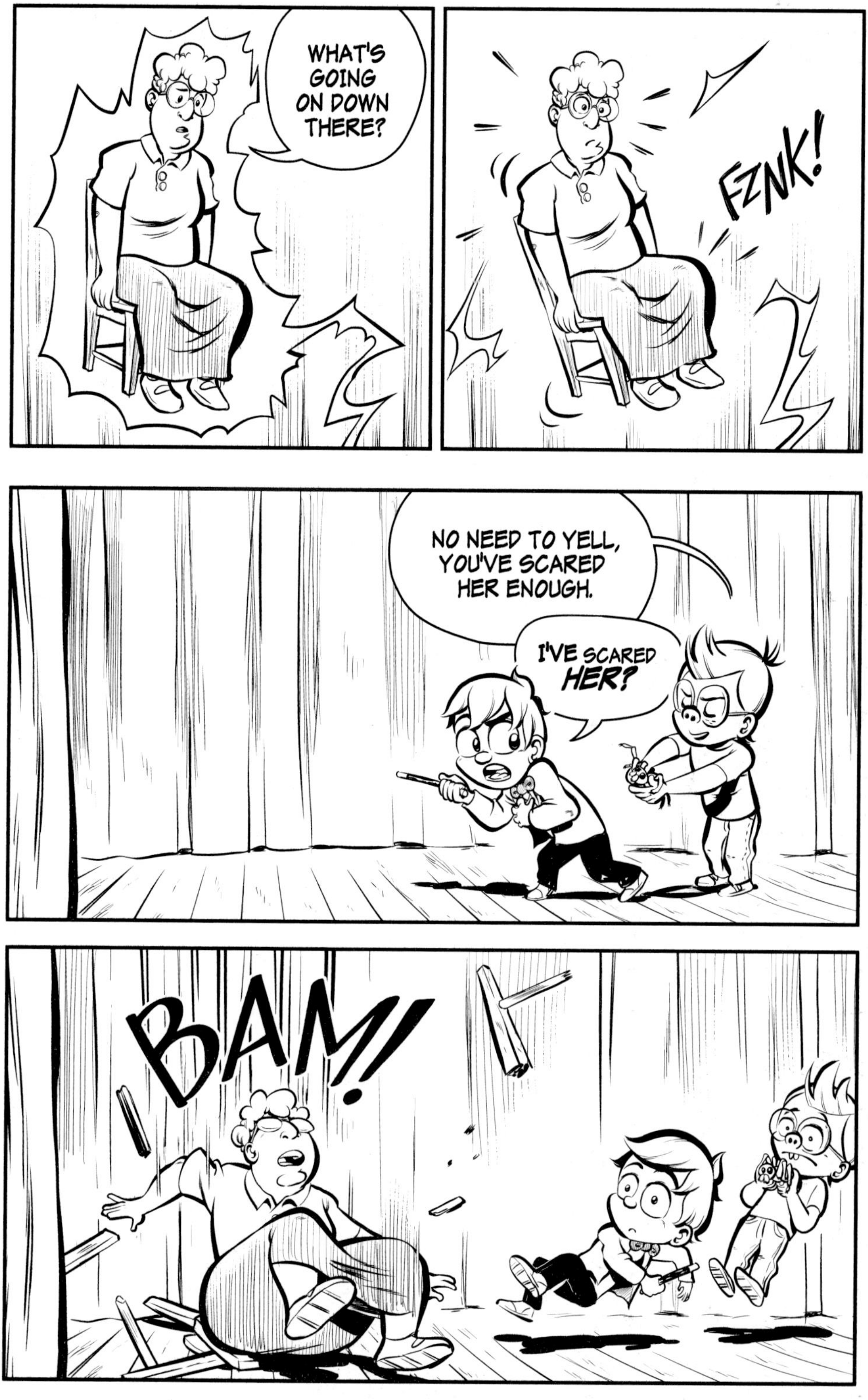
WHAT'S GOING ON DOWN THERE?
FZNK!
NO NEED TO YELL, YOU'VE SCARED HER ENOUGH.
I'VE SCARED HER?
BAM!

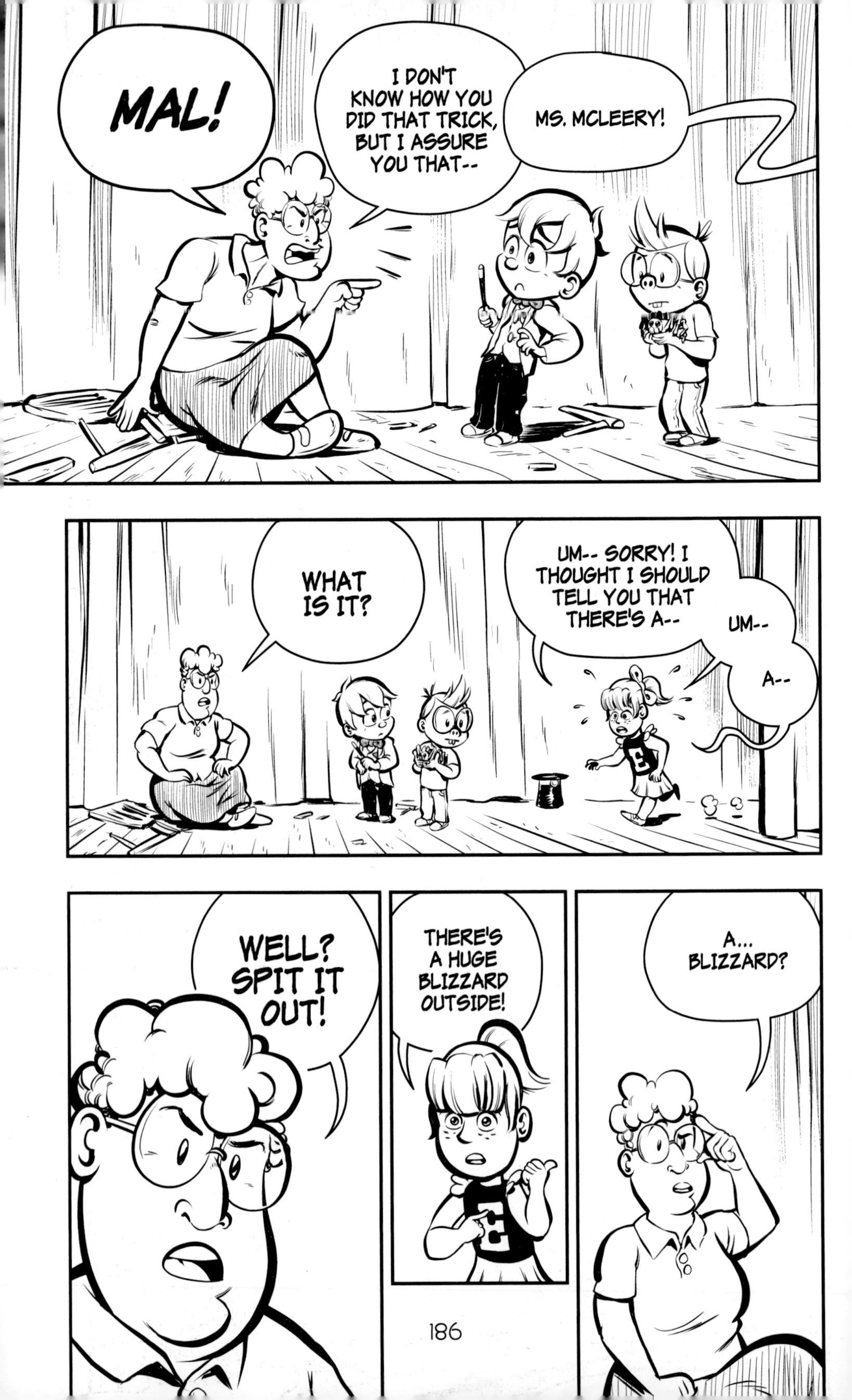
MAL!
I DON'T KNOW HOW YOU DID THAT TRICK, BUT I ASSURE YOU THAT--
MS. MCLEERY!
WHAT IS IT?
UM-- SORRY! I THOUGHT I SHOULD TELL YOU THAT THERE'S A--
UM--
A--
WELL? SPIT IT OUT!
THERE'S A HUGE BLIZZARD OUTSIDE!
A... BLIZZARD?

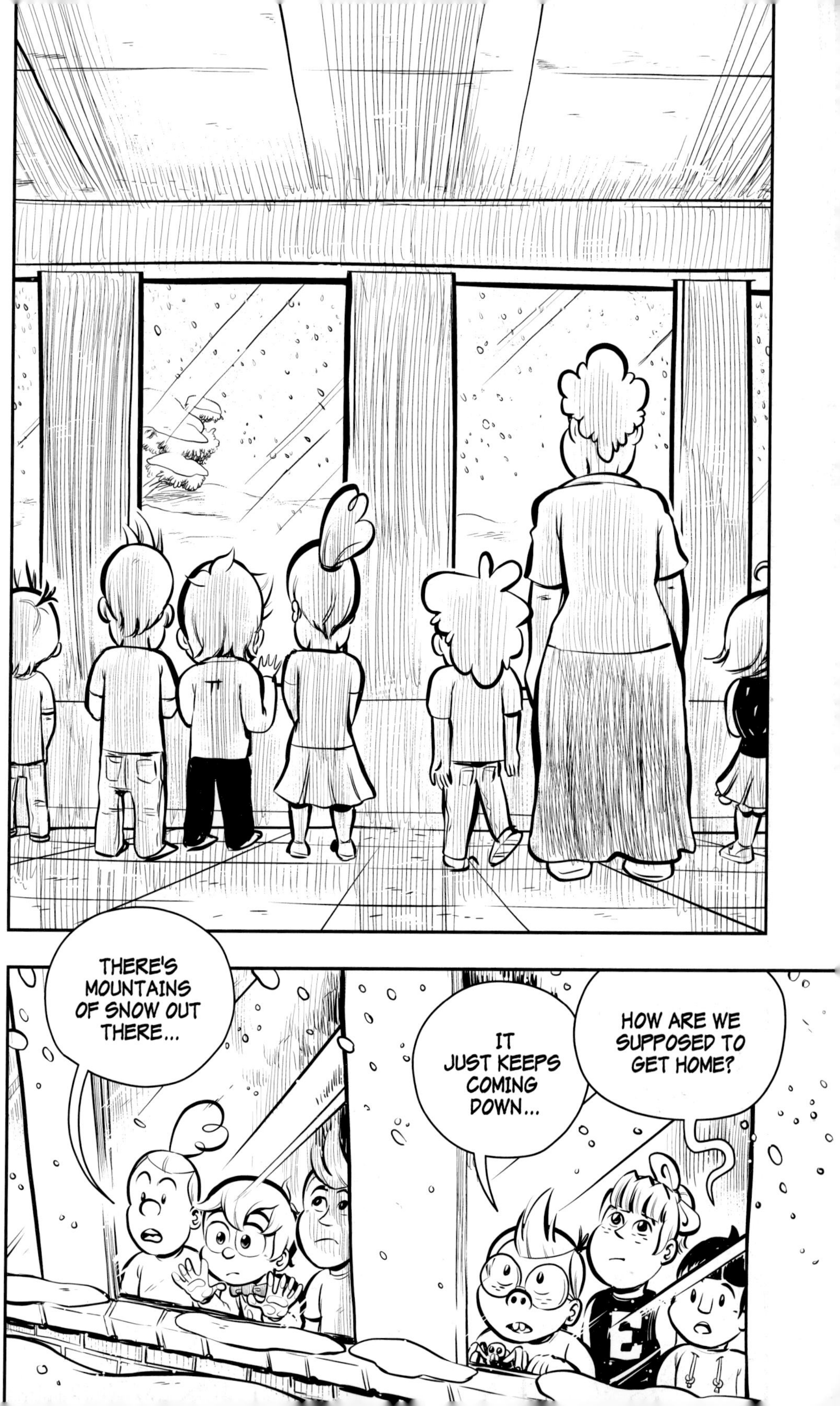
THERE'S MOUNTAINS OF SNOW OUT THERE...
IT JUST KEEPS COMING DOWN...
HOW ARE WE SUPPOSED TO GET HOME?

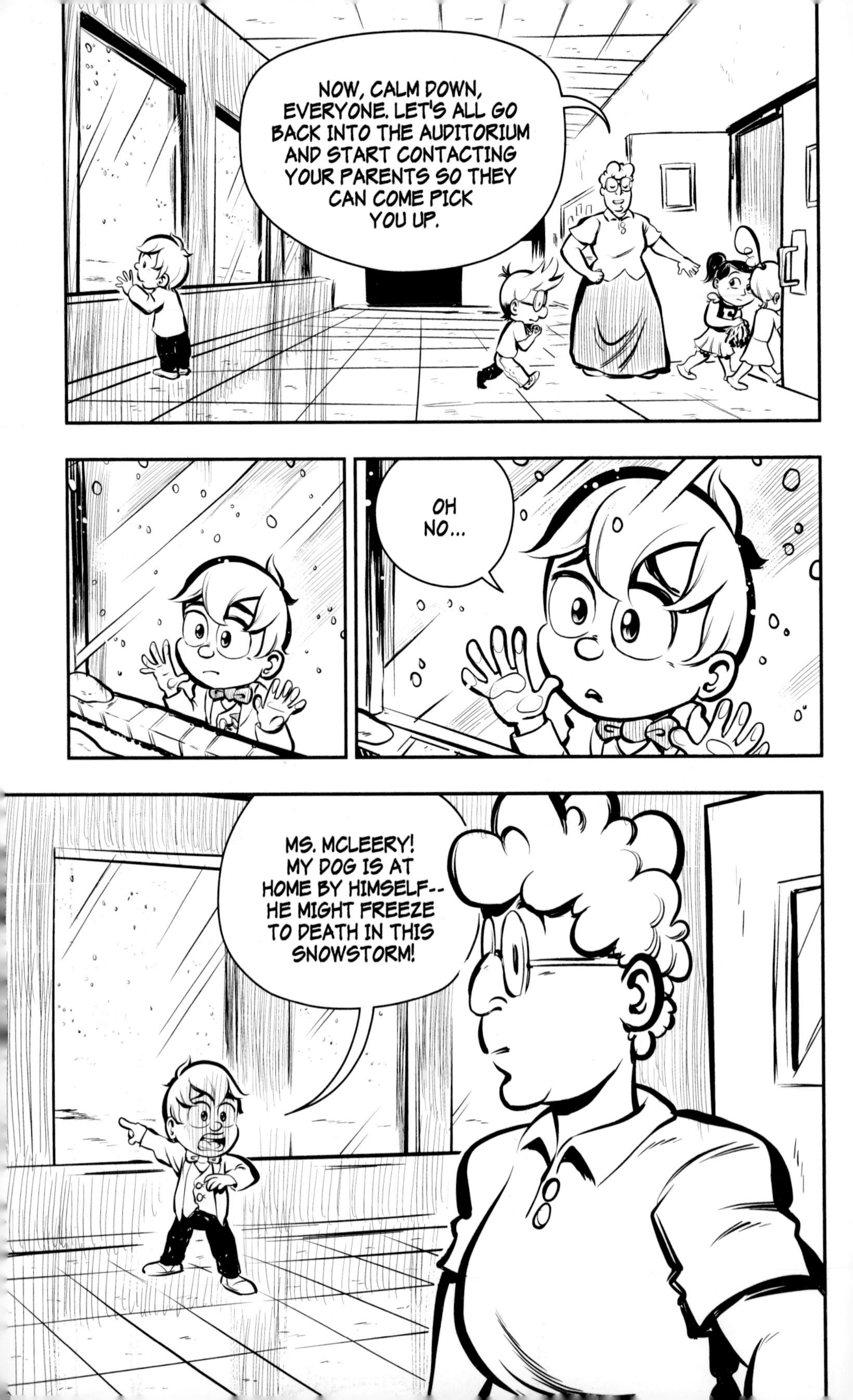
NOW, CALM DOWN, EVERYONE. LET'S ALL GO BACK INTO THE AUDITORIUM AND START CONTACTING YOUR PARENTS SO THEY CAN COME PICK YOU UP.
OH NO...
MS. MCLEERY! MY DOG IS AT HOME BY HIMSELF-- HE MIGHT FREEZE TO DEATH IN THIS SNOWSTORM!

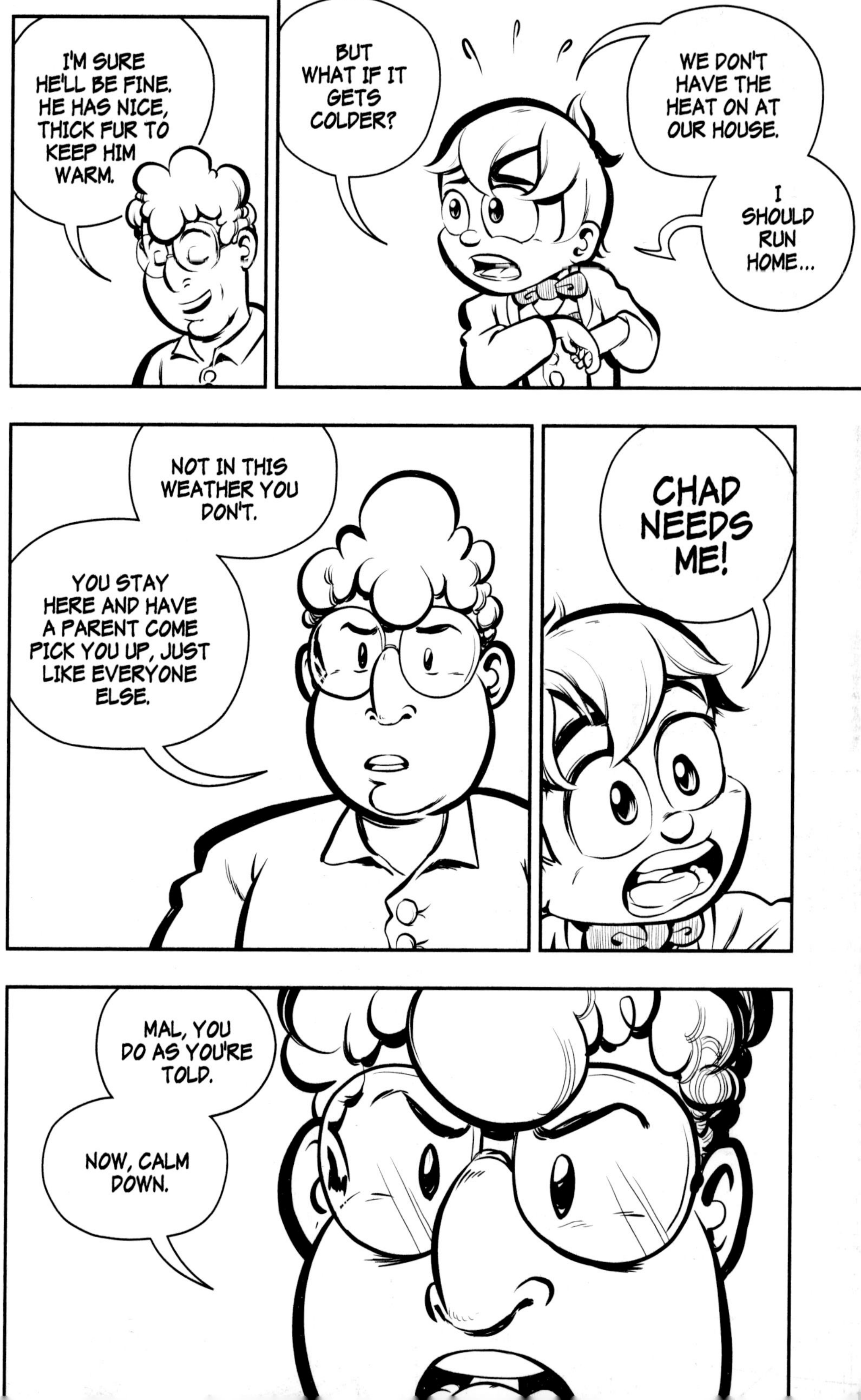
I'M SURE HE'LL BE FINE. HE HAS NICE, THICK FUR TO KEEP HIM WARM.
BUT WHAT IF IT GETS COLDER?
WE DON'T HAVE THE HEAT ON AT OUR HOUSE.
I SHOULD RUN HOME...
NOT IN THIS WEATHER YOU DON'T.
YOU STAY HERE AND HAVE A PARENT COME PICK YOU UP, JUST LIKE EVERYONE ELSE.
CHAD NEEDS ME!
MAL, YOU DO AS YOU'RE TOLD.
NOW, CALM DOWN.

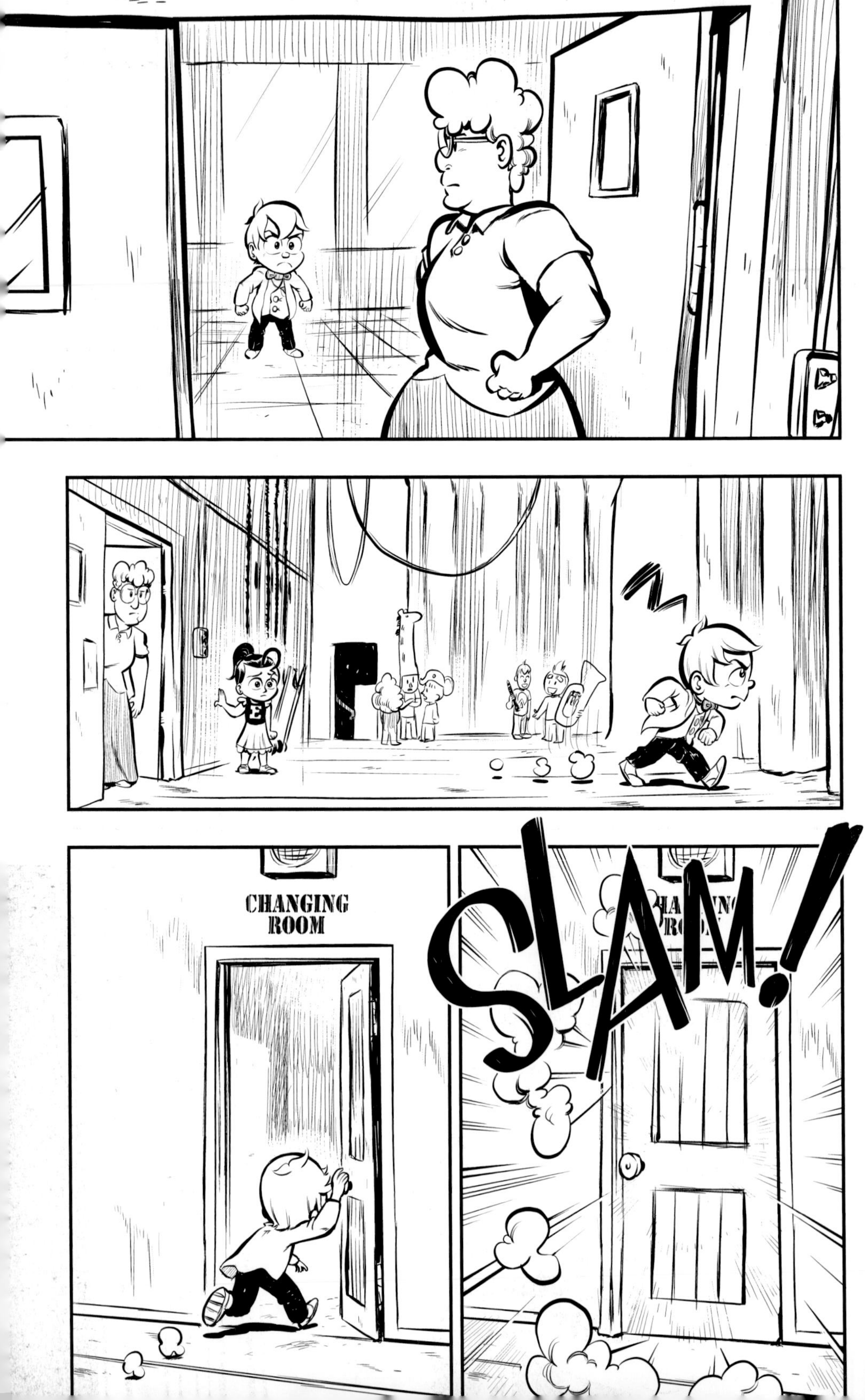
CHANGING
ROOM
SLAM!

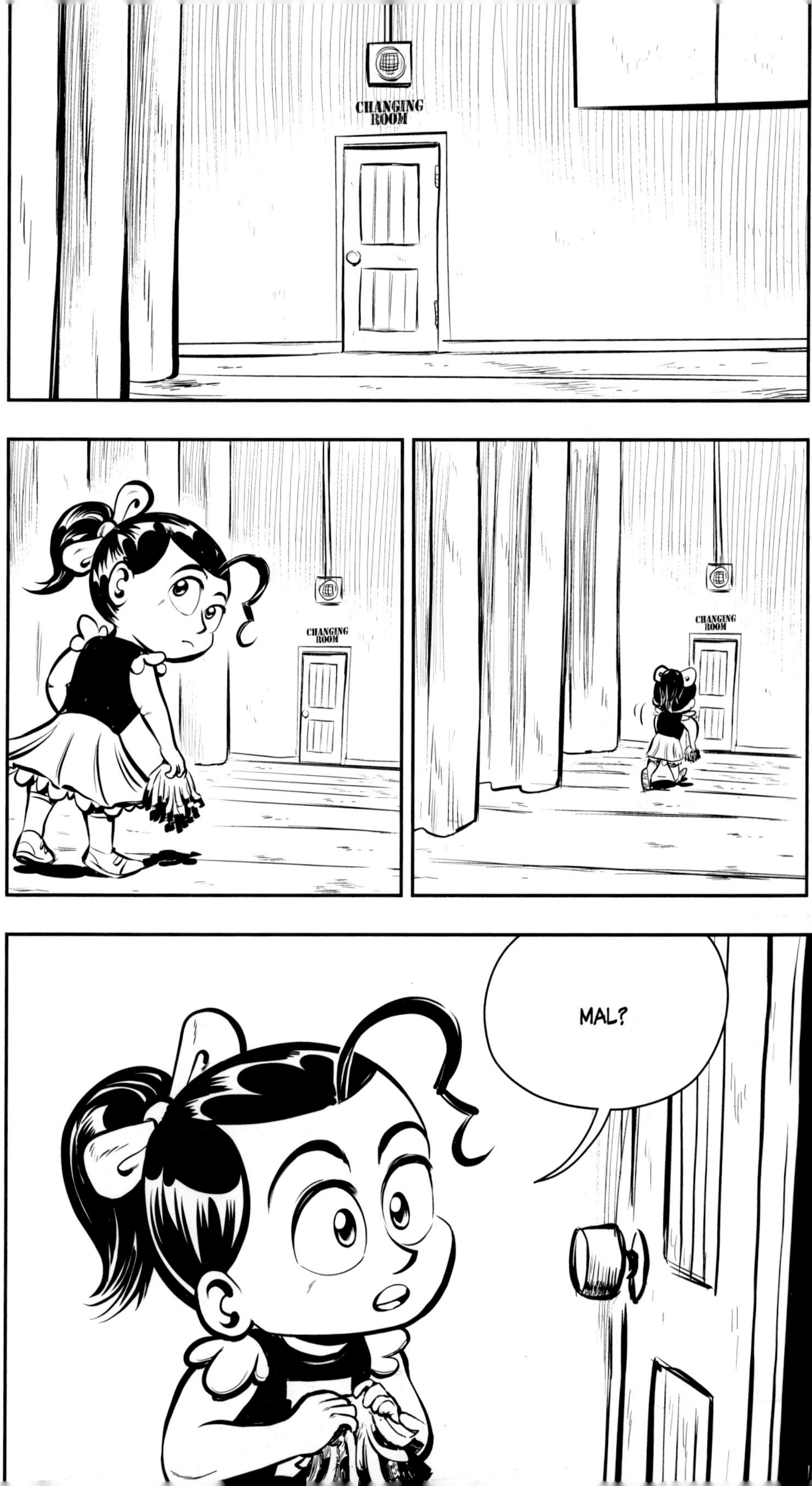
CHANGING ROOM
CHANGING ROOM
CHANGING ROOM
MAL?

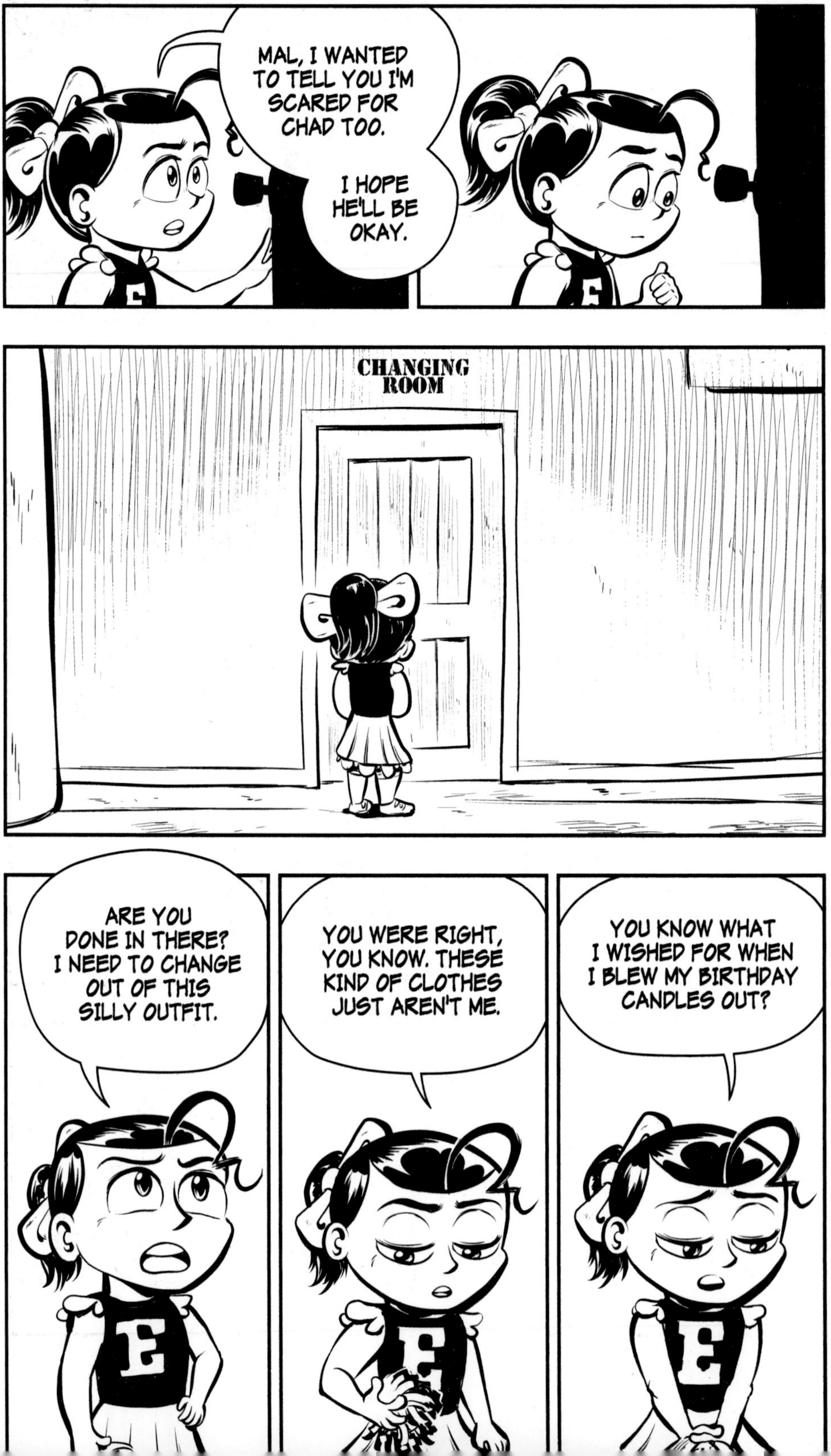
MAL, I WANTED TO TELL YOU I'M SCARED FOR CHAD TOO.
I HOPE HE'LL BE OKAY.
CHANGING ROOM
ARE YOU DONE IN THERE? I NEED TO CHANGE OUT OF THIS SILLY OUTFIT.
YOU WERE RIGHT, YOU KNOW. THESE KIND OF CLOTHES JUST AREN'T ME.
YOU KNOW WHAT I WISHED FOR WHEN I BLEW MY BIRTHDAY CANDLES OUT?

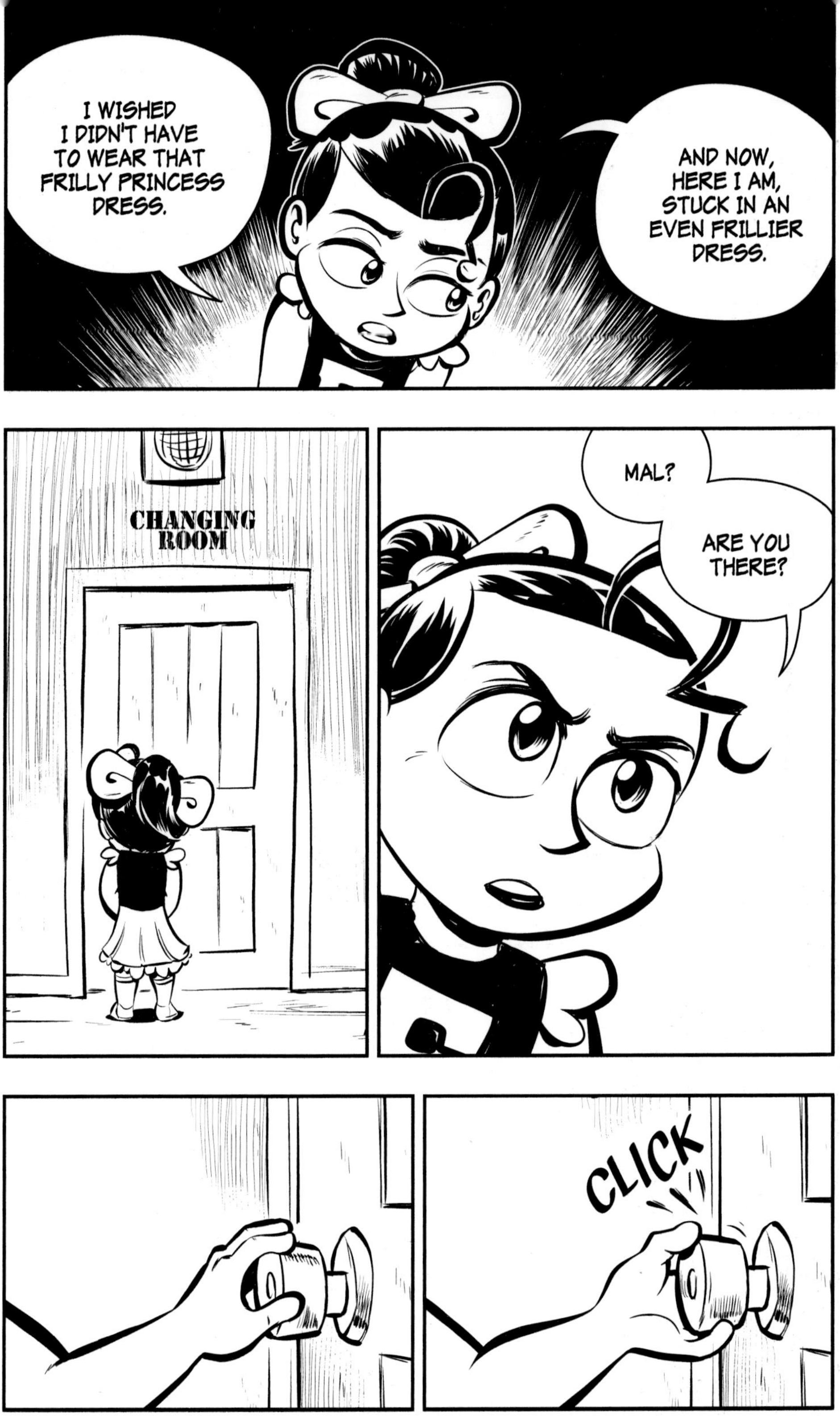
I WISHED I DIDN'T HAVE TO WEAR THAT FRILLY PRINCESS DRESS.
AND NOW, HERE I AM, STUCK IN AN EVEN FRILLIER DRESS.
CHANGING ROOM
MAL?
ARE YOU THERE?
CLICK

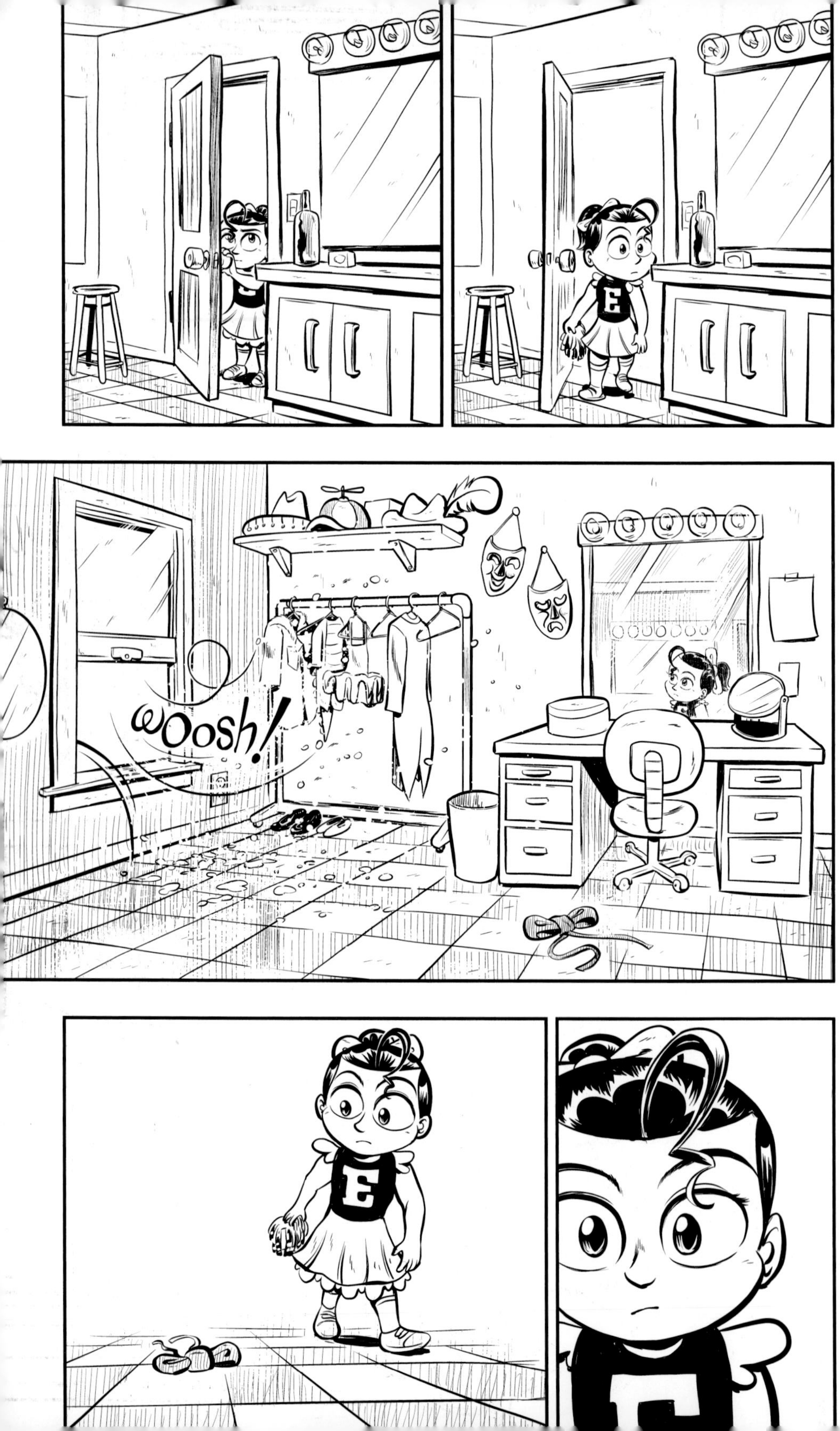
wOosh!

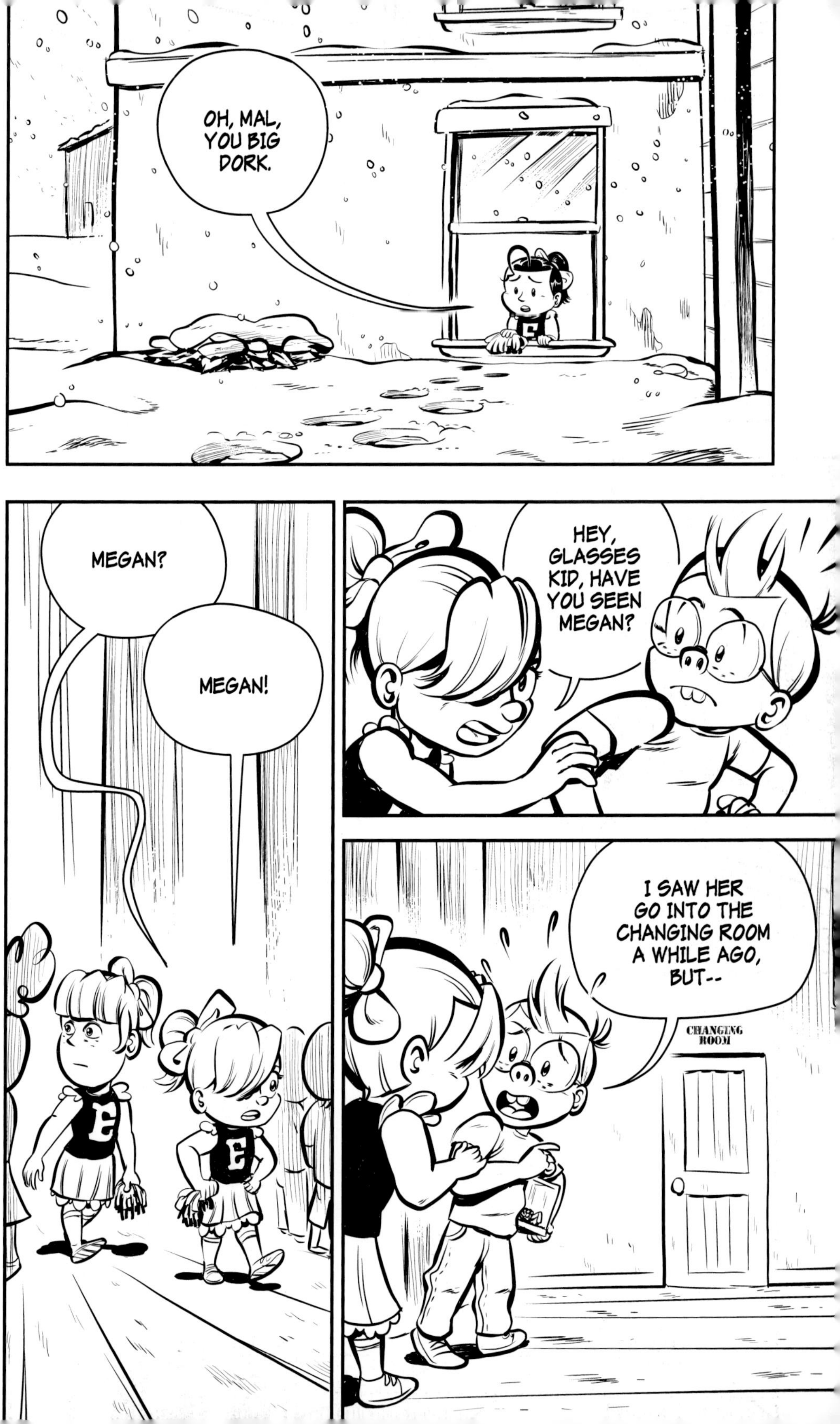
OH, MAL, YOU BIG DORK.
MEGAN?
MEGAN!
HEY, GLASSES KID, HAVE YOU SEEN MEGAN?
I SAW HER GO INTO THE CHANGING ROOM A WHILE AGO, BUT--
CHANGING ROOM

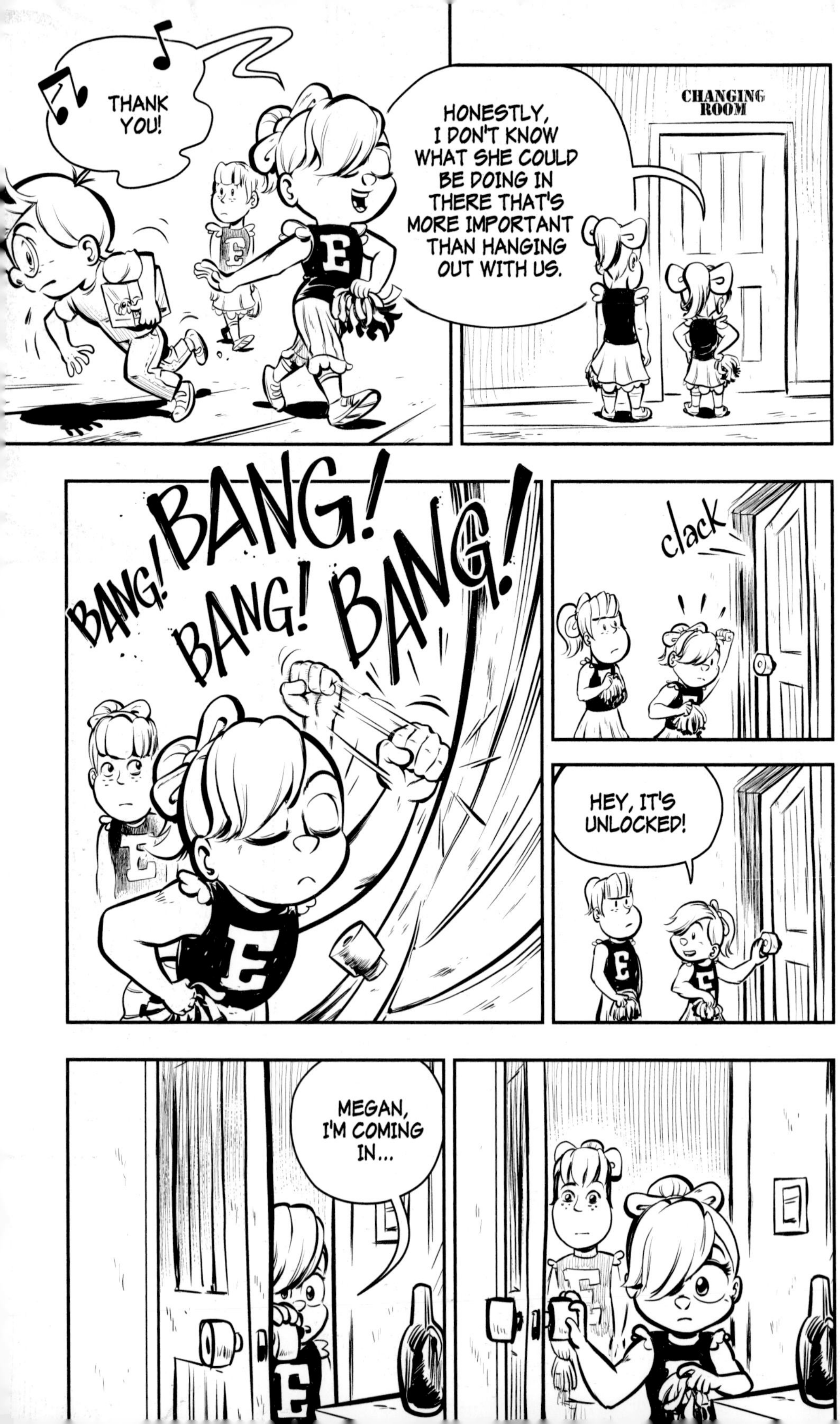
THANK YOU!
HONESTLY, I DON'T KNOW WHAT SHE COULD BE DOING IN THERE THAT'S MORE IMPORTANT THAN HANGING OUT WITH US.
CHANGING ROOM
BANG! BANG! BANG! BANG! BANG!
clack
HEY, IT'S UNLOCKED!
MEGAN, I'M COMING IN...

THERE YOU ARE!

WHAT ARE YOU WEARING ALL *THAT* FOR?

WELL, I CAN'T VERY WELL WEAR A CHEERLEADER OUTFIT IN THE SNOW, CAN I?

IN THE SNOW--

WHERE ARE YOU GOING?

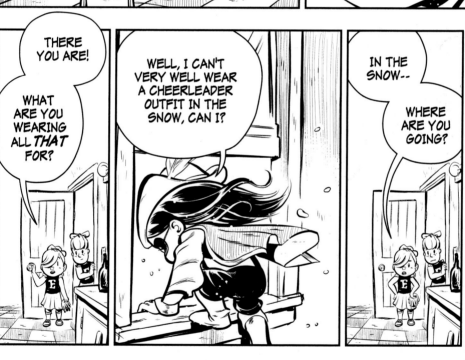

KNCH!

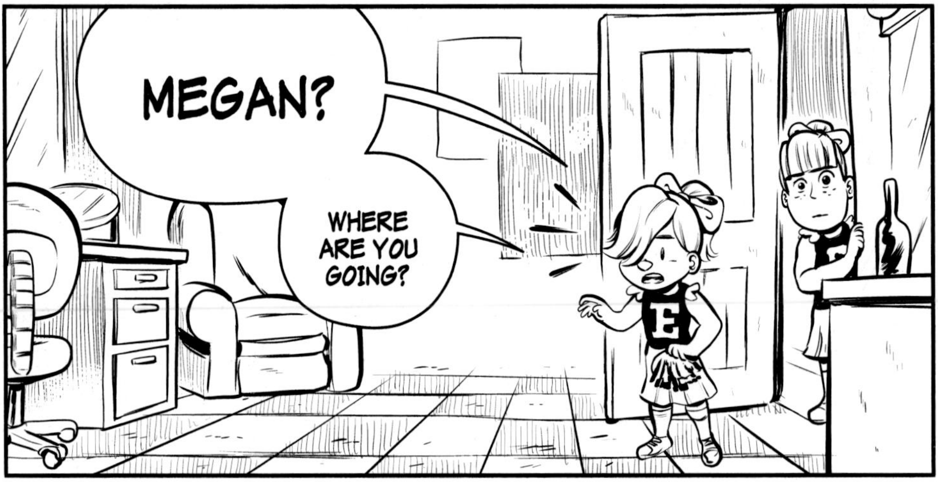
MEGAN?
WHERE ARE YOU GOING?

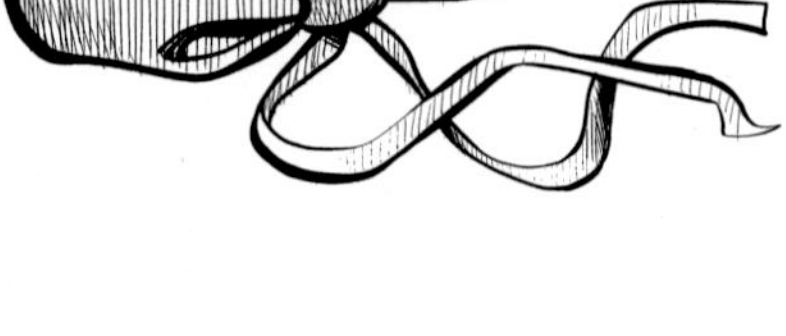

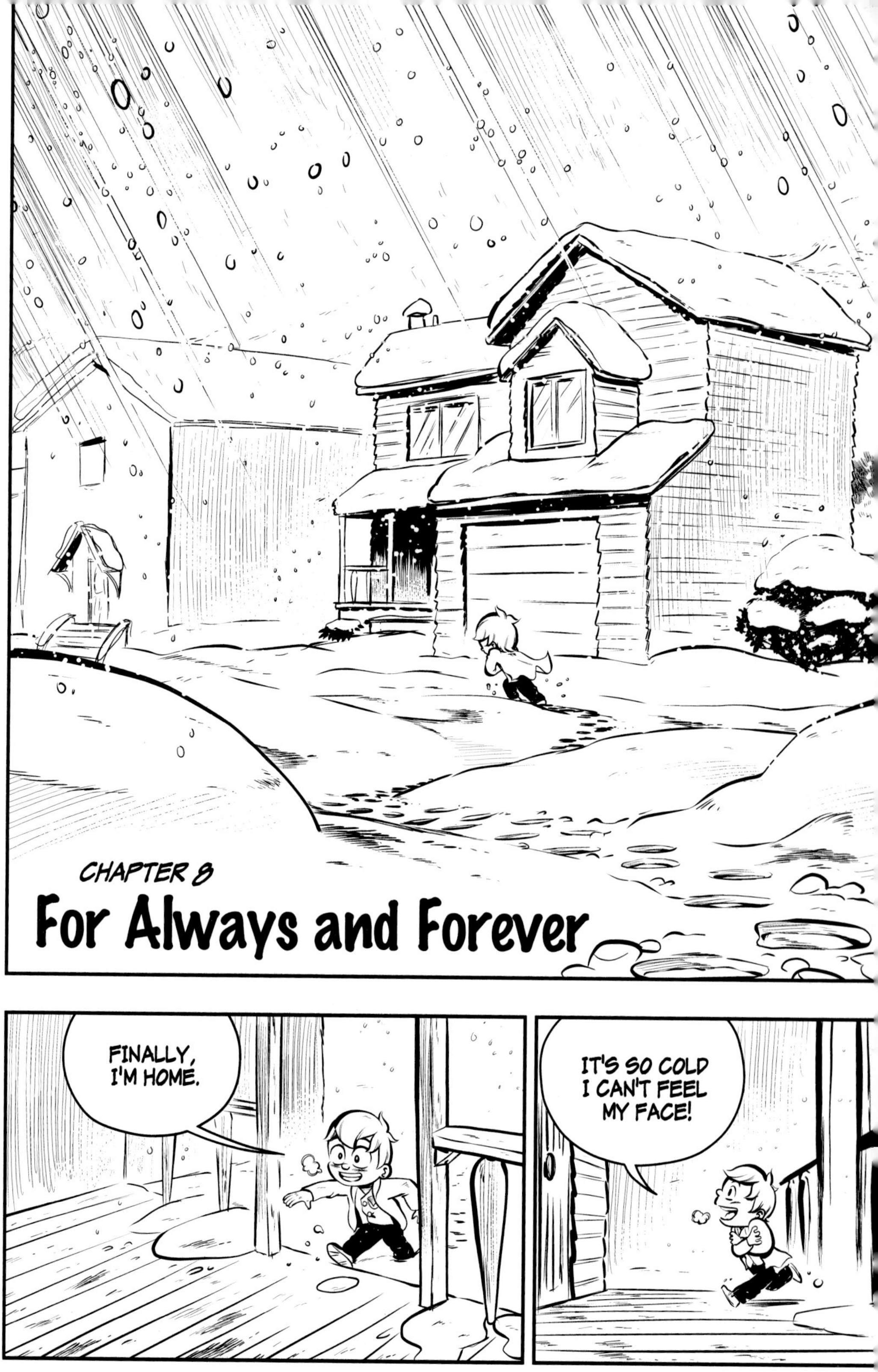
CHAPTER 8
For Always and Forever
FINALLY, I'M HOME.
IT'S SO COLD I CAN'T FEEL MY FACE!

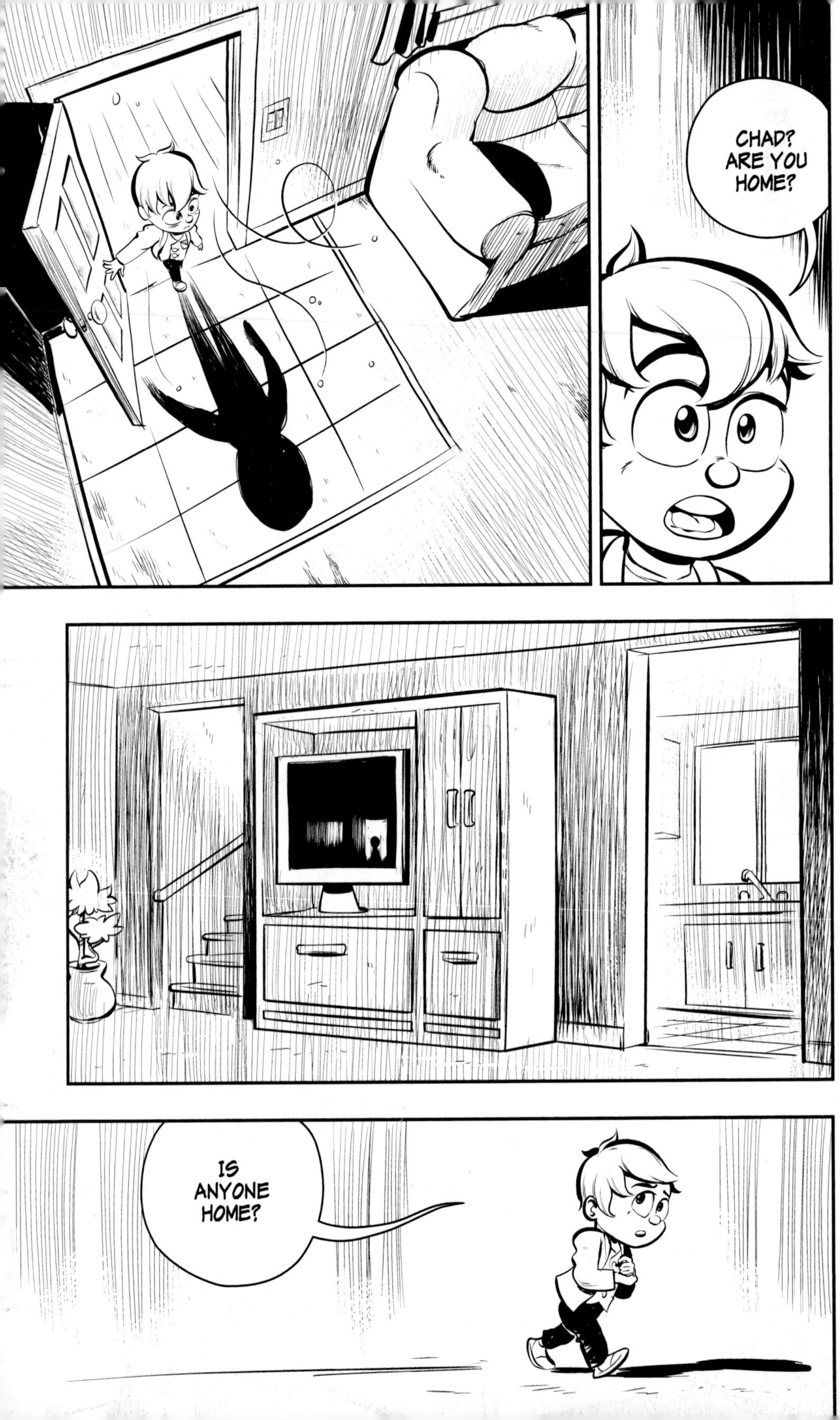
CHAD? ARE YOU HOME?
IS ANYONE HOME?

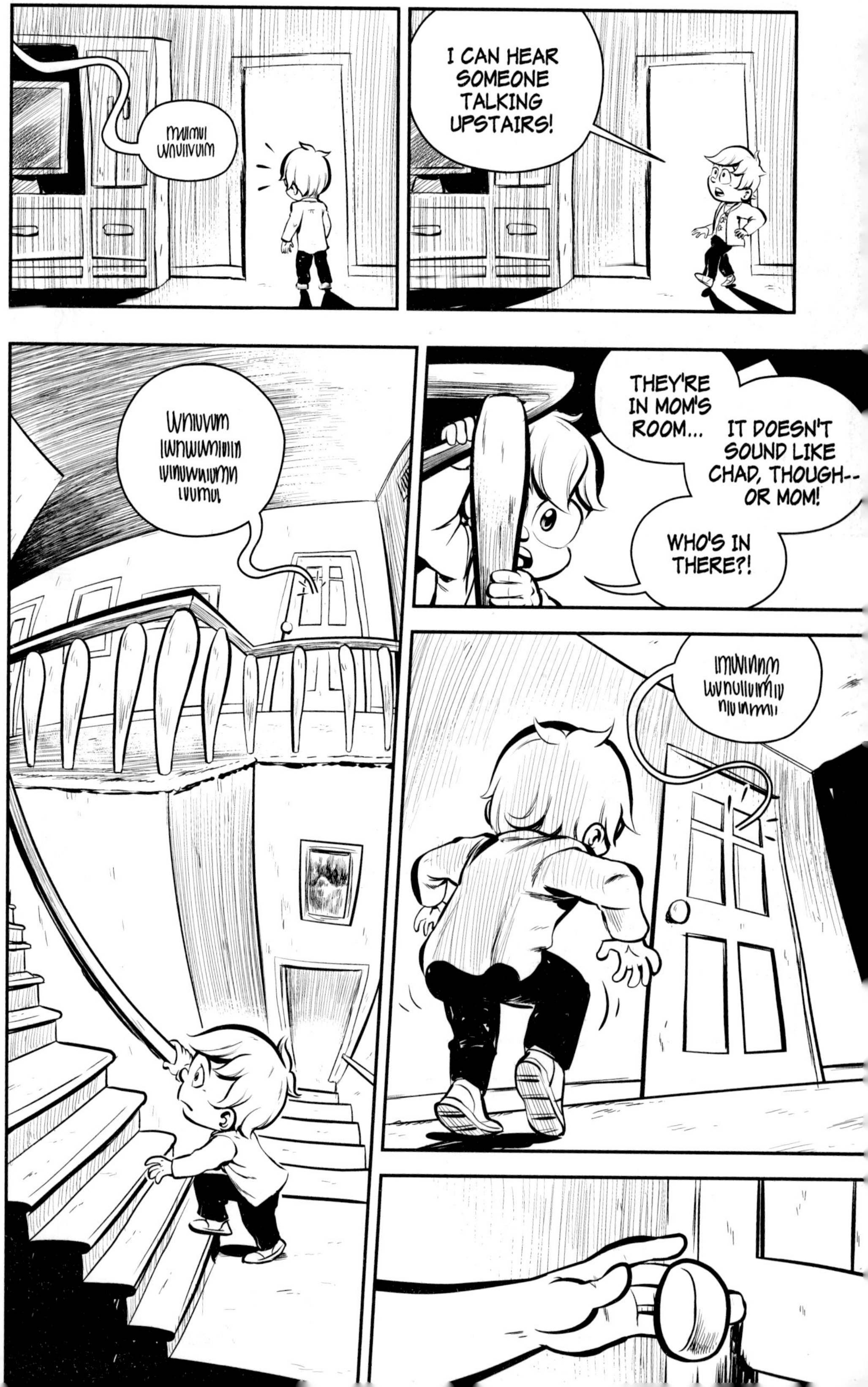
I CAN HEAR SOMEONE TALKING UPSTAIRS!
THEY'RE IN MOM'S ROOM...
IT DOESN'T SOUND LIKE CHAD, THOUGH-- OR MOM!
WHO'S IN THERE?!

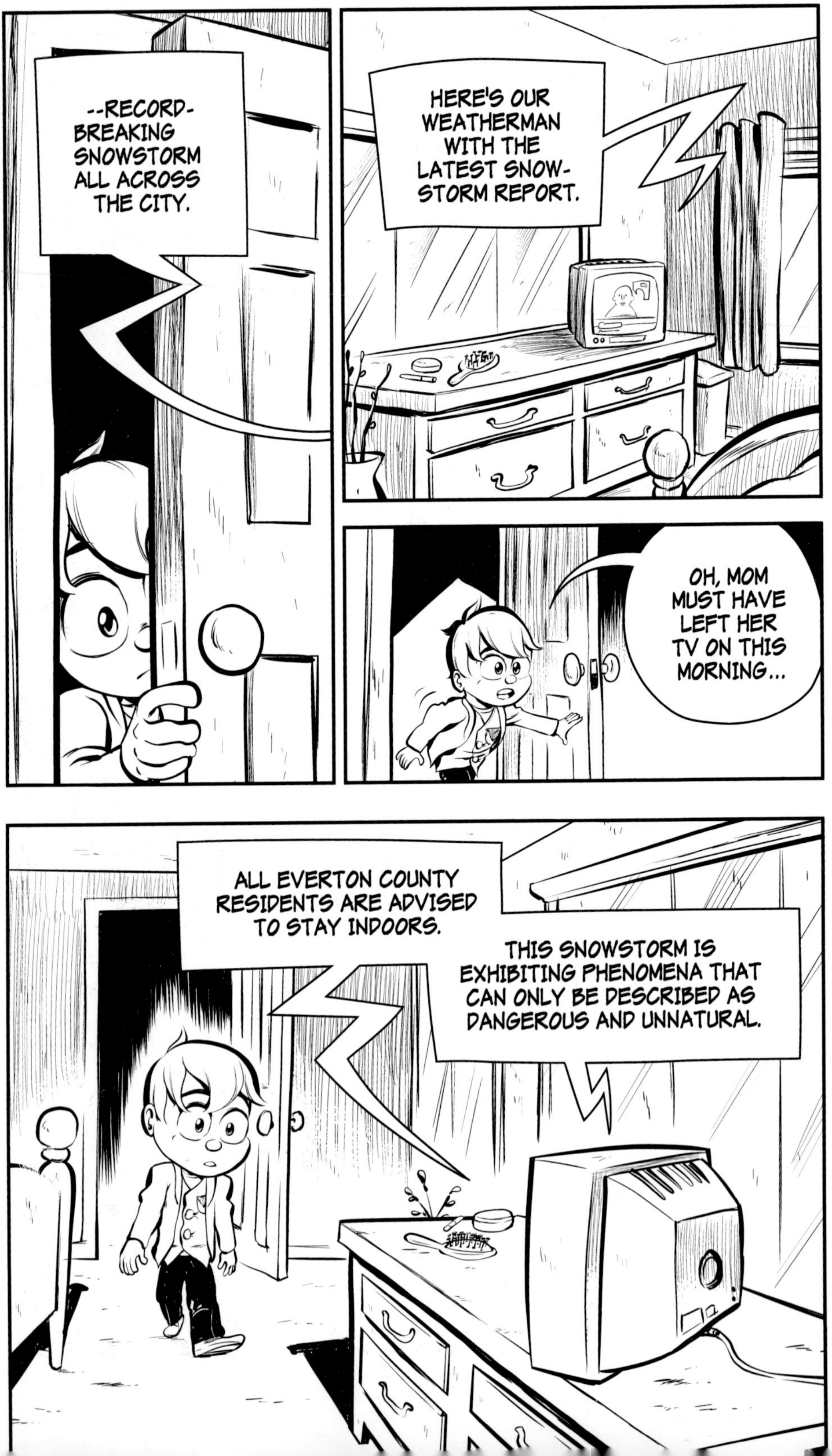
--RECORD-BREAKING SNOWSTORM ALL ACROSS THE CITY.
HERE'S OUR WEATHERMAN WITH THE LATEST SNOW-STORM REPORT.
OH, MOM MUST HAVE LEFT HER TV ON THIS MORNING...
ALL EVERTON COUNTY RESIDENTS ARE ADVISED TO STAY INDOORS.
THIS SNOWSTORM IS EXHIBITING PHENOMENA THAT CAN ONLY BE DESCRIBED AS DANGEROUS AND UNNATURAL.

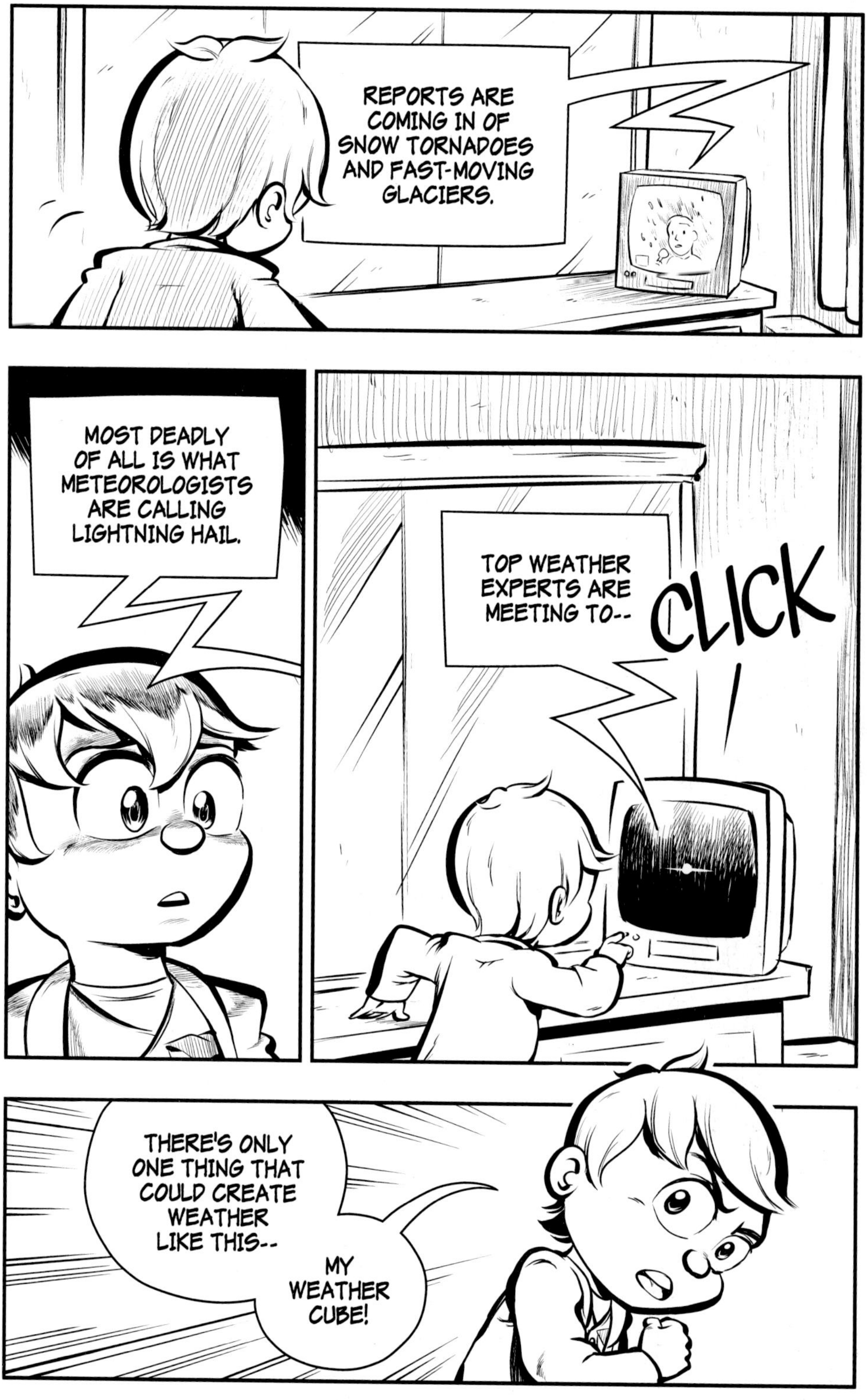
REPORTS ARE COMING IN OF SNOW TORNADOES AND FAST-MOVING GLACIERS.
MOST DEADLY OF ALL IS WHAT METEOROLOGISTS ARE CALLING LIGHTNING HAIL.
TOP WEATHER EXPERTS ARE MEETING TO--
CLICK
THERE'S ONLY ONE THING THAT COULD CREATE WEATHER LIKE THIS--
MY WEATHER CUBE!

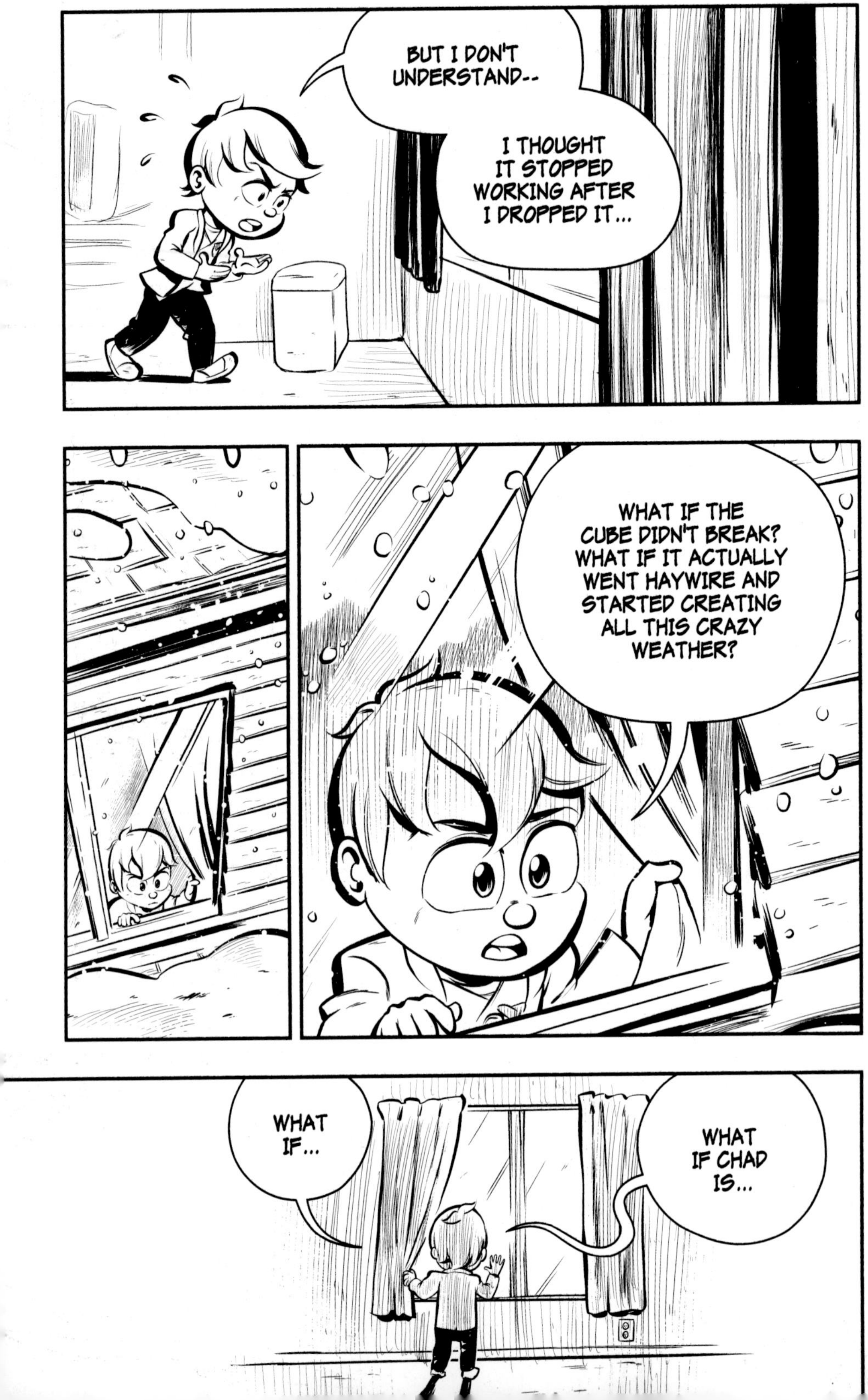
BUT I DON'T UNDERSTAND--
I THOUGHT IT STOPPED WORKING AFTER I DROPPED IT...
WHAT IF THE CUBE DIDN'T BREAK? WHAT IF IT ACTUALLY WENT HAYWIRE AND STARTED CREATING ALL THIS CRAZY WEATHER?
WHAT IF...
WHAT IF CHAD IS...

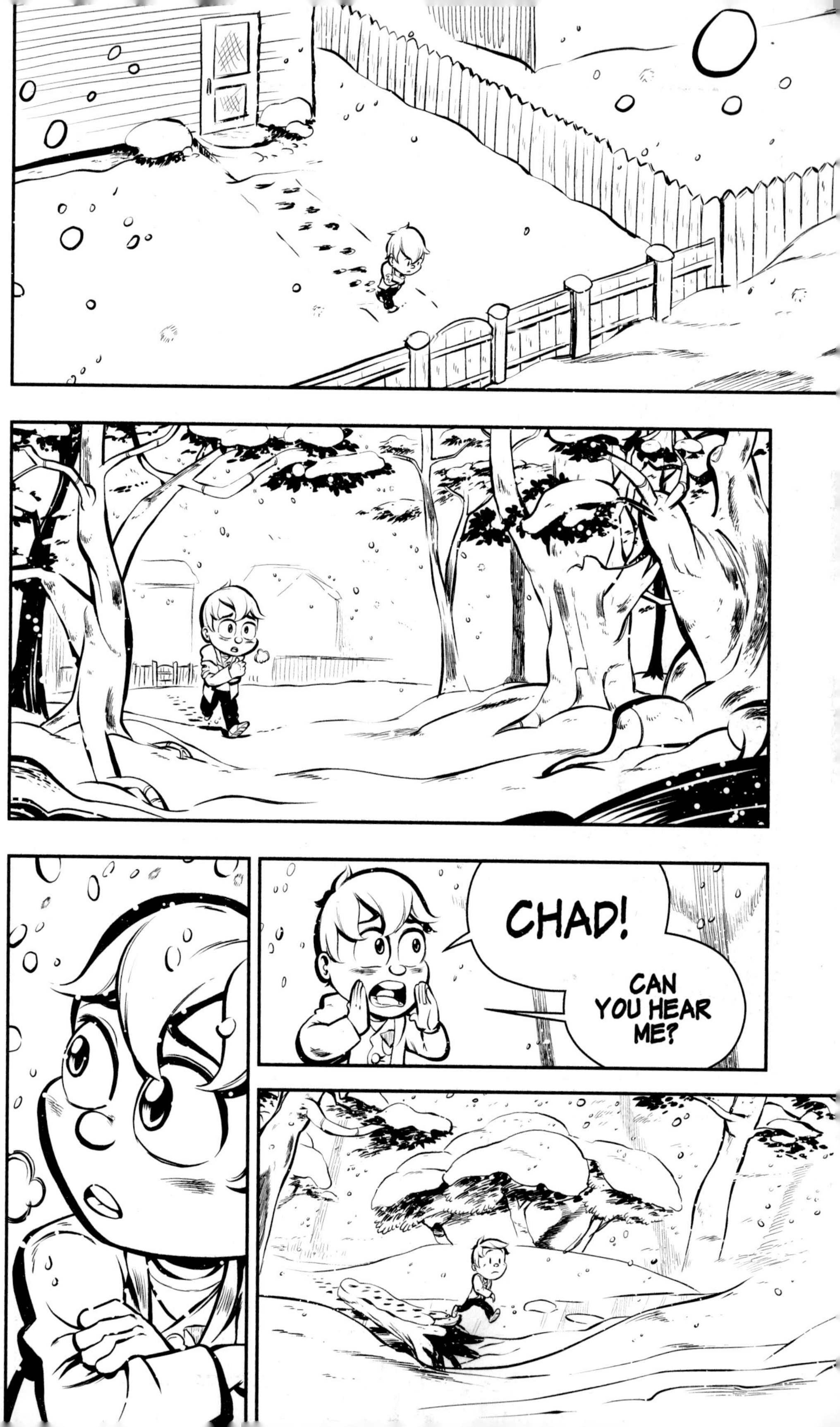
CHAD!
CAN YOU HEAR ME?

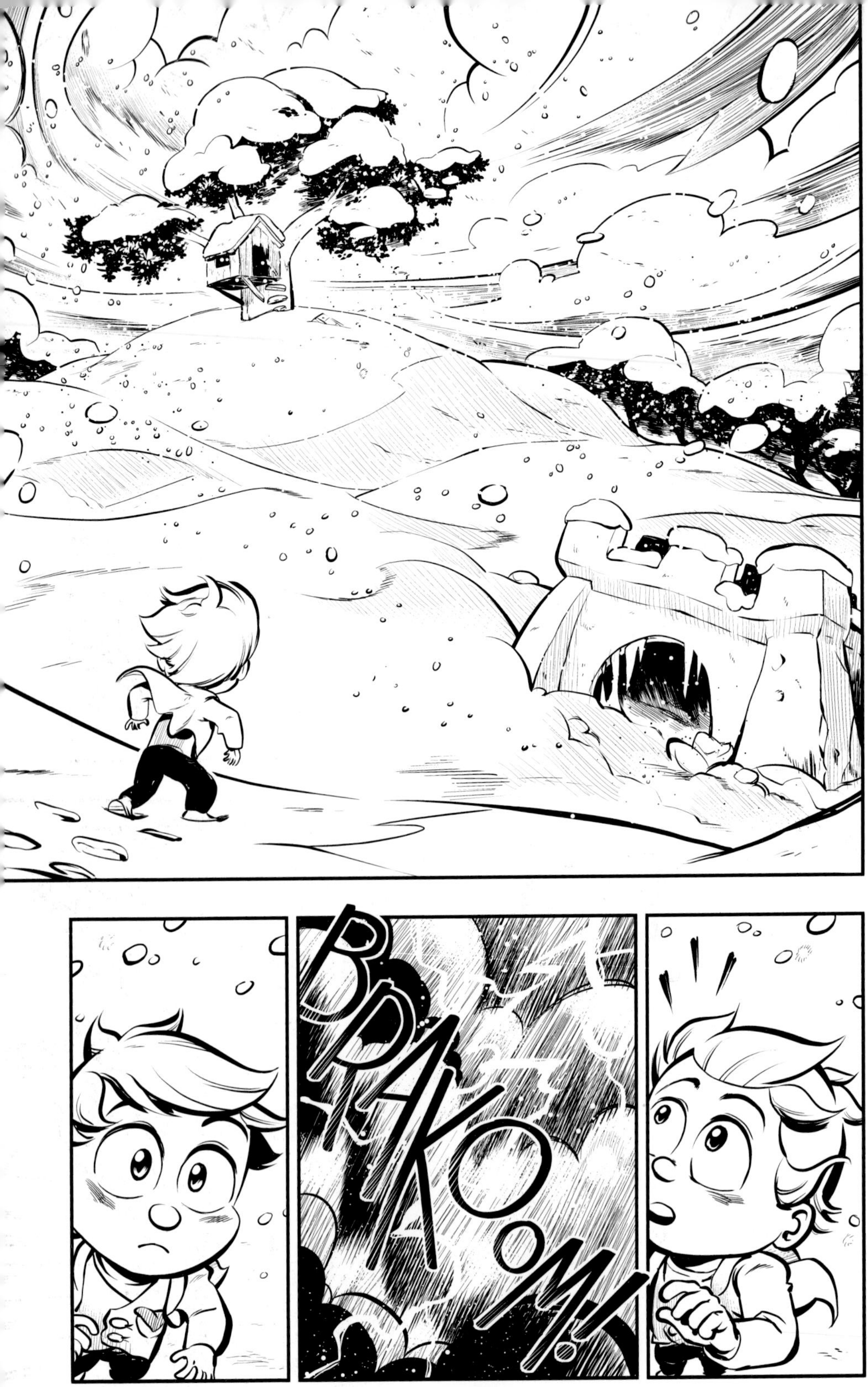

BDAKOOM!

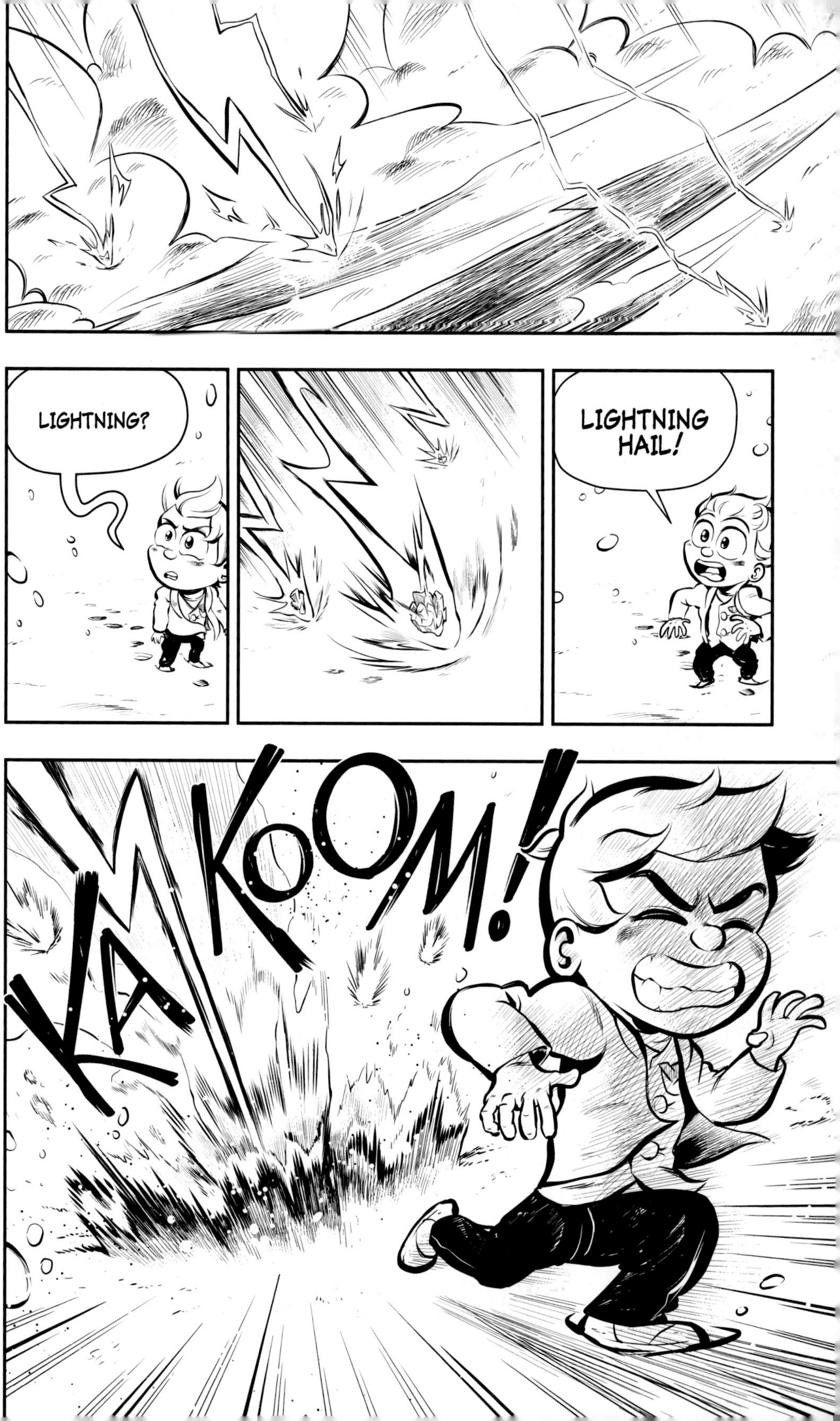
LIGHTNING?
LIGHTNING HAIL!
KA-KOOM!

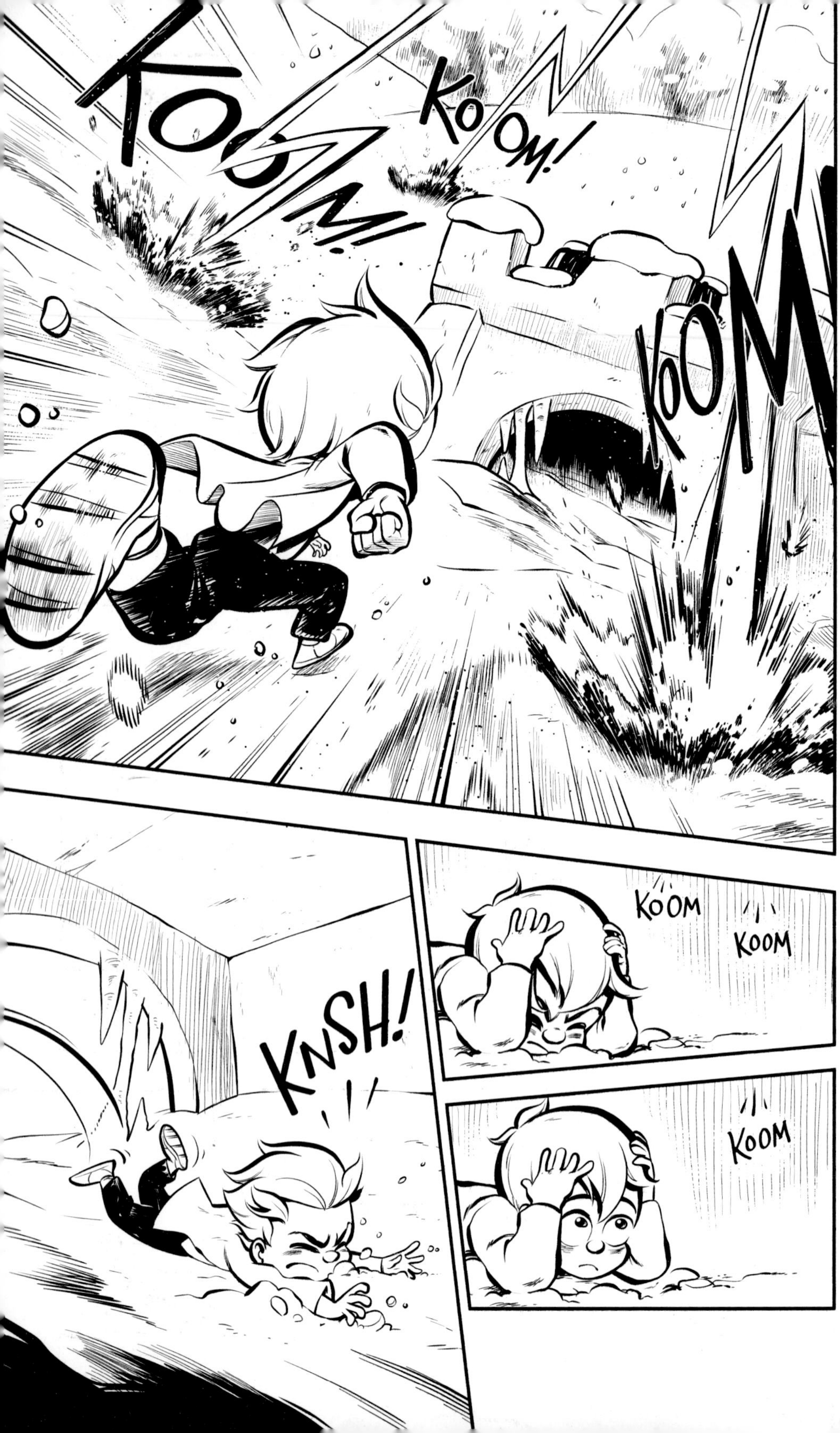
KOOM!!
KOOM!
KOOM
KNSH!
KOOM
KOOM
KOOM

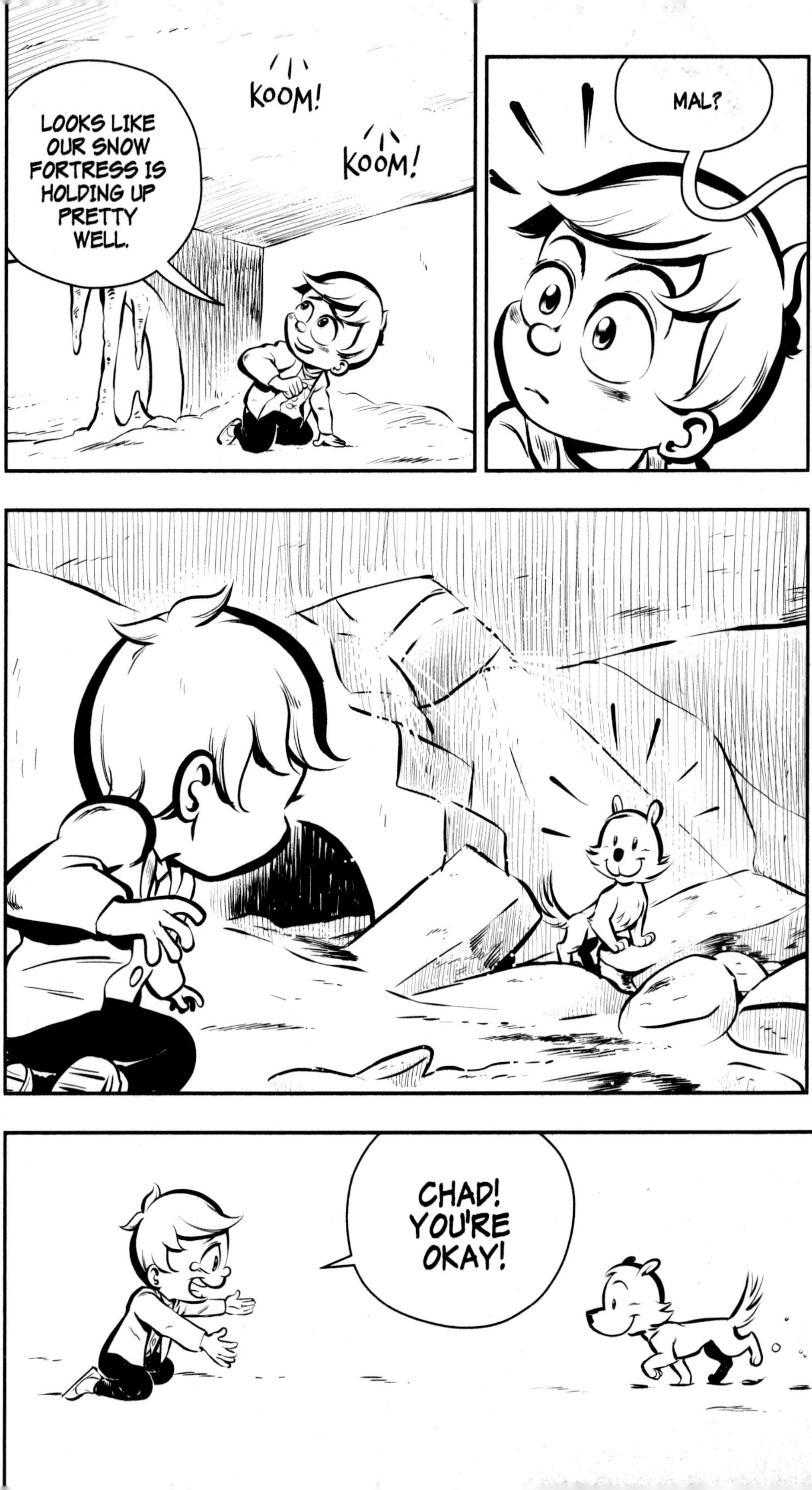
KOOM!
KOOM!
LOOKS LIKE OUR SNOW FORTRESS IS HOLDING UP PRETTY WELL.
MAL?
CHAD! YOU'RE OKAY!

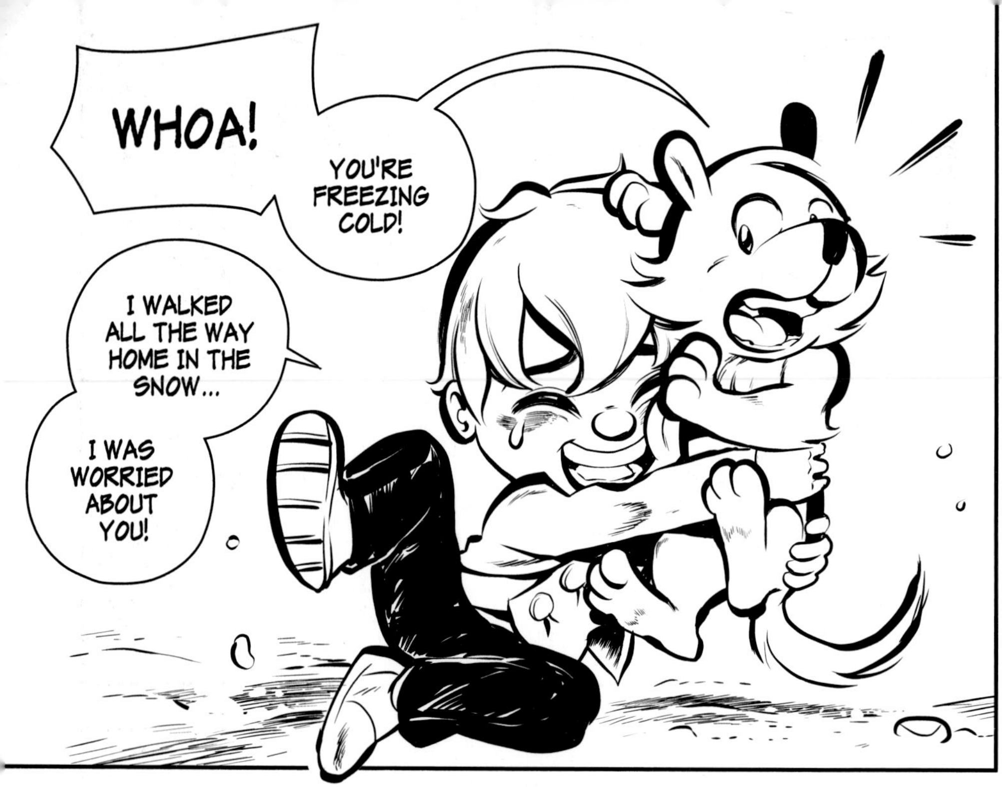
WHOA!
YOU'RE FREEZING COLD!
I WALKED ALL THE WAY HOME IN THE SNOW...
I WAS WORRIED ABOUT YOU!

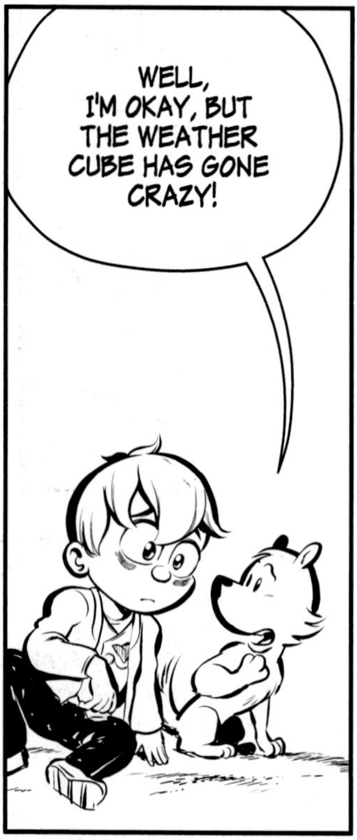
WELL, I'M OKAY, BUT THE WEATHER CUBE HAS GONE CRAZY!

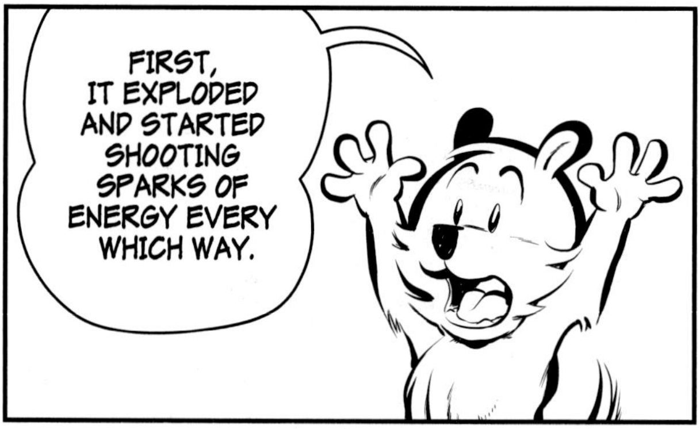
FIRST, IT EXPLODED AND STARTED SHOOTING SPARKS OF ENERGY EVERY WHICH WAY.

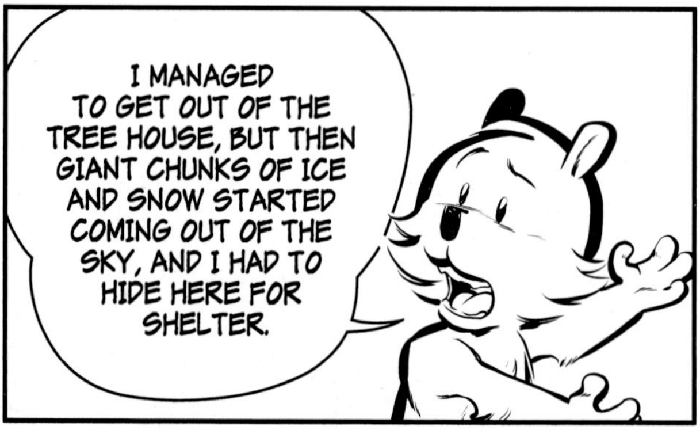
I MANAGED TO GET OUT OF THE TREE HOUSE, BUT THEN GIANT CHUNKS OF ICE AND SNOW STARTED COMING OUT OF THE SKY, AND I HAD TO HIDE HERE FOR SHELTER.

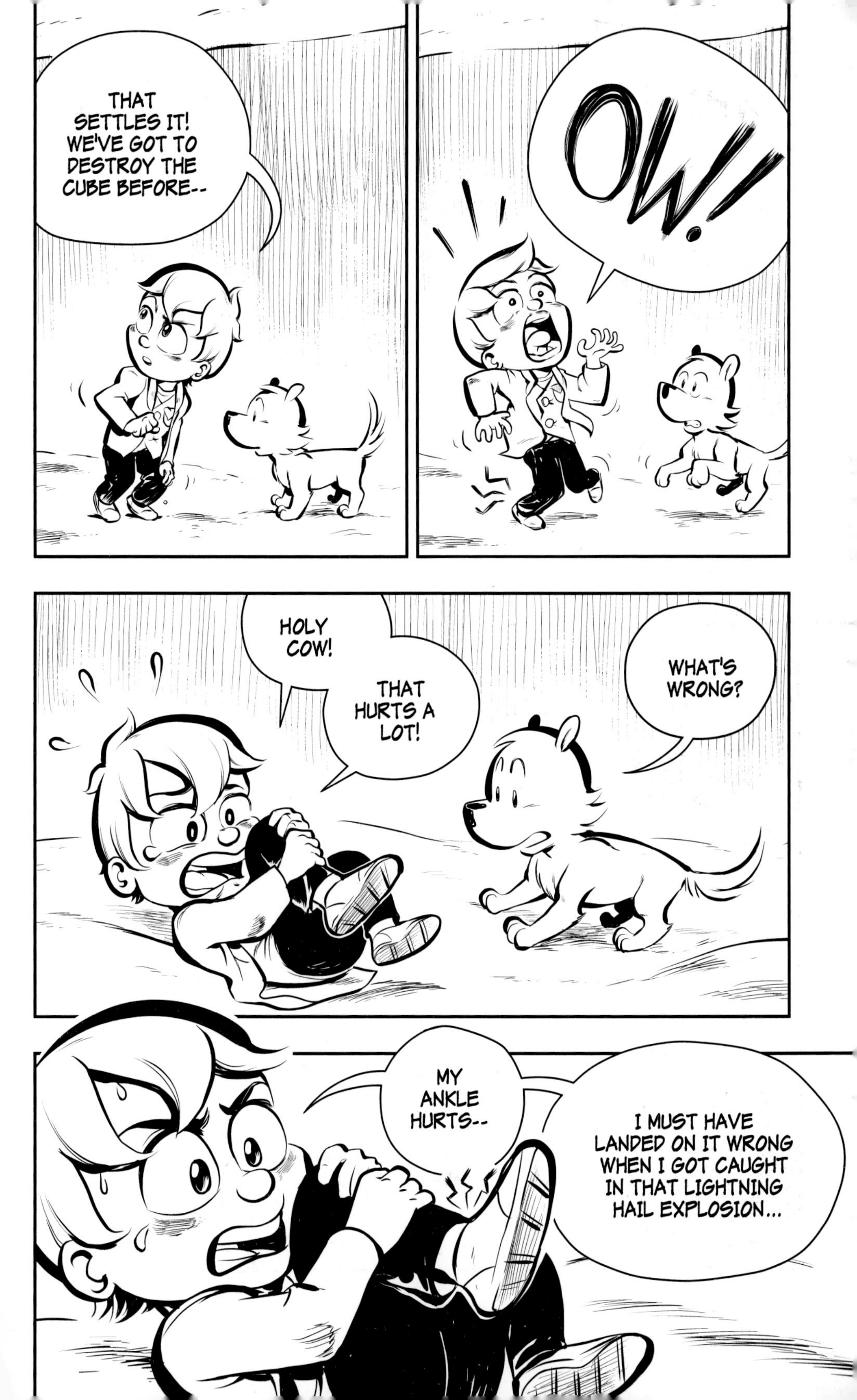
THAT SETTLES IT! WE'VE GOT TO DESTROY THE CUBE BEFORE--
OW!
HOLY COW!
THAT HURTS A LOT!
WHAT'S WRONG?
MY ANKLE HURTS--
I MUST HAVE LANDED ON IT WRONG WHEN I GOT CAUGHT IN THAT LIGHTNING HAIL EXPLOSION...

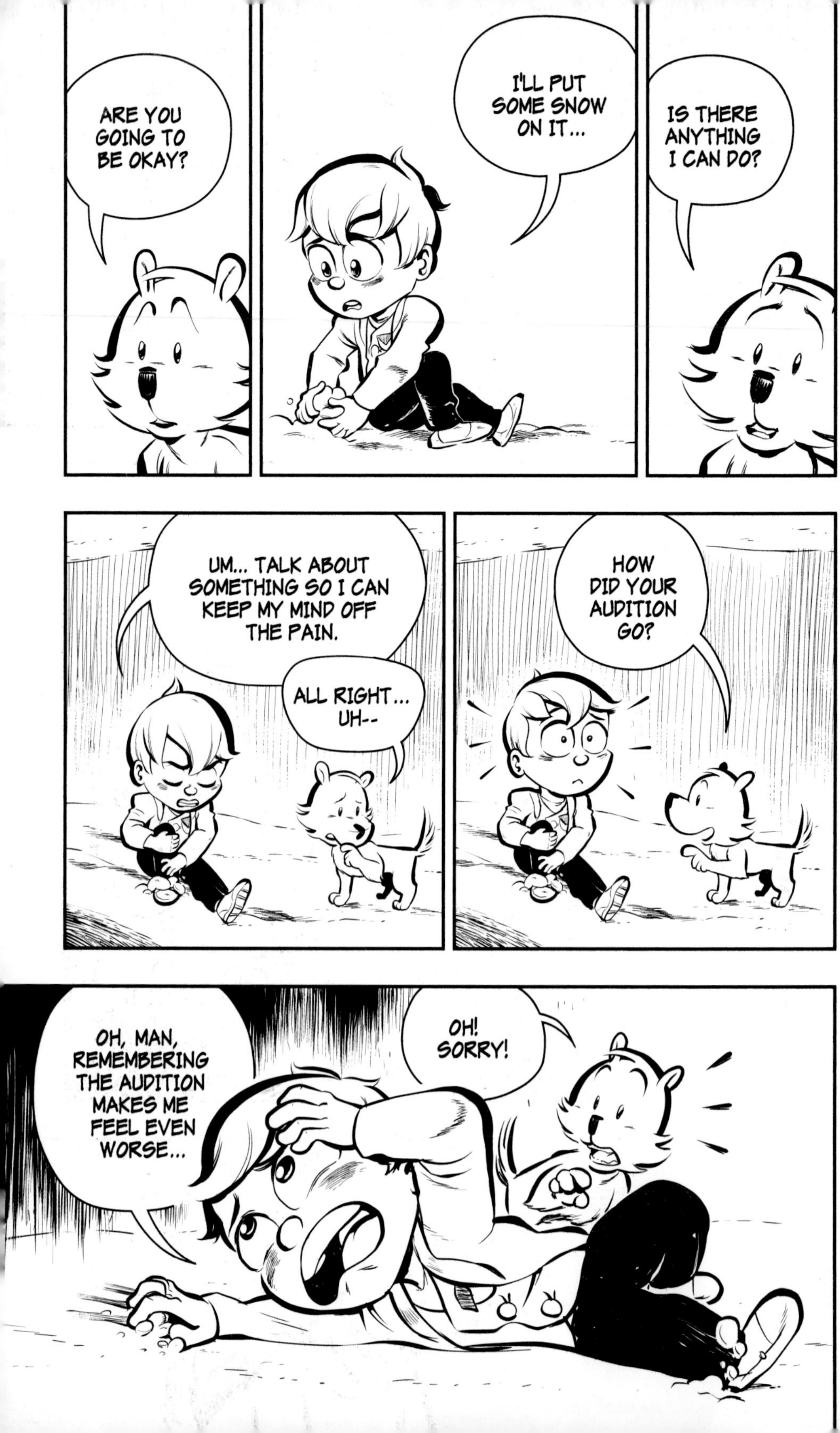
ARE YOU GOING TO BE OKAY?
I'LL PUT SOME SNOW ON IT...
IS THERE ANYTHING I CAN DO?
UM... TALK ABOUT SOMETHING SO I CAN KEEP MY MIND OFF THE PAIN.
ALL RIGHT... UH--
HOW DID YOUR AUDITION GO?
OH, MAN, REMEMBERING THE AUDITION MAKES ME FEEL EVEN WORSE...
OH! SORRY!

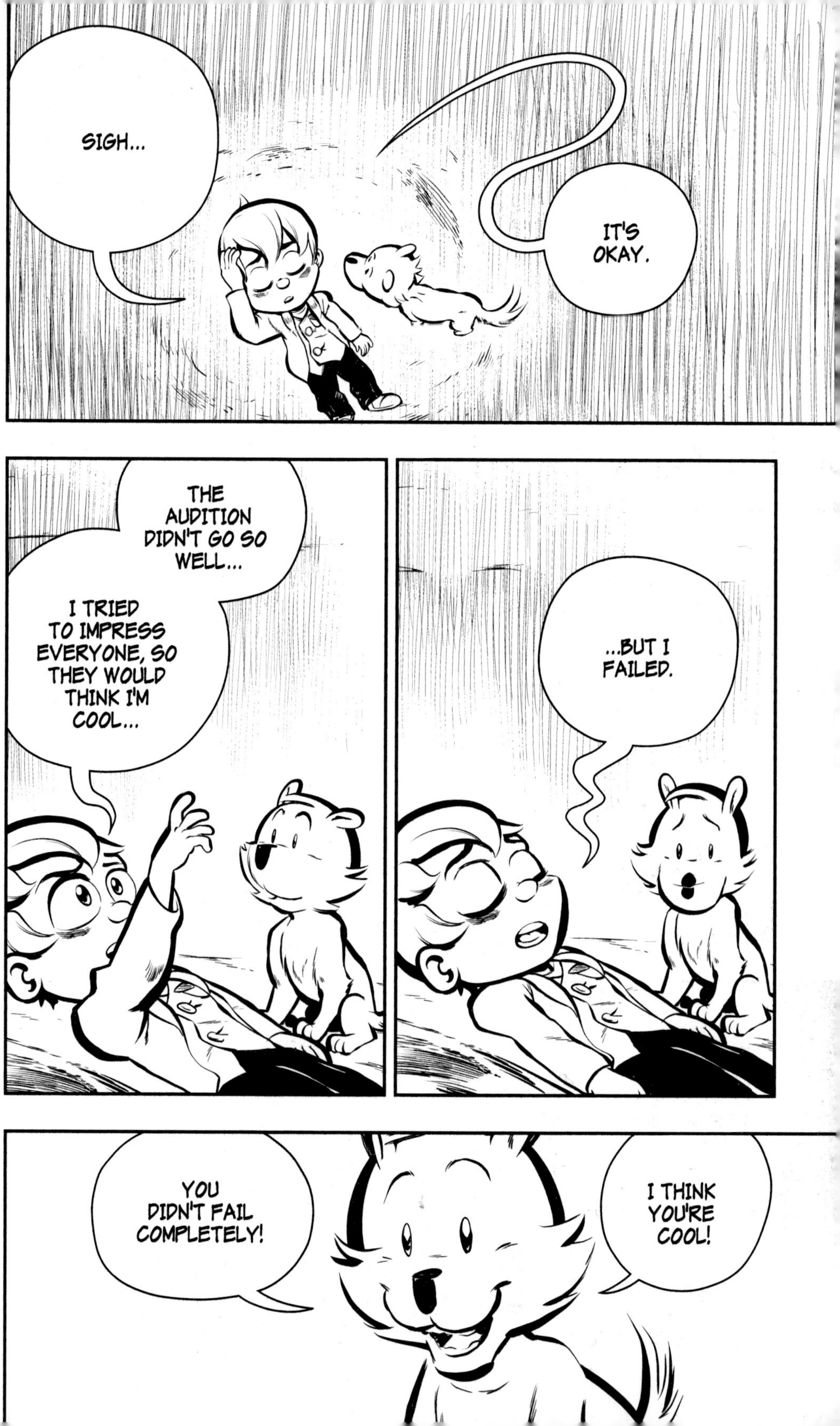
SIGH...
IT'S OKAY.
THE AUDITION DIDN'T GO SO WELL...
I TRIED TO IMPRESS EVERYONE, SO THEY WOULD THINK I'M COOL...
...BUT I FAILED.
YOU DIDN'T FAIL COMPLETELY!
I THINK YOU'RE COOL!

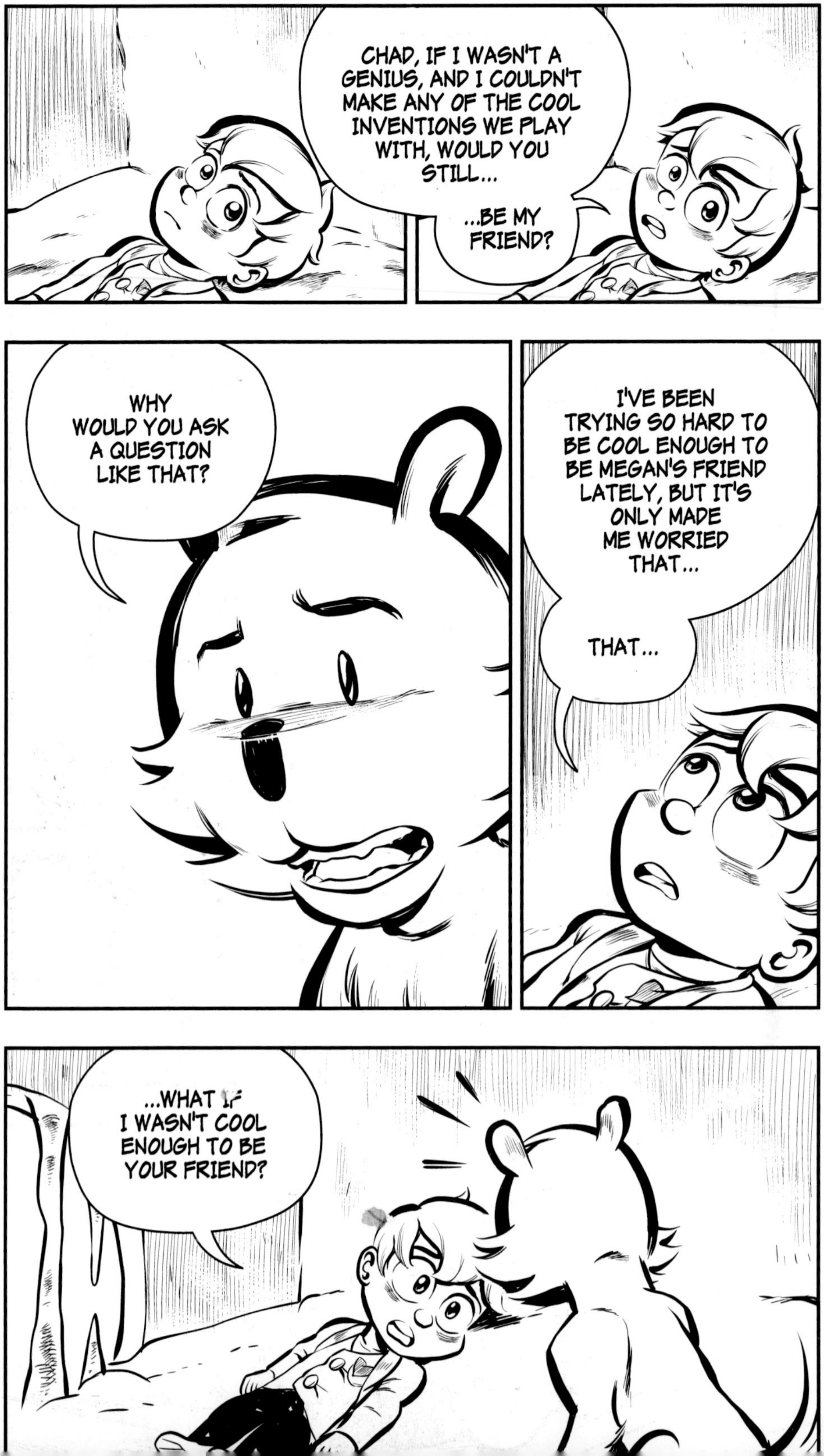
CHAD, IF I WASN'T A GENIUS, AND I COULDN'T MAKE ANY OF THE COOL INVENTIONS WE PLAY WITH, WOULD YOU STILL...
...BE MY FRIEND?
WHY WOULD YOU ASK A QUESTION LIKE THAT?
I'VE BEEN TRYING SO HARD TO BE COOL ENOUGH TO BE MEGAN'S FRIEND LATELY, BUT IT'S ONLY MADE ME WORRIED THAT...
THAT...
...WHAT IF I WASN'T COOL ENOUGH TO BE YOUR FRIEND?

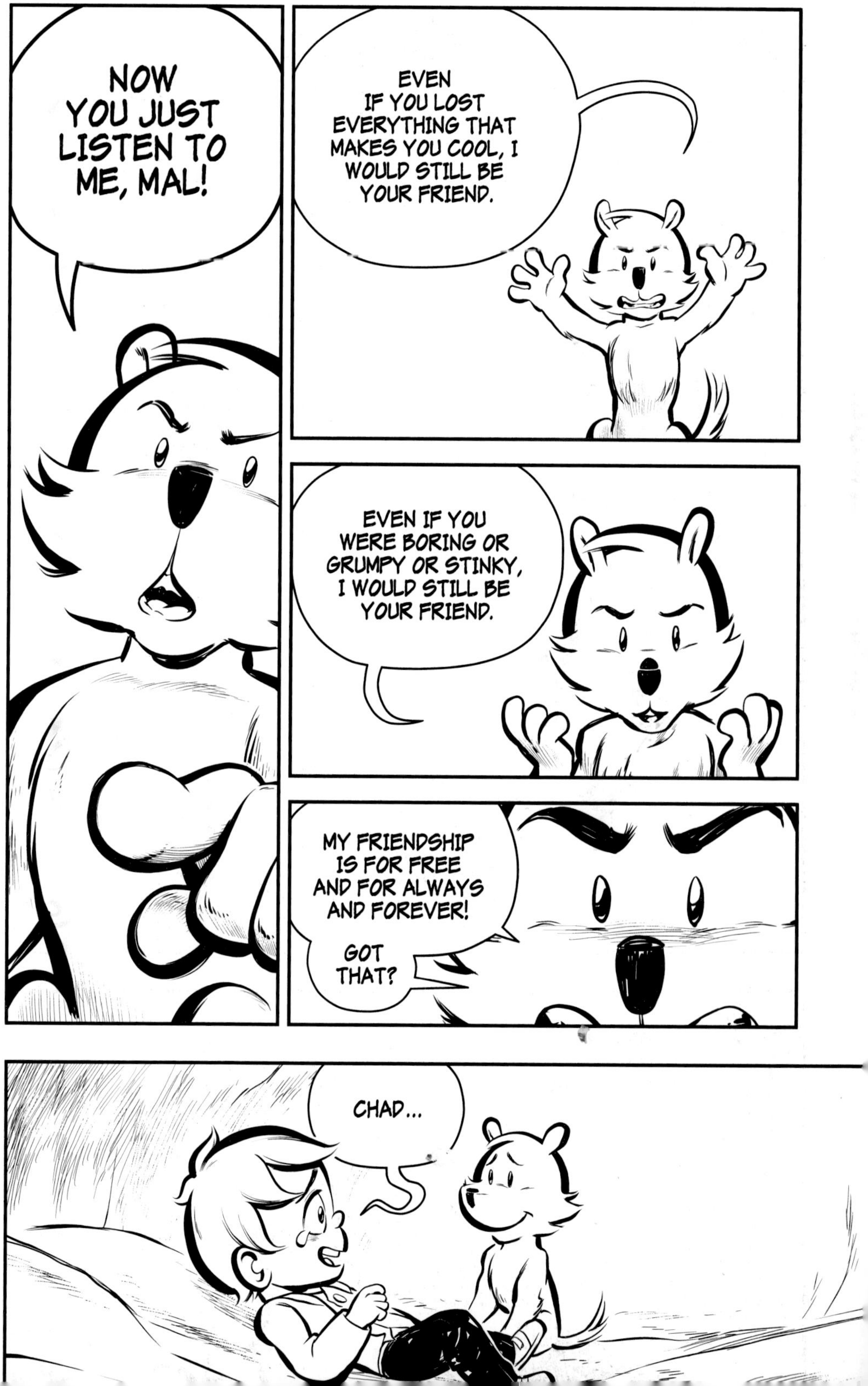
NOW YOU JUST LISTEN TO ME, MAL!
EVEN IF YOU LOST EVERYTHING THAT MAKES YOU COOL, I WOULD STILL BE YOUR FRIEND.
EVEN IF YOU WERE BORING OR GRUMPY OR STINKY, I WOULD STILL BE YOUR FRIEND.
MY FRIENDSHIP IS FOR FREE AND FOR ALWAYS AND FOREVER!
GOT THAT?
CHAD...

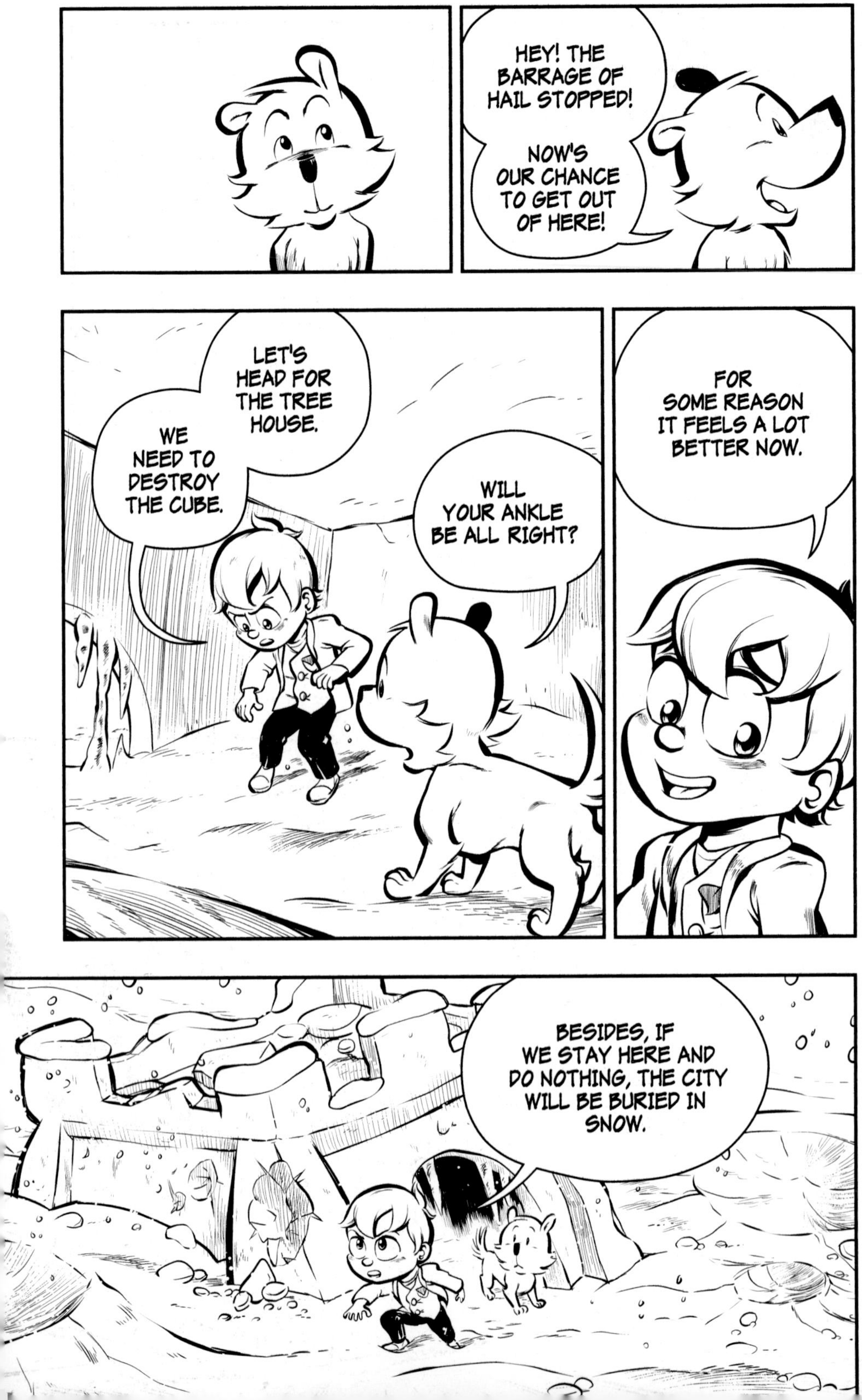
HEY! THE BARRAGE OF HAIL STOPPED!
NOW'S OUR CHANCE TO GET OUT OF HERE!
LET'S HEAD FOR THE TREE HOUSE.
WE NEED TO DESTROY THE CUBE.
WILL YOUR ANKLE BE ALL RIGHT?
FOR SOME REASON IT FEELS A LOT BETTER NOW.
BESIDES, IF WE STAY HERE AND DO NOTHING, THE CITY WILL BE BURIED IN SNOW.

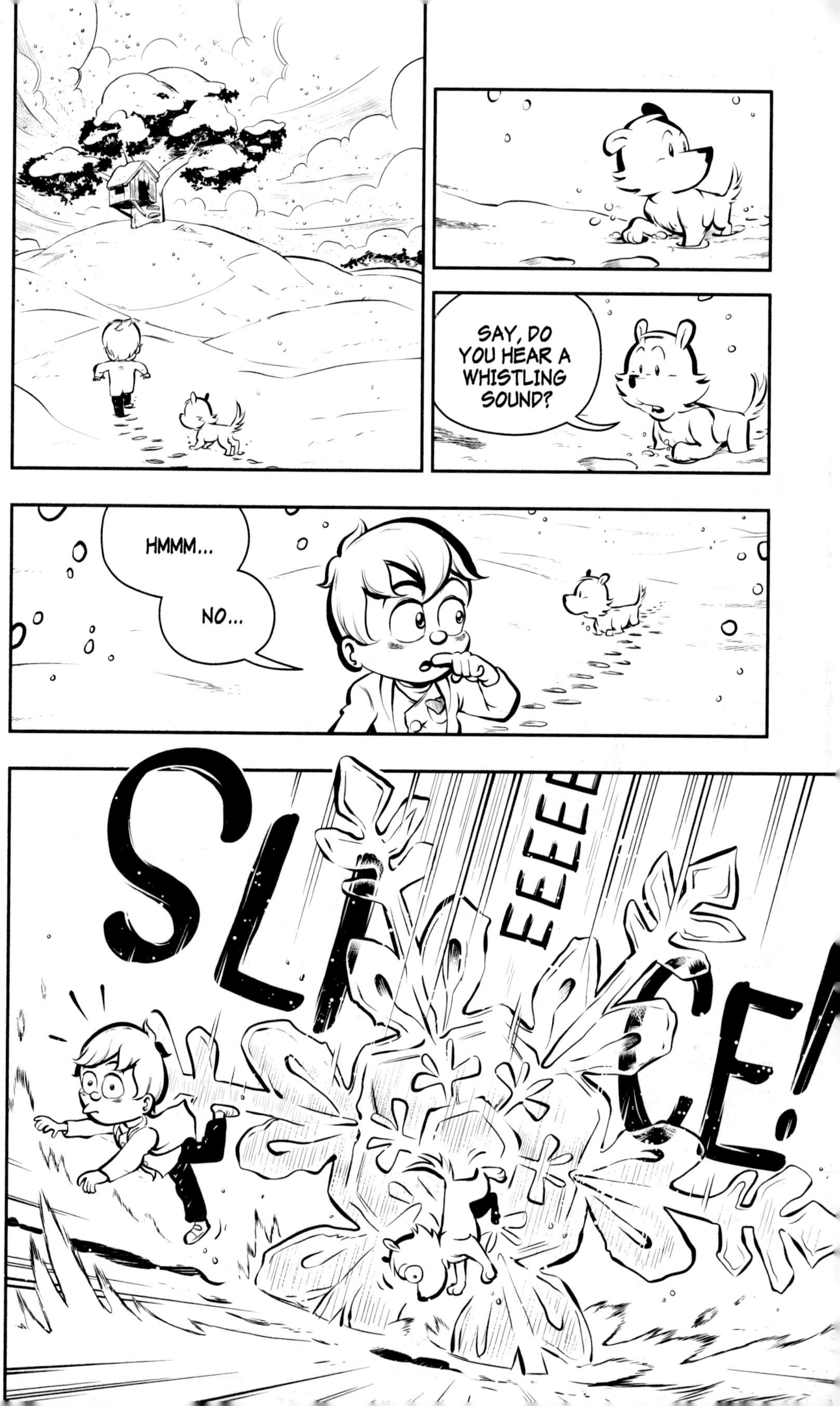
SAY, DO YOU HEAR A WHISTLING SOUND?
HMMM...
NO...

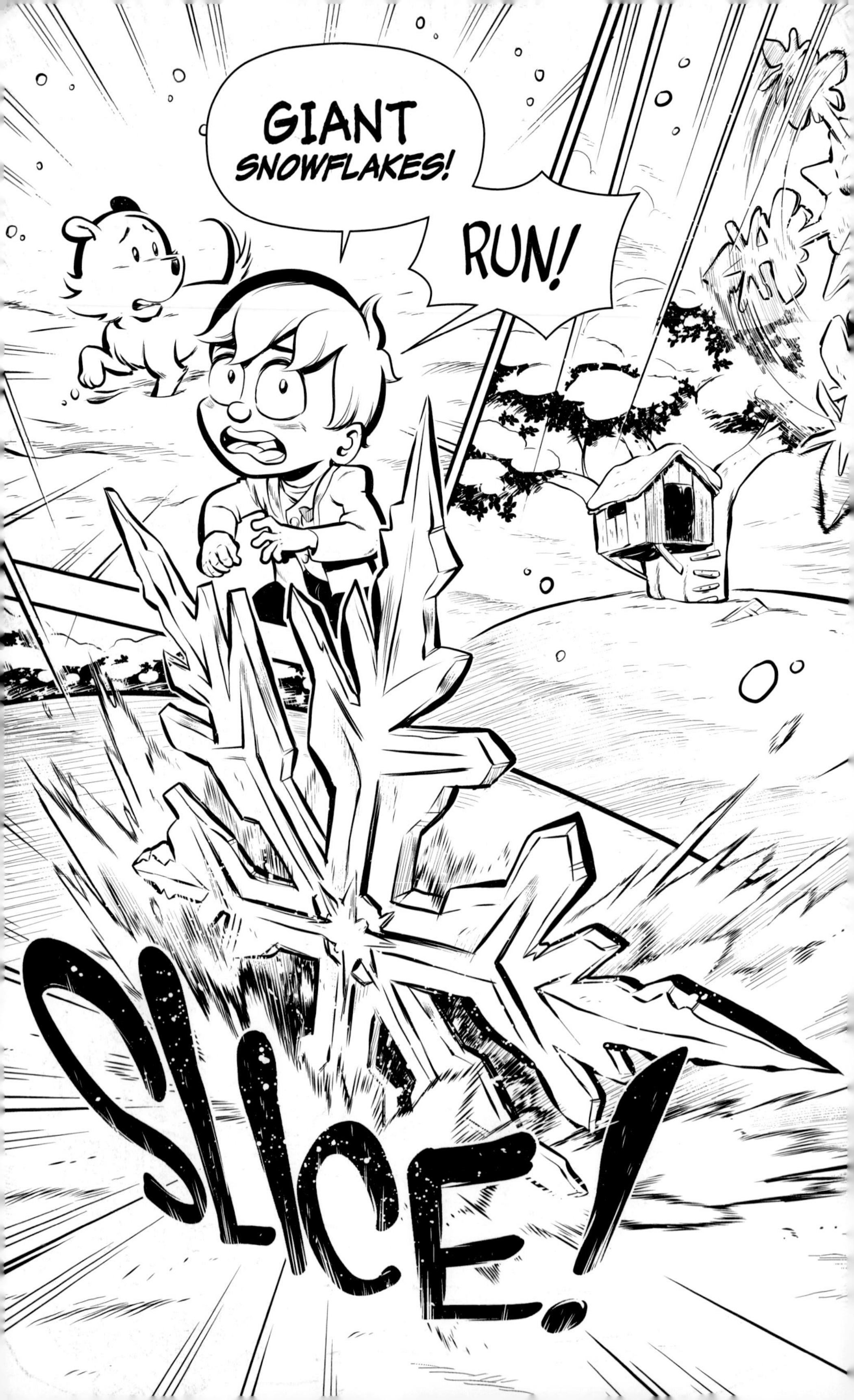
GIANT SNOWFLAKES!
RUN!
SLICE!

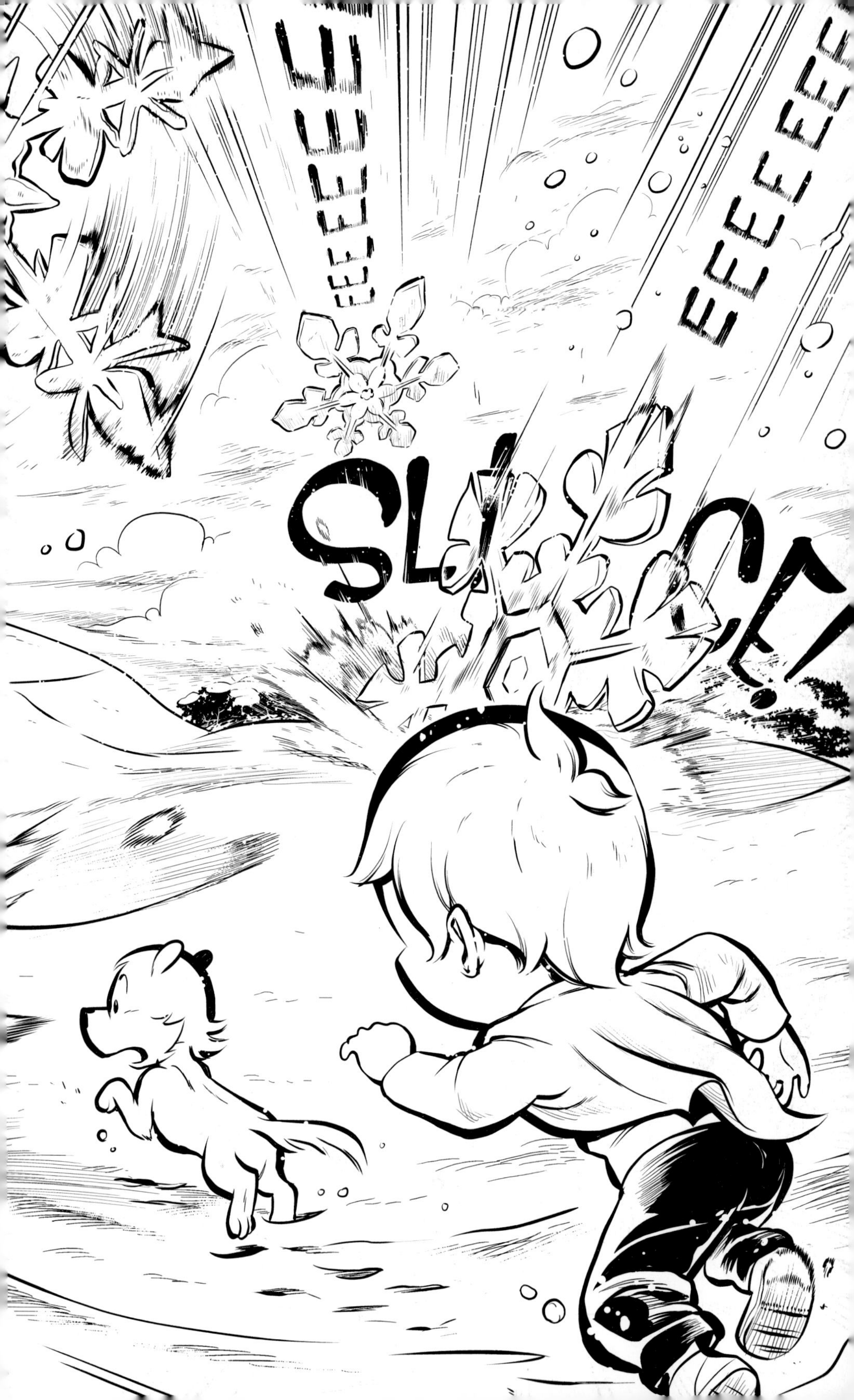
EEEEEEE
EEEEEEE

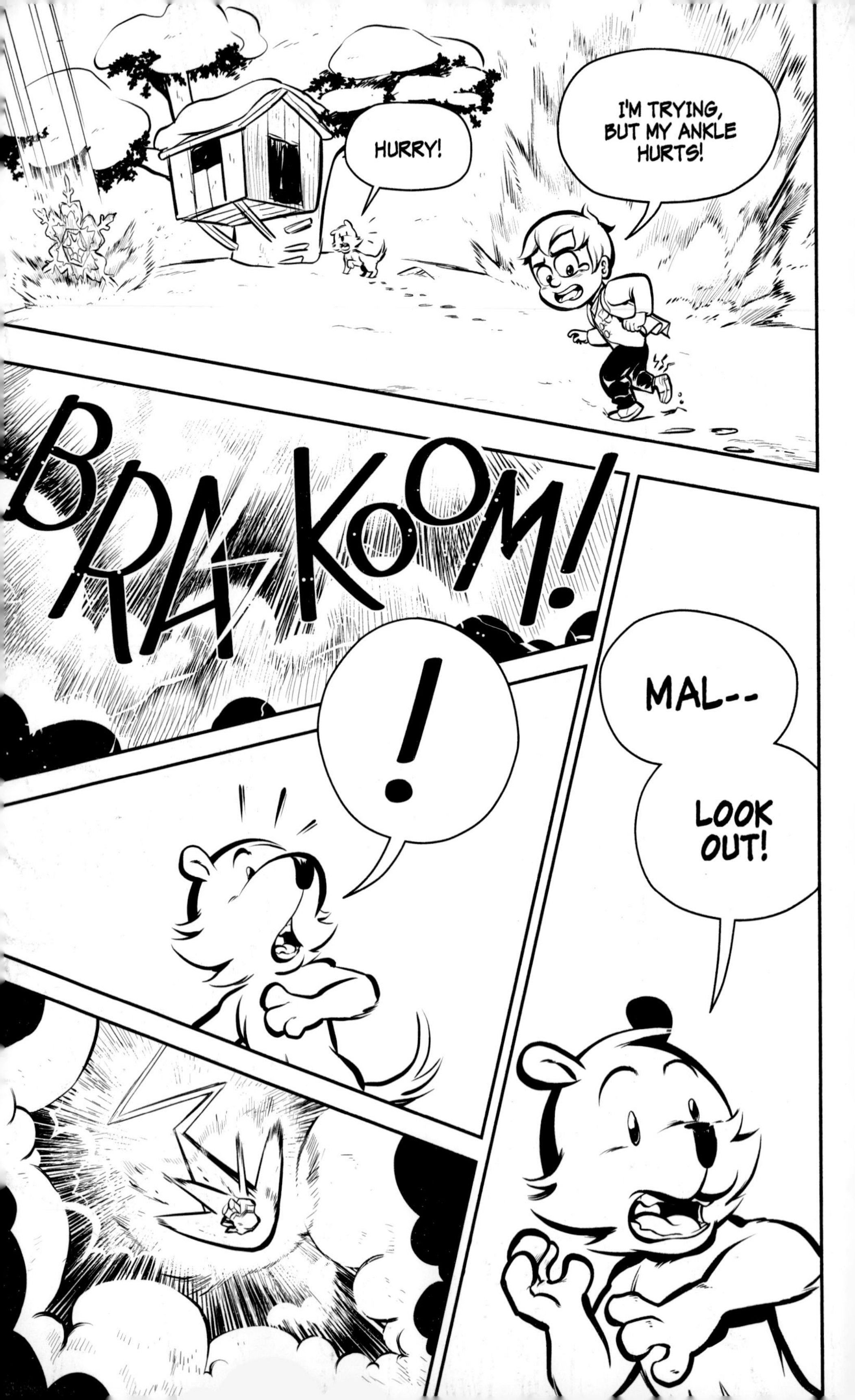
HURRY!
I'M TRYING, BUT MY ANKLE HURTS!
BRRAKOOM!
!
MAL--
LOOK OUT!

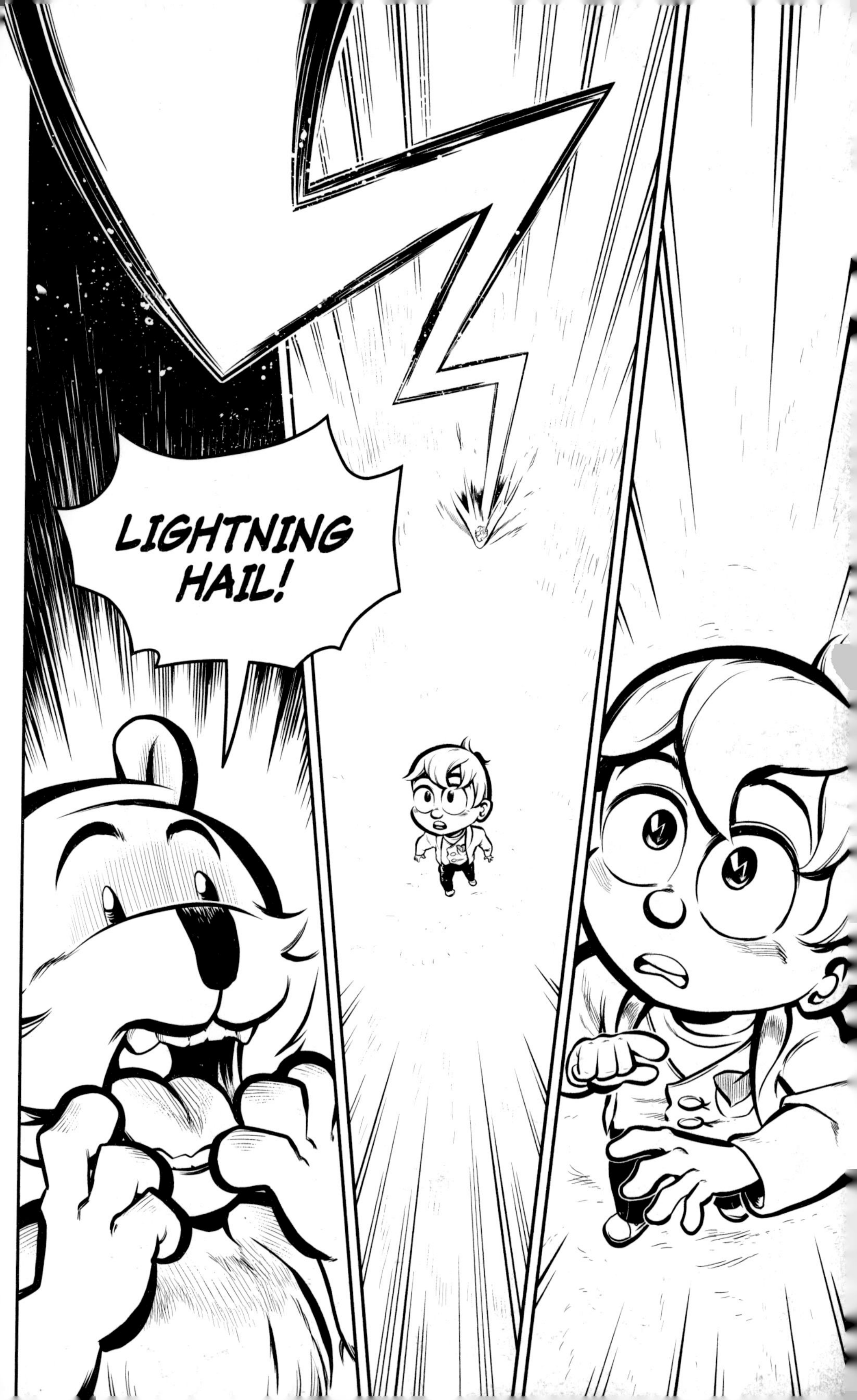
LIGHTNING HAIL!

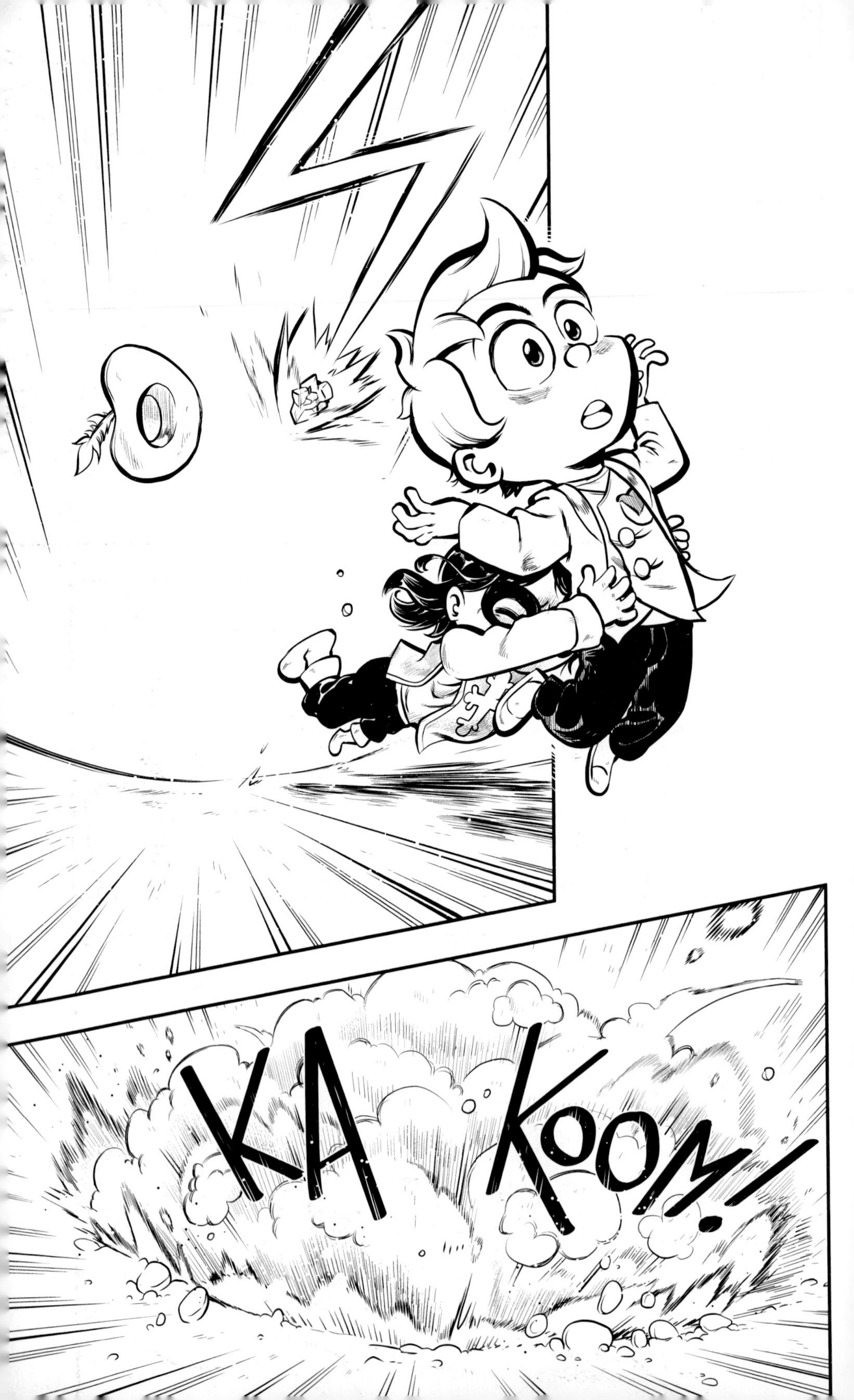
KA KOOM!

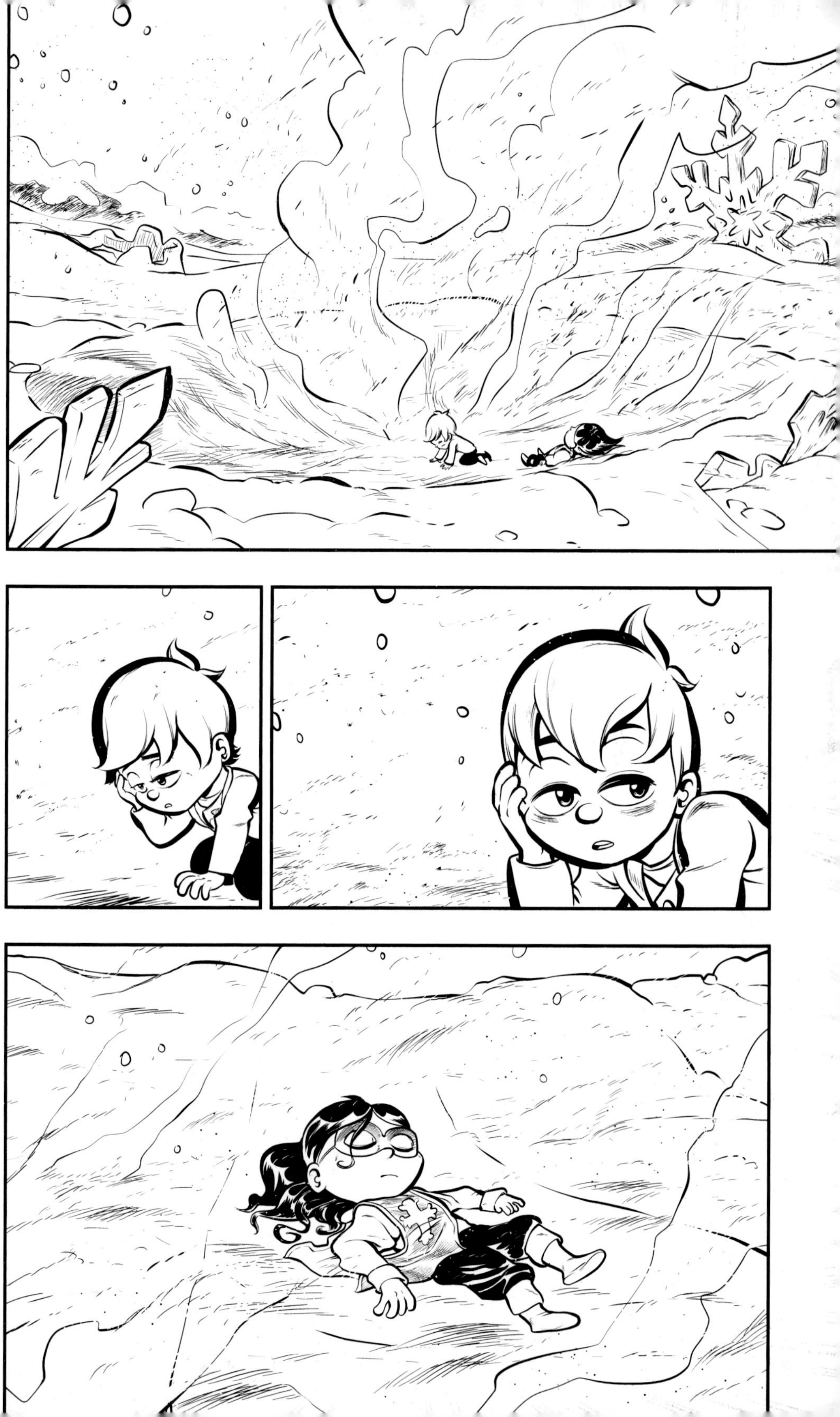

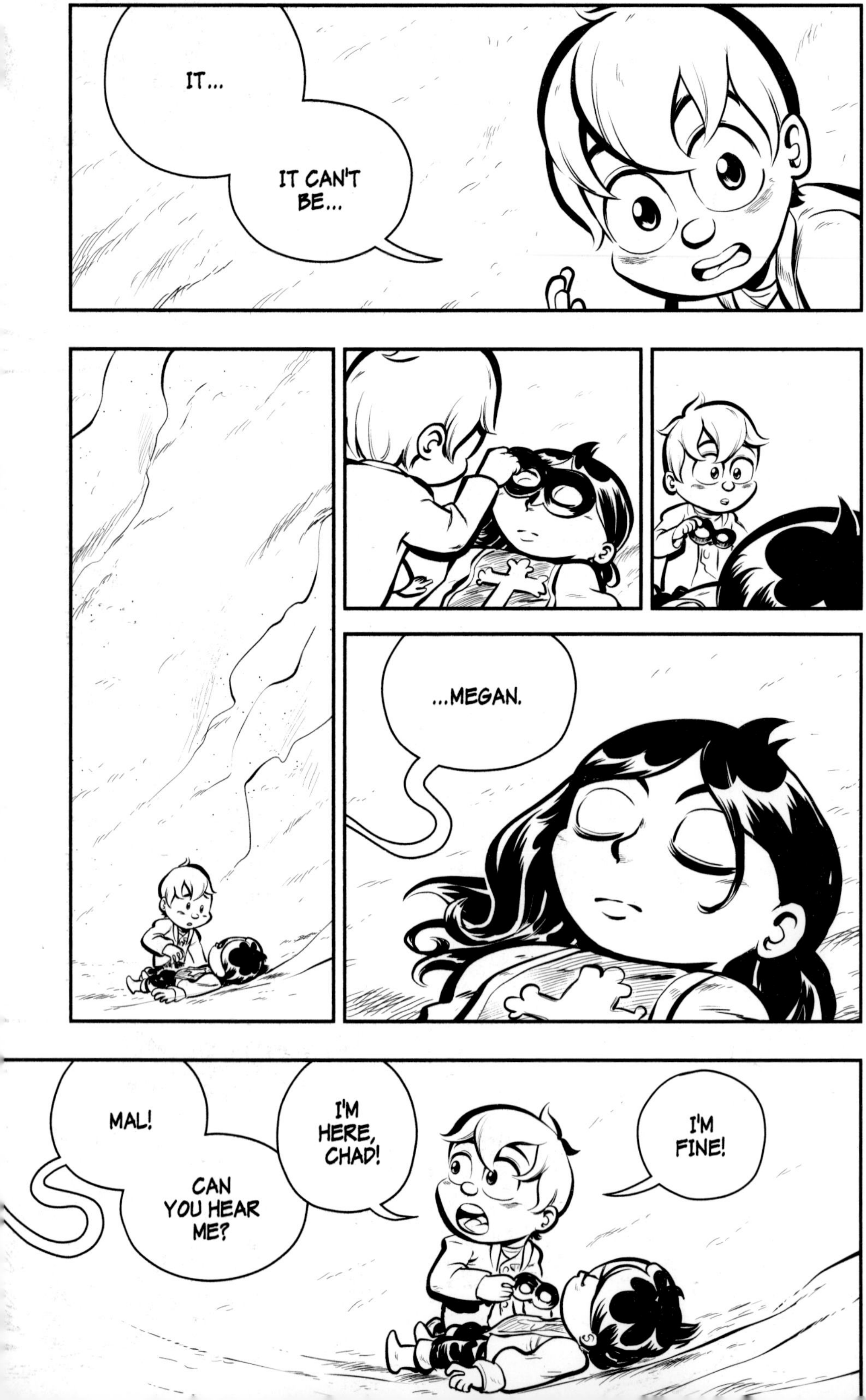
IT...
IT CAN'T BE...
...MEGAN.
MAL!
CAN YOU HEAR ME?
I'M HERE, CHAD!
I'M FINE!

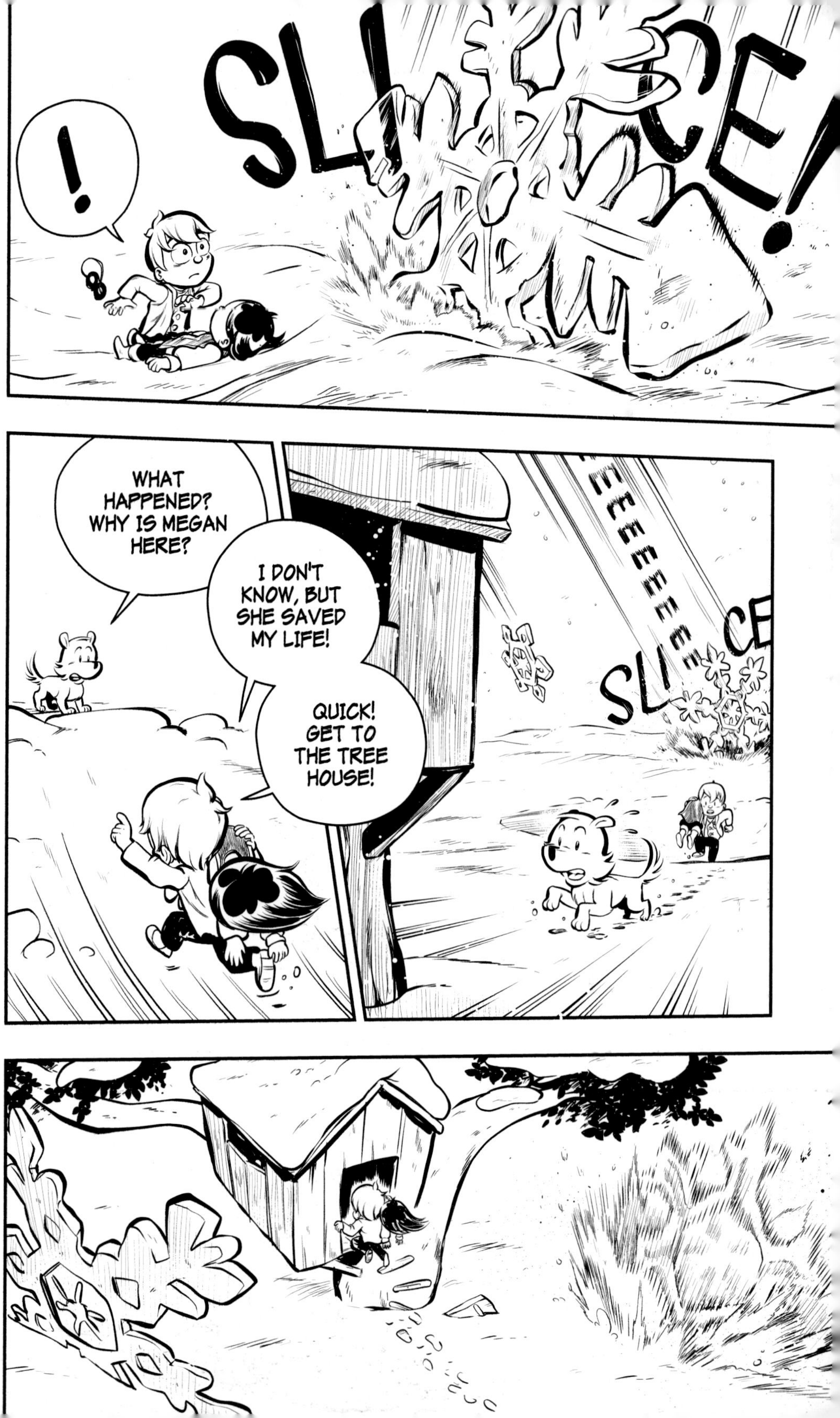
!
WHAT HAPPENED? WHY IS MEGAN HERE?
I DON'T KNOW, BUT SHE SAVED MY LIFE!
QUICK! GET TO THE TREE HOUSE!

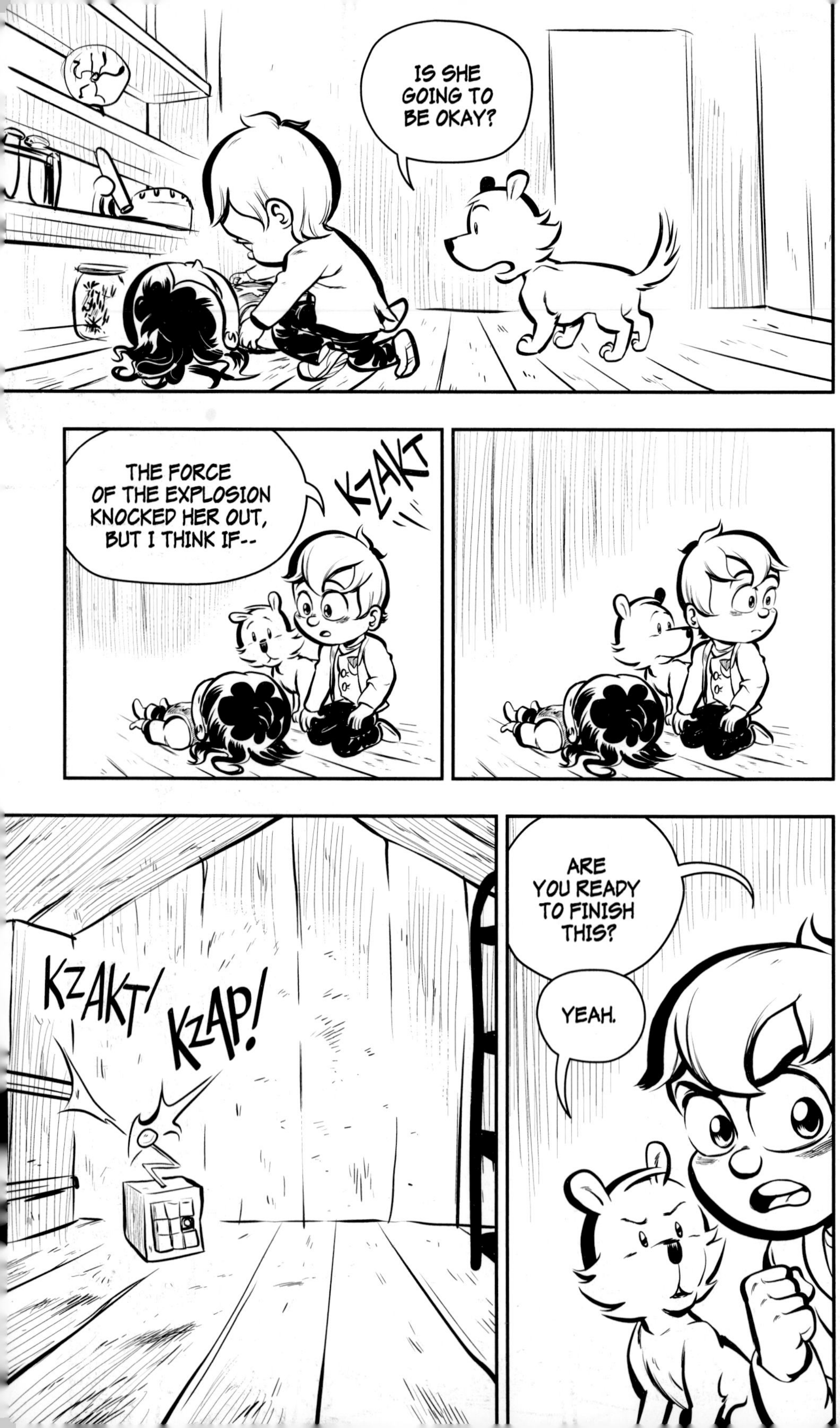
IS SHE GOING TO BE OKAY?
THE FORCE OF THE EXPLOSION KNOCKED HER OUT, BUT I THINK IF--
KZAKT
KZAKT!
KZAP!
ARE YOU READY TO FINISH THIS?
YEAH.

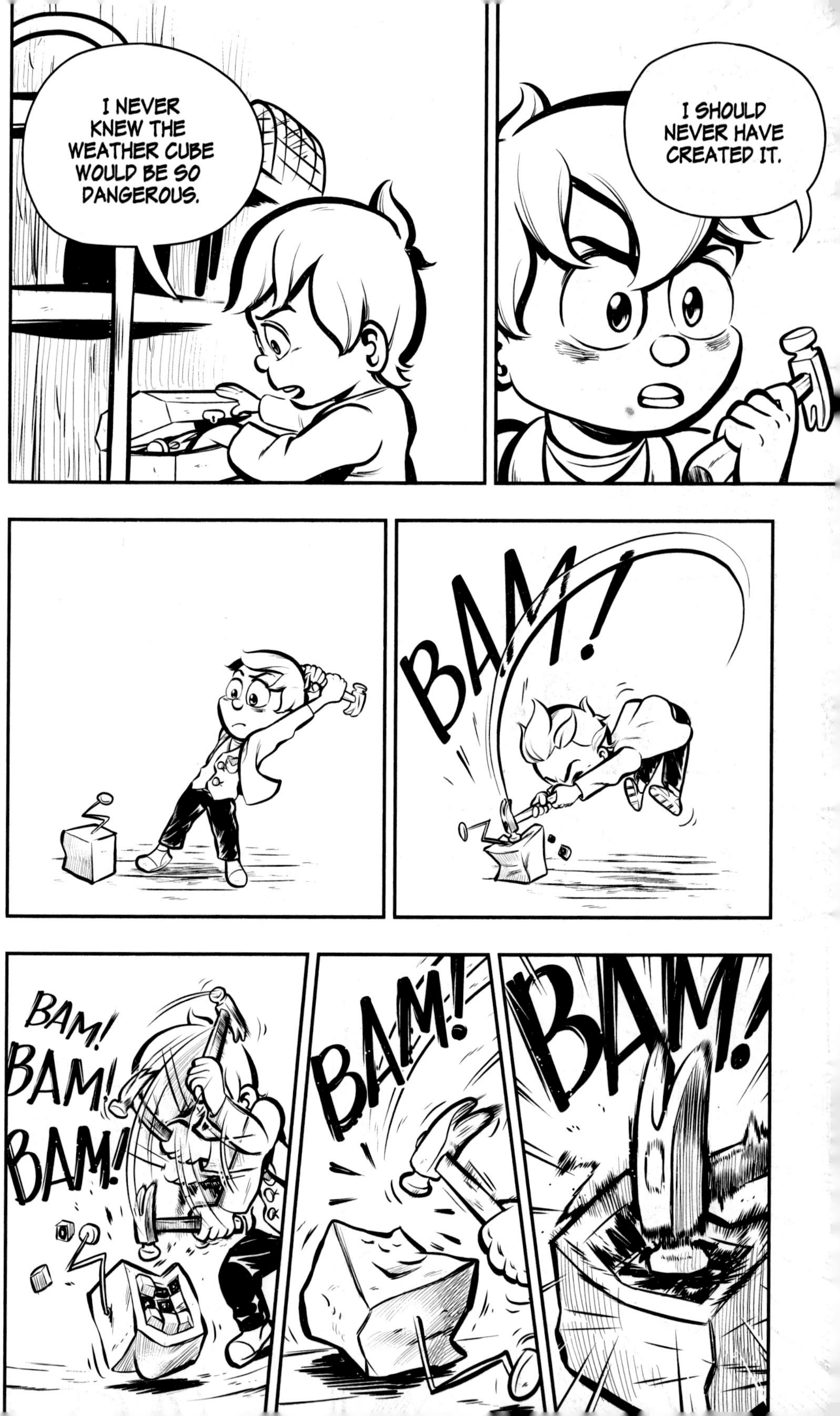
I NEVER KNEW THE WEATHER CUBE WOULD BE SO DANGEROUS.
I SHOULD NEVER HAVE CREATED IT.
BAM!
BAM!
BAM!
BAM!
BAM!
BAM!

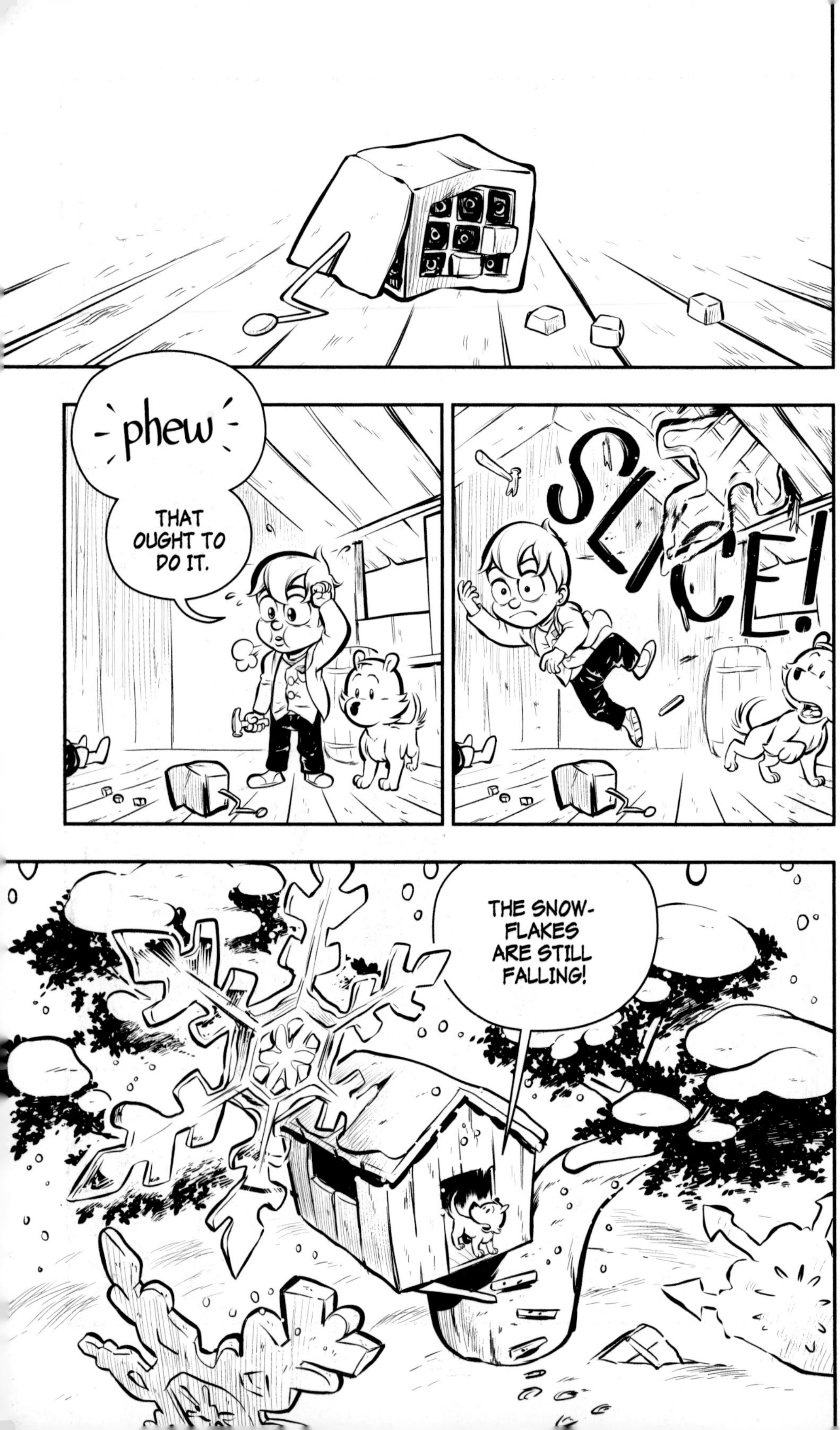
phew
THAT OUGHT TO DO IT.
SLICE!
THE SNOW-FLAKES ARE STILL FALLING!

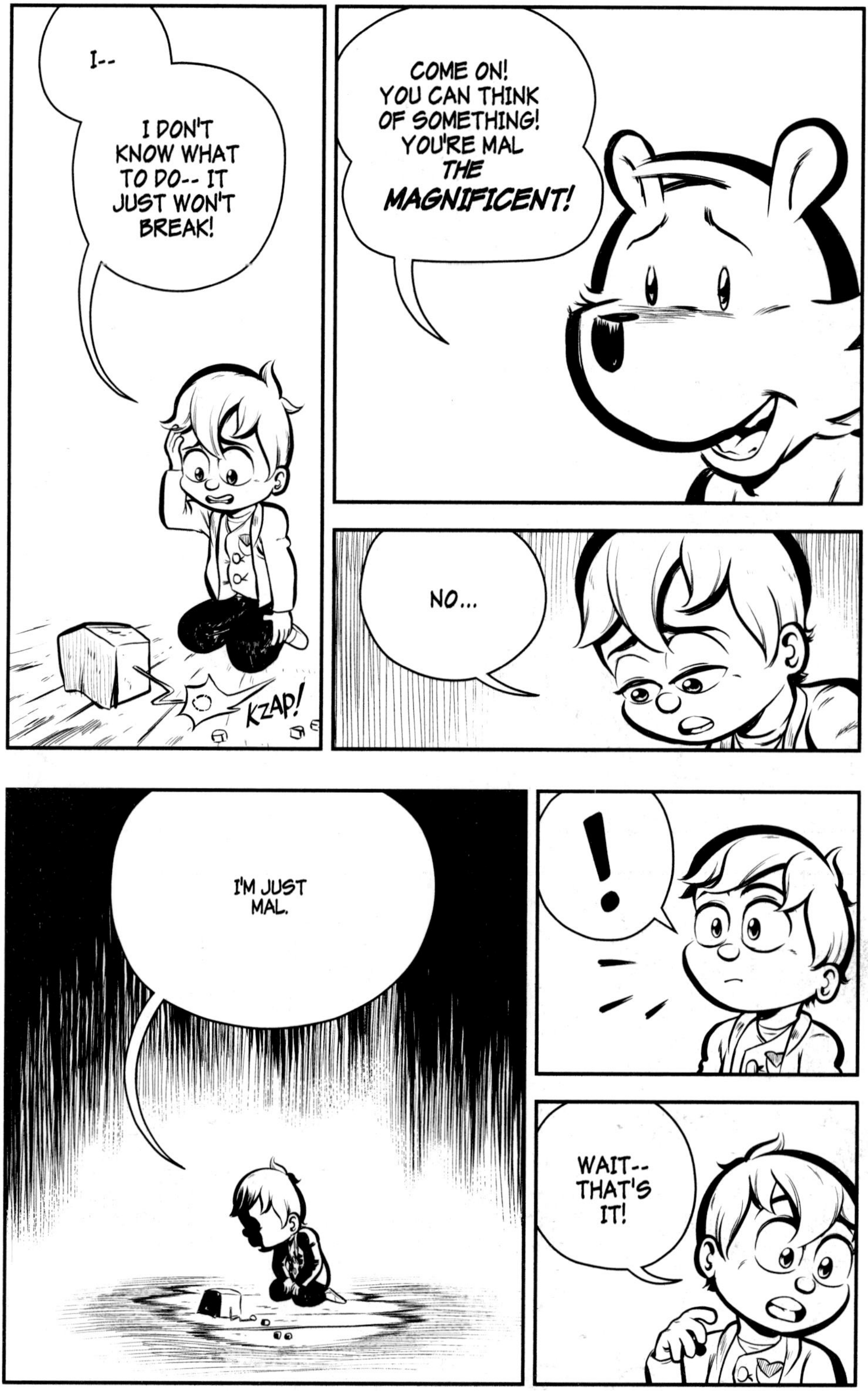
I--
I DON'T KNOW WHAT TO DO-- IT JUST WON'T BREAK!
KZAP!
COME ON! YOU CAN THINK OF SOMETHING! YOU'RE MAL THE MAGNIFICENT!
NO...
I'M JUST MAL.
!
WAIT-- THAT'S IT!

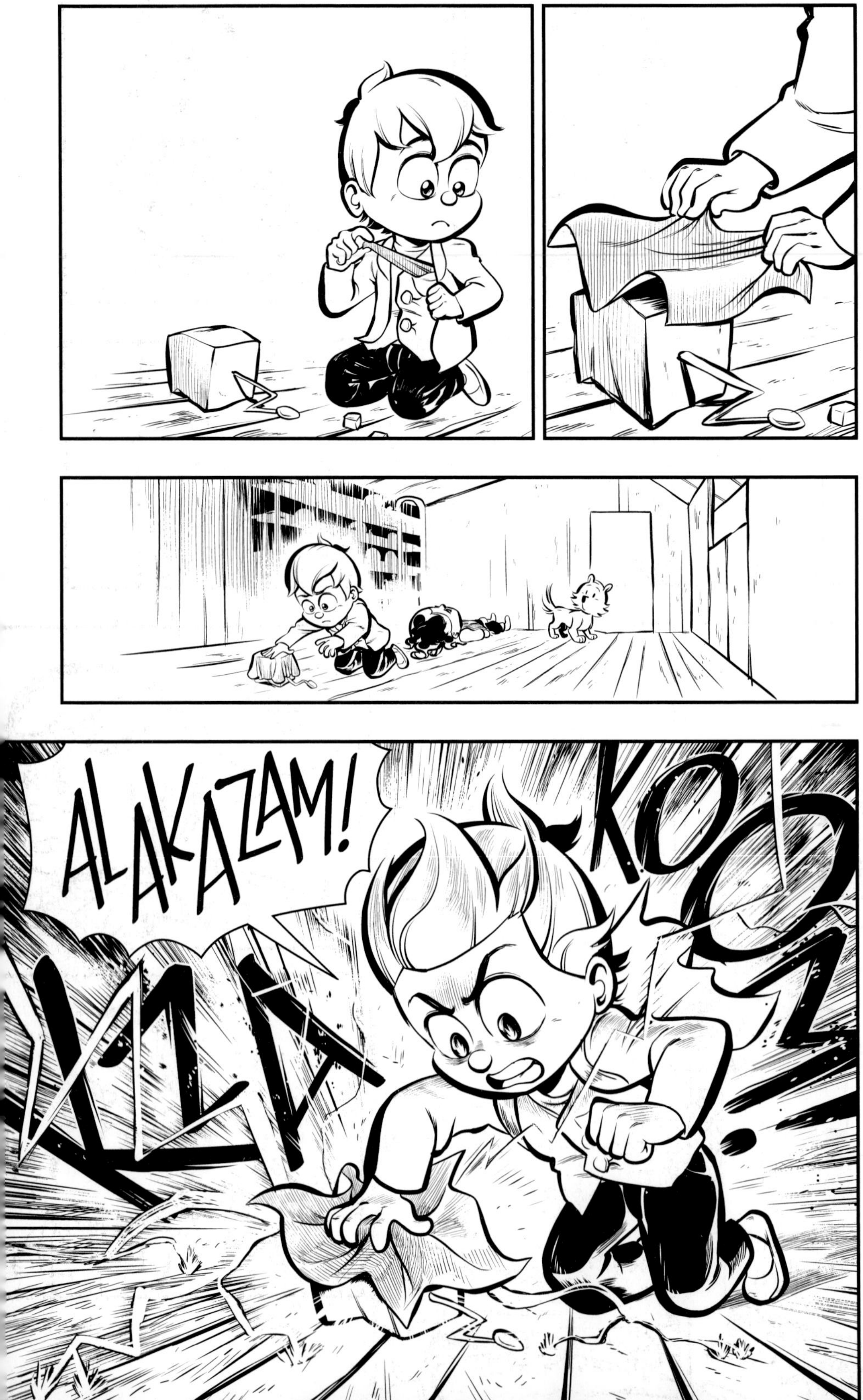
ALAKAZAM!
KA

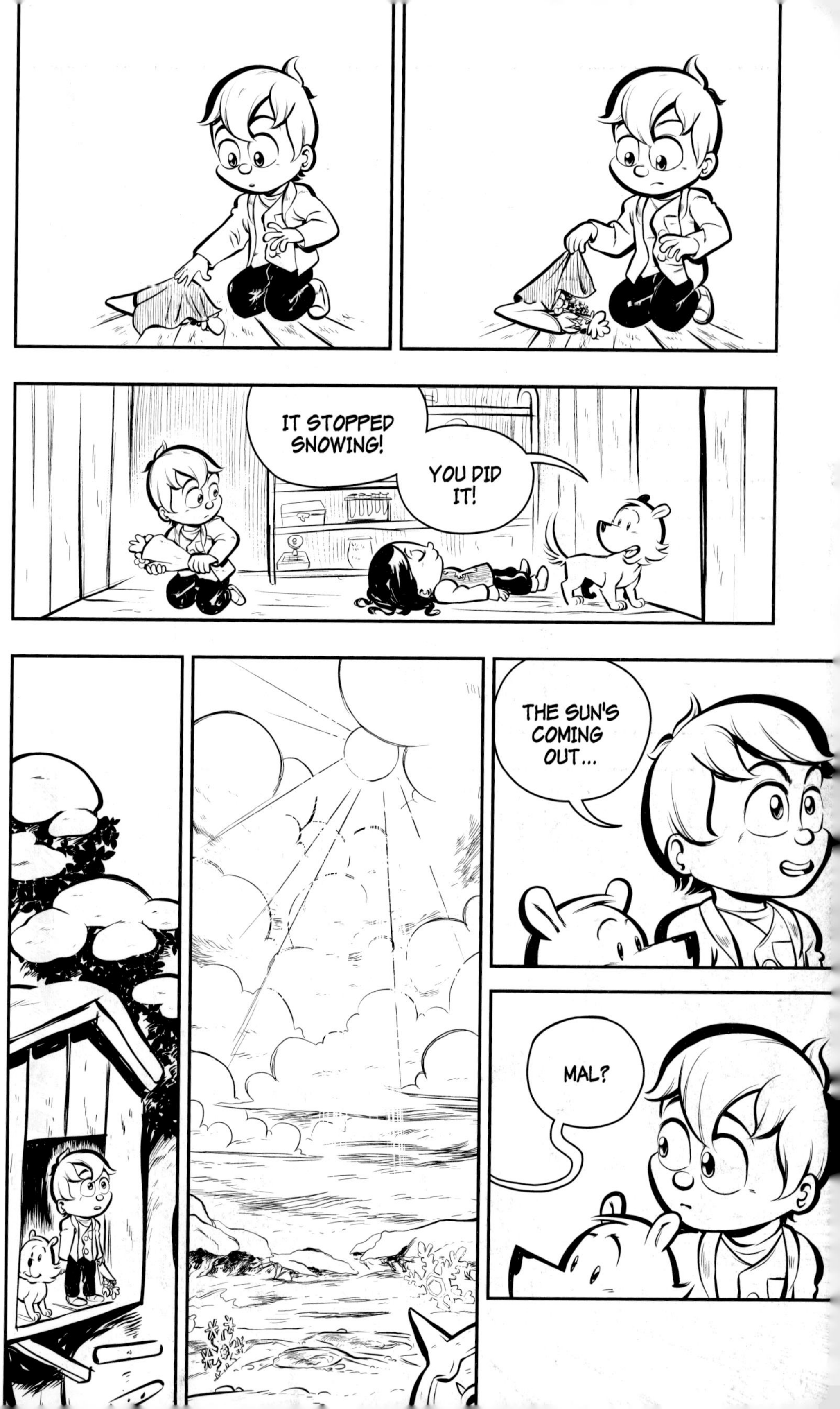
IT STOPPED SNOWING!
YOU DID IT!
THE SUN'S COMING OUT...
MAL?

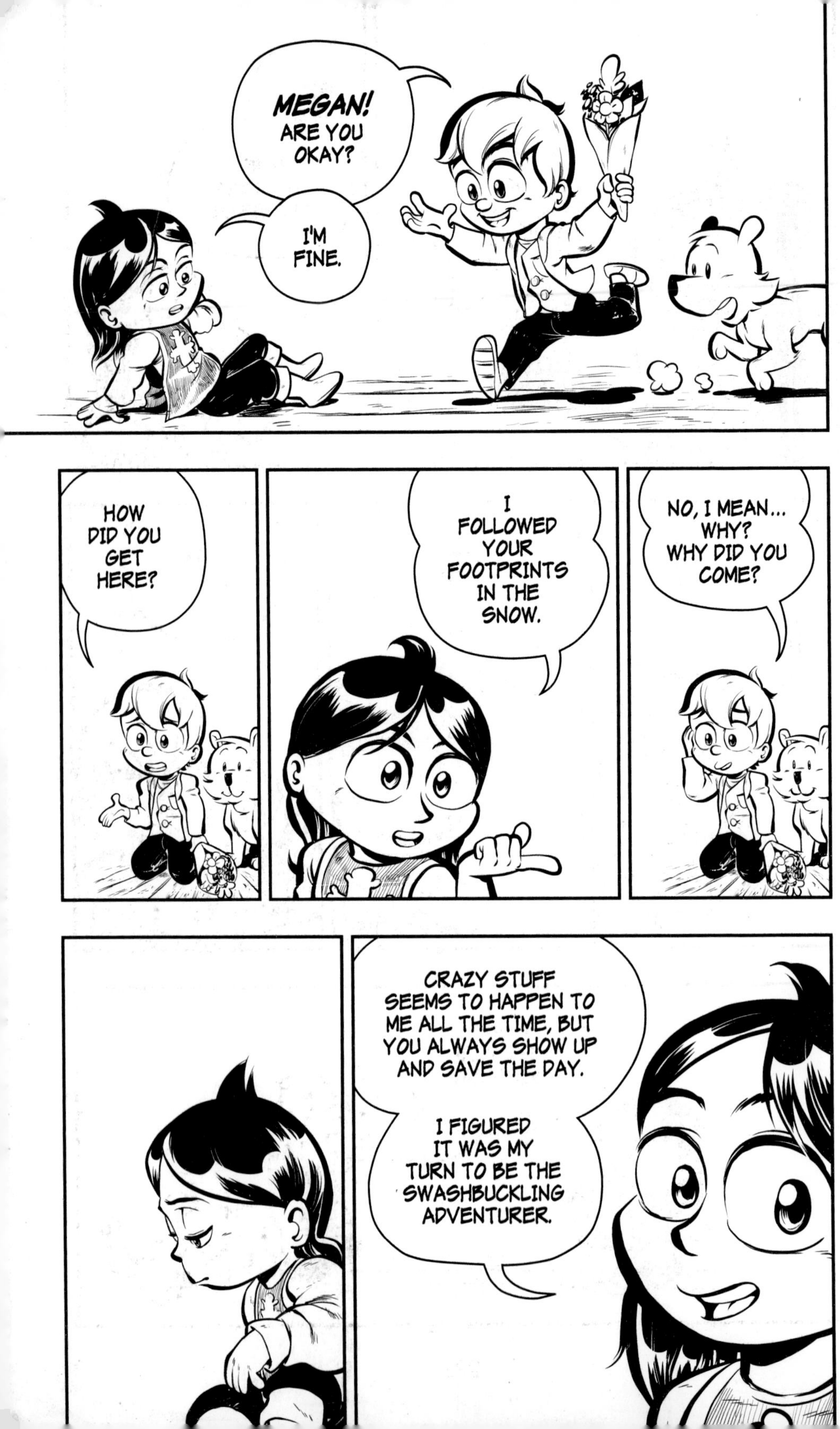

MEGAN! ARE YOU OKAY?
I'M FINE.
HOW DID YOU GET HERE?
I FOLLOWED YOUR FOOTPRINTS IN THE SNOW.
NO, I MEAN... WHY? WHY DID YOU COME?
CRAZY STUFF SEEMS TO HAPPEN TO ME ALL THE TIME, BUT YOU ALWAYS SHOW UP AND SAVE THE DAY.
I FIGURED IT WAS MY TURN TO BE THE SWASHBUCKLING ADVENTURER.

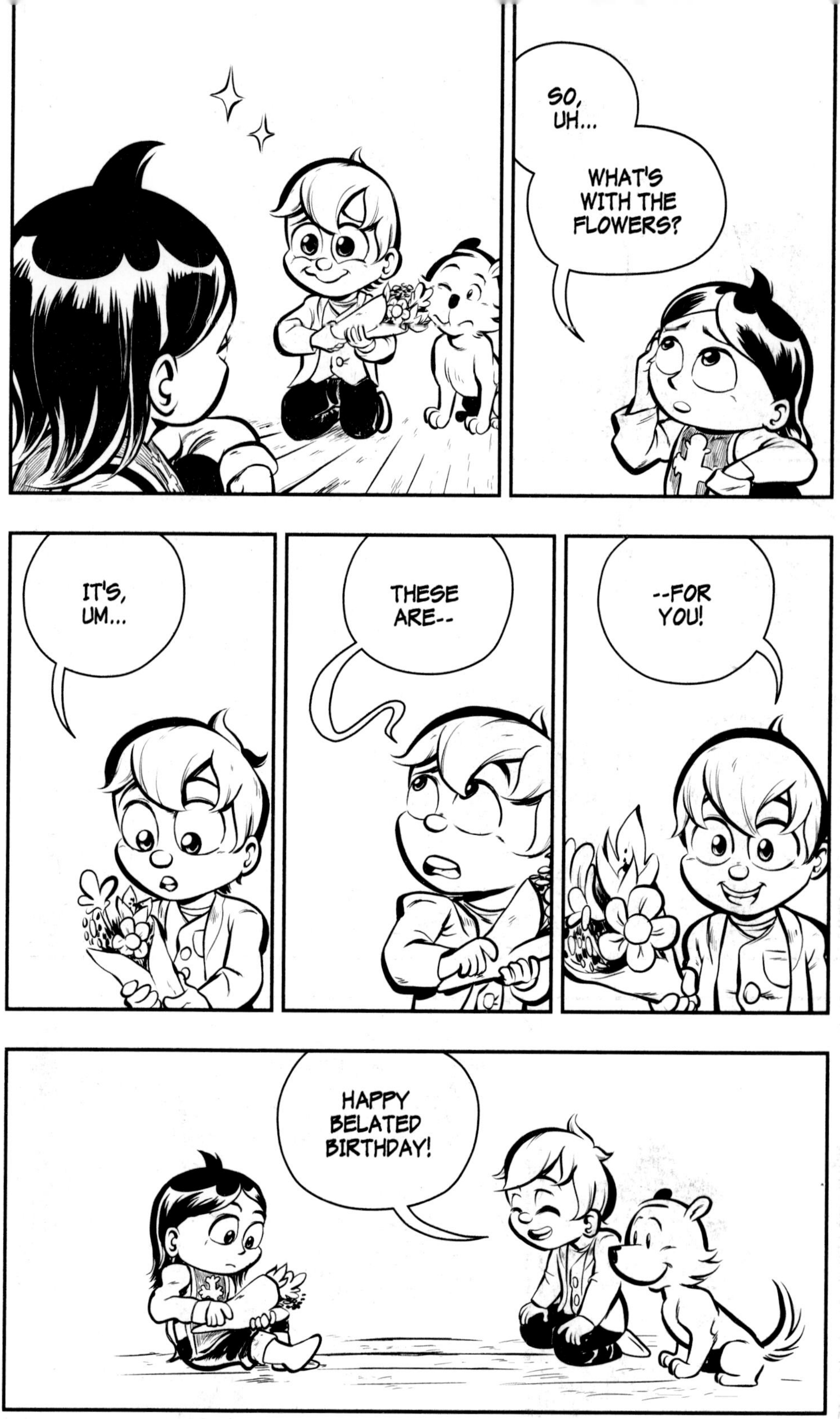
SO, UH...
WHAT'S WITH THE FLOWERS?
IT'S, UM...
THESE ARE--
--FOR YOU!
HAPPY BELATED BIRTHDAY!

the
end